To my good friend Bill

Larry

Pure Vision

Be a part of The Vision.

Perri Birney

PURE VISION

THE MAGDALENE REVELATION

a novel

PERRI BIRNEY

Pure Vision Communications
High Falls, New York

PURE VISION: *The Magdalene Revelation*
© 2009 by Perri Birney

This book is a work of fiction. With the exception of a few historical characters, including Walter Stein, names, characters, places and incidents are products of the author's imagination.

Photo credits:
Karmapa Flag - 16th Gyalwang Karmapa
Heilige Lanze (Spear of Longinus) - Kunsthistorisches Museum, Wien
Meditative Woman - Devyani Saltzman
Woman in Jerusalem - Reuters
Kalachakra Symbol - Larry Birney
Cover Design - Angelina Birney

Song lyrics from Raising Cain and All the People copyrighted by Pure Vision Communications, Inc. All rights reserved.

Library of Congress Control Number: 2008926921
ISBN: 978-0-9817482-2-1
ISBN-10: 0-9817482-2-8

Published by
Pure Vision Communications
P. O. Box 481
High Falls, NY 12440

Website: www.purevision.us
e-mail: purevision@peoplepc.com

PRINTED IN THE UNITED STATES OF AMERICA

For all the people in the world.

ACKNOWLEDGMENTS

Many thanks to all those who inspired the writing of this book, including Trevor Ravenscroft, author of *The Spear of Destiny* and John Michell, author of *The Temple at Jerusalem: a Revelation*. Both of these books are published by Samuel Weiser. Quotations from the *Spear of Destiny* appear on pages 66, 75 and 163 of *Pure Vision*. A quote from *Jesus Lived in India*, written by Holger Kersten, is cited on page 252.

The *Sefer ha-Zohar*, the thirteenth century Kabbalah classic, is one of the world's most profound spiritual masterpieces. A passage from the Pritzker edition is included on page 141.

An acknowledgment of appreciation also for the pioneering efforts of Nicholas Roerich who helped convey the Shambhala myth to the West. The excerpt on page 270 is from Roerich's *Altai-Himalaya*.

For readers who would like to learn more about the great prophet, Jeremiah, Jack R. Lundbom's translation and commentary in The Anchor Bible series is a treasure trove of information.

And finally, the author is especially grateful to all those teachers and spiritual friends who have helped bring this novel to life. This includes a special thank you to a dear friend, Frank Didero, whose generosity and encouragement will always be remembered.

The spirit of truth and falsehood
Struggle within the heart of man.
Born out of the spring of Light is truth
From the well of darkness, falsehood.
Accordingly, as a man inherits truth
So will he avoid darkness.

—Manual of Community
The Dead Sea Scrolls

PROLOGUE

IN THE DARK NIGHT OF INDIA, within the courtyard of the Temple of Vimala, the silent stone statues sat like watchmen. Their gaze fell upon all who entered the holy grounds. Unseen among the shadows, Sri Kailas waited patiently until the last elder left the temple. Once alone, the young Brahmin priest crossed the garden grove, closing the massive iron gate behind him as he entered the main chamber. The *one flame* was still lit—a large open oil lamp that cast light throughout the room.

The slate floors were cold, but the priest removed his shoes as always. With each step, the chill heightened his senses. Shadows of the statues, Vishnu and Krishna, Lakshmi and Saraswati, moved across the floor like gods in a cosmic dance. *They have always watched. They have always seen,* he thought.

Kailas reached his hand under his shawl, nervously removing the small chisel and mallet he had hidden beneath his garments. At the feet of Vishnu, in the corner of the stone edifice, he tapped the chisel firmly in a straight line several inches from the edge of the base. A thick layer of stone fell away to reveal an opening. Trembling, he reached his fingers inside and pulled out a thin leather pouch, knowing it contained the precious document.

A creaking from the gate and the sudden approach of voices startled him. Kailas leapt to his feet and moved quickly, securing the pouch under his robe. Just as he dashed behind a wide marble pillar at the back of the temple, a *sadhu,* the Hindu high priest, entered. A tall, dark-skinned gentleman followed just behind him. Dressed in a dark blue suit, the man bore the air of a dignitary. Holding his breath, Kailas watched as the two men walked to the foot of the Vishnu statue. The sadhu's body stiffened and his eyes widened with alarm when he saw the hole at the base.

"Kyā!" the high priest yelled, a look of disbelief on his face. His eyes darted across the room. *"Sac!"*

"Kyā bāt he?" the gentleman with him responded angrily.

Unable to hold back any longer, Kailas acted quickly. He turned and rushed through the long narrow corridor that led out the rear of the temple. Angry voices shouted for him to stop as he raced across the grounds, over the low stone wall and into the forest. Running hard, as fast as he could, Kailas felt the speed bestowed to him by the *nagas* of the woods. *The gods must protect the protector.*

With his breathing in sync with every stride of his powerful legs, Kailas kept his destination in mind. Now the secret, hidden by the Apostle Thomas in Madras nearly two thousand years ago, would travel to another land, and he, an emissary of *the Way,* would guard it on its journey.

Five thousand miles away in Vienna, in the dimly lit recesses of the Shatzkammer Museum, Ladislaus Almasy sat at his massive mahogany desk unable to take his eyes off the simple object before him. Resting on a red velvet setting was the ancient relic—a dark, iron blade. Silver, gold and copper wire threaded around the tarnished metal, securing a long nail within a shallow notch on its surface.

The Spear, thrust into the side of Christ by the Centurion Longinus, and the nail was from the true cross. Almasy could scarcely believe it. For the first time since he had become director of the Imperial Treasury, the lance was out of its protective display cabinet, where he could touch it. He didn't dare.

Tonight the Holy Lance, the Spear of Longinus, was to be taken to the university so metallurgy tests could be performed—all part of a television documentary. *Some more ridiculous maneuvering by the Board,* Almasy thought, smirking. *How little they knew about security.*

In fact, it had actually been Almasy's decision to transfer the blade late at night, secretly. He knew his subordinates thought he was being excessive, but after tonight, none of them would question his decisions again.

He glanced at his watch. It was almost time—midnight. There was a soft knock at the door.

"Herr Director?"

Almasy closed the leather case over the blade and placed the container inside an aluminum attaché case. He spun the tumbler locks and fastened the handle to his wrist with a security strap. *Where the Spear goes, I go.*

Almasy strode out of his office, his long legs propelling him forward through the Treasury hallway. Upon seeing him, the two armed guards waiting for him in the corridor scurried to catch up. According to plan, they would exit together through the Reichkanzleitrakt and the apartment once used by Emperor Franz Josef.

The night air was brisk as the three men emerged from the rear of the building. Across the street, in front of the *Burggarten* entrance, three sleek black armor-plated BMW sedans and their drivers were waiting for them. *Good,* Almasy thought when he saw them. *Everything is in place.* As soon as he climbed into the middle car, doors slammed, tires squealed and the convoy raced past the Mozart Memorial onto the Ringstrasse toward the University of Vienna, only fifteen minutes away. A smile of contentment crossed Almasy's face as he leaned his head back and closed his eyes.

Moments later, as the sedans turned into the dark Volksgarten Park, the sound of crunching metal and screeching brakes breached his countenance. *A plan within a plan.*

Almasy's driver reacted quickly, slamming down on the brakes and bringing their car to an abrupt halt. His heart racing, Almasy gripped the door handle and peered through the window. Jagged beams of light slashed across the central fountain ahead. He then saw the lead sedan laying on its side, smashed by a massive dump truck.

Several men rushed Almasy's convoy. The black metal of small Uzis shone by the car windows as the men flanked the vehicles.

"Aus, aus!" A heavyset man, stout like a bull, aimed a remote control at the cars.

The locked doors of the sedans snapped open.

"You! Come with us!" the man ordered as another armed gunman pulled Almasy from the car.

Barely on his feet, Almasy heard several short rounds of gunfire as he was shoved into a van. Just before the side door was slammed shut, he glanced at the crushed BMW, a rear tire spinning aimlessly, the Ingolstadt name on its bumper. *An appropriate sign,* he mused, since Ingolstadt, Bavaria was also the home of the renowned, grotesque figure known as Dr. Frankenstein as well as of the secret order of the *Illuminaten.*

Almasy smiled to himself. *Monsters and mystics.* After tonight, the only monsters and mystics the world would require would come through P2, and he would be part of it.

As the van sped away from the scene, Almasy stared into the grave-like park grounds. The headlights from the abandoned BMWs cast eerie traces of red and yellow beams across the baroque-sculpted gardens, while in the distance, the sound of sirens bellowed, initiating what he knew would be a futile pursuit.

Now, sitting amidst the watchful eyes of his captors, Almasy knew what was expected. He removed the wrist strap and spun the tumblers, unlocking the aluminum case that held the precious treasure. He then handed the case to the formidable man across from him. "As you promised," Almasy insisted, "I go where the Lance goes."

"Of course." The leader, a small but powerfully built man, smiled in confirmation. "Your plan worked excellently, Signore Almasy."

"Thank you, Captain Volpi." Ladislaus Almasy was pleased. The patience that had been his virtue for so many years would now bear him fruit.

Volpi opened the attaché case and the leather box within. Appearing satisfied, he looked up and nodded at his huge bullish bodyguard.

Before he knew what was happening, Almasy felt a garrote-style noose tightening around his neck. Choking, the fear raged through him as he struggled desperately against the inevitable. All the while he stared into the cold vacuum of Volpi's eyes, horrified that it would be the last thing he would see on this earth.

CHAPTER 1

MICHAEL SONADA WAS SIPPING his morning coffee and squinting at the world when the telephone rang. He groaned and shook his head. Gazing out the window of his Brooklyn apartment onto the sunlit trees of Pierrepont Street had provided some buffering. The last thing he needed was to jabber on the phone and have his headache elevated into a hangover.

Michael glanced half-heartedly at the caller ID. *Area code 32—somewhere in Europe.* Now curious, he answered. "Hello."

"Doctor Sonada?"

Michael hated the title. Doctors were healers, not Ph.D.s in History and Middle Eastern Studies.

"Speaking."

"I'm calling from the Office of the European Union in Brussels. Please hold."

Who in the world could be calling from the EU?

"Michael." The crisp voice was cool and cosmopolitan, with barely a trace of accent. "Giovanni Mabus. I'm glad to catch you at home. Do you remember me?"

"I certainly do." The president of the European Commission and one of the richest men in the world—it was hard to forget him.

"Excellent. I wonder . . . I'm flying to New York and would like to meet with you if I may. It's rather important. I should say it's rather *historically* important."

History—the key word. Michael's first novel, *Africa's Fox,* an adventure based on the life and undoing of General Erwin Rommel had been on *The New York Times* best-seller list for the last five months. Writing it had been a welcome departure from scholarship and analysis. Prior to his escape into fiction, Michael had spent fifteen years as a senior member of a translation team studying the Dead Sea Scrolls.

"I have a parchment fragment that I would like you to examine," Mabus announced.

"In that case, I can recommend several qualified scholars." Michael had tried hard to escape that tedious and dry academic world. His desire now was to bring history alive through adventurous fiction.

"I can make it *well* worth your while."

The baiting in Mabus' voice gave Michael pause. He had turned down a couple of projects recently, no longer letting money be his deciding factor. "No, thank you, I'm—"

"It concerns the Third Temple," Mabus added quickly.

Michael's curiosity was instantly piqued.

"Preliminary examinations say the author might be Jeremiah."

Shocked and fully awake, Michael sat up alertly in his chair. "You already have a translation?"

"Yes, but I'd like you to be part of the confirmation process."

The importance of such a find, if it was real, was too great of a lure. Michael found himself giving in to the inevitable. "When would you like to meet?"

"I'll have a driver at your apartment at seven thirty this evening. I look forward to seeing you, Dr. Sonada."

Michael heard the click from the other end of the line before he could provide his street number. No doubt, though, that a man of Mabus' connections knew where he lived. He already had his unlisted phone number.

The principal stockholder of Mabus International, one of the largest oil and petrochemical firms in the world, calling me personally. Talk about a bolt from the blue. Nearing the end of a five-year presidency of the European Commission, Mabus was also a driving force behind an upcoming peace conference in Jerusalem.

Michael took a sip of his coffee. *A parchment . . . the words of Jeremiah actually found.* He was still reeling from the possibility. Jeremiah was one of the most powerful of the Old Testament prophets, an outspoken advocate of the individual's right to a personal relationship with God. Openly critical of the Temple hierarchy, he predicted the destruction of Solomon's Temple. Jeremiah also prophesied that the children of Israel would be "fed wormwood and given poisoned water and then scattered among nations." In the end, he was driven into exile for his efforts. Michael was not alone among scholars in his fascination with the man and his revelations. If the parchment was authentic, he would be reading the words of one of the greatest of all prophets.

Jeremiah and Mabus. What curious energy had drawn them together? *Jeremiah and Jerusalem.* A twenty-five hundred-year-old link. Was a new, significant chapter unfolding?

Looking up at the clock, he remembered the eleven thirty talk being given at Riverside Church by Maggie Seline. Her book, *Pure Vision: The New Jerusalem,* had created a great deal of controversy and discussion. Her bold premise proposed Jerusalem itself to be the Third Temple and advocated internationalizing the city. The idea had stirred powerful emotions, attracting both advocates and detractors from around the world.

If it had not been for his association with Maggie's father, Michael might have passed on even reading the book. He remembered the interview he had given David Seline, the *Washington Post* correspondent, while he was in Israel reviewing some documentation on the Dead Sea Scrolls. Now it was Seline's daughter, Maggie, who was receiving the acclaim.

Only two days ago, Michael had gotten an e-mail from her.

> *Dr. Sonada,*
>
>   *I hear you're writing a book on the Longinus Spear. I'm doing some research on it myself, as well as on its connection to the Grail and Shambhala myths. I'd like to talk to you. Could we meet this Saturday?*
>
>   *Maggie Seline*

He was flattered, surprised that she had contacted him, especially since he knew nothing about this *Shambhala* myth she referred to. He went ahead, though, and made the arrangements with Seline's assistant to get together after her talk at the Riverside. He had to admit meeting her would be intriguing enough.

As Michael grabbed his copy of Maggie's book and headed out the door, he couldn't help but wonder: *What would Jeremiah have to say about a woman like this?*

CHAPTER 2

LOOMING OVER the Upper West Side, the Riverside Church stood like a gothic sentinel. The surrounding streets were closed to traffic and overflowing with people as Michael made his way toward the towering cathedral. A crowd of protestors, confined to the area of Grant's Tomb, were deep in the throws of battle, yelling and stamping their feet.

"The kingdom of God is upon us! The kingdom of God is upon us!"

Scattered within the large group were several people vigorously waving Israeli flags. One young man mounted the steps of the tomb and set up a tall wooden cross, his message written on it in bold black letters.

THE RAPTURE IS NEAR

On the same corner, a choir sang fervently. "Mine eyes have seen the glory of the coming of the Lord. He is trampling out the vintage where the grapes of wrath are stored." A large poster of Haram al-Sharif in Jerusalem that omitted the Dome of the Rock mosque and instead sported a huge new Temple leaned against a tree beside them.

Across the street, below the Women's Porch of the church, Maggie Seline's supporters were chanting the lyrics of *Give Peace a Chance*, while overhead, the stone figures of Mary, Martha, and the Angels of the Apocalypse oversaw the spectacle. Four hundred feet above them bearing witness, looking toward the four quarters of the midday sky, were the four archangels: Gabriel the messenger, Raphael the guardian, Uriel the interpreter of prophecy, and Michael the protector, with his spear thrust firmly into a dragon.

New York's finest kept a firm divide between the two groups. Mounted police rode their horses down Riverside Drive while their colleagues on foot stood beside bright blue barricades marked *Police Line*. Michael guessed that church officials had requested the police presence.

They're not taking any chances.

When he finally reached Claremont Avenue on the east side of the church, Michael found it teeming with patrol cars and media vans. All along the street, technicians were wrestling with thick cables—informational arteries bundled like reeds—while reporters prepared notes and practiced presentations for their cameramen and producers.

Following the steady flow of the crowd, Michael weaved his way into Riverside Church and found a seat in one of the long pews toward the back of the nave. There, he sat quietly, feeling a sense of timelessness as he watched the sunlight pour through the stained glass windows. In this otherworldly space, Michael observed as one by one the rows filled with people eager to hear Maggie Seline . . . *the lady prophet . . . the naïve dreamer . . . the pot stirrer.*

By eleven fifteen, the unreserved seats in the nave were already full, and many people around him, Michael noticed, had actually brought along Seline's book. As he began paging through his own copy of *Pure Vision*, he felt a bit amazed. His initial reservations had actually shifted. He was becoming more intrigued by Maggie's bold solution to the Middle East crisis—the creation of an international city belonging neither to Israel or Palestine, a global spiritual community protected by the United Nations. Everyone would be welcome to visit the holy sites of the three major world religions. Spiritual tolerance and brotherhood would be the foundation of the city, ultimately making it a haven for *all* religions and spiritual traditions.

After all, Michael thought, *Maggie's ideas were rooted in the original proposal made by the UN back in 1947.* Michael marveled at the changing scope of his opinions. Was it the holy atmosphere of the Riverside that gave him the inner freedom to entertain the possibility. *Can you really create a field of dreams?*

Paging through the book further, he stopped at some passages he had highlighted in yellow:

> Religion is our link to the divine. You are returning back
> to the spirit, be it through Christianity, Islam, Judaism,

Buddhism, Hinduism, or any other form. In essence, all
viable religious teachings are paths to the ultimate truth,
reconnecting us back to the divine nature of all things.
Religions are tools, skillful means, but not ends unto
themselves. Once you begin to use religion as a pretext
for hating and harming others, you have broken the
connection. You are no longer practicing your religion.
You are no longer linked to the divine.

The nations of Israel and of the world are all
broken, like pieces of shattered glass. It is time for all of
us to come together and start anew, not with old ideas
about buildings that need to be erected and divisions
that need to be marked, but with the new idea of
restoring ourselves to unity with God and one another.
The Messiah is not coming while we destroy each other
and this world in the process, but only when we unite in
peace. Then we will be worthy of a Messiah because we
will have realized the greatness of our humanity.

When Michael had first heard about Seline's book, he thought it
was a naïve attempt to place a Band-Aid on a gaping, bloody wound.
Peace in the Middle East had been the goal of the greatest of leaders.
How could a woman reporter, with nothing but her vision and passion,
offer so much hope, create so much turmoil, and shake the political pundits off their high horses? Was Seline only stating Jerusalem's unfulfilled
destiny, or was hers just a cry in the dark?

He would have to see.

Maggie Seline sat quietly in the second row of the first floor Christ
Chapel of the Riverside, a place where Nelson Rockefeller had taught
Sunday school. Soon she would be speaking from the very pulpit where
Martin Luther King, Jr. had railed against segregation and taken his
controversial stand against the Vietnam War.

How did I even get here? she wondered.

As she faced the altar, staring at the stone *reredos* that portrayed
the Last Supper and the Transfiguration, Maggie felt the stirrings of her

Catholic upbringing—the grammar school full of nuns, the parades of children, herself among them, marching through the streets singing . . . *This little light of mine, I'm gonna let it shine* . . . Catholic High School . . . when the nuns stopped wearing the traditional long habits, instead winning certain freedoms . . . knee-length skirts, even contemporary hairstyles.

Yet even back then, none of it seemed to matter. Maggie had realized early on that the Church could never fill her need. There had to be more to Christ than endless homilies and outdated dogmas. Didn't even *He* go beyond religion, deep into the spirit to find truth and awareness?

Her own spiritual aperture dilated during the summers she spent with her father in Jerusalem. Throughout those visits, she could see for herself the sufferings of the Israelis, the proud nervous Jewish soldiers, the wide-eyed vulnerability of the Palestinians—all living with tragedy, all desperate for a homeland to call their own.

Her father, forever the advocate, wrote about the injustices suffered by peoples throughout the world. In the last twelve years of his life, David Seline concentrated mainly on the Israeli-Palestinian conflict, a dilemma that weighed heavily on his mind.

The last time she had seen him, they were sipping lemonades at an outdoor café in the Gaza Strip, where they often sat watching the passersby. Her father reminded her then, as he had so often, that the world would never be at rest until the Middle East had found peace.

"This is such a volatile place, Mag, yet so many are connected to what's happening here." His simple words would one day prove to be the impetus behind her own actions. "A city of peace is what we need."

Her father the visionary . . . her father the torchbearer. Had he foreseen his own death that day?

As Maggie began to refocus her mind, she paid inward homage to the fact that it was his work and his powerful feelings that had influenced her so much, until she found herself doing the inevitable: writing with a purpose.

Maggie looked up toward the stone carvings on the chapel wall. Surrounding the depictions of Christ's life were images of the prophets of the house of Jesse. In particular, it was Isaiah who held the most meaning for her. He had also prophesied about the appearance of a Messiah.

A shoot will spring from the stem of Jesse, and a branch
from his roots will bear fruit. This Messiah will bear
the spirit of understanding, wisdom, counsel and
strength. He will judge not what he sees or hears but
will decide with fairness and the words he speaks will
slay the wicked. A sign of his coming shall be the wolf
dwelling with the lamb and the leopard laying with the
goat.

But Maggie knew she was not of the "seed of Jesse." She wasn't even Jewish. What right did she have to prophesize about Jerusalem? By whose authority did she cast her vision among all those . . . men? Wasn't that part of the problem . . . not only were they all men, they were all dead?

This new Jerusalem was *alive*—it was *now*. Not a vague prophecy for future generations but a here-and-now proposition for action. Maggie felt the pain of the mothers . . . mothers who had lost their children to war. She spoke for those weary of violence. She neither sought nor feigned justification for her prayer. It was simple, from the heart. Pray for peace, and let Jerusalem be its capital.

A stately black gentleman dressed in a light gray suit entered the chapel. The pin on his lapel, a small white dove, caught Maggie's attention. He nodded for her to rise, indicating the pastor of Riverside was about to introduce her to the audience.

Michael's eyes were riveted as Maggie Seline stepped out from the rear of the altar. Dressed simply in a light green blouse and black slacks, she strode toward the front of the two hundred-foot-long nave. The morning sunlight, filtering softly through the circular stained glass windows, seemed to further accentuate her elegance. Tall, fair-skinned, with light brown hair and green eyes, she was at once formidable yet accessible. Michael sensed an open-heartedness, a *simpático,* that immediately drew him.

It had only been several months ago that he caught her interview on *Good Morning America.* Gone was the seductive, voluptuous, earthy vitality that had so disturbed women and intrigued men. In its place was an aura of calm certainty and a radiant strength that inspired contemplation and dignity. This was a woman who had succeeded in life by rousing deep emotion in the people she interviewed. Now, quite the opposite, her presence brought forth a stunned silence.

"Hello, I'm Maggie Seline."

Maggie spoke softly, but the microphone pinned to her lapel picked up her resonant voice, amplifying it clearly throughout the nave, the assembly halls and the streets outside the church.

"I am told by those I've heard on television that I have been engaged in prophecy, which is the domain of men. Perhaps I should return to sorcery for which women are reputed to have a certain notoriety in the last two thousand years."

Amidst the laughter, Maggie heard a bit of snickering ascent. No matter what the sentiment, all eyes were upon her.

"One thing's for certain. Whether prophecy or sorcery, I am convinced we all have an obligation. That obligation is to take our collective heads out of the sand. We need to help each other become more aware of the problem that exists in the Middle East and make it our problem—not something simply happening over there somewhere," she said, waving her hand into the distance, "but something real and present and just as dangerous for everyone in our world today, including ourselves here in New York and in the United States, as it is for the Israelis and Palestinians. If we do not become more aware, then we are missing the boat."

Maggie allowed her eyes to sweep over the crowd for a moment. Was she connecting?

"Communication is the key. That is why I am here today. I will not waste your time or mine, so I'll come right to the point. There can be no political, economic or military solution to the problems existing in the Middle East. The only solution is a spiritual one. The holy land of old Jerusalem must become an international peace zone, not belonging to any one country or government . . . a spiritual community for all nations. The home of three great religions—Judaism, Islam, Christianity—must be protected as a refuge for those seeking God and enlightenment no matter what their religious or spiritual tradition. Then Jerusalem will fulfill its own destiny and become what it is meant to be. A city of turmoil will finally become the City of Peace."

Maggie believed it with all her heart. Passion and commitment had to be the key.

"That is why today our voices must cry out, *No more!* No more will we stand by and allow governments to murder, commit genocide in the name of religion or with racial superiority as their justification. We must stand together to face the demons. Those *demons*, first and foremost, are our own prejudice and hatred. When we're able to face them down, then we'll have a chance of creating peace."

"Ms. Seline!"

Maggie heard the voice from the crowd. She had wanted to invite questions or comments later, but the young man wearing the *Youth for Christ* shirt was insistent.

"Are you saying, Ms. Seline, that the Israelis don't have the right to protect themselves, or that the Arabs should just stand by if someone from their family is being murdered? If you have the power to destroy your enemy, shouldn't you?"

Maggie had been asked the question before. Emotions were always hot and complicated around the issue and the answer never came easily to her. Yet, every time Maggie answered it, her resolve grew stronger. "So your question is 'Why not use the ring?' "

"Pardon?" the man stared, baffled by her response.

"Why not use the ring?" Maggie enjoyed referencing Tolkien's classic. "Like in *The Lord of the Rings*, sir."

Nods of recognition came from fellow admirers of the heroic volumes and the film.

"In the book, there is a character called Boromir who came from one of the lands being attacked and overtaken by an overlord. Although Boromir was a good man at heart, he was suddenly consumed by the power of the ring, an object which had been formerly used by the enemy for their own gain and power, conquering whoever stood in their way, including Boromir's people."

"I still don't see your point," the young man said drily.

"The point is," she said, keeping her cool, "just because you gain possession of the ring, it doesn't mean you should use it. If you have the power to kill others, you shouldn't just go ahead and do it. Acquiring power for its own sake, so you can dominate and abuse others for your own gain is the oldest schemata on earth. Revenge is not the answer.

Perhaps the wisest thing would be not to use the ring, but to get rid of it."

Maggie expected some form of contention, but instead the man was silent. Apparently out of steam, he slouched back into his seat.

"Maybe they all need to be killed!" The stinging statement came from the back of the church. A tall man wearing black from head to toe stood in the aisle defiantly.

Another mind set in stone, Maggie thought, taking a deep breath. She surveyed the faces in the crowd, most looking disturbed and appalled.

"Sir," she addressed him, "how will we attain peace if the killing doesn't stop?"

"Israel is being terrorized," he answered vehemently as he started up the aisle toward her. "Arabs wish us dead. And you . . . you are a dangerous simpleton!" The man's voice echoed through the nave. "Dangerous to the Jewish people of Israel."

Several security officials, spurring into action, moved quickly down the aisles.

"You do not know what you speak of," he accused. "You know nothing of the suffering of my people."

As the man reached the front of the church, two of the security officers grabbed hold of him and began tugging him back toward the exit.

"Fighting for what is justly ours has been the only way. You wish to give away what you do not own." As the guards pulled him through the door, he cried out in torment. "You do not own Jerusalem! You have no right to her!"

A stunned silence enveloped the crowd. Maggie stood at the pulpit quietly wondering how much the man had suffered to make him hate so much. *Did he lose his wife, a brother, a child?* Finally, she was able to speak.

"There has been incredible suffering," she said softly. "Most of you, including myself, can never know the depths of the persecution and loss the Jewish people have faced. The Arabs, too, have gone through great atrocities. But do we keep on killing to avenge previous deaths? The question is: When will it end? How do we put a stop to it? We cannot change the past, so we must make a leap at some point."

Maggie's voice began to quiver. "What other way? I ask you. What other way?" A tear rolled down her cheek. Maggie slowly wiped it away.

The small release of emotion allowed the trembling in her legs to subside. Some degree of equilibrium steadied her mind.

Maggie sensed the breath of a collective sigh move through the crowd. She recognized that her genuine emotion was a source of relief.

"Let's face it," Maggie continued, a renewed strength in her voice. "The United States is still the most powerful nation on earth. We have a tremendous responsibility to use that power wisely. This is why it's the people—every man and woman—who need to take their own power back and question the dilemma we face in the Middle East. We must use our own minds to come to rational conclusions and not depend upon government-issued opinions that seem to have been concretized back in the Stone Age. We cannot hold a dogmatic view upon entire races of people and expect any wisdom to come of it."

Her words struck a chord. Maggie was only telling them what they already knew.

"Let us begin simply with our own individual integrity," Maggie appealed, "so we can stand up and begin to speak out to denounce the injustices and atrocities, so we can unite in a stand for peace on humane terms, based on common sense. Even back in 1948, when the Universal Declaration of Human Rights was proclaimed by the United Nations, they recognized that 'disregard and contempt for human rights have resulted in barbarous acts which have outraged the conscience of mankind.' This is all too true. I have personally witnessed children, barely twelve or thirteen-years-old, trying to attack a Jewish settlement with some knives and a grenade. This is what it has come down to—a people so degraded and terrorized that young children are willing to fight, willing to die in order to be freed from such horror. Can we stand by and watch this occur any longer?"

A young blond woman raised her hand.

"Yes," Maggie acknowledged.

"I know you're asking everyone to act, but with all of our so-called progress, women still don't have enough influence. It seems to me it's really the men who have screwed up."

"Yea . . . that's right . . . you said it . . ." Several listeners concurred.

"You're right about one thing," Maggie said. "We definitely need more balance. More women need to be in places of leadership and responsibility. Aggression is what has brought us to this calamity, and it's now time to allow the pendulum to swing back toward the feminine—toward nurturing rather than destroying, understanding rather than fighting."

Maggie paused. Although filled with more than a thousand people, the nave was like a deep, silent well. "Today, I call upon all women to stand up and help guide the direction of our world with the wisdom that it so desperately needs. It is time for the feminine energy to prevail and establish a new age, a dawning that will bring peace and tolerance in our time. The fact is, there is no time left. If we do not change direction now, away from aggressive patriarchal policies, we are going to self-destruct."

In front of her, suspended above the gallery, was a twenty-foot high Ascendant Christ gilded in gold. Below that, the long pipes of the Trompeta Majestatis organ reached out into the divine space. As she stood within the mandala of the church, Maggie felt enraptured. In that sacred space, she believed in the pure vision of her mind. She believed in its ability to invoke a *new* Jerusalem and hoped all who heard her would imagine the same.

"Our time has come as one people, of many faiths, to offer Jerusalem to God, whose voice we have invested so much energy in ignoring. Let us call upon the peoples of Israel and Palestine to lift their hearts and tell the creator that the long battle between Cain and Abel, Isaac and Ishmael, is over. Then the Third Temple will be complete. The city of Jerusalem shall itself be our shrine."

Although there were undertones of disapproval, the vast majority of the crowd overwhelmed the nave with loud applause. Many stood in ovation, including the Rev. Robert Milstrom, who had witnessed some of the most impassioned speeches in American history. As he moved toward Maggie with outstretched arms, she detected a glimmer of hope and inspiration emanating from his eyes and a look on his face that posed a question.

Could it be?

CHAPTER 3

ONCE HER TALK WAS OVER, Maggie was escorted down the center aisle of the nave. She had definitely exposed a nerve, she sensed, as she made her way through the dense maze of people all discussing her message passionately. At once angry, hopeful, exuberant, tense, haughty, even cynical, all the voices seemed to have been strongly affected by the event.

She moved quickly through the building's large entrance foyer now awash in photoflash and television camera lights. Reporters anxious to file their stories were pointing their microphones like swords at some of the diplomats and celebrities, who were all too happy to add their spin to the event.

"In reality, the Palestinian people have suffered long and now will . . ."

"The idea is brash and arrogant. Typically American . . ."

"Jerusalem belongs to the nation of Israel . . ."

"An interesting idea. It deserves careful consideration . . ."

"Stupid and naïve . . ."

Just as several journalists were dashing over to her, she noticed Michael Sonada standing in the crowd just outside the entrance. She ran up to him and grabbed him by the hand.

"Dr. Sonada," she said, noting the look of surprise in his eyes. "Sorry to be so forward, but I'm about to be ambushed with questions. Could you please come with me?"

"Of course," he said, nodding sympathetically.

Maggie pointed across the street and the two sprinted.

When they reached the other side, Michael turned to her. "How did you know about my research on the Spear?"

"The *Enquirer*."

Michael stopped suddenly in his tracks. "What the—"

"Come on," she urged, pointing at several reporters who had seen their escape.

Maggie guided Michael around the corner and down a side street. She glanced over her shoulder, making sure the reporters hadn't turned down the block, before leading him through a narrow doorway and up a flight of stairs.

"Can I ask where we're going?" Michael questioned, tripping behind her.

"We're almost there," she replied as they hurried up the creaky wooden steps to the second floor.

When they reached the landing, there it was. *MOZAMBIQUE.*

Maggie was glad to see the same worn indecipherable sign hanging over the door. Her little hideaway in the city, dimly lit with alcove seating, the offbeat European-style café seemed the perfect place for a clandestine meeting.

After they found a table and placed their order, Maggie took note of Michael's looks for the first time. *Mid-forties, attractive, a little rough around the edges.* His brown eyes met hers as she began to speak.

"Dr. Sonada . . . "

"Michael, please," he said, smiling. "After holding hands, we should be on a first-name basis."

Maggie felt the blood rush to her cheeks. She liked him immediately. Her mentor had said that Michael Sonada was a man who could be trusted. Soon, she would find out.

"Before you even begin," Michael said, looking at her quizzically, "how in God's name did you find out that I was doing research on the Spear of Longinus . . . and from the *Enquirer* of all places?"

"Well apparently, you were seen in Vienna several months ago. The reporter following you there found out from one of the museum guards that you were questioning the curator about the Spear, so the article states."

"And *you* read the *Enquirer?*"

The look of astonishment on Michael's face made her laugh out loud. "You'd be surprised," she said. "The truth manages to leak out of the strangest places."

Michael shook his head.

Maggie was prepared for resistance. *If you think that's strange, wait till you hear the rest.*

"I've been investigating an energy deal," she said, "between Mabus International and an inventor, Stephen Einsof."

"Wait." Michael looked confused. "I thought this was about the Spear of Longinus. You mentioned the Grail myth and something called *Shambhala*. Was that the name . . . *Shambhala*?"

At that moment, the waiter arrived with two cappuccinos. Maggie waited until he set them down and was out of earshot before answering.

"Yes, that's right," she said, keeping her voice low. "But if you'll let me explain. There seems to be some kind of bizarre connection between them all. Apparently, during the vice president's international tour this year, one of his stops was the Hofburg Treasure House in Vienna."

"Where the Spear is housed."

"Exactly."

Michael took a sip of his cappuccino and looked up at her, amused. "Okay, so you've proven that he has an interest in artifacts."

"Just listen," Maggie insisted. "It goes further. Vice President Bohmer took a very *special interest*. He asked if the U.S. might sponsor the Spear being exhibited here in America. It turns out that the curator was up in arms."

"Okay . . . you have more of my attention," Michael said, his tone measured.

Maggie needed him to understand. After all, she had been told Michael was an important key. "The vice president tried very hard to cut corners and get the Spear to the U.S. but failed at his attempts. After it was all over, when he was asked about his special interest in the Spear, he just laughed it off as simply an interest in World War II memorabilia. Curiously, it was during this trip that the vice president also met with Wilhelm Pretzsche."

Michael's eyes lit up with recognition. "Are we talking about a relative of—"

"Ernst Pretzsche."

"He was an occultist who helped Hitler."

Maggie's voice fell another notch. "And was directly linked to Karl Haushofer."

"The Nazi occultist who was the head of the Luminous Lodge." Michael was visibly spooked. "The man was the spiritual advisor to Hitler."

Maggie nodded, the chilling association made her place her hands around the warm cappuccino cup. "He was the one who planted the seed that eventually sprouted into Heinrich Himmler's formation of the Nazi Occult Bureau—the *Ahnenerbe*. Those guys launched expeditions for Hitler, all in the name of finding and claiming ancient relics." She paused. "They wanted the Spear."

"And they knew exactly where it was . . . in Vienna." Michael's face became grim.

"Hitler was also searching for the Grail," Maggie added, "but in ways that were a lot more remarkable. He even commissioned Haushofer to send teams of explorers to Tibet."

Maggie could see that Michael was trying to process all the information. He looked up. His eyes searched hers.

"I know it's a lot to take in," she offered, "but what I really want to talk about here is a specific link that's been bothering me. The vice president, according to my source, is involved in the development of a radical energy system, something that would vie the petrol industry— threatening their stronghold, to say the least. It turns out that the final stop the vice president made in Europe was at the recent World Energy Forum held in Rome—the one co-sponsored by Giovanni Mabus."

Michael stared at her, knitting his eyebrows.

At that moment, Maggie realized she probably didn't sound as coherent as she would have liked. "In any case, the article I've written will expose Bohmer's connection, not only to the alternative energy system itself—developed under Mabus' auspices—but to its monopoly. It'll be printed in tomorrow's edition of the *Times*. I've gotten a heads up, though, that some White House officials are trying to throw up roadblocks."

It was now Michael's turn to scan the café. "So you believe that all of them . . . the Spear, the vice president, Mabus . . . are linked."

"Call it reporter's intuition. The hook-up with Pretzsche, the Spear business, the meeting in Rome . . . I can't draw direct lines yet, but I just know they're connected."

"And why would you need me?"

Maggie had tried to prepare herself for this very moment. As she braced herself for some backlash, she felt her stomach tightening. "Well, actually . . . I need you to find something out from Mr. Mabus."

The look of astonishment on Michael's face quickly turned to anger. "What the hell . . . ? The man just called me this morning. How would you even know—?"

"I told you I have my sources. This one's from Jerusalem. You can't try to do something as incredible as building the Third Temple without a few outsiders finding out about it."

Michael's eyed widened.

Do I tell him now? Maggie hesitated. After all, she really didn't know this man. Even though he had been highly recommended by her mentor, there was no telling what kind of character he could turn out to be. But there was little time left for pondering. Maggie decided to reveal her hand, just a little.

"Michael," she whispered, "what I've been researching now could blow this whole New Temple proposal right out of the water. It's what I call the Shambhala theory. There is apparently a document—" Maggie stopped short. Her heart began to race as she recognized the dark-eyed man who entered the café.

Michael couldn't imagine what was going on with Maggie Seline. She looked like she had just seen a ghost.

"Darling," she said playfully.

Now he was *really* bewildered.

"I'd love to go to that play. Pick me up around seven tonight, okay?" Seline got up and leaned across the table, planting a warm kiss on his cheek. As she nuzzled against his face momentarily, she whispered in his ear. "Gotta go. The man to your right's been following me for a week. Play along. I'll get in touch with you."

"Okay, sweetheart," he replied as she pulled away. "I look forward to it."

Michael watched as Maggie sauntered away. She was acting, as far as he could tell, yet he couldn't help feeling attracted.

After she was gone, Michael drank more of his cappuccino and looked about the room nonchalantly. The man who had been watching them quickly averted his eyes as Michael made contact. *Dark complexion, shoulder-length brown hair, mid-thirties perhaps.*

Michael took in as much as he could about the mysterious stranger before leaving the café. He moved quickly down the stairwell that led to the street, all the while turning to see if he was being followed.

What the hell is Maggie Seline getting me into?

Once outside, he felt nagged by a sense of dread. He hurried to find the nearest subway entrance and dashed down the steps into the tunnel. Suddenly, as the train roared into the station, he remembered he would be meeting with Giovanni Mabus that evening.

Oh for God's sake, he thought.

It was turning into the longest day of his life.

CHAPTER 4

B ACK IN HIS BROOKLYN HEIGHTS apartment, Michael
Sonada was annoyed with himself for an uncharacteristic in-
ability to decide what to wear. *Damn, it's not like visiting the
home of one of the world's richest men should be a big deal.* He settled on
casual slacks, a cashmere pullover and a sports coat, even taking the time
to make sure his socks matched.

Michael opened his closet door to view himself in the narrow, full-
length mirror. As he ran his fingers through his wavy brown hair, he
was certain he detected a few more grays. He sighed at the thought of
the color fading out of his life, but decided to cultivate the idea that the
strands made him look more distinguished. At least his eyes still retained
their soft brown hues, although today the whites of them were lined
with red, a testament to the little drinking party he had with himself the
night before.

At exactly seven thirty, the doorbell rang and Michael found himself
being escorted by a sporty-looking Italian chauffeur to a black Mercedes.
"Signor, this way to Mr. Mabus," was all the man said as he pointed to
the car door.

As Michael was whisked over the Brooklyn Bridge into Midtown
Manhattan, he recalled the night in Libya several years earlier when he
had met Giovanni Mabus. Michael had been in Tripoli doing research
for his novel about General Erwin Rommel and was invited to attend a
reception hosted by the Libyan government. Most of the guests, he had
been told, would be trade representatives, in the country for an electronics and communications fair.

The site of the event, the Al Mahari Hotel, overlooked the harbor and was the cosmopolitan showpiece of the city. Upon entering the
main ballroom, Michael found it was elegantly decked out with all the
refinements necessary, except of course, alcoholic beverages. Since the

revolution in 1969, there had been a strict adherence to the letter of the Quran regarding intoxicants.

Despite that, the guests were giddy. A rumor was circulating that Colonel Muammar Qaddafi himself would attend. Michael was anxious to observe him firsthand. Was he sane? Rational?

Across the ballroom, Michael noticed a group of trade show attendees jockeying to get close to one of the guests. A dark-eyed Mediterranean decked out in a radiant, white silk suit seemed to be the focus of all the attention. The man had a vulcan-like self assurance, surveying the scene around him with the ruthless ease and incisive eye of a Wall Street baron. Heads turned and eyes darted in his direction as more people became aware of his presence.

Michael turned toward one of the few other Americans present. "Who's that?" he asked, indicating the man in question.

"You mean the Modigliani sculpture?" Envious disdain was apparent in the American's voice. "That's Giovanni Mabus. He's said to be a key player in Qaddafi's circle. His father, Abu Nai'im, was the oil minister before Colonel Qaddafi's coup in 1969. The Italian wife and children, including Giovanni, were then semi-exiled to Italy ."

"Quite an interesting background," Michael said, drawn by the link to Qaddafi.

"Yes indeed," the friendly informant eagerly agreed. "The father, Abu Nai'im Mabus, rejoined the family after several years of 'captivity' so they say. In reality, his knowledge of the Libyan oil interests were simply too extensive to be cast aside by the fledgling, radical regime. Perhaps Qaddafi was captivated by the senior Mabus' mystique from his days in the Afrika Corp as native aide to General Rommel."

"He was Rommel's aide?" Michael hadn't acquired that bit of info.

"That's right, as well as an influential member of the Muslim Brotherhood. Abu Nai'im was said to have been one of the commandos who fought against Israel in the 1948 war as a member of the Special Order of the Brotherhood's militia. Like his father, the son reveals little of himself or his past."

Although he was drawn to meet Mabus, Michael resisted the pull to join the panting circle around him. He stepped outside instead, onto the hotel terrace. Refreshing himself with the cool harbor air, he watched as a magnificent sunset stirred across the horizon, magenta and crimson clouds seeming to fill the sky with flames. The scene only underscored the evenings events as Michael sensed that another movement in the long-running drama of the Mediterranean was about to unfold.

"Spectacular, isn't it?" A voice addressed Michael in flawless classical Arabic, the scholarly language of the Quran, as incomprehensible to most native speakers as Sanskrit would be to an average Hindu.

Michael turned to find Giovanni Mabus beside him. "*Ai'wa,*" he answered.

"Dr. Sonada, I was told your Arabic is quite good. I'm impressed." Mabus offered Michael his hand.

"Mr . . . ?" Michael played ignorant, but was certain Mabus wasn't fooled by the pretense.

"I apologize. Of course you don't know me," he said, playing along. "Giovanni Mabus."

"Of Mabus International?" Michael questioned.

"The same."

"Then I should apologize, quite careless of me."

"No need, Dr. Sonada, since I'm about to mix a little business with your pleasure. I'm told you are well-versed in Arabian studies."

Here it comes. Michael tensed. *Another job offer. Literary careers have floundered on lesser shoals than these.*

"I could use a man knowledgeable in research such as yourself," Mabus said. "It can be difficult for Arabs, especially Libyans, to communicate with Americans."

"You seem to be doing quite well."

"Ah." A charming smile spread across Mabus' smooth face. "What can one man do alone, as you say." He raised his hands to emphasize the question, exposing gold cuff links and a Patek Philippe watch. "You are here researching a book?"

"Yes, I am."

"History, or perhaps fiction?"

"Both—an historical novel about Erwin Rommel." Michael was hoping perhaps Mabus would mention his father's experience with the Desert Fox. "I find it's easier to tell the truth when you disguise it as fiction."

"That is quite true. Perhaps in your book, you'll be able to convey Libya's rich history as well as its culture with some authenticity." Mabus pointed across the harbor toward a large, flat-roofed squat structure. "Of course, you are familiar with the castle of the Barbary Pirates."

"From the halls of Montezuma to the shores of Tripoli," Michael responded.

Mabus smiled. "Beyond that, most western people are clueless as to the depth of our heritage. They are unaware that even long before the Romans built Leptis Magna, the world's culture included North Africa."

Just then, a young, sleek Arab gentleman almost as dashing as Mabus himself stepped up to Mabus' side and whispered something inaudible in his ear.

Mabus turned toward Michael. "I will have one of my associates provide you with all the necessary contacts during your visit." He bowed in a gesture of departing. "Now, if you would please excuse me . . . ."

Michael's musings ended when the chauffeur-driven Mercedes pulled up in front of a nondescript skyscraper on Fifth Avenue next to St. Patrick's Cathedral. Two men, well-tailored and definitely over-dressed by Michael's standards, quickly walked toward the Mercedes. One of them opened the car door for him while the other continuously surveyed the sidewalk.

"Dr. Sonada, this way please."

Michael was escorted around the corner, away from the Armani Exchange at the front entrance of the building. Inside a service entrance, beyond the Onassis Atrium, one of the men began to search Michael for weapons when his cohort stopped him. "The boss said no."

As they entered the elevator, Michael noticed it was richly apportioned despite its entry being in a service area. He understood why when he saw the guard push the lone button on the panel: PENTHOUSE.

After the elevator ended its climb, Michael exited with his silent companions and was ushered through the front door of the penthouse suite. The living room, where he was left to wait, was huge, spanning the full depth of the building. The Scandinavian furnishings were simple, yet elegant. No camel saddles or brocade leather ottomans for this Libyan. The south "wall", Michael noticed, was actually a thick smoke-colored glass window that reached from floor to ceiling, which allowed a clear view of the Manhattan skyline—including the Empire State Building topped in red, white and blue, the rocket-nosed Chrysler building jutting into the sky like an obelisk, and several blocks away, the domino-shaped Secretariat building of the UN.

Michael turned in time to see Giovanni Mabus walking down a gold-colored spiral staircase in the foyer. Wearing a pastel shirt, light tan slacks and canvas boat shoes, Mabus appeared as if was heading out to the beach or a polo match. Looking alert and fresh, nothing at all like a man who had flown in from Europe that afternoon, he entered the living room, his hand extended in greeting.

"Monsieur Mabus, *ahlan wi sahlan.*" As Michael greeted him, he felt his host's dark eyes surveying him intensely.

"*As-Salam alaikum,* Michael. Thank you for coming on such short notice."

Mabus then directed Michael to take a seat on the couch. "I have begun reading your new book, *Africa's Fox.* You include a lot of information I myself didn't know about the Afrika Corps."

Michael laughed. "Don't believe everything. It's a novel."

"No, no. I see how you work. You may play with the personal details but the historical details, never."

It was true, Michael went to painstaking lengths researching his book. Erwin Rommel had always fascinated him—everything about the man personally as well as the forces that finally drove him to participate in the plot against Hitler.

Just then, a houseboy swept into the room carrying a carafe on a large brass tray.

"Coffee, Michael?" Mabus invited.

"*Qahwa* is fine, thanks," Michael replied.

Mabus nodded, giving the young man approval to pour.

Well, I'll be up for the night now, Michael thought, knowing Arabian coffee to be the epitome of a super espresso. At the same time, he was grateful for the rush of clarity it gave him as he took a sip. It would help him to remember the life of a genius.

Since the time of their meeting in Libya, Michael had made a point of following Mabus' career as it was reported in the press. Few men would have been willing to walk away from a billion-dollar empire for five years, but Mabus did just that when Prime Minister Berlusconi had asked him to represent Italy at the European Commission, the organization that administers the day-to-day work of the European Union. He had also been charged with oversight of the EU's spending, treaties and laws. Now his term was coming to an end.

Giovanni Mabus is a true universal man, Michael had concluded. He embodied the principal characteristics Michael hoped to champion in his novels—he was decisive, brilliant and tough.

After taking another sip of coffee, Michael placed his cup down on the table. Mabus, he realized, had been politely waiting for him.

"Let me start by informing you that I was able to convince the European Parliament this week to co-host the upcoming Peace Conference in Israel," Mabus revealed. "The vote was taken in secrecy, so I suspect it will be a lead item in tomorrow's papers. This Peace Conference lies at the heart of the reason I asked you to meet with me."

Mabus paused and looked down at the palms of his hands. Michael waited silently for him to continue.

"I apologize for the short notice, but something has come up that may impact heavily on the conference, and I need the opinion of someone I can trust."

"Why would that someone be me?" Michael asked. Surely, Mabus wouldn't include him in his confidence based on a single conversation they had years earlier.

"For two reasons. You are an authority on ancient Hebrew and Aramaic texts. Quite well-respected, I might add. I have made inquiries, and your name carries the highest regard. Secondly, your writing displays a sensitivity to Arabian cultures that is both refreshing and sadly lacking in America."

"I'm flattered, but I'm quite fatigued by that world. The issues involve bickering over tiny shreds of evidence and then projecting large scenarios based on biased conclusions." Michael wanted nothing more to do with it.

"Well in that sense," Mabus said, "both the ancient texts as well as the regions they are from have not changed in the last three thousand years. But, *ins'Allah*, in this particular case, there might be a ray of hope. I only ask that you review the parchment that's been discovered before making a determination.

"Consider this," Mabus' tone grew heavier. "For five years I struggled every way I knew to bring the Palestinians and the Israelis together. I may have finally found the answer." Mabus picked up a briefcase next to his chair and set it on the table. "Professor Binah of Hebrew University and Doctor Mizrahi of the Egyptian Office of Antiquities have developed a theory that will allow the Third Temple to be built in Jerusalem. Yes, on Haram al-Sharif, the Temple Mount."

Michael took another sip of coffee. *Fat chance. What shaky evidence could they present?*

"I can see you are skeptical." Mabus accurately assessed Michael's thoughts. "I don't blame you."

"They feel the Temple can be built without displacing the Dome of the Rock?" Michael wondered what kind of fantasy he had wandered into. "That sounds like a formula for war, not peace."

"Many Arabs, myself included, feel Muslims and Jews are one people," Mabus said. "Two nations, one people, both descendent from Abraham. If allowing Jews to build a temple will lead to peace, then Allah will be served."

Mabus voice became more measured. "What I tell you now is confidential. I have persuaded the *waqf* authority that administers Haram al-Sharif to consider the idea of a Judaic presence on the Mount. In return, I have a tentative approval from the Israeli prime minister to consider relinquishing the entire area of the West Bank captured in 1967—settlements and all."

Michael let out a low whistle. "How were you able to do that?"

"By following the power lines," Mabus leveled. "The evangelical movement in America has been one of Israel's staunchest supporters, a posture that also allowed Clinton and Bush to contribute vast sums of money and support without need for reciprocity. The whole situation has been fueled by the fact that for two hundred years a continuous succession of Protestant ministers have been predicting an apocalypse. That means the pressure is on—either produce Jesus or lose their following. Since they haven't succeeded in triggering Armageddon, the next best thing is to build a Third Temple in the hope this will fulfill prophecy. To maintain their support, a skeptical Israeli government is willing to allow the conference to go forward."

Michael shook his head. He couldn't imagine them doing anything of the kind.

"These are only agreements to *consider* these issues," Mabus added quickly. "The clincher is that the United States would assume control of the West Bank from Israel until a further agreement becomes possible. This would also be a necessary condition in order to sell the plan to the

Israeli settlers. Needless to say, none of this can be discussed publicly until the Peace Conference is under way. If it leaks, radicals on either side could torpedo it."

Michael was finding this hard to believe. What Mabus was outlining would radically rewrite the face of Palestine and Israel. "Other than headaches, what does the United States get?"

"A long-awaited win." Mabus stared at him coldly. "The civil war in Iraq and the unstable governments in Afghanistan and Jordan have left the U.S. with only Morocco and Egypt as allies in the Muslim world. The former has no influence, the latter no credibility. Even Saudi Arabia's friendship is a myth. That leaves you with a War on Terror in tatters. Eventually even neo-cons must learn that poker without cards is a bad deal. And, like the Israelis, they need evangelical support."

Mabus paused, allowing Michael time to reflect on what he had heard. Meanwhile, he opened his briefcase and removed a manila envelope and a thick, hermetically-sealed glass case. Visible within the glass frame was a yellowed parchment approximately six-inches long and four-inches high. Mabus handed the case to Michael. "This was obtained for me several months ago at St. Catherine's Monastery at Mount Sinai."

If there was any plausible place on earth to discover a "lost" prophecy, it was in the sixteen hundred-year-old sanctuary. Michael was familiar with the monastery and its jealously guarded secrets. The site was so old and venerated that Muhammad himself issued a decree for its protection, a copy of which was still in the monastery's possession. Nonetheless, the monks' wall of secrecy about their treasures was penetrated in 1860 when a German, Constantin von Tischendorf, got one of the librarians drunk and smuggled out the *Codex Sinaiticus*, the oldest known copy of the New Testament.

In spite of his trepidation, Michael felt intrigued and excited being presented with what was possibly the written word of a man who had been dead for over twenty-five hundred years. It would have been easier to walk away from an idea, but he couldn't disregard tangible evidence. Without hesitation, he accepted the large magnifying glass Mabus handed him and began examining the parchment.

"You have a translation prepared?" he asked.

"In the envelope, along with a full copy of the scholars' theory and evidence. Also, there is a color photograph of both sides of the parchment." Mabus took back the glass case. "I will keep the original."

"You said this was found in the Sinai?"

"Yes. The jar it was in was still intact. Doctor Mizrahi himself broke the seal."

How convenient. Michael's natural suspicions were roused. *The author of the Temple plan was also the principal witness affirming the evidence vital to his case.*

Mabus eyed him as he continued. "Doctors Mizrahi and Binah feel that this text may be part of the lost scrolls of the prophesies of Jeremiah destroyed by King Jehoiakim."

"That would make this discovery equal in importance to anything found at Qumran."

"More importantly," Mabus added, "if their translation is correct and these are Jeremiah's words, it will go a long way toward possible Orthodox acceptance of the Third Temple. The carbon dating and paleographic examinations have been made. The results are early, but they show this document to be approximately twenty-two hundred years old."

"Carbon dating is at best rough and can only date the parchment, not the writing." Michael's intense training in analysis took over. "Paleography is *guesswork* that is only as good as the guesswork done on the writing to which you make a comparison."

"I'm asking you to comment on the translation only," Mabus asserted, unflinching. "There is no need for you to verify or refute the authenticity of the copy. If you feel it could be from Jeremiah, then that will add credibility to the upcoming Peace Conference. Of course, speed and secrecy are imperative.

"We must achieve peace." Mabus' voice became impassioned. "The flames of Palestine have already engulfed Iraq, Syria and Lebanon. Iran will soon follow. Jerusalem, *Yerushalayim*—Vision of Peace—is Isaiah's mountain. We all believe in prophecy, all the children of the book. We simply can't agree on which prophesies and what they mean."

Michael believed in one prophecy—Murphy's. If it could be screwed up, the human race would find a way. All people want health, peace and happiness. Unfortunately, for too many dreamers, one man's vision was another's nightmare. But on the other hand, Michael felt that if he could contribute in some small way toward resolving such a complicated and long-running struggle, he must.

"Very well." Michael finally conceded to the intrigue. "I will study this and get back to you."

"I need an answer in two days." Mabus responded to Michael's raised eyebrows with a smile and a shrug before planting the final seed. "You see those buildings?" he asked as he pointed out the window toward the UN complex. "The United Nations has been our symbol of hope for the last sixty years. With limited success and many setbacks, the world's nations have maintained a continuous dialogue because of it. I've no doubt the Assembly's approval for the Peace Conference is forthcoming."

Not knowing what to say, Michael remained silent.

"And with the UN behind us," Mabus added, "we will finally attain what has been so elusive—peace in the Middle East."

After Michael left, Mabus poured himself some sherry. As was his custom, he swirled the light red liquid around the crystal and enjoyed the aroma as he brought the glass to his lips, allowing the first sweet drops to settle on his tongue. *Use all the senses and extract all the pleasure. Wasn't that the objective?*

Just then his phone rang.

"Yes," Mabus answered.

"Do we have him?" It was one of the *Fratineri*. The man's voice betrayed his fear.

"He's a bit skeptical, but I'm not worried,' Mabus answered. "I'm certain Sonada's involvement will give us the impetus we need."

"What if he doesn't vouch for the parchment's authenticity? We cannot afford confusion."

Mabus was angered by the suggestion of failure. *Dealing with this fool now was necessary, but afterward . . .*

"There will be no confusion. Sonada's past credentials will prove the asset we need to succeed, and after all," Mabus added sarcastically, "he is an American."

The voice on the other end laughed. "Americans. Give them a title and there are no bigger fools. I apologize, Giovanni, for any glimmer of doubt."

"We are past doubt," Mabus said, knowing there was no turning back. "Now let us continue as planned."

CHAPTER 5

JUSTIN ERICKSON, Managing Editor of *The New York Times*, stared at the old ceiling fan he retained in his office. Air conditioning, although essential on hot, sweaty New York days, was a bit too insulating for Erickson's taste. He preferred the fan's Casablanca motion, easy and smooth, enough breeze to cool off the situation while still keeping you in touch with the atmosphere. Who ever heard of so much heat in mid-April anyway?

Earlier that evening, he had received a phone call. The official government big leaguers from Homeland Security seemed to know his office habits. As he sipped lukewarm coffee from a plastic cup, he wondered what they were up to. *Those bastards don't know when to stop.*

The buzzer on his desk went off. Erickson looked up at the clock on his wall. 7:46 P.M. A moment later, two gentlemen in dark gray suits entered his office. The elder, obviously in the lead, walked in as if shot by an arrow. The rookie following him, short but built like a boar, emitted the aura of a defensive tackle there to support his superior. Erickson's radar for trouble was immediately amplified.

"Mr. Erickson, I'm Chief Inspector Richards." Intense and eagle-eyed, he nodded at Erickson. "And this is my associate, Special Agent Benedict Greer."

Erickson pointed at the two chairs in front of his desk. "I hear the secretary of Homeland Security is not pleased about an article we plan to publish in tomorrow's Sunday edition."

"You've heard correctly, sir." Richards laid it on the line. "We're here to ask you not to run it."

"It's a legitimate piece," Erickson defended, "well-researched, with an unquestionable source. I see no reason not to print it."

"We do."

Erickson didn't like the sternness in Richard's voice. "And what does that mean?"

"It's your journalist who's in question," Richards declared, tapping on the editor's desk. "The DHS does not wish someone who is under investigation to be writing articles that are not only inflammatory, but make accusations that can directly result in a possible threat to national security."

"Woa, just a second here." Erickson was taken aback by the ridiculous accusation. "You're saying Maggie Seline is being investigated? On what grounds?"

Richards nodded toward Greer, directing him to speak. Erickson had come aground on the younger man's turf.

"There is now evidence," Greer announced definitively, "that Al Qaeda operatives have gained further support and momentum due to Seline's siding with Arab dissent and hostilities. They have issued another video to Al Jazeera citing that if Israel persists in refusing to pull out of the West Bank and to stop terrorizing Arabs in the region, and the U.S. government continues to support Israeli interests, there will be several attacks in the forthcoming weeks. Al Jazeera has decided not to air the video because of the potential chaos it would cause."

"How considerate of them." Erickson had learned the tricks of the trade long ago. It wasn't the first time federal officers had tried to put the kibosh on an important story. "It seems rather convenient that the Qatar-based TV station would suddenly be sensitive to the needs of the U.S. Department of Homeland Security. It's also interesting that you have evidence that Seline's somehow associated with an Al Qaeda threat."

Steely-eyed, Richards ignored Erickson's sarcasm. "In essence, the woman's been a propagandist for the Arab cause, and we have her linked to a specific known terrorist in Jerusalem. We've been given a directive straight from the White House. The *Times* should give serious regard to our national interest."

Erickson remained quiet. He drummed his pencil on his desk, looking up occasionally. He had been in the army once, Vietnam, and knew that often the best tactic was silence.

Rolling his chair back from his desk, Erickson stood up. "I appreciate your stand. Now let me tell you mine. Although you come into this office making accusations, you have not offered me a shred of evidence to back your claims. This newspaper has a reputation of presenting truthful accounts based on factual evidence. We are not in the habit of killing off legitimate, well-researched articles founded on sound sources that are written by impeccable journalists. The answer to your request is an emphatic *NO*. The story runs."

The two men rose from their seats. Greer's smile could not have appeared colder.

"Here then." He tossed a document onto Erickson's desk. The bold letters **FEDERAL COURT ORDER** appeared at the top of the page. "Since you're unwilling to comply with your government's request, we have no choice but to issue this order. You will not run the story or the *Times* will face the consequences."

Erickson knew there was nothing left to say. They had him in a corner. "Well, since you all are so determined, I'll pass this on to my publisher." Erickson grimaced as Richards and Greer walked out of his office. *But this isn't over,* he thought.

Erickson had put on a poker face for the bullies from Homeland, but now alone, he faced facts. He knew Josephs, the *Times'* publisher, would take the matter to court, but only after putting a stop to the article being printed. There's no way he would jeopardize the paper with a lawsuit or risk being thrown in jail.

Erickson pressed the buzzer on his desk. His secretary, Chelsea, walked in and gave him a questioning glance, apparently aware that he had just been worked over.

"Yes, Justin."

"Get Seline on the phone. Tell her I want to see her right away in my office."

"Sure thing."

"After you talk to Seline," Erickson added, "get a hold of our commander in chief, Josephs. It seems we have a problem with our government."

Chelsea, with raised eyebrows, silently left the room.

How long will these fascists put a stranglehold on the media? Newspapers, Radio, Television . . . Erickson pondered the question that had been rearing its head over the last several years with more force. There came a time when Joseph McCarthy had wrapped the U.S. government around his little finger, instilling fear in the nation, terrorizing citizens until a group of reporters decided to expose him for the fraud he was.

Maybe it was time to face the enemy again, head on.

But Erickson realized his bold thought was like a lone buoy bobbing in the ocean. He sank back into his chair. The days of gutsy reporting had gone the way of television antennas and hard-line telephones.

This doesn't look good.

When Maggie entered Erickson's office, she could tell by the weary look on his face that whatever battle he had been waging had been lost.

"We're killing the Mabus story."

The words from Erickson's lips landed on Maggie like a ton of bricks. She had been warned by her source that Homeland might come after her, but she had expected Erickson to keep his backbone.

"What are you talking about?" In an instant, she felt the blood rush from her face.

Erickson stood by the large glass window behind his desk, looking down on Forty-third Street below, his normal self-assurance shaken. Maggie knew he liked watching the masses, referring to the people pulsing along the avenue as currents of electricity that charged the whole city. The spectacle was a meditation to him, and it appeared he needed it now.

He turned toward her, an uncharacteristic softness in his eyes. "Just what I said. Sit down and let me—"

"What do you mean sit down? I'm not sitting down."

Erickson's voice dropped to a calm monotone. "They have a court order, Maggie." He handed her the bold-faced document.

As Maggie read it, she shook her head. "This is unbelievable. Let's get a judge—"

"I've already talked to Josephs," he interrupted. "Despite the edge on this, I thought I had a chance of convincing him the story was worth running. I pulled everything out of my hat—media responsibility, guts in reporting, references to Edward R. Murrow. Nothing worked." He sighed, shaking his head in disgust. "It stops here . . . at least for now."

"Justin, you know how much time I've put into this. My source is thoroughly reliable. It's a *huge* story."

"Well, *they've* got a story of their own."

Erickson proceeded to tell her the details of the Bureau's investigation of her.

"This is crap." Maggie wished she had been face-to-face with the Homeland reps. "These people will say and do anything to stop this information from getting to the public. The link to Senator Denton is undeniable."

Maggie leaned over Erickson's desk, bringing her face close to his. Her voice was low, but intense. "The trail leads to the *vice president*, Justin. It's explosive. The ramifications of what these men are doing reach global levels. Do you realize how dangerous it is for everyone if only a handful of people are in control of an energy monopoly?"

Erickson's obvious frustration conveyed that he knew all too well. "I hated giving into those government bullies, but this one's out of my hands. We're going to have to find a way to convince Josephs . . . "

But Maggie was no longer listening. Choking back her anger and disappointment, she walked out of the editor's office without another word.

CHAPTER 6

IT WAS AFTER TEN when Mabus' driver dropped Michael off in front of his townhouse. Despite the serious issues Mabus had presented, Michael found his thoughts focused once again on old memories, ghosts he wished he could shake.

Once inside, he found Rachel was waiting for him. Or rather, remnants of their long-running relationship were still embedded in his mess. She had ended their on-again, off-again romance before dashing off several months ago. To India this time, on the trail of ancient mysteries and probably sharing a swinging hammock with a real-life Indiana Jones or Swami Megabucks. Perhaps one of them had financed her trip, otherwise Michael wasn't sure where the money had come from.

Rachel had been capable of creating complex clutter—clothing trails and standing book mounds—and some of the remnants of her sojourn in Michael's life were still present. He often wondered how an archaeologist, normally so level-headed and balanced, could be so attracted to the intangible world of metaphysics. Yet, anything with hints of mysticism or magic seemed to turn Rachael's head and the evidence lingered—material on Tibetan yogis, pyramid theories, past-life cognition, psychic phenomena, telepathy. All of it, hodge-podge to him, enthralled her.

Although Michael was drawn to Oriental and Eastern expression, the orderliness of his mind settled more easily into forms like the intricate arabesque calligraphy of Islam's *shahada*. *There is no god but God and Muhammad is the Messenger of God.* He was even mesmerized by the title page of his sixteenth-century copy of *Sefer ha-Zohar*, meditating at great lengths on the neatly-formed Hebrew script—as if the letters themselves held the key to the mystery within, which of course they did.

But tonight, there is another mystery to unravel.

Michael headed into the kitchen. He took two bottles of Becks from the fridge and his ice cold Hamburg stein from the freezer and settled into his reading chair, the only one not buried under books, sweaters and magazines. He snapped the remote for the CD carousel. First up, Miles Davis and Sketches of Spain. Perfect.

Looking down at the desk, the title page of the Jeremiah thesis glaring at him, Michael turned his mind to the work at hand, knowing he had a long night ahead.

THE NEW TEMPLE

PROFESSOR BINAH - HEBREW UNIVERSITY
DOCTOR MIZRAHI - EGYPTIAN OFFICE OF ANTIQUITIES

The authors believe we have discovered the exact location of Solomon's Temple. In addition, a recently discovered parchment found in St. Catherine's Monastery in the Sinai has shed new light on the possible dimensions for a Third Temple in Jerusalem. There is strong reason to believe this document to be a portion of the lost oracles of Jeremiah.

Before explaining the possible location and size of a New Temple as well as our conclusions as to where the original temple stood, it would be helpful to review some history.

Moses secured the culture founded by Abraham, and the Temple was its symbol. Solomon, the son of King David and Bathsheba, had the First Temple built in Jerusalem one thousand years before the birth of Jesus. It took seven years to construct, with stones so well-fashioned that no iron tools were used in its erection. The entire inside was overlaid with gold, and chains of gold secured the inner sanctuary that housed the Ark of the Covenant.

And so it stood for four hundred years, a powerful testament of God's covenant with the Hebrews.

Then came Jeremiah, prophet without honor in his own land. Jeremiah was an outspoken advocate of the personal God, the right of an individual to his own relationship with spirit. He was *ne'um-yahweh,* an oracle of God. His was the voice through which God spoke.

His most profound prophecies concerned the New Covenant. "Look, days are coming—oracle of Yahweh—when I will cut with the house of Israel and with the house of Judah a new covenant . . . I will put my law in their inward parts, and upon their hearts I will write it. And I will be God to them, and they, they will be a people to me. And they shall not again instruct each person his fellow and each person his brother saying, 'Know Yahweh,' for they, all of them, shall know me, from the least of them to the greatest of them."

Jeremiah was also an open critic of both the Temple and its priests. His prophecies were written down by the scribe Baruch and delivered to King Jehoiakim who had them burned in a fit of anger. Jeremiah again dictated his predictions and again the king had the scroll destroyed. No copies of either scroll have been known to survive, until now.

An open critic of both the Temple and its priests . . .

Michael looked up at the picture hanging on his wall, one inherited from Rachel. The image was that of a wild and dangerous-looking creature whose blood-red eyes peered at him menacingly. *Mahakala,* the great protector of Tibetan yogis. Rachel had told him the deity offered a form of tough love. Perhaps Jeremiah was a bit like this *Mahakala,* Michael mused, not so much a nice guy, but someone fearless enough to get the job done. He allowed the thought to linger as he read on.

After the destruction of Solomon's Temple, Ezekiel had
a vision of a new Temple. Living in captivity in Babylon,
he saw "between the porch and altar of the Temple of
the Lord were twenty five men with their backs to the
Temple and their faces toward the east." So it would
seem that during Herod's reign, the Second Temple
would have been built facing east.

Certain rituals also are in keeping with this
assertion. No person could enter the Temple who had
touched or even been in a room with a dead person. The
only way to remove the impurity was to sprinkle them
with the ash of an unblemished red heifer, the sacrifice
of which was held on the Mount of Olives. The priest
performing the burning was required to maintain his
gaze on the entrance of the Hekhal, the sanctuary of the
Temple, while sprinkling the blood. Thus, the Temple
would have been in direct line of sight with the Golden
Gate through which the Messiah must enter Jerusalem.

An east-west line from the Mount of Olives to the
Golden Gate passes directly over the small Dome of the
Spirits on the Temple Mount. Disregarding the outer
court, which was for the Gentiles, the Temple could
be rebuilt without disturbing the Dome of the Rock.
Although there is scholarly disagreement on exactly
what constitutes a "cubit" by which the original Temple
was laid out, the accompanying parchment will lay that
discussion moot.

Found at St. Catherine's Monastery, this parchment
has been carbon dated to within one hundred years of
King Herod. There is evidence that it is the first known
copy of Jeremiah's scroll. One of the fragments, in
particular, concerns the Temple.

woe to him who builds a house of dimensions
for the Righteous One ... woe to him who seeks
righteousness through spacious rooms ... by the
spark of impenetrable darkness shall the waters
be aligned and define the LORD's house ... self-
created, its courts shall not be measured by man
... alone of itself, defined by the rock, aligned
with the Golden Gate ...

"Woe to him who builds a house of dimensions for the Righteous One ... woe to him who seeks righteousness through spacious rooms." These lines, of course, closely parallel the twenty-second chapter of Jeremiah.

"By the spark of impenetrable darkness" refers to a nebulous size, without set definition, neither length nor breadth nor height. This means that the Temple shall not be limited in size, nor should it be limited by its lack of size. It may be smaller than either of the original Temples. This is a central point. As long as its relative dimensions remain proportional, a new Temple may be any size.

"Self created, its courts not limited by man," also refers to a lack of defined space. "Defined by the rock" means the altar location is defined by a rock.

Our conclusion is that the Temple must have been constructed on an east-west axis. The Golden Gate,

believed to be the entry point of the Messiah upon his
arrival, falls directly on this line. For the Lord said to
Ezekiel, "This gate shall be shut; it shall not be opened,
and no one shall enter by it, for the Lord God of
Israel has entered by it; therefore it shall be shut." This
Biblical confirmation points to the fact that the gate is
an entrance for the *Shekhinah*—the divine presence.
Therefore, although basically sealed for fifteen hundred
years, the Golden Gate is a main point on our axis.

In addition, the only rock aligned with the Mount
of Olives and the Golden Gate is not *as-Sakhrah*, the
sacred rock under the Golden Dome, but that which lies
to the north of it under the Dome of the Spirits, a site
once known as the Dome of the Tablets. The flat rock
under this dome is the only other stone still visible on
the Mount. We believe it was originally within the *Debir*,
Holy of Holies, where the Ark of the Covenant was once
located.

Therefore our proposal is to build a Third Temple,
smaller than the first two, with its Holy of Holies
located over the present site of the Dome of the Spirits.
This will not affect the Dome of the Rock in any way. In
fact, in the spirit of Moses, the "Temple" could initially
be an open tent Tabernacle of the Congregation as it was
at Shiloh.

Finally . . . after twenty-five hundred years . . .
Were these the words that had caused Jeremiah to be exiled by his
own people?

It was close to midnight when Michael finished reading the thesis
summary and the attendant technical data relating to the dating and
authenticating process. He then turned toward the multiple high-res-
olution photos Binah and Mizrahi had included in their presentation.
Michael spread the photos out on the desk and sat quietly, letting the
document speak. If the voice was an ancient one, Michael would hear

it. *Shema. In my name.* When his mind was sufficiently calm, he would examine them one by one.

Beginning with the photo which showed the full parchment, he half closed his eyes and let his breathing settle into an easy rhythm as his mentor, Napesh Samuels, had taught him. It was Professor Samuels, in fact, who had given Michael his introduction to Hebrew at Columbia University. It certainly wasn't something he had picked up from the nuns at St. Pancras Grammar School in Queens, New York.

"Begin your studies with *lamed,*" the Professor would say. "Everyday begin with *lamed.* The tallest of the letters, it symbolizes study. It is shaped like a *shofar,* the ram's horn trumpet. It stands straight, symbolizing man reaching upward. Halfway it bends forward, representing God reaching down to man. At the top is a small hook, the eye of God, which resembles the *nada* found atop Sanskrit letters. *Nada* represents the nondual nature of man's relative and ultimate self."

It was that nonduality, it turned out, which made it hard for Michael to believe in the existence of God. If any of the nuns of St. Pancras had ever found out, Michael was certain they would have keeled over in horror.

Placing his reminiscing aside, he picked up the copies of the parchment Mabus had given him and looked the pictures over carefully. The parchment was similar to one from *Deuteronomy,* the Book of Second Law, that had been found at Qumran. So similar, in fact, Michael was tempted to consider it a forgery.

Keeping his doubts in check, he held the photos under his large illuminated magnifier. The Hebrew was in full script, using all the vowels, without the dots, which became common at a later date. The lettering and style also looked similar to that of a 4Qjer scroll Michael had worked on, one of the four Jeremiah scrolls found near the Dead Sea. The oldest of those had been dated approximately 200 BC. If authentic, it was possible this present find was at least as old.

For now, he decided, he would accept the dating of the parchment. That meant if the paper of the original document was two thousand years old, it would be impossible to write on it recently without detection. As he examined further, Michael could see the lettering was smoothly assimilated, which indicated it had been applied when the parchment was new. He also noted the repetitive phrasing, reflected in the translation, was typical of Jeremiah.

As he continued scanning the parchment, Michael reminded himself that understanding of prophecy often depended as much on the original context of the source as on the literal meaning. He looked at each letter and every syllable. As he formed his translation, each phrase seemed a mystical code intended to be broken. Finally, satisfied he had a rough approximation of the text's meaning, he placed his pen back down on the desk.

Could these be the words of Jeremiah, his lost prophesies? The first two lines, especially, had a style that was consistent with Old Testament metaphors. But did that just mean that the author had been a clever forger or was the parchment truly derived from Jeremiah's scroll? The originators of this theory, Binah and Mizrahi, must provide further evidence. Had they seen more of the contents of the jar? Michael would certainly not certify the author, but the parchment itself was quite old. *Perhaps over two thousand years old.*

Michael stared at his translation, noticing it differed subtly from that of the scholars.

Woe to him who builds a house
of dimensions, Righteous One.
Woe to him who seeks righteousness
through spacious rooms.
The House of the Lord shall be illumined
by the spark of impenetrable darkness
as water is measured in the hand.
Self-created, its courts cannot be measured
by man . . . incomparable, interpreted by the rock,
and aligned with the Golden Gate.

Michael furrowed his brow as he contemplated. *Can this actually be referring to a new Temple?* He wondered about Binah and Mizrahi's conclusions and felt there were certainly other possible interpretations. It seemed to him the words were pointing toward something beyond the scope of physical dimensions, cautioning not to attempt to contain the mind of God in some form.

Still, Michael noted, *the parchment does refer to the rock and the Golden Gate . . .*

As he pondered the meaning, another thought took precedence, a thought that had been trying to break through for hours. It was a comment that Rachael had made in one of her notebooks. Where was that thing?

Finally, after searching under the coffee table, he found it—a leather journal, marked with her favorite emblem . . . *a gold and black monarch butterfly.* She had insisted that he keep this particular volume. It dated from the time she began the research which was now culminating in her Indian explorations.

After flipping through, he found the excerpt he was looking for.

> Beneath the mount, within the sand, calling to us from time beyond time, the mystery we search for beckons us. We answer her call, some by refusal or doubt, others by surrender. The voice belongs to Lazarus, the mount to Solomon, the seed to Abraham—we journey on—Lapsis Excellis guides our trail . . .

As Michael read on, he was aware of a feeling of recognition, but of what, he couldn't put his finger on.

> Jerusalem is the point at which our journey begins and ends, through Persia to Ladakh, the land of the lamas. Prof S called today. We talked for an hour. I told him of my discovery in the archives of the Met. He vaguely reminded me of a conversation we had last month. What was it he said? Try as I might it escapes me.

Damn the old coot—he won't even give me a
hint beyond "cepha." He just laughed knowing
it would drive me crazy until I figured it out.
When I did, I still didn't know what he meant.
The word means rock in Aramaic.

Michael turned the desk lamp off, allowing the darkness to relax his mind. He sat quietly for a long while wondering what Rachel could have possibly found in the Met that would make her seek the Professor's help and have her careening to the mountains of Asia, half a world away.

CHAPTER 7

MICHAEL WOKE UP late that Sunday morning. Wanting to lighten his mind after a night of translation and analysis, he put on some jogging gear and headed out the door.

New York Harbor was brimming with sailboats and kayaks by the time he reached the Brooklyn Heights Esplanade. There, his jog turned into little more than a walk as his gaze spanned across the water toward Manhattan. Buffered between the bay and the deep blue sky, the island seemed as if it were suspended in space.

An optical illusion or is that just the way I feel?

"Michael!" A tall, blond man wearing shorts and a N.Y. marathon shirt joined him as he ran along the walkway. "Thought I'd catch you today. Sorry I missed last week."

"Okay, Jarrett, tell me your bosses at the FBI sent you to infiltrate the White House and conduct a criminal investigation and all will be forgiven."

"How'd you know?" Jarret answered, giving him a pat on the back.

Thank God, Michael thought, grateful to be meeting up with a friend who had some earthy common sense. *Someone with his feet on the ground.*

Jarret Williamson carried himself like a soldier. An army lieutenant in Vietnam, he was drawn to special ops, espionage, undercover assignments and all that reeked of mystery. After the war, Michael was not surprised when his friend found a home at the Federal Bureau of Investigation.

"Actually, I was hoping you'd show up today," Michael said. "I know we haven't talked much shop since I worked on those Guantanamo translations, but I have a special situation developing. I want to get some info on Giovanni Mabus."

"The EU guy?"

"The same."

Jarret gave Michael a curious stare. "Well . . . actually, he's someone we've had our eye on of late."

Michael sensed Jarret's reluctance to speak. "Is there anything you can tell me that wouldn't compromise you? You see, Mabus has asked me to do some work on a parchment for him."

"Religious artifact?" Jarret asked.

"Yes. He's got some notions that are tied to it that are a bit off the charts. I wanted to get more background on him, other than what I've heard in the news or read in *USA Today* the last few years."

Jarret took a moment to assess the situation. "Well it's difficult for me to say anything right now. I'm sure you've heard about the Peace Conference Mabus is trying to set up in Jerusalem."

"He's told me a few things about it," Michael answered, not wanting to convey how much he knew.

"We've been looking at the particulars—who's involved, the when, the where. So far we haven't come up with much." Jarret paused, turning around as he continued to jog, making sure no one was in earshot. "The Libyan connection has got us concerned, of course," he whispered. "We're watching him closely."

"So you're not buying this peacemaker business?"

"Who knows?" Jarret shrugged. "It's a long shot if it's true, but we have to continue the investigation. Have you talked to the *wizard* yet?"

Michael smiled at the reference. The *wizard* was Michael's mentor, Professor Napesh Samuels, a legend in the FBI and Pentagon circles, known as a walking *facts machine* about the inner workings of both the Nazi and East German governments. What many of his Pentagon admirers did not know was he was even more knowledgeable about myths and legends—the accounts of Popul Vuh, the mysteries of Thoth, the legendary lands of Atlantis and Avalon. If there was a myth involving lost civilizations or ancient relics, Professor Samuels was tracing it.

"You know," Jarret pointed out, "it's possible Samuels can get info on Mr. Mabus and his *strange fascinations.*"

Michael noticed Jarret cringe as soon as he made the statement. "What are you talking about?" he asked.

"I've started to ramble." Jarret now avoided answering. "Let's just leave it be for now. If I can, I'll tell you more in time."

Strange fascinations. Michael wondered what they could be. He pondered the notion silently as he jogged alongside Jarret until reaching his turnoff on Montague Street. "You know, for a spook, you're an okay guy, Jarret," he said, slowing down to almost a halt.

"I love it when you compliment me." Jarret waved as they parted. Then turning and jogging in place, he called out. "By the way, Mabus is in the *Times* this morning. The man's name is everywhere."

Michael jogged down Montague, stopping in front of the twenty-four hour Korean deli. He veered straight to the news rack and picked up the Sunday edition of *The New York Times*. There it was, the Mabus story, centered on the first page:

> BRUSSELS — The European Parliament, in a nearly unanimous vote on Friday, authorized support for the upcoming Peace Conference in Jerusalem. The driving force behind the conference is the New York-based Council on Mideast Affairs, which is largely funded by Mabus International. The council, which is a coalition of religious, business and NGO groups, has been a strident advocate of alternative visions in the region for several years.
>
> From Washington, Senator Denport, Chairman of the Senate Foreign Affairs Committee said the upcoming Peace Conference in Jerusalem sponsored by the European Community is a pivotal event in Middle Eastern affairs. He claims it would be in the best interests of the United States for this administration and Congress to lend its full support to the endeavor.

So the PR work begins . . . Michael shook his head in dismay. When the whole agenda hit the public arena, he was certain there would be hell to pay. *A new temple on the Mount.* Michael wondered what Professor Samuels would say about this Third Temple fantasy? Was history about to repeat itself?

Michael recalled the first time he had seen Samuels walk into the World History lecture hall at Columbia and stride across the stage toward the podium. Late fifties, tall, thin, his wavy brown hair falling across his forehead, the Professor swept his powerful gaze across the auditorium taking everything in at once. After placing his notes on the lectern, he walked to one of two giant chalkboards mounted on wheels and wrote his name in large letters.

Then without missing a beat, he swung into action.

"He who does not understand history is *doomed* to repeat it," the Professor stated emphatically with a cultured Bavarian accent. "Our government and business leaders do not understand history, nor do they make any effort to do so. The primary focus of this course will be to convince each of you, or those of you who wish a passing grade," the Professor said, stopping for a moment to let the laughter subside, "that history is not linear. There is no yesterday to be subdivided from tomorrow. Borrowing from physics, we will understand time as a curve, or sphere, forever wrapping around itself. Events and decisions made long ago are just as relevant as the schemes our president and his co-conspirators have dreamed up this week."

Professor Samuels had been right. History had proved itself not to be linear at all, and perhaps it was winding into another knot around this *new temple* issue. If it weren't for Michael's pledge of confidentiality to Mabus, he would call Samuels immediately to discuss the parchment with him and get his take on the whole Peace Conference agenda.

But circumstances dictated otherwise. Michael sighed as he realized his life would have to be put on hold. It would be some time before he would be conferring with Professor Samuels or even be able to get back to his own writing, a novel based on the work of the Professor's uncle, Walter Stein.

Stein, the Viennese philosopher who had fought for Austria in World War I, had been an advisor to Ataturk and King Leopold before serving with the British Intelligence against the Nazis. Professor Samuels was in possession of all of his uncle's notes, which detailed Stein's ominous encounter with Adolph Hitler and the Nazi leader's bizarre beliefs. Talk about history repeating itself.

But today, Michael realized as he headed back toward his apartment, his work was to analyze facts and apply science.

Fiction and myth and novels would have to wait.

CHAPTER 8

MAGGIE HAD SPENT the day in her office staring at the Sunday Times, dwelling on one disturbing fact—her story was missing. The last thing she wanted to feel was powerless or overcome, but found herself fighting both. That was until her editorial assistant, Rema Phillips, shook Maggie out of her chair and insisted on taking her home

Now, as Rema drove them through the dark Manhattan streets, Maggie realized her protégé was not about to let her off the hook. The young, black woman was about as strong-willed and determined as Maggie herself. Being ground through the same mill together at *The New York Times'* National Security Desk, the two had grown close, often joking about their friendship. *Camaraderie from the trenches*, the two women called it.

"So what are you going to do?" Rema glanced over from behind the wheel. The traffic light's glare reflected off her rich, dark eyes.

Maggie returned the glance with a wide stare.

"Oh come on, Maggie. This whole damn thing reeks of a cover-up."

"And it looks like it's working."

Rema was incredulous. "Do you think Mabus really has that far of a reach?"

Maggie shrugged, not knowing who to blame. "One thing's for certain. There are bigger fish to fry. Someone in the White House doesn't want the story to come to light. They're protecting Mabus for a reason."

"And what could that be?"

"Maybe they owe him."

The light turned from yellow to red. Rema stopped the car and turned toward her.

" 'Maybe they owe him?' " Rema repeated the words, her eyes beginning to question her friend's grip on reality. "What are you driving at?"

Frustrated, Maggie dug out a low-carb chocolate bar from her purse. "I don't know, but they must owe him *big*."

Rema's look of annoyance quickly changed to one of concern. "Maggie, I think you better back off here. If you're being investigated, you could get into a lot of trouble."

Maggie was no longer listening to her. She took a bite of her chocolate.

They owe him, alright.

Maggie looked into some far-off place in her mind, barely conscious of her surroundings. What was it that Einsof said during their interview? *Using the earth's natural forces and electrical charges, we could create enormous amounts of energy with minimal cost.* You basically reduce the amount of energy needed to make something work. Harmony creates less friction, less friction means greater efficiency. *No electrical lines.* Within ten years crude oil consumption could be reduced by fifty percent—a death knoll for the oil business.

Mabus International had the first option to buy the rights . . . Vice President Bohmer, once a lobbyist for OPEC, was now involved with this new energy development. *The petroleum connection is there.* If the oil magnates were eventually going down, the vice president would make sure his boat was kept afloat while everyone else's was sinking.

As the light turned green, Maggie resurfaced, catching the end of Rema's soliloquy of warning.

"Look, why don't you let the whole thing blow over," Rema said, "just concentrate on something simpler for a while? How about that excerpt from the new book you're working on? Is Jackson going to use it?"

Maggie sensed Rema's fear and allowed her friend to direct the conversation to calmer waters. "The last time I tried to get the story taken seriously as a short series in the Travel Department, Jackson nearly chewed my head off."

The travel editor, Jackson Pallet, was a prickly old hard-edged reporter, believing in the traditional standbys in travel reporting that were reminiscent of *Wild Kingdom* and *Animal Planet*. He was not too keen on Maggie's venture into the world of the traveling mystic.

"*The Shambhala Myth* might make it as a book," Maggie ventured, "but I'm not too sure an excerpt is going to make it as a interest piece in the *Times.*"

" 'Not too sure it's going to make it,' " Rema parroted. "Why the roadblock?"

"Trying to convince Jackson that readers in today's climate would definitely be interested in the adventures of the likes of Notovitch, Nicholas Roerich, and Edwin Bernbaum, and their quest for another Shangri-La, is turning out to be a hard sell. Jackson almost hit the roof with it, telling me people would question my credibility if I took on that kind of a piece."

Maggie recalled her last bout with Pallet about running the article. Pursing his lips, eyes bugged out, his cynicism simmered to a low boil as he drove home what he pronounced was his final decree.

"Are you crazy? Do you expect anyone to take your reporting seriously after a whimsical tryst into the fantastic? This department is not about to turn dipsey doodle because you've decided to *enlighten* people about hidden lands in the Himalayas." Hands on his hips, Pallet glared at her, his gravelly voice growing louder. "People want fun, excitement, a good tan! For God sake, I want articles on Barbados, Cancun and the like, not this far-out stuff on remote regions in Ladakh and Tibet." He tossed the story onto a pile on his desk. "Besides, I thought Tibet was swallowed up by China."

Maggie had left his office rolling her eyes, determined to approach the editor-in-chief if she had to. *My article will be printed. Pallet can keep his travelogues for the rich and insatiable.*

"Hey," Rema said, her voice insistent. "Hellooo. You'd think that after writing a best-seller that a colleague on your own paper would let up a little."

"Pallet's worried about his precious reputation," Maggie replied. "You know, he likes to toe the line. Besides, he can't look like he's bowing down to me or anything like that. At this point having a book out is actually making it harder to appeal to anyone's senses."

"Why don't you just quit?" Rema questioned, looking impatient. "You don't need this anymore."

Maggie had toyed with the idea. "Well, it looked like the natural course for a while, but you know . . . how would I have had access to all of those places I wrote about in my book and seen the atrocities, spoken with the people, found the sources so directly had it not been for investigative reporting? It's the reason I could write *Pure Vision* in the first place."

Rema tried to sound encouraging. "I'm sure you're father would really be proud. A daughter who writes for the *Times*, a best-selling author."

"Probably." Maggie heard the insecurity in her own voice. "I think about what he would say these days, though, especially after all his years with the *Washington Post*, wiring home stories from Israel."

"And your point?" Rema asked in a disapproving tone.

Maggie caught the message. *Stop being insecure, and STOP putting yourself down.*

"My point *is* I'm working from a belief first and moving through to find the evidence," Maggie explained, "instead of the other way around."

"So what?" Rema asked. "As long as your conclusions are ultimately based on sound facts, what difference does it make how you get there?" The pragmatist in Rema shone through. "Besides, maybe it's time people listened to their hearts and believed in some possibilities for this world, instead of lowering their sights and not having any vision at all."

Maggie held out the last piece of her low-carb chocolate for her friend. "Did I ever mention you are quite inspiring when you're pissed off?"

"Tell me about it." Rema pretended an air of superiority as she bit into the chocolate with relish. She stared at the wrapper on the dashboard. "Only three impact carbs. Don't you love it when you pay a lot of money to get conned?"

On West Eightieth Street, Rema slowed down and pulled up to the curb outside Maggie's apartment building. "Remember, call me before the Harper Crow thing," she urged. Maggie had agreed to a showdown with the right-wing talk show host.

"Don't worry, I will," Maggie assured her.

As the blue Chrysler pulled away, Maggie dug into her purse for her keys, pulling out everything but—scraps of paper, her wallet, candy bar wrappers, a hair clip. She shook her head, thinking how the familiar scenario was like a comedy routine at this point. Then she touched the front of her jacket. *Of course.* Smiling, she slipped her hand inside her pocket and retrieved the elusive keys.

"Whew mamaaa, what we have here? You the bitch." A young white punk, hair slicked back, earring through his nose, called out from a top-less Chevy as it slowed down in front of her building. He turned toward the driver and the three other white hoods in the back. "Hey, it's the bitch, *the peace lady*. You need a ride, mama? I can give you a *ride.*"

The other guys in the car started laughing, loud and sputtering, almost as annoying as their burnt out muffler.

In her hurry to get the front door open, Maggie dropped her keys. Nervously, she bent down to pick them up.

"*Whoa*, you got some piece of ass. You better keep your love for Jew boys and Arab towel heads in line, lady. We white men don't like to see our women protecting the scum of the earth."

Maggie unlocked the front door as quickly as she could and stepped inside the hallway. Now more angry than fearful, she spouted back toward the men in the car. "Funny statement coming from the likes of you."

"What she say? Wha—"

Maggie slammed the front door shut, heart still pounding, and raced up the stairs to her second floor apartment. A pile of mail was awaiting her just outside her door, no doubt placed there by her Irish super who liked to look out for "the lass" who lived alone in the city. She picked up the letters, went inside, and then locked and double-bolted the entrance.

Still anxious, Maggie flipped on the lights and made a bee-line to her fridge. *May wine should do the trick*, she thought. She poured the light pink liquid into her favorite Castilian glass and sank onto the sofa.

Slowly, with each sip, Maggie's mind began to settle. It had happened several times now since the release of her book—remarks made to her on the street . . . verbal assaults. After some threatening phone calls, she had her number changed and blocked all unidentified ones. Tonight was another straw on the pile. Maggie wondered what the final straw would be.

There in the softly lit room, she saw her dilemma through the gold and brown hues of shaded lighting. Staring into space, she took another sip of wine. Her eyes settled on the coffee table where more mail, and lots of it, had sat unopened for days. Frustrated with all the work she faced, Maggie found it hard to shake off another *Why me?* moment.

Sighing, she turned toward the pile. A large manila envelope stood out. Picking it up, she noticed no return address, only her name scrawled in thick black ink. She undid the clasp and pulled out what looked like a photograph.

Suddenly, Maggie felt her hand go limp. "Oh my God," she whispered as the picture slipped from her fingers and fell to the floor.

CHAPTER 9

FOR THE NEXT hour, Maggie turned her apartment upside down but couldn't find what she was looking for. *Where could I have put them?* Her father's notebooks . . . passed on to her after his death. She could barely look at them back in '92, when the odd-looking box had been mailed to her from Israel. One of her father's colleagues had sent them to her with a note: *Your father would have wanted you to have these.*

Pulling open her huge closet doors, she started throwing clothes, hangers and all, across her bed. Finally, there under a thick afghan, she found a cardboard box imprinted with red felt markings. *DAD'S.*

Grabbing hold of the carton, Maggie got off her knees and walked over to the bed. She flipped off the lid, and there they were—old black-and-white notebooks, filled with her father's descriptions of his time in Israel—his ideas and ideals. She drew out one of the notebooks and began to read, hoping to find a passage, anything that would tell her about the strange lettering she had seen on the photograph.

P2

P2 . . . What was P2?

She combed through the books, until finally she saw an interesting inscription on one of the pages.

Fascist Infiltration.

Slowly, as she read, turning page after page, the story unfolded, more bizarre and complex than she could have imagined. Mossad agents, U.S. government officials, British military commanders, Italian politicians, even Arab oil moguls—together they had formed a strange and formidable brotherhood that quested for power and land, oil rights, energy monopolies . . . all the while breeding right wing political ideals that would make even conspiracy theorists reel.

The world thought it had closed the book on the mindsets that had brought about World War II, but according to her father's findings, the neo-fascists had lived on, many under the cover of legitimate businesses. Here was a list of names, for years practically under her fingertips, in notebooks that she had been too emotional to even look into.

Was there some connection here to this P2? Whoever or whatever it was, why would they announce themselves to her now? Could it tie into the popularity of her book, focusing in on the Middle East crisis and all the elements that she had tried so hard to bring to light? Or was it simply arrogance, pure and simple? One thing was clear—the threat was apparent. *Your father's fate could be yours.*

Maggie continued her search but could not find any mention of P2 anywhere. Had she just missed it? She decided to go through the notebooks again, combing through line by line this time. After nearly an hour, she came across something interesting.

> My article on Propaganda Due will show
> the powerful influence this group still has as a
> pseudo-freemason society . . .

Propaganda Due . . . P2.

Maggie switched on her computer and logged onto the internet. Her fingers moving quickly, she keyed in the words.

SEARCH: Propaganda Due

A list of names popped up on her screen. She clicked on the website for San Francisco Bay Guardian.

> **Propaganda Due, also known as P-2, a
> nominally Masonic lodge. For decades P-2
> virtually ran Italy from behind the scenes,
> while the front men in Rome traded cabinet
> posts back and forth dozens of times in
> what they laughably called "changes in**

government." For a while, with the help of
U.S.-born gangster-priest, Paul Marcinkus,
P-2 ran the Vatican Bank. It was during this
era that the Vatican Bank was caught red-
handed laundering counterfeit paper for the
Gambino crime family.

P-2's longtime Grand Master (cappo de
tutti cappos) was a man named Licio Gelli.
Gelli, among other things, attended the
inaugural ceremonies of Presidents Ford,
Carter, and Reagan, and called himself a
friend of George Herbert Walker Bush.

Other sites brought up more information . . . claims of P2 helping the CIA finance the Bolivian Cocaine Coup . . . attempts to take over the Italian government . . . a membership that included over a thousand leading political financial and government figures.

A right-wing fascist outfit . . .

Maggie also discovered that under Gelli, the Grand Master of the outcasted Masonic lodge, P2 became the most powerful, violent, political organization in Italy, working at times with the CIA and MI5. Government officials, military officials, and important businessmen and financiers became members of this secret society.

Obviously, fascist sentiment was the cornerstone of Propaganda Due, but what was the foundation for this Gelli character's takeover of the ousted Masonic lodge? Maggie continued surfing, trying to rake up more information until finally, she found what she was looking for at masonicinfo.com.

Licio Gelli was born in 1919 and when
17 years old, volunteered for the fascist
expeditionary force sent by Mussolini to
Spain. Thereafter, he became a liaison officer
with the army of the Third Reich. When the
winds changed, he joined the ranks of the
U.S. Central Intelligence Agency where he

**apparently mixed business with personal
interests, becoming rich in the process . . . .**

Another hit brought Maggie to freemasonrywatch.org where Gelli's tactics were elucidated further.

**P2 was a secret cell for the preparation of
a right-wing coup like those which engulfed
Greece in 1967 and Chile in 1973 (in Chile's
case, to overthrow President Allende, who
was a communist Freemason of an "irregular"
Masonic order). Gelli hosted frequent P2
meetings where the politics of destabilization
and subversion were discussed by police
chiefs, army generals, security service
bosses and appeal court judges.**

Pensive, Maggie sat back in her chair and drew a long breath. Had her father found some connection between P2 and the Israeli-Palestinian conflict? It certainly wasn't a farfetched notion, considering P2's history of using infiltration and destabilization to gain power and monetary spoils for the group and its members.

When Maggie turned her attention back to the screen, she soon learned that Propaganda Due's agenda today was reputed to be no different. With a new Grand Master at the helm—Guiseppe Volpi—the organization's reach was frighteningly widespread.

An unholy citizenship of men, she thought. Like an intricate web, the circuitry involving the likes of Propaganda Due had created a global kinship among the rich aficionados of power, their main concern being to preserve their own financial interests and power domains throughout the world.

Maggie wondered about all these links. What else had her father discovered, what were the ties to the U.S. and other countries, and what were the global effects of these "secret cells," P2 being only one in a web of interconnected organizations?

One final internet passage she found on the site hit a nerve. It reso-nated well with the diplomacy of arrogance that Maggie had seen used so brilliantly in international relations.

Gelli believed in the "weapon of fear." He believed that fear was the instrument by which real power could be masterfully employed, and he believed fear was most useful when cloaked in silence . . .

Terrorism, attacks on national security . . . playing on the fears of the American people, using real events to promote secret aims. The driving forces in this world . . . *who are they . . . what are their ultimate aims?*

The ringing of the phone jarred Maggie from her thoughts. She walked over to the credenza and picked up the receiver.

"Hello."

"Have you opened your mail today, Ms. Seline?" The male voice on the other end spoke in a low whisper.

"Who is this?"

"Remember your father," the caller warned.

The line went dead.

Maggie laid down the phone, her pulse racing, and looked toward the picture still lying on her living room carpet. She had not been able to pick it up all this time, but the image left no doubt. Sprawled out on a dirty floor, a bullet hole in his forehead, her father lay in a pool of blood. After all these years, Maggie was now brought face-to-face with the stark truth.

David Seline had been assassinated.

CHAPTER 10

INSIDE HIS HOME in Rhinecliff, New York, Professor Napesh Samuels dwelled like a hermit in a cave. Surrounding him was a protective circle of books and manuscripts, paintings and sketches—a mandala of spiritualism and mythology. His practice—to forgo dogma for the mystical and the esoteric—had brought him to the secret teachings of Christianity and Judaism, where he found both.

Now, as he sat within the confines of his library, Samuels looked out his huge portico windows wondering where his old student Michael Sonada had run off to. After coming up to the Professor's Hudson Valley retreat almost every weekend for nearly four months, Michael dropped out of sight. It was just like him, the Professor thought, to apply himself so diligently and then cool his efforts.

Michael had been studying the notes left by the Professor's uncle, Walter Stein, a man obsessed with ancient holy artifacts, sacred talismans, and Grail lore. Michael especially concentrated on the Spear of Longinus, the famous lance that was used to pierce the side of Christ. Professor Samuels could not imagine him staying away for too long. Stein's encounters with Adolph Hitler would make any writer salivate.

Tonight, the Professor was overcome by a strong urge to look over the notebooks himself. Although he had read them numerous times, he always felt there was something he was missing. With an air of anticipation, he unlocked his desk drawer and pulled out one of the old leather journals.

As the Professor turned the frayed pages slowly, his uncle's writings swirled into life, creating images that appeared like photographs in his mind. Samuels closed his eyes and sat quietly. Like a monk in a cell, he meditated, allowing himself to move deeper into the recesses of his spirit. The history of all mankind, he knew, lay deep within the mind—a history of all of man's highest good as well as his darkest obsessions. It was in the vast ocean of this knowledge and space that Napesh Samuels receded, and time, past and present, melded to form the pictures and to tell the story.

AUSTRIA, 1912

In the mid-afternoon, in the city of Vienna, a young man meandered down the narrow dusty halls of the occult bookstore, glancing at titles. As he walked, the dirty old wooden floors creaked, making him all the more self-conscious of being the only customer in the store. Outside a church bell rang, a slow hollow sound, tolling the approach of midday.

So, what have we here, Walter Stein wondered as he allowed his fingers to pass along the hard covers. Although he studied science and philosophy at the University of Vienna, his passion was his interest in mysticism and the occult.

For the past year he studied the legends of the *Grail*. What the Grail was, no one knew—a cup, a platter, a bowl . . . or perhaps a jewel, a transcendent experience. *And what does it matter*, thought Walter Stein, *the message is not the object itself but what it stands for—enlightenment, awakening.*

The corner of a book caught his eye. The old brown binding protruded high on a shelf above his head. He reached up and took it down. It was a copy of *Parsival*, the magnificent tale of the quest for the Grail by Wolfram von Eschenbach. Flipping through the pages, he saw that someone has scribbled on almost every one of them. Different ideas were jotted down as if the reader wished to explain every passage to himself. As Walter read on, he became more and more fascinated with the commentator's insights. How keen was this mind that it could find such meaning in the poet's verse. Even the script of these jottings was intriguing, swirling like waves across the page.

In an excited hurry, Walter quickly brought the book up to the store owner, a most unnatural sort of man. Small, glassy brown eyes peered at him, squinting as if they hurt to look upon his bright young face. At first, Walter thought the man's poor vision was due to the dim lighting and dark shadows that fell in every corner. But the squalid man, who lived in these shadows and called the back room of his shop *home*, was not responding to any physical light.

The proprietor took the *hellers* that Walter handed him and placed them in an old wooden box on the countertop. "You've an interest in the occult, young man?"

"Yes, I do," Walter answered. "Mysticism and the occult have always fascinated me . . . the Grail legend in particular. Seeking the divine opens up the magic of this world, I believe."

"Magic is as it is, my young sir, whether divine or unholy." The man's sallow complexion and hollow eyes made him appear like a ghost in the shadows.

Walter's distaste for the bookstore owner grew more pronounced with each passing moment. "Thank you," he said with cursory politeness. He took his newly purchased book from the storekeeper and walked briskly out of the shop.

Once outside, a light cool breeze blew through him, shaking Walter free of the dark cloud of dust. He strolled through the old city streets, the precious treasure in his hand, stopping just outside a café. *Demel's,* read the sign above the doorway. He went inside and sat at a large picture window that looked out onto the busy market street. For a few moments he watched the hustle and bustle of Viennese women grocery shopping, mason workers building an archway for the church across the way, and the children playing in the sun at the corner market. But none of it would be enough to hold his interest today, Walter knew.

After placing an order of coffee with the young waitress, Walter focused his attention on his newly acquired possession. He was excited to find more comments and was impressed by the previous reader's knowledge of Eastern religions and mystical traditions. But as he read on, Walter's excitement and admiration transformed into something quite different. The reader began to describe the Grail romance and the knights within the story with disdain. "These men betrayed their pure Aryan Blood to the dirty superstitions of the Jew Jesus—superstitions as loathsome and ludicrous as the Yiddish rites of circumcision."

Surprised and disturbed by the remark, Walter became even more distressed when he read the mysterious commentator's response to the description of the Grail in *Parsival* as a *precious stone*. The reader concluded that this *stone* referred to the pineal gland—the third eye—and must be opened.

Was this position being asserted by a student of the occult? Walter felt the shudder of an uneasy fear, since opening the eye could be done by the sinister as well as by the benevolent.

Reading the Grail poem further, Walter discovered something more. The desire for power over destiny was centered around a *Spear*. No ordinary lance, it was the one known to have pierced the side of Christ, been held by the mighty emperors and kings of the world, and which presently resided quietly in the Treasure House of the Hofburg in the very city where he now sat reading.

The Spear of Longinus.

Held by those moral or unjust, it was a symbol and source of pure power to be used for either good or evil—dangerous in its own right, since history had chronicled that the quest for power had led many men down the darkest of paths. By its very nature, Walter knew, the Spear was quite different from the Grail, which appeared to guide the seeker toward a path of clarity and light, unattainable by those who chose power for power's sake.

With the turning of each page, Walter's mind grew heavier. He looked up and glanced out the window of the café, suddenly feeling as if he was being watched. The waning afternoon sun shone upon a figure standing at the edge of the sidewalk, the man's icy blue eyes staring directly into his. Walter quickly turned away and closed the book. Although what he had read unnerved him, now something else—something unnamed—disturbed him even more. He placed money on the table and left the café.

Once outside, Walter noticed that the odd man was still watching him. He was a dirty sort of fellow, disheveled, with dark hair hanging down upon his forehead and a short handlebar moustache shading his mouth. Not knowing why, Walter gravitated toward him. The man, an artist, was selling watercolors. Walter picked up a few at random and gave the sorry soul some coins.

Several blocks away, he nearly dropped everything when he took a closer look at the sketches he had bought. One of the pictures was a drawing of the very Spear he had been reading about—the Longinus Spear! Even more astonishing was the artist's signature, the same name scrawled in his copy of *Parsival*.

Adolf Hitler.

For two weeks, young Walter Stein frequented Demel's Café daily but saw no sign of the wretched young painter. One morning, while sitting anxiously sipping his coffee, he decided to revisit the occult bookshop. Perhaps that strange, pouting man who owned the store knew something of Hitler's whereabouts.

"Ah, the young scholar," Ernst Pretzsche said as Walter entered. He put down the sandwich he was eating and pried a piece of bologna from the roof of his mouth. "What kind of magic book are you looking for today, young master?"

"None, actually. I'm here regarding the former owner of the book I bought from you a couple of weeks ago. Would you by chance know anything about him? Adolf Hitler is his name."

Pretzsche did not have much in the way of eyes, but those he had grew larger than the red gumballs sitting in the dirty bowl on his counter. "Come," he said, and guided Walter to a doorway at the back of the shop. "This is my office."

As Walter stepped into the room, his nose curled from the foul stench of stale air and old food. Pretzsche turned on two lamps and took a seat behind his desk, beckoning Walter to sit on a tattered green chair across from him.

It took his eyes a moment to adjust, but when they did, Walter found that the smell in the room was not the only ominous sign. Pentagrams, swastikas, Jewish slurs, obscene photos—the walls were covered with them. In the midst of it all, a picture of the infamous German occultist, Guido von List, was hanging on wall behind Pretzche's desk.

Germanic Pride. Pretzche, this reptile, is swollen with it.

"I have not seen Hitler in several weeks, but I find him a penetrating and intelligent young man. I think he will go far in our cause." Pretzche stared at Walter, his dark eyes intense. "The Aryan German race must come into power, and it will."

Walter turned his head away for a moment, not wanting to betray his disgust. "Sir, I am sorry I cannot stay," he remarked, "but if you could tell me where I can find this Mr. Hitler, I would most appreciate it."

"Ah yes, yes," Pretzsche muttered, searching through the top drawer of his desk. "Here it is." He then gave Walter the address of the hostel where Hitler was living.

"Much obliged, much obliged." Walter rose quickly, nearly knocking over the pencil cup on the side of the desk. Having obtained what he came for, his only desire was to escape the devious creature's presence.

"I could teach you some things, young sir, if you care to learn them."

Without turning, Walter mumbled his goodbye, hastily rushing out of the shop.

But it would not be at the hostel that he would see Adolf Hitler again. Walter found him outside the Hofburg Museum, painting and trying to sell his watercolors.

"Pardon me," Walter said tentatively.

Hitler turned toward him, a scowl on his lips.

"I don't wish to bother you, but I believe I've a copy of a book you used to own."

Upon seeing the title, Hitler's eyes flared with anger. "That book should not have been sold to you. I pawned it and meant to buy it back."

"I'm sorry," Walter apologized. "I was so fascinated by the notes I found in them about the Grail and the Spear of Longinus that I simply had to buy it."

A flash of camaraderie sparked in Hitler's eyes. Wanting to learn more about this strange soul, Walter was encouraged by the kinship the man felt toward him. Perhaps this Hitler saw him as being another great intellect that could appreciate the magnificence of the work of Wolfram von Eschenbach.

Walter listened in amazement as, one by one, Hitler recited the names of the historical figures that had once claimed and eventually lost the Spear—*Landulf of Capua, Constantine the Great, Justinian, Charlemagne,* and especially the German emperors such as *Otto the Great* and *Frederick Barbarossa,* among others.

"Follow me, and we shall see it together," Hitler said as he led the way up the stairs to the Hofburg Schatzkammer.

Hitler's gait was sure as he planted each foot firmly upon the steps leading to the entrance. Each stride was purposeful, as if driven by the intent to achieve an end that Walter, at present, could not even guess.

Finally, Walter found himself standing before a glass case with his unlikely companion. Just inside, the infamous Spear lay on a red velvet cloth, its point still looking sharp although darkened with age. Small golden crosses and the wings of a dove were inlaid on its base, and secured to the blade with gold, silver and copper threading was a nail from the cross of Christ.

As Walter looked upon the Spear, his heart began to ache. Pain, suffering, compassion, love . . . all moved through him like the blood coursing through his veins. Feeling strangely awakened, he now understood why so many had been drawn to the ancient talisman. An awesome power permeated it.

But there was something else Walter was beginning to sense. His ears pricked, and he felt a cold shiver move through him. Apprehensively, he turned toward his companion.

Beside him, Hitler was standing in a rapt trance like a medium in a séance. His face looked like that of an apparition—eyes that were luminous, shining forth a ghostly light. "That Spear will be mine one day," Hitler declared, his words echoing in the chamber.

Filled with trepidation, Walter realized he now stood witness to an evil presence.

How evil, he could not fathom.

With each passing year, Walter Stein watched as new seeds of hatred sprouted and flourished. The failed artist, Hitler, along with his fellow propagandists, took refuge in their lack of esteem and wounded pride. Defeated in World War I, their seeds of disdain had grown into powerful towering trees, roots deeply inlaid and spreading across Germany, draining any last hope of decency from her soil. And now Austria would be next.

One quiet summer evening, when Walter Stein returned to the house he shared with his sister in Vienna, her youngest son, Napesh, was waiting for him on the front steps.

"What's this?" The eight-year-old leapt to his feet, brandishing a small frayed book in his hand.

Walter recognized it immediately. *How stupid*, he thought to himself. A gnawing anxiety had kept him up during the night, and he had taken up reviewing the old volume. He must have forgotten to bring it back to his room.

"Napesh, give that here."

"No, not until I look at the pictures."

"There are no pictures," Walter spouted, annoyed.

He usually treated Napesh like a younger brother, unwittingly encouraging a little too much mischief. But tonight, his tone conveyed there would be hell to pay if Napesh didn't heed him.

"*Parsival.*" With a sheepish grin, the young boy read the title. "What's that?"

Walter took the book from his nephew's outstretched hand. "One day, I'll let you read this book, Napesh, and I'm sure you'll understand exactly what it means."

Walter clenched the book tightly as he walked to his room. It had been over twenty years since he had gained possession of Hitler's copy of *Parsival* and stood with him in the Shatzkammer. Today, he had heard that the Führer would be entering the city of Vienna once again.

Walter shuddered. Hitler's return to the city could mean only one thing . . .

VIENNA, 1938

His black Mercedes arrived in the city, driven with the dignity and honor he had long deserved.

As Adolf Hitler sat in the back seat looking through the closed window, he was pleased to see the crowd's fervor. Anxious to behold their German messiah, people were crying out passionately, all the while their eyes searching his vehicle. Screaming uncontrollably as if possessed, some even fainted when they saw him.

Devotion, Hitler realized. *They are possessed by devotion.*

He smiled, tensing his mouth to control his emotions. Tonight, his bid for power would bear the sweetest fruit. Was it not said that the anticipation, the journey that takes you to a place, can sometimes be just as fulfilling, if not more, than actually attaining your goal? It was both in this case. Hitler knew how much power he had already acquired, and once the Spear was in his hands, the channels that may have been blocked before would flow freely. Then the pure power of the gods would course through his veins unrestrained.

The Spear belongs to me. Soon, I shall claim what is mine.

But Hitler realized that for the sake of security, he would have to be patient. According to plan, he commanded his driver to make haste and was whisked to the opulence of his hotel room at the Imperial. He would wait until the midnight hour, after darkness had descended upon the city.

A deceptive evening calm enveloped Vienna. When the long-awaited moment finally arrived, Hitler was driven to the Hofburg, his car slowly pulling up before the museum steps. He exited the vehicle and stood for a moment before the majestic edifice, imagining himself as he once was, the failed artist who had dreamed that one day he would hold the Spear. Tonight, he would realize his wish.

Hitler moved forward then and climbed the stairs to enter the Treasure House. Beside him, laboring to keep up with his stride, was his trusted henchman, Heinrich Himmler. Himmler, who founded the Nazi Occult Bureau, Ahnenerbe, had a pleased smile on his face. Hitler knew he was elated, for the Spear was truly a magnificent relic to possess. The only prize that could possibly surpass it was the Grail itself.

As Hitler and his men walked the hallowed halls, the only sounds echoing in the silence were the tapping of their heels against the floor. His entourage knew to be silent as he was led to the open glass case that held the treasure. Entranced, Hitler picked up the Spear and ran his fingers along the blackened metal. He placed his index finger on the point, savoring the thought that this was the instrument that had pierced the side of Christ.

Standing in the shadow of the hall, Adolf Hitler felt the heat rising in his body. Soon the Spear would be taken to Nuremberg where it had rested previously for five hundred years. Hitler would return it to its rightful home, and dominion and power would be Germany's once again.

Now, with the sacred talisman in his hand, the Führer could not resist his moment of glory. "Heil Hitler," he whispered.

APRIL 30, 1945
NUREMBERG, GERMANY

Bombs burst like fiery dragons across the sky, and crimson and gold sparks ignited into dazzling lights. Blood ran red through the streets of Nuremberg, all the arteries of the last fortress of the Nazi regime open and bleeding. Lieutenant Randolph Black smelled victory for the American Seventh Army. He and his soldiers were coursing the battered streets on sheer adrenaline. They were riding high on the knowledge that Hitler's army was on the brink of defeat.

The city lay in ruins. Piles of brick and concrete rubble covered the streets. As the American soldiers scoured through them, unaware of what lay hidden beneath, Lieutenant Black and his men rounded one of the old gabled houses in the *Oberen Schmied Gasse*, the Upper Blacksmith's Alley, and came upon the blown open entrance to a tunnel.

"Hey, Lieutenant, I think we've got something here!" one of his privates, Hanneson, called out.

Lieutenant Black slid over a pile of rocks with his attendant, Corporal Biers, following suit. When they reached the private, he was pointing excitedly. Just ahead, Black saw a hole in the rubble gaping at them like an open wound.

"L.T.," Hanneson addressed him, "what do you suppose is in there?"

"Don't know, but we can sure find out. Give me a hand."

The lieutenant laid down his rifle and his men did the same. All three worked together, bare hands pushing away loose stones and debris.

"One more." Black angled himself along the edge of a huge rock while the corporal and private each got a good grip. Together, they heaved up the boulder, and after scuttling a few feet, dropped it heavily onto the ground.

"Whew, lookie here!" The young private's eyes were like giant brown walnuts, nearly bulging out of their sockets.

"Give me a flashlight," the lieutenant commanded.

Corporal Biers dug into his knapsack. "Here, sir."

Lieutenant Black took the flashlight and angled himself through the opening. Once inside, he straightened up and looked around. "It's a tunnel! " he yelled up to the men.

Black walked the length of the cavern, until the light from his flashlight bounced off a shiny surface. He blinked several times, uncertain he could trust his own eyes. He was standing in front of two large steel doors.

"Holy shit," he whispered, staring at the dial setting and lock next to the handle. "The damn thing looks like a bank vault."

—-—

Word got around fast, the lieutenant knew. The soldiers of the American Seventh Army were brewing with excitement over the secret passage that held something of grave importance to the Nazis. Now, several hours after discovering the tunnel, Black returned with U.S. Intelligence officer, Lieutenant Walter William Horn and two captured Nazi members of Nuremberg's City Council—Stadtrat Heinz Schmeissner, a building expert and Dr. Konrad Freis, who had been in charge of air raid safety measures. Freis held the key and Schmeissner knew the five-digit code that opened the vault.

After their prisoners unlocked the steel doors, Lieutenant Black could see that his troops and Horn were just as astonished as he to discover what had been hidden in the tunnel's dark recesses. The whole room was piled with precious regalia stolen from countries all over Europe. One magnificent piece in particular caught Lieutenant Black's eye. He moved toward a huge, beautifully carved altar.

"That belongs to the Church of St. Mary's," Lieutenant Horn informed them.

But it wasn't the altar itself that drew Black's eye. It was an old, battered leather case that captured his attention. He picked up the case from the red velvet cloth it was resting on and opened it, removing what appeared to be an ancient spear. As Black stared at the gold-embossed crosses on its handle, a powerful sensation gripped him . . . one he did not want to release . . . one which would not let him go.

Instantly, Lieutenant Black knew.

History was in his hands.

The Professor lifted his eyes toward the sunlight streaming through his library window.

And on that very day, within hours of those Americans finding the Spear, the almighty Führer, Adolf Hitler, committed suicide, shooting himself in the head with his 7.65-mm Walther pistol.

Samuels had been sitting for hours. Finally, after a long stone silence, he walked over to a shelf of books and took one from its niche.

Mein Kampf by Adolf Hitler.

A bookmark lay between some pages. Professor Samuels opened the text there and found the quote he had written down long ago, attributed to Hitler himself.

> There is a legend associated with
> this Spear that whoever claims
> it, and solves its secrets, holds the
> destiny of the world in his hands
> for good or evil.

The words of Adolf Hitler held even more meaning for the Professor now. Although he didn't know what it could be, he was sure his dark ruminations meant there was something foul afoot.

CHAPTER 11

NEARLY EIGHT THOUSAND miles away, as the train moved slowly out of the Madras station, Kailas likened it to a caterpillar inching forward through the grass.

"*Chai! Chai!*" A young Indian boy with tin canisters yelled above the clanging bells, trying to sell tea to the passengers.

It was almost like a comedy, Kailas smiled to himself, the way the dangling arms reached through the open windows of the moving train— if you could even say it was moving. He watched as the young boy poured cup after cup, each one disappearing for a few moments, then returning empty, only to be quickly rinsed with murky water.

"*Chai!*"

Kailas thought that perhaps tea would help him stay awake for his journey. He should not sleep, he thought, with such a prized possession in his care. Kailas took a cup from his satchel and let the young boy fill it. Wishing to pay, he looked for a place to set it down, but the train's filthy floor repulsed him.

"Shall I hold it for you?" The female voice addressing him was soft, encouraging.

Kailas did not like to look at women, but found himself turning toward her. She was not from Kerala, not of Indian descent. Her skin was olive, of the Mediterranean, her eyes wide, like green opals smiling at him. He noticed her dress then, a long green and white tunic that reached her ankles.

"Your cup," she said, holding out her hand.

It's only for a moment, he thought. "Would you? Yes, that would be kind." He handed it to her and reached into the small purse in his satchel. Removing some rupees, he gave them to the boy.

"Six rupees," the boy said, still holding out his hand.

Kailas had only handed him five.

"One more rupee," the young boy insisted.

Kailas guessed it was a ruse the child played on all the sadhus, hoping to squeeze another rupee out of them. "Here, I'll give you two more."

The boy smiled widely, baring two broken teeth. He snatched the coins and hurried away.

Kailas turned again toward the young woman. "Thank you, madam," he said as she handed him the cup.

She smiled, and he felt her trying to hold his gaze. Kailas averted his eyes quickly with the motion he had learned and used so often around women. Instead, he turned to look out the window at the rolling plains. The April sun had already turned the grass a lush green, and the fields and countryside were blossoming.

Kailas closed his eyes, now wishing to draw his attention inward. Following the steady rhythm of his breath, he focused his mind once again on his purpose and on the Brotherhood.

The *Guardians* of *the Way* were an ancient union of men and women, dating back even before the time of Christ. They bore the knowledge of the secret teachings as well as the parables and prophecies of those disciples who had lived and walked with Jesus in Jerusalem, Egypt and India. They were called by many names—the Templars, the Rosicrucians, the Masons . . . and others lost or hidden. They were divided in sects but united in passion and purpose—to guard and protect the teachings of the Grail. Theirs was a world of the privileged . . . of secrets hidden . . . of ancient knowledge.

In the Indian tradition, within the Hindu sect to which Kailas belonged, they had always honored the prophet. *The Twin* they called him. Some of the men who came to the temple to pray, making offerings of sandalwood and lighting oil lamps, also considered themselves *Thomas Christians.* A disciple of Christ, Thomas had brought the teachings of Jesus to India, planting them like seeds within the people's hearts, upon the rich soil of the eastern land.

For the one is in the many, and the many are one.

The story of old was that Jesus took Thomas aside and revealed only to him the deepest and most secret of his sayings, but Thomas was not allowed to tell the other disciples or to write them down. Christ had conveyed that these sayings were powerful, and those who were able to discover their true meaning would not experience death.

Kailas remembered the first time he had heard of Thomas and of his secrets. *The Guardians of the Way* protected these truths—keys to unlocking the deepest mysteries of enlightenment, of creating a heaven on earth—bestowed upon mankind by the divine light through the great messengers.

I also know the truth, Kailas thought, *for with my own eyes I have seen the great guardians in India, and with my own ears I have heard the oral teachings passed through the generations, watched over by the elders.*

Kailas remembered as a young boy being trained in the language and precepts of *the Way*, he had been allowed to attend the sacred meetings of men and women. From the great lands they had come. The American statesmen, the European masters and scholars, the wise clerics of Palestine and Libya, the rabbis from Israel, and the Coptic clergy from Egypt. From all over the world they gathered together in secret, for the light was to be hidden and guarded, he was told, until the moment it could be revealed.

CHAPTER 12

MICHAEL OPENED THE curtains in front of his balcony. The morning sky was marred by clouds, making him all the more weary after another long night of analysis. Already feeling skeptical after his talk with Jarret the previous day, contacting Mabus seemed a dreaded chore.

One that can't be avoided, Michael realized. He picked up the phone and dialed.

"I was hoping I'd hear from you this morning," Mabus greeted, anticipation in his voice. "What are your findings?"

"Based on photographs alone," Michael answered reticently, "the writing seems to have been done when the parchment was new. Judging by the lettering, grammar, and vocabulary it's also consistent with known pre-Masoretic texts. In other words, it pre-dates the Christian era. I've also prepared my own translation. It's more literal, perhaps less poetic. But on such short notice, I can stand by it."

"Fair enough," Mabus replied. "I promise not to hold you to an assessment, but do you see this as an authentic document?"

Michael did not like giving this type of rapid-fire analysis. "Without question, I would not ascribe the text to Jeremiah. There simply isn't enough evidence to suggest that. Without certification of the author, I think you're going to have a tough sell using this to justify building a new Temple."

"I expected no less from you, Michael. Although I'm sure if you were given more particulars about the discovery, you might be convinced." Mabus' voice conveyed no disappointment. "Would you be willing to meet the authors of the proposition, Professor Binah and Doctor Mizrahi?"

"Actually, I would like to speak with them," Michael answered. Although he was surprised at Mabus' reaction, Michael felt compelled to discover more about the St. Catherine find.

No stranger to the Sinai monastery, Michael had visited St. Catherine's long ago through Professor Samuels' urging. The religious establishment, named after a young girl beheaded for opposing the early persecution of Christians, was a place he found mesmerizing. Its huge and mysterious library contained the most ancient Old and New Testament documents in existence, and its Basilica of the Transfiguration, dating from 550 AD, was filled with some of the oldest icons in the world. Many times during his stay, Michael found himself sitting under the arched ceiling of the refectory copying icons like *Christ Pantokrator—* Christ Omnipotent—while black-robed monks sat around the oak tables eating in silence.

"There is a meeting of the Council on Mideast Affairs this afternoon at two." Mabus was not a man shy about his requests. "If you can attend, you can meet both scholars at that time. I'm sure they'll be happy to tell you the details of their discovery."

Several hours later, Michael found himself hurrying along Eighth Avenue, weaving through the mass of lunch-hour pedestrians. It was just rounding two o'clock when he reached the Milford Plaza Hotel, where the council meeting was being held. He entered the ornate lobby and was directed to a large conference room that was brimming with people—a welcome sight since a full house meant he could melt into the background a lot easier.

"Dr. Sonada."

No such luck.

Michael turned. Standing in front of him was Sheikh Wayani of Saudi Arabia, an elderly gentleman whose noble face was always framed by a carefully groomed white beard. His keffiyah, tied around his head, flowed down his back.

"*Ahlan wa sahlan*, Sheikh." Michael had not known that the Sheikh, a close friend of Professor Samuels, would be in attendance.

"What brings you into our midst today?"

"Giovanni Mabus invited me."

Sheikh Wayani smiled. "And what part have you to play in his conference agenda?"

Michael, not about to reveal anything about the Jeremiah document, cloaked himself with humbleness. "I'm not a player, Sheikh, merely a consultant."

"Oooh?" Sheikh Wayani cocked an eyebrow in mock disapproval. "For a man behind the scenes, Michael, you have learned our game of politics very well. Never show your cards, even to a friend."

"You know me well enough, Sheikh. I'm engaged in research at the moment, and I never divulge information without the plaintiff's consent."

The Sheikh's eyes narrowed with suspicion. "Now Mr. Historian becomes Mr. Attorney. I hope you are not involved in this energy issue."

Michael shook his head. "That's just a rumor gone belly up, from what I've heard."

The Sheikh lowered his voice. "Don't believe everything you're told. I read some initial reports about the energy project Mr. Mabus is involved with. But now everything has gone hush hush. You must have heard about the work of Stephen Einsof?"

"The environmental engineer?" Michael had met him ten years earlier when Einsof had come to Qumran. He had been part of a research team trying to determine how the Dead Sea community, living in the area known as the Salt Sea two thousand years ago, had managed to provide themselves with drinking water. As Einsof related at the time, that stupendous feat, occurring in the lowest and most arid region in the world, had made the study all the more provocative.

"The same. Supposedly, he has developed a radical plan that will—" The Sheikh stopped abruptly, turning a stern gaze past Michael's shoulder. "Let's talk more about this later."

Michael turned to see that Mabus had entered the room. Apparently, Sheikh Wayani was not particularly fond of the council's leading man. Michael wondered what created the tension.

As Mabus began to make his rounds among the guests, the Sheikh directed the conversation to a new subject. "You're aware that there's another idea that has generated public interest. Maggie Seline's proposal has brought the matter of the internationalization of Jerusalem to center stage. I bring it up in light of Mr. Mabus' proposal for building the

Temple. I do not know if his ideas will be as influential now that her book has created such an uproar."

"Yes, I suppose Mabus has his work cut out for him," Michael noted. "She's certainly getting her picture on a lot of magazine covers."

"And?" the Sheikh asked, trying to elicit his opinion.

Michael's political savvy dictated he wait before offering it. "Sheikh Wayani," he said, bowing deferentially, "what do *you* think?"

"Ah," the Sheikh sighed resignedly. "Brilliant, timely, and a public invitation for a martyr's death."

Michael was surprised by the Sheikh's candor. "Actually, I think Maggie Seline has opened a new chapter for dialogue about the Middle East, but as for internationalizing Jerusalem . . . " Michael shrugged. "That will be a tough sell."

"Tough indeed," Mabus said, appearing at Wayani's side. His forced smile revealed displeasure at Michael's remark. "Sheikh, I see you have met my esteemed author friend."

"Oh, yes," the Sheikh answered. "Michael attended some seminars I gave on Middle Eastern history some years ago at Columbia. We also have some mutual friends."

"Like yourself, Mr. Mabus," Michael added.

"And Professor Samuels," Mabus offered.

The Sheikh acknowledged the acquaintance. "Of course. There isn't a scholar in the field who hasn't been influenced by the esteemed Professor."

Michael noticed Sheikh Wayani hadn't mentioned he was a close friend of the Professor's nor that he had seen Michael at Samuels' home on several occasions.

"My authorities have arrived," Mabus said, looking toward the door. "Excuse us, Sheikh."

Michael had hoped to speak further with Sheikh Wayani, but Mabus steered him toward the two scholars.

"*Shalom*, Professor Binah. *As-Salam alaikum*, Doctor Mizrahi," Mabus said, greeting his main speakers. "This is Dr. Michael Sonada."

Professor Binah, tall, with graying brown hair, stood next to the comparatively shorter, less distinguished looking Dr. Mizrahi. They both gave Michael a perfunctory smile, but their eyes betrayed suspicion. Michael was not surprised. In the world of scholars, discoveries that were proclaimed after laborious efforts were oftentimes quickly debunked by competitors.

"Mr. Mabus told us you would be here today, Dr. Sonada." Professor Binah addressed Michael courteously. "Thank you so much for reviewing the assertions that we're presenting today to the council. It is comforting to know there will be at least one sympathetic set of ears."

Michael recognized the polite rhetoric. He was about to respond when suddenly a voice boomed from the front of the room.

"Gentlemen and ladies." Omar Murzug, the well-known Lebanese journalist was addressing them. "We must begin. Our normal meeting will be shorter today since we have a presentation on the Third Temple proposition. First, we shall hear from Mr. Mabus."

As he stood at the podium, Mabus' commanding presence filled the room. "In less than a month the Peace Conference we have all worked so hard on will take place in Jerusalem. This has been a momentous undertaking. It comes at a time of renewed peril and pessimism.

"The war in Iraq has reduced the prestige of the United States to its lowest level in history. This is true not only within the Islamic world, but in Europe and Asia as well. America has been weakened, and this weakens our efforts to find solutions."

Michael listened as Mabus treaded on delicate ground. There were plenty of Americans who didn't want to hear that their country could be at fault.

"Israel is facing a crisis," Mabus stated emphatically. "If it hangs onto the occupied territories, it will either be an apartheid state or a democracy with an Arab majority. If it begins to disengage from these areas, it faces civil war. The fact that many of us have warned of this danger for thirty years does not make any difference now. The so-called friends of Israel have encouraged a self-destructive path for too long. Yet Israel cannot continue to exist as it has up to this point."

Even with his momentum building, Mabus' face was impassive. "Iraq is involved in a civil war, and we have just seen the governments shaken in Syria and Jordan. Perhaps Lebanon will be next. Egypt is a limping giant, heavily in debt and overpopulated. Saudi Arabia has become so dependent on the American economy and military that her own people are beginning to rebel in shame."

Several of the council members nodded in agreement. Michael wondered how Mabus would win over the resistors.

"In what direction should the Middle East go as a region?" Mabus continued. "What is needed? Every person in this room issues from the spiritual family of Abraham. We need to pray together as a family to find an answer. In fact, perhaps we have already found one. One of the more radical ideas that has come out of this forum in the last few years is for a Third Temple to be built on Haram al-Sharif. It now appears there may be a way to accomplish this. Our guest speakers today will explain."

"I hope this doesn't involve any of the crazy ideas of the whore mouthpiece of Hamas," a shrill angry voice called out.

"My friend, Mr. Netsah Karlbach." Sheikh Wayani softly cut him off. "I have known you since you were a child, before you entered the Knesset. I knew your father before there was an Israeli Parliament. Let us not be silly. We are men here. Not all friends, but all men."

Michael darted a glance at Karlbach expecting him to snap back. Instead, Karlbach, holding his tongue, glared hostilely as Sheikh Wayani continued.

"Maggie Seline has some noble ideas, albeit naïve," the Sheikh said. "But I believe they spring from her heart and generous spirit. To present her as a Palestinian puppet is an insult to my intelligence as well as your own. She has traveled tirelessly and spoken to representatives from every possible point of view. So it is easy for your CIA or Mossad to plaster the world's press with photos of her meeting clandestinely with members of Hezbollah or Hamas. But where, I wonder, is the photo I saw last year in the *Jerusalem Post* of her talking to a group of young Jewish settlers?"

"She has low moral values," Karlbach barked, his long jutting chin pointing toward a copy of the *Washington Times*, "lovers in every city she visits. She is a disgrace, an unmarried sow. Here." He threw the paper so it landed in front of Wayani. "There's an article there about her liaison with a known Palestinian terrorist."

"Propagandists in Washington. What a surprise," the Sheikh said with an exaggerated voice.

Sheikh Wayani's feigned look of astonishment made Michael chuckle.

"The Reverend Moon loves to support Republican agendas in his newspaper, Netsah," Wayani said condescendingly. "Don't believe everything you read."

Netsah Karlbach would not be dissuaded. "Seline wants to voice her ignorant beliefs and calls for women, even Jewish women, to join her in her blasphemous schemes."

"So what? Who among us can deny her views the attention they deserve on their own merit?" The Sheikh nodded toward his assistant who was sitting at a small desk with his laptop connected to a video projector. With the press of a button, an image appeared on the screen at the front of the room.

"Look at the facts," the Sheikh said, pointing to the map. "As for your claim that she attempts only to undermine the Israeli government, you know well that her effort to internationalize Jerusalem only concerns the Old City, perhaps from Mt. Zion to Jaffa Gate over to Herod's Gate then around to Absalom's Tomb. You may keep your Knesset, do what you will.

"I tell you this," the Sheikh was standing now, his face stern. "If she is not invited to the conference as a member of the American delegation, or as an independent, then she will be invited to be a member of the

Saudi delegation. If that is not acceptable, then my government will not attend, and nor will, I suspect, any reputable Palestinians."

Although the Sheikh directed his remark at Karlbach, Michael knew he meant it for Mabus as well.

Hod Nastar, an Arab representative in the Knesset, then stood up and nodded her agreement.

The Sheikh then motioned to his aides to gather their papers as he started toward the door.

Acting quickly, Mabus positioned himself, blocking the Sheikh's exit. "I am quite sure, Sheikh Wayani, that your arguments will be sufficiently convincing." He turned to Netsah. "Will they not?"

Netsah shrugged his shoulders as if he did not care whether the conference took place or not. "Why should they be? These problems are far too complicated to be solved by dreamers. Israel will not allow the topic of Jerusalem's internationalization to be placed on the agenda." He gave Mabus a smoldering stare. "We have made too many concessions already."

The old Sheikh stared coldly ahead and motioned toward his attendant, who turned off the projector. With swift efficiency, the young man placed his gear in a leather case.

"I will be down the hall when you are done. My colleagues can continue in my absence," the Sheikh said, bowing his head. "*As-Salam alaikum.*"

He walked out the door.

The old fox, Mabus thought quietly to himself. *The time has come for the House of Saud to return under the rocks, with the lizards and scorpions for company. And that woman, Seline. Her simpleton views have caused me enough trouble.*

Mabus realized another need was presenting itself.

CHAPTER 13

"LET US CONTINUE," Omar Murzug said. "The council recognizes Amy Fry, representing the Christian Peace Cause."

"Now, perhaps we can take another look at the issue presented at our last meeting—the injustices against Palestinians and the resultant suicide bomber attacks." The young woman spoke with a soft but determined voice. With her brown hair tied in a single braid and large, owl-like glasses perched on her nose, she looked more like a librarian than a freedom fighter. "We need to search our souls and ask why. Why, especially in God's name, would anyone strap explosives to themselves?"

"You have no right to speak of injustice. Only an animal would blow up women and children," the yeshiva scholar, Rabbi Neveh, exclaimed.

Sava Hawali, a Sufi cleric, stood and paused for a moment before he spoke, as if waiting for communication from a higher power. "Islam has no role for suicides. They are not even permitted burial and will be damned for eternity."

Rabbi Neveh began to protest again, but Sava paid no heed. "However, with the blessing of some Iranian clerics these suicides are being praised as acts of martyrdom—a ploy that has a long tradition in all our faiths." Sava nodded at Bishop Angelico, the Papal representative, who smiled gratefully, looking pleased to be acknowledged.

"How can anyone condone blasting innocent children with bombs packed with nails?" the Protestant minister, Reverend David Smythe implored, wringing his hands.

Mustev Ari, a Lebanese reporter stood up defiantly. "Israel itself was founded on terrorism. Just ask the families of the British soldiers murdered while policing Palestine. Their crimes were innocence, their sentence death," he declared. "And what about Count Folke Bernadotte, the Swedish UN diplomat who helped negotiate a ceasefire in the 1948 war—killed by the Jewish Stern Gang. His crime? Urging Israel to allow Palestinian Arabs to return to their homes."

"The Achille Lauro." Josh Ralson, the well-known and self-important *New York Times* editorialist weighed in. "A bunch of PLO terrorists wheeled a crippled American tourist off the ship's deck."

"The King David Hotel," Hod Nastar volleyed back. "Ninety innocent people killed by a Jewish bomb in 1946."

"Remember the Stern Gang? They hung two British sergeants in the same year, then booby-trapped their bodies," contributed the ruddy-faced reporter, Reginald Buckwald, from the UK's Independent News Service. "And on January 7, 1948 a young biology student, Uri Cohen, rolled a bomb from the back of a stolen police van into a crowd of Arabs waiting for the number three bus in Jerusalem. Seventeen people died, including the wife of Hameh Majaj." He paused. "It was her wedding anniversary."

"Eleven dead Israeli athletes at the Munich Olympics." The Reverend Smythe, a look of righteousness on his face, would not be undermined. "That isn't holy war. It's unholy hell."

"Do you have any right to spout such nonsense?" Hod Nastar shot to her feet, looking intently at the American preacher. "How many innocent children died in Vietnam? Was *that* war? How many of your own people died from handling Agent Orange? Who are you to tell us of hell, holy or otherwise?"

"This isn't Vietnam, madam."

The minister's holier-than-though tone did not dissuade her. "No, in Jerusalem we've been fighting for thousands of years," Nastar fired back.

"That just means you are more practiced at fighting," the reverend remarked snidely.

"*Arabs and Jews.*" Amy cut through the crossfire. She gave Smythe a silencing stare.

"Brothers," Nastar added.

Reverend Smythe looked around the room. Appearing cornered, he answered, a feigned reasonableness in his voice. "I suppose the longer the bitterness flows, the longer it will take to stop."

"We *must* stop it," Mabus interjected, crowning the exchange, "otherwise we all fail. Agreed?"

The group fell abruptly into silence.

―――

Perfect timing, Michael thought. Like a great showman Mabus knew the right moment to enter and take credit with a bow.

"Agreed?" Mabus asked again.

"Yes, yes. Agreed, agreed," most of the members exclaimed vehemently. Others, still visibly doubtful, gave perfunctory nods in the name of peace.

Then, during a break in the meeting, Prince Sharif, the Sheikh's nephew, approached Michael.

"Dr. Sonada," he whispered, pointing down the hall, "if you have a moment . . . "

Michael welcomed the change in venue. The stamina these people showed for grudges was as impressive as it was depressing.

Michael followed Sharif to a small conference room. Sheikh Wayani, just finishing his afternoon prayers, stood and turned.

"My friend." The Sheikh grasped Michael's hands. "These are troubling times. Our worlds are colliding. Christian and Jew . . . Islam and the West. None of us may survive."

Michael sensed urgency and hesitation in the Sheikh's words. Although he appeared driven to reveal his fears, Michael knew that Sheikh Wayani was also constrained by generations of Bedouin reserve. Understatement, an ancient curse, had not served the Arabs well in a fast-moving world. Michael waited.

"What do you know of this Peace Conference and this evidence for building the Third Temple?" Sheikh Wayani finally asked.

"Very little," Michael replied.

"Ah. Perhaps you have performed some service for our Mr. Mabus that seals your tongue." He smiled when Michael made no response. "I see. You know that this Third Temple idea is a powder keg. Anyone who claims the Muslim world will watch calmly is either foolish or foolhardy."

"Or both."

Sheikh Wayani's face lightened at the remark. His voice lowered to a whisper. "Perhaps this time, our prophet wears the dress of a woman. Find out more about this Maggie Seline. She has also unearthed information about Einsof and the financial backing for his new energy system. Mabus denies any monopoly. He says he no longer funds Einsof, but my government is certain he does."

"Why wouldn't he admit it?" It made no sense to Michael. Usually, financial tycoons were only too happy to have their names attached to grand ideas. Mabus was certainly not shying away from the Peace Conference publicity.

"I don't know," the Sheikh replied, "but the two together—the development of Einsof's energy ideas and the formidable task of organizing this Peace Conference . . . a handful even for someone with Mabus' reach."

Michael had to agree. The whole thing seemed an impossible dream. When he returned Wayani's gaze, he found the Sheikh was studying his face carefully.

"You must get back now," the Sheikh directed. "If you discover anything suspicious, contact the Professor. He will know how to reach me."

Michael got back just in time to hear the Temple presentation. Afterwards, he approached the two scholars.

"I was the one present when the jar was opened," Professor Binah stated. His dark eyes hinted of antiquities seen and mysteries perceived.

"It was only a 'discovery' by definition. The monastery has been rumored to have a copy of Jeremiah's lost prophecies since Pope Leo III sent his crazed, iconoclastic minions charging around destroying anything of religious value seven hundred years ago. At that time, an old rabbi and his grandson found their way to St. Catherine's. The rabbi was anxious to preserve his heritage so he left the monastics several sealed jars for safekeeping."

"Without telling anyone what was in them?" Michael asked. "Whatever happened to him?"

"He never returned. No one knows whether he revealed what was in the jars to the abbot or how the rumor started. Soon the story being told was that the jars contained the lost prophesies of Jeremiah. Some even thought it was just the dream of an old monk. At the base of Mt. Sinai, the voice of God is loud and men start hearing what they want to hear."

Michael was fully aware of the Sinai's mysterious nature.

"I first visited St. Catherine's in the years when Israel occupied the Sinai," Binah continued. "Perhaps the army, in an unusually lucid moment, thought a religious scholar might be just the right person to liaison with the monastery. It proved to be the right decision. I found the abbot, Father Barsanuphios, was of a rare, intellectual breed. Even though he lived in isolation in that desert locale, it had not stopped him from being versed in world affairs. Being a great admirer of the former UN Secretary General, Dag Hammarskjöld, the priest offered me his favorite quote. 'Understand through the stillness. Act out of the stillness. Conquer in the stillness.' "

As Binah revealed his memories, his demeanor saddened. "A few months ago I got a call from Father Barsanuphios. He said he was old and his time was drawing near, so I flew down to Nabi Sâlih as quickly as I could. When I arrived, he told me of a dream: The old rabbi had returned and he wanted the world to have the scrolls.

"The abbot was certain it was a portent. He decided the time had come for the jars to be opened. I just hoped the old man would not be disappointed. For much of his life his wish had been to see the words of Jeremiah for himself. Even so, the abbot would not invent a dream for his own sake. Men who need gratification do not live in the desert for eighty years."

Binah paused, his eyes appearing to search Michael's for resonance. "Soon, a jar was brought into Father Barsanuphios' cell. It turned out that all the other vessels had been lost or had vanished in the last seven hundred years. This particular jar that remained was made of clay and its lid was still secured—covered by a thick layer of wax embedded with two seals."

Intrigued, Michael's eyes widened. "What did the seals look like?

"One of them had three letters embossed on it," Binah answered, "*Tzadee, dalet* and *kof.* Together that spells *tsadek,* which as you know, means righteousness. The other seal was an Eastern Cross, with two cross members at the top and a third slanting crossbar representing the foot piece."

A Jewish and a Christian seal. Michael found the combination intriguing.

"As I continued examining the vessel, the abbot sat quietly in his chair, his lips moving in prayer. Knowing that these would be the last few hours of his life had moved me greatly. I would gladly not have broken the seals if it meant he would stay. Finally, he lifted up his dark eyes, feeling my hesitation. 'My son,' he said, and indicated that I should proceed to open the jar."

Binah paused, a look of regret in his eyes. "Of course, I did as he wished. Carefully, I slid a knife under the wax around the lid and lifted it off. One of the monks shone a light into the container while the abbot and I looked inside. Several tightly rolled scrolls were packed loosely within. I retrieved the center one and laid it on the table. The leather binding strap was brittle and snapped when I attempted to untie it. Yet, after I removed the linen wrapping, I found the parchment itself was surprisingly supple and was able to partially unroll it. I placed it before Father Barsanuphios so he could see it while I took some preliminary photos. Then the monks and I left the father alone for an hour."

Binah dropped his gaze and took a deep breath. "When we came back he was dead—still sitting upright with his eyes fixed on the parchment."

Michael swallowed back his own sentiment. He, too, had met Father Barsanuphios and had been touched by the saintly monk's presence.

"The following day," Binah continued, "I called my friend, Dr. Mizrahi of the Egyptian Antiquities Department, and asked him to come to the monastery and begin examining the scrolls with me."

Michael looked toward Mizrahi who had been silent during the rendition. "So what evidence do you have that this is the work of Jeremiah?"

"Nothing concrete," Dr. Mizrahi stated, now explaining their stance. "We have actually only fully studied the one section you were shown. The rest of the scrolls are presently in Cairo, all being carefully opened, photographed and placed in protective cases. Thus far, what we do know is that because of the use of *scriptio plena*, the texts predate the Christian era."

Professor Binah, having regained his posture, spoke slowly now, keeping his emotions in check. "We're aware of your reputation, Dr. Sonada, and value your opinion. I admit to you, I want very much for this to be Jeremiah's words—for Father Barsanuphios' sake."

Dr. Mizrahi put his hand on the professor's arm. "We have been working on our calculations for the original Temple site for some time. This scroll was only opened very recently."

"And that's when I became involved."

Michael turned to find Mabus at his side. Engrossed in the story, he hadn't noticed that Mabus had joined them.

"Since I have been funding their work," Mabus stated with an air of authority, "it is also my wish to see these efforts proceed without regard for politics and budgeting delays. Because Dr. Mizrahi and Professor Binah are the authors of the New Temple plan, we need outside confirmation that authenticates the Jeremiah document as well as someone who I can trust to be discreet until we can lay this out publicly at the Peace Conference. If this leaks too soon, chaos will result."

Michael took a deep breath. He realized he had a lot to consider. "Well then, I will take a fresh look at the material based on what I've heard. In the meantime, of course, I will not discuss this with anyone."

Mabus' demeanor lightened with the promise of a fresh assessment of the parchment. "That's all I ask, my friend."

With the agreement made, they shook hands. As Mabus escorted Binah and Mizrahi to a table of interfaith delegates, Michael looked on, unable to cast off his uneasiness. Was this Mabus a man of peace, he wondered, or a fool about to create an even bigger rift?

CHAPTER 14

THE SOUND BOOTH of the *Harper Crow Studios* was lined with a vinyl brickface paneling—so far from looking like the real thing it would have been laughable if Maggie wasn't feeling so apprehensive. In fact, she hadn't felt this nervous since her first interview on *Good Morning America* a couple of months earlier.

Nervously, Maggie fingered the opal pendant hanging from her necklace. Just touching it gave her a sense of calm. She remembered the day her grandmother had given it to her long ago—the day of her mother's burial.

Only four years old, Maggie had stood shivering in the cold autumn breeze, watching as her mother's casket was lowered into the earth. Afraid, she shut her eyelids tightly and tried to envision her mother's soft blue eyes once again. When she realized she couldn't, her fear deepened. *Why can't I see them anymore?* she wondered. *Why did mommy leave me?*

A loud thud startled her and she opened her eyes. They were covering the wooden box with dirt. Her father was crying—something she had never seen her dad do. The little red lines in his eyes spoke to her of pain and loneliness..

"Mommy is gone," he said. His voice was soft, almost a whisper.

"Where?" she asked. "Where did she go?"

"With the angels."

Maggie saw a golden face, bright wings, beckoning compassionate eyes. This was the image she held of death, but wondered where the angels had taken her mother. She was told heaven, but heaven was not a word she could understand. *Where there are no troubles and there is peace.* But how could there be no troubles? Was there really a place like that?

Later that morning, her father led her down a familiar path, now strewn with brittle reddish-brown leaves. Maggie walked up the brick staircase—the same rough stone she would tread for nearly twenty-two years—steps that led her to her grandmother, Laurel Seline, and to the chain with the opal pendant.

Now, as she sat silently in the sound booth, Maggie wondered. *What would my grandmother do today if she knew her only son had been targeted so maliciously?* Maggie would never tell her about the photograph or the threat. It made no sense to create more grief. Laurel had believed her son had died in a suicide bombing in an Israeli café. Wasn't that difficult enough?

"Ms. Seline."

The voice came from behind her. Maggie turned to see a young production assistant poking his head from behind the studio door.

"Starting in one minute," he announced, before disappearing again.

Moments later, her two male adversaries entered, smiles on their faces and ready for action. Maggie took a deep breath. *Well, here we go.*

She heard the numbers being rattled off over her headphones. "Four, three, two, one . . .

"Good evening. This is Harper Crow and the Christian Witness Radio Program coming to you live from New York. My guest tonight is Maggie Seline author of *Pure Vision: The New Jerusalem.*"

Full of self-importance, Harper heralded himself a spokesman for the entire Christian faith. Maggie was aware the man saw no contradiction between his so-called beliefs and being paid large "consulting" fees by the Republican Party or the pharmaceutical and gun lobbies.

". . . and Jack Bailey of Fox News' *The Bailey Report.*"

God help us, Maggie thought. Jack Bailey, Mr. Fair and Balanced himself. Bailey's constant use of phrases like *OH REALLY, get off of it . . . OH REALLY, I suppose all women should have a voice in American government, OH REALLY, OH REALLY . . .* had caused his show to become known in comic circles as *The Oh Really Report.*

"Now Maggie. May I call you Maggie?" Harper Crow's wide head and fleshy face was crowned with a large radio headset. It appeared to Maggie that his equally large body threatened to topple out of his swivel chair at any moment. "You have proposed a radical plan to make Jerusalem the international capital of the world."

"Spiritual capital," Maggie corrected.

"Okay, spiritual capital, but to a lot of Christians and Jews that sounds like an idea to reward Palestinian violence."

Maggie knew she had to jump right in.

"Israelis are not simply the good guys and Palestinians the bad guys, Mr. Crow. This is not the Middle East version of cowboys and Indians. We need to have an intelligent view of the situation. Would we as Americans—for that matter, would we as New Yorkers—wish to have our town invaded by foreigners, have our land taken away from us, our homes trespassed, be hoarded into refugee camps or killed in the streets, or at best be unable to move about freely during the day, but instead be subjected to constant humiliation and tyranny? Would we as Americans stand for this? Not for a second. You bet we'd fight. Let others call it terrorism, but we would fight tooth and nail. We are not going to let anyone trample on our fundamental human rights and do nothing about it. So, if a Palestinian who has been oppressed for the last fifty years decides to fight back or do something as crazy as become a suicide bomber— which by the way is their own brand of retaliation that really began in the 1990s—then why should we be surprised? If the world turns its back on you while you are screaming for your life, perhaps you would use something louder than your voice to get heard."

Harper Crow, normally high-strung and verbose himself, looked surprised by her long-winded discourse. Maggie began to wonder if she had even taken a breath.

"Yet, I am not in any way condoning suicide bombings," she added.

"*Oh really*, Ms. Seline." The accusing tone, the mock sense of the audacity of it all, came from none other than Jack Bailey.

Ignoring him, Maggie repeated her statement. "I do not in any way condone suicide bombings, Mr. Crow, another horrendous act of war. What I *am* doing is trying to understand why some people might resort to such an extreme measure. It is surely shocking to find out that a young college student, or an eighteen-year-old woman about to be wed, would feel so hopeless and degraded that he or she would be willing to give up life itself. It's the ultimate form of weeping—where there is nothing left to live for, where life is no longer precious and death is welcome." Maggie paused. "We have reached a point where we should all hang our heads in shame."

Crow started coughing profusely, as if he was choking on the mere thought that he would have anything to be ashamed about. He gulped down some water. "And why would you think that?" he asked with exaggerated disbelief.

"Because our country was founded on principles." Searching her memory, Maggie hoped she wouldn't stumble over the words. "Let me quote our own Declaration of Independence: *We hold these truths to be self-evident, that all men are created equal, that they are endowed by their Creator with certain unalienable Rights. That among these are Life, Liberty and the pursuit of Happiness. That to secure these rights, Governments are instituted among Men, deriving their just powers from the consent of the governed.*

"If we investigate our own history, we will find that the original thirteen colonies were under the tyrannical control of England's King George III. He had been using the British army to attack his own people in the Americas." She paused. "The colonists finally reacted with violence."

"We're talking about terrorists, Maggie, not freedom fighters." Harper let out a loud sigh for his listeners.

"Semantics," she retorted. "We're standing here today because the revolutionaries who founded our country fought back against a government that had turned against its own citizens. In today's terms, those revolutionaries would be known as *terrorists.*"

"This is a bunch of baloney," Bailey chimed in. "You bleeding hearts, so liberal in your views toward enemies of our country." Mimicking benevolence, he placed his hands together in prayer and pleaded mockingly. "Let them go free. Oh please, don't hurt them. They're our brothers." Rolling his eyes and crossing his arms across his chest, he bellowed in a voice filled with exaggerated frustration. "OOH . . . REEALLY!"

"Gentlemen, I hear your concerns," *unintelligent as they may be,* "but I still believe it is the path of *reconciliation* that we need to follow here. I know that you both like to pray, don't you, gentlemen?"

Taken by surprise by the question, both men could only go down one road on a live radio broadcast. "Of course. Certainly, we do."

Maggie had them.

"So then let us say a prayer now for the children," she said. "More aptly for bits of children, pieces of tiny flesh splattered across charred concrete, gunpowder-singed fingers severed from hands that will clutch for their mothers' breasts through eternity."

"My God!" Harper, raising his hand toward his throat, gestured with the cut sign.

Maggie was certain the producers would do no such thing. They would love the contention, she knew, since it would probably send Harper's ratings through the roof.

"Let us together imagine collecting these severed heads, hands and feet and offering them as sacrifices to our gods," she continued.

"Oh shut up!" Bailey shouted.

"The gods of territory, the gods of pride, the gods of ethnic purity. Let us not forget the gods of financial gain. Is that not the greatest of the gods worshipped by most nations." Maggie's voice dropped to a whisper. "Does this sound cruel?"

"But the children are Israelis." Beads of sweat flowed down the sides of Harper's forehead. Maggie watched as he dabbed himself with a hanky while he desperately tried to maintain control. "Killed by suicide bombers."

"Yes, they are," Maggie agreed. "They are Israeli children killed by suicide bombers. They are Palestinian children killed by air raids and retaliation squads. But in the end, these are our children, yours and mine. Children don't understand nationality."

Bailey was glaring at her hostilely. "So what are you suggesting?"

"If we can't do better than this, then we are no different than the civilizations that before us offered human sacrifices," Maggie answered. "Throughout the world we feed human beings to faceless terrorists and military squadrons hiding behind aircraft, armament and plastic explosives. And who profits from these cowardly acts? The chemical companies who design the explosives. The nationally subsidized corporations that produce the bullets that splatter the brains of mothers and children alike."

"Ms. Seline, I believe that's enough!" Harper yelled. Maggie thought he was about to explode. His face was beginning to look like an overblown balloon.

Undeterred, she continued. "Will it stop without intervention? Of course not. Throughout the world we worship murdered ancestors daily by sacrificing those we hold responsible. Instead, let us turn the tide.

Let us pray to a different God. A benevolent God. A healing God who wishes us to acknowledge others as our brothers and sisters."

"Oh, in the name of Christ," Bailey blurted, pursing his lips.

"We can begin today, now, by uniting together as children of *one* family. We can say *No More* to the human sacrifices by planting a powerful seed—an aspiration for the internationalization of old Jerusalem."

A look of excitement lit up Harper's eyes, and a smile spread slowly across his face. "That all sounds very wonderful, Maggie," he remarked with sugared hostility, "but how does this affect Israel? Jerusalem is *their* capital."

Here it comes, Maggie thought. *They're gonna love this.*

"No, Jerusalem is a city under siege. Captured in the 1967 War, it has been held hostage for too long. The original United Nations resolution for Israel called for the creation of an international de-militarized zone in Jerusalem. This resolution would not *only* be for Arabs or Jews. The world needs to stop the killing. Palestine, the Sudan, Kashmir, Bosnia. What's the difference?" Maggie stared at her host. "Mr. Crow, it's this simple: Do you believe in the message of Jesus?"

Harper's jaw dropped. "What right do you have—?"

"Simple. Yes or no?" Maggie cut him off.

"Who are you to take it upon yourself to question the followers of our Lord?" Bailey's voice shook with anger.

Maggie standing now, spoke calmly. "I see plenty of self-appointed ministers and politicians, up to the highest levels, who propose themselves as representing a man who was condemned to death as a criminal." She smiled, narrowing her eyes. "Yes or no? Do you believe in the message of Jesus?"

"Of course I do," Harper Crow bellowed.

"Then you know, *Blessed are the peacemakers, for they shall be called sons of God.*"

"Matthew five verse nine," Crow squawked.

"Don't give me chapter and verse. *Google* can provide that." Maggie was enjoying herself, slowly walking back and forth, pacing to the extent her headset cable allowed. "There's a lot more to Christ's teachings than the number slapped on Bible verses. Look a little deeper. Aren't the Beatitudes the central message of this man?"

"Jesus was not a *man*. He was the Son of God. The only Son." Harper was twisting the microphone wire with his fingers. Maggie thought he probably wished he had it wrapped around her neck.

Bailey smoothed a hand over his grayish white tufts. Looking almost nauseous, he sputtered, "Jesus will return to this earth very soon, Ms. Seline, within our lifetime."

"Your problem, gentlemen, is that neither one of you believe in the message of Christ. Not really. Deep down, you haven't accepted the challenge of the *Sermon on the Mount*."

"I resent that, Ms. Seline." Harper Crow, accustomed to guests wilting under his bombastic arrogant style, looked surprised Maggie wasn't playing along. Reduced to gibbering like a scolded kindergartener, his voice became boyish. "I accept Jesus Christ as my savior, my lord, my—"

"What you do not accept," she injected, her voice strong and unmoving, "is the responsibility that goes with the teachings. *Blessed are the poor in spirit, for theirs is the kingdom of heaven.* Have you reached out for the poor, the underprivileged? Your radio ministry has raised millions of dollars to support politicians who work tirelessly to deprive those in need of life-sustaining government programs.

"*Blessed are those who mourn, for they shall be comforted.* No people on earth have suffered more heartache than the Arab and Israeli families who've seen loved ones blown apart and dismembered. What have you done besides urge our government to send more arms and money to Israel knowing that will fuel the fire? Praying for Armageddon comforts no one, nor will it hasten the return of Christ.

"*Blessed are the gentle, for they shall inherit the earth.* Isn't it plain, Mr. Crow, that the victims of your doomsday scenario must in the end be victorious? Otherwise, the words of Jesus must be false?"

"That's not so. Why you bi—" Harper caught himself just in time.

Smiling, Maggie bombarded him some more. "*Blessed are those who hunger and thirst for righteousness, for they shall be satisfied. Blessed are the merciful, for they shall receive mercy. Blessed are the pure in heart, for they shall see God. Blessed are the peacemakers, for they shall be called sons of God. Blessed are those who have been persecuted for the sake of righteousness, for theirs is the kingdom of heaven. Blessed are you when people insult you and persecute you, and falsely say all manner of evil against you because of me. Rejoice and be glad, for your reward in heaven is great; for in the same way they persecuted the prophets who were before you."*

Maggie took a deep breath and leaned toward the two men. "Let us, Mr. Crow," she said, her tone now softening, "you and I and Mr. Oh Really . . . I mean Bailey, put aside our differences for a few moments and pray that we might experience the inner meaning of Christ's message."

Both Harper Crow and Jack Bailey, both surprised by the directive, had no choice but to agree.

Maggie knew radio stations hated dead air. It was synonymous with media suicide, yet no one moved or touched a dial or whispered instructions to Harper. In that moment of silence, the spirit of compassion and love was allowed to flood the air waves.

Suddenly, the door to the studio crashed open. A stout man dressed in black, his face covered with a stocking mask, burst in. Maggie could see the pistol in his hand.

"Hey, you can't come in here!" Harper jumped up in fear, throwing off his headset.

"Get down," Bailey yelled at the others. He dashed around to the back of his chair, taking cover.

As she bolted for the exit, Maggie lost her footing and fell. On the floor stunned, the emergency lights blinking in a nervous panic above her head, Maggie tried to get her bearings. With no time to lose, she started scrambling to her feet just as Harper and Bailey began screaming bloody hell behind her.

That's when the shots rang out.

CHAPTER 15

A S SHE SAT in her living room listening to Maggie's interview, Laurel Seline heard the gunshots blaring over the radio. She jumped on the phone. For the next couple of hours she tried without success to get through to the Harper Crow Studios, all the while staring at the television screen to see if she could find out anything about her granddaughter.

Other than some initial reports of the shooting, the news stations were only replaying audio accounts of the incident. Nonetheless, Laurel kept snapping the remote, bouncing from one channel to the next. Finally, she found a live report.

"According to Police Detective Ronald Rohan," a female reporter outside the studio entrance on Thirty-third Street informed, "a lone masked gunman, who escaped the studio, fired several shots at Harper Crow and his guests Jack Bailey and Maggie Seline. Mr. Bailey is unharmed. There are some reports that Mr. Crow is being treated for shock and is about to be removed from the building into this awaiting ambulance."

At that moment, ambulance attendants in white jackets and pale blue shirts moved briskly as they rolled a stretcher out onto the pavement. Just as they were about to place it into the back of the emergency vehicle, Laurel saw the look of fear and confusion on Harper Crow's face.

"As you can see," the reporter relayed, "they are placing Mr. Crow into the ambulance right now, and we are told that they will be taking him to St. Vincent's Hospital. As of this time, there have been no other reports concerning Maggie Seline or her whereabouts. Sources say that Ms. Seline raced outside, apparently looking for the assailant. Sources also say more shots were heard on the street and suspect further foul play. The FBI has also been called into the investigation since there is fear of a possible kidnapping. We will keep you informed of further developments as they occur. Reporting live from Thirty-third Street and the Harper Crow Studios this is . . . "

Fearing the worst, Laurel muted the set. *What happened to my granddaughter?*

Laurel remembered watching Maggie leave after visiting the previous weekend. A storm was beginning to brew just as Maggie was headed down the path toward her car. Although lightning ripped through the dark gray clouds, no rain had fallen. Even then, Laurel sensed that something powerful was moving toward them—an unseen force that was intensifying the winds.

This evening brought a similar feeling. Laurel walked onto her porch and looked up into the sky. Above, the clouds were moving quickly, sweeping past a nearly full moon. All day there had been a threatening aura of rain, but none had come. Laurel was certain now that it would.

The night wore on—a restless one. When Laurel finally looked at the clock again, it was 5:22 A.M. She had been up most of the night deep in thought, her body working on sheer adrenaline. Feeling fully awake, Laurel walked outside and stood for a long while watching the oncoming storm. Like the force of the wind, Laurel's determination mounted as it approached, and with the first clap of thunder, her resolve was set in place.

Finally, the great breath of wind sighing across the Catskills brought in the rain. Laurel felt relieved, like a heavy burden had been released. When the downpour ceased at daybreak, the sky was cleared of clouds— a stark blue.

It was time to go.

After filling her old leather backpack with some essentials for her journey, Laurel got dressed, making sure to put on a pair of tough walking shoes. As she headed toward the door, she stopped in front of the mantelpiece and glanced at the picture of her son, David. His face was determined . . . his smile soft . . . his intense green eyes were looking at her from behind the glass.

A pain stirred in her heart as Laurel felt the bond of commitment. What she was about to do she would do for him, for her granddaughter, Maggie, and for what they both believed in.

Once outside, Laurel locked her front door and turned over a worn oak sign so the big, black letters faced outward:

GONE WALKING

And that Laurel would do. She would walk the mountain trails down to the river valley as she had done many times before, but this time she wouldn't turn back.

CHAPTER 16

LAUREL WALKED, her final destination uncertain. She had always loved to venture along the winding mountains paths that led to the river, so it seemed fitting to begin her journey in the same way. As she moved forward, she found a sense of stillness, a quiet center that would clear her mind. Movement, she knew, was the key.

At least Laurel was aware of where her walk would lead initially, to the middle of Manhattan, the hub where the world met. *Perhaps even to the United Nations.* One thing was for certain, Laurel would not sit at home, watch her television set, and be spoon-fed by a media bought up by corporate giants. No one knew where Maggie was. That was the only fact. Now it looked like they wanted to kill Maggie's message as well, but Laurel was determined not to let them.

Every step she took brought more shape to Laurel's plan. She would follow the Hudson River downstream . . . toward those news crafters who had created so much difficulty with their fears. She laughed aloud at the thought, wondering if she had gone mad. She then pictured herself confronting them with the truth even as they tried to deny it. Laurel could barely imagine what she would say if she had the opportunity and was certain she would probably look the fool. But it didn't matter any longer. Maggie was missing, and the world of appearances was meaningless.

Laurel finally arrived in the heart of Woodstock at the Goldstar Creativity Center, her friend's home and crafts store.

Lonnie will understand, won't she?

She walked up the cobblestone path that led to Lonnie Hersch's front door. Multi-colored flags flapped in the wind as she knocked. "Anybody home?"

A voice from the back of the house called back. "Laurel, is that you? I'll be right there."

Laurel glanced at the small sculptures for sale on the porch and the Picasso-like drawings and paintings lining the outside wall of the entranceway. The swirling colors created a vibrant field on the canvases—energy in motion.

Lonnie walked onto the porch. In her sixties, her attractive wide face made her look a lot younger. Once crowned *Belle of the Hudson Valley* when she was seventeen, she was also a veteran of the 1969 Woodstock Music Festival. But that was all before Laurel had met her. These days, Lonnie's life had taken a less frivolous turn. Head of the Woodstock Chapter of *Gold Star Families for Peace*, she had helped turn Woodstock from a theme park for artists and wanna be hippies to one of the foremost centers for the current day peace movement.

"You're joking?" was her response when Laurel announced her plan, which now definitely included walking to the UN.

"No, Lonnie, I'm not."

"Do you think they'll really listen to you?"

"I have no idea." Laurel's tone was sober. "All I know is that it's what I've got to do. I have a voice. We all do. It's high time we make it known that some of us have seen through the lie." Laurel had lost her only child, Maggie's father, to the insanity spawned in the Middle East. She was not going to lose her granddaughter, too, and allow all of Maggie's work, her vision, and her proposition for the Middle East to die without a fight. "I'm walking to Manhattan, and if they won't let me talk at the UN, then I'll speak out on every street corner."

"Don't think I'm going to let you do this alone." Lonnie's tone presented more of a statement than a question.

"Well, actually . . . I came here to ask you to join me."

Lonnie took a moment to respond. All of her actions these days centered on whether or not they furthered her mission. *Bringing home the troops, not supporting the killing, ending an illegitimate war.*

Aaron, sent home in a box two years ago. Lonnie immediately thought of her son, his tour in Iraq, and the senselessness of his death.

Now confronted with Laurel's urgency, Lonnie finally answered. "There's no doubt that the more people you have along with you, the stronger your message is going to come across. I believe in a *new* Jerusalem, too, Laurel, and the more voices that speak out for a referendum on making Jerusalem an international city, the better. We've got to start somewhere."

Jules knew something was up when she saw her Aunt Lonnie and Laurel Seline walking down Tinker Street, each with a backpack and Lonnie holding a *Gold Star Families for Peace* sign. She was used to her aunt's eccentricities and spur-of-the-moment decisions and imagined seeing her with Laurel meant whatever they were up to had to do with Maggie Seline's disappearance.

After running up to the women and digging for some answers, she found out she was right. "*What* are you two doing?" she asked, wanting to make sure she had heard correctly.

"We're walking to the United Nations. We're bringing Maggie's ideas to the big boys," Lonnie said flatly.

A philosophy and political science major at Marist College, Jules had read Maggie's book and was impressed with the ideas, finding herself in agreement with Maggie's conclusions that political and military solutions were a dead end to the problems in Jerusalem. It would be a leap for mankind, Jules recognized, to create a solution that would actually resolve the situation on a spiritual basis. The bottom line—any movement toward healing, true peace and tolerance was the ONLY answer.

A couple of summers ago, after graduating high school, Jules had spent a month in Israel—an experience that only heightened her sensitivity to Maggie's plan. While there, she had a bird's eye view of all the senseless fighting. *What insanity, a nation armed to the teeth and living in denial.* What if the American south had continued to deny integration? What if South Africa refused to recognize apartheid? Wasn't that what this was about? A holy land with a third of its citizens considered unholy, even inhuman? *How holy is that?*

After hearing more of Laurel's ideas on the referendum, it didn't take Jules long to decide.

"New York? The UN? I'm in."

As the three women walked down the road toward Kingston, Laurel noticed some familiar faces among the drivers. Questioning glances and amused smiles let on that some of her neighbors thought she had probably cracked, a reaction to Maggie's disappearance.

It's a reaction alright, and there's a lot more to come.

The honking of a horn brought her attention to a passing car, the driver waving and giving a thumbs up toward Lonnie's sign. As they walked on, more people noticed them, some stopping to ask what they were up to. Finally, several hours later as they reached the outskirts of Kingston, they were greeted by a large green neon sign that buzzed steadily at them as they approached.

The Kingston Motel & Diner.

Laurel decided to give way to her aching feet. "Let's stay here for the night."

Hungry and tired, Lonnie and Jules readily agreed. They entered the diner and chose a table by the counter. After ordering their meals from a rather surly waitress, they were approached by a slim, light-haired fellow in a mauve pullover, a look of determination on his face.

"Hello ladies, my name is Eric Derckson. I'm a reporter for the *Daily Freeman.*"

Oh Lord, Laurel thought. She nodded politely, acknowledging him. "Good afternoon."

"I couldn't help noticing ma'am, but you and your friends seem to be walking quite a bit. I saw you this morning in Woodstock, then on Route 28 in West Hurley. A couple of hours later I saw you again walking through Ulster. Now here you are in Kingston. I don't mean to pry . . . "

Yes, you do, Laurel thought.

"But are you ladies in need of assistance? If you're headed over the bridge, I could give you a ride. I live in Rhinebeck."

"Didn't you see the sign?" Lonnie said, pointing toward her Gold Star Peace sign.

"Actually, no," Derckson replied.

"You didn't hold it up every second, Aunt Lonnie," Jules admonished.

"We're walking." Laurel hoped her abrupt tone would prompt him to leave.

"Yes, I see that ma'am." Derckson nodded, looking for more. "But where are you walking to?"

"To the *city*." Lonnie's interjection was met with a sidelong glance from Laurel.

"You're *walking* to Manhattan?" Derckson raised his eyebrows. It appeared he was going to keep on fishing. "Why would you ladies be doing that?"

"*We're walking toward the NEW JERUSALEM.*" Laurel's emphatic outburst caught the reporter by surprise. His wide eyes questioned what he had heard.

"It's symbolic," Laurel explained. "Actually, I'm walking to the UN. My granddaughter is Maggie Seline. I am walking to further her ideas on a resolution to the Middle East crisis."

"So the author of *Pure Vision* is your granddaughter?" A flash of recognition passed across Derckson's eyes. "Did she ask you to do this, ma'am?"

Perhaps it was meant to be. Laurel felt her juices flowing again. *Isn't this why I set out, to speak up?*

"Ma'am," Derckson repeated, "did Maggie *ever* ask you to initiate this walk to Manhattan?"

"No, she didn't," Laurel replied.

"She didn't direct you to go to the United Nations before her disappearance?"

"You could say that her ideas are what have now inspired me to make this walk. Maggie says that a direct approach is needed, and I believe she's right. People need to voice their concerns to their leaders. Not only here in New York, but throughout our entire country. Not only in the U.S. but throughout the world."

Laurel watched as Derckson scribbled furiously.

"The world is stuck, repeating the same mistakes over and over again. Government leaders, with their heads buried in the sand, have only exacerbated the problem. It is time for women to breathe some fresh air into the situation. A feminine perspective is imperative. New versions of Sharon and Arafat—men without sense—are not what the world needs now."

"Tell me more," Derckson prodded. "Where do you see all this leading?"

Laurel's voice grew stronger as she answered his questions. She felt energetic, even surprisingly at ease. Wondering at the change in her demeanor, she let her eyes shift toward the remaining sunlight shining through the glass windows. It refreshed everything on the diner's counter—the meringue, chocolate, strawberries, the vanilla icing—making every morsel look delicious and vibrant. Even the young reporter, his face open and attentive, seemed to resonate with her thoughts.

Not wanting to miss a word, Eric Derckson listened carefully as Laurel spoke. The more he heard, the more intrigued he became. His reporter's ear was starting to burn, and he sensed the heat of a growing story was at hand.

The grandmother of Maggie Seline, Eric kept thinking, *walking to the United Nations.* His reporter's instinct told him this story would keep getting bigger . . . and he would be the first to break it.

CHAPTER 17

GROGGY AND DAZED, Kailas was startled by the sudden lurch of the train as it pulled into the station. Had he been asleep?

"Gaya, next stop. Next stop, Gaya," the conductor called out over the loudspeaker. "Bodhgaya connection. Gaya! Gaya!"

He looked at his watch. Kailas could scarcely believe he had been so tired—a day's travel and he had fallen in and out of sleep throughout the ride. He felt drained of energy.

Squinting at the daylight, Kailas slipped his tunic off his shoulder and tied it around his waist. They had traveled several hundred miles north of Kerala to Bihar, and the temperature had dropped. Still, Kailas grew hotter and more uncomfortable with each moment. Perhaps once off the train, he would regain his senses.

After all, he still had a task to perform.

Kailas touched the satchel around his waist. Within, the sacred parchment lay hidden. It was the key that would unlock the secret, known only to a chosen few.

As he gripped the satchel closer, he felt the connection he shared with the great Brotherhood—a belief in the divine nature of all beings, in universal truth. If you were a man or woman of faith you entered *the Way*. It did not matter what faith that was, for it was divine inspiration that was necessary to guide a man's life on earth. How it came, the path it took, was not paramount. Only its source had any meaning. From the lineage of ancient masons, the Brotherhood would join together in prayer, concentrating on God—*the great architect of the universe*—and not on their differences.

Kailas lifted his hand up to the rack above his head and pulled himself up. He turned toward the window and saw the dry earth turn into a metal platform as they pulled into the station. Just then, familiar tunes of Hindi music drifted through the cars, along with the voices of young men who were yelling, "Chai, newspapers, bidis, cigarettes!" as they moved like ocean currents through the disembarking crowd.

"Gaya! Last call!"

Kailas felt a wave of nausea moving through his body. His throat grew sore and scratchy and he felt he might fall over from the heat. Focusing became harder, but he managed to get past the young woman next to him. As he attempted to push his way forward, he felt her moving up against him. His body stiffened. Perhaps she was using him to part the crowd for her as well.

When Kailas exited the train, he could barely keep his balance. As he reached the stairs at the end of the station, a man stepped out from behind one of the columns.

"Do you need some assistance, sir?" the man asked.

Kailas smelled the scent of stale cigarettes. "No, I am fine," he answered, swaying to avoid him. But before he could get past, Kailas felt a hand shove into his side, pushing him behind the corner of the platform.

"Get it! Get it from him!"

Kailas could barely stand, but he recognized the voice of the young woman who had been sitting next to him on the train.

"Where?" her menacing companion asked, pulling on Kailas' tunic.

"Try the satchel," she commanded.

Though he felt dizzy and faint, Kailas held tightly as the man pulled hard, almost ripping the satchel from him.

"Give that to me!" the assailant demanded.

Kailas heard the sound of a switchblade snapping open. Suddenly, the man lunged, and Kailas was knocked down to the ground. Just then another man, lean and wiry, wearing glasses and a red jacket, jumped from behind a pillar, stunning Kailas' attacker. Grabbing the assailant by the arm, he knocked the knife out of his hand. The young man then slammed his fist hard into the attacker's face, knocking him down to the ground.

Surprised to see her cohort defeated, the woman turned and ran into the crowd. The assailant soon followed, scurrying to his feet and disappearing down the platform.

"*Kya hal he?*" the young man who had saved him asked.

What is your condition? Kailas was so dazed he could hardly speak. "I can barely stand."

"We can't stay here, sir. Let me get you to my house. It's not far, and you can rest there." The man pointed to a motorized buggy.

"You're a rickshaw driver?" Kailas knew he couldn't stay in the area. "Get me to the Stupa."

"But the gentleman is not in any condition—"

"Just do it."

Kailas took hold of the stranger's arm and moved forward, swaying and tripping like a drunk. The young man helped him into the rickshaw.

They sped along the road, the shops and stalls appearing as if rushing past them in a whirling haze. All the while, Kailas held his head in an attempt to stop his mind from spinning. "I can't understand why I'm so dizzy and woozy."

"Looks like drugs," the driver said over his shoulder.

"What!" Kailas said incredulously. Then he remembered the tea he had let the woman hold for him. *My God,* he thought, *drugged.*

They zoomed down the busy street, the rickshaw weaving in and out of oblivious pedestrians like an electric toy car run amok. Soon, they were out of the city and heading along an isolated country road toward Bodhgaya. Twenty minutes later, just as they were entering the town, the rickshaw driver turned down a narrow road.

"You must rest and recover," he said before Kailas could protest. "You can stay at my home tonight. I live close to the Stupa and can take you there in the morning."

Kailas found himself giving in, his head still aching. "What is your name?" he asked his rescuer.

"Sajjid."

Kailas noticed a prayer rug leaning against the lower panel at the side of the driver's seat. His savior, he realized, was Islamic.

Sajjid reached back toward Kailas, a large plastic bottle of water in his hand. "Drink as much of it as you can. You need to wash out the poisons."

Kailas took several swigs. Slowly, his mind began to clear, although the pounding in his head had barely subsided.

"Do you know who those people were who attacked you?" Sajjid was looking at him in the rear-view mirror.

Kailas shook his head. No, he did not know who the assailants were, but he remembered what the elders had told him.

The dark prophet would also be sending emissaries. *The greater the light, the darker the shadow.* Any knowledge that shed light upon his plans was often thwarted. The dark one's power was without limit, or so it seemed. He stood against *the Way* and all it protected, but he did not stand alone. His legions also believed in the supremacy of the rich, the sheltering of the privileged. Theirs was a world of "Do unto others before they do unto you."

The guardians had reminded him that this dark prophet did not strive for peace or unity. Compassion and understanding were not his aims. Yet, so many listened when he spoke of doing God's work and helping the world, of bridging differences. They did not know his goal was to create more of a divide—polarizing peoples, faiths, nations.

Kailas quivered in the backseat of the rickshaw.

No, I do not know my attackers, but I know who sent them.

CHAPTER 18

NEARLY TWO DAYS had passed, and Maggie Seline was nowhere to be found. Michael was still distraught and tired, his nights filled with images that seemed more real than his waking life. Dark patterns from his mind wove themselves into the appearance of reality, and it was becoming hard to tell one from the other. He was amazed by his turmoil—the *why* of it bothered him as much as the pain itself. Why would he feel so close to someone he barely knew?

Maggie's ideas had begun to affect Michael far more than he realized. Intimate, nurturing, spiritual—he could hear her voice still as it sounded on the Harper Crow Radio broadcast before being silenced by the shrill sounds of gunfire and screams.

As the early morning clouds moved in across the bay, Michael found himself staring at the Manhattan skyline. There was only one question in his mind, the same question that had the city officials and police in a tailspin: Where was Maggie Seline?

Frustrated, Michael left his apartment and jumped into his car. *Just drive,* he thought.

A light rain falling, he headed over the Brooklyn Bridge into Manhattan where he found the city far more awake than he was. Although traffic was still light, taxis whizzed by as usual, and vendors pulled their carts along the streets, hustling to their work posts before the morning rush.

Without knowing why, Michael drove to Thirty-third Street and parked his car across from the Harper Crow Studios. As he stared at the studio entrance, he remembered Sheikh Wayani's comment. The Sheikh had called Maggie's quest a public search for martyrdom. Was that what had happened to her? Was it the course of those who cared about this world to be doomed to the same fateful end?

Michael climbed out of the car and began to walk. New York City was cast in a wet drizzle, yet somehow nothing seemed to dampen its spirit. A place that believed in vision had provided millions from around the world a refuge—where their hopes and dreams had a chance if they were willing to work hard to attain them. Yes, New York was definitely a city of vision, so what was so hard about conceiving a city of peace?

Absorbed in thought, Michael bumped into an old man as he rounded the corner.

"Good morning to you, too," the gentleman addressed him, re-adjusting the fedora Michael had nearly knocked off his head.

"Excuse me," Michael apologized. "I didn't see you there."

"No, I suppose not. You being in another world and all," the man said, staring at him with large bulbous eyes. He leaned back against the wall of the skyscraper as if he were leaning against a pole, using his umbrella for balance.

Michael thought the man, in his dusty black overcoat, looked out of place. "You're out early, sir."

"I'm always here around this time of day. I like coming when there's not many people. Early morning . . . it's the best time for bums and old people." He laughed at Michael's dumbfounded stare. "Actually," he said, "it's a good time to remember the old days."

"Did you work around here?"

"I did—as an architect for International Engineering & Architecture." He tapped the building behind him.

"You worked in *there*?" Michael asked. The massive structure behind them stretched up into the sky, hovering above all the other buildings on the street. A few amber street lights, still on, gave the walls of the stately stone building a glow.

"Until a couple of years ago," the man answered nostalgically. "It used to be the best place in the world to work until the merger. After it was taken over, they never changed the company's name or the management. That's why only a handful of people actually know about it. Damn shame, though. The ideas that were germinating here . . . " He gave a low whistle. "International Engineering would have stood in the forefront of design and building. The whole world could have changed, if only those greedy bastards would have allowed it."

The old man's anger made Michael curious. "What company did they merge with?"

"That swanky Libyan's company. You know, the one with the big villa in Italy."

Michael couldn't believe what he was hearing.

"Oh, lots of people in the company were so impressed. The European Union guy, the head honcho of that big conglomerate—Mr. Mabus himself of Mabus International—interested in appropriating our firm. You could see the dollar signs in the CEO's eyes." The architect shook his cane. "I knew it would only mean trouble. The ideas sprouting here . . . brother, they were unbelievable. You want to talk about changing the face of technology, creating new energy systems. But now . . . ," he said, shaking his head, "everything is just a secret, kept under wraps, so the public won't know."

"What do you mean?" Michael asked.

"Everything about the takeover was secretive," he whispered, "very quiet, conducted in closed meetings. Me, I was too old school, ready for retirement they said. But I saw some of the plans before they forced me out."

"What plans?"

"Energy producing plans—solar and electrical energy. Would have annihilated our dependence on oil and gas and moved this world into another era, almost overnight in the scheme of things."

On instinct Michael asked, "Do you know Steven Einsof?"

The old man took a step backward, his eyes narrowing tensely. "Why do you want to know?" He drew his umbrella in front of him. "I can't help you. I haven't seen him for months."

"Wait," Michael pleaded as the man began to walk away. "I just want to find out what happened."

"Mabus. *He's* what happened," the man sneered, tensing his mouth as if he were ready to spit.

"But he's working for peace. From what little I've heard, Mabus is funding Einsof's energy project and helping to manifest his ideas."

The architect's gray eyes glared at him icily. "You'd better wise up, son. Mr. Mabus is not a peacemaker. He's an oil magnate. Ideas that can have a great impact on humanity should never be entrusted to the likes of a *Giovanni Mabus*."

The biting words took Michael aback.

"What is your name?" the old man asked.

"Michael Sonada."

Without another word, the gentleman turned abruptly and walked away, tapping his umbrella like a cane as he hurried down the misty street.

CHAPTER 19

MICHAEL COULD NOT get the old architect out of his mind. He had been thinking about the strange and confusing encounter throughout his drive back to Brooklyn. It was as if the man's words were following him like the dark clouds that passed across the bay. *Everything is just a secret, kept under wraps, so people won't know.*

No sooner had Michael entered his apartment than the telephone rang. For some reason it sounded louder than usual. He wouldn't have answered except for wanting to put an end to its insistent jarring.

"Hello."

"Is this Michael Sonada?" the voice asked.

"Yes."

"This is Stephen Einsof."

Michael felt as if someone had thrown a bucket of cold water on his head. "Mr. Einsof . . . "

"I hear you wish to speak to me."

"I do. Can we meet?"

"Yes," Einsof said simply. "I'll meet you at the entrance to Central Park, Fifth and Fifty-ninth."

"When?"

"Now."

Keys still in his hand, Michael ran back out and into his BMW. He sped over the Brooklyn Bridge, suppressing the urge to complain to himself about the drive back to the city. He maneuvered up FDR Drive to Fifty-ninth Street and parked along the tree-lined block. Fifth Avenue turned into one long stream as he ran across the cement pavement and over the pitch black granite. Finally, Michael could see the statue of General Sherman ahead. Close to it, sitting on a bench under an oak tree, was Stephen Einsof.

Michael ran up to him.

"Michael Sonada?" Einsof stood and stretched his hand out toward him. His determined blue eyes were steady, but the dark circles underneath them told a different story.

"Mr. Einsof." Michael was nearly out of breath from his sprint.

"Stephen," Einsof replied, his eyes scanning the street. When he seemed satisfied there was nothing out of the ordinary in view, he turned toward Michael, gesturing for them both to sit.

Before Michael could ask any questions, Einsof wearily closed his eyes, appearing to be gathering his thoughts. As he studied his companion, Michael noted Einsof's long angular features only accentuated the gauntness of his face. He wondered, *How long has it been since this guy's had any sleep?*

When Einsof opened his lids, Michael found himself staring intensely into his stark, penetrating gaze.

"I think we can help each other," Einsof announced.

Michael was surprised at the directness of the remark.

"You want to know about the energy plans, and I need someone I can trust," Einsof said, his eyes unwavering. "I'm aware of your work, Michael. That's why I know you couldn't have all the background info, see the implications, and still be a part of this so-called Peace Conference Mabus is planning."

Michael felt his nerves tighten. "What are you talking about?"

"For several years, my friend Tod Rahamim and I had been developing a new approach to energy management. When we were studying some ancient sites in Great Britain, we discovered some new applications for what are essentially age-old secrets." Einsof took on a pedagogic tone. "Simply put, the earth has a resonant frequency that can be coupled with solar energy and gravity, which can then be used, for example, to oscillate large synthetic crystals. The energy produced by these crystals can be transmitted without wires, initially for low energy needs."

Einsof smiled, a hint of pride in his eyes. "In essence, we combined the ancient technology of the Druids with the high-tech wizardry of Nikola Tesla. Tod and I were convinced that our idea, which we called Einsof-Rahamim Energy—ERE—could be expanded to higher-power applications, but we needed funding."

"Don't tell me," Michael said. "Something you got from Giovanni Mabus?"

Stephen's eyes opened further. "You know?"

"Rumors. But what does this have to do with the Peace Conference?"

"Two years ago, Mabus agreed to fund our project. He gave us an unlimited budget for equipment, material and manpower. We set ourselves up in upstate New York and operated in total secrecy. We agreed not to contact anyone about what we were doing or where we were. We even took code names so our security guards wouldn't know our actual identities." Einsof wiped his face wearily with his hand. He unclasped the water bottle he had fastened to his belt and took a swig. "Initially, I couldn't have asked for better results. Our first two prototypes worked more efficiently than expected. Mabus brought some engineers to see us, and they were amazed at our results. Within six months we were generating hundreds of amps of power and transmitting it a distance of several miles."

"Without transmission lines?" Michael was impressed.

"Absolutely. But then things got weird. A few times we found our equipment had been rearranged. Then our original security people were replaced one by one by a Libyan intelligence team." Einsof gave him a wary look. "We didn't let on though that Tod, with his Lebanese background, could understand and speak Arabic. We stuck with our code names, thinking Mabus had not divulged our true identities, even to the new security team. Tod, even more suspicious than I at the start, began spying on them like it was a game. The game got uglier, though, when it became apparent that someone with engineering skills was manipulating our experiments."

Michael was trying to keep up. "Why would they do that?"

Einsof shrugged and brushed his hair back with his fingers. "Someone understood our system enough to attempt redirecting the energy, so rather than broad transmission it was directed narrowly. Targeted, you might say."

"Like a laser?"

Einsof nodded and took another sip of water. "We were determined to find out what was going on, so Tod set up a parabolic microphone and a voice-activated recorder aimed at the guardhouse. The security team spoke in Arabic so he had to interpret for me. The word *Longinus* kept coming up, as if they were referring to some sort of event."

Longinus . . . the Roman centurion who held the Spear. Michael remembered what Maggie Seline had told him about Vice President Bohmer's interest in the relic.

"Last week, several of the guards accompanied Mabus to Brussels. Tod decided to use that as an opportunity to sneak into their quarters and poke around. I was against it. 'Leave it alone,' I told him. But he was determined to find out what they were up to."

Einsof finished off his bottle of water and took a deep breath. "I never saw him again. The cops found him in a ditch at the bottom of the mountain the next morning. His car was totaled. They said he was drunk and that they had found several empty beer bottles at the scene." Einsof cast a look of doubt as he shook his head. "Tod and I had been friends for years. He was a devout Muslim. He *didn't* drink. At that point, I didn't know what to do, so I acted as if I had no suspicions. Yesterday, I came into the city for Tod's wake. Then today, I got a call from a friend who said you'd been asking about me."

Michael nodded.

Einsof turned toward him with a worried look on his face. "Tod found a list of names and addresses last week." He paused. "Yours was among them. It appears you're being watched closely."

Now it was Michael's turn to feel uneasy.

"As soon as I heard you were on the Peace Conference team doing some kind of translation," Einsof continued, "I started to get suspicious about all the links. Since I met you in Qumran and knew your work to be legit, I took the chance in trusting you."

Einsof's story had snapped Michael from his doldrums. He remembered Sheikh Wayani's comment that although Mabus was clever and focused enough for his ventures to run parallel, his current undertakings were so extraordinary they would be enormously painstaking to accomplish. In that case, why coordinate a peace conference in Jerusalem while still developing Einsof's theory of ERE—a venture that would require vast amounts of time, ingenuity and money to harness and manage properly? *Danger and headaches vs. power and wealth.* It just didn't make sense.

Michael felt he was being led in a new direction. He turned toward Stephen. "Where is this secret site of yours upstate?"

"In Olive," Stephen answered, "not far from Woodstock."

Michael knew the area. It was close to Peekamoose Gorge, where he and Rachael had rented a cabin and gone hiking. "Let's go. I want you to show me what you're doing with this energy project."

Looking eager, Stephen got up from the bench. "Good. You can see for yourself how powerful this thing is."

CHAPTER 20

J ACK SHULTZ HAD been keeping his post on the Kingston Bridge for nearly fifteen years. He had seen nutjobs before, even a couple of people doing headers off the bridge, but not a liberal, pot-stirring old granny about to do the unthinkable, and on his turf.

Nobody walks this baby.

And where was this Seline woman and her friends walking toward anyway? What the hell did they mean by a *New Jerusalem*? The anger in him mounted. He just hated the audacity of this stupid woman, questioning the U.S. government, the most powerful force on this earth. He slammed his newspaper down on the counter and grappled with the phone as he punched in his fellow toll-collector Maureen's number. After all, it was stupid to think you could change the world with a new idea.

How preposterous. How downright moronic!

Maureen Donaldson didn't need Jack's phone call to inform her who was walking toward the bridge entrance. She had read the article in the Daily Freeman that morning herself. Maureen glanced down at the newspaper still sitting on her counter.

BEARSVILLE WOMAN 'WALKING TOWARD THE NEW JERUSALEM'

Kingston, NY—Laurel Seline and companions are en route to the international center of the world, the United Nations, to voice their support of Maggie Seline's proposition of the internationalization

of Jerusalem. The women are also urging a civilized end to the current wars in
Iraq and ...

Laurel Seline . . . now that's a lady with courage, Maureen thought.

With her phone now ringing off the hook, Maureen looked to her side toward Jack's booth. He was waving his arms frantically, motioning for her to pick up.

"Yes, Jack," she answered.

"What are we going to do about this?" he asked snottily.

Jack was a pain in the ass, but Maureen knew he followed protocol. Still, she had five years seniority.

Maureen's thoughts moved quickly. Her own granddaughter, Katie, was only five. If she was kidnapped, Maureen would be paralyzed with fear. Here was Laurel Seline actually doing something about her granddaughter's disappearance. Not only that, she was keeping Maggie Seline's ideas in play.

Finally, someone with the backbone to stand up for common decency. Not like some of our leaders, living the lives of petty thieves . . . like some people I know.

Maureen gripped the phone firmly. *Sometimes it takes the sense of a woman to wake a man up.* "Well, Jack," Maureen answered slowly, looking at him through the glass booth. "I think we're going to do absolutely nothing."

"What!" Jack yelled so loudly that several of the drivers in his lane reared their heads up toward him.

"You heard me."

"I'm gonna call this in myself then, Maureen. Don't think I'm gonna just stand here while some sniveling old broad stands up for that unpatriotic bitch of a granddaughter and decides to use my bridge as a pass over to that kingdom of heaven of hers."

Maureen laughed out loud into the phone. This clod, who was normally about as eloquent as a moose, was so furious he sounded like a ranting poet.

When her laughter subsided, Maureen answered. "Remember that little incident, Jack? Oh . . . about a month ago. We were short a few hundred dollars at day's end. I found out and reported it to Bill at accounting."

Dead silence on the other end. Maureen knew she had his attention. "Then a few days later it turned up. You remember, 'Someone put it in the wrong envelope,' you said."

"I told you, Maureen," he whispered into the phone. "It never happened before. I put it back, right? You promised as long as I put it back and never do it again . . . "

"That's right, and I normally keep my promises," Maureen threatened. "But if you don't back off and let these women pass, you're going to have to start tap dancing quickly, because I'm going to rat your ass out to Bill and to anyone else in the free world who'll listen."

Maureen saw the grimace of hatred and resignation that crossed over Jack's face.

"Are we clear?" Maureen knew she had already won.

"Very."

With the click of the phone, Maureen smiled silently to herself. She relished her part in the picture. Would it be a big picture or a fluttering image? *Who can tell.*

In any case, it was another notch for womankind.

Laurel sensed good fortune was with them as the two toll keepers looked preoccupied collecting fares from the oncoming cars. She thought the people in the booths had seen them, but they showed no signs they had. Laurel was not about to question their lucky star as she, Lonnie and Jules began walking along the bike lane over the bridge.

"It's like walking into the sky." Jules' voice vibrated with excitement as she peered over the railing.

Barely taking her eyes off the pavement, Lonnie's fear of heights betrayed itself. "Oh please, tell me about it."

But Laurel felt a sense of growing freedom, like a bird unleashed to soar to the heavens. She became fascinated by the bridge itself, spanning high above the flowing expanse of the Hudson—a brilliant concept brought to reality. She knew that literally taking the first steps across it had already broadened her perspective.

Protecting life and human rights cannot just be a local affair, she realized, *but a global, a universal condition.*

Walking the bridge, she could feel the link between one side of the river and the other. More bridges were what mankind needed, linking sides around a central theme. *Peace and human decency based on spiritual truths.*

Honking horns then brought her mind back to the oncoming traffic. Waves, smiles, angry grimaces, stern glares, startled awareness, surprise. Whatever the face behind the wheel conveyed, Laurel kept on moving.

A carload of students drove slowly past them. "Alright . . . yeah." Two young women, each sticking her head out a window addressed them.

"I think it's a great idea," a young black woman called out.

"Can anyone walk with you?" her friend asked.

"Yes, anyone can walk." Laurel's role was swiftly metamorphosing. "But I am particularly encouraging women to join us in any way possible."

"Move it!" A loud voice yelled from the diesel truck behind them. "Get going!"

"Shut up!" one of the young women shouted back. "Good luck," they said together as the car pulled ahead.

"I'm with you, ladies." A young, scholarly looking man in a rusted Oldsmobile that was plastered with Bard College stickers slowed his car down to a near halt. "Are you really headed to the UN?"

"Of course," Lonnie retorted before Laurel could speak.

The car behind him honked. The man in the Oldsmobile gave them a wave and smiled as he moved forward.

"Get off the bridge," someone else yelled above the loud rock music coming from his car radio.

"No!" Lonnie barked back, waving him off.

"Lonnie, please. Whatever you do, don't respond negatively."

Lonnie's face contorted with anger, making her appear as if she were about to go into a tirade. After a few deep breaths, she seemed to think better of it. "For you, okay. If you think we shouldn't respond, I won't."

"I think we shouldn't respond," Laurel answered.

When they finally reached the other side of the bridge, a sign on the road read DUTCHESS COUNTY, ROUTE 199. They took a side street that wound through Fernwood Forest and led them into Rhinebeck. There, in front of the Beekman Arms—*the Oldest Inn in America*—a flurry of commotion at the hotel's entranceway caught Laurel by surprise. Several men and women came dashing toward her, pens in hand. Just then the door to the Inn flew open. Laurel recognized the man exiting as a reporter from the local news network RNN. His eyes fixed on hers as he strode toward her, his cameraman hurrying by his side.

Flanked by Lonnie and Jules, Laurel stood her ground and braced herself. *There's no turning back now.* Apparently, several members of the regional press corps had picked up Eric Derckson's lead and had gathered there awaiting her arrival.

Just as the reporters were about to descend upon her, several women carrying *Women in Black* and *Gold Star Families for Peace* signs appeared by her side.

"Lonnie?" Laurel suspected her friend had made a few calls.

Lonnie just smiled at her and nodded. "Yes."

"Mrs. Seline!" It was Derckson himself, yelling with the rest of the reporters.

Laurel motioned for them all to settle down. "It's Laurel, by the way," she said, as she pointed toward the *Freeman* reporter.

"Laurel, have you heard from Maggie?"

"No, I haven't." It was hard for Laurel to believe it had been less than forty-eight hours since Maggie's disappearance. It felt more like an eternity.

Derckson shook his head sympathetically. "So then, what exactly do you plan on doing?"

"First, my companions and I plan to reach Hyde Park and the Franklin Roosevelt Library." Laurel paused, sensing that she would be leaving town with more people than she had arrived with. "We're bringing the *Big Deal* everywhere."

A number of people in the crowd began to laugh.

"And what's the *Big Deal?*" the RNN reporter questioned.

"Women."

Cheers broke out. The female reporters laughed and applauded, as did the women working at the hotel desk who had stuck their heads out the front door to listen.

"The Big Deal is women," Laurel reiterated. "FDR gave us the Four Freedoms: freedom of speech and expression, freedom to worship God in our own way, freedom from want, and most important . . . *freedom from fear.* It's time for women to take hold of all of them."

A petite woman standing with *Women in Black* spoke up. "And you still plan on continuing on to the UN?"

"Yes, I do," Laurel answered. "I have to. Wherever Maggie is, whatever happens, I will carry her message forward."

"What exactly is that message?" asked a female reporter who was waving an ABC mike.

"There's a chance for peace in Jerusalem. There's a chance for peace in the Middle East," Laurel replied. "The fighting and warring have got to stop. The mothers of those men and women who are dying have had enough. Americans and Iraqis, Israelis and Palestinians. We say *No More* to war. Eleanor Roosevelt herself declared, 'No one won the last war, and no one will win the next war.' I agree, and the women on this street agree."

Clapping hands and stomping feet drowned out the laughs. "Let's go. Hyde Park. It's just down the road."

That was it. It didn't take Lonnie long to comprehend that her shy friend, Laurel, had become a media star in front of the lobby entrance of the Beekman Arms on the second morning of their walk.

As they moved forward, Jules began singing the words to *Let Peace Begin With Me*, while Eric Derckson, keeping pace beside her, simultaneously called in the story on his cell phone.

Walking behind them, Lonnie found her thoughts turning toward her son. She remembered how handsome Aaron looked in his Marine uniform after boot camp. She had been so proud of him although anxious for his safety. When he left for Afghanistan, she hoped that his tour would be a short one—that Osama bin Laden would be caught quickly and the Taliban would be annihilated. Not the case. Years later—no bin Laden and the Taliban had reemerged. When they shipped Aaron's body back from Iraq, it was as though her life had ended as well.

Let this walk be for Aaron and for all the others, she thought.

As the group moved forward out of Rhinebeck, Lonnie saw it clearly. They were walking together to honor the past, as well as to invoke the future.

CHAPTER 21

INITIALLY, WHILE DRIVING Einsof out of the city Michael had been quiet, trying to digest everything the scientist had told him. Now, finally heading up the New York Thruway, he began to regain his equilibrium. "Tell me," he asked, breaking the silence, "what is this ERE exactly?"

Einsof sat up in his seat. "You want to know the whole story that led to its conception, or do you just want the short deal?"

"Give me the long version," Michael ventured, although he was certain Einsof's riddles would take him a while to figure out.

"Okay then," Einsof began, taking a deep breath. "It all started during my architectural training at Oxford. I made numerous visits to ancient sites throughout England, returning frequently to Glastonbury where I became engrossed with the myths and legends surrounding the Tor—the large cone-shaped hill east of town. It was obvious that the megalith society that developed Glastonbury, as well as those that developed Stonehenge and Malta, were aware of the earth's energies in ways we've lost.

"This energy is based on the *ley* of the land. Ridiculous . . . that's what many of the super-scholar, head-in-the-sand types thought about my interest in the sacred science, but there were others, scientists and historians as well, who had already begun to take a new look at the science of energy meridians along the earth."

So, Stephen Einsof is another one of "those" scientists.

"L-e-y," Einsof laughed, as if reading Michael's thoughts. "Not l-a-y. *Ley* are the earth's natural energy meridians. The Chinese call them *lung-mei*, dragon lines, an expression of *feng shui*. Alfred Watkins, an Englishman, coined the term *ley* after a mystical experience traveling through Herefordshire in 1921. He had a moment of realization when he actually saw the lines of the earth's energy stretched out before him and realized they were aligned with standing stones and mounds that ran for miles. Carlos Castaneda described the same thing in his books."

Castaneda, Michael recalled, was one of Rachel's favorite authors. She would love this Einsof guy. Smart enough to change the world and wacky enough to try. "Did you ever have a similar experience yourself?"

"I did. In Scotland on the Isle of Arran," Einsof divulged. "It was sunset, and I was standing within the Circle of Stones at Tormore when I actually felt the energy rising from the earth. It was as if the stones themselves were magnifiers sending the energy upward. All the while, the sky around me was thunderous and the air crackled with electricity." Einsof paused, a look of excitement in his eyes. "It was such a powerful moment that afterward I read everything I could on the subject of terrestrial geometry and dedicated myself to finding a modern use for this ancient science. That's when I became equally fascinated with the findings of Nikola Tesla."

"The father of alternating current and electric motors."

"Exactly," Einsof acknowledged. "Tesla built generators that produced millions of volts. What originally caught my attention was a picture of Tesla sitting beneath one of his generators reading a book as sparks crackled thirty feet through the air."

Michael smiled. "That photo was staged."

Einsof appeared to admire the audacity of such a trick. "I know—a time exposure. I found that out much later, after I was already convinced of Tesla's genius. When I got back to the States, I was determined to work with his ideas, so I moved to Boston and hooked up with Tod who was working on his doctorate at MIT on ball lightning."

"Which is?" Michael asked.

"Ephemeral balls of plasma. They can appear suddenly, float slowly, and then vanish. It's a phenomena witnessed occasionally in passenger planes. Nikola Tesla claimed to have found a way to create them at his laboratory in Colorado Springs around 1900. Yet, no scientist had ever been able to duplicate his feat or discover how he did it."

"Don't tell me," Michael asked, stupefied, "that you guys found a way?"

Einsof smiled. "Well, let's just say Tesla's philosophy and his intuitive knowledge of electricity were the spark. When Tod and I began talking, I convinced him that modern efforts neglected to take into consideration *ley* lines and *feng shui*. No doubt, in Colorado, Tesla had gravitated toward a natural energy resonance in keeping with his character. So that's why we set up our test lab in the Catskills on High Point Mountain. At over 3,000 feet and overlooking the Ashokan Reservoir, High Point is a natural antenna that concentrates the energy of the entire Hudson Valley and Catskill region and transmits that power as well. If you watch the Weather Channel like I do—it's my favorite station—you will notice that the Hudson Valley consistently has the fewest natural disasters and the healthiest weather in the western hemisphere."

Michael fell into a long silence. He tried to soak it all in. *Far-fetched, extraordinary, genius, nuts.* He found no shortage of adjectives to describe what he thought of Einsof's theory.

Before he knew it, the Catskill Mountains came into view along the northwest horizon. Suddenly, the mysterious mountains that spawned the legend of Rip Van Winkle seemed a fitting backdrop for Einsof's extraordinary and unearthly experiments.

CHAPTER 22

AFTER EXITING the thruway in Kingston and heading west toward the mountains, Michael and Einsof finally reached the Ashokan Reservoir. Driving past the reservoir's edge, Michael gazed out the window at the deep clear water, mountains and clouds mirrored on its surface.

"*Lung-mei,* dragon current—here you see it clearly," Einsof said. "Earth, fire, water, wood, and metal meet the sky at this point. A perfect balance." He pointed toward one of the peaks. "That's High Point. The mountain itself, while pyramidal, is slightly rounded. If it was craggy and pointed, it would create a conflicting energy."

Michael found that despite his reservations, he was becoming intrigued.

"Instead, it is the perfect transmitter," Einsof said with a sense of awe. "Humble, not too high, rounded at the top, which creates complimentary *feng shui.*"

With Einsof directing him, Michael drove along a rising, winding road toward High Point. When they were finally past the tree line, Michael could see the awesome panorama of the reservoir valley. But Einsof wouldn't let him stop for a moment. He seemed determined to reach their destination before being spotted.

"We turn here," he said, directing Michael onto an old fire watch road. "It's a back way. I doubt the snoops know it. Tod and I trekked these mountains for six months before selecting our location." Several miles down the road, he told Michael to park. "Now we walk."

Climb would have been a more accurate word, Michael thought, as they maneuvered up the mountainside. Twenty minutes later, they arrived at a small meadow.

"There it is," Einsof said. "Our first prototype." He pointed to a round wooden barn sitting in the middle of the field.

And it's surrounded by twelve standing stones . . .

Seeing Einsof's concept actualized, Michael felt as if he was walking into a separate reality . . . as if a threshold was being crossed.

Continuing forward, finally reaching the barn, Michael brought his focus to bear again. The structure, he could see, had a fifty-foot high steel tower protruding from the center of its cupola, just like those designed for ham radio. At the tower's peak was a large copper octahedron—two, four-sided pyramids joined at their base. A copper pipe from the bottom apex extended down through the tower and into the roof of the barn. Amazingly, there was no tarnish or discoloration either on the octahedron or the full length of the pipe. They glistened as if they had never been exposed to weather.

After following Einsof into the barn, Michael was surprised to find it almost bare. The center column surrounding the antenna tower was paneled and painted a light yellow. Evenly spaced around the interior walls were square panels that emitted a bright, but pleasantly muted light. Yet, there were no wires, switches or devices of any kind in view.

Michael stared in dumbfounded amazement.

Einsof laughed. "The few people who've seen this have had the same reaction, even Mabus. 'How is this done?' they ask."

"How *is* it done?"

"*Ley* and Tesla. The earth's own magnetic field is channeled through the standing stones surrounding the barn. The octahedron above acts as a receiver and sends a magnetic current down the copper tubing into quartz crystals which oscillate. The lighting panels are made from gallium-selenium crystals which produce light when pulsated by the frequency of the quartz. These lights will stay on as long as the stones and the antenna remain in place."

Astonished, Michael stood moot as he listened to Einsof's wizardry.

"We know from Plato's writing that even during his time there was a realization of the energy inherent in the volume created by shape. In his *Timaeus* discussion of the cosmology of geometry, he listed five sacred shapes and their relationship to elements. The cube relates to earth, the tetrahedron to fire, the octahedron to air and the icosahedron to water. The fifth element is elemental energy itself, known in Sanskrit as *prana,* to the Chinese as *lung* and to Einstein as *aether. Lung* is held by the dodecahedron," Einsof explained, barely stopping to take a breath.

"In fact, Plato's listing may be a catalog from the Pythagorean school. There have even been stones carved in these shapes—dated to be thirty-five hundred years old—found in Neolithic sites in Britain."

Michael's mind was spinning with all the information. "So, are you saying this relates to the octahedron above the barn?" he asked, trying to keep up.

"Yes. The octahedron both captures and amplifies the natural field created by the environment," Einsof said matter-of-factly. "This transference of energy keeps the copper atoms resonating at such a pure rate there is no available bond for oxidation. Therefore, no discoloration."

"And so how does Tesla's work figure into all this?

Einsof's eyes widened with admiration. "Tesla devised a plan to create high-power transmitters that could send electricity through the air wirelessly. What Tod and I discovered is that it's not even necessary to have the transmitters powered by generators—the earth's own field is sufficient. And better still, it can be done through local stations at a significantly lower power level."

Michael was awed not only by Einsof's discovery but by the unfathomable genius of his predecessor. "Seems like this Tesla was some sort of electrical magician."

"That's not even the half of it," Einsof said, smiling. "He was known to walk around his Greenwich Village laboratory holding a gas-filled glass tube, illuminating it through high-frequency oscillators." Einsof paused. "Now that's a wizard."

Michael saw a radically wild element within Einsof's otherwise scientific nature. *Genius or madman?* As history had shown, there was often a fine line of distinction between the two. *Einstein, Oppenheimer, Van Gogh, Beethoven.* Great artists and scientists who had made sweeping intellectual strides in their field . . . strides all simultaneously accompanied by far-reaching, intuitive leaps that basically opened up new dimensions of experience, some profoundly beneficial and some extraordinarily deadly.

Michael shook his head as the ramifications began to sink in. "Tell me you didn't sell the patents to Mabus?"

"No, not exactly," Einsof explained. "He insisted on a development agreement that gave him first rights to purchase the patents in return for the money to build prototypes and perfect the system."

"Which must have cost millions," Michael added.

"As of now, hundreds of millions. Our larger systems are scattered about the side of the mountain. The newest is quite sophisticated. This looks primitive in comparison."

Michael felt concerned. "But Mabus will still get the rights eventually?"

"Not if I can help it." Einsof smiled thinly. "He didn't take into consideration that I would be willing to license the rights for free. Something I never considered until Tod's death."

Suddenly, the sound of an approaching vehicle startled them, and he and Stephen raced to a window. A black Humvee was moving across the meadow toward the barn.

"Here they come," Einsof warned anxiously. "It's better if you're not seen. Stay here until I'm gone."

Einsof casually walked out of the building and toward the Humvee. When it pulled up next to him, he exclaimed, "There you are!"

Michael couldn't hear the passenger's response but he was able to see the driver's profile—a sunken forehead, protruding jaw and dark features.

"No, I walked up. Give me a lift back," Einsof said. He got into the back seat, and the Hummer drove off down the hill.

Michael waited several minutes until the vehicle was well out of sight before making his slow descent back down the mountain.

The long walk gave him time to think. What Einsof had showed him could revolutionize the world. Mabus' motivations were definitely questionable, and Michael was now determined to unearth his agenda. After all, should such technology be under Mabus' control?

CHAPTER 23

GENEVIEVE LIAN MISSED the Sixties like a child would miss a secret hiding place. She could name most of the students involved in the Columbia University takeover and the Berkley Free Speech movement. She could even recite every act of the opening day at Woodstock starting with Richie Havens through to Joan Baez.

Trouble was the Marist College student hadn't been born until 1989.

But today, sitting in her dorm room, Genevieve knew her day had arrived. The political science senior had just seen a live report on Laurel Seline's march toward Manhattan. Her friend, Jules, was standing right up front alongside Maggie Seline's grandmother!

Genevieve was excited. She had read *Pure Vision* twice and had filled the margins with notes, as had lots of her friends and classmates. From the seed of Maggie's book, new roots of awareness had taken hold among them. All semester long, she joined with other students, gathering on the Marist campus lawn to hear perspectives on the Middle East from the greatest of political minds—Noam Chomsky, Dilip Hiro and disciples of the late Edward Said. But their burgeoning awareness, Genevieve knew, was already starting to turn to frustration. Students were beginning to feel they needed to do something more than listen to lectures.

Suddenly, a light went off in the Marist coed's head.

Laurel will be walking past the campus, she thought.

Genevieve grabbed her cell phone and started punching in numbers.

She had a plan.

With Lonnie and Jules at her side, Laurel walked down the long, tree-lined driveway that led to the nation's first Presidential Library. There on the lawn of the Roosevelt grounds, amidst the fuchsia rose bushes and tall gray-barked Beech trees, the museum and library staff were waiting.

But before she could reach them, Laurel was cut off by a group of reporters. It appeared that since her short talk in Rhinebeck, more network news representatives had been dispatched to cover her story. As microphones and cameras emerged, Laurel realized her little *walk* was getting bigger by the minute.

"Madam, I understand that you plan on walking to the UN. What exactly do you wish to accomplish?" The young woman asking the question was one of several reporters who had walked with her from Rhinebeck.

"As I've previously explained," Laurel began, "there is a need for Americans to voice their opinions in responsible ways that will get them heard. We must bring the issue of human rights violations directly to the organization that is sanctified to protect and uphold these rights as well as to bring to justice those who violate them."

Laurel had seen the devastation caused by the Second World War. As a child in Italy, she had experienced the fascist fear mongering of Mussolini. But war was more of a gummy event back then, something you could chew on and suck the juices out of, not like it was today where it resembled instant soup. Just boil the water, throw in the powdered ingredients and, presto, you had ready-made disaster. Laurel felt that kind of potential to destroy made it even more imperative to act responsibly.

"The Middle East *peace process* does not exist," she emphasized. "It never has. But together, we can create one. First we must put out the fire before we all explode. We can do this by shedding light on the real problems in the Middle East—problems that have grown out of fear and ignorance.

"That's why Eleanor Roosevelt means so much to me. She was fearless. She used her eyes, she used her brains, and she got off her duff and tried to change things that were wrong."

Laurel felt surprised at how easily the words were coming to her. "As Adlai Stevenson once said of Eleanor, 'She would rather light a candle than curse the darkness.' That's the kind of wisdom we need today, especially after hearing the same ominous chants for years. *We must be afraid*

... *We have enemies* ... *We must strike first.*" Laurel paused. "Striking first is a death wish. Instead, let's light some candles of our own."

A woman nearly Laurel's age, walked up to her deferentially. "Mrs. Seline," she said, "on behalf of the FDR Library, I want to present you with this small token." The woman's light-gray eyes conveyed a sincere appreciation. Laurel recognized the loneliness within the sincerity, a look she had picked up in Maggie's eyes from time to time.

When Laurel saw the gift she was being given, her belief in the power of thought was solidified. The librarian was holding out a small blue and white pamphlet.

The Universal Declaration of Human Rights.

CHAPTER 24

THE HUDSON RIVER, slow moving, steady and serene was a quiet companion as the women traveled south—a deep blue sky and warm sun confirming the confident tone Laurel's talk had set. Laurel now felt particularly encouraged as many members of the press chose to forgo their vehicles and join the marchers, at once witnesses and participants.

The grandmother, the painter, and the philosopher continued their journey, but now they were joined by housewives, secretaries, cashiers, students, writers—everyday people. Having started the walk alone, Laurel found she was now buoyed by a steadily growing number of supporters. Not surprising, most of them were women. The several men who had joined them understood—the walk was not meant to exclude men but to show support for women and their role in creating peace.

By the time the group reached Marist College, there were nearly a hundred people walking together flanked by several police cars. A loosely formed welcoming committee greeted them at the Marist entrance, ready to serve everyone tea by the roadside. With the sun low in the sky, Laurel knew they had reached their limit. She slid into one of the several folding chairs set up on the lawn, ready to call it a day.

Soon, several coeds approached her. Laurel listened as they talked in excited bursts about what was happening at Marist as well as at other nearby colleges like Bard and Vassar. The students, she learned, were rallying and holding open forums. Some were even organizing to join Laurel's walk.

She was about to respond when, suddenly, the doors to the Lowell Thomas Media Center flung open. Out poured a group of more than fifty coeds all dressed in black pants and white T-shirts.

"What in the name of heaven . . . ?" Lonnie tugged on Laurel's sleeve. "Do you see what I see?"

As the flock of students reached them, she saw it clearly. "Oh!" Laurel exclaimed.

"That's excellent, girls," Jules added with a tone of familiarity.

"Mrs. Seline. Ladies."

A voice addressed them, but Laurel couldn't take her eyes off the shirts that the students were wearing, all imprinted with the same saying.

"There's a number of us who would like to walk with you into Manhattan. Can we join you?"

Finally, Laurel looked at the leader who was speaking, a brown-eyed young woman about nineteen. Her small diamond nose ring, long gold-streaked braid and tawny Jamaican features gave her an island girl look, but her accent was notably upstate New York. Before Laurel could answer, the young woman handed her a bundle of white shirts.

"My name is Genevieve Lian and on behalf of all of us, I offer you ladies these T-shirts. As you can see, they're like the ones we're all wearing."

Laurel smiled effusively, touched by the young woman's gesture. She gave a shirt to both Lonnie and Jules before putting one on herself.

Solidified, Laurel's group now voiced a definitive statement.

WALKING TOWARD THE
NEW JERUSALEM

Several hours later in the Yemin Moshe section of Jerusalem, Muriel Lumina thought she must be dreaming when she saw the photo of the American women, wearing their printed T-shirts, which appeared in that morning's edition of *Ha'aretz*. Along with her husband Isaac, a retired and notable military hero, Muriel was a peace activist and leader in the cause for reconciliation in Israel. Tireless in her own efforts, she couldn't help but admire the women's audacity and gumption. Besides, Laurel Seline's message was just the kind she liked—simple, loud and clear.

Muriel recognized opportunity knocking. Not caring that it was the middle of the night in New York, she picked up the phone.

A personality in the entertainment world for forty years, Rosa Manus could not escape the feeling of being on stage, not even now in the roof-top garden privacy of her West Side, New York apartment.

At that very moment, as the waning moon was casting a faint glow over the vast expanse of Central Park thirty stories below—*birthing and dissolving the world*—Rosa realized a new beginning was upon her. The recording artist, Hollywood star and Kabbalah student did not need to speak with her astrologer to know this. Of course, she would call Deborah in the morning for zodiac details, always a phenomenon she found as much confusing as thrilling.

Let there be me'orot, lights—the moon . . . Numerologies and calculations of equinoxes, solstices, and intercalations derive entirely from the mystery of the moon, no higher. So it was written in the *Zohar* and so Rosa believed. The moon shone in the sky above, mysterious, alone and aloof. All power below was only a reflection of the feminine principle that governed all realities, both esoteric and mundane.

Rosa had spoken out, she believed, as the voice of this principle for many years. Her fans and friends looked to her for guidance on issues of morality and truth. In conservative circles, she was viewed as a flake or left-wing fruitcake. Rosa knew this and didn't care, better a nut than a conscience-dead shell of life.

Tonight, the moon, stars and deep black emptiness of the sky enveloped Rosa with expectation. The moment had arrived. The divine feminine within was arising, ready for birth, awaiting the lifting curtain of yet another performance.

The sound of her cell phone ringing brought Rosa back from the expanse. A private number, she wondered which of her friends was calling at this late hour. "Hello?"

"Rosa," the familiar voice said. "This is Muriel in Jerusalem."

CHAPTER 25

BY LATE AFTERNOON the following day, Laurel and the other women reached the Hudson River's narrowest point. There, the Bear Mountain Bridge, spanning from sheer rock cliffs, passed over the flowing river several hundred feet below.

Laurel sensed the group, now almost two hundred in number, needed a break and decided they should pause at a nearby lookout point. To her dismay, when they arrived she saw several police cars were already in place waiting for them. Immediately, an athletic-looking trooper approached her, his blonde hair and hazel eyes making him look more like a surfer than a law official.

"Ma'am," he addressed Laurel, "your group won't be allowed to pass this narrow band of road. Too dangerous."

"But I'm sure you realize that we're not simply on a stroll." Laurel's heart sank as she stared at the officer.

"I'm aware of what you're doing, ma'am. But my orders are to make sure your group complies."

Laurel decided then that the Beach Boy was fast losing his charm. "So how do you suggest we continue our walk?"

"I don't have much of a suggestion really." The trooper shrugged, scanning the marchers. "All I can tell you is we can't have a large group of people obstructing the road. We have a lot of fast moving vehicles and it's pretty obvious there's no room for pedestrians."

"Then I suppose we'll have to find another way," Lonnie injected caustically.

"There's one more thing," the officer added. Laurel thought she heard a hint of sympathy in his voice. "Peekskill is the governor's home-town. The local politicians don't want him embarrassed. They are refusing to grant you a permit to walk on the roads."

"Why those sons of—"

"Lonnie!" Laurel grabbed her friend's arm firmly. "We've got the message, Officer. Thank you." As Laurel steered Lonnie away from the trooper, she whispered in her ear. "Time to regroup."

Genevieve walked up to her then, a sly smile on her face. "The Light of Christ Baptist Church."

Laurel stared. "Yes, what about it?"

"I know the choir director, Corinne Cutting. She may be able to help us," Genevieve said confidently. "Let me give her a call."

Jules took a long look at the barricades up ahead. *No use in feeling defeated*, she thought.

She jumped up onto one of the picnic tables. Dylan's *Blowin' in the Wind* came to mind and Jules began to sing. A few moments later, Genevieve, banging two aluminum cans together, began keeping the rhythm. As more voices joined hers, an unlikely accompanist—a woman in her forties, dressed in a tailored jacket and skirt, who appeared to be a corporate executive—walked over with a guitar and started strumming. All the while, more cars pulled into the lookout area dropping off passengers.

Suddenly, Jules heard another voice alongside hers, a voice both comforting and familiar. When she turned, she was astounded, unable to take her eyes off the woman who had appeared next to her. High cheek bones, full lips, thickly-bunched golden brown hair . . . *Is it really her?*

Elsie Howe of CNN News jumped to her feet. The other television crews around her, noticing Rosa Manus as well, quickly began filming, forgetting all about their coffee and danish, the damp weather and their boredom. Rosa Manus was a star. She was news. Best of all she had been a recluse for several years. Now, here she was in public, belting out a song with her Carnegie Hall-quality, soprano voice.

Watching Rosa, Elsie felt mesmerized, as if through the star's presence the great movements of the Sixties that ended segregation and the war in Vietnam were fast-forwarding into the present.

Hearing a countdown from her producer, Elsie snapped into form. "Live from Peekskill, New York, this is Elsie Howe for CNN. In response to Maggie Seline's disappearance, her grandmother, Laurel Seline, has led her intrepid band of feminine warriors down the Hudson past West Point to a lookout just beyond the Bear Mountain Bridge."

Elsie's cameraman panned his camera from her face to the large group of women sitting on the boulders.

"Activist-actress Rosa Manus arrived moments ago and is already lending her voice to Laurel's campaign. For many years, Rosa had been the embodiment and face of protest. So, to no one's surprise, she is here with Laurel Seline today."

So glad, so strong . . . finally. It seemed to Rosa a moment, long awaited, had arrived. This was not just about politics or the disgraceful actions of a greedy government. This was life itself. Voices of women singing loudly and clearly beside this great river—it was a song that needed to be sung.

Rosa's life as an artist had been defined by the issues—some of those, she sadly realized, as inane as the people who had created them. Who in their right mind would have crafted Vietnam or Iraq? No one, of course, not in their *right* mind.

But now the Divine Mother is with us. We are free, and in her image, we will overcome. As they reached the end of Dylan's song, Rosa smiled as it dawned on her. Perhaps the answer wasn't blowing in the wind after all.

An outburst of cheering and clapping brought her attention to the road. Large yellow buses with the words *The Light of Christ Baptist Church* emblazoned in black were pulling in.

It looked as if the barricade had turned into a blessing in disguise.

Thank God, Rosa thought as she let out a sigh of relief. She had to admit that although she loved the idea of protesting, she hated the idea of walking.

CHAPTER 26

ELSIE HOWE NOW FELT more like a member of Laurel's team than a CNN correspondent. She could sense Laurel's reluctance to give up on the idea of literally walking all the way to the United Nations. Yet, riding in a bus for thirty miles to Spuyten Duyvil was certainly not going to be considered a break in trust. Elsie didn't want to elaborate, but the truth was apparent. For all of her courage and spirit, Laurel was a seventy-six-year-old woman who had walked over sixty miles in a few short days. On top of that, she had given several public talks and appearances under a glare of publicity that would tax even a younger and more experienced speaker.

"Laurel needs to rest," Elsie had voiced to Rosa. "Maybe you can accompany her in my RV. I have a bed in my dressing room." Elsie had not risen through the CNN ranks without learning how to corner a news item. She was going to see to it this became the *grand* mother story of her network.

Once Laurel was settled comfortably in the dressing room of the RV and they were on their way, Elsie turned her attention to Rosa, who had accepted Elsie's invitation to join them, making her scoop even more exclusive.

"Rosa, can this really be effective—women marching to the UN with an agenda of internationalizing Jerusalem?" Elsie was all about practicality. It was her trademark approach to issues. *What are the nuts and bolts of a story?*

"Sure it can." Rosa, sitting comfortably in the captain's chair at the front of the camper, swiveled to face the interior where Elsie was seated. "In the last forty years, I've seen some major turnarounds, all due to the power of determination. Certainly a group of unarmed women can at least turn some heads with such a radical idea."

Rosa gave her a smile, but Elsie sensed uneasiness in her tone.

"Seriously though," Rosa continued, "the issue is at once complex and simple. Zionism has worn two hats since its inception. Some dreamed of a land where Jews could live normal lives. Others expanded upon this vision with the idea of a unique nation heralding Hebraic culture—a super race so to speak."

Elsie didn't get it. "How does that impact this story?"

"Neither of these groups was religious," Rosa explained. "Originally, Israel was not conceived as a religious state but as a cultural one. The first difficulty was obvious—what to do about all the Arabs who stubbornly insisted upon hanging around a land where they had been living for a thousand years." Rosa took a sip from her dark green bottle of Perrier. "They still haven't figured that one out. But the issue of Jerusalem never came up initially. Real Zionists back then were content to view Tel Aviv as the capital of their country, and the Orthodox had long considered it to be a violation of God's will to force a return to Palestine until the Messiah arrives. Even though those views have changed, if these two groups could be convinced to be a part of declaring Jerusalem an international city, it would solve some big problems. It would also calm the Muslims worldwide and still make it possible to slip Palestinians over the border every day to lay brick, roll pita and pick oranges."

Elsie wondered how tenable Rosa's view really was. "You make it all sound easy."

"Oh, it's not easy," Rosa conceded, her tone assertive. "There's another group . . . the kooks, the settlers . . . the same group that revolted against Rome two thousand years ago. They won't rest until this homeland has been destroyed as well."

"And now this woman from Bearsville . . . " Elsie said.

"Walking to promulgate her granddaughter's ideas." Rosa finished the thought, admiration in her voice. "She's set in motion forces that will influence the destiny of the world's most famous city."

It still was unclear to Elsie. "You believe that was Laurel's intention?"

"Not Laurel's—Maggie's." Rosa spun her seat around to face the road. "Laurel is the conduit. Maggie, though, may be the one the Orthodox and Evangelicals are waiting for," she said quietly, "except they wouldn't know it."

Elsie felt amazed by what she was hearing and fell into a long silence. She realized that younger fans, like Jules, would probably not comprehend the subtleties of her discussion with the singer or its importance.

Rosa Manus represents an awakened Israeli conscience.

Elsie had been in high school when Rosa had her first starring role in a major film. The actress played a young Israeli woman who joined the army as a man during the Six Day War just to prove that women were tough enough for combat. The role personified Rosa herself—strong and high-spirited—a character Americans related to easily.

For years afterward, Rosa enjoyed fame, being the public face of Israel in America, until a powerful and disastrous event in 1982 added another dimension to her life.

The Israeli invasion of Lebanon. Rosa's peace activism began then and was solidified by the September horror of that invasion, when over seventeen hundred Palestinian men, women and children were massacred by Lebanese Christians while Israel's army stood by, both complicit and complacent. Rosa then became a spokesperson for protest, so much so that younger people believed she had always been a radical. Not so. It was that ungodly war and the monstrous way it was conducted that had turned her into an activist as well as toward mysticism.

Now, sitting quietly next to the actress, the RV barreling down the highway, Elsie recalled a quote of Rosa's she had read years ago. *God neither recognizes or confers citizenship, and humanity recognizes no national boundary.* Elsie made a note to include it in her live report tonight. Better yet, see if she could get Rosa to say it herself on camera.

Swaying comfortably with the rhythm, Laurel awoke easily, at first uncertain where she was. In a half daze, she remembered the Pullman sleeper cars she traveled in as a young woman.

I am no longer young. The thought brought her a sense of finality, but not sadness. Everything had to come to a close. *Then I must find closure for Maggie as well. Don't let it end for me without knowing she is safe.*

An opening door lifted the darkness. Rosa slipped into the small dressing room and pulled the window curtain aside. "Laurel," she said softly, "we've just passed over Spuyten Duyvil. We're in Manhattan."

Laurel's mind turned back to the reality at hand. *The march.*

"We'll stop and rest for the night," Rosa added, "then in the morning, we can start walking again."

As Rosa turned to leave, Laurel stopped her. "Don't go," she said. Laurel found that instead of renewed confidence, sleep had brought with it a nervous edge. "Is this all madness . . . what we're doing?"

Rosa sat down next to her on the bed. "The only real madness is losing faith," she said, taking Laurel's hand. "But that's not what you meant though, is it?"

"I think it's exactly what I meant," Laurel said regretfully. "My generation came out of the Second World War numb. All we wanted was Ford and Maytag. For years we had a sense of protection. Vietnam ended that."

Rosa looked at her with an air of confession. "Only for a time. Eventually, all of us found some sort of a shell to hide in. I came out of mine after 9/11. For a few months, there seemed to be a chance the world would unite . . . fight violence, face terror and find a better way. Then we invaded Iraq and all the horror came back, only multiplied." Rosa stood up, the sadness in her eyes changing to hope. "But Maggie's proposal offers something new. I could never have imagined that solution—to internationalize Jerusalem—but it makes sense. Her talk at the Riverside has become one of the defining moments of my life. Your granddaughter is truly someone special, someone we've been waiting for."

Laurel heard the words but could not digest the meaning.

"Maggie is one of those chosen to help us all make the leap." Rosa's voice trembled with emotion. "I know she is alive and safe, Laurel. I know it."

Laurel heard what she wanted to hear. *Maggie is alive, safe and alive.* Although Laurel knew Maggie was special, calling her one of the chosen sounded a bit too prophetic. Visionaries, after all, could be found everywhere. It was the ones who made their vision a reality who were hard to find. Laurel knew, in that respect, Maggie was extraordinary.

CHAPTER 27

FTER A DAY alone in a mountain cabin, Michael's mind was now settled.

Overwhelmed by everything that Einsof had told him, as well as by Mabus' Jeremiah parchment and Peace Conference agenda for Jerusalem, Michael felt he had been put on overload. Instinctively, he had retreated to the single place he knew he could find solace and be away from any further sensory bombardment. The cabin in Peekamoose he had shared with Rachel on their hiking jaunts proved to be his best refuge.

Now, as he left the rustic confines of his hideaway, Michael's destination was certain. His head had cleared enough for him to realize there was only one person who could possibly untangle the unlikely web of characters and events that had snared him.

The early evening sun reflecting off the rearview mirror was almost blinding as Michael crossed the Kingston Bridge over the Hudson. He snapped his sunglasses off the visor and put them on. Their amber tint cast the Catskill Mountains into a golden light as he drove toward Rhinecliff and Professor Samuels' house.

Once across the river, he turned south toward Ferncliff Forest where the towering oaks and groves of white birch loomed over the road, forming a gateway as he drove. With each passing mile, the street narrowed further until, finally, granite boulders appeared like silent sentinels—something like the Professor himself—questioning, staunch, immovable.

Michael recalled how he and Rachel, making numerous visits to Samuels' home over the years, jokingly began to refer to it as "the hermitage." In some respects, they even considered it a reflection of the Professor's life work . . . an ironic notion, considering he was one of the most prominent experts on myths, legends, and the occult—a reputation he had gleaned for himself during the forty years he spent teaching History and Ancient Civilizations at Columbia University.

The evening shadows were darkening when Michael came upon the brick gateposts adorned with silver eagles—the entrance to the Professor's driveway. He turned in, still unable to see the Professor's stone house through the trees. Finally, reaching the end of the long gravel drive, there it was, covered in thick ivy, resembling a miniature medieval cloister.

Michael exited his car and approached the granite porte-cochère in front of the Professor's home. As he stood in front of the dark oak doors, he felt apprehensive. He took a breath and lifted the large brass knocker.

It fell with a thud.

Michael stepped back from the entrance and waited. He gazed up above the doorway, where an inscription was etched in the stone. *VOCATUS ATQUE NON VOCATUS DEUS ADERIT.* One of the Professor's favorite quotes, he had carved it himself. *Summoned or not, the gods will be there.*

As Michael reached again for the knocker, a light went on in the vestibule. The door swung open and the Professor's statuesque, ebony black Ethiopian assistant, Ebed-melech, was standing in front of him, silhouetted against the muted light of the hallway.

"Good evening, Michael, the Professor is expecting you," he said, motioning Michael in. Taking long sweeping strides, his dark blue tunic billowing behind him, Ebed-melech glided down the hallway toward the library. Michael followed in his wake. When they reached an open door, Ebed-melech gestured for him to enter.

Once inside the Professor's familiar and comforting hideaway, Michael felt relieved. He noticed the fire place was alight and new carvings had been set upon the granite mantel—runes, bits of coral, chiseled wooden figures. The bookshelves were brimming as usual, lined with the rarest of books . . . some even handwritten, chronicling the history of man's continual search for meaning. Michael knew that although there were several other libraries in the house, this one held a special place in the Professor's heart.

When Michael turned, he saw Professor Samuels standing at the west end window. Looking worn, he appeared as if he had aged a century in the last several weeks. There was a stoop in his normally tall stature, and his white hair, now shoulder length, shrouded an unusually somber expression.

"Michael. I'm glad you've finally arrived." The chill that came from the Professor's long bony fingers as they clasped Michael's hands sent a shiver through him.

"I'm truly sorry, but—" Michael began to explain why he hadn't called.

The Professor waved off any need. Instead, he motioned with his deep-set, dark eyes for Michael to turn to his right.

Michael caught his breath. There, sitting on a sofa on the other side of the room, her face highlighted by the warm glow of the fireplace, was Maggie Seline.

It took several seconds for Michael to realize his mouth was hanging open. Besides being surprised and happy to see her alive, he felt a protective feeling, fiery and fierce, a reaction beyond any he would have expected.

Maggie's light green eyes locked into his as she stood.

"I'm told you have met my house guest." The Professor was the first to break the silence.

"Ms. Seline," Michael said, aware of how awkward he must look.

"I believe we went beyond formalities at our first meeting, Michael." Maggie extended her hand. A woman both formidable and vulnerable, her firm eyes were equaled by her soft touch. "Since I've known him, the Professor has spoken highly of you."

"Nonsense," Samuels said in mock denial.

Michael let out a long sigh of confusion. "Maggie, I don't get it. How do you two . . . ?" Then he remembered the article, a profile Maggie Seline had written on Professor Napesh Samuels. The exposé documented Samuels' knowledge of Nazi occult tactics and rituals as well as the mythological archetypes used by Hitler and his henchmen, including Himmler, in their process of carrying out Hitler's goals for the SS. Maggie's research and work had been extensive. Quite a feat, in Michael's eyes.

Still, he felt as if an emotional dam had broken. A wave of anger began to override his feelings of relief and protectiveness. "Are you aware that everyone's up in arms? They think you've been shot, kidnapped, even killed. What the hell are you doing *here*?"

Maggie challenged his angry look with a bold stare.

Michael was amazed at her arrogance, her apparent belief that she was above accountability. *Just who does this woman think she is?* "Excuse my bluntness," he said, "but don't you think you should let people in on the fact that you're alive?"

"It's better that she doesn't," Professor Samuels interjected before Maggie could answer. "This is no time for media hoopla and sensation. There's too much at stake."

"Too much at stake! What's at stake?" Michael could now feel the blood pulsing through the carotid artery in his neck.

"Michael, calm yourself and listen," the Professor directed force-fully. "Maggie's life is at stake. Proposing that the old city of Jerusalem be internationalized has definitely hit a nerve—a big one."

Article titles flashed through Michael's mind. *The New York Post*—**MAGGIE SELINE TIED TO AL QAEDA TERRORIST**. *Time Magazine*—**SELINE: ARAB SYMPATHIZER**. *The Christian Chronicle*—**A WOMAN OF IMMORAL MEANS**. Confusion about Maggie's past beset Michael, yet nothing in her manner even suggested the slurs against her were real.

"You're talking about the accusations," Michael said. "Muslim bias . . . possible ties to terrorist organizers."

The Professor remained silent.

"Do you believe them?" Maggie asked.

Michael thought he heard a hint of anxiety in her voice. He turned toward her then. "I don't know . . . These charges came up so quickly, and you haven't made any public denials."

"And I won't."

Michael furrowed his brow. "I'm confused as to why."

"Because the issue is the future of Jerusalem, not my nor anyone else's personal reputation."

"Bullshit," he countered. "An accusation of being party to terrorism is a serious matter. If public suspicion about you grows, the future of your campaign for Jerusalem will be irreparably harmed."

The Professor placed a calming hand on Michael's shoulder. "Let's everyone sit down and quit this standoff."

Michael took a huge breath, relieved to fall back into a plush armchair.

The Professor joined Maggie on the sofa, folding his hands together in a thoughtful mudra before continuing. "Michael, this isn't about

Maggie or Hamas. This is about our vanishing opportunity to bring peace and sanity into the Middle East before the entire region explodes. There are plenty of sane respectable leaders who believe in the internationalization of Jerusalem. I believe in it." He paused, looking deeply into Michael's eyes. "But apparently, Giovanni Mabus has another plan he wants to put into play."

"You mean you already know about—"

"Mabus' fairytale resolution? Yes, I do." The Professor gave him an uneasy smile. "How reasonable is it to even suggest building a Third Temple alongside the Dome of the Rock? Even the slightest marring of the area will be enough to start World War III."

"It's monumentally stupid," Maggie interjected. "The Muslim world will never accept having the Temple built on the Mount, no matter how many scholars defend the rationale. War will be inevitable."

"That's your opinion," Michael said, "based on the conclusion that the Muslim world will rise in arms—a catastrophic *jihad.*"

Maggie rose from her chair swiftly. "Not my opinion. Fact. Any effort to build atop the Mount will unite Muslims in an unprecedented manner. This scares the Arab governments as much as it does the Israeli government. For over sixty years Arab regimes have used the vague threat of Jewish Palestine to distract their people from larger issues at home, all the while paying lip service with hush money to the Palestinian cause. If the fantasy starts looking real, then Arab citizens may find themselves not only fighting a religious war but a civil one as well."

"This type of rationale is getting awfully close to looking like a doomsday scenario," Michael said, irritated. "I find it hard to believe you've reached such a dire conclusion."

"Apparently," Maggie said facetiously, "I'm not the only one whose conclusions are dire. Mabus seems willing to push this Temple issue to the point of no return."

Michael had to admit she could be right. He quickly gave them both a rundown of his involvement in translating the Jeremiah parchment and Mabus' plan for its use.

The Professor leaned forward. "Ask yourself why then, Michael? Why is Mabus aligning himself with forces that will inflame the deepest paranoia of the Muslim world? Is it simply because of a prophecy made thousands of years ago?" The worry lines on Samuels' forehead creased deeper. "Mabus' dice are loaded, and they may explode before the end of the roll. All the more reason to hurry down a different road."

Michael felt uncomfortable. *All of this prophesying, this apocalyptic babble.* He had come to see the Professor because of Stephen Einsof's fears. Now he felt like a cornered pawn on a chessboard. Michael hated admitting it, but he was afraid that if he let go of his rationality, he would sound like a lunatic—granted well-educated, but out of his mind. Yet, he couldn't help but wonder . . . *Are the Professor's assertions feasible?* Unable to hold back any longer, Michael blurted out the information Einsof had given him.

"The project he's working on is a source of incredible power." Michael found himself standing, an anxious sweat breaking out on his forehead. "As you suspected, Maggie, Mabus seems to be gearing up to monopolize the technology. The whole thing is so far-out, but I can't dismiss Einsof's concerns. What if they're true?"

"All the years we've been fighting in Iraq—the whole thing has always been about energy." The Professor stared at the burning embers in the fireplace as he spoke. "Up until now, of course, our focus has been oil. But if a new energy system is brought on line, it would blow the oil companies, the corporations built around them and their government stooges right out of the water."

"That's true," Michael conceded. "No more big bucks to line political pockets with."

"And no more government backup to help the oil conglomerates and corporate heads skim the top off all their profits," Maggie added.

The Professor's eyes narrowed. "Like P2." His ominous tone hung in the air.

Michael knitted his brow.

"P2 . . . Propaganda Due," the Professor elucidated. He removed a walnut pipe and bag of tobacco from his lapel. "Also known as the *Fratineri* and as the *Black Friars*. They are a powerful and violent group based in Italy."

Michael now recalled hearing a little about the group in the Eighties—a scandal involving the Vatican Bank and mob associations. "They're some kind of Masonic group, right?" he asked.

"An aberration, I'd say," Samuels asserted. "The actual Freemason lineage adheres to the highest code, accepting all men of faith whatever their race and whatever their religious beliefs. Christians, Jews,

Muslims—all are part of the brotherhood. Believe me, their idealistic order has nothing to do with the Black Friars—a group of thugs whose aims revolve around political supremacy and money. Power and greed, all the way."

Professor Samuels paused to puff on his pipe. Rings of smoke, like clouds of mystery, were still drifting through the air as he resumed. "They are right-wing politicians," he said. "Generals, military men, journalists, bankers, financiers . . . and mobsters. They work against what they conceive of as leftist ideas and want to subvert any kind of parliamentary government that exists. One of their most potent leaders, Licio Gelli, even tried to move Italy toward a presidential dictatorship."

Michael looked over at Maggie who had fallen silent. She was staring into space, her face drained of color.

Maggie felt herself tremble.

Propaganda Due.

Professor Samuels and Michael were worried enough as it was. To hear she had received a threatening note from P2 . . .

Maggie stood up and moved toward the liquor stand to pour herself a brandy. She took a sip, realizing her nervousness must have been apparent as the two men eyed her curiously.

"My father covered the Gelli story himself in Washington," she said, intimating a knowledge of the group through David Seline. "Gelli was a guest of honor during the inaugural ball for Ronald Reagan."

"Political allies, eh?" Michael questioned.

"Of sorts." Professor Samuels took a draw from his pipe. "Let's not forget something of special import here," he said as he leaned his head back to release the smoke. "Our friend, Giovanni Mabus. His father also had, shall we say, clandestine associations with Propaganda Due."

"But what about the traditional Masonic order?" Maggie asked, returning to the couch. She deliberately kept her voice to a journalistic monotone. "Haven't they always had a hand in political agendas? It's documented that some of the original patriots, including George Washington, were Masons. And now we're finding out that plenty of other big-time politicians have belonged to the group as well."

"Yes, that's true," Samuels said, raising his thick eyebrows as he spoke. "In fact, several of our presidents have been Masons, Franklin

Roosevelt among them. Even his vice president, Henry Wallace, was part of the order. Actually, it's specifically because of those two gentlemen that the U.S. has a very powerful tie to the Shambhala myth."

Michael sighed, looking confused. "Again with this Shambhala myth. What does a legend have to do with the affairs of a government?"

Samuels gave him a cutting glance. "Don't dismiss the powerful connection between politics and spirituality," he said, his voice fiery. "Entire empires have been run through their interplay. It just so happens that a Russian poet and artist named Nicholas Roerich, a true believer in the Shambhala myth, had quite an influence on Vice President Wallace and thus on Roosevelt himself. Even one of Roerich's expeditions into the Himalayas in search of this enlightened hidden kingdom was actually initiated through Wallace with Roosevelt's approval."

Michael, looking dumbfounded, shook his head. "Professor, I have to tell you, this stuff is hard to swallow. Are you telling me that these men were riding on the tails of some sort of spiritualist?"

"Life is not as black and white as you often paint it, Michael. Wallace and Roosevelt were Masons of the highest order. They took their posts in life seriously. What they saw in Roerich was a man of great integrity who was trying to realize a powerful truth. Roosevelt even put his signature to the *Roerich Pact*, an agreement initially among twenty-one nations to protect the cultural, artistic and historic treasures of all countries during times of war or peace."

"I had no idea," Michael said.

"Most people have no idea," Professor Samuels retorted. "That's the problem. Perhaps if they did their homework, they wouldn't be duped as often as they are. They'd realize that men in power have their own secret beliefs, ones that will influence the fate of a nation."

Michael responded with silence. Maggie knew his respect for the Professor finally had him thinking.

"Still," Maggie argued, "you have to admit the Masons have had their share of negative press over the years."

"Just think of it this way." Professor Samuels took on a lecturing tone. "Besides the fact that there a number of Christian sects, being a Christian doesn't mean you're a good person or for that matter, that you even believe what other Christian do, now does it? Yet, all these different Christians from various sects can still stand underneath the auspices of one huge—"

"Christian umbrella," Maggie said.

"Precisely. So don't be so quick to judge everything by a label," the Professor admonished. "The Masons are a far older lineage than you think . . . or will ever know. Part of *the Way,* they are guardians of the secret teachings."

Part of the Way. Samuels' intriguing tone struck a deep chord in her. Maggie felt a sudden awakening, as if the veil of mystery the Professor cloaked himself in had lifted for a brief moment.

Looking worried, the lines on Michael's forehead grew deeper. "Okay, so even if the Masonic order is basically an honorable one, obviously there are these lodges that are aberrations, as the Professor put it. And if there is some connection between Mabus and these P2 guys, the question is *how far does it go?*"

"The chain has many links." The Professor's dark eyes were piercing. "Oil, power, money and politics."

CHAPTER 28

J UST THEN, the telephone rang.

"The devil's mouthpiece," the Professor grumbled, not wishing to take the call. Instead, he allowed his answering machine to kick in.

"Professor Samuels," the caller said in a German accent. "This is Inspector Kliener of the Vienna Police. I'm sorry, but in spite of your warning, we were too late."

The Professor hurried to the phone and picked up the receiver.

"Yes, Inspector." The voice on the other end sounded solemn. *Did the Inspector just say what I think he said?*

Professor Samuels sank down onto the couch, the grim news draining him of energy. "When? Several days ago? I see . . . Do you know who was involved? Please let me know what occurs. Yes, yes, thank you. Good bye."

The Professor's mind raced. He quickly assessed the ominous turn of events. "So it's begun," he whispered.

"What's happened?" Michael asked. "Who was that?"

"That was my friend, Inspector Kliener, the commander of the Vienna Police force." The Professor looked at both Michael and Maggie aware of his dismal appearance. "The Spear of Longinus was stolen from the Hofburg Treasure Museum in Vienna."

Both Maggie and Michael stared at one another and then back at the Professor, each looking too stunned to speak.

Michael finally broke the silence. "What do you mean," he asked, "*it has begun?*"

"One of the great secrets about World War II," the Professor explained, "was Hitler's interest and mastery of the occult. He was not satisfied with military and political conquests. You're both aware of this, especially you, Michael."

The Professor decided additional pressure was called for. *Michael has to remember sooner or later.*

"The Spear," he emphasized, "was one part of a much larger puzzle. That's what Rachel discovered. She had found a link between Hitler's occult power and a powerful secret in the east."

"Rachel?" Michael was now looked totally confused.

"Who's Rachel?" Maggie asked.

"An old student of mine and Michael's friend. She called me from India shortly before she left to travel into Nepal," the Professor said. "She told me she discovered an ancient Tibetan text during her dig in India. A one-thousand-year-old relic. While translating it, she found unmistakable references to the Spear and the Holy Grail."

Professor Samuels watched Michael's confusion turn to surprise.

"How can that be?" Michael asked. "The Grail is a Western myth."

"Quite true," he responded, smiling at how unfathomable the link was. "Rachel also said the text referred to prophesies made in India and a parchment left by the Apostle Thomas that concerned Jesus and Jerusalem. It also spoke of the Grail as representing the path of enlightened compassion and the Spear as a power object, symbolizing the path of sovereignty alone."

Although Maggie appeared fascinated, Michael gave him a questioning glance.

"There's something you both need to understand," Samuels related. "The apostle Thomas was, like Magdalene, extremely close to Jesus. In 1945, when his gospel was found in Nag Hammadi, Egypt, the world was given a much different perspective of Christ and his teachings. This gospel was specifically filled with Christ's secret sayings. Interpreting their deeper meaning is key to understanding the path that Christ taught."

Now all the tumblers are falling into place. "Within his gospel," Samuels continued, "Thomas himself indicates that Christ took him aside and told him three additional sayings which he was to keep completely secret. Thomas was not to tell any of the other disciples. There are those of us who believe that it is through the discovery and understanding of these three sayings that the Grail will be found. We also believe that the Thomas parchment holds the clue to their discovery."

Michael gave him a speculative glance. "Even if you're presenting another theory about the Grail," he said, "I'm still not getting the link. Why a Western myth discovered in a Tibetan document?"

"Why, indeed?" Samuels questioned in turn. "The clue lies in the fact that the document Rachael found was a Shambhala text."

"Shambhala." Maggie's voice was barely audible.

Samuels could see the light of realization in her eyes. He turned toward Michael to explain further. "This is where the Shambhala *theory* comes in. Specifically, the text describes the path of enlightenment and links the Eastern myth of the Wish-fulfilling Jewel and the Western myth of finding the Grail, or Lapsis Excellis. In essence, these myths are basically one and the same. That's the theory."

Michael suddenly looked up curiously at the Professor. "*Lapsis Excellis*. Rachel wrote that in a journal entry that I found."

"It's another name for the Holy Grail," Maggie added.

"Literally, it means precious jewel or precious stone," the Professor explained, "and is used to refer to the Grail itself."

Maggie had already surmised the conclusion. "Precious Jewel . . . Wish-fulfilling Jewel. Do you see the similarity?" She was staring at Michael with a look of anticipation.

Michael's eyes were like pinballs darting back and forth. Samuels recognized the look and knew his protégé was beginning to put some pieces together.

"One second here." Michael suddenly took a step back. He furrowed his brow. "What about the fact that the Grail is usually known as the Cup of Christ?"

The Professor realized he was being called upon to explain the unexplainable.

"Yes, it's commonly symbolized as a cup," he acknowledged, "but it is also depicted as a stone or a bowl. Today, we even have those who claim it's a bloodline." Samuels shook his head in disbelief. Although he understood why the possibility of finding a descendant of Christ would be exciting to many, the idea that it had anything to do with the Grail path of enlightenment was amiss.

Maggie smiled knowingly, appearing to agree.

"In the end," Samuels added, "it's not the Grail's form that's significant, but what it does to us. In searching for it we go on a personal voyage, deepening our awareness and becoming fully human. We are literally searching for something beyond our wildest dreams. Our minds, our hearts, are forever changed."

The dark mahogany wood of the library became even richer to the Professor's eyes. *Where will it eventually lead? What will be the outcome of discovering the mystery of the Grail?*

Samuels had come to know, without doubt, that the myths he spoke of had emerged from the same source. "The path of finding the Grail and the path of finding the Wish-fulfilling Jewel are like two sides of the same coin. Being so, one side is equal to the worth of the other." He paused. "Both represent the quest for enlightenment."

A look of concern suddenly passed across Michael's eyes. "There seems to be another kind of strange connection here," he announced. "Steven Einsof said he overheard Mabus' men using the word *Longinus* as if it were some kind of code."

Disturbed, Samuels allowed the implications of Michael's words to settle in his mind. He took a long draw on his pipe before addressing him. "The text Rachel found also spoke of prophecies declaring that someone with great authority and influence would attempt to combine the power of the Spear and the Grail, unconcerned with the dangers of making such an attempt. That's what Hitler was trying to do by going after these power objects."

"Power for power's sake," Michael concluded.

"A deadly venture," Samuels added. "That is why, in light of what you have just told me, I can only come to one conclusion. I believe the theft of the Longinus Spear is somehow related to our Libyan peace broker."

Michael's face was immediately drawn. "Mabus?"

Professor Samuels needed to push the envelope. *Will Michael eventually see?*

"Just think about it," Samuels urged. "The Peace Conference in Jerusalem, the proposal to build the Third Temple on the Mount, the Spear of Longinus stolen from the Hofburg . . . There's only one person or group of persons who could benefit from the synchronicity of these events."

The light of awareness grew in Michael's eyes.

Samuels walked over to the hearth and shuffled the logs in the fire. Hissing, they sent small waves of light to the corners of the room. "As legend states, after Christ's death, Joseph of Arimathea was held captive in a tower because he openly professed to being Christ's follower and so was seen as a traitor by the Sanhedrin, the organization of Jewish leaders to which he belonged. It is said Joseph survived on the strength of the Grail and eventually made his way to England. The Spear, though, did not arrive with him." Samuels paused as the fire blazed higher. "It resided somewhere in quiet obscurity for several hundred years before appearing again at the end of the third century. Perhaps those it served during its years of repose were only interested in matters of the spirit. Or perhaps they did not know what they had. Now I fear someone like Mabus has discovered this old hiding place, and by returning the Spear to that mystical spot, its power will be infinitely greater than anything Hitler may have known."

"What you are saying only leads us to one conclusion," Maggie said, "that if someone were to attempt to find the Grail at this time it would be a significant threat to anyone in possession of the Spear."

"Quite significant," the Professor acknowledged as he sat down again beside her.

"So when Rachel became interested in the precious stone . . . " Michael mused.

"That's when she must have become a danger to someone . . . or possibly to some group, jeopardizing their hidden aims," the Professor concluded, his chest tightening. "Those who are in possession of the Spear are occult obsessives of some kind. I can't begin to judge how they became who they are, but I do know they are people without conscience, who would readily commit atrocities without blinking an eye."

Michael's face grew even more sullen.

"You see, Michael," Samuels said, leaning toward him as he explained further, "the evil intent which is forming before our very eyes is more than just a mental state that can be reduced to psychological terms. If Mabus is involved, those who are working with him have created one massive web, a spiritual vortex of negativity."

"Spiritual?" Maggie asked.

"Yes, spiritual," Samuels said firmly. "Don't be fooled into thinking that negative entities do not attempt to influence man's destiny, that someone like Hitler can be explained as simply the product of a mismanaged childhood. Oh, my dear friends, if you think about it, you can clearly see the absurdity of it."

"But psychological factors are a part of us," Michael responded.

"Of course, but that does not explain how someone can slaughter his fellow man as extensively and brutally as Hitler did. What was it in his childhood that set him up to be the incomparable mass murderer that he was, sending millions to horrifying deaths surrounded by the dark forces of his SS and Gestapo?" Samuels paused. "Don't you see? There are other forces at play here. It is also no coincidence that at the exact moment of the Spear's discovery by U.S. troops, Adolph Hitler killed himself in an underground bunker in Berlin."

Samuels turned toward the end table and pulled open a drawer. "Here," he said, retrieving a black hardbound book. He turned a few pages until he found the entry. "Hitler himself describes what he felt while standing before the Spear of Longinus in the Treasure House of the Hofburg." Samuels read the passage aloud:

> *The air became stifling so that I could barely breath. The noisy scene of the Treasure House seemed to melt away before my eyes. I stood alone trembling before the hovering form of the Superman—a spirit sublime and fearful, a countenance intrepid and cruel. In holy awe, I offered my soul as a vessel of his will.*

A silence filled with darkness and shadows followed his words. Samuels eyed Michael and Maggie, realizing time was of the essence. "You must both go to India and find the Thomas parchment Rachel mentioned," he announced then. "The key is in Bodhgaya."

"What?" Michael asked incredulously. "Go to India?"

But something in the history scholar's eyes told the Professor that he was already packing.

"Remain with me tonight, both of you," Samuels said authoritatively. "In the morning, you can make arrangements for your trip, and I will share with you what I can of this mysterious journey."

CHAPTER 29

ONE HUNDRED MILES away in Manhattan, Giovanni Mabus stepped out of his chauffer-driven sedan onto Fifth Avenue, readying himself. He was not fond of entertaining, but when he did, he took the perspective that each instance was more of an elaborate ruse than a social event. Mabus had noted long ago that the world was made for and of appearances. For this reason alone, he dressed in Pierre Cardin suits and always sported a Patek Phillipe watch. This evening, especially, called for elegant manipulation. He made sure he looked the part.

As Mabus was escorted into the Sherry-Netherland Hotel's private ballroom, he noticed the many foreign diplomats, corporate CEOs and wealthy entrepreneurs milling about nervously, hoping to learn more about the dinner's true purpose. In fact, few of the night's select guests were even vaguely aware that Mabus was their true host. The European Commission had made the arrangements for the European-American Friendship Dinner, issuing the invitations in the name of Felix Kersten, the incoming president of the European Commission.

But Mabus had seen to it that all the invitees received hints that tonight's event was much more than a diplomatic dinner honoring Mr. Kersten. Therefore, no spouses had been extended an invitation to the black tie event. The few women that were actually present had earned their attendance, having satisfied Mabus' requisite criteria. In fact, he had selected the several hundred candidates himself—power and money being the common thread—as part of an initial screening for those he hoped to invite into his grand plan.

Among the eclectic group of invitees . . . Senator Malcolm Denport, representing the United States Congress, although he was under strict orders to avoid being seen with Mabus . . . mega-wealthy stockholders—some from multinational software and computer firms that started up in garages . . . and on-line vendors, film producers and media moguls on a never-ending quest for sponsors. All were eyeing each other warily, like animals that had suddenly found themselves in the same cage.

After dinner, brandy and cigars were served, and the room was cleared of all hotel staff. Mabus' security people guarded the doors as well as monitored the area for eavesdropping devices. All the while, seated at a secluded table in a darkened corner, Mabus himself sat watching. He was patiently awaiting the arrival of his own special guest, one who would not be seen by the other attendees.

The time finally arrived for Finland's Felix Kersten to make his address. Mabus' true motives remained unknown to the honored speaker, whose honesty and trusting nature were the very qualities that had led Mabus to steer his selection as the next president of the European Commission—a position that Mabus himself would oversee, of course. Kersten was only aware of his task: to deliver a warning and a hopeful message to America's economic elite. He did not know that secrecy and discretion had been exacted from each attendee even before an invitation was extended.

And their curiosity has brought them all to this dinner like moths to a flame.

Mabus watched as, through a sea of diners shrouded in darkness, Kersten approached the low stage at the front of the ballroom and stood at the podium.

"America is no longer at the crossroads," Kersten began. "The United States has entered an era as dark as was faced by Europe in the 1930s. The invasion of Iraq and the poorly conceived military strikes against Iran have left the Middle East in turmoil. Gasoline is selling for an average of five dollars a gallon, and illegal migrants have taken over the construction industry. The disparity between the super rich—yourselves—and the average family has reached a tipping point."

Mabus heard some nervous snickering. *Kersten is hitting a nerve.*

"Due to the military adventures of the last administration," Kersten declared, "public debt in America has destroyed the country's future. Foreign governments are beginning to seek ways to leverage their debt at America's expense. Capital is no longer available to your corporations at levels that are profitable. Unemployment is rising." Kersten paused. "In fact, your plight has affected the world. For instance, in Germany, overall unemployment is ten per cent. But in the former East German areas, unemployment is over twenty per cent. Therefore, it is no surprise that in the eastern section, the neo-Nazi parties have received over ten per cent of the vote, a worrisome and dangerous development."

Kersten most definitely had the group's attention. As they listened, each face now posed a similar question. *Where is this going?*

"Without health care and retirement benefits, the average American family lives in a state of continual crisis." Kersten scanned the crowd as he spoke. "What does this all mean for you? I will tell you. America is poised at the edge of a social revolution, without the benefit of Europe's social safety nets."

Mabus smiled to himself. *Because you bastards stole those benefits and emptied the pension funds.* Little did his loyal, stealth bureaucrats scattered throughout the European Commission know, they had inspired the speech Kersten was delivering—the theme of which was designed to serve Mabus' purpose.

"My esteemed American colleagues." Kersten now delivered the final punch, one Mabus had designed from the start. "It is time for the United States to join the European Union."

When his guest finally arrived ten minutes later, Mabus changed his venue, moving to a penthouse suite specifically for his meeting.

"You can't be serious," Vice President Richard Bohmer scoffed.

Mabus stared at the man sitting across from him. Judging from appearance, he was amazed that someone with such closely set eyes and such a thick neck had inspired enough confidence in anyone to reach the office he held. Bohmer was, in truth, too stupid to be entrusted with anything other than a podium and teleprompter.

Mabus felt pleased watching Bohmer squirm. With Kersten undoubtedly coming to the end of his address twenty stories below, the web was nearly sewn.

"Mr. Vice President, Richard, you are the product of the finest integrity voting machines can buy." Mabus narrowed his eyes and focused his attention on the worm in the chair across from him. "America has no choice. China is poised to call in your loans. They have already begun pressuring the remaining oil-producing states to restrict sales to the United States."

Bohmer stared at him scornfully, his silence daring Mabus to go on.

"Your foolish air strikes on Iran resulted in a cascade of terrorist strikes against oil refineries, wells and pipelines throughout the Middle East. When you get elected president next year, your first order of business will be a treaty with the European Union setting America on the road to membership."

"I can't do that," Bohmer spewed. "The party will never approve."

Mabus chuckled. "Don't make me laugh."

Bohmer was squirming again in his seat.

"Your party has two constituencies," Mabus said. "The men downstairs represent one, and the other is the evangelists who will do whatever their ministers say. Those ministers tell their flock what I *pay* them to tell them. So don't tell *me* that the party won't approve."

Bohmer stared deeply into his brandy snifter as if the way out of the mess he had made of his life lay in a bottomless glass.

"The truth is simple—you have no option," Mabus stated. "Your last administration left America in debt as well as with a tattered, demoralized military. Rich Arabs are fleeing the Middle East with suitcases full of gold bullion and the hopes of their own people. The Chinese are surveying Times Square, Fisherman's Wharf, and everything in between."

Bohmer looked like he was about to curse. "So you think a speech at a fancy dinner party is going to offer the decisive blow?"

"Tonight is only the opening bell," Mabus declared. "They may not like it, but the men and women downstairs will not forget what Kersten has told them. The American political leaders already know it's true. They just haven't been able to admit it. Plus, they haven't known how to address it. As smart and as rich as they are, they really want to be told what to do."

"And I'm to assume you're going to be the one to do just that," Bohmer said.

"You need not assume anything." Mabus paused, eyeing him coldly. "Just remember who you're beholden to."

Mabus had Bohmer cornered. The latter couldn't look him in the eye, because without the monies from Mabus' corporation backing him, Bohmer's presidential hopes were finished before they began.

CHAPTER 30

A T THAT MOMENT, half a world away, Kailas sat in the backseat of the shaking rickshaw as Sajjid motored past the pedestrians on the road. It was still early morning but the streets of Bodhgaya were already bustling with pilgrims and tourists.

Kailas' mind was clear. Whatever the strange substance was that had intoxicated him, it had been purged from his body. If it had not been for Sajjid, he felt certain he would now be dead.

As Kailas pondered the unforeseen shifts of his fortune, Sajjid drove through the crowded streets, finally stopping at a tall gate in the center of town. Once out of the rickshaw, Kailas found himself standing before a magnificent sight—the Bodhgaya Stupa—a towering manifestation of enlightened mind. Next to it, beneath the great Bodhi tree, the Buddha Shakyamuni had attained enlightenment over twenty-five hundred years ago.

Kailas looked up in awe at the fifty-meter structure that now commemorated that event, allowing his gaze to move down the length of the pyramidal tower, taking in the fine details of its design. Amazed by its stature, he stood amidst the crowd of people walking through the stupa garden. It appeared he was not alone in his admiration as, even this early in the day, there seemed no end to the flow of travelers and pilgrims entering through the iron gates.

"Another Mecca," his Muslim friend, Sajjid, remarked.

Kailas smiled and gestured for Sajjid to follow him into the Stupa temple. Once inside and his eyes had adjusted to the dim light, Kailas saw a large gilded statue. *Shakyamuni Buddha, his hand touching the ground in the earth-touching mudra.* Seventeen hundred years old, the sacred image faced east on the site claimed to be where the Buddha himself had meditated, sitting with his back to the Bodhi tree.

Kailas stood quietly amidst the swirling mass of pilgrims. Finally, he turned toward his companion. "Can you stay and sit with me?"

Sajjid shook his head, his eyes sweeping across the crowd. "I must go. Work still waits," he replied. "Will you be alright?"

"Yes, yes. Thank you, my brother, for helping me reach my goal," Kailas said, trying to hand Sajjid some rupees.

But the driver refused to accept payment. "Allah is the God for all. I cannot be paid for giving service to another in need."

"Then let me offer this prayer for our friendship," Kailas said. "Dear God, the Great Architect of the Universe, we thank you for our fellowship. Always let us see our interdependence, one faith upon the other, with the aim of illumination and unification in mind. Let us and all of our brethren throughout the world spread your light to others. May we always keep aware of ourselves as moral beings, living with each other in peace."

What better place, thought Kailas, *than this site of illumination and enlightenment for such a prayer.*

The warmth of friendship in his eyes, Sajjid bowed and silently took his leave.

His legs still a bit shaky, Kailas walked out of the stupa and past the gates. As he weaved cautiously through the sea of people, he wondered what he would say to the Bodhi Temple guardian.

Upon reaching the Temple Management building, Kailas found that in his weakened state, the tall iron gates in front of the structure were hard to open. Finally pushing them ajar, he walked onto the grounds and entered the main building where he discovered a lone monk in saffron robes standing behind a desk. As Kailas approached him, the man looked up and peered over the rim of his gold spectacles.

"My brothers of *the Way* have sent me." Kailas spoke up quickly. "Their instructions have brought me here to you."

Appearing to understand immediately, the older monk hurried Kailas into a small room behind his office and closed the door.

"You are Ananda?" Kailas asked.

"Yes," the monk replied, his eyes filled with anticipation. "Do you have it?"

Kailas removed the shawl from around his shoulders and undid his belt. From the inner pocket of his robe he pulled out the thin leather pouch.

"May I?" Ananda's voice softened reverently with his request.

Kailas understood and allowed Ananda to take it from him.

"It is safe then," the monk whispered.

Ananda had heard the legend before, but to hold the legend . . . this was something different. He had studied and mastered Pali, the language of the original Buddhist texts, then Sanskrit, in order to comprehend the great Hindu and Buddhist scriptures. But nothing could surpass touching the legend itself—the gateway to the mystery—beyond all texts, all language, and all words.

The Way had drawn him. Filled with great thinkers abounding in wisdom, its tradition and doctrines spoke of insight and integrity. This brotherhood accepted all those of virtuous intent no matter where the seeker was from or what language he spoke . . . no matter what his religion. *Enlightened activity.* The heart of every religion lay within it, beyond any scripture or text.

Now, feeling the powerful relic in his hand, Ananda could not resist inquiring about the parchment's destiny. "Where will you take it?"

"You know I can't tell you." Kailas held out his hand, indicating it was time to return the sacred treasure. It was understood that each had his part to play—a piece in the puzzle. No one but the high-level initiates could know the whole, and they were but a few. Yet still, although Kailas was firm and resolute in his beliefs, it was hard to resist opening the pouch.

"Could we not look for a moment?" Ananda urged.

Kailas did not anger easily, but he felt a flush of heat rise to his face. "I have come for the key," he said, controlling his feeling. "From this point, I will complete my task. I thank you, brother, for helping me."

With an accepting nod, Ananda reached under his shawl into the pocket of his shirt and produced a tarnished silver key.

Kailas took it from him and placed it in his satchel.

"You must be careful," Ananda cautioned as Kailas was about to leave. "Heed my warning."

Kailas nodded in response, feeling Ananda's watchful eyes upon him as he left.

Once outside, Kailas closed the outer gates and walked back out onto the road. As he hurried through the crowd, gripping the satchel at his side, he had but one thought.

It is almost done.

Now, he need only wait for the cover of darkness to complete his task.

CHAPTER 31

A NOTHER MORNING, another chapter.
Laurel understood their story had only just begun.
Besides newspapers that noted their arrival in Manhattan, the
morning brought with it coffee, bagels and several hundred more supporters. Laurel and the *Seline Marchers*, as they were now being called by
the media, walked beside the majestic Hudson once again, but now even
stronger in number and more invigorated.

Heartened, Laurel felt a surge of energy quickening her steps. They
really were encroaching upon a dream. Yet, she realized it was much
more than a dream. An idea that had only been a thought in her head
several days earlier had been pounded into the pavement. That idea was
now as real as the street beneath her feet.

Laurel glanced up ahead. Towering almost four hundred feet into
the hazy sky, the Riverside Church awaited them like a fortress. As she
walked forward, astounded by the number of people surrounding the
church and on the sidewalks on both sides of Broadway, it appeared to
her as if half of Manhattan had anticipated their arrival. She could tell
that a large group of Columbia University students and professors were
there as well, making themselves known with colorful signs and banners—*Jerusalem Walk, Freedom from Fear*, and Laurel's favorite, *Mind
over Money*.

Laurel proceeded up the church steps, humbled by the thought
of the many noble minds who had traversed them before her. *Nelson
Mandela, the Dalai Lama, Martin Luther King, the Reverend Jesse Jackson.*
The list was long and noteworthy. When she reached the top, Reverend
Robert Milstrom, Riverside's senior minister, smiled and greeting her
warmly before turning toward the crowd.

"We meet here today," Reverend Milstrom began, "as a congregation of diversified groups. Although many of us have taken different

paths—Jewish, Islamic, Christian, Hindu—our destination is the same. Union with the Divine, fellowship with all human beings, and seeing with an awakened heart."

As he continued to speak, the reverend turned toward Laurel for a moment. "Our grandmother, Laurel, is helping us to do just that—to awaken hearts that have been asleep for too long. Intellectual approaches to solutions, devoid of human compassion, are lopsided to say the least. At their worst, they are extremely dangerous, providing us with endless rationalizations for our behavior. That's why, by separating our minds from our hearts, we've been able to weave intricate webs—to justify genocide, if you can believe that, or to make cases for our cruelty. Together, we may act as conspirators, but our hearts do not lie. Our hearts know the truth. The eyes of the heart balance wisdom with compassion."

His jaw set firmly, his eyes piercing and direct, a look of determination crossed Reverend Milstrom's face. "May this walk, inspired by Maggie Seline, be an offering of unity. Together, we can attain our desire for peace in the Middle East and throughout the world by realizing one thing above all else . . . If we want to go to heaven, we must build it here on earth."

After speaking briefly to the crowd assembled outside the church, Laurel walked down the steps hoping to escape any contact with the media. She quickly realized her wish was no more than a fantasy when, at the bottom of the stairs, she was greeted by a television reporter and his camera crew.

"Mrs. Seline. Mark Alvarez of Channel 5 News," the reporter said with a rush. "They're accusing you of pointing your finger too much. Being self-righteous."

Laurel stopped to answer him. "Who's 'they'?"

"Congressman McGrath for one," Alvarez divulged.

Laurel greeted his answer with a huff. "Perhaps that's better than finger wetting."

"Finger wetting, ma'am?"

"Yes, Mr. Alvarez," Laurel said. "McGrath's a politician always raising a wet finger in the air to determine which way the wind is blowing. If the wind is blowing south, Congressman McGrath likes to blow with it. He says anything he believes his constituents want to hear, pressing buttons that inflame voters in order to derail them from concentrating on the more serious and pervasive issues."

"And what issues is he avoiding ma'am?" Alvarez blurted his question in return.

Laurel smirked, knowing that reporters had to have quick tongues to stay in the running. "Well, perhaps he should be talking about starting wars, sending innocent young men and women to their deaths for oil, not tending to the poor and disenfranchised in our own nation, and turning this country into a land of zealots devoid of compassion, who disregard their fellow man and sell their own souls for a big dividend paycheck." She paused, hoping her words were providing a challenge. "McGrath should practice some of the loving kindness taught in the Gospels he claims to be such a spokesman for."

"That's a lot to say." With a quick flick of his wrist, Alvarez brought the mike to his own lips and back to Laurel's.

"And I've lived long enough as an American citizen to say it." Laurel turned her back and started to walk away.

"Just one more thing," Alvarez said, running behind her.

Laurel turned her fierce gaze back at the reporter.

"If Congressman McGrath is finger wetting the public to determine, as you say, which direction the winds of opinion are blowing, then just what is it that you're doing?"

"Changing it."

"What?"

"Changing the wind's course. It's not just me, but thousands of others." Laurel wanted to throw this little brat a verbal punch. "Perhaps a media spokesman like yourself would like to make a change, too. You know, maybe try some *real* fair and balanced reporting."

She flashed a charming seasoned smile and took her leave.

Alvarez turned toward the camera as Laurel walked away. "This is Mark Alvarez, Fox News, reporting from outside Riverside Church."

"Jack." Alvarez addressed his cameraman as he grappled with his microphone clip. "You know that's a cut-and-paste job. Let's make sure we get rid of the fair and balanced remark. Did you get the angle I wanted, shooting down at the old girl?" Alvarez felt pleased when he heard his cameraman answer in the affirmative. "Okay, good. Just cut out the Congressman McGrath lines and keep in the rest of her rant."

Assured, Alvarez smiled to himself. He would have Laurel Seline looking like a nutty old bat in time for the six o'clock news.

CHAPTER 32

HEAT, FLIES, BLOOD, *sand, and sweat.*
Only the sweat is mine. The heat belongs to Jupiter. As king of the gods, the sun is his. The sand and the flies are the living symbol of this stinking land to which my Caesar has sent me. A narrow dunghill perched between three seas . . . one dead, one red, and one which leads back to Rome.

Rome, the land of my birth, yet here I am, my arms no longer young and tireless, my eyes weakened by a white film that increasingly robs my sight with each passing year. A centurion still, but for how long? Only my many years of loyal service to Pilate have left me with my sword.

The blood?

The blood belongs to the man on the cross, the Rabbi. For two years, at Pilate's request, I have followed his trail. In Capernaum, I saw lame men walk. In Cana, I drank wedding wine. Beside the sea of Galilee, I heard him speak as we shared loaves and ate fish.

Surely this is a dream. No, a nightmare.

This most honest of men, full of giving and joy, now naked and streaked with blood. How can I look? How can I cast my eyes aside? A lifetime of battles, seeing broken bodies with guts spilled like wine, has still not prepared me for this savage sight.

The Rabbi's hand twitches. Drop by drop, the blood drips from the ugly black metal spikes which pin him to the cross.

In anguish my horse rears back, as if contemplating flight from this god-cursed land. Sharply, I pull his bridle and move closer to the man. Atop the horse, my head is even with his waist. Against my will my eyes move toward the Rabbi's face. Still alive, barely, he returns my gaze. His dark eyes have lost most of their shine and the fire I have grown to admire.

Again, my horse kicks up its legs causing my head to turn. A small band of men are carefully picking their way over the rocks, maneuvering past the growling packs of dogs that live on the rotting corpses left on their crosses. Now what? The sight of the men makes me heave, but still, I must face them. Their presence can only mean trouble.

"Centurions, arise!" I yell at my men who have grown accustomed to sleeping, gambling, or just picking their teeth while waiting for crucified men to die. This is no time for them to turn their backs. I intend to make sure this rabbi at least dies with a dignity his last few hours have lacked.

"Centurion Gaius Cassius Longinus, move aside." It is the temple guard, Caiphas' police, who addresses me. The elder in front who speaks carries a long spear held aloft . . . the spear which is the Temple stamp of authority, forged by Phineas, and once thrown at young David by old King Saul.

At last I have a face to which I can assign my anger. I kick my horse sharply in the side and gallop towards the group. The elder guard jumps back when I reach them, but before he can turn and run, I yank the spear from his hand.

"No!" He yells in frustration and rage, almost equal to mine, as I gallop back up the hill to the cross.

The Rabbi is watching me. What keeps this man alive, I wonder? For twenty-four hours he had been beaten and whipped without water or food. My men, louts, had then placed a crown of thorns on his head. Now he has met his cross.

Although it pains my failing eyes, I look up at him. "Forgive me, Rabbi. I will help in the only way I know how." I shove the spear into his side. Blood shoots out from his wound and covers my eyes.

Blackness. The sun seems to have left the sky. Wiping the blood away from my face, I look around in disbelief. The cloud from my eyes has lifted, and I can see even more clearly than when I was young.

But the signs do not look good. Dark clouds move quickly across the sky . . . the wind is wailing . . . a mighty thunderous rumbling arises from the ground. Slowly, the Rabbi closes his eyes. His head drops limply to his shoulder.

Silence.

My ears strain to hear even the faintest of sounds but there are none, until I hear the mournful cries of his mother and her companions. For a moment, I do not heed their grief. I am overwhelmed by what the Rabbi has given me . . .

My sight.

———

Michael awoke in a flush of heat, his heart racing. He had never experienced a dream so vivid before. His first instinct was to find Samuels.

He threw on some clothes and darted down to the kitchen where he found Ebed-melech washing up breakfast plates. Confused, Michael glanced up at the clock above the stove. *10:06 A.M!* Why didn't anyone wake him? When Michael asked the Professor's whereabouts, he was told Samuels was already out in the garden. Ebed-melech watched him with raised eyebrows as Michael grabbed a piece of toast and headed out the portico doors.

Once outside, Michael noticed how the unusually warm spring had already transformed the Professor's garden into an earthly paradise. Pink and yellow begonias hung from trellises, and tall mimosa trees had scattered some of their flowers onto the grass, adding a touch of the romantic renaissance to the otherwise oriental flavor found in the stone statues along the path. Buddha, Krishna, Shiva, Christ, even a meditating Moses lined the walkway. Michael thought it fitting that the artistry of civilizations long past would find a home in the Professor's garden.

When he reached the rose garden at the end of the path, Michael found Samuels seated on his favorite bench. He sat down beside him, and in a rush of words, told the Professor about his dream.

"Your life seems to be turning around for you," Samuels said abruptly, "and it's time you recognize that you are being initiated."

Michael took a breath, surprised. "Initiated into what?"

"I can't really say. Maybe you're ready for something new, something less narrow and opinionated, something—"

"Something different from the life of an accomplished but frustrated scholar."

The Professor smiled knowingly.

"Why would this all be happening now? It's not like I wanted or invited it." In fact, Michael knew, he had been hiding for years from his own intuition. The realm of adventure and drama—life on the edge—was a fantasy best played out by actors like Harrison Ford on a movie screen.

"You had to," Professor Samuels stated firmly. "We never just stumble into situations. It's not possible. Somewhere in your past you longed for this to occur and now it has. The precious jewel calls to you, and you are bound through your own bidding to search for it, which makes the journey toward awakening inevitable."

"Okay, so even if I had some hidden desire," Michael said, "I certainly wasn't aware of it."

Samuels laughed. "But you're becoming more aware, and there are ways to help yourself along."

"Like what?"

"Through preparation. You prepare by dedicating your life and making compassionate activity your cornerstone. It is the only way to self-knowledge. Without compassion there is no true quest, just an aberration. A black magician like Adolf Hitler would never be able to find the Grail. His lack of humanity and intentional malice made it an impossible feat. It was due to a total absence of compassion that Hitler was able to wield raw power with such evil intent."

"Do you think it's truly possible that Mabus is planning to use the Spear with the same kind of malevolence?"

"It's possible," the Professor answered. "And it appears as if it may actually be happening. He's already established tremendous trust through his management of the European Commission. He's also positioning himself not only as a peacemaker in the Middle East, but as *the peacemaker*, period." He paused to look at Michael. "Move by your intuition. There isn't time left for anything else."

With sudden clarity, Michael realized where his intuition was leading. "Rachel."

The Professor, looking pleased, nodded. "If you follow in her footsteps, you will be taken to a land far away, so deep and rich in lore that it will stir you to the depths of your soul. Rachel followed the clues that led her from the holiest city of India into the wild, mountainous region of Nepal." He leaned closer, his penetrating dark eyes brimming with another revelation. "Rachel said she discovered something else in that ancient text . . . the key to the location of the mythical land of Shambhala."

"Why didn't she tell me anything about it?" Michael asked, perplexed. "She only mentioned *Lapsis Excellis* in a notebook entry. I never heard anything from her directly, especially about this Shambhala."

"Perhaps it was because she knew what your attitude would be—doubtful, not particularly supportive." The Professor's tone was admonishing.

"I would have told her to forget it, that the journey was uncertain and wasn't worth the danger."

"So there you have it . . . the reason why she didn't confide in you. As far as you're concerned it's only a wild goose myth."

Michael gave Professor Samuels a thin smile, uncertain what to believe anymore. Legends, prophecies . . . who could tell what was real?

"Into the Himalayan range. That's where Rachel was headed, and if you want to find out what happened to her and understand the connection between the Spear and the Grail, that's where you'll have to go, too."

Michael realized the Professor was not letting up. "And just how am I supposed find a *mythical* city?"

"Don't worry. You'll be guided."

"By whom?"

"I have no idea," Samuels answered with a smile. "Perhaps one of the old ones . . . one of *the Way*, will find you."

Before Michael could ask him what he meant, the sound of an approaching car caught his attention. Professor Samuels stood up abruptly.

"I am expecting a visitor this morning, Michael," Samuels said, his voice edgy. "Please excuse me."

As soon as Samuels left, Michael strolled toward the other side of the rose garden, passing through a stone archway. A series of arbors and connecting trellises laced with English ivy hid him from view as he stealthily moved toward an iron fence that looked out onto the driveway. Trying to remain discreet, he peered through the foliage just as a black Mercedes pulled up in front of the house.

A dark-skinned man, wearing a suit and carrying a briefcase, walked up to the front door and knocked. He looked to be in his thirties. As he waited, he scanned the courtyard, unaware he was being watched.

The front door opened and Professor Samuels indicated for the man to enter. Meanwhile Michael, still hidden behind the trellises, decided to get closer to the house. A few moments later, Samuels and his visitor, coffee cups in hand, reappeared out the back door and sat under one of the garden arbors.

Seeing their position, Michael worked himself toward a massive juniper hedge just behind them. Just then, a movement from above caught his eye. Maggie was standing at the window, glancing down at the two men. Appearing to be just as sneaky as he, she concealed herself behind a curtain.

After some polite references to the Professor's work, his guest handed him a document. Placing his coffee cup aside, the Professor began to read the material, an impassive look on his face. Meanwhile, the man lit a cigarette and waited.

Crouching behind the bushes, Michael was having a hard time not groaning. He was thankful when the Professor finally looked up and began to speak.

"I'm sorry I won't be able to help you, sir," the Professor said as he handed the papers back. "Mr. Mabus and Ambassador Singh seem to think I am more informed than I actually am regarding the activities of my former students."

Michael's whole body tensed when he heard Mabus' name.

"Yes, I have heard of a certain archeological find regarding the Apostle Thomas, texts recorded and the like, but I'm unaware of anything else about the matter." The Professor paused to sip his coffee. "Why such an interest now?"

"Professor Samuels," the man said as he flicked his cigarette. His Middle Eastern accent suggested a British upbringing. "We believe that Dr. Kumari is in illegal possession of an artifact which was found in an archaeological dig in the area of Bodhgaya several months ago. He denies this on all counts, but we have reports from several of those associated with his American colleague, Rachel Prescott, that she discovered an ancient document at the site. Dr. Kumari did not report it as part of the find."

Michael caught his breath. *Why would Mabus be interested in what Rachel discovered?*

"The Indian government has legal rights to all artifacts found on her soil and any findings must be declared to the Bureau of Indian Antiquities," the man insisted. "And now the American archaeologist is missing. Even the American Embassy has not heard from her."

Missing! Michael steadied himself behind the bushes. As he peered through the leaves, he could see that Samuels' face was drawn, yet his dark knowing eyes were glaring straight ahead.

Finally, Samuels broke his silence. "As I stated before, I have no information with regard to that particular field trip. My dealings with

Dr. Kumari are limited. He was a student of mine once, but it's been several years since we've spoken."

Michael knew the Professor well. When he heard the nervous tinge in his mentor's voice, Michael felt his own anxiety mushroom. At that moment, Professor Samuels stood up, indicating the meeting was over. His bearings quickly grew unsteady, and he reached down toward the arm of the bench for balance. The man watched without concern as the Professor slumped down to his knees, his coffee cup falling from his hand.

Alarmed, Michael bolted from behind the bushes and rushed toward the Professor. The man, upon seeing him, took off through the garden toward the driveway. As Michael lowered Samuels fully to the ground, he could see the Professor was having trouble breathing. Just then, Maggie came racing out of the house.

"He's just pulling out," she yelled as she ran toward them. "Hurry. Get his license!"

Michael got back to his feet and ran into the courtyard just as the Mercedes screeched forward. The car's angle made it impossible to see the license plate. Just before peeling out into the driveway, the man turned his intense, black eyes toward Michael. Then he was gone.

When he returned to the garden, Maggie was holding Professor Samuels' head in her hands. Ebed-melech, who apparently had heard the commotion, was kneeling beside her.

"I'll call an ambulance," Michael said. He started running toward the house.

"No," Ebed-melech commanded as he nudged Maggie aside. "Go. You must both go."

"What?" Michael turned toward Maggie who looked just as surprised by the directive.

Ebed-melech pulled a cell phone out of the side pocket of his shirt. "I'll take care of this. It's too dangerous for you to stay," he said, his voice shaking. "You must go immediately. Do whatever Professor Samuels told you to do. Just go! Now!"

CHAPTER 33

A
FTER HAVING LEFT the Fox reporter in her wake and being bombarded by questions from other news media corre-
spondents fixating on her mission to keep Maggie's message
alive, Laurel found herself once again revamping her vision. Her coffee
klatch crew that had started with Lonnie and Jules was now a troop of
over fifteen hundred women. She was beginning to feel their road didn't
have to end at the U.N. A bolder thought—*just an idea*—was beginning
to take hold.

As Laurel and the marchers walked down the sidewalks of Broadway,
it became apparent to her that the word was out. *Walking Toward the
New Jerusalem* banners and shirts were everywhere. Laurel could see that
savvy New York entrepreneurs had been busy through the night.

Nearly two thousand people marching down Broadway.

It was the kind of spectacle one would expect in New York City.
As they proceeded down the street, a group of unsavory looking men
gave her a round of applause in a show of support. Even some homeless
people huddled under a construction overhang yelled, "Go, grandma!"
as she walked by. Laurel felt the raw power of emotion as people watched
or joined the mass movement of marchers.

The city was alive, bustling with electricity. Colorful streamers,
flamboyant reds and vibrant yellows, flapped feverishly in the wind.
Local residents in Washington Heights and Harlem came to their windows bearing U.S. flags, some securing them from posts, some emerging on the stone steps of their apartment building to wave them as she
passed. More flags emerged—red, white and blue; red, green and black
of Jamaica; green, white and red of Mexico; Cuban flags, flags of the
Dominican Republic, of Venezuela. Here they were, the united nations
of American citizens, part of the throngs of the city, living together in a
maze of nationalities and cultures.

Encouraged by the cheers, Laurel felt a surge of energy. But then some new voices emerged from the crowd.

"You're traitors, all of you."

"Terrorist supporters."

Batons in hand, police moved quickly through the crowd. Several men who had been waving their fists menacingly backed away as the patrolmen advanced. Laurel heard them begin to yell, and before she knew it, several people were scuffling in the street.

Looking frightened, Lonnie grabbed her arm. "Let's move!"

As they hurried down Broadway away from the disturbance, Laurel tried not to look back. *We're so close,* she thought. But experience had taught her that anything could happen, no matter how fervent your hopes.

Joseph McNaughton had been working security at the United Nations for nearly twenty years. Before today, he had never encountered anything that stirred so much confusion among UN officials. He heard there were about two thousand people moving toward First Avenue and Forty-second Street, the home of the United Nations, and was certain that by the time they arrived and others heard of the gathering, it would be at least four times that many.

No sooner did he have that thought, than the lights on the control panel of his desk started blinking like fireflies.

Great, McNaughton thought, *every department head in the whole UN complex will be calling me.*

He braced himself for the deluge.

After finally reaching Times Square and turning down Forty-second Street, Laurel decided theirs would be a symbolic arrival. Once they reached Lexington Avenue, she headed to Forty-third, leading the marchers down United Nations Way, where colorful miniature flags of different nations cascaded off the light poles that lined the block.

Then, as Laurel looked further down the street, the courage she had felt throughout the march suddenly waned. With the United Nations, her destination, now in sight, she felt her body swoon at the thought of descending upon it. *More like ascending to it*, she realized as she reframed her thought.

Her fear seemed to be justified when she saw several UN security guards waiting on the landing above Ralph Bunch Park, right by the steps that led down to the street in front of the UN. Several other gentlemen wearing dark suits, and crisp, dark blue ties were standing with them. Their piercing eyes stared at her and the group as they approached.

Laurel breathed deeply and tried to forget the aching in her feet. She kept her game face on as she propelled herself forward, each step feeling slightly heavier than the last.

"Laurel Seline?" A deep, grainy voice came from the eldest of the men waiting at the stairway landing.

"Yes," Laurel answered.

"Captain McNaughton, Head of Security." The officer introduced himself curtly. "Come this way, madam."

Worried that the security team was sent to stop the marchers from protesting, Laurel readied herself for a confrontation. "I should be allowed to speak. I was told we have permission to gather here for a speech and rally."

"Change of plans." The broad-shouldered security official, apparently a no-nonsense type of individual, didn't blink.

Some of the protestors from the crowd behind her began to yell. Laurel lifted her hand, gesturing them to remain silent. The security team wouldn't be given a reason to make any arrests, not when the group had come this far.

"What's this about?" she asked the captain.

"As I told you, ma'am." McNaughton's eyes grew stern. "I have been instructed to escort you below.

Laurel saw no other recourse but to agree to his directive. With the captain leading them, Laurel and the marchers descended the steps to First Avenue. On the way down, she saw the inscription on the wall beside her, the words of the prophet Isaiah:

They shall beat their swords into
plowshares. And their Spears into
pruning hooks: Nation shall not lift
up sword against nation. Neither
shall they learn war anymore.

With the rest of the marchers following, Laurel entered Ralph Bunch Park. The small garden and sitting area that looked on to First Avenue was buzzing. In fact, to Laurel's surprise, the street was filled with people, all awaiting their arrival. Finally, tearing her gaze from the crowd, she looked across the avenue, taking in the amazing sight for the first time.

Flying from poles along First Avenue in front of the United Nations complex were the flags of the member states, one hundred and nine-ty-two, all positioned in alphabetical order. The first flag belonging to Afghanistan started at Forty-eighth, and the last, the flag of Zimbabwe, ended the row at Forty-second Street.

McNaughton and the other guards parted the crowd and brought her to the edge of the street. There, two barricades had been placed per-pendicular to First Avenue, creating a pathway up the middle that led straight to the UN complex.

Laurel's surprise quickly turned to excitement.

They're letting us in!

Laurel, with Jules and Lonnie by her side, walked between the bar-ricades followed by the hordes of supporters they had picked up during their one-hundred-mile journey. The marchers now included men and women, old and young, students, migrants, day laborers, truck driv-ers and even some *suits* that had skipped out of their office to witness Laurel's arrival.

Astounded, she moved forward. The number of newspaper and television reporters jostling behind the barricades was mind-boggling. Now, it appeared both national and international press were in full swing. Reporters thrust their microphones and vaulted questions at her as she passed.

"Laurel, do you believe in the reconciliation policies presently in effect in the Middle East?"

"After all of their suicide bombings and terrorist acts, do Palestinians *really* have the right to expect help from anyone?

"What about Israel, Laurel? Are we being fair to those people in Jerusalem of Jewish descent who wish to keep their hold on the city of God?"

They were all questions that had the right to be asked, Laurel mused. But still, the important matters, the inquiries that could lead to civilized answers were not being posed. *Why don't they ask questions aimed toward resolutions?*

The answer, Laurel realized, was simple.

No one wanted resolutions, just a story.

Rosa glanced at the signs in the crowd as they walked between the barricades.

No more war . . . A Call to Sanity . . . Give us Peace . . . Living as One . . .

Idealists, thank God! Rosa always found it amusing how that word had gotten so much bad press. Without idealists none of them would be standing there today, able to express their thoughts and opinions. Without idealists the United States of America wouldn't exist!

Honor, love, peace, brotherhood, and yes, ideals. Words of beauty—words of power. The small-minded liked to force their hand and pick up a gun to get their messages across—a lazy man's option. But idealists did not subscribe to that luxury. In fact, the best idealists were often realists. They understood that people needed to create a secure space where they could talk to each other and attempt to understand their differences and concerns. It was a key factor in reaching a fair agreement. Otherwise . . . back to the Stone Age.

There's still room for sanity, Rosa thought, thankful they had reached this moment. Confidently, she walked forward. The flags snapping in the wind seemed like welcoming hands, beckoning them to enter.

CHAPTER 34

IN A MATTER of moments, Laurel and the Seline Marchers who had walked with her from upstate New York and throughout Manhattan were crossing a border—separate from the city itself—into international territory. With its own security force, fire department and even its own postal administration, the United Nations complex was an international zone belonging to all member states.

The gates, normally only opened for the delegates and those working for the UN, had been parted for Laurel and her comrades. The member states representatives who had walked through them earlier that day were now gathered in greeting as Laurel and her troops passed through security posts set up at the entrance for their arrival.

Surrounded by television communication equipment, as well as radio and newspaper reporters, Laurel kept telling herself to settle down and to move gracefully like the dancer she had once been in her youth. *No time for too much thinking. Just stand tall and talk straight.*

She and the other marchers walked onto the complex, stopping in the circular plaza in front of the Secretariat Building. As Laurel reached the fountain area, a hand reached out to help her step up onto the platform. She looked up. Surprised and elated, Laurel recognized the smooth brown skin, the black oval eyes, the graying black hair and elegant stance.

Akanis Arran, the soft-spoken leader from the Republic of Benin knew the world of devastation well. On the continent of Africa, his own country had deployed peacekeeping forces to the Democratic Republic of Congo, a land savagely raped by warring tribes, government overlords and roving bands of terrorists slaughtering women, children and thousands of civilian men. Now, as the United Nations secretary-general,

Arran felt he was finally in a position to hold out his long arm, an extension of peace that he hoped would inspire those who assembled with him.

As he helped Laurel Seline onto the podium and watched the marchers gather before him in the plaza, Arran was pleased to see how quickly the seeds of peace were sprouting. He knew his own power within the UN, as well as how tremendously influential that body's support would be in utilizing the growing movement toward Middle East peace that Seline's walk was spreading throughout the U.S. and the world.

Sometimes the universe bestows upon man moments . . . doorways through which the greater mind of the divine can enter into the affairs of the world.

Steadying his mind, Arran prepared himself. Time and space had created an opening, and doorways, he knew, could be sealed.

"Ladies and gentlemen," he said, addressing the onlookers, his voice resounding over the loudspeakers lining the plaza and First Avenue. "We have all gathered here today for one purpose, to acknowledge a vision, and to acknowledge those messengers who have the forbearance to bring that vision to our doorstep. So I will not delay in introducing the woman who has encouraged its growth. I give you . . . Laurel Seline."

Laurel gave Arran a nod of appreciation. When she turned toward the sea of faces, she realized she had envisioned this moment all along. "I thank the United Nations for welcoming me onto these international grounds and allowing me to speak. As you can see, everyone here with me today has added their steps to this journey. Walking side-by-side, we have been both praised and criticized, but no matter. Our opportunity has come nonetheless. I speak for all of us when I say we want our fellow citizens to be aware we have done it in honor of our country and for the great values for which it stands—liberty and justice for all.

"Today, we come before you as voices for peace, wishing to express our concern about the troubling state of international affairs. It seems we have enough energy to dedicate to wars and suppression rather than toward resolutions? How can that be? How can political leaders, including those of my own country, suppress ideals of peace and unity and replace them with unconscionable lies?"

Laurel took a deep breath, allowing the moment to shape her thoughts.

"One resource we were able to depend upon has now failed us. That is why I make a special plea today to the world media, especially that of my own country, the United States. The role played by television, radio, and the press is so vital and important," she asserted. "Why? Because you affect the events you're reporting. So please understand that *how* you cover an incident is just as important as *what* you cover. Are you acting responsibly, or are you inciting more hatred by what you focus on? Is the heart of your reporting geared toward helping create solutions, or are you part of the problem?" Laurel paused. "Just remember, the rest of us are depending on your integrity and good judgment."

As she spoke, Laurel scanned the bay of reporters. Several began pulling back their microphones while camera lights around them went off. Laurel found herself actually feeling sorry for them. As journalists, they had to be extremely frustrated working for networks that kowtowed to corporate overlords who were all to willing to pull the plug in an instant.

Laurel drew a long breath. There were enough lights and microphones still on, and as long as even one remained, she wouldn't stop. It was time someone spoke bluntly, without mincing words and without fear of repercussions.

"And so . . . here as the voice of my granddaughter, Maggie Seline," Laurel continued, "I call upon women, from *every* nation, to unify and meet with me in Jerusalem as the mothers of the world—protectors, guardians, nourishers. Together, we can foster the birth of the holy city, where the spirit of man is honored and will reach new heights. We declare this land should be owned by no one, but rather should come into its own as an international zone of peace, a global center that by its very presence preserves, honors and supports all genuine religious and spiritual traditions."

As Laurel motioned toward the thousands of onlookers before her, she felt the force of her own words. "This river cannot be held back. It will be carried forward by the current of ideals and the power of faith. We will flow with it into the Holy Land. Let us meet there and pray for an end to inhumanity and for peace to prevail."

Laurel smiled with appreciation as the crowd encouraged her with a rousing ovation. She hoped that the cheers and the overwhelming show of support she was witnessing weren't just part of an old woman's dream, destined to fade.

Just then, Laurel caught sight of Rosa, her red handkerchief in hand, beckoning the crowd.

"Where are we going?" Rosa prompted.

"All the way!" they answered.

"*Where* are we going?" she repeated.

"All the way!"

"*WHERE* are we going?"

"*All the way to Jerusalem!*"

CHAPTER 35

THE *FRATINERI* had trained him well.

Swiftly, slithering through the darkness, the lone figure scaled the high iron fence surrounding the Bodhgaya Stupa and dropped onto the grounds inside. With scores of small stone stupas all around him, the man crouched behind a four-foot high structure and waited.

It had been a while since he had spoken with his contact in Nepal, but the instructions he had been given were clear. The man smiled to himself as he thought of the cleverness of his employer and about the task he was commissioned to perform.

How ironic that the wind should shift in such a place, he thought. *The Way, believed to be so impenetrable, will be surprised by a far greater brotherhood tonight.*

The moon, half full, cast dim shadows along the ground as Kailas moved stealthily through the darkness. Quietly, maneuvering along the fence that surrounded the great Stupa grounds, he peered between the iron rails. Several butterlamps were still flickering around the edges of the great Stupa itself, but all else was still. When he reached the back gate, Kailas retrieved the key Ananda had given him and opened it, careful not to awaken the sleeping guard posted at the end of the path.

Had it not been for the deep quiet of the night, he would not have heard the snapping twigs. Kailas' awareness shifted then to the shrubs and smaller stupas to his left, but he kept his gaze pointing straight ahead. Quickly, he moved toward the side of the great temple and into the shadows.

What the elders had warned him of was coming to pass . . .

The secret place, he thought suddenly, remembering. Kailas felt for the key they had given him.

The hooded man, laying low in the bushes, was about to spring when he saw Kailas suddenly head toward the other side of the Stupa. The man then dashed between the small stone statues and ducked behind the Bodhi tree, knowing he would be able to surprise the young Brahmin when the priest emerged from the other side.

But what should have only taken moments stretched into minutes. Suspicious, the man began to wonder.

Where is the Brahmin?

Finally, the shadow of the young priest emerged from around the corner of the building.

No sooner had Kailas reached the Bodhi tree, than a hooded figure lunged at him in the darkness. Kailas caught sight of the shining surface of a knife a moment before its sharp edge cut across his arm. As he cried out in pain, he felt another slash across his hand. The leather pouch he had been holding fell to the ground.

The assailant's gleaming black eyes widened. Swiftly, he reached down and picked it up, still pointing his knife at Kailas. "Don't move, or I'll kill you."

Kailas stood motionless as the man pulled on the strings of the leather pouch with his teeth. After opening it, the culprit glared up at him, an explosive look in his eyes. He turned the pouch over. Several small pebbles fell to the ground.

"What's this?" he questioned angrily. Suddenly the knife was at Kailas' throat. "Where did you put the parchment?"

There was a moment where both life and death met, and Kailas knew he was there. But his oath was deeply inlaid, like a jewel set in gold. Nothing and no one could cause him to break it.

"Where is it?" his assailant screeched.

Kailas remained silent.

The man's response was iced with cold hatred. "Then you have chosen." Swiftly, he plunged the knife into Kailas' side, then turned and ran through the courtyard and out of sight.

Kailas fell to the ground as the pain seared through him, yet he did not cry out. Writhing, he applied pressure to his wound, but the warm red blood continued to flow.

Before long, his head lightened and an odd sensation overtook him, as if his breath was no longer his own. The flicker of burning butterlamps receded as he lay on his back and looked up into the night sky filled with stars. One in particular attracted him, and he allowed his mind to move freely with it across the heavens.

Is this the one, he wondered, *the Star of the Mother of the World?* He had been told it traveled through the heavens toward the earth, bringing with it a new era . . . an era prepared for by *the Way,* and as foretold, guarded by it as well.

As his awareness expanded even further, one thought in particular filled his mind.

"It is the woman," he murmured.

The light was drawing him now. With his eyes still transfixed upon the brilliant star, Kailas allowed his mind to soar toward it, into infinity.

CHAPTER 36

WHEN MAGGIE AND MICHAEL arrived in Delhi it was already late evening. They connected to a train and traveled throughout the night, finally arriving in Patna at dawn. After waking up a sleeping rickshaw driver at the station, they traveled the rest of the distance in what Michael referred to as an *electric buggy*, little more than a small, motorized cart. Maggie was quite familiar with that style of vehicle and was used to the jittering lurches and spurting coughs that went along with the ride.

The morning light was stirring across the sky, a crimson orange crest rising from the east. All around them, the terrain of rich, sandy soil appeared like a course beach as they rode. Soon the earth turned a warm brown and shoots of milky green grass enriched the landscape. Having barely slept, everything looked surreal to her—as if she had entered a Picasso painting—a world swirling and full of color.

She turned toward Michael, who sat beside her dreamily canvassing the scene. "You'd probably be having the same sort of otherworldly experience even if you weren't exhausted," she assured him.

Michael took a look at his watch and sighed. "I suppose so, but traveling like a bat out of hell certainly hasn't helped," he said grumpily.

Finally, they entered the town of Bodhgaya where the chai shops were already open and local merchants were readying for business. When the rickshaw came to a stop in front of the Stupa, Maggie exited the small cab feeling lightheaded, her footing unsteady. Apparently feeling the same, Michael stumbled out of the vehicle behind her.

As they approached the great Stupa, Maggie gazed at the familiar sight. Colorful prayer flags waved in the wind, and stone monuments protruded from the earth, their formidable presence giving her steps more solidity and substance. Even there at the entrance, men and women were prostrating, praying and chanting.

What they encountered next, though, was something totally unexpected.

The courtyard was filled with police, batons in hand, who had already cordoned off the square around the stupa itself. The majestic grounds of the Buddha's enlightenment felt charged with fear and confusion. The locals were moving quickly, eyes filled with alarm and dismay, looking at one another in an endless chain of disbelief.

Maggie and Michael walked over to the side of the Stupa. Before she could say anything to him, Michael grabbed her hand and stopped dead in his tracks. Unable to see above the crowd, Maggie didn't know what he was witnessing that had him so disturbed. That's when the line of police parted, and she saw the body.

Within several yards of the Bodhi tree a man lay prone, his eyes still open and directed up toward the branches. It was as if he was relaxing on the grass and gazing at the playful light on the leaves. The scene would have been one of rest and repose had it not been for the blood stains on his shirt and the pool of blood by his side.

No sooner had she seen the body, than a bald-headed monk wearing saffron robes walked out from behind the line of police. Maggie barely recognized Ananda when she saw him. Besides age, apparently the strain of a harrowing morning had further lined his face. His sagging, puffy eyelids spoke of little sleep.

"Ananda." She said his name as she stepped up to his side.

He turned toward her looking shocked by the nightmare he was witnessing. The pain in his eyes sent a surge of anxiety through her.

Ananda had been dealing with the police since early that morning. A local guard, after opening the gates, had found the horrifying scene. Before mass hysteria took hold, the guard ran to the Temple Management office to tell the monk of his discovery.

Now, standing in the stupa garden, Ananda could not believe the scene before him. *The young emissary has been struck down.* Of all places, it had happened right in front of the Bodhi tree. *The Way* had failed. It was possible that the dark prophet had obtained the document. Between that serious implication and an actual murder on the Stupa grounds, Ananda, normally so stalwart, found his legs growing weaker.

"We must speak," he said to Maggie, as he eyed Michael suspiciously.

"It's okay," Maggie assured him. "This is Michael Sonada, a friend of mine."

Ananda nodded, his eyes drawing them both closer. He quickly filled them in on the encounter he had with Kailas. "What has this world come to?" The monk's face was lined with pain. "Killing another human being . . . on such sacred grounds."

Unfortunately, Maggie thought sadly, *people have been doing that for millennia.*

"In all the years I have lived in Bodhgaya and worked for the Stupa Committee, I have never encountered anything so terrible." Ananda shook his head and cradled his forehead in his hand.

Although Maggie also felt disturbed, she knew they had to work fast. "Did he tell you anything? Did the priest reveal where the parchment would be hidden?"

Ananda shook his head. "No, it is all very discreet. I do not even know if he managed to hide it at all. Each man is alerted of his role, and we hardly know anything about what the next will do."

"Who was he?" Michael asked.

"I had never even met this young sadhu before," Ananda replied. "His arrival was foretold to me by one of the highest in *the Way*."

Maggie stared at him for a moment. "Professor Samuels?"

"Yes." Ananda gave her a long knowing look. "He told me of the great mission concerning the parchment of the Twin, the disciple Thomas, and instructed me to give the Brahmin priest the key to the Stupa grounds so he could carry out his task. The Professor also told me, Maggie, that you would be coming from America. He said you would know what to do."

"He said *what?*" Maggie couldn't imagine what the Professor meant.

"He said that you would know where to find the document."

Maggie turned and stared at Michael in disbelief. She felt the riddle growing in proportion. *All this way, without a clue as to what to do next.* Her body tightened as she tried to get a grip on the situation. "Okay, one possibility is that the priest was able to hide the document on the grounds as he planned."

Michael looked determined as his eyes moved across the garden and throngs of people.

"He didn't give any indication where?" she pressed the monk.

"No. He would say nothing," Ananda replied. "That is *the Way*."

Maggie watched Michael's gaze turn hazy. A familiar look. She realized he was frustrated by the mystery.

"Why not just give it to us when we arrive?" Michael questioned flatly.

Ananda shrugged. "That was not his instruction. Throughout history it has been like this." The scholar in him surfaced. "Sacred relics have been secretly removed from their hiding place, sometimes under the noses of those who have been their caretakers. It has always been important that only a handful of the Master initiates know the whole story. The rest are to carry out their mission."

At that moment, one of the stern-faced detectives waved at Ananda, indicating he wanted to speak to him. The monk bowed and walked reluctantly toward the police line.

"So now what?" Michael turned toward Maggie, searching her eyes for an answer.

"I've got to think," she said. Maggie probed her mind to uncover any clue Samuels might have left her. "The Professor would never have sent us here without giving us some kind of inkling where to begin," she insisted.

"But there's nothing," Michael groaned. "The only thing he told us was to get to Bodhgaya. He indicated that the wheels were in motion and that someone from *the Way* would *find* us."

"You just don't understand," Maggie said, exasperated. "Professor Samuels often works clandestinely. Sometimes I don't understand his methods, but—"

Maggie placed her hand in her pocket and felt a wad of paper between her fingertips. Now, as she retrieved it and read the contents, a ripple of excitement moved through her. "This could be meaningful," she said. "The Professor motioned for me to take this from his vest pocket after he collapsed. I thought he wanted to write something down but lost consciousness before he had a chance."

"Why didn't you mention it before?" Michael questioned, an irritated expression on his face.

"Before now, I didn't think it had any significance. It was just a crumpled piece of paper, and with us racing out of the country, it totally slipped my mind."

Michael stepped closer to take a look. "Looks like poetry and some sort of dimensions. What on earth could it signify?"

Maggie remained silent as she stared at the note in her hand.

"And what about the Professor's statement, 'The key is in Bodhgaya.' We don't even have a clue what that means either." Michael sounded frustrated and uneasy. "In any case, I still don't get why everything is so mysterious. Why not just tell us what to expect?"

"Because if we're intercepted," Maggie explained, figuring out the Professor's rationale, "it would be impossible to get any concrete information out of us. We simply wouldn't know enough. So the process has been encoded through language and image."

Maggie stared off into space as she began to murmur. "The key is in Bodhgaya . . . the key is in Bodhgaya . . . the key—" As the words sunk deeper, a light suddenly went off. "Oh, of course, of course!"

Michael was staring at her like a crazy woman now.

"*The key is in Bodhgaya!*"

CHAPTER 37

C HIEF OF DETECTIVES, Rajiv Shanawar, was astounded to see the woman Ananda had been speaking with only moments before, now running toward the police lines. The burly, rather overweight officer hurried over and blocked her passage. Still, he was awed by the strength she emanated—her bold stance, the fierceness of her green eyes. She was like a tigress ready to spring into action.

"Miss, you cannot enter," he commanded.

"It's still a holy site, right?" the woman questioned curtly.

Astounded by her audacity, Detective Shanawar took another intimidating step forward. *These foreigners, especially these Western women.* "Madam, we are investigating a murder here," he said in his most condescending tone. "You will remain outside these lines or you will be arrested."

Maggie stood head to head with the detective. In no time, Michael was at her side. She was about to make a brash reply, when Ananda stepped forward, still having enough wits about him to notice the confrontation and come to her aid.

"Excuse me, Ms. Seline," Ananda said, affecting an apology. Turning to the detective, his tone remained formal. "Detective Shanawar, do you know who this is? This is Ms. Seline from America's Asia Society, and this is her husband, Lord Michael of the Royal Academy of England. They are here for the yearly meeting of the Bodhgaya Stupa Committee, part of the Council of Trustees that care for these sacred grounds."

Maggie could barely believe her ears.

The detective, hard-nosed and looking agitated, raised his eyebrows and held his mouth in a sneer. Maggie thought she heard him mumble something that sounded like *religious fanatics.*

"Is that so?" Shanawar shot back caustically. "May I remind the superintendent that any criminal activity that takes place within this confine still falls under the jurisdiction of the Gaya police?"

"Yes, and with all due respect, Detective, I believe both Ms. Seline and Lord Michael's presence here will prove helpful to your investigation since they have witnessed the aftermath of this unfortunate incident and can prepare all proper reports for the Committee and its many very generous supporters. That also includes Director General Sanjay Awadhara."

Maggie could see that the mention of the highest ranking police official in Bihar made the thick-necked detective turn from a forbidding rhinoceros into a swooning pelican.

"Well then," the detective said, still trying to emit a tough demeanor, "if it means facilitating a written representation of the scene to the director general, then you may proceed onto the compound." As the detective stepped back, allowing the threesome to walk past the barrier, he added one last directive. "But none of you are to interfere or by any means disrupt this investigation."

Maggie noted his hostility was meant for her.

"Of course." Ananda bowed as they took their leave.

As they ventured forward past the guards and behind police barricades, Maggie whispered, muffling her excitement, "Ananda, the key."

His eyes questioning, Ananda appeared confused.

"The key to the room upstairs in the Stupa. Please, give it to me."

Ananda reached inside his shoulder bag and pulled out a large silver key. Taped to it was a label initialed with the letters BTM—Bodhgaya Temple Management.

"I can't believe I didn't remember this sooner," Maggie said. She took hold of Michael's arm and directed him through the Stupa's entrance toward a staircase.

"Where are we going?" Michael questioned, looking distraught as they moved upward.

Maggie sensed that Michael Sonada was not fond of surprises. "There's a room, a meditation area, that's been closed to the public for a number of years," she explained. "It was Ananda who first let me use it . . . gave me the key. It turned out to be my own little private hideaway right here in the Stupa. Professor Samuels must have remembered the story. That's what he was referring to when he spoke to us, but I hadn't realized it."

Michael's eyes lit up. "So that's what he meant by his cryptic remark, 'The key is in Bodhgaya.' "

"Exactly," she said, "he was giving me direction, even though I couldn't see it at the time."

Once up the stairs, they walked outside onto the Stupa's upper terrace and stopped in front of a tall, heavy door. Maggie placed the key in the lock and wriggled it around several times until she heard a loud click. Then, thrusting her shoulder against the door, she gave it a hard push and flung it open.

As she entered the room, Maggie reached over to the wall beside her. "The lights are out," she said as she flipped the switch back and forth. "Typical."

Michael could see some light entering from the windows above, enough to enable them to make their way around.

"Watch out," Maggie warned, pointing toward a ladder and some tools that lay by the doorway.

Michael stepped over the material. As he looked up, he could see a large Buddha statue, its eyes peering down at them from the front of the room. Suddenly, feeling like a trespasser, he averted his gaze from the Buddha's, which appeared to be following their every move.

"Now those dimensions are beginning to make more sense," Maggie said as she pulled out the notepaper that bore the Professor's message.

"What makes you conclude they're dimensions?" Michael wondered how she could be so certain.

"What else could they be," she answered brusquely. "Here, take a look again."

Michael took the small piece of yellow notepaper from her hand and stared at the numbers.

$$7 \times 12 \times 8$$

Then, once again, he read the poem the Professor had written beneath.

Within the seven

Twelve tribes return in due course

From high above, the eight rests

Naturally in its source

"Okay," Maggie whispered, "we know that the Professor wanted us to come to this room. So if these numbers are dimensions, they have something to do with this area."

"If we're going to make that assertion, then let's start with the obvious." Michael scanned the room. He walked back to their point of entry. "Starting from the door here, if we pace out seven feet . . . " He measured the distance, placing one foot in front of the other.

Maggie gave him a wide-eyed stare.

"Size-twelve shoes." Michael glanced down at his loafers. "What? I've got big feet, okay?"

Maggie smiled, obviously holding back a laugh.

"Twelve across," he said firmly, not seeing what was so humorous about his shoe size. "Then eight up."

The measurement brought them midair in the center of the room.

"No good," Maggie noted.

Michael walked over to the opposite wall. "Okay, then let's start from here." Once again he paced out the same dimensions. Still nothing.

After another two attempts, Michael slumped down to the thinly carpeted floor. He could feel a wave of cynicism overtake him. *Damn the Professor's Masonic puzzles. Why must everything be a riddle?*

Maggie, looking equally tired and frustrated, joined him.

If this was a puzzle, at least they had some of the pieces. Michael realized then the Professor was counting on his insights as well as Maggie's.

"Hold on." He suddenly saw his error. "We've been looking at this too simply. Knowing Professor Samuels, the dimensions are in cubits not feet—Hebrew medium cubits to be more precise."

"What are you talking about?" Maggie asked.

"It was the Professor who first introduced me to Hebrew and the measuring system. What we normally measure as one foot, converted into the Hebrew medium cubit, would measure 2.0736 feet. To make it easier the Professor would round that to two feet for us. So the actual measurements wouldn't be 7 x 12 x 8."

"It would be double that," Maggie declared, catching on.

"Right. 14 x 24 x 16."

Both Michael and Maggie jumped to their feet. Michael turned to find Maggie looking at him, anticipating what he would say next.

"We need to pace it out again," he said, "starting from the entrance."

When they wound up facing another wall, Michael knocked on it looking for a hidden compartment. Again, their venture turned up empty. "Are you sure we should be in here?" Michael began to wonder if Maggie's initial interpretation had been correct.

"I'm positive. This has got to be the place." She turned slowly, examining the room from different angles. Finally her eyes moved upward, fixating on a point where the ceiling met the front wall.

Once more she returned to the Professor's poem, reading it aloud.

Within the seven

Twelve tribes return in due course

From high above, the eight rests

Naturally in its source

"Holy shit!" Maggie exclaimed.

Michael was surprised and amused by her sudden outburst.

"Oh, excuse me," she said, appearing to remember where she was. Her voice then returned to a reverent whisper. "It's not from below, it's from above." Maggie's eyes now sparked with insight. "The line reads 'from high above,' Michael. 'From high above, the eight rests.' We've been measuring from the floor up. We need to measure from the ceiling down."

Michael's mind grabbed hold of the revelation.

Fourteen feet from the door. Twenty-four feet to the front wall. At this point Michael found himself standing in front of the large Buddha statue. He used his eyes to measure the distance down from the ceiling. *Sixteen feet down.* That brought them to a point right behind the Buddha itself. Michael now looked with amazement into the same eyes that had been following him around the room since they had arrived.

"If I'm right," he proposed, "then there may be some sort of hiding place in that wall, approximately behind the Buddha's neck."

They moved toward the side of the sitting Buddha. There was a narrow space between the back of the Buddha and the wall itself.

Michael grabbed one of the ladders lying on the ground and placed it up against the wall as close to the statue as possible. He climbed up and tapped gently on the wall again and again. "There doesn't seem to be any hollow spots at all. And there's no indication that the wall's been opened up in anyway."

"Let me take a look," Maggie said.

Michael acquiesced. After he was down on the ground, Maggie climbed up the ladder to take a look for herself.

"It's dark. You might not—"

Before he could finish, she pulled a penlight out of her pocket. Michael could see a small beam of light as she flashed it behind the Buddha's head.

"What are you, a jack of all trades?" he asked, impressed by her resourcefulness.

Maggie didn't answer. Instead, she continued to survey the wall. Finally, she reached over with her hand to tap the concrete.

"Ouch," she muttered, pulling her hand back suddenly. Michael could see the small cuts that now lined several of her knuckles. Blood began to trickle down her hand. She didn't stop though, and immediately shone the light behind the Buddha again—no longer on the wall, but directly on the statue itself.

"Michael."

The excited resonance in her voice made him move closer. "What is it?" he asked.

"There seems to be something protruding from behind the Buddha's neck—a metal lip."

Michael craned his neck and watched as Maggie began pulling delicately on a thin piece of steel. Finally, the lip gave way, opening like a small drawer. Maggie shone the light into the compartment. Looking fascinated, her eyes were aglow.

"What? Is there something there?" Michael could barely stand the wait.

Without saying a word, Maggie reached in and appeared to be removing an object. She climbed down the ladder smiling, a thin leather pouch in her hand.

With a rush of excitement, they hurried to one of the windows. Even in the dim light, Michael could see Maggie's eyes widen as she pulled on the strings and opened the pouch. Delicately, she inched inside with her fingers and removed a thin wooden case.

Maggie pried it open. There, protected behind sealed Plexiglas, was a parchment. It appeared to be a rudimentary map—geographical markers, some indistinguishable due to the age of the paper, placed on what looked like mountain ranges.

Below the map were words written in a language Michael recognized. "Aramaic," he announced. "May I?"

Maggie carefully handed him the case. After a few moments of interpreting the meaning in his mind, Michael looked up. "Write this down," he directed.

Maggie quickly retrieved a pen and small notepad from her pocket. She jotted down his words as he spoke.

Moving to the Mother Harvest
The words lay hidden
beyond the cave of the lakes
We bow and make journey
for the warm healing waters
At the beak, behind the misty veil,
the final word is revealed
Within the pure land of the sun

Michael felt an unparalleled excitement. Had they actually found the Thomas parchment the Professor had spoken of? Michael couldn't even begin to understand what the passage meant, or how it would lead them to the three secret sayings. He looked toward Maggie to see if she had a clue. "So," he said, "you're the one with the Christian-Buddhist connection. What does it mean?"

"I haven't the faintest," she responded.

It was not the answer Michael wanted to hear.

"Actually, there's someone I know who might be able to help us figure it out," Maggie said, smiling at his wariness. "And I believe it's time to pay him a visit."

CHAPTER 38

MAGGIE STARED OUT the window onto the dry dusty terrain. It had been nearly two hours since she and Michael had left the Bodhgaya stupa site. Their driver, a friend of Ananda's, had agreed to take them directly over the border and into Nepal, a two-hour excursion. Thankfully, aside from the rocking and jostling provided by the 1950s Checker cab that left their necks feeling like rubber, their ride was going without incident.

Sitting silently, thoughts of the Professor began to fill her mind. Could he have survived? Without his guidance, would they actually be able to continue their journey?

"Thinking about Samuels?"

Maggie returned Michael's sympathetic smile. "Yes. I just hope he's alright." Anxious and concerned, Maggie's fear for the Professor had been gnawing at her since their hasty departure from his home.

As Michael held her gaze, the empathy in his eyes told her that he, too, was hoping for the best. "You never told me how the two of you came to know each other," he said.

"Actually, we met in Jerusalem of all places. Professor Mullenstein of the Tami Steinmetz Center for Peace Research introduced us. Professor Samuels had just traveled from Kerala in Southern India, where he had been doing research on the Grail legend."

"The Grail legend . . . in India. That still seems a little out of sorts."

"Tell me about it," she replied with a knowing side-long glance. "He had explained at the time that he was in Jerusalem to do further research on the Grail but did not give me any specifics as to what that entailed." Maggie shook her head with the same frustration she had felt back then. "To say he was cryptic about it would be putting it mildly. The Professor has his secret side."

Michael returned her gaze, displaying his familiarity with the Samuels mystique.

"In any case, I was fascinated by what he was doing," she continued, "and the feeling was mutual. He seemed to think his research resonated with the work I was involved with at the time—focusing on the process of reconciliation among the city's religious communities."

Maggie envisioned Napesh Samuels in her mind, such a spiritual light and strength coming from him. He had taken a special interest in her from the start, especially after she told him of her own adventures in India. Maggie had to admit she liked his fatherly concern. *Mein daughter*, he would call her from time to time in a show of warm affection. As their relationship grew, he began relating to her his understanding of the Grail . . . that he believed it to be the path of enlightenment—the opening of the chakras and the movement of spiritual energy through channels to a higher source. Professor Samuels had definitely struck a chord. The mystical, spiritual thread that linked them compelled her to call on him several times even recently. Each time, he welcomed her knowingly, seeming aware of the reasons why she sought his counsel.

By this point, all Michael could think of were the questions he wanted to ask. He had read news accounts making accusations against Maggie, as well as heard them within Mabus' circle. The most damaging was her link to Hamas.

"What do you want to know?" Maggie asked.

Startled, he looked at her.

"You've got a question mark stamped on your face," she laughed.

"Well, I was wondering about—"

"Before we start, I want you to agree that I'm innocent until proven guilty, got that?"

"Got it." Michael caught a serious thread in her lighthearted tone.

"So," she said, "what's on your mind?"

Michael took a deep breath. "Well, the lowdown on you mentions that you were once involved in a protest that broke out into violence which was linked to PLO radicals, that you are connected to Ahmin Khalidi, a renowned Hamas agent, and that you had dealings with him as recently as a several weeks ago."

Maggie shook her head and smiled. "Who's putting together this information? I'm guessing it's someone who may not like me much."

"Well, it's—"

"You know," she interrupted, raising her hand, "don't even tell me. I think I can guess. Your sources have managed to weave an interesting cover story. Yes, I was in a demonstration that broke out into violence, and the PLO was behind that violence. I was seventeen, attending a rally in New York against the West Bank occupation. What was a peaceful protest that voiced our concerns was infiltrated by a few students with PLO connections. The rest of us had no idea what they were up to. The situation turned volatile quickly, and suddenly out of nowhere people were swinging clubs. My friends and I tried to run, but the police swarmed the scene in no time. We were all taken to jail. We explained our part, the police believed us, and it was over. But *not over*, you know what I mean? Not over for the kids beaten up, not over for the guys who did the beating. I tell you it's a sight I'll never forget."

"There's no mention in the file of your being exonerated."

"An insignificant detail, I suppose," she said with a wry smile. "Of course, in reality that doesn't matter as much as we might think. By bringing up the whole incident, doubt is fostered, and that's the point."

"Look, I . . . " Michael hesitated. He was starting to get uncomfortable with his own questions, but he continued to press. "I just want to get at the truth here. What about the tie to Ahmin Khalidi."

"Okay, there is a connection. We've been friends for a while. We met in Israel when I was visiting my father one summer. At the time, he was a young student. Brilliant. Someone who could have done a lot for his people."

Not the remark he expected. Michael responded to her candor with silence.

"But that only addresses part of your question," Maggie added. "You should get your information from a more reliable source. Ahmin is an activist, *not* a terrorist. He's never even associated with Hamas, or the PLA for that matter. He and his family have had to live through a lifetime of abuse—his town decimated, his home razed. Because he speaks out against the injustices faced by the Muslim community in Israel, it doesn't make him a terrorist."

"But why the current link?" Michael probed.

"I was writing my book, and I needed information from an insider—someone who was living it out—to give me the Palestinian view. I didn't want to use dry facts or polarized rhetoric. Instead, I wanted direct feedback from both sides about the conflict being waged. When I asked if he would let me interview him for the book, he agreed."

"Why's that?"

"Perhaps he trusted me." The sunlight streaming through the cab's window accentuated the sadness on Maggie's face.

Michael wanted to believe her, but there was something more that was bothering him. "But you're still talking to this Ahmin, aren't you? Reports say you spoke with him several weeks ago."

Her eyes avoided his. "Not at liberty to divulge that."

Michael shook his head, uneasy with her reply.

"Look, Michael, I'm not putting people's lives in jeopardy in order to defend myself from accusations being made now," Maggie said as she lowered her head, "or your doubts."

CHAPTER 39

A S THEY ENTERED Kathmandu, Maggie found herself breathing a sigh of relief. She looked over at Michael who had gone silent for the last half hour. Despite his apprehension, he appeared mesmerized by his first journey into Nepal.

She understood the feeling. As the cab weaved through the busy streets, women wearing multicolored saris and adorned with golden earrings watched them curiously as they drove by. Men, some walking hand in hand, strolled down the street while others, smoking thin *bidis* stood around candy and cigarette stands where music blasted from amplifiers that looked like trombones. Honking cars and the rickshaws maneuvering between them all deferred to the cows, whose sacred countenance gave them superior rights to the road. Amidst it all, holy temples stood next to fruit stands allowing pilgrims devoted to Shiva, Krishna, Saraswati and other Hindu gods to pay their homage and do their shopping in one shot.

Nepal, Maggie thought, *the land of ancient mysteries and modern distractions.*

"Who's this friend of yours we're staying with?" Michael asked, interrupting her reverie.

"Lama Jampal. He's an old Tibetan man who runs a clinic on the outskirts of Bodhnath. I spent some time helping him out."

"How did you wind up there?"

"After college I took six months off and went traveling throughout India and Nepal, visiting lots of monasteries and temples. During my wanderings, I met plenty of spiritual teachers . . . some turning out to be not so spiritual. Eventually, I wound up in Bodhnath where I found Jampal. The old lama was eating an ice on the stupa steps." She smiled. "I like him right away. So I spent some time with him and got some meditation instruction. It was a time of spiritual opening really."

With a mischievous gleam in his eye, Michael looked like he couldn't hold back his comment. "So, Lois Lane went Hindu mystic."

"Very funny," she retorted.

"Look, I'm sorry. I've never been much for personal journeys, I suppose. Not much of an adventurer. Who knows, maybe after this escapade with you . . . "

Veiled within Michael's amusement, Maggie caught a hint of sincerity.

At that moment, she saw the turn she was anticipating and directed the driver onto a quiet country road. High trees swayed in the breeze as they drove between wide fields where men and women walked alongside muddy streams, carrying bundles of bamboo on their heads. Just as they rounded a bend, a team of oxen pulling a wooden cart obstructed their passage. Their car now moving slowly, Maggie could hear music. A woman was sitting on a boulder on the side of the road playing a vina— a string instrument with a long bamboo neck and a large gourd at both ends. As she sang, the woman's high-pitched tones made Maggie's body vibrate.

"Calling to the gods," she remarked, turning toward Michael.

He eyed her. "What gods?"

Maggie could count on her companion's display of doubt. "I don't know. A personal God, the beauties of the natural world, the spirits within the elements." She smiled, amused. "Do you have *any* spiritual beliefs?"

"I'm a Democrat."

They both laughed. Maggie guessed that ultimate truths were not Michael's forte. He studied mankind alright—by analyzing data and working behind the scenes. But what kind of feeling did he have for it all?

After they turned back onto the main road, they were again immersed in a sea of shops and people. Maggie leaned up toward the driver and told him in broken Nepali to pull over.

"We stop here," she informed Michael.

"Where are we?" he questioned, stepping out of the cab after her.

"Bodhnath, at the stupa."

"You're kidding? Another stupa?"

Maggie didn't want to hear it. "Don't worry we're not going in, just around it. Jampal's clinic is on the other side."

They walked alongside the stupa, the two blue eyes painted on its surface peering down at them. As Maggie pulled Michael along the path, groups of people spun prayer wheels and whispered chants while others talked and laughed. It wasn't long before Michael's face took on an unusually peaceful quality. His eyebrows, normally furrowed in some kind of analytic thought, relaxed for the first time since they had left New York. It was apparent that he, too, was struck by the faces and the scene before him.

Nepal's magic is working on him, Maggie realized. All around, people were displaying a simple faith. Life might be hard, but faith wasn't.

When she turned toward him, she found Michael smiling at her curiously. He appeared to be enjoying this side of her, the wanderer, the seeker.

"Should I be bowing?" he asked.

She chuckled. "Who knows? It might be good for you. For the time being, just be grateful I know my way around India and Nepal. Whenever I'm back, I feel like I've come home."

Michael smiled. His cynicism appeared to have waned considerably since they had arrived.

"When I'm tired and worn down," Maggie said, "I think of the sacred places of India and Nepal, and I find some peace. It's something beyond religion . . . you know, a pure spirituality."

As he gazed at her, the look of ease on Michael's face turned to concern. "Do you think it's worth trying to convince some hard-line nationalists that *pure spirituality* is what they need, that Jerusalem could be the starting point?"

"I don't know," she answered honestly, "but I'd certainly like to try."

Maggie realized how idealistic and naïve she sounded, but now, standing in a land where miracles were still possible, she didn't give a damn.

CHAPTER 40

THE HOT DUSTY AIR made it hard for Michael to breathe as he stood beneath the large Kathmandu Clinic sign. He took a swig of bottled water, hoping to alleviate the dry bitter taste in his mouth. Suddenly, the front door of the clinic swung open. Maggie walked toward him, shaking her head as she approached.

"Lama Jampal isn't here. There's some kind of special ceremony at his monastery."

"So, what next?" Michael asked.

"We get back in the cab."

Maggie spoke to him as if he were a child. That controlling tone in her voice would creep in from time to time, and Michael was getting irritated with it.

"This is the last area Rachel was seen," he informed her, "and there's no way I'm leaving here without having a look around first."

"Okay," Maggie said, acquiescing, "if you're going to insist on this, let me at least check out the government office. It's just across the street there."

Michael looked toward the gray, fortress-like stone building. He sensed a fruitless inquiry was at hand.

"I'll ask some questions and see what I can find out. Just wait here," she directed.

"This must be your *master complex* taking over." Michael's remark appeared to have caught Maggie off guard. "Don't worry," he added before she could reply. "I'll be here when you return."

As Maggie crossed the busy thoroughfare, Michael saw his opportunity.

Thirty minutes. Before she knows it, I'll be back.

He turned abruptly and walked toward the Gopal Hotel. Anticipating Maggie's reaction, Michael had decided not to tell her about the meeting he had arranged with Dr. Rajif Kumari when he found out they were heading into Nepal. Kumari was a Nepalese archaeologist, one of Rachel's colleagues who had worked with her in Bodhgaya. He would know more than anyone what Rachel had been up to.

Kumari had given Michael the hotel's location during their hurried phone conversation—the bottom of Gopal Hill, only a five-minute walk from the center of Bodhnath.

Michael took the winding dusty path that led past several make-shift temples and candy and chai shops. No sooner had he rounded a curve in the road when he saw a large, yellow crescent moon sign hanging from a tall iron gate.

Gopal Hotel

The sound of a car engine and tires rolling over the gravel path caused Michael to turn abruptly. A lime-green coupe slowed down and stopped beside him.

"Michael!"

Through the car's open window, Michael could see a man stretched across the front seat. He wore an old Yankee cap, a white NY insignia printed on the front. Short tufts of wavy black hair curled up from beneath.

"Dr. Kumari?" Michael was surprised. *Is this guy psychic?* The man had arranged to meet him at the hotel this morning, but to pull up in a car at that very moment . . .

"Yes," he answered, removing his cap. "Glad you found this place. Hop in. We can talk while we ride."

With dark mocha hair and a creamy brown complexion, Kumari looked younger than Michael expected—mid-thirties perhaps. Except for the scar on his cheek giving him a bit of a rough edge, he had an air of privilege. Private schools . . . cricket leagues . . . expensive women.

"Thanks for meeting me," Michael said as Kumari pulled away from the hotel. "I don't have much time, and I thought you might have some idea what's going on. Someone has harmed Professor Samuels . . . someone who also seems to know a lot about Rachel's last dig in India. She supposedly found some sort of document . . . "

Kumari looked stunned. "Yes, she told me about it when we last saw each other, but she took it with her into Nepal. I never saw her again. I'm not sure how much help I can be."

Michael tried not to give in to his feeling of dismay. "Since you were her colleague, I was hoping you could tell me more about the circumstances of her disappearance."

"I wasn't on that leg of the expedition, so I don't know anything about the boat accident."

Michael needed a moment to let the words sink in. *Boat accident . . .* "What are you talking about?" he asked, shaken.

"They didn't tell you?" Kumari gave him a look of disbelief. "Rachel . . . well there is some speculation that her craft went under on the Kali Gandaki River. No one knows for certain, Michael. That's the last place she was seen."

Michael couldn't believe it was true. He searched his heart, and knew it couldn't be so. Rachel had to be alive. "I'll find her." His voice rang with determination. "Whatever her discovery, it was important enough for her to venture into Nepal and to drop enough bread crumbs for me to find out what she was up to. Professor Samuels believes this as well."

"What did he say?" Kumari asked.

"That Rachel was drawing near to finding an object of profound importance and that it was linked to the disappearance of the Spear of Longinus. He said it was imperative that I make this journey, that the destiny of the unfolding of future events were all tied into it somehow."

"He was always a bit dramatic," Kumari said as he pulled a cigarette out from his shirt pocket. He lit it and took a puff. "Are you sure you want to go forward with this?"

"What do you mean by that?" Michael didn't like Kumari's condescending tone.

"Well, we really don't know *what* happened to Rachel. And she was an experienced archaeologist."

Michael felt an angry heat rise to his face. "So you think I can't handle it?" Although Kumari was actually echoing Michael's thoughts, it didn't make it any easier.

"If there are dangerous forces at play . . . " Kumari tapered off. His tone then turned conciliatory. "I hate to say this, but Rachel may be dead, and now Professor Samuels has been poisoned. There is still time to back off."

Michael took a moment, trying to remember. *Did I mention poison?*

The roar of an engine made him look up suddenly. In the side view mirror, he saw a car making a fast approach until it was almost right on their bumper.

"Police?" Michael turned around in his seat to take a better look.

"No, not police," Kumari said, squinting at his rear view mirror.

Kumari slowed down and waved the car on. It pulled out to the side and sped past them.

"Hard to imagine," Michael smirked. "Reckless driving on Nepali roads."

"More reckless than you can imagine," Kumari replied.

As they continued driving down the road, Michael viewed the surrounding landscape like a dream—a grand illusion filled with road-side shrines and Hindu holy men, faces lined with colored vermillion, on the way to *pujas* at the ancient streams and rivers. It seemed like only a moment ago he was on a 747, and the next, staring at men who could have stepped out of the tenth century.

"Where are we going?" Michael asked, suddenly realizing they were near the outskirts of town. "I need to get back."

"I'm sorry. I forgot to mention," Kumari apologized. "After you called I contacted the Archaeological Commissioner. He is connected to the Nepalese Ambassador who has also showed great interest in Rachel's expedition."

"Has he?" Michael's sensors were up. *Why would that be?*

"The commissioner will be able to tell you a great deal more about Rachel's last whereabouts than I can," Kumari said. He took a final puff of his cigarette before flicking it out the window. "Actually, both the Indian and Nepalese embassies are quite interested in hers as well as other recent expeditions into Nepal and Tibet. Other groups too, like the Chinese and certain European teams, have already begun treks into the Himalayan regions in search of lands that were previously considered . . . undetectable."

Michael immediately thought of Mabus.

"What would the president of the European Commission have to do with all of this?" Michael asked.

"What do you mean?" Kumari's face tightened.

"Giovanni Mabus." Michael spoke the name firmly. "What's his connection? The man who came to Professor Samuels' home mentioned Mabus and his interest in Rachel's work."

Kumari's vibrant face seemed to flatten.

Michael probed, sensing Kumari was assessing what to say. "I mean how is he tied into Indian and Nepalese politics?"

Kumari took a moment before answering. "Mr. Mabus and those who work for him have managed to create a network with an international range that is phenomenal to say the least. With corporate liaisons throughout the world, his influence carries great weight politically and economically. India and Nepal are no exception. He has managed to gain the trust of a number of political leaders, and not only by baiting them with the usual fare—money—but by acting as a liaison, infiltrating as a peace broker if you will."

"Infiltrating—interesting word."

"Yes, Michael. What other way? By invitation?" Kumari said sarcastically. "Mr. Mabus has done a lot of good for the economic community at large, but it seems he has not forgotten his own people. He knows it's through becoming more powerful that the Middle Eastern countries will have a strong position in any world government or alliance. His convening of the upcoming United Nations Peace Conference in Jerusalem is a stroke of genius. It will give him and those close to him inconceivable power."

Exactly right, Michael realized, *inconceivable power.* Professor Samuels had said anyone who had tremendous power would need great strength to be able to resist the inherent temptations. Would Mabus be able to do that?

Kumari suddenly turned the car down a side rode. To Michael's relief, he slowed down as they reached a lone house set back from the street. Kumari then turned into a dirt drive and pulled up alongside another car that was already parked under a grove of trees.

They walked up the stone path, all the while Michael praying he would learn something significant about Rachel's disappearance and wasn't just headed for a fruitless double talk session.

Once inside the house, Kumari directed him to an overstuffed gray couch strewn with papers. "Please sit," he said. "I'll let my friends know we've arrived."

Michael cleared some of the clutter, placing the papers on a table next to several half-filled coffee cups. As he sat waiting, he noticed that other than the essentials—an HD-TV, a DVD player, several iPods and a few extra chairs, the room was barren. *What else would a man need?*

The sound of voices coming from the next room made Michael turn.

Kumari reappeared followed by two dark men, both in suits, who walked into the room like delegates entering a symposium. The first man—definitely not an emissary of friendship—remained expression-less as he approached. The second, wearing a brown vest, smiled as he walked toward him with a small folder.

Michael's nerves began to tingle and a feeling of panic overtook him. He stood up. The man he had seen running from the Professor's home addressed him casually.

CHAPTER 41

"HELLO, HELLO, my friend. So we finally meet face-to-face. Let me introduce myself. Raciam Heloff. And of course we already know who you are."

Before Michael could react, the well-dressed goon that had walked in with Heloff knocked him to the ground. As he pinned Michael down with his knees, Heloff walked over and stood above them.

"Now, now Dr. Sonada, no resistance," Heloff said. "No resistance and all of this will go as smooth as silk."

Michael winced as his wrists were bound together tightly behind his back.

Heloff then nodded to his assistant. "Khan, please show our guest to his seat."

Khan grabbed Michael by the shoulders and roughly brought him back to his feet. No sooner did Michael find himself standing, when he received a shove that sent him reeling backward onto the couch.

Kumari lit a cigarette and sat in the chair opposite him. "Mr. Heloff has been wishing to meet with you, Michael."

Heloff, a thin cool smile on his lips, took a seat beside Michael on the couch. His narrow eyes and long arched nose gave him a shrewd, hawk-like appearance. "We are aware of your work with regard to the upcoming Peace Conference," he said, his tone patronizing. "Of course, we are also most grateful that you have been able to assist your American journalist friend as well."

Heloff waited silently, but Michael chose not to respond.

"We also understand that you have a great interest in a text recently discovered in Bodhgaya. A document describing a hidden land. Supposedly, there is a secret place somewhere in the Himalayas where great treasures have been concealed." Heloff paused. "Do you believe that, Dr. Sonada?"

"It's possible, I suppose." Michael replied curtly.

Heloff smiled. "That text describes a stone, a jewel of some kind. Ever since its discovery by your lady friend, the archaeological community has been chomping at the bit trying to pin down its whereabouts."

Michael's body tensed at the reference to Rachel. "What exactly do you want with me?" he asked.

"Since you are not to be deterred," Heloff said, his eyes narrowing, "we have decided to share this expedition with you. Surely you are in need of assistance for your search. It would be difficult for you to find alone, and our team is also determined to see this endeavor succeed."

"Look, I think you're talking to the wrong man. Ask Kumari here. I'm not a field researcher, never was."

The three men stared at Michael intently. Bound and surrounded, Michael felt the possibilities for escape looked nil, yet his fear prodded him to come up with something and fast.

"We are not going to harm you," Heloff said calmly, "nor did we harm Rachel, even though she was in illegal possession of a document that belongs to the Indian government."

"You have no proof of that," Michael shot back angrily as he looked toward Kumari who avoided his gaze. "Even if she had the document, it was her right to fully research her find before reporting it."

"True enough," Heloff replied, "but she left the country with it."

"Did she? How do you know that your Dr. Kumari isn't in possession of it?" *What was Kumari seeking to gain by cooperating with these men and revealing information about Rachel's findings?* "And you know very well that I don't have it. I wouldn't have contacted Kumari if I did."

Heloff sighed impatiently, ignoring Michael's accusation. "What we actually want is to find this hidden land, this Shambhala, and the stone."

"Rachel and I were friends as well as colleagues," Kumari interjected. "I had nothing to do with her disappearance—none of us did. She undoubtedly died in that river accident. That's all we know. It is unfortunate to have lost such a valued archaeologist, but we go on."

"What do you mean *we*?" Michael asked.

"Can't you see, Michael?" Kumari said, coaxing him. "What's important now is that we find this jewel. It would be Rachel's wish as well. Frankly, without us you'll never make it, and we are willing to admit that without you, we may not find the stone."

Bullshit, Michael thought. "That's ridiculous, why should you need my help?"

Kumari put out his cigarette and shot a quick glance at Heloff before continuing. "It's a another twist in the story, I suppose. Just last evening, I was contacted by Mr. Mabus. He feels quite strongly that you must be a part of our expedition." He paused, eying Michael. "He says your name is on the stone."

Michael stared blankly at the men. *What could that mean?*

"Perhaps you didn't know Mabus was funding us?" Kumari smiled, showing pleasure at Michael's surprise. "It was through his organization that Rachel and I received the monies for the dig in Bodhgaya."

Foggy thoughts began to crystallize as the meaning of Kumari's words dawned on Michael. *The discovery of the ancient text in India. The expedition into Nepal to locate the mythical Shambhala.* The funding had all come from one man. Mabus.

"So we venture together, Dr. Sonada," Heloff said. "You know that there is little time left before Mr. Mabus goes forth with his plans for the Third Temple Peace Project."

Michael remembered what Professor Samuels had said. Anyone who was able to bring the Spear and the Grail together would have inconceivable power. *Is that Mabus' goal?* Michael was frightened by the thought.

Suddenly, he felt connected to another kind of force . . . the ambitious thrust of treasure seekers . . . Mabus and Propaganda Due, all dreaming along historical lines, working tirelessly to unearth talismans of power.

"Do you even understand the issues at stake here?" Michael heard his voice shake as he searched Heloff's eyes for a sense of reason.

"I know what I'm here for, and that's *Lapsis Excellis*, the precious stone."

Michael caught his breath at Heloff's reference to the Grail.

Heloff was staring at him condescendingly now, as if he were speaking to an impetuous child. "Your Peace Conference—Israeli Jews and Palestinians reconciled—the pipedream of a woman who has never grown up, are all well and good, but not my concern. I work for Mabus in order to obtain the jewel of all prizes."

Michael couldn't believe what he was seeing or hearing—Heloff, in his Armani jacket, appearing as civil, privileged and debonair as Mabus himself, speaking like a brainwashed disciple.

"Just think," Heloff's eyes bore into his. "This will be one of the greatest finds known to man, and we have the opportunity now to attain it. Without Mabus, there would be no chance in hell of that happening."

At that moment, Heloff's cell phone started ringing. He nodded at Khan who had been standing guard at the door. The two men left the room without a word.

Kumari turned toward Michael then, his voice barely a whisper. "Come on, Michael, give it up. We can find this thing together," he said with a feigned sense of camaraderie. "With the help of Mabus' people, nothing can get in our way."

"You seem so sure of yourself." Michael's fear began to fuel his anger. As he spoke, he maneuvered his hands slowly, trying to work them free. At this point, his wrists were burning from scraping them against the rope.

"The gods are on our side." Kumari's delusions of grandeur inflated as he spoke. "I may have been educated in the U.S., but I'm a Hindi man at heart. The time is ripe to find the Grail, and you and I, Michael," he said, grinning, "are players on the field. We've been chosen to discover it."

"Cut the mumbo-jumbo talk," Michael blurted, tired of Kumari's audacity.

"You don't believe in a power beyond yourself?" Kumari questioned. "It looks as if you don't believe in anything much at all."

"My beliefs aren't the issue here," Michael shot back. "I know that the Grail, whatever it is, cannot fall into Mabus' hands."

"And who's to say it will?" Kumari said, leaning toward him.

Michael was surprised by the confiding tone in his voice.

"I told you the only issue for me is the Grail," Kumari whispered. "If I free you, will you work with me? Together we . . . "

Kumari fell silent as Heloff and Khan entered the room. Michael grew more fearful as he watched Heloff walk toward him. His captor was staring at him with a penetrating gaze, his eyes set like hard black stones.

"Get up now," Heloff commanded. "We're leaving. There's no time to lose. Looks like your lady friend has gone ahead without you, Dr. Sonada."

Michael found that hard to believe.

"Our men went to pay Ms. Seline a little visit and found she had left the clinic for some unknown destination," Heloff sneered. "You thought she would wait for you, Dr. Sonada. It seems your friend, Maggie, has some ideas of her own."

"We don't need that woman," Kumari said. "I tell you we can find the Grail. Between Sonada and myself we can find this place."

Heloff's voice hissed with hostility. "Mabus thinks otherwise. Let me remind you who's in charge here." He then nodded a silent command at his henchman.

Khan's movements were quick as he pulled a gun from his lapel and pointed it at Kumari.

Heloff smiled maliciously. "Let's just say, ours is not a democracy. It is more of a dictatorship. You're here to assist us Kumari, nothing more."

"I was promised—"

"All prior agreements are null and void."

Before Kumari could react, Khan was upon him about to make the same cattle-wrestling move he had made on Michael. But Kumari was quicker than Michael would have expected. As Khan tried to get a hold of him, Kumari swung his clasped hands, hitting Khan across the side of the face and throwing him off balance.

The sound of a gun blast as Khan fell to the ground brought Michael to his feet. At that moment, having managed to free his hands from the loosened rope, he leapt across the coffee table and knocked Heloff down onto the couch. With Heloff pinned beneath him, Michael caught sight of Kumari as he swung his foot up and smashed Khan against the shoulder in a karate-like move that caused Khan's gun to go flying out of his hand.

Just then, the front door swung open.

A shot rang out.

Michael looked up along with the other men who, from their various unsettled positions, took in the peculiar sight. It was Maggie, standing framed against the doorway, Khan's .357 magnum in her hand pointed up to the sky.

She lowered it slowly and aimed it directly at Heloff. "Move and I'll blow your brains out."

Like Ma Barker ready to shoot 'em up, Maggie stood as poised as any gun slinger. Michael couldn't figure out who was more shocked—him or the rest of the party. Kumari, still unaware that his mouth was hanging open, got up off of Khan who could do nothing more than stare in disbelief. Heloff, immobilized by the sight of her, stood transfixed as if a holy apparition had just appeared.

"You three," Maggie ordered, "stand with your hands behind your heads. Michael, check these guys for any more weapons."

As Michael was frisking Heloff, he found a small Beretta pistol wedged beneath his belt. He removed it and pointed it at the men. Although it wasn't the first time he held a gun in his hands, he found himself trembling.

Kumari, in a bold move, walked toward him.

"Stop!" Michael yelled. "Don't come any closer."

"I—"

"Just shut up!"

Although Kumari had been in the same danger as he only moments before, there was no real reason for Michael to trust him now.

"Give me that, Michael, and tie them all up," Maggie commanded, holding out her hand.

Michael handed her the gun. After binding the men's hands and feet and making sure the ropes were secure, he took back the pistol. Now it was his turn to play High Plains Drifter.

"You," Michael said as he pointed the gun at Kumari who was struggling to get to his feet. "Stay down."

"Look," Kumari pleaded, trying to convince the two of them, "I'm in as much trouble as you are right now. These guys aren't exactly friends of mine."

"Just think," Michael said, "if you're able to get free before they do, you'll at least leave here alive."

"Don't count on that," Heloff commented.

Kumari's mouth fell open at the remark.

Maggie gave Michael a silent nod and started backing out the front door. Meanwhile, Michael, keeping an eye on the three men, confiscated their car keys before making a hasty exit.

Once outside, Michael stared for a moment in disbelief. A dirty yellow cab was blocking the driveway.

"Don't just stand there," Maggie said, already in the front seat. "Hurry up and get in." She slammed the door on the driver's side as Michel hopped into the passenger seat. Maggie then quickly revved up the car and sped down the rough driveway onto the road.

Michael gripped the inside door handle as they pummeled down the street. "What the hell did you do, steal a cab?" he yelled.

"No, I didn't *steal* a cab," she admonished. Michael guessed Maggie's adrenaline was pumping as she floored the gas pedal. "I'm barely inside the government building for a minute. The guy I needed to see was unavailable. I come out and you're gone. I start heading up the street, and I see you just as you hop into a car." She turned her head briskly toward him. "Are you nuts?"

Before he could answer, she was back in a tirade.

"I saw a cab running, key in the ignition, and no driver. I jumped in."

"You *have* stolen a cab," Michael said matter-of-factly.

"No, I did not. When the driver ran over to me, I gave him four hundred rupees and told him to pick up the cab at the northeast edge of town. I admit the guy was upset, but what was I supposed to do? If I hadn't acted immediately and followed you, in a matter of seconds you and the car you got into would have been out of sight. There's no way I would have found you."

Michael took in Maggie's unusually disheveled appearance. "You look like a wild woman."

Maggie was now incredulous. "After I saved your skin, is that all you have to say to me?"

"Thanks. I mean, thank you."

"It's about time," Maggie huffed.

The cab careened down the narrow road, the woods growing darker around them. All the while Michael gripped the door handle hoping they wouldn't crash. Suddenly, at the sight of a small roadside stupa, Maggie jammed down on the brakes.

"This is it," she blurted, flinging open the car door.

Michael stared into the thick woods. "Where the hell—?"

But before he could finish, she jumped out.

CHAPTER 42

CRASHING THROUGH the massive rhododendron bushes, Maggie and Michael ran as fast as they could, trying to avoid any soft soil that would reveal their direction. As they ascended up the rough incline, Maggie scanned the overhang above hoping she hadn't taken the wrong path. She breathed a sigh of relief when the glistening gold roof of Lama Jampal's monastery came into view. At that moment, Maggie realized Samuels knew all along she would seek Jampal's help. No one would know the mountainous terrain and gorges of Nepal better than the rugged lama.

Soaking wet, they moved deeper and deeper into the dark, waxy maze. Michael stopped abruptly, looking like his lungs were ready to burst.

"Michael," Maggie whispered urgently, pulling him by his jacket into the brush. "There's no time to waste. We have to keep moving. Those men know too much already. Soon they'll begin to sense our direction."

"How in the world would they sense that?"

"Hunters know."

Moving quickly ahead, they reached a stream, where Maggie signaled for Michael to follow. With rocks shifting beneath their feet, they both tripped more than once before finally reaching the other side.

"Just a little further," Maggie urged, her breath labored. Her side was beginning to ache from all the running. She glanced toward Michael. The frustrated look on his face gave way to despair, but he didn't speak.

The land continued to slope upward. Jutting rocks and loose gravel made it a treacherous climb. Maggie and Michael forged through the harsh brush, scratching their skin against the bristling vines, all the while trying to keep their balance.

Over the ridge, the land leveled out once again, and a remote settlement, previously hidden, came into view. Prayer flags, tied to trees and across roof tops, flapped feverishly as the rushing wind cascaded down from the surrounding plateaus. Directly across the grounds in front of them, several old Tibetan men wearing mitts on their hands prostrated themselves on the hard dry earth, rising and falling like caterpillars.

Maggie's breath deepened when she saw the monastery sitting atop the ridge at the center of the plateau. Silhouetted by high mountain ranges, its golden roof shone brilliantly against the azure sky, and its pale sandstone colored walls rose fluidly from the rocky ground. Maggie sensed the power of the elements permeating it—a wide airy spaciousness and a rough earthy solidity—the ingredients of spiritual potency. Like a beautiful ancient castle, the monastery housed within it the knights of the order—a host of Tibetan monks who guarded the old texts and practices.

Some young initiates were sitting in front of a large white Buddha statue as Maggie and Michael approached.

"*Avalokiteshvara*," Maggie said, indicating the statue. "Otherwise known as Chenrezig, the *bodhisattva* of compassion."

Michael peered at her, a questioning look on his face.

"A *bodhisattva*," she explained, "is a selfless guide. An awakened being."

"Awakened to what?" Michael asked.

As she answered, Maggie's eyes were drawn to the beautiful glistening gem sitting in Chenrezig's palms. "To the fact that helping others is the main goal."

The sound of laughter made Maggie turn as a group of young monks ran up to her.

"*Maggiela*." The boys repeated her name several times, smiling in recognition.

"*Tashi Delek*," she greeted them in return. "Is Lama Jampal here?"

"Yes, he's in his room," one of the young monks answered in English. "Come."

Maggie then noticed the costumes they were holding, especially the masks—ferocious black faces trimmed in red, gold and blue.

Maggie and Michael followed several of the monks up the stone steps and into the monastery. As they walked through the dark halls, the smell of burning butterlamps and incense permeated the air. All the while, images of the mythical and historical figures of Buddhist lore—friendly and compassionate, sublime and all seeing, powerful and dreadful—stared at them from the stone walls.

They stopped in front of a narrow doorway where the youngest of the monks pulled aside a heavy, blue and white curtain, motioning for Maggie and Michael to enter. As she did, Maggie saw Lama Jampal smiling at her from across the room. Although nearly seventy, the old Tibetan lama looked extraordinarily healthy. His ruddy brown face was vibrant, and his hair, almost white except for a few remaining streaks of black, lay thick and full down to the nape of his neck. His large brown eyes, steady and penetrating, scanned them both silently as they approached.

"*Lamala,*" Maggie uttered respectfully.

"*Ah, tashi delek, tashi delek,*" Lama Jampal addressed her in greeting.

"*Ku suk de bo yin be, Lama?*" Maggie moved toward him with her arms outstretched. They reached for each others hands and touched foreheads.

Maggie started to smile as Michael positioned himself with an outstretched hand. She could almost hear him comparing the common Tibetan greeting of touching foreheads to the congratulatory head butting of football players during a game.

"This is Michael Sonada," she said.

The elderly man reached out and clasped Michael's hand. Spared, relief passed over Michael's eyes as he received a good old American handshake.

"Maggie, Michael, please sit," Lama Jampal said, pointing to the thick, hand-woven rug on the floor.

Maggie sat down on the carpet, allowing herself a moment to soak in the texture of the lama's quarters. Deep reds and golds lined the lush rich brocades that draped over the gold statues. Water glistened in silver bowls as offerings to the Buddhas while oil lamps, glowing with the light of dancing flames, flickered on the shrine. *Thangkas,* images of Tibetan deities, black and monstrous, brandishing cutting knives, hand drums, bells, and lavish jewelry, glared at her from around the room. Maggie then noticed the most vibrant and finely designed of them all was hanging directly behind the lama.

Vajrayogini.

The female deity, red in color, stood haloed in flames like a powerful angel. Wild and fierce, she held a knife and skullcup and wore a crown of five skulls. The deity trampled a human body under her foot, symbolizing the destruction of ego and transcendence of the spirit.

A powerful female, Maggie thought. *How long can they keep her spirit under wraps?*

Maggie realized Lama Jampal was waiting for her to speak. Unraveling their tale, she told him why they were in Nepal and about the dilemma they now found themselves in, including being pursued by Mabus' men, hoping she sounded at least somewhat coherent. Jampal occasionally nodded, but made no comment. Finally, Maggie opened the pouch. Delicately removing the wooden case, she placed it on the meditation table in front of him and opened it.

Lama Jampal's eyes widened. "Where did you get this?"

"It was brought to Bodhgaya by a young Brahmin priest," Maggie replied. "I think he was from somewhere in Kerala."

Michael pulled out his translation and began to read.

Moving to the Mother Harvest
the words lay hidden
beyond the cave of the lakes
We bow and make journey
for the warm healing waters
At the beak, behind the misty veil,
the final word is revealed
within the pure land of the sun.

A hint of recognition crossed Lama Jampal's face. He took a few moments to comprehend the translation as he stared at the parchment in front of him. "The map of the Twin," he said. Jampal's voice held no doubt. "We have kept it hidden for two thousands years."

Maggie's mind moved quickly. Investigative reporting had thrown her into many spheres, but this? This was beyond comprehension. She turned toward Michael who appeared as astonished as she was. Were they actually deciphering the words of the apostle Thomas?

"Moving toward the Mother Harvest," Maggie said aloud, the words resonating like a mantra.

"Mother Harvest," Lama Jampal repeated, looking at Michael. "What do you think it means?"

"Could be the name of a temple," Michael guessed.

"That might be true," Maggie said, reminded of her research. "At the time of Christ there were plenty of Hindu temples around."

"Or," Michael said glancing over at the crude map, "it might have something to do with the ley of the land."

Maggie knew his scholarly tone meant there was an explanation involved. "You're talking geography," she assessed.

"Well, to a degree, yes. Ley, l-e-y," Michael said, spelling out the word, "the energy lines of an area, also refers to some extent to the lay, l-a-y, of the land—its geographical features. In this case, it seems to relate to the topography of Nepal, or at least what was known of it at the time. Even one of the markings on the map appears to reach into what later became Tibet."

Michael maneuvered himself next to Jampal. "Let's start connecting the dots," he said, using his finger to show direction. "Here's a point on the map—Bodhgaya—the origination point. The course that appears here runs north, across what's now the border of Nepal, then northwest along what looks like a river."

Maggie wondered where Michael was leading, but Lama Jampal didn't allow too much time for speculation.

"At the time of Jesus," Jampal stated, "there were some settlements in the Himalayan foothills where certain spiritual masters lived and practiced."

"What are you saying?" Michael asked.

The embers of a long-held secret glowed within the lama's eyes. "That Christ's spiritual journey was also a physical one. He understood the universal spiritual energies and how certain places acted like magnets and generators, in other words, that they were sacred. The great Himalayas were a focus for him. The Son of Man moved through this region as he also moved through the desert of the Middle East. These areas themselves were wellsprings of the spiritual, where a man could be alone with the divine, with his God, as you would say, and understand his deep connection with all of life." Jampal paused. "You see, Jesus realized the divine in his own heart. Today, Buddhists would call him a great *bodhisattva*, an awakened being."

Lama Jampal's eyes rested upon the parchment once again. "He told his disciple Thomas of his journey. This map marks the path that Christ followed through the Himalayas and the words direct the bearer to a great discovery."

"You're saying that the essence of his teachings can literally be found?" Maggie could barely absorb the thought.

"I'm saying that words in themselves have great power." Lama Jampal leveled his gaze at her. "They are the sounds of the universe. The directions that Christ left with Thomas reveal the *ley*, the spiritual energy lines that must be followed to reach the source of his teachings."

Michael looked confused.

"You need to understand that the *Mother Harvest* is not only the direction, but also a powerful force manifested on this earth . . . a place." The lama was now eyeing them both. "The Mother Harvest is the *Mother Mountain*."

"Oh God." Maggie's heart beat faster with recognition. "Why didn't I see it before?"

"It's the first area we are directed to," Lama Jampal stated confidently.

"Yes, yes," Maggie said, her excitement growing. "It's Annapurna!"

CHAPTER 43

A T THAT MOMENT the sound of drumbeats, loud percussive rhythms, resonated through the monastery's well of silence. Drawn to the window, Maggie watched as monks adorned in maroon and gold robes carried large drums across the courtyard. Just then, a lone monk standing on the rock face at the eastern end of the monastery held a conch to his lips. Long, low moans issued from the large seashell, indicating a ritual was about to commence.

BOOM . . . tap, tap . . . BOOM. The drumbeats grew louder.

"The dance begins," Jampal stated.

"What dance?" Michael asked.

"The dance of *Mahakala*, the great black one . . . the power of time."

Michael got up and joined Maggie by the window.

Just then, a loud bellow came from the *radungs* as two monks, cheeks puffed widely, drawing air through their noses, blew hard into the huge instruments. The horn's eight-foot long stem and wide mouth resounded as distinctly as any foghorn calling out to ships at sea. The call, Maggie knew, invoked the protectors to the monastery to attend the ritual dance and meditation.

"If only Harper Crow could see this," Michael whispered as he leaned over toward her. "If anything could give small-minded Christian impersonators the heebie-jeebies, this would be it."

"*Om Sri Mahakala, sapari wara argham, padyam, pupe, dupe, aloke, ghende, newide, shabda . . .* "

Maggie felt the deep low voices of the monks resonating through her body. Instinctively, she knew it was time to leave. When she turned to tell Lama Jampal, she saw that he was gathering some provisions into a large, sheepskin knapsack. Already dressed in a thick pair of khaki jeans and a yellow woolen pullover, he cloaked himself in a burgundy shawl and with a nod, indicated he was ready. Jampal then quietly led her and Michael through the monastery's wide sullen hallways and into the courtyard.

Once outside, they hurried down the path, passing a group of women dressed in elegant chubas, their hair tied with colorful ribbons and all adorned with their finest jewels—turquoise and mother of pearl necklaces, golden lockets, silver chains, and long coral earrings. Maggie noticed them turn, a look of surprise sweeping over their faces as they saw the lama accompanying the two *English*.

With the rhythm of the chanting driving them forward, Jampal hurried them through a narrow gate in the stone wall. Luckily, besides the few women at the main entrance, they had not been noticed.

Outside the monastery's perimeters, the brush quickly turned into thick woods. They traversed down the slope, sliding on wet rocks and earth, until they eventually came upon an old trading route that paralleled the road below. As they quietly moved along the stony path, Maggie glanced across at Jampal. The lines across his face seemed to have deepened with the afternoon shadows.

"The sun will be going down soon." She tried to keep the worry out of her voice, but Maggie knew she wasn't kidding anyone. "We can't continue on this route. If Mabus' men are persistent, they'll find us."

Jampal's only reply was to quicken his pace. As she tried to keep up behind him, Maggie was surprised by his agility. He had always moved so slowly, as she recalled, nothing hurried or rushed. Now, leaping across boulders and crouching and scurrying along the twisting paths, he looked more like a man in his thirties rather than a normally sedate, seventy-year-old lama. He turned toward her and smiled, as if aware of her thoughts .

Once they were down the hill, they came upon a couple of sherpas sitting on top of an old Nissan station wagon. Jampal approached them, and Maggie could see by their head nods and hand gestures that negotiations were in play. He then turned and motioned for both Michael and Maggie to hurry over.

"Give me some money," Jampal said, addressing Michael.

"Excuse me?"

"Come on, let's go," Jampal whispered urgently as Michael reluctantly pulled out his wallet. "And turn around when you take your billfold out. Haven't you been to Nepal before?" Jampal searched Maggie's face for some kind of answer.

She shrugged.

Michael slapped a twenty-dollar bill into one of the sherpa's hands. Both men, giggling with delight and obviously pleased with their haggling abilities, motioned the threesome to get into the back of their vehicle.

"They want the money for their whiskey supply," Jampal informed.

"Oh, great. Don't tell me we're about to be driven by a couple of drunks."

Maggie had been through this before, and there was little time for explanation. "They're perfectly sober, Michael." She smiled and couldn't help adding, "These guys are law-abiding citizens, you know."

"Right," Michael replied, sarcastically.

"They'll be living it up later tonight," Maggie said, enjoying his annoyance, "but they are serious when they're on the job."

Michael rolled his eyes. "So where are we going?"

"We're headed to Pokhara," Lama Jampal replied as he stared out the car window.

"Isn't that place filled with bold, rugged Europeans and Americans living out a kind of trekking nirvana?" Michael asked.

"Just be glad we're getting a ride there," Maggie said.

"Wait. Spiritual seekers are supposed to walk the path, right, not use a cab?"

She grinned. "Very witty. Just a little over a week until the conference. We need transportation as much as possible."

"Actually," Michael confessed, "I'm glad. These shoes—"

"But don't worry," she interrupted, "you'll get your fair share of walking later on."

"Driving to nirvana," Michael sighed, sinking back into his seat. "Too good to be true."

Dropped off by the sherpas at the western outskirts of Pokhara, they were greeted by a sight of exquisite beauty. Michael lifted his eyes up toward the mountains and took a deep breath. The Himalayan peaks jutted into the serene blue sky with stunning, icy fierceness.

The Annapurna range.

But Jampal was not one to linger. He quickly led them out of the town and away from the wandering tourists. Over an hour later, with the sun beginning to set, Jampal finally stopped. He looked at the stars while rolling a long string of beads in his hand. After a moment of quiet, he looked toward Michael.

"Tonight, we sleep here—close to the perimeters of the hidden land."

Here, Michael realized, was in the middle of the brush. Before he could object, Jampal took a long knife out of the sheath attached to his belt and began cutting away the growth. Maggie, following his example, started tearing at it with her bare hands. Seeing her fervor, Michael sighed reluctantly and joined in. Soon they created a small clearing, just enough space for the three of them to stretch out.

"If we keep the space small, it'll be hard to see us," Maggie explained to Michael. "Even though Mabus' men can't know our exact route, they have a pretty good idea which direction we headed."

Fearing detection, starting a fire was out of the question. Instead, the moon was their only source of light. They sat quietly while Jampal prepared "dinner"—dried meat and some hard bread he retrieved out of his sack.

When Michael was finished devouring his meal, Jampal leaned toward him, his face barely visible in the moonlight. "There is something I need to tell you. A woman named Rachel came to see me before she started her expedition into the Himalayas."

Stunned, Michael stared, waiting for Jampal to continue.

"Napesh Samuels sent her to me. Rachel told me of a document she'd found in Bodhgaya and that she needed direction into the mountains. She also warned me about a man she'd been working for—Mr. Mabus—the man you say is trying to harm you. Rachel said Mabus was not what he appears and was frightened that he would send men looking for her."

What Jampal was saying coincided with what Kumari had told him. Their expedition had been funded by Mabus.

"Did Rachel say anything else?" Michael implored.

"She asked me to get word to you somehow through the Professor. She wanted you to come to Nepal, Michael." Lama Jampal paused. "She was looking for the hidden land . . . Shambhala."

Despite his resistance and doubt, Michael was beginning to feel compelled to find this place. "Beyond the myth, why is finding Shambhala itself so important?"

"It's not only important, it's imperative." Lama Jampal was insistent. "Rachel understood that. All the signs point toward finding this hidden land and bringing forth its treasure."

"And what would that be?" Michael asked.

"The Wish-fulfilling Jewel that Christ left there." Jampal uttered the amazing words. "What you call the Grail."

Astonished at what he was hearing, Michael found his mind racing to put together both past and present information.

"She also learned something about Mabus' connection with certain caves in Tarhuna, near Leptis Magna," Jampal said. "Whatever she found out drove her all the more to locate Shambhala."

"Tarhuna." Michael wondered about the significance. He had traveled through that isolated place several years ago while doing research for his book. "It's just a small oasis in the mountains in Libya."

What was in Tarhuna that made finding Shambhala so important? Michael looked up to meet Jampal's eyes.

The lama was watching him curiously. "Your own dreams brought you here to find out what happened to your friend . . . and to find the *termas*."

"The *termas*?" Michael had not heard the word before.

"Sacred treasures, objects of power," Maggie interjected, breaking her silence. "Jampal knows the land well and says he has been given the task to guide us to the hidden site."

Michael turned to meet the lama's intense gaze. "Are you actually telling me that the Grail is something real, that we're actually going to find it in this mysterious Shambhala?".

"You'll find out soon enough," he answered. "The path and the destination are the same."

Michael was unhappy with Jampal's cryptic reply. "I'd like to know *now*."

Disregarding Michael's impatience, Jampal started to chant in deep whispered tones. He held his mala in his wrinkled hands and moved the sandlewood beads gently, without hurry. As he watched him, Michael wondered if the lama even knew the word anxiety existed.

Tired and frustrated, Michael quietly prepared himself for sleep and stretched out on his make-shift bed—a shawl as a sheet and his knapsack as a pillow. Maggie lay a few feet away. He turned toward her to speak, finding it hard to keep the weariness out of his voice. "How do you know so much about all this? Just what kind of investigative reporting are you doing these days?"

Maggie smiled as she leaned toward him. "I've been working on a piece about actual journeys people have made trying to find the sacred, hidden land of Shambhala. Several professional explorers as well as some adventurous amateurs received guidance from lamas in Nepal and Tibet who had access to special texts describing the place and how to reach it. The lamas spoke of Shambhala as a place, tangible and of this world, as well as being something that was symbolic, an inner journey that led you to an enlightened state. These studies fascinated Professor Samuels. He kept trying to find out just where my research was going."

The excitement in Maggie's voice quickened. "What I was able to find out was truly profound. After studying the texts on the apostle John's *Book of Revelation* and his vision of the New Jerusalem, I looked into ancient legends originating through various cultures all over the globe, especially the legend of Shambhala from the Tibetan Buddhist tradition. What surfaced was a striking similarity between the religious lore. Shambhala, as described in the ancient Tangyur text of Tibet, is a place like the Jerusalem of the Revelation, one filled with peace, harmonious living, and fellowship—an enlightened society. The people of this land dedicate themselves to a spiritual path that furthers their own enlightenment and secures that of the community in which they live."

"You're saying people have *actually* been looking for this place?" Michael still couldn't wrap his head around the thought.

"*Actually*, I am." Maggie smiled. "Of course, in the end, no one knows if a land like Shambhala ever existed or if it exists today, but the scholars all agree on one thing. The symbolism inherent in the myth. Shambhala is a pure state of being, a pure realm manifesting in the world. In this way it resembles the vision of the New Jerusalem. Put simply, it's basically the creation of a heaven on earth where all peoples of all nations live in spiritual harmony and truly come to the *Kingdom of God*."

As Maggie spoke, Michael couldn't help thinking she looked like a Renaissance fresco. In fact, her beauty seemed to be a reflection of her words. Framed by lush waves of hair, her long, oval face glowed angelically in the moonlight, and her beautiful haunting eyes, almost otherworldly, penetrated his.

She's a Mediterranean dream, he thought.

"I've been studying a lot of the ancient Tibetan texts," Maggie said, betraying no awareness of his reflection. "In particular, those of the *beyul*."

"*Beyul?*"

"The hidden lands," she replied.

Michael envisioned treks of bandana-wearing hippies and adventure seekers staking a claim in Shangri-la. "Come on, you're an educated woman. You've lived in Jerusalem, seen fighting in the streets, traveled abroad for years doing investigative journalism. You're not telling me you actually believe this Shambhala exists?"

"What I believe, Michael, is the vision. Places like the New Jerusalem, Shambhala, the Kingdom of God, Mecca. They are the power of man's vision of decency and beauty on earth." Maggie's voice was filled with emotion. "Through believing wholeheartedly and truly desiring it, then anywhere you are can become a pure land."

Despite his outer casing of cynicism, Michael recognized the ideal of a visionary. No matter how far-fetched, no matter how unlikely, it was the dream that always created the reality.

His heart warmed as he watched Maggie, her breath beginning to slow as sleep descended. Something deep within him stirred as he sensed there had been a former connection.

Somewhere . . . sometime.

CHAPTER 44

LAMA JAMPAL was the first to put his pack together the following morning. With little sleep, he found himself beginning to worry. The trek itself was dangerous and the text on the beyul was a strange mixture of the material world and the mystical. His heart felt heavy as he thought of the obstacles they would face.

Then he remembered the words of his own teacher. *There are no obstacles.*

With that new thought in mind, he buoyed himself, knowing that the rugged mountains were not sympathetic toward the weak or foolish. He then directed Michael and Maggie to break up camp while he plotted out the course of their morning trek. Although he was old, he would continue to lead them on the path that Thomas had set down in writing.

Beyond the cave of the lakes.

Jampal felt strongly he knew what that meant.

Between the rustling of their footsteps, the cooing and songs of the birds, and the intermittent calls of the monkeys from the trees above, there came a stream of sound—light and melodious music drifting in the breeze.

"What's that?" Maggie asked.

The old lama cocked his head and turned a large, spiral-shaped ear up to the sky. "That is a bamboo flute, *bansuri*." He pointed straight ahead. "Over there. Must be a village close by."

Maggie saw nothing but the large looming trees. The sound emanating from the woods was like an imprint carried by the breeze . . . still searching for whomever had called it forth. The beautiful tones continued as they walked on the path, resonating a mysterious longing.

Soon they were headed into thick foliage that made it nearly impossible to see more than a few feet ahead. As they walked beneath some bamboo and banana trees, they were assailed by loud screams as a family of monkeys taunted them through the leaves.

Nearly an hour later, the brilliant blue sky grew darker. Gray-black clouds arose and were soon hanging over them like a veil. The air became heavy and a mist descended just as Jampal ushered them into a thick grove of trees. Clutching her backpack, Maggie stared into the dark shadows of the forest, a growing paranoia moving through her.

Suddenly, loud rumbling thunder shook the ground. A moment later, Michael was standing beside her, a protective hand on her shoulder.

"I've walked through similar areas before," she said, "but I've never experienced anything like this."

Jampal peered into the shaded forest, a knowing look on his face. "The dark ones are here, the shadow people."

They walked slowly ahead, following what looked like a mere outline of a path. It finally opened out into a small settlement. A young woman, her garment soiled and gray, saw them and began yelling. Others, alerted by her cries, came out of their clay huts and ran to her aid. Alarmed and frightened, some of the people began to yell in a language that was clearly not Nepali or Tibetan. Maggie didn't recognize it. Soon the odd group of men and women were waving their arms and making clicking sounds at them in warning.

"Not too friendly, are they?" Michael asked nervously.

"No, not friends," Jampal said.

They kept walking, but more quickly now.

Then several of the men began to move toward them, clapping their hands frantically. A toothless woman, her hair in messy braids, began to throw stones.

"Let's go," Lama Jampal urged, taking off into a run.

Throwing stones and clicking their tongues, the villagers chased the three of them into a shallow creek. As they splashed across, Maggie grew dizzy. She was finding it hard to focus as she treaded across the slippery rocks. Then, within the flash of a moment, the world blurred and reappeared. The whole landscape appeared to have changed. She saw herself in a strange land, the images flashing quickly through her mind . . . *a young woman, a man, a soldier, all running fervently from a hostile crowd. Soldiers pursuing them as they race through the gates of a city, hiding in shadows.*

As quickly as they had begun, the images ceased. Again, she was running with Jampal and Michael, splashing across the creek. They reached the bank on the other side and scurried toward the trees.

Suddenly, Michael called out behind her. "Wait!"

Maggie turned to see the chase had ended. As if prevented by a mysterious boundary, their pursuers did not venture through the shallow stream, but instead halted at the water's edge. Making ugly angry faces at them, they stood for a while waving their fists and clicking until, finally, they ceased their hostilities and departed once again into the woods.

Sighing, Jampal motioned for her and Michael to follow, and they proceeded into the thick forest. After they were safely distanced, they came to a halt under a long rock overhang.

Maggie took a moment to breathe deeply. She looked at Michael who appeared perplexed and shaken. Had he experienced the same images as she?

Familiar scents, haunting sounds, and long-forgotten memories rustled with the leaves. The old lama stared at them both, a calm assurance in his manner. "You will remember when it's necessary," Jampal said.

"Remember what?" Michael asked.

Maggie noticed the reserve in his voice.

"The images you have just seen, yet already forgotten." Jampal looked at them both for a moment, a slight trace of a smile on his lips.

Maggie felt a strange familiarity with their surroundings. "This is the exact spot we need to be at this time," she said with certainty. "It's where the first opening lies."

"The first opening?" Michael asked.

"A point in the path, a spiritual center," Jampal enumerated.

Maggie felt a presence and looked up toward a huge boulder looming on the edge a cliff about hundred feet above them. A young leopard was prowling on the rocky heights, her large, tawny eyes scanning their camp. She stared down at them for a few moments, then stealthily climbed over the ridge and disappeared.

"Good sign," Jampal said. "We follow her."

"Do you think that's wise?" Michael asked.

"She will take us toward the water." Jampal shaded his eyes as he peered up at the ridge. "That means the cave we are looking for, the *Cave of the Five Lakes*, will be nearby."

Maggie felt her patience running thin. "Let's get moving then. We still have a way to go, and it appears we're in for some nasty weather."

As Jampal guided them upward, scaling the boulders where the leopard had been treading, the sky, already dark, grew more ominous as swirling clouds signaled the rain to come. Finally, they came up onto a road. Across the way, Maggie could see a large cave cut into the granite slope of the mountain.

Suddenly, a flash of lightning streaked across the sky. An explosive clap sent them bounding forward just as the rain began to fall.

CHAPTER 45

"**G**UPTESWAR," LAMA JAMPAL announced, nodding with certainty as they arrived inside the narrow opening.

Wet, and not particularly happy about it, Maggie stood for a moment, allowing her eyes to adjust to the dim light. Suddenly, she heard a voice that made her turn.

"Five rupees."

A thin, middle-aged Hindu man, red vermillion on his forehead, approached them from around a corner on the opposite side of the cave entrance.

Stunned by the oddity of it, Maggie stared at the man, then at her companions. Soon, her practical mind kicked in. With all the trekkers and tourists around the Nepali mountain range, holy sites, although still revered, had been turned into commercial commodities.

Smiling to herself, Maggie pulled out some money from her knapsack and paid the entrance fee for all of them. Then she, Michael and Jampal flicked on their flashlights and ventured forward into the cave.

"Where do we look?" she asked overwhelmed by the prospect of searching the long tunnel. "This place seems huge."

But her companions appeared to be in their own world. Michael and Jampal walked ahead, using their lights to scan the walls. Following them, Maggie was beginning to doubt Jampal's interpretation of the parchment, when the cave opened up into an alcove. There, in the dusky light, Maggie glimpsed the shimmering reflection of water.

"Well, we do have water here so I guess it's a good sign," Michael said, not sounding particularly hopeful. "Yet, even if one of the sayings was ever hidden in this cave, it could have been removed hundreds of years ago."

"No one said it would be easy. We are following a path, moving through areas that Christ traversed himself thousands of years ago." Maggie tried to display an encouraging tone. "We can't be sure of what we'll find, but anything is possible."

Jampal, undeterred by the outer environment, was already setting up a practice site on the rough ground. "This cave is nearly three miles long." Lama Jampal opened up his satchel and removed his *pechas*—a leather-bound text of dharma chants and teachings. "We prepare first."

Maggie admired his tenacity and decided to join him.

"Protector practice," Maggie whispered in response to the questioning look on Michael's face. "We are at the outer circle in our movement toward the hidden land and are invoking the guardians' protection."

A thunderous rumbling resounded throughout the cave. To Maggie, it was like the fierce growl of the protector, resonating through their refuge hole. The intense and powerful sound heightened her focus as they began to chant.

Hung Tuk je nyur day chen ray zi

Nak po chen po sha dru pa . . .

Michael sat on the ground listening as Maggie and Jampal continued chanting. After a while, Jampal pulled out a small, gold embroidered box from his bag and opened it. Inside, some old dried-out leaves, cracked with age, were laying among a group of gemstones—jade, turquoise, opals. Thin red strings were bunched together in the corner of the box.

"Protection cords," Jampal said, eying him.

As Michael leaned over the box, the smell of sandalwood, jasmine and unknown spices stirred his imagination, conjuring images of faraway places and ancient mysteries. A feeling of longing overcame him, and he reached out impulsively.

He touched the beautiful object.

At that very moment, his senses began to heighten. Within the dark quiet, he could hear the wind blowing outside the cave and the gurgle of moving water from an underground stream. The sounds invoked a timeless serenity that belied the danger Michael knew to be following them.

Now, with the scent of incense lifting his mind, the natural flow of water and wind created their own aqueous rhythm.

A young man approaches the gate of a monastery and speaks to a monk who allows him to enter. The man comes from a strange land. "From Judea," he says to the abbot, "in the west." His heart has led him to this place.

The abbot directs him down a dark wide corridor, the air scented with the smell of burning butter. On the walls are textured prints with strange images, black and red caricatures, wrathful and frightening. On shelves and within niches are scrolls and texts, words of realization, teachings which he longs to study and practice. The many secrets . . . what are they? Secrets he touched long ago, in other times and places.

When he turns the corner to another corridor, an old lama appears. The lama's large eyes meet his. The face of the lama seems both grim and pleased as he searches the silence for knowledge. Deep and profound, the stillness speaks to them both, as the disciple accepts the master, and the master, the student.

As Michael removed his hand from the golden box, he looked up at the same face he had seen speaking to the young man in his vision.

Jampal was watching him, his eyes luminous even in the dim light. "The box has been in my family for a long time. It may look small, but it holds much more than you might guess. These cords were worn by the man who came from Judea, who lived among my people long ago and learned the spiritual ways—the meditations and yogas—from the old masters." He paused and pulled out one of the long red strings. "When a man is enlightened, then everything he touches is blessed."

As Jampal handed him the chord, Michael felt surprised that the lama would give him something so precious. Touched, he accepted the gift. "What do I do with it?"

"You wear it," Jampal said as he placed the golden box back into his bag. "Tie it around your neck for protection."

Michael placed the chord around his throat and secured it with a knot.

Looking pleased, Lama Jampal smiled. "Now you're ready."

Michael wasn't sure for what, but he had to admit it. He felt emboldened, empowered.

Suddenly, the sound of voices brought them both to their feet. Maggie, apparently having heard it too, was soon by their side. A moment later, Heloff, Kumari and Khan came rushing through the cave opening, moving in full force.

Jampal's face tensed. "Let's go!" Sprinting forward, he led them deeper into the cave.

With Jampal constantly urging them to hurry, they raced through the narrow passageways. Soon, the tunnels began opening up into caverns, one after the next, all shimmering with small bodies of water.

The lakes.

With their flashlights searching the darkness, they ran for what seemed like a mile, hugging the cave walls surrounding each body of water, all the while looking for a way out.

Finally, at the edge of one of the pools, the cave floor sloped upward, and they came upon a low narrow opening in the rock wall.

"We enter here," Lama Jampal said, pointing ahead.

"You must be kidding." Rooted to the spot, Michael stared at the hole in the cave wall. It looked about two feet wide. "I'm not going through there."

"There's no way to go but forward," Maggie insisted, removing the pack from her shoulder.

"But we don't know where that hole leads," Michael pleaded.

"There is something ahead that you'll want to see, Michael," Jampal said. "You think you can go back, but you can't. Back there are only Mabus' men and the shadow people."

Not much of a choice, Michael thought.

The sound of running footsteps made the idea of choice a moot point.

Michael took a few steps toward the edge of the lake. "Both of you go ahead. I'll be right behind you," he told them.

Maggie was about to protest, but Michael cut her off. "Just go!" he yelled.

Jampal and Maggie fell to their knees and started crawling through the black space in the rock.

Michael recognized Heloff's voice echoing through the shadows. Then suddenly, across the cavern, all three men emerged from the darkness. Kumari caught sight of him first and motioned to Heloff and Khan. As the men started racing around the pool, Michael realized he needed to make a move or his fear would do him in.

His breath quickening, he crawled into the hole, never feeling more frightened of anything in his entire life. As he wedged his body between the rocks, barely able to drag himself forward, he wondered if things could possibly get any worse. The answer came quickly when he heard Kumari and the others clamoring to enter the hole behind him.

Finally, as the tunnel grew even narrower, the space became so cramped that Michael came to a dead stop. His nightmare of being stuck alive was becoming a reality. Paralyzed with fear between the voices behind him and the darkness ahead, he heard the distant sound of Maggie's voice but couldn't understand what she was saying. Just then, the sound of scraping started up behind him, frightening him even more.

Now, pinned between the walls, Michael was beyond desperate. His lungs were aching.

"Michael."

Finally, soothing and clear, Maggie's voice sounded close.

"Come on. Just let go," she coaxed. "Don't be afraid. Now ease your breath and relax your shoulders. Yeah, that's right."

Michael felt his breathing beginning to normalize as he wedged his shoulder and his upper body forward. Maggie's hand took a hold of his then, soft and comforting, leading him forward. Feeling grateful, he realized she had crawled back into the rock face to get him.

"Come. Just keep moving forward," she said gently. "It's not far."

As Maggie crawled backward, Michael kept inching himself ahead.

"That's it," she urged. "Come on, keep going."

It was as if the rock was releasing its grip on him, or so it felt.

Suddenly, a hand clutched him by the ankle. Michael kicked his leg backward, jabbing his foot into what felt like a shoulder. A voice cried out. *Kumari's.* Michael dragged himself forward as quickly as he could, until finally, the rock opening widened and he was able to crawl out of the passage.

Totally exhausted, Michael collapsed onto the cave floor only to find Maggie stretched out next to him, panting. As he lay there, spent and weak from his ordeal, he recalled descriptions of the many hells one could enter upon death.

He felt certain he had just been through one of them.

But Jampal did not give him much time to ponder. Looking anxious, the lama helped him to his feet. "No time," was all he said.

Suddenly, a scream came from behind them.

Michael realized Kumari was now stuck in the tight passage himself.

"Sounds like the rock didn't let him go," Jampal said, listening to the wails of the trapped man.

Michael shuddered, still feeling the asphyxiating clutch of the cavern walls.

"That should keep them at bay for a while," Maggie said flatly.

Jampal took a deep breath. "Let's hope it's for a long while."

CHAPTER 46

A S THEY EXITED the cave, Michael saw the same beautiful leopard they had encountered earlier, moving gracefully along the far side of the ravine. He glanced over at Jampal wondering how the lama was translating the event. After all, Tibetan lamas were no strangers to interpreting the universe. *Signs and omens, as they say.*

They climbed down the slope only to head back up a steep incline until they reached level ground. After passing through a thin grove of trees, they encountered the ruins of an old building—dark gray stone, moss growing in niches in the rocks, an arched doorway, a weathered wooden door with one remaining tarnished brass handle.

As they got closer, Michael could make out Arabic writing carved into the stone. "Akbar," he said, recognizing the name. "He was the moghul leader who attempted to unite India under one religion."

Maggie raised her eyebrows. "Must be the remains of a Muslim temple then," she said, moving toward it.

Michael could see an alcove-like, prayer niche made of stucco and marble which was pointing to the east. *A shrine.* He assessed it was a modern addition to the grounds.

Just then, from behind the only standing wall, an old man emerged. He wore a tattered white turban that seemed to be molded against his small skull. His *lungi*, a long cotton cloth skirt, was draped around his body, falling about mid-calf. He eyed the threesome, looking more curious than frightened.

Just as he began addressing them in Nepalese, a quick assessment, like a flash, appeared in his eyes. "What do you want here?" he asked in English, gazing at them curiously. The man spoke in an educated manner.

Michael answered. "We were just looking at the ruins of the mosque." He pointed to the saying. "Moghul Akbar."

"Yes, the Moghul. He created many such mosques. This one was destroyed almost a hundred years ago, but I still carry on the tradition of my family—upheld by my father and grandfathers, and their fathers before them. My family has guarded this site ever since the Christians abandoned it."

Michael asked him to explain.

"Long before the Akbar came, this temple was a Christian pilgrim site." The caretaker pointed. "You see?"

Etched above the remaining archway was Arabic writing that Michael hadn't noticed before. He walked up to the wall and took a closer look. "Maggie, Jampal. Come see this."

They came up beside him and stared at the strange writing.

"I'm clueless," Maggie said, squinting. "What does it say?"

The old Muslim looked at her as if she should know. "It says *Issa!*"

Maggie's eyes lit up. Michael could see it was definitely a word she understood.

"*Issa,*" she whispered. "Jesus."

Michael gaped in astonishment as he read the words inscribed on the stone. "If this is what I think it is . . . " He leaned against the archway for support, "then we may have just found one of the secret sayings."

Her eyes wide with excitement, Maggie grabbed a pen and notepad out of her backpack. She took a deep breath. "Now," she said slowly, "tell me what it says."

Michael carefully read the words on the stone wall, all the while aware that Maggie was waiting impatiently. Finally, ready to give his interpretation, he spoke slowly as she wrote:

Jesus, peace be with him, said:
The world is an overproud house.
Take this as a warning, and do not build on it.

When Maggie finished scribbling, she looked up expectantly.

"An agraphon," Michael explained. "A saying of Christ not included in any of the four gospels."

Maggie appeared mesmerized as she moved closer to the archway. "So this was probably handed down from the early Thomas Christians."

Michael nodded, concurring. "Thus far, it seems to fit the pattern. In the Gospel of Thomas, the words *Jesus said* begin many of the lines. *Jesus, peace be with him, said* is probably the Islamic version of the same initial introduction.

"In Tibet," Lama Jampal was quick to add, "we also have heard of the sayings. In some of the monasteries, such as Hemis in Ladakh and in Lhasa at the Potala, there have been texts that speak of the holy man from Judea. Tibetans know of him through the Pali texts that came from India and Nepal—writings that describe the time he spent in these lands, arriving as a boy and leaving as man."

Maggie stood on a large rock by the archway, her hand touching the last letter of the inscription. "But can this really be one of the secret sayings? What about what was stated in the Thomas Gospel . . . that the sayings were not to be written down because they were so secret?"

"Not written down in any gospels or texts," Michael reminded her. "Thomas wasn't supposed to tell the other disciples, but what about his own? Just as Christ passed them on to him, it would be natural for Thomas to eventually reveal them to the few who were worthy enough to understand their meaning."

"As I told you before," Jampal stated, "Christ's words are powerful. They will find their way to those who can realize their meaning."

"If that's true, then we're following more than a map," Maggie said emphatically. "We're following a stream of consciousness—one that is meant to lead us to the lost secret sayings. If this is really one of them, then I believe its meaning must *somehow* be connected to what's happening in Jerusalem." She paused and took a deep breath, her tone softening. "Perhaps I'm seeing what I want to see, but I think the meaning is obvious. It's an impassioned directive. *Do not build on it.*"

All the while Michael had been staring at her. Now a glint of conviction replaced the resistance in his eyes. She knew he agreed.

"Since we've been directed to find these sayings, we need to look at the bottom line," he said. "What started us on this journey in the first place is the convergence of three extraordinary factors. Mabus' Peace Conference, the question of the old city of Jerusalem being turned into an international peace zone, and the possibility of rebuilding the Third Temple."

"As I said," Maggie declared, "the directive is clear. *Do not build on it.*"

"So you believe that means that another Temple should not be built—not a physical one, that is," Michael enumerated.

"It is not only that the Temple should not be built," Jampal added, "but the world itself is an overproud house. There has been a prophecy from long ago that says this earth will almost be destroyed—that wars, hunger, earthquakes, floods, fire will kill many—and that this will become an empty world, a wasteland."

Maggie glanced at Michael who was listening intently.

"There were men from the old time who knew this was coming," Jampal continued, "and that living creatures would not really be able to live in this kind of a world. The old ones gave us this message. Christ was one of them, but we have not listened. Because of our arrogance we have turned our faces from the truth."

Darkness was beginning to fall, ready to envelop the world once again. Maggie knew there was a lot to think about as she looked at the old Muslim man standing in his ruined temple garden. His life would remain the same, but for her, for the whole world, nothing would be the same again.

Using a tarnished silver urn, the old man poured water over the archway. As he cleansed the holy remains of the temple, Maggie recognized the short prayer he recited—a prayer to Allah for purification and thanks. When he was finished, the man motioned for the three of them to follow. He led the small group through the trees to a boarding house in a nearby village, about a quarter of a mile away.

Maggie made no complaints when she saw her bare room with its canvas mat on the dirt floor. As if being greeted by a goose-down mattress, she laid down and fell into a deep sleep.

CHAPTER 47

THE NEW MORNING emerged like a beautiful dream, a passing mirage of golden sunlight brightening up the vast expanse of light blue sky. Now, miles from Pokhara and heading toward Beni, they moved forward into the mountainous jungle.

The majestic view of the Annapurnas soon left them. Instead, towering trees blocked the sun, darkening their path. As they proceeded, stringy green vines entangled themselves in their hair and clung to their shoulders and gear. Michael soon found they were sloshing through ankle-deep water, fearfully watching for snakes and pulling off leeches.

"Damn these slimy creatures," he cursed in distaste.

Maggie moved closer to him, half smiling. There was something about the way she looked at him now, as if she was seeing him for the first time. "You'd better start viewing things a bit more clearly if you want to see a pure land," she said, pulling a leech from his shirtsleeve.

Michael grimaced as she dropped it into the shallow water. "Keep dreaming. There is no way I'm going to see those slimy creatures as pure."

As they traveled further along the shallow creek, the tree line opened up. Salamanders sat peacefully on rocks above the waterline basking in the heat of the sun. Michael could see their beady eyes watching them curiously as they walked by.

As he watched the strange sparks of light glimmering in the afternoon sun, Michael could only express the experience as being elemental. The world was a place of magic and illusion. All sounds were sharp, all colors clear, all sensations distinct. The gurgling brook, bounding before him, spoke of soon-to-be-found treasures and aligned him with something counter to his nature—a flowing, moving reality.

Michael's silent world was suddenly penetrated by the sound of Jampal's voice.

"What are you thinking about?" The lama was now walking beside him.

"He's thinking about a hot bath and a bottle of beer," Maggie chided.

"Yes, that's definitely true," Michael confessed, "about that and a lot of other things."

Maggie's eyes widened. She was obviously amused by his serious overtones.

"Are you also questioning your doubts? If some things you didn't think existed, actually do?" Jampal held his gaze. "Perhaps you are wondering if there really is a hidden land."

Maggie looked like she was working hard to suppress a laugh. Feeling a bit slighted, Michael gave her a dismissive glance. After all, he was an intelligent scholar, perfectly capable of having a discussion on spirituality.

"Okay, yes," Michael admitted. "Some of my beliefs, or lack of beliefs, are being challenged."

Jampal was silently studying his face, waiting.

"I'm also concerned about Rachel, about finding out what really happened to her."

"Do you think you'll be able to?"

Jampal's question surprised him, and Michael remained silent.

"If it's a powerful wish," the lama added, "then maybe you will."

The afternoon sun sent a shimmering light through the leaves. As they walked, Michael remembered the last time he had seen Rachel before she left for India, eyes radiant, a look of expectation on her face. He was touched to see she was wearing a necklace he had given her. *A small gold butterfly with a diamond chip glimmering at its wings.* As he thought of her, the pang of loss cut through him.

"It's like everything we see." Jampal motioned around him. "How do you think we can possibly perceive a place like this? The mind is magical, miraculous. It is spacious beyond any sky, beyond space itself. Did Rachel die? Will you die? Perhaps within our usual experience, yes, you will die. But what about what most of us can't perceive beyond our normal limited awareness? What if I were to say, you can never actually die, that there is no death as we have perceived it?"

"I don't understand."

The old man studied Michael quietly for a moment before speaking again. "The mind goes on. This awareness that we call 'I' continues on and on, Michael. We have already been all things to each other, experienced endless relationships, and we will continue like this until we break the links in the chain." Jampal's eyes searched his. "This entire world, every single one of us, is ready for a leap. Ready to move away from seeing things as so solid and substantial. There is so much more, so much inside of us. Who will go past their fear and make the journey?"

"It's like an adventure," Maggie added.

"Yes," Jampal said nodding his head, "a great adventure. And spiritual realization is the treasure."

The sound of echoing voices made them all turn.

"I think those men have found us," Jampal said, looking unexpectedly calm. He started to pick up his pace and indicated for them to follow.

"I'm tired of running," Michael said, stopping in his tracks. He was fed up with the whole affair. "There's probably only two of them at this point. What if I just try to talk to them. They said they wanted my help."

"These men won't listen," Jampal replied gruffly. "They are controlled by Mabus."

Having barely eaten, his nerves on edge, Michael was worn from the constant pushing. He felt a physical need—an actual craving—for comfort and peace. Now, falling into the haze of disturbing thoughts, he felt as if he was caught in a dust storm, blinded by his own anger.

"Dr. Sonada!" Hearing Heloff's voice was like hearing the sound of crashing glass. He was standing with Khan on a bluff opposite them. Apparently they had left Kumari behind. "You can't run forever."

Michael fought hard to resist the urge to respond. Jampal shot him a quick glance, his eyes fierce.

"Let's move, Michael," Maggie urged, tugging on his arm. "We'll lose them."

"Those guys aren't letting up, Maggie." Michael felt the anger welling up inside, but Maggie was insistent.

"We *can't* give up," she pleaded. "We just can't." Her eyes were intent on his, expressing her feeling clearly without words. *I need you.*

Michael felt the change instantly. As he looked at her, he was un-prepared for the understanding that dawned on him. Call it protective-ness, loyalty, devotion, whatever. *If it wasn't for Maggie*, he thought.

With Heloff and Khan beginning their descent into the narrow ravine, Michael realized he had already made his decision.

He treaded with Jampal and Maggie up the muddy slope and didn't look back.

CHAPTER 48

A FTER CLIMBING THROUGH a thick rhododendron grove, their ascent was steep as they skirted Ghorapani. Before long, the trail began to drop once again and they found themselves descending.

The Kali Gandaki Gorge.

Maggie let her focus shift from the path momentarily and move across the deepest gorge in the world. Soaring ahead, a black and white Himalayan vulture moved easily through the air, its six-foot wing span making it appear almost as if it were suspended in space. The sky, an ethereal blue, sketched the snow-laced summits of Nilgiri and Annapurna, while just below the snow line, a wispy thread of clouds seemed to suggest a natural barrier above which mortals should not venture. *The realm of the gods.*

The serenity of the scene brought Maggie's thoughts to bear on their journey.

The map and the quest. The secret sayings given to Thomas the Twin.

Local legends—words in the wind or carved in stone—seemed to appear at those moments when despair dominated hope. *Had Jesus, known as Issa, come this way?* Would they find in these mountains what had eluded the Christian community for two thousand years?

Finally, reaching the perigee of their mountainous orbit at Ghar Khola, the steady roar of the Kali Gandaki River replaced the sound of the wind. The air, filled with the scent of apple blossoms and distant orange groves, soothed their senses.

After walking past a terraced hillside, they came across the edge of a rock cliff. As Maggie turned the bend, she took a deep breath.

The trail led toward a towering flat face of solid rock about a thousand feet high. At the base, an inverted **V** had been worn into the stone wall, and through it the white capped, frothing Kali Gandaki poured.

Over the water, a narrow bridge of hand hewn planks was the sole access to Tatopani.

Jampal placed his hand on her arm. His warm calming touch immediately soothed her.

"Now come, the two of you," Jampal instructed. "If you're afraid, well . . . don't worry."

"Oh, right. I won't worry," Michael said sarcastically, backing away. "I don't think I can cross that."

This time, Maggie had to admit, she was with him all the way. The idea of crossing the suspension bridge gave her the feeling that her Lara Croft adventure was about to get real. She got close to the bridge post and looked down. The Kali Gandaki River showed no mercy below.

Jampal frowned at the both of them. He grabbed onto the ropes on both sides and walked forward onto the planks.

The sight of the jagged cliffs on the other side of the bridge made Maggie all the more wary. As she was trying to decide what was worse, death or humiliation, Michael placed his arm around her, securing her by the waist.

Before she could utter a word, he said, "Believe me, I'm doing this as much for myself as I am for you. Whatever you do, don't yell, okay, or you'll scare me to death."

Maggie would have laughed if she wasn't so terrified. As they started to walk across together, she could only think one thing. *Don't look down!* But nearly halfway there, she found she couldn't resist any longer. A quick glance at the moving water was enough to make her swoon.

"Are you okay?" Michael gripped her harder, hurting her abdomen.

"Yes, yes." There was nothing else but the affirmative. Maggie realized it was the only way she could keep going. *I can collapse when I get to the other end.*

The wind moaned, a wailing sound that did not make the walk any easier. Breathing deeply and keeping her eyes raised upward, she concentrated on the curious-looking green birds, more brilliant than the sky itself, gliding through the dizzying heights above their heads. When they finally reached the other side, Maggie felt her legs give way and she fell to the ground. Feeling the rough granular earth beneath her gave rise to a sudden burst of relief.

"Are you crying?" Michael asked as he sat down next to her.

Maggie tried to hold back, but in fact it was all catching up to her now. Several warm wet tears trickled down her face. She brushed them aside quickly. "I'm fine," she said. "I'm just a little overwhelmed, I guess."

Michael stood up. "You're a lot braver than I am," he said, giving her hand a squeeze as he helped her to her feet.

Maggie became aware that Jampal had been watching them both quietly. He took a long drink from his canteen and gazed up the path. "Come," he said. "We're almost there."

The torrential sound of rushing water grew louder as they walked forward. Maggie felt as if a magnet was drawing her in, attracting her to what lay ahead. Without thinking, she left the others behind and moved quickly through the trees and brush.

Green and vibrant, the large wet leaves were almost luminous as she brushed them aside. She soon discovered why she was so compelled. A beautiful cascading waterfall lay before her. Magnificent, white foaming waters fell about forty feet into a brilliant blue-green pool. Maggie immediately felt refreshed and awake. She moved along the water's edge, until she found another standing pool glistening in the mist. Before long she was wading waist deep.

A moment later Jampal and Michael arrived. As Maggie looked up toward the lama, she saw a smile moving slowly across Jampal's face.

"*Tatopani!*" he announced.

Michael eyed her, looking concerned. "What are you doing, Maggie? Leeches. Remember them?"

"Not to worry," she replied. "None at all."

"Just feel," Jampal assured him, dipping his hand into the pool. "The water is warm."

Michael sank his hand into the water. His eyes widened, and he turned toward Jampal with a questioning look.

"*Tato* means hot and *pani,* water," the lama explained. "The place of hot springs."

Maggie allowed their voices to fade as she basked in the serenity of the healing waters. They were lucky, she knew, to be in the quiet outskirts of town. The center of Tatopani would be filled with people, crowds of tourists using the municipal bathing pools. Here, by the riverbanks lined with apple and orange trees, they could at least enjoy some comfort and peace.

"Blessing water from the earth's womb," Jampal said, splashing into the water fully clothed.

Michael followed him in, albeit more gingerly, and soon the tension began to dissipate from his face.

Smiling to herself, Maggie leaned back into the warm water, feeling grateful. Soothing nourishment was what they all needed.

Mother earth to the rescue.

Feeling renewed, Maggie and the men ditched their dirty wet jeans for new ones bought at a local store. Now, wearing her Tibetan pullover sweater and Nepali cap, Maggie felt more natural. She smiled when she saw Michael and Jampal both wearing their hats as well.

"We look like a bunch of sherpas," Michael said, adjusting his cap proudly.

Jampal gave him a smile but quickly turned to the matter at hand. "We must look carefully while we are here. The map points us to Tatopani for a reason."

"Any idea where to start?" Michael asked.

"Well," Maggie assessed, "my inclination is to search on the outskirts of town, somewhere around the natural hot springs and just see what we can find."

"Keep your eyes peeled for a sign. Remember the archway we found by the Cave of the Five Lakes," Michael reminded them.

As they walked along the riverbank, a film of clouds began to fill the sky. The light filtering through the haze created a feeling that was almost supernatural.

Before long, the dusty path inclined and led them to a rickety picket fence. The unpainted and forlorn boards appeared one blast of wind shy of collapse. A small plaque on the gatepost caught Maggie's eye.

MISSIONARIES OF CHARITY

A glass-framed picture of Mother Theresa hung beneath the sign. Wearing a light blue and white veil, the nun's gnarled hands were brought together in prayer just below her face. Although faded, the photo radiated Mother Theresa's strength and power.

Right underneath it, a brief mission statement was written in Hindi and English:

To Serve the World through Love and Understanding

Orphanage
School
Clinic
Senior Outreach

"I'm going in." Maggie pushed the metal gate aside and stepped through without a glance at her companions. She headed up the sloping path toward the unassuming collection of stone and mud plaster buildings.

"What are you doing?" Michael asked, as both he and Jampal hastened to follow.

"I'm visiting the sisters," she replied matter-of-factly.

The work of Mother Theresa had always been of special interest to Maggie. *Mother* had been in her forties when she heard a calling to strike out on her own. After obtaining the Church's permission, that's exactly what she did, and she began to aid the dying peoples of India, literally rescuing them off the streets and giving them shelter—a place to live out the rest of their lives in the presence of love and compassion. Mother Theresa's lifetime of dedication inspired women around the globe, many of whom joined her in her efforts, helping her to start and uphold the Missionaries of Charity, the very place they had found.

Scattered fruit trees and delicate, blue-leafed poppies did their best to brighten the sparse rock-strewn grounds as Maggie and her companions walked through the complex. All around them, an eclectic group of devotees strolled down the paths—Hindu sadhus, Buddhist monks and Catholic nuns. A few scholarly-looking Westerners, mostly older men and women, sat together on benches.

Maggie saw there was a school up ahead, and next to that an orphanage, the *Orphanage of the Blessed*. Outside, children were playing tag, running on the concrete pavement. Some young boys in cricket uniforms were walking toward a narrow field, carrying bats and wearing mischievous smiles.

All the while, with every step she took, Maggie felt more at home, intrigued by the peaceful aura surrounding them.

As they passed the outer courtyard, something ahead grabbed Michael's attention. Fatigue and annoyance forgotten, he stared. A tree, about fifteen feet high with bright glossy leaves, pink and white buds sprouting along its branches, was just beginning to bloom. It was enchanting. The ground beneath it and the space surrounding it spoke of a living presence.

Mother Theresa.

Maggie slowed her stride, then turned to join him.

"A peach tree?" Jampal queried.

"No, *saqed*, an almond tree." Michael's voice quickened. "It's a sign."

"You believe in signs now?" Maggie jested.

Not answering, Michael looked up into the branches of the tree, lost in his own knowledge. "We call Jeremiah a prophet, from the Greek *prophetes*, one who speaks for another. The one for whom Jeremiah spoke was God, who addressed him as *ne'um Yahweh*, Oracle of Yahweh. When he was given his call as a young boy, he was told, 'Before you came forth from the womb I declared you holy, a prophet to the nations I made you.'

"Jeremiah responded, 'I do not know how to speak, for I am only a boy.' Yahweh's response was, 'Do not say, *I am only a boy*, for on all that I send, you shall go and all that I command, you shall speak. You must not be afraid because of them, for I am with you to rescue you.' "

Michael was enjoying his rendition, finally feeling in his element. " 'Look I have put my words in your mouth. See, I have appointed you this day over the nations and over the kingdoms: to uproot and to break down, to destroy and to overthrow, to build up and to plant.'

"Then Jeremiah was asked, 'What do you see?' Jeremiah responded, 'An almond branch, I see.' And Yahweh said: 'You are good at seeing, for I am watching over my word to do it.' "

Maggie and Jampal looked astounded as they listened intently, eyes riveted on Michael as he spoke.

"And ever since," Michael concluded, "the blossoming almond has been a sign of God watching over his children."

"You seem to know your Old Testament."

They all turned toward the unfamiliar voice. The speaker was a blue-eyed, fair-skinned woman robed in white, her head wrapped with a blue and white veil. She moved toward them, a steady but forbidding countenance. "And as Jesus said, 'There is no good tree which produces bad fruit, nor, on the other hand, a bad tree which produces good fruit.' "

Michael nodded respectfully in concurrence.

"I am Sister Marie Bernarde," she said. "This almond tree is indeed special. Not only does it speak to us of fearless obedience to a calling shown by Jeremiah but it also breathes the limitless love of a mother for her children. It was planted here by Antoinette Pierre, a French woman from the Pyrenees Mountain region. Disenchanted with Western life, she came to India in the late fifties seeking holiness, *ganja* and adventure. With Gandhi and Alexandra David-Neel as her heroes, she studied yoga, Khatak dancing and Tibetan Buddhism with the early émigrés."

Sounds like Rachel, Michael thought, his sad reverie quieting his mood.

"Then, as the years progressed," Sister Marie continued, "Antoinette heard of Mother Theresa's work. She moved to Calcutta and became a lay volunteer at *Nirmal Hriday*—Pure Heart—the Mission of Charity Home for the Dying. For ten years she washed and changed bandages for the wretched of the earth."

"Following in the Mother's footsteps," Maggie added.

"As do we all," the nun replied, her eyes moving over the three of them. "Now, how can I help you travelers today?"

Maggie fidgeted. *There's something here.* She was sure of it. Issa had left his mark.

"We are pilgrims," Lama Jampal replied, "here to visit your holy grounds."

"Then perhaps you would like to visit the Durga Nath temple site?" Marie Bernarde's smooth round face and dark eyes revealed a hint of mystery. "I think you will find it interesting."

As they proceeded forward, Maggie positioned herself in front of the group, traversing the increasingly rough path as if she had done it before. Suddenly, the slope crested and she walked up to the edge of a shallow pool, the dark water mysterious and quiet. Just to her right was a small temple, or what Maggie could see of it. Moss and age had conspired to make it appear as if it had sprouted from the hillside. When her gaze moved upward, Maggie saw several spires were rising from its flat roof, while on each tier below, crows, like guardians, were watching them with an air of authority and defiance.

"As part of the arrangement we made with the previous landowner, Mr. Narendra, this area—Durga Nath—is managed by his family," Sister Marie informed them. "His son, who lives in Calcutta, raises the funds and provides for the priest."

Sister Marie directed them forward toward an archway that framed a set of massive teak doors. One of them was ajar. Just as she was passing through, Maggie grimaced when she saw the severed goat's head, dyed orange and hanging from a spike near the door, greeting them with its macabre presence. The goat's eyes were open and set looking directly toward the entrance.

The nun, obviously familiar with the sight, brought them inside without batting an eye. As they all stood silently within the temple's dimly lit foyer, Maggie felt as if a presence was drawing her forward. She was about to speak when she heard Sister Marie's voice.

"I will see you when you are finished."

Surprised, Maggie turned quickly, barely catching sight of the nun's white robe as she exited the door.

CHAPTER 49

"SHE NEVER STAYS." A voice from the shadows offered. "But she has an unfailing knack for knowing which of her visitors Mother wishes brought here."

A young man stepped out of the darkness, slight, dark-skinned, wearing a long white Punjabi shirt that draped over his black pants. "I am Vishnu," he said introducing himself. "I preserve the temple. Actually that is an illusion."

Everything on the Indian subcontinent falls under that category, Maggie thought, wondering who or what might step out of the shadows next.

"Durga is the wrathful element of Mahadevi, the great goddess," their mysterious guide offered. "This Annapurna region is sacred to her, as Mt. Kailas is to Shiva, her consort. Shiva the destroyer and Mahadevi the *shakti*—the creative power—belong together." Vishnu looked squarely at Maggie. "Come, Mother is waiting for you."

Maggie expected to be led further into the main chamber, but Vishnu turned toward the door and directed them back outside just as a crowd of devotees was entering. He circled the building and led them into a grove of ancient brown oak trees—*khasru*—their branches spread wide and low. As they walked, a curious misty fog began to settle onto the grounds, each tiny droplet looking distinctly visible, appearing to be chasing after the next.

"The home of the Mahavidyas, the Mother's ten faces," Vishnu announced, stopping just in front of them. "This is the oldest building on our temple site. Its origin lies beyond any time we know, perhaps even before the time of the Swayambhu stupa. It is guarded by *nagas,* serpents of the hidden world."

Maggie could barely see a stone wall ahead, the thick mist obscuring anything she couldn't reach out and touch. Then, in the next instant, a shaft of sunlight pierced through the fog, casting a golden haze into the grove.

Now as they walked forward, forms began to take shape. What Maggie had thought was a random piling of stones turned out to be a tightly woven tapestry of massive boulders, each fitting together almost seamlessly—a dome of glistening black rocks.

After leading them to a stone stairway, Vishnu motioned for them to follow him down. Once at the bottom, they were faced with a forbidding doorway through which Vishnu vanished. As she stared into the darkness, Maggie wondered why he hadn't said anything. She decided to enter. Finally, when Vishnu turned on the lights, she realized she was standing in the middle of a huge shrine room.

She turned toward Michael and Jampal who had followed her in. They all stared at Vishnu who regarded them with the slightest hint of a smile.

"The gatekeepers of light and darkness, *Dvarapalas*," was all he said.

In the middle of the far wall, a life-size brass statue of Durga seated on a lion dominated the shrine. With six arms and wearing a jeweled tiara on her head, the deity was a formidable presence, her beautiful face and fierce gaze pervading the room.

Maggie glanced at the side walls, each decorated with vividly-colored murals . . . a wrathful *Tara*—the female liberator—dark blue in color, wearing a lion skin and a garland of skulls, standing atop a flaming funeral pyre . . . another protector, *Chinnamasta*, dancing with a sword in one hand and her own severed head in another.

Then as if on cue, Vishnu pointed toward the ecstatic image of yet another female deity. Beautiful and seductive, she was fully naked, her long black hair flowing over her full breasts.

Michael moved closer, giving the picture a shy glance.

"This one is *Bhairavi*, the essence of sexuality," Vishnu revealed. "She is the source of the *Vedas* and kundalini shakti. She is known . . . "

Vishnu's voice began to fade as Maggie left the group and wandered alone through the maze of hallways that splintered off from the main room. She wound her way through the building, until she came upon a passage that led to several other shrine areas. As she was about to turn back, she noticed one last door at the end of the dark hallway.

Maggie ventured forward. Upon entering the room, what she saw in the muted light made her stare in disbelief.

In front of her, in a niche chiseled into the rock surface, was an unmistakably Greco-Roman style, wooden statue—a woman, wrapped in a red and green robe, standing with her right hand extended in a gesture of blessing. In her left hand, she held a carved image of a scroll marked with faint, barely discernable lettering.

"In here!" she called out excitedly. "You guys, hurry!"

A few moments later, she heard the men's voices along with their clamoring footsteps. When they entered the room, Maggie pointed toward the three-foot high sculpture. Vishnu, looking pleased with her discovery, gave her a broad smile. Jampal, on the other hand, cocked his head to one side, appearing uncertain what to make of it. When she turned toward Michael, his eyes were wide with amazement.

"It looks like a statue of Mary," Maggie said.

Michael moved even closer to examine the carved figure. "I think you're right. The question is, which Mary?" he asked. He squinted as he tried to make out the words on the scroll.

"Ne desperetis vos qui peccare soletis, exemploque meo vos reparte deo." Michael translated. " 'Those who have strayed, follow me to God.' Perhaps one of the Thomas Christians brought this sculpture. The Gnostic texts, including *Pistis Sophia,* speak of Thomas as being one of the disciples who most closely understood Jesus." Michael paused. "Of course, the texts also speak of another . . . "

Maggie began to see where he was going and her pulse quickened. *If this is what I think it is . . .*

"There's more," he said, as he traced his finger along a faint carving in the rock below the niche. *"Apostola apostolorum.* A title given to Mary Magdalene by Hippolytus in the second century after Christ's death. *Apostle to the apostles."*

Maggie shivered as she stood in the cold underground recess of the stone temple. But feelings of familiarity and recognition soon displaced any discomfort. This room, this image, these words had called to her from the moment they left Ghorapani. *Apostola,* one sent out, a messenger.

When Maggie moved closer to Michael, she suddenly saw what had been hidden within the shadows. Alongside the niche were letters nearly an inch high carved carefully into the rock. The whole wall was filled with words! Despite its obvious age, the dry interior of the room had preserved the script.

"Are you seeing this?" she asked, grabbing Michael's arm.

Michael had been staring at the statue intently until now. When he turned to his side to look at the wall, his mouth fell open.

Jampal came up beside them then. After taking a few moments to peer at the inscription, his head reared back. "Pali, very old style," he said. "I cannot understand it, though." He glanced down toward a block of letters placed at the bottom of the wall. "Wait," he said, his eyes lighting up with amazement. "It says . . . Issa."

As Michael turned toward her, Maggie felt her heart leap.

"I will read it for you," Vishnu offered. As he read the words off the rock surface, his slow melodic translation was entrancing.

> *"Reverence woman, mother of the universe. In her lies*
> *the truth of creation. She is the foundation of all that is*
> *good and beautiful. She is the source of life and death.*
> *Upon her depends the existence of man, because she is*
> *the sustenance of his labors. She gives birth to you in*
> *travail. She watches over your growth. Bless her. Honor*
> *her. Defend her. She is your only friend and sustenance*
> *upon earth. Love your wives and honor them, because*
> *tomorrow they shall be mothers, and later—the mothers*
> *of the human race. Their love ennobles man, soothes*
> *the embittered heart and tames the beast. Wife and*
> *mother—invaluable treasure. They are the adornments of*
> *the universe.*
>
> *"As light divides itself from darkness, so does woman*
> *possess the gift to divide in man good intent from the*
> *thought of evil. Your noblest thoughts shall belong to*
> *woman. Gather from them thy moral strength, which you*
> *must possess to sustain your near ones. Do not humiliate*
> *her, for therein you shall humiliate yourselves. And*

*through this shall you lose the feeling of love without
which naught exists upon earth. Bring reverence to thy
wife and she shall defend you. And all which you do
to mother, to wife, to widow or to another woman in
sorrow—that shall you also do to the Spirit."*

Vishnu turned toward them, his face serene. *"These are the words of
the one called Issa."*

Astounded, Maggie took a deep breath. After a long silence, she
looked up. "It's incredible," she stammered, "a lot more elaborate than
the last saying. Do you think it could really be the words . . . ?"

"Legend says they were spoken by the man from Jerusalem," Vishnu
told them. "They were derived from a fifteen hundred-year-old manuscript preserved by our brothers in Tibet."

*The lost wonders of the world . . . Gospels, Islamic sayings, Tibetan
texts.* Maggie wondered how many more pieces of evidence existed that
had been buried or tossed aside—accidentally or intentionally—by nar-
row-minded guardians of dogma.

They had found the second saying, Maggie knew. It was Christ's
directive to uphold the feminine, to listen to the wisdom of the heart.
The nurturers of the earth would save the earth.

As Jampal bowed his head in deference, Michael walked up to the
carved figure, and in an unusual move, reverently touched the scroll in
her hand.

It was then Maggie felt the *tendrel,* the powerful connection she
had to these men and to finding the secret sayings. She, too, found herself humbled by the beautiful woman who blessed the earth.

CHAPTER 50

ELATED BY THEIR DISCOVERY Maggie, Jampal and Michael set out the following morning toward upper Mustang. Jampal was convinced that the cryptic description on their map matched a location known as *the Beak*.

Walking alongside the Kali Gandaki gorge, with the peaks of Dhaulagiri and Annapurna rising formidably into the sunlit sky, they crossed yet another suspension bridge as the roaring river slithered through the chasm below.

On the other side, alongside a high waterfall, they came across a guesthouse. Michael walked up to the front window where he could see a display case filled with an assortment of baked goods. Although he was amused by the oddity of finding the little bakery in the middle of nowhere, he was most definitely tempted by what was behind the glass—a tantalizing array of chocolate cakes, frosted cookies, donuts and tarts.

Hanging just above the case, a handwritten message on a wooden sign gave a directive:

> Eat dessert first
> life is uncertain

Michael couldn't agree more. Despite being teased by Maggie and Jampal about his sweet tooth, he fortified their supplies with confection-sugared goodies.

Now, we're ready to forge ahead.

Michael soon realized that although eating chocolate donuts was uplifting, their journey that day would prove as hard as any other.

Through Kalopani and Marpha, the threesome waged war against the wind and dust. To Michael's dismay, Jampal barely wanted to stop on this final leg of their venture. Maggie was no help to his cause either, as she consistently backed Lama Jampal's insistence that they keep moving. Finally, it appeared that relief was in sight. The long cavernous trail opened out into a living, breathing market square, and various shops and vendors came into view.

"We've reached Jomsom, the regional headquarters." Lama Jampal's voice was quivering with excitement. Michael had seen Jampal stern, formidable, friendly, even amused. But childlike . . . this was a first.

So this is the district headquarters of Mustang.

Michael soon learned that Mustang had previously been a forbidden kingdom. Isolated and barren, the area had remained untouched for centuries even though it was located on what was once one of the major trade routes.

"Salt and wood flowed from Tibet into Nepal and India, while goods like rice came from the regions to the south," Lama Jampal informed them. "Also, butter, tea, *chang*—"

"*Chang* . . . that's beer," Maggie poked at Michael, smiling.

"I know," he answered dryly.

" . . . as well as dried and smoked yak meat and wool," Jampal added, conveying a sense of pride in Asian commerce as heavily laden horses and ponies with jingling bells carried their loads past them.

When they ventured further, they came upon an amazing sight. *An airport!* Michael turned toward Maggie, who let out an audible sigh. *The sound of regret,* he thought.

"There was probably a flight here from Pokhara." Maggie, her hair disheveled, her blouse hanging loosely over her jeans, looked longingly at the few small planes on the runway.

"What's this?" Michael ribbed. "Is Lara Croft regretting her adventurous journey on foot?"

Maggie gave him a wry smile.

"We go to Kagbeni," Lama Jampal directed, maintaining his full-speed-ahead manner.

Michael sighed. *There's no stopping him.*

They followed the rocky bank trail next to the river, sharp precipices protruding like arrowheads above them. Jampal explained that their next destination, Kagbeni, was located on top of the highest cliff that guarded the entrance into Upper Mustang. There, the rivers of the Kali Gandaki and Jhong Khola met.

Rocky dry mountains surrounded them as they walked for what seemed like forever. Finally, after passing through several wheat and barley fields, they approached another mountainous ridge.

Maggie stopped suddenly. A look of discouragement crossed her face as she pointed ahead. "Look," she said.

In front of them, the Kali Gandaki River flowed into a massive, naturally-formed rock tunnel and disappeared. It would be impossible to follow.

Lama Jampal, after assessing the situation, gave his directive. "We must climb up the rock gully. There is a small hotel at the top where we can stay."

Hotel? Cursing to himself, Michael nodded at the lama despite his reluctance, not wanting to betray he was finding it hard to keep up. In any case, he longed to rest, so any "hotel" would do at this point.

Yet, he had to admit, now even he felt driven to arrive at their final marker in Mustang—Lo Manthang.

As Michael had suspected, the hotel Lama Jampal mentioned didn't turn up until a couple of hours after they passed Kagbeni and proved to be barely more than a shack. After a fitful night of sleeping on what Michael would have sworn were rice sacks, they headed out at the crack of dawn to continue their trek.

Now, several hours later, definitely not feeling bright-eyed or bushy-tailed, Michael was glad to finally see their arduous climb prove fruitful as they crossed the pass at Nyi La. A gentle descent through the valley under ochre and gray cliffs eventually led them to another make-shift wooden bridge. Seasoned by their previous experience, they ventured forward, shaky but determined, passing over the waters of the Tangmar Chu.

But as it turned out, challenging fate paid off. Michael was transfixed by what they encountered on the other side—a three hundred meter long *mani wall* made of stones, inscribed endlessly with the Tibetan mantra, *Om Mani Padme Hum.*

As he turned toward Jampal to express his astonishment, the lama just smiled and pointed ahead, the stupendous wall not swaying him in the least. Even still, Michael thought Jampal was finally beginning to show signs of wear. His hair, soaked in sweat, lay clinging to the sides of his neck. The bags under his eyes appeared fuller, and his shoulders, normally pulled back and proud, were now slumped forward from fatigue.

"Almost there," Jampal said, breathing heavily.

Michael no longer believed him. No sooner did they reach the top of a ridge, than Jampal had them descending another path, crossing a stream and back up another incline. When they crested the top, Michael nearly doubled over from fatigue. After taking a moment to regain his breath, he straightened up and found himself staring straight at what looked like a medieval fortress.

The walled city! In that instant, he realized where he was.

"Lo Manthang, the Plain of Aspiration," Jampal said, raising his arm as if greeting an old friend. "There is a single gated entrance." He turned and pointed. "There, at the northeast corner."

Immediately upon entering the city, Michael felt they had passed through a door to an ancient kingdom. A tight, unpaved road packed with mud brick houses was filled to the brim with people. Small knots of men, their faces ruddy and rogue-like, eyed their approach with incisive stares. Michael could see their long sheathed daggers, hilts crested with turquoise and coral, dangling at their hips. Unnerved, he found the men's raw and natural presence both awesome and frightening.

"These guys don't look particularly compassionate," Michael observed.

"Ah, they're pussycats," Maggie jested.

But Michael took in the fact that she kept her distance.

Jampal, appearing to be oblivious to their banter, nudged him, pointing.

Michael could see that just ahead, bareheaded monks clad in ceremonial robes were waiting, instruments in hand, while brilliantly clad men and women formed a line behind them at the end of the wall. Suddenly, the monks started beating huge drums, the driving force of the rhythm drawing more people to them.

Just then, several lamas dressed in golden tunics and pointed hats who were standing at the head of the procession, began to walk forward. Immediately, attendant monks dashed toward them and raised colorful umbrellas above the lamas' heads. The crowd followed, chanting *Om Mani Padme Hum*, while spinning prayer wheels and carrying banners—tributes to the wind, *the lung*. Everywhere, brightly colored prayer flags, hanging from houses and carried on poles, flapped graciously in the breeze.

"We seem to have arrived on a special day," Maggie noted.

"They're celebrating *Saka Dawa*, the day of the Buddha's enlightenment." Lama Jampal was now in his element.

As the crowd, dynamic and vivid, proceeded onto a barren field, the three of them decided to follow. Michael found that once out under the stark blue sky, the colorfully-clad men and women with their reddish brown cheeks, long greased hair and black eyes looked even more striking.

Michael then noticed that one lama in particular presided over the function. Sitting on a high throne, his head was crowned with a tall, broad yellowish-gold hat.

"It's called a Gampopa hat, named after a high lama of the Kagyu lineage. You've never heard of it, I assume," Maggie quipped.

"No, Your Magnificence, I haven't."

"Ah, there's so much for you to know," she said, winking. "So much for you to discover."

Michael stared at her. "What's gotten into you all of a sudden? You seem especially lighthearted. Did you buy an airline ticket at Jomsom for the trip back?"

Maggie smiled at him. No longer joking, her eyes penetrated his, conveying an appreciation and warmth. Touched by her sincerity, Michael shyly lowered his head, a rush of heat moving into his face.

The subtle winds of the desert-like landscape added to the mystery as Jampal focused on the scene unfolding before him. A group of the largest, fiercest-looking men began tugging hard on a thick braided rope that was attached to a stout-looking pole around thirty-feet long. As the pole raised higher with each jarring effort, the crowd cried out with excitement.

Michael moved toward him then, a questioning look in his eyes. "What's the significance of all this?"

Jampal was happy to find him interested in the ritual. "The people believe it is an auspicious omen if the pole can be made to stand pointing toward the sky," he explained.

Just then, like an army captain, an older, gnarly-skinned Khampa stepped forward shouting directions, every word followed uniformly by the infantry hoisting the pole. Finally, with one loud *aaah* from the crowd, the pole stood erect in the middle of the dry barley field, an image of the Buddha Shakyamuni waving victoriously at the top.

Everyone burst into cheers.

Great effort, unity, drive, passion, lifting the burden upward, to move it with the wind.

Jampal smiled quietly. When he turned toward Michael and Maggie, he saw they were both overcome by the power of the moment.

Now the Buddha's enlightenment could be celebrated with even more happiness and abandon. Jampal watched as broad smiles, pats on the back, and *chang* began to flow through the crowd. Soon, several young monks appeared, pulling a cart onto the field. They placed their precious cargo—a gold statue—atop a large rock close to the base of the pole. It was an image of a Buddha sitting on a lotus, his large face emanating loving kindness.

"The future Buddha . . . Maitreya," Jampal said, holding his hands in prayer mudra. He was about to speak further when, suddenly, he felt his throat tighten at the sound of a familiar voice.

CHAPTER 51

"JAMPAL!" The voice was gruff and forceful.

Reluctantly, Jampal turned. "Norbu Lama," he greeted, his tone reserved. Of course they had to meet up with the last man on earth he wanted to see.

"You are finally back, after two years." Norbu extended his hand in greeting. A short stocky lama in his sixties, he held his mouth in a tense purse.

Jampal cringed internally but took Norbu's hand despite his misgiving. After all, better to eat honey with your enemies. "I have come this time as a guide," Jampal said. The half-truth would do for now.

Norbu turned, eyeing Maggie and Michael with suspicion. "Americans?"

"That we are," Michael replied, giving Jampal a concerned look.

Norbu, short on niceties and decorum, directed his gaze back toward Jampal. "We must talk."

Jampal walked aside with him, dreading what was about to come.

Norbu took a deep breath as he turned toward him. "We waited for your reply," he said sternly. "Why wouldn't you speak with us?"

Jampal's voice fell to a whisper. "You know I will not be a part of any uprising, either here or in Kathmandu."

"We find that position troubling. Do you realize your loyalties to the lineage are now in question?"

"Who thinks I'm not loyal to my own lineage?" Jampal challenged. "A bunch of demons who pervert the meaning of the Dharma they teach?"

Norbu set his jaw angrily. His nostrils flared.

Jampal's first impulse was to walk away from the *yo-gyu* lama. But he realized, although deceptive and shifty, Norbu might be able to help them find their final location. "Perhaps we can talk later," he said in his most conciliatory voice. "I am here for a few days."

At that moment, Maggie and Michael joined them.

"Let us at least drink like in the old days," Jampal cajoled. "Any differences we have can be settled, Norbu. After all, don't we both still believe in the same things . . . freedom for Tibet, for our people?"

Norbu eyed the others. "What about your friends?"

"Don't worry. They both like a little whiskey now and then." Although Jampal no longer drank, he would put on the face of a guzzling revolutionary if it meant attaining their goal.

Norbu gave Michael a hard slap on the back and smiled at Maggie condescendingly.

"Yes, that's right," Maggie crooned. "You know us American women. We can take it like a man."

An uproarious laugh bellowed from his unsavory old cohort. Obviously amused by Maggie's remark, Norbu appeared less apprehensive now. He ushered them out from the midst of the crowd. "The Nepalese Army checkpoint," he said, nodding toward a large stone structure appearing to be an old fort. "Those soldiers have eyes like hawks. They sent me to bring you to them."

"Sent *you?*" Jampal was alarmed by the remark.

"Yes, me. I work with them now. "

Jampal cocked his head, surprised at the blunt admission and the direction his old comrade, a Tibetan loyalist, had taken.

Norbu looked at him unfazed, his dark eyes piercing. His gaze then shifted toward Maggie and Michael. "All cultures have a similar saying, I believe. Keep your friends close, but your enemies . . . "

"Closer." Maggie finished the phrase.

"Yes, that's right." Norbu's mouth was held in a sneer, his distaste for women becoming more apparent.

"My friends are on a research expedition," Jampal said. "They are looking for a special area—the Precipice of the Beak."

Norbu raised his eyebrows with a sense of recognition. "Why? What is so special about *that* place?"

Jampal realized Norbu wasn't about to divulge any information without first finding out if there was any monetary gain to be had.

"It's purely for historical reasons, I assure you," Michael interjected. "I am writing a novel and was told about this area from some friends who did a trek up here several years ago. They referred to a special cave, possibly used by the great yogi, Milarepa."

"A history novel," Norbu concluded.

"We will pay you well, Norbu, if you can direct us to it." Lama Jampal knew the time for more cajoling was at hand. It went a long way in Tibetan culture. "Perhaps you will even be mentioned in Dr. Sonada's book."

Michael darted a glance at Jampal. "Uh, yes, yes, that's right. Of course, an honorable mention."

"And some compensation," Norbu was quick to add.

"Yes." Michael reached into the small travel pack around his waist. "Here's a twenty."

The Tibetan stared blankly at him.

Michael then pulled a fifty-dollar bill from his money belt. He added it to the "compensation" before zipping the pack back up, indicating he had reached his limit. Norbu, maneuvering his palm over Michael's as if in a handshake, took hold of the cash.

Slippery fingers, Jampal thought.

Seventy American dollars richer, Norbu's manner turned from sour to sweet. "Of course, I can show you. You can see it from here. Look." He pointed beyond the outskirts of the city where a large precipice jutted from the side of a cliff. Even from that distance, it looked like a sharp pointed triangle, hanging over the barren land below.

"The Precipice of the Beak." Jampal looked at it with wonder. "I was told of the place when I traveled here last. I never knew it was so close."

Maggie's eyes were alight with excitement. "It looks like there's a small gompa there."

Jampal saw she was right. Perched back on the precipice, a monastery had been built around a cave entrance.

Maggie shaded her eyes from the glare as she surveyed the area. Looking frustrated, she turned toward Norbu. "How do we get up there?" she asked.

"You go nowhere before coming with me to the checkpoint." Norbu was tired of this Western woman. He didn't like the self-assertion he heard in her voice. Even some Tibetan women were beginning to open their mouths a little too much.

Women's rights!

They forget it is *men* who fight for them, who will win them their freedom. What more did they want? *Give them the yaks and give them the children* was the motto he professed.

"Well then, let's get on with it, shall we?" Maggie decided to push the little Tibetan rat around. Checkpoint or no checkpoint, she wanted to lose this Norbu character as quickly as possible.

Jampal headed their anxious group as he walked with Norbu toward the army post.

Soldiers everywhere. Gray uniforms, green berets. Maggie realized it was just a new scene built upon the old. For years, Mustang had been a central district for guerilla operations in the Tibetan fight against the Chinese. The *Khampas*, from eastern Tibet, had waged their war along this so-called "border." The remnants remained. Sadly, although skirmishes at the crossroads entering Tibet had practically ceased, some attempts at fighting were still made by those who couldn't forget their homeland.

Maggie felt a sense of foreboding as the group approached the checkpoint. Several soldiers were straddling the fences around the old stables. Some were smoking their little bidi cigarettes, puffs of white smoke hovering above them in the cool air.

The border patrol.

Norbu led them up some narrow stone steps and into the armory. Then, without saying a word, he took several steps back, pointed ahead, and turned to leave.

Great. Maggie thought. *So much for fearless Tibetans.*

The group walked down a long dimly-lit hallway, arriving at a door flanked by two lean young soldiers armed with rifles. Both eyed them suspiciously as they entered the small dank sovereignty of the captain's office.

The checkpoint guardian apparently presided over his terrain with, what seemed to Maggie, little respect or care. As if coming out of a stupor, he roused himself at the sight of their presence. As he stood up, he ran his fingers through his hair and placed a Nepali beret squarely on this head.

"Permits." The one word directive from the captain didn't sound welcoming.

"Sir." Jampal was quick to the forefront. "We did not intend to trek this distance. I'm an old lama, sir. We became lost and then just followed the pilgrims who were coming here for the Shakyamuni feast and to celebrate this holy day. If you would allow us to show you our credentials . . . "

"We have our passports." Michael pulled his out of his side pocket.

The captain snapped at Jampal in Nepalese. Maggie, getting the gist of what was being said, stood by quietly.

"Yes, of course," Jampal said, nodding deferentially. He turned toward Michael. "Give me more money."

"Holy shi—"

"Do you want to continue this journey?"

"I don't have anymore. Just some traveler's checks I haven't cashed."

The Nepalese soldier seemed to understand the course of their conversation. "No money, then no permit."

"But I can assure you—" Michael pleaded.

"You can assure me nothing," the officer barked back. "You Americans think you are so privileged. You think you can walk into any land and act like you own it. You are on Nepali soil within a restricted kingdom. You either pay or you shall find your justice at our Kathmandu military headquarters."

Jampal tried to halt what appeared to Maggie to be an oncoming train. "But sir!" Jampal implored.

"Mahend! Ramir! Get in here!" In a flurry of anger, the unyielding captain called out to his inferiors. "Take these people back on the next transport to Kathmandu. They have illegally entered the District of Mustang and must face proper penalty." He came out from behind his desk and stood before them menacingly. "All of you will go with these men."

On that note, Jampal nodded at both Michael and Maggie to comply without complaint.

"I'm *not* leaving," Maggie announced sternly. She thought both Michael and Jampal would keel over from shock.

Clearly furious, the captain took several steps toward her. She had upped the ante, and from the look on his face Maggie realized, *This guy's not gonna fold.*

Eyes blazing with anger, the captain's body tightened. "Take them out now!" he yelled at his officers, practically spitting as he spoke.

With the two soldiers behind them, the three companions were escorted from the fort toward a gravel road. As they walked down the incline, loose slippery gravel beneath their feet, Maggie was distracted by the blaring horns of several trucks just entering the compound at the bottom of the hill. No longer watching her footing, she lost her balance and fell to her side, scraping her arms on the sharp stones.

Suddenly, a loud snarl made them all turn. From her vantage point on the ground, Maggie saw the leopard. Tawny gold and white-fanged, her beauty quickly took a back seat to her ferocity. The leopard reared and sprung upon a boulder about ten feet away.

Jampal started to step back slowly and motioned for her and Michael to do the same. Cautiously, Michael helped her to her feet, and the two of them began to back away.

Ramir, who had been standing petrified, was now fumbling with fright. He barely managed to lift his rifle when the leopard changed her course and scurried up the boulders, reaching the crag just above their heads. Frightened by the animal's sudden move, Ramir, still shaking, dropped his weapon. In a bold move, Maggie came up behind him and kicked it, sending the rifle sailing down over the loose dirt onto the rocks below.

"Crazy woman! You're crazy!" The wiry young soldier began to crawl backward to get down to the convoy when the cat leapt across a narrow ravine on his left and onto level ground not far from the group.

Meanwhile, Ramir's companion, Mahend, muttering curses, kept his eyes glued on the leopard, who made no other move but to pace and growl continuously, occasionally peering over the side of the ridge at Ramir's descending figure.

Then, apparently realizing it was no match for a leopard attack, Mahend threw his rifle to the ground. Looking both frightened and angry, he fell onto his belly and began sliding down the slope, following Ramir's flight.

All the while Michael, Maggie and Jampal had been slowly retreating, making no sudden moves that might alarm the animal. Frightened, Maggie was breathing quickly, yet she couldn't help being awed by the leopard's grace and power.

"Stop," Jampal suddenly directed.

The leopard's gaze had been fixed steadily on the two men. Now, with Ramir nearly at the bottom of the slope and Mahend following closely behind, the cat leapt gracefully to the higher rocks. She moved around the edge of the ridge and disappeared from view.

At that moment, Maggie felt a sense of raw power—her own. The leopard appeared to have emboldened Michael as well, as he ventured to walk alone, looking toward the ridge where the ferocious cat had stood only a moment before.

Jampal walked toward them, his eyes flashing with a fierce determination. "Let's get to the Beak." Not waiting, he sprinted forward before either one of them could reply.

Maggie glanced quickly at Michael. A split second was all she needed to see his reserve had turned to courage. Then without a word, they ran together, following Jampal back toward the forbidden kingdom and the temple cave.

CHAPTER 52

J AMPAL LED THEM east, just out of Lo Monthang, into an area that few trekkers had ventured. Now, as they reached the base of several cliffs, Jampal finally indicated they should stop.

"There," he said, pointing up to a ledge hanging about one hundred meters up.

It had become harder to see the gompa as they had gotten closer to the precipice, but now from their new angle, Maggie could see its base. Sandstone pillars upheld the blood-red mud bricks that surrounded the sacred cave.

"The question still remains. How do we get up there?" Michael grimaced, not appearing to relish the idea of trying to scale the dangerous rock face.

"Somewhere there's got to be a path," Jampal said, looking determined. He began beating his way into the brush.

Michael, resigned, tugged on her arm and they both started tearing at the low branches. They hadn't been searching long, before Jampal suddenly cried out.

"Here!" he yelled, pointing.

Maggie saw he was standing before a narrow footpath that had been hidden from view only moments before. The path wound up the side of the cliff toward the gompa.

Jampal immediately started the ascent. Following right behind him, Maggie found she needed to lean forward to brace herself on the jutting rocks as they scaled higher. Thirty minutes later and with a few more scratches for the wear, she reached Jampal's side at the cave entrance. Michael, breathless from the climb, came up beside her.

"You first," Maggie said, eyeing Michael with a hint of daring.

In front of them was a notched plank walkway that connected the lower opening of the cave to the actual entrance.

Expecting a teasing jab in return, to her surprise, Michael obliged with a smile. As he led the way across, she hurried to follow, Jampal, his hand on her shoulder, walking right behind her. After reaching the other side, she found they were standing in front of a single doorway, the wooden door already ajar.

With Michael still leading them, they entered the temple cave. Butterlamps were flickering on the shrine at the back of the cavern. By their light, Maggie could see that the rough rock walls were covered with murals of Indian and Tibetan yogis. Although the artwork was worn with age, Maggie could still make out much of the detail. *Quite an accomplishment for its day*, she thought, guessing *its day* to be somewhere around the twelfth or thirteenth century.

There was something about the cave, though, far beyond the artwork, that felt extraordinary. Maggie sensed a powerful energy, the presence of the *siddhas*—the yogic masters—who had dedicated their lives to reaching enlightenment. Caves were their havens in the past. Perhaps several had meditated in this very one . . . maybe even the great Tibetan yogi, Milarepa. In fact, she had no doubt.

From the shadows another source of light appeared. A young monk carrying a large, silver butterlamp entered the room. Walking in just behind him was a strikingly tall lama, wearing a white shawl over his traditional red robes.

The room, lit by the surrounding flames of the butterlamps, was now brightened further by the addition of the large lamp. Light danced upon the walls as the older monk, appearing to be in his thirties, began to speak.

"Tashi delek, I am Lama Rangjung. Welcome." He opened his white shawl and bowed graciously, then covered his shoulder with it once again. "You have come to visit us on quite an auspicious day. The day of the Lord Buddha's enlightenment. It is also on this day that we honor the Buddha to come, *Maitreya*."

As the younger monk placed the large butterlamp on the shrine, the dancing firelight shone on a golden figure. Michael looked toward Maggie then, the light of recognition in his eyes. The statue was the same they had seen brought before the crowd in the barley field where the huge prayer pole had been placed. Maggie felt her mind lifting as her eyes settled on the image of *Maitreya*, the awakened Buddha.

Jampal turned toward Rangjung, breaking the silence. "Lama, following the path of Issa, we seek Shambhala. Our search has led us here."

In a thoughtful silence, Rangjung looked at the three of them before answering. "Reaching Shambhala is the great human destiny, the highest of human attainments. It has been known by many names, through many faiths. It is both heavenly and earthly. It appears and it is nonexistent. The best of humans, the greatest of minds, the highest of character, the purest of hearts . . . all seek Shambhala."

"We have been searching for the secret sayings of Christ." Maggie, impassioned by the moment, addressed the monk. "We wish to bring his lost words, the sounds of peace, back to the world in order to restore it, to heal old wounds and open hearts."

"Each river has many tributaries," Rangjung said. "They are enticing, leading us down streams to myriad worlds. Some do not want to stay the course of the river, but for those who do, they find the source of the light. Those of *the Way* are messengers of that light. The community of Shambhala also exists within the world. Even today they live in all corners of the earth . . . rays of hope and enlightenment."

As she listened, Maggie thought of Professor Samuels, Ananda, and the young Hindu priest. There were, undoubtedly, countless others.

Rangjung smiled at her softly. "The Kalachakra, the wheel of time, is a sacred teaching that has been protected and practiced in the pure land of Shambhala. A spiritual system by which a heavenly kingdom is created by the power of the mind, it is the Wish-fulfilling Jewel . . . the great *Chintamani.*"

The word resonated in Maggie's mind. *Chintamani.* Samuels had told them the Grail was the *Lapsis Excellis*, the precious stone. The correlation between the precious stone of the Grail and the Wish-fulfilling Jewel of the Shambhala myth was becoming even more palpable.

"This Issa . . . this Jesus so venerated in your world, is the Christ whose heart was open, enlightened, compassionate. Yet, some people have created different "christs." Fantasies replace reality. Childish veneration replaces true discipleship. All sides claim to have God on their side in the wars they create. This God must be a divided one indeed, yet division is not God. Only unity is divine."

Michael eyed the monk curiously. "But in reality there isn't unity. There are different religions, different doctrines, different cultures all vying for their version of the truth to prevail."

Rangjung smiled, the light in his eyes never faltering. "Which truth, relative or ultimate? Are the gospels themselves Christianity? The Kabbalah, Judaism? Or the Quran, Islam? Or are they aspects of enlightened mind springing from the same source? Can it be that all truths emanate from vast, divine enlightenment, from nowhere else, so all truths that are taught spring from this one divinity?"

Rangjung moved toward a large thangka on the wall, a picture of the future Buddha, *Maitreya*, holding a double *dorje* in the form of a cross. Maggie immediately understood its meaning. Indestructible truth . . . emptiness . . . compassion. Standing before Maitreya in the picture were the gathering peoples of all nations—Hindus, Muslims, kings and commoners—all the peoples of the world bowing before the spirit of truth.

As Rangjung's eyes filled with compassion, Maggie felt he understood what they were seeking. Like others before and others to come, the hearts of humans yearned for the highest good, searched for a place created by the wisdom of their own minds.

A pure land.

CHAPTER 53

RANGJUNG MOTIONED FOR THEM to follow him into an inner chamber. They entered a cavern within the cave, its high domed ceiling covered with the images of Tibetan yogis. *The Eight Mahasiddhas.* Michael remembered the term from one of Rachel's texts. The yogic figures were all looking down upon a small Tibetan stupa, a *chorten*, which sat centrally within the space.

Rangjung lit a stick of jasper incense and placed it in the burner. As Michael watched the smoke swirl upward toward Maitreya's gaze, he sensed something unusual. It was as if he was watching the essence of his own mind, finally free, moving into the unknown world of Shambhala.

The beautiful woman with the flowing black hair moves forward. Her hands are the color of blood as she touches the man's feet. They have taken him from the cross after his death so the family can hold him. The old man, Joseph, has brought his servants to carry the body to a grave belonging to his family.

"Longinus, don't go."

A whispering voice comes from behind me. A loyal Roman soldier, Demetrius, urges me to stay with my men.

"The man is dead. Let him go," he says.

Instead, I follow the women and the old man down the hill and watch as they progress through the streets.

"What do you want?" Joseph turns suddenly, questioning.

"You are Joseph."

"Yes, what is it that you want?" he asks again.

"I wish to follow the Rabbi."

"He is dead. You witnessed it."

I look toward the woman whose hair is as black as her cloak, who I have seen many times at the Rabbi's side. The one called Magdalene.

She turns toward me. The face I have viewed from afar looks pale. Yet her blue eyes are like piercing bands of light.

"Let him come," she tells the old man.

"But he is a Roman soldier," he warns.

"I saw his compassion." She walks ahead leading the women.

When we reach the burial cave, they lay the Rabbi's body gently upon a smooth stone, wrapping him in a shroud. The Sabbath will begin soon, and the women are concerned that they will not be able to anoint the body with oils.

"Now is not the time," Joseph tells them.

Magdalene turns toward the others. "It grows dark. We must come after the Sabbath. Please take Mary home, comfort her and tend to her needs. I must go and meditate and prepare. Now teachings on death must be practiced."

Her stately gaze falls upon me. Is she the Rabbi's main disciple? Where are the men I have seen him with in the temple and on the streets? None have come but this young one, John. He begins to lead the Rabbi's mother and the other women away.

I wish to go with them, but Magdalene's eyes give no such approval. "You must go now," she says.

I touch her shoulder. "How will I find you?"

"I live here in Judea. You can visit me whenever you wish," she says. "Then, when it is time for me to leave, you will come with me." The shadows of the evening fall upon her face as she turns and walks away.

There is no question in my mind that I will.

Several days later . . . commotion, accusations.

Are they lying? They must be, some of the soldiers and some of the Jews are saying. But others, like me, believe. Did the Rabbi rise? Is he enlightened as some say? I believe it, and Magdalene knows it.

The women of the village come to Magdalene's home, and some of the young men have started coming as well. They listen as she tells them stories in the evenings, while the small iron kettle heats above the fire pit. Cups of tea are made and wine is also offered to quench the thirst of those who come. The Master taught through stories, and now, so does she. Sometimes people come who she takes special interest in. She walks in her small garden with them, separating them from the rest, divulging deeper knowledge. I know this to be true, since I am one to whom she speaks in this way. I am always hungry for more, but she will only give me morsels of teachings, enough for the time. When the right moment comes again, she says, then more will be given.

One evening, while sitting on the old wooden bench in her garden, I hear them arrive. It is Peter, and the tax collector they call Matthew is with him. Peter calls Magdalene out into the garden and speaks to her without restraint.

"Who are you?" he questions, standing with her under the olive tree in front of her door. "Do you think you can teach without speaking to the rest of us first?"

"I know that I can teach. The Master said—"

"Don't tell me what he said!" Peter shouts angrily. "I was there with him as well. I ate with him and lived with him. He taught all of us."

"But differently," Magdalene says, lowering her eyes.

"What are you talking about?"

"He gave us all the same teachings when we were together, but separately he gave some of us . . . different teachings. There's nothing for me to explain. I do what I am commended to do."

"Woman, are you saying that we all should be listening to you?" Peter's voice cracks with anger and pain.

Crying, Magdalene does not answer. I know she feels his wound.

"If the Master said she is the first disciple," Matthew says, intervening, "then who are we to say she is unworthy? He knew Magdalene's mind, Peter. That is why he loved her more than he loved us."

"Now you're crazy, too!" Peter reproaches him. He again turns toward Magdalene. "You will not teach about visions and self-knowledge, or about things which lead the people to act according to their own wishes and not abide by the teachings and rules of our church. You cannot just speak to anyone, especially those who are not Jews. Maybe in time, but this is all too soon. It must stop."

Magdalene draws her shawl further around her shoulders. The evening shadows are growing longer and some stars are noticeable in the sky. She looks at Peter directly, with sorrow but with determination. "I do not wish there to be a rift between us, but I will teach as I do. The Master is with me."

"Then maybe you should do it elsewhere."

"Peter!" Matthew's voice betrays the shame he feels. "Please, let us go," he urges.

Peter quickly turns to leave. Matthew glances sorrowfully at Magdalene before following him into the darkness.

Under the olive tree, Magdalene stands quietly. The other apostles have been like her brothers, even though some of them have been jealous of her and of her wisdom and angered by her closeness with the Master. Still, they have always stood together. Now she will have to stand alone.

The next morning, a young woman in a gray and maroon dress knocks upon my door in a way which implies hurry. "Magdalene says she is leaving."

That is all I need to hear. I gather my belongings in my sack and fasten the beaten leather sandals around my feet. I place the spear in the leather looped belt tied around my waist. An old tan shawl covers it all as I wrap myself in it.

I hasten through the streets, no longer feeling my age, the film once obscuring my sight now gone. I see them both, the old man and her, walking in the light rain, moving along the damp road on their way out of the city.

Where to go from here?

They stop at a house and Magdalene enters. Joseph stands alone by the pillar of the doorway as I approach.

"I'm coming with you," I say.

Joseph holds out his hand and takes mine. "I am not going. Make sure she remains safe."

"What will you do?" I ask.

"They wish to speak to me . . . the Sanhedrin," he discloses. "I knew it was time for Magdalene to leave."

I am distressed to hear the temple rulers have summoned him.

Joseph dismisses my look of concern. Instead, he pulls out a large wooden cup from his satchel. The Master's. It is plain, made of dark olive wood, strong and sturdy.

"What does it look like to you?" He holds it up closer to me.

Why ask such a question, I wonder. "It's a cup."

"Really?" he remarks curiously.

"Why do you speak with so much mystery?"

"It appears as it should to the one who is perceiving."

Strange answer, but I have no time to ponder his meaning as he places the cup back into his bag. Magdalene appears then, a large brown satchel strapped across her back. She is strong and no stranger to carrying burdens.

Joseph signals to us both that he is leaving. He bows his head toward Magdalene and looks at her with eyes that convey they will meet again.

"Why didn't you leave Judea sooner?" I ask her as we walk away. "It's been dangerous."

Her eyes sweep over me, acknowledging my wish to protect her. "I wanted to be with the others for a while to help them understand the meaning of the Master's message," she says, as we hurry along the dark wet streets. "But some of them were angry with me for receiving more teachings and for being his companion. Peter will not rid himself of his jealousy."

"They wouldn't let you stay?"

"No, they would never let me be a part of them. After all," she says, "I am only a woman. Isn't that so? I must go elsewhere to teach . . . somewhere where I am not known to anyone."

The flickering of lanterns draws our attention to a small ship docked at the pier ahead. Chilled and wet from the rain, we head up the plank. A man appears on the deck and motions us to hurry on board. He looks to be from Africa—skin as black as night, his nose full and broad. With rings in his ears and wearing a cloth of green, white and red, he is a curious mix of brilliance illuminated in the lantern light.

"When do we leave?" Magdalene asks as she steps under the shelter of a canvas canopy.

"Right away. We have been waiting for you to arrive." The man looks toward me then.

"This is Longinus. He is traveling with me," Magdalene says. "Longinus, this is Captain Mantiag. He will take us to Leptis Magna on the African coast."

The captain nods firmly at me. I notice his eyes are fierce, but also knowing.

Soon the boat heads out to sea, and the flickering lanterns on the dock grow dimmer.

"I loved him," she says, speaking of the Master.

"I know," I reply.

Days later, in the early morning, we finally reach the coast of Tarabulus and the safe waters of Leptis Magna harbor. Once upon the shore, the warm desert wind is the first sign of hope. I am happy to feel the solid earth beneath my feet again. My soldier's legs are made for horses or dirt, not ships.

I don't know what to think when I first encounter the strange men wearing barracans and keffiyahs—their robes and headdresses—riding beautiful stallions across the stirring sands. A young one, learned and assured, approaches and speaks to us in Latin. It is not long before Magdalene and I find ourselves upon their powerful steeds, moving like the wind through the canyons. As dusk approaches, the sky darkens with clouds, and an unexpected cold rain falls. It chills me, but I cannot complain while I am following her. Hair folded within the dark cowls of her shawl, she rides through the night upon her black mare with the intensity of her spirit—chased out of Judea, onto the dark sea, and now into the dusty wind.

The young man, who calls himself Ibrahim al'Mabus, halts our party at the edge of a rocky hill. He tells us to follow him and he will brings us to the elders, the leaders of this tribe of desert men. I watch him as he speaks and notice that the sand, which has blown across our faces and left scratches upon our skin, has not harmed al'Mabus in the least, as if the sharp, fine sand was unable to etch its mark upon him.

He leads the way toward a passage in the rock, keeping a distance between himself and Magdalene. The women walk behind in this land, I notice, faces covered by dark veils, not to be seen by men other than their husbands. It is a culture, jealous and possessive.

Inside the cave, the elders of the tribe sit before a fire. They watch us as we move closer. Softly, al'Mabus speaks to them. He then motions for us to sit across from the men whose faces I see clearly now . . . foreheads and cheeks lined in black, faces stony in appearance but for their eyes, which appear glassy and soft, like shifting waters in a lake. They are not eyes fixed on the present appearance of things, but seem to see deeper, far below the surface, penetrating the mystery beyond the world we know.

The men draw strange symbols in the sand, triangular shapes that lie atop one another. Then, within a deep silence, they meditate. After some time, the oldest motions with his staff for food to be brought to us.

Magdalene removes her cowl from around her head. Her long, black hair cascades down her back, and her eyes take on a sensuous softness in the firelight. There is something both divine and radiant about her. She speaks to the men through al'Mabus. "Tell them I know who they are, and that I wish to stay here with my companion for a while in their care. I am aware that they knew the Master."

Surprised, I stare at Ibrahim al'Mabus. Had he met the Master, too?

Their eyes meet then. Magdalene and al'Mabus look at one another as if they share a secret, each knowing of the other in some undefined way.

A moment later, al'Mabus breaks their silent connection when he turns to the elders. Translating her words, his manner now betrays resentment. I wonder, will it ever end for her, this stupid fear and jealousy?

At least, deep underground in the Tarhuna caverns, we are safe for now. I glance around at the figures who sit and move around us, their faces half hidden by their cowls.

The Brotherhood of the Sand.

For so many years I have heard rumors of their mysterious activity from Morocco to Persia . . . shifting, shadow-like, ever present protectors of spirit. They guard the old temples and ritual grounds, the great pyramids and statues, and they watch over the lonely pilgrim who may be wandering through the land.

Months pass before we hear word that Joseph has arrived. He is brought directly to us.

"Do you have the spear?" Joseph asks, his eyes searching mine.

"Longinus has not let it leave his sight," Magdalene replies.

The old man reaches beneath his robe and retrieves a small bundle wrapped in white silk. After the cloth is removed, I see he is holding a simple wooden cup.

"Is that . . . ?" Magdalene begins to question, a look of recognition in her eyes.

"Yes," he answers. Joseph looks toward me, his hand extended.

I reach within my tunic and remove the blade I had used to hasten the Rabbi's death. Reluctantly, I hand it to him.

As Joseph holds the cup and the spear in his hands, a shaft of sunlight enters the cavern making the limestone walls glisten. "This cup by itself has only sentimental meaning, but for many of us it has come to symbolize the mind and spirit of the Master."

The old man's voice barely penetrates the thick fog engulfing my brain. I hear but cannot quite comprehend.

"The spear is power," he says, "the cup, compassion. Power without compassion is deadly. Compassion devoid of power robs you of victory."

Magdalene moves closer to me. The sound of her voice clears away any remaining confusion. "The cup and the spear symbolize the esoteric teachings of compassion and wisdom . . . teachings the Master gave to only his closest and most trusted students, the very essence of his practice. They are what we must preserve and protect at all costs." Her somber tone alerts me. "We cannot allow them to be lost or distorted."

At this moment, the light illuminating the stone walls dims. Quickly, I reach my hand out and retrieve the spear from Joseph, readying myself for a fight. Some movement from across the room then catches my eye and my body stiffens. A member of the brotherhood is standing in the shadows beyond the entrance of the cavern watching me closely, but I cannot make out who he is. My hand instinctively tightens around the lance until he steps forward.

Ibrahim al'Mabus.

One season seems to flow into the next, and a steady stream of believers visit us in Tarhuna, drawn by the power of Magdalene and Joseph's presence. Without regard for their own comfort, they see everyone, giving each person the teaching they require. After every powerful transmission, Magdalene appears weary but translucent, as if some bond between her life and this world is loosening. I understand she is leaving by degrees.

Perhaps I am fading as well. My steps grow heavy. It has been a long time since my youth has ended, long before I had even entered Judea. But as a soldier, I refuse to submit to the thought of old age.

As the days progress, I realize that each sunrise holds the possibility of being my last. The Master's image pervades my mind as witness to the many battles, the thousands of miles of dirt roads, and the forgotten and meaningless campaigns that led me to the Judean wilderness and my new life.

"Who will protect you now?" I ask Magdalene. I look up into the comforting blue of her eyes as she leans over me, placing a wet cloth to my burning forehead.

"You have been my good friend, Longinus, and have protected me ever since the Master's death. Now the brotherhood will help me to keep the teachings safe. Don't worry. Just let me care for you now."

The mist returns to my eyes . . . the mist that the Master's blood had once removed. Across the room I barely make out al'Mabus watching me. He holds the spear within the long sheath at his side. It is he who has been entrusted to guard it now that I am no longer able. I do not wish it to be, but it is. With great difficulty, I turn my head away from him.

I try smiling at Magdalene. I want to lift my hand to wipe the tears from her eyes as she bends over me, but my arm will not move. As if sensing my need, she takes my calloused, old soldier's hand and holds it to her face. Her tears flow freely now, washing my spirit one last time.

Michael felt as if he was awakening from a deep sleep. He lifted his gaze to the wafts of smoke still rising from the incense burner. *Had Maggie and Jampal experienced it, too?* When he turned toward them, the look on both their faces left no doubt.

But before anyone could utter a word, the sound of scurrying feet and voices shattered the silence.

CHAPTER 54

"L AMA! The soldiers, they are here!" the younger monk warned as he came running into the cavern.

"This way." With no time to waste, Lama Rangjung didn't hesitate. "All the signs indicate that the opening is to be revealed once again. Hurry."

Maggie sensed a surefootedness about the lama as he directed them quickly around the small domelike cave through yet another opening.

"Look there," Rangjung said, pointing toward the rock ceiling.

In a dark recess at the corner of the cavern, Maggie could see a sudden shift in the level of the roof.

"It is a secret passage," Rangjung whispered, his eyes penetrating hers. "No one can enter the sacred mandala if they do not belong."

At that moment, the younger monk hurried to their side with a ladder.

"Go up, then into the water," Rangjung instructed. "At this time of year, the river is low. Follow it, and you will find the beyul—the pure land."

There was no time to ask questions. Maggie climbed up first but couldn't see anything other than hard stone. She moved her hand around until she felt a lip in the rock—an opening that curved slightly upward. She stuck her head through it for a moment and saw there was enough room for them to maneuver.

Suddenly, she remembered the Cave of the Five Lakes. *Déjà vu all over again*, she thought. Curling her head back in from under the ledge, she yelled, "Push me!"

Michael looked a bit embarrassed since her rear-end was the only part he would be able to get his hands on.

"Don't worry," she assured him. "I'll pay you back later."

After a good heave, she pulled herself into the chasm and crawled forward on her stomach. Michael and Jampal followed close behind. They continued on their bellies, grappling and sliding across the damp surface. Soon, the narrow tunnel began to slope downward until finally it widened, and one by one they dropped down into the darkness.

The next thing she knew, Maggie was standing in ankle-deep water. *This is where Rangjung said the river flowed.* As she clutched at the wet walls for balance, Maggie realized their good fortune. The tunnel did indeed look passable.

The three of them followed the current further into the darkness. Their sojourn seemed endless, and before long Maggie began to question her initial assessment. The water was beginning to rise. Feeling edgy now, she wondered how long they would have to wade before finding an exit. Finally, with water up to her knees, her nervous impatience turned to fear.

"What's that?" Michael blurted.

Maggie couldn't see a thing. "What? What do you see?"

"There," he said.

Maggie felt him grab hold of her shoulder, aiming her in the darkness. She saw it then, a faint flicker of light, barely noticeable.

"I see it, too," Jampal said. "We must be coming toward an opening."

Soaked and sore, Maggie felt chilled to the bone as they forged ahead. The light became more visible, growing brighter, until it was a beam dancing off the flowing water.

Maggie breathed a sigh of relief. *Thank God*, she thought. With her wet and weary companions beside her, she followed the river into the misty sunlight.

CHAPTER 55

MAGGIE FELT as if she were awakening from a dream.

Suddenly, a little girl in blue overalls appeared out of the mist. Maggie thought she looked about seven, but something about her seemed timeless. The little girl's face, delicate and soft, was shining like the sun. In her hand, she dangled a chain that held a golden incense burner. Tufts of smoke rose from the censer, filling the air with the smell of sandalwood.

She didn't speak a word, but her gray-blue eyes were wide, beckoning them to approach. At that moment, the wide arc of a rainbow became visible in the eastern sky.

Maggie felt compelled to follow as the girl turned and walked through the wheat field behind her. Maggie noticed that the young girl's hair was golden like the wheat stalks, and blew long and curly in the breeze. Her feet were bare, but she was surefooted. Maggie on the other hand, felt just the opposite as she stumbled to keep up, all the while beckoning Michael and Jampal to follow.

The landscape was quiet and still. Even the moving wind was silent, and like a deep well seemed to draw them in further. When they finally reached the end of the field and stepped out into the open, the young girl was nowhere to be seen.

Instead, Maggie found they were standing at the edge of a soft green meadow, a ring of mountains shimmering with glaciers framing the valley on all sides. Before them, a river flowed easily, glistening with tones of aqua and green, its banks lined with white stone. All around them, clusters of wildflowers were swaying in the wind like misty pastels, while above, the sky, a swirling blue and white, was brightened by the warm yellow-orange glow of a sun like no other. The moment Maggie lifted her face up toward its soothing healing rays, thoughts of danger and harm dissolved. *How can any harm come to us here?*

A natural buoyancy made walking effortless. Maggie found it easy imagining herself soaring along with the brown-gray sand hill crane overhead, which seemed to be leading them forward with only an occasional easy flap of its wings. Sound was neither present nor absent, but rather, a deep pervasive awareness spoke through the silence.

Maggie sensed her mind unified with Michael and Jampal's. The simple ability to almost hear thoughts did not feel unfamiliar. It stirred childhood memories of *knowing* . . . knowing the thoughts of her father, her friends, feeling at home in her mind, feeling one with everything.

Initially, the smooth dirt lane they were walking on seemed ordinary. The first house they saw, small and white, was well-trimmed, a light yellow pastel lining its window frames. It was what was glistening atop the steep thatch roof that was extraordinary—a metal antenna crowned with an octahedron, fashioned from seamless copper.

Across the field Maggie saw another house, then another, each with the same anomaly . . . *All the houses have the strange octahedron shape on their roof.*

"Greetings."

A voice to her right startled her. She was even more astonished to notice that a small open jeep had pulled alongside of them on the road. The vehicle's approach had been so quiet none of them had heard it. Behind the wheel, a young man with a rugged tanned face and close-cropped hair scanned the group with interest.

Maggie, struck by the oddity of the situation, took a step toward the driver. "We are looking for *Shambhala.*"

"Well, you've found it," he said casually. "It's surprising, actually. Not many people know about this place, and most of the people who do haven't been able to find it." The man took another moment to study their faces. Appearing satisfied, he added, "I suppose that makes you unusual."

Michael stepped forward. "Unusual?"

"Yes," the man answered. "You are *un* . . . usual. That means special, not in your *right* mind. To seek the truth—that's a pretty crazy venture for most people."

Tell us about it. Craziness was the least of it. Maggie realized that time was running short and they needed to work quickly. Suddenly, she felt like an angel who wasn't allowed to enjoy heaven . . . *a working class angel.* She smiled to herself.

"Your name?" Jampal asked.

"James, but actually everyone calls me Jim."

Jampal leaned toward the driver. "Jim, there's someone we're looking for. I think you know who I mean."

Maggie stared at Jampal. *What is he talking about?*

Jim nodded in the affirmative. "I'll take you to him," he said. "Hop in, there's plenty of room."

Maggie took the front passenger seat as Michael and Jampal climbed in the back. As he started to drive, she noticed the small steering wheel almost disappeared beneath Jim's large hands.

The car moved forward, accelerating to thirty miles and hour easily and noiselessly. Confounded and amazed, she turned toward Jim who smiled at her baffled stare.

"Solar and hydrogen," he said. He pointed at the hood, which was a quartz-like panel with what appeared to be a small propane-type cylinder protruding on one side. "All it takes is water and sunshine. On a cloudy day, water alone will do."

Maggie sat back, allowing her mind to absorb what she was experiencing. *Natural energy—clean and sustainable.* Already, Shambhala was offering a certain easy rhythm. Michael and Jampal were quiet, undoubtedly experiencing it, too. *Michael would probably say we are in sync with the ley*, she thought, smiling to herself.

Suddenly, the air was filled with an intoxicating scent, like the powerful aroma of incense. Maggie thought it was coming from the woods across the road. "What's that over there?" she asked.

"The Malaya," Jim answered. "Some know it as the Cool Grove. That whole park is filled with sandalwood trees."

"Are we going in there?" Michael asked.

"No, some other time. Right now I want to get you to Kalapa."

"Kalapa?" Maggie furrowed her brow, trying to remember where she had heard that word before.

"It's our capital," Jim said.

They reached a cross in the road, and Jim turned the jeep to the right. Maggie saw that the road before them ran through a meadow filled with wildflowers. Trees, their tiny mimosa blossoms fluttering, dotted the edges of the path.

"It's a peaceful place," Michael said, appearing to be enraptured by the countryside's beauty.

"It is," Jim affirmed. "The land is rich. Sustainable agriculture provides an ongoing source of food of all kinds. Energy is produced naturally, so there's no conflict over resources. It makes the whole concept of creating peace highly intelligent, yet incredibly simple. Also, the people who live here help each other whenever they can. They understand the importance of one thing in particular that most humans like to remain ignorant about."

"What's that?" Maggie asked.

"The power of the mind." The expression lines on Jim's face deepened as he smiled. "Everyone has the capacity to love and to heal. Happiness, health, peace, all the wealth in the universe . . . it all begins in the mind."

Jampal leaned forward from the back of the jeep. His face was close to Maggie's when he spoke. "Meditation and compassion—two powerful tools. They practice them both here, right?"

"They are the only reason why Shambhala even exists. A pure land can only be created by our own innate goodness."

"Something like heaven," Michael added.

"Not something *like* heaven," Jim corrected. "Exactly like heaven. The higher the mind, the more powerful and pure the experience."

As Jim drove them further down the road, they passed some circular arrangements of standing stones ranging from two to twelve feet high. Maggie thought they were markers especially laid at the city's entrance. Soon the road widened, and houses and tall buildings lined the street. The road eventually led them directly to a circular civic center, itself marked by a distinctive, power-generating *chorten*.

"My God!" Michael exclaimed, grabbing Maggie's arm. "This whole place is powered by electromagnetic radiance—the same energy that Stephen Einsof has been tapping into in his experiments."

The chorten's cubic base, painted a bright yellow, measured about twenty feet per side. Above it was a white hemispheric dome crowned by a towering red spire that reached fifty feet above the street, making it taller than any other building in the area. Atop the spire, naturally, was a copper octahedron.

Maggie sensed that Jim understood their awe and excitement. Like a skilled guide, he addressed them in a quiet, yet deliberate voice.

"All of the technology and science that we have developed, whether it's been in medicine, astronomy, engineering, or any other scientific field has had but one end, and that *end* is enlightened activity." Jim brought the jeep to a stop. "We're here."

When they all got out, Maggie turned to see if he would follow.

"No," Jim said, appearing to know her thoughts. "I'm going to be moving on. I think you have some business to tend to, though." He smiled and with a slight nod of his head, drove the silent jeep down the road.

Jampal and Michael moved toward the chorten, drawn to it as much as Maggie was. She couldn't help but feel that the nuclei of their karmic universe had brought them home to the center—the heart center—from which their minds had sprung. Now it was time to enter. Indeed the door was ajar, inviting them in.

Maggie felt the shift in energy as she walked through the chorten's entrance. She peered up at the pale blue ceiling of the hemisphere. Two large skylights embedded in its surface seemed to magnify the iridescent sky above. When Michael and Jampal reached her side, they too were transfixed by what they saw.

As she lowered her gaze, Maggie glanced toward the right side of the room. There, set in the corner, was a surveyor's transit mounted atop a tripod. The table next to it was strewn with colored pencils, compasses and drawing paper.

"Oh good, you've come," a voice rang out.

Maggie turned, thinking it sounded youthful, well-educated and . . . familiar.

Across the room, a man about six-feet tall was standing before a sloped drafting table. "Maggie, Michael, and of course, Lama Jampal. Welcome." Behind wide oval glasses, a pair of brown eyes regarded each of them intently.

Michael voiced their confusion. "How did you . . . ?" He trailed off as if he didn't know quite what to say.

"I am Matt, a geomancer," the man said, introducing himself. "I'm glad you've arrived. I could use some advice on my new project."

Maggie thought his eyes were the lightest brown she had ever seen. The prominent arch of his brow gave him an intense and curious look.

"I am designing a city," he explained, placing a pencil in the pocket of his blue cambric shirt.

Maggie could also see the edge of a miniature protractor protruding out of his shirt pocket as well. With Dockers and desert boots, Matt looked the part of an engineer.

"Did you say geomancy?" Michael's natural curiosity kicked in. "That's based on energy systems, right?"

Matt nodded. "Geomancy is the science of environmental design. What the Chinese call *feng shui* and the Tibetans *sache*. Just as gardeners create a garden by control of water, soil, sun and shade, a geomancer protects society by observing the earth and allowing for the natural accumulation of positive energies and the dispersal of less favorable ones. There are no negative forces, only displaced or obstructed energies."

"Look at this," Matt said, standing aside so they could view his drawing.

The three of them walked over to the drafting table. Under the bright glow of a solar lamp, Maggie saw the print clearly: A large domed structure on a hill dominated the urban center surrounding it. A tower topped with an octahedron stood atop the dome. Lightly drawn radiant lines extended from the octahedron to the city below, while even more energy lines emanated from the standing stone columns that were interspersed throughout the city.

"Is that structure creating the energy?" Maggie asked.

Matt shook his head. "The octahedron does not generate electricity or energy of any kind. Rather, it channels existing energy. The whole system is based on allowing subtle energies to move freely. Remember, the subtler the energy, the more powerful. Our whole human existence depends on the flow of these subtle energies, even though most of us don't even realize it. As individuals we exhaust ourselves fighting unseen foes and unnecessary battles. If we would only allow our minds to relax and our emotions to flow smoothly, we would have much greater energy to accomplish our desires."

Maggie's interest was piqued. "Are you saying that this type of energy is already available for us to use? By the look of your drawing, it seems remarkably powerful and efficient."

Matt smiled. "Now you're getting it. Any society or city, or for that matter any single dwelling, can operate on the same principle. Channel the earth's energy and any activity requires less effort. Properly accomplished, this would allow something as small as a double-A battery to light your home. Of course, that is the design perfected, but aren't we *supposed* to be striving toward perfection? That is our nature as humans."

Jampal, having kept his silence for a while, suddenly spoke up. "But for human beings there must be training, there must be dedication, there must be clear intention."

"Absolutely," Matt agreed. "And motivation means everything."

"It's like acquiring the knowledge of nuclear physics," Michael added. "Do you use it to create an energy source or to blow up the world?"

Matt nodded. "That's why it's important to have this work done by persons with the proper training. If an unqualified individual wired a home he might harm himself or cause a fire. This is where the problem lies today. Within the world at large, you have allowed life to be regulated by persons with no knowledge of *ley* lines or *lung-mei*, dragon lines. So your lives and your energy are depleted."

Maggie couldn't help but wonder. If the *lung*, as Matt described it, was being weakened, then what could be done about it?

It appeared Matt sensed her state of frustration. "Ignorant minds ignore the obvious and declare themselves authorities," he said, walking toward her. "It is up to us to restore the emperor's clothing."

The sudden clinking of bells made them all turn toward the door.

"The Franklin bells," Matt announced.

"The what?" Michael asked, looking mystified.

"Come with me." Matt gestured for them to follow as he walked outside.

"You see this?" he said, pointing toward a copper wire.

Maggie noticed the wire was split in two. Each end, about five inches apart, had a little bell dangling from it. A small brass ball held up by a silk thread was moving between the bells, striking them.

"We're talking Benjamin Franklin here?" Michael asked as he walked up to the device.

"That's right," Matt affirmed. "It's basically an alarm system. Lets us know that lightning is on the way."

Maggie was amazed that such a simple-looking device was able to signal an impending storm. She reared her head back and looked up toward the sky. There were some clouds moving in their direction, but nothing that looked too threatening.

Matt picked up on her doubt. "Believe me, a storm is on the way. The Franklin bells haven't let me down yet." He paused. A look of concern spread across his face. "My daughter."

Maggie suddenly remembered the little girl they had seen when they entered Shambhala. The feeling of being compelled consumed her once again.

"You'll look for her," Matt directed, his eyes never wavering from hers. "Take Jampal with you."

Jampal didn't even hesitate. He started walking away without her.

"Hey!" Maggie called out, but the lama paid no heed. She turned back toward Matt, uncertain where to start looking. "How will I know where to find your daughter?"

Matt wasn't listening either. A look of excitement flashing across his eyes, he headed for the door on the other side of the chorten.

CHAPTER 56

"COME ON," Matt called out, indicating for Michael to follow. "We're always preparing for storms in this area. Lightning likes to hit high places."

Matt led him to a small cottage just outside. He walked over to an old tool bag lying on the porch, retrieved a lightning rod and some wire, and began climbing the wooden ladder that was leaning against the side of the building. He stopped midway, looked at Michael, and pointed toward a shovel that was laying on the ground.

"If you could give me a hand," Matt said, indicating a spot at the base of the building. "We need to place another grounding plate. You can start by digging right there."

Just as Michael began shoveling, a flash of lightning and a loud clap of thunder startled him. He looked up. Across the sky, dark clouds were rolling toward them like waves.

Matt didn't seem to miss a beat. "Here comes life itself," he said. "A whole lot of energy heading our way."

"Well if a whole lot of energy is heading our way, shouldn't we go inside?" Michael didn't find the prospect of being hit by lightning too appealing. Matt, on the other hand, looked like he enjoyed playing with fire.

"I put these conducting rods around the house," he said, ignoring Michael's anxiety. Matt touched the tip of one of the rods. "As you can see, they all come to a point. Since electricity is attracted to the highest spot on an object first, it makes the rod more effective."

Michael's eyes searched the sky. Despite his trepidation, he resumed shoveling. "So I guess whenever you get a thunderstorm around here you're protected."

"That's right," Matt said as he attached the rod to the side of the cottage, "but even when there are no clouds in the sky, and apparently no storm brewing, you can still get lightning."

"And how's that?" Michael felt he was dipping into foreign waters.

"Because energy is everywhere," he explained. Matt started climbing down the ladder, a wire in his hand. "And there is always electricity in the air. The earth is like a huge battery, not only emitting electricity, but receiving it from the atmosphere as well. All over the world, thunderstorms are constantly waging their powerful magic. That's the atmosphere giving back electrons to the earth." Matt paused, smiling. "Actually, it's an ongoing balancing act. Thunderstorms are a way to replenish the electrons that the earth is constantly giving away."

As if for the first time, Michael looked across the meadow. The blades of grass were vibrant, radiating with energy.

As he walked over to him, Matt gave Michael a knowing look. "*That's* electricity."

"What exactly?" Michael asked.

"What you're looking at," Matt said as he pulled a copper plate out of his tool bag and dropped it in the hole. "The blades of grass, tips of leaves, tops of flowers. They give out electrons all the time. If it were dark out we might see a corona, like a halo, surrounding some of these plants here. But right now, these thunderclouds coming are pushing more electrons toward us than the earth is pushing towards them. These clouds become so charged that sooner or later the pressure gets too great and there is a burst of energy. That's lightning."

Enthusiastic was hardly the word to express Matt's reverie. "You can't imagine," Matt said with awe, "how much electrical current is passed between a cloud and the earth when lightning strikes—millions of volts. Then we hear the explosion, right? *Thunder!* A sudden expansion of air that's literally being pushed aside."

Matt's eyes shone with brilliance. *Electricity*, Michael thought. He couldn't help but admire Matt's extraordinary intelligence.

"This energy has always existed!" Matt continued passionately, "even before life began on this earth. And the most amazing quality of all is that it's all the same. There is only one kind of electricity. It just comes at us with more or less force."

"So then utilizing this force is the key," Michael concluded. "But how do we begin?"

Matt's eyes bore into his. "Like I told you before, *lightning will follow the path of least resistance.*"

Michael got the feeling Matt was trying to tell him something far beyond the obvious, but at the moment, it was more than he could fathom.

CHAPTER 57

MAGGIE FOLLOWED SILENTLY as Jampal led her into the woods. The uplifting scent of sandalwood created a curious meditative ease as she walked through the forest, now being darkened by the shadowy clouds overhead. Within the intense quiet, all she heard were the rustling of leaves as the wind strengthened from the oncoming storm.

Then the sound of thunder, like the rumbling of a distant train, broke the stillness. Jampal stopped suddenly. Maggie walked to his side wondering what had made him come to such an abrupt halt. Jampal's eyes scanned the dark corners of the forest as he turned slowly. Maggie stared into the shadowy trees, trying to follow the direction of his gaze. She came up empty.

"What is it?" she asked.

Just then lightning streaked across the sky, illuminating the forest. In the flash of a moment, Maggie saw her, the little girl, running through the trees. *Matt's daughter.* She was no longer carrying a censor. Instead, the child was holding a large lantern.

Jampal started moving quickly. "Hurry, we must follow her."

Another crash of thunder sent Maggie scurrying forward. Jampal took hold of her arm as she reached his side. Now, walking beside him, barely able to see in front of herself, she felt the storm strengthening as the forest darkened further.

Fear and awe. The mysterious force of thunderstorms—the howling winds, brilliant lightning, ferocious thunder—had always elicited those feelings from her. Now, as the treetops swayed above her, Maggie came to the quick conclusion she would rather be watching the storm while cozily sipping tea in Laurel's kitchen. Not so today.

Droplets of rain began to fall. *Great.* It was hard enough seeing as it was. As she stumbled forward with Jampal still holding her arm, Maggie wondered where in God's name the child was leading them. Jampal grabbed her harder then, motioning for her to stop.

It was at that moment that she realized where they were. Scattered gravestones were all around them. *A cemetery.*

Maggie followed as Jampal moved carefully between the headstones. When he reached an eight-spoked metal wheel wedged in the ground, he knelt beside it. Placing his hand on the rim, he peered at the Hindu lettering etched into the large rock behind it.

"Sanskrit," Jampal announced, his eyes beaming brightly. He looked up at her and broke into a hearty laugh.

Maggie thought he looked a tinge mad.

Still chuckling, he got up to his feet and grabbed her arm again. "We are entering it," Jampal declared, beside himself with elation.

"Entering what?" Maggie was in no mood for enigmas. Although there had only been a few droplets of rain thus far, Maggie was certain that a cloudburst was at hand and they would soon be drenched.

Jampal still hadn't answered.

"Entering what?" Maggie asked again.

"Look there," Jampal directed, pointing to a light in the distance.

Maggie's frustration softened as she recognized the warm glow of the lantern. They were close.

Then, with a thunderous roar, the sky let loose. As the rain poured down heavily, they stumbled through the trees and into a clearing. Coming to a stop, Maggie's mouth fell open when she saw what was standing at the center of the field. Within the circular grounds before her was the most magnificent structure she had ever seen.

Five stories high, each level a different color, with eaves lined in pearls and emeralds.

As Maggie's gaze moved upward she saw her . . . the little girl, still holding the lantern, standing on the uppermost balcony.

"Where . . . " Maggie was finding it hard to even form words. "Where are we?"

"We are in the mandala. Can't you see?"

Maggie turned and faced outward once again. Colored stones formed concentric circles all around them. *Yellow, white, pink-red, grey-black and green.* As the realization of where they were took hold, she whispered, "My God." Amazed, she looked back toward the structure. Matt's daughter, her golden hair blowing in the wind was beckoning for them to join her.

Jampal seemed to recognize what to do. "We go in through the eastern door," he said. "That is tradition."

Maggie raised her eyebrows, realizing she was treading unfamiliar waters. *If tradition dictates, then so be it.*

Jampal held her hand as they entered the pagoda gate.

Once through the gateway, they found themselves standing on the first level of the outer stairway. The granite-colored marble foundation was solid, giving the entrance a stately strength.

Four pillars stood across the front, two on each side of the doorway.

Stone lions flanked the borders of the walkway.

Maggie also noticed various shapes painted on the walls before her. *Yellow squares, white circles, red triangles, gray bows, greenish blue spheres.*

Curiously, although they had reached the first level, they were still not inside the structure itself. The outer perimeter was like a long breezeway that squared around the entire building.

As Maggie stood alongside the white ledge, a large white crane came flying overhead and swooped down onto a sandalwood tree across from her. It perched itself on the longest limb and watched, appearing to be just as fascinated with her as she was with it.

"This mystic circle was built for the people of Shambhala," Jampal said, walking up beside her. "The mandala itself is an expression of the enlightened mind."

Maggie hugged her arms. Jampal's words, like the cool damp wind sweeping through the breezeway, seemed to rush through her. With her gaze still settled upon the crane, she remembered the Shambhala prophecy and what it foretold.

It was said that during the degenerative times, conditions in the world would become so negative that people would be motivated mainly by greed and ambition. Human dignity and concern for others would be undermined as material concerns for money and power became widespread. Truth, justice, spirituality, religion would bear little meaning as the lust for domination grew.

Throughout it all, a powerful and evil ruler would instigate an era of fear and terror based on arrogant and self-important beliefs. When he eventually discovered the land of Shambhala, he would wish to conquer it as well. But a great warrior leader would then arise from that land to fight against him and for the ideals of an enlightened society, restoring the world to peace and allowing decency and dignity to flourish.

Maggie smiled. *Nice story,* some people might say. But was it more than that? She wondered about Jampal's words.

The mandala was built for the people.

Yes, Maggie was certain it was. Yet, if the people remained unaware of it, if they couldn't see or know it, then how in the world could they experience it?

Maggie snapped out of her thoughts as the crane spread its long gray wings and glided out of the tree. It swooped over the top of the building and out of sight.

"Today, the signs are inviting," Jampal observed.

Maggie met Jampal's sobering gaze. He pointed to the steps in front of them. They curved like a bridge, inclining to a higher level.

"Today, we reach the top," he declared.

Side by side, Maggie and Jampal stepped forward, walking under the arch of another small pagoda-like roof. It was only then that she noticed the thunder had subsided. Now, rising from the damp surface of the ground was the light veil of a mist.

As if moving through a dream, they followed the path to the next level. The intense, fiery-orange marble floor created a sense of warmth and alertness. Maggie felt as if the space around her was magnetized with power. This time, she and Jampal encountered a glass wall designed with multi-colored painted forms of beautiful women, *yoginis,* holding musical instruments. Symbolic of the power of speech, Maggie could almost hear their melodic voices.

"Are you ready to go further?" Jampal asked.

Maggie had almost forgotten the little girl. But how could she? She wondered what had happened to her sense of urgency.

"Don't worry. Not everything is meant to be hurried." Jampal eyed her keenly as he took her hand.

A huge, golden-spoked wheel flanked by two deer—an image Maggie had seen many times before on her sojourns to monasteries in Nepal and Tibet—adorned the next portico entranceway. She and Jampal walked beneath it and followed the marble stairs that bridged them to yet another level. The foundation there, a light blue in color, was like an airy sky, creating a sense of openness that pervaded Maggie's mind. Small bells, hanging from the eaves at each corner, were moving gently in the breeze.

This time, there was no wall to greet them. Instead, a golden platform about fifteen-feet wide was centered on the floor, filling the space with brilliance. Its perimeters were lined with clear glass vases, each filled with exquisite, fully-bloomed lotuses.

Jampal started circumambulating the room, disappearing behind the raised platform. Maggie could still see his image, though, in the small, brass-framed mirrors hanging from the eaves. Each angle, in fact, gave her a new perspective of him. Curiously, as her eyes swept the room, the images flowed one into the next, like a silent movie. A few moments later, Jampal walked from behind the other side of the platform and was standing in front of her once again.

"Within the mind," he said, "there is tremendous potential. The body is your support . . . the speech, how you create and communicate . . . and the mind, where all creation begins."

Where all creation begins.

Maggie looked up to the final level—a dark blue platform, in each corner, an auspicious object . . . a *white conch, a red wooden gong, a black wish-fulfilling jewel, a yellow wish-granting tree.*

And in the center of it all, resting on a black onyx table . . . a huge stone!

She stared at its surface . . . a gold relief symbol, lined with effulgent colors . . . *blue, green, red, gold, white and black.*

"The symbol of the Kalachakra." Jampal reached over and squeezed her hand. His eyes wider than she had ever seen them, he whispered softly. "This is why we've come. *Chintamani*."

Chintamani. Maggie felt herself tremble as she remembered the meaning. *The Wish-fulfilling Jewel . . . Lapsis Excellis!*

Everything in the room took on a special aura. With the storm now over, the clear light of the sky entered the open mandala space and fell upon the stone. At that moment, the young girl stepped out from behind the table. Her eyes were the essence of the sky . . . a blue, light and luminous. In her hand, she now held a gleaming silver butterlamp. Maggie felt riveted to the spot, captivated by its warm enriching glow.

The little girl placed the butterlamp on the table next to the stone symbol, then walked out to the edge of the platform and held out her hand. For the first time, Maggie saw the child was wearing a necklace . . . *a butterfly pendant suspended from a gold chain, a tiny diamond chip set between its wings.*

Jampal prodded Maggie lightly with his fingertips.

Maggie ascended up to the mandala's highest level. As she stepped onto the blue foundation, the girl took her hand and made her turn to face the Kalachakra stone. Maggie felt as if the child was waiting. For what, she had no idea. They stood together for what seemed like an eternity, until finally the little girl let go of her hand.

Without knowing why, Maggie was overwhelmed by a strong urge to touch the stone. Her hand, as if not even a part of her body, moved forward. With her fingers outstretched, at the moment there should have been contact, Maggie found there was none. Her hand moved through the rock as if it were moving through space, yet the stone itself still appeared solid.

Shocked by the fact that she was no longer seeing her hand, Maggie lost her footing and lunged forward. Suddenly, she felt a long cool object between her fingers. She tightened her grip and stepped back.

A vase! Opaque . . . the color of lapis lazuli . . . shining with a clear light!

Maggie turned toward the child, but as mysteriously as she had appeared, the girl was now nowhere to be seen.

Jampal moved quickly up onto the platform to reach Maggie's side. Although he was not a man who showed emotion easily, he looked beside himself with joy. Without a word, he moved forward, appearing intent upon discovering the secret of the stone.

Again and again, he tapped its surface with his fingers. Finally, after a long moment, Jampal turned toward her, his eyes wide with wonder. "It's as solid as a rock."

CHAPTER 58

MATT AND MICHAEL were standing at the drafting table when Maggie and Jampal came rushing through the door.

"We found this," Maggie announced. She had gingerly carried the vase back from the Malaya woods. Maggie now made a place for it on a tall workbench that was otherwise covered with Matt's diagrams.

Jampal was quick to qualify her statement. "She means *she* discovered it."

"Discovered it where?" Michael ran his fingers along the vase's exterior.

"At the Kalachakra mandala."

Maggie spoke rapidly, giving them a brief account of her and Jampal's venture into the mandala and of finding the stone.

Matt's eyes flashed with recognition. "A *terma*."

Jampal nodded. "Yes."

Maggie knew the word and what it meant, but the idea that she had discovered some sort of hidden spiritual treasure was hard to comprehend.

All four of them stood around the workbench, eyes transfixed on the vase.

"You have not opened it," Matt said, as he eyed the container.

It was plain to see that the blue glass top was still melded onto the vase.

"I wouldn't know how. The top is wedged tight," Maggie said. "I thought I should bring it to you."

"Ah, engineering . . . my specialty." Matt walked over to a tool drawer and pulled out a small wooden mallet.

Maggie couldn't imagine what Matt had in mind. Certainly he wasn't about to simply break it. Matt turned the vase on its side. Before she had a chance to think, she realized that was exactly what he planned to do.

With a swift light blow, the vase shattered. Horrified, Maggie couldn't believe what she had seen. She could have easily done that herself.

"Don't look so surprised," Matt said, giving her a provocative grin. He began to pick through the glass pieces. "Sometimes you just have to deal with matter in a matter-of-fact way."

Michael and Jampal chuckled.

"Okay," she bellowed, "so I expected the extraordinary. It's been a day for that you know."

"Indeed it has," Matt agreed as he picked up what looked like an emerald.

"Is that . . . a jewel?" Michael asked.

"Yes." Matt was quick to answer. One by one, from between the glass shards, he removed gemstones about a half inch in diameter—amethyst, emerald, ruby, among them. When he was done, he was holding twelve stones in his hand. He lined them in a row on the drawing table.

ཨོཾ་ཧ་ཀྵ་མ་ལ་ཝ་ར་ཡ་སྭཱ་ཧཱ་ཨེ་ཝཾ

As Maggie came closer, she saw that each stone had an etching on it. *Looks like Sanskrit letters,* she thought, peering at the markings, but she didn't have a clue to their meaning. Maggie glanced at her two companions. Michael had a strange, confused look on his face, while Jampal, excited by what he was seeing, reached out to touch the stones.

"*Om Ham Ksha Ma La Va Ra Yam Sva Ha.*" Matt recited the Sanskrit. He then pointed toward the last two stones. "The syllable *E* is the Kalachakra deity, representing compassion, and the syllable *Vam* is Vishvamata, the consort, symbolizing wisdom."

"The mantra," Jampal said, looking toward Matt.

Matt drew a long breath and nodded. "Well, Maggie, it looks like you have made quite a discovery. Someone has etched Sanskrit lettering onto these stones. Together, they form the Kalachakra mantra."

"And what have we here?" Michael asked. He pushed aside a long piece of glass and picked up a tightly-rolled piece of vellum. He moved his hand toward the thick string that held it bound. About to undo it, Michael hesitated, then motioned to Matt to take it from him.

Instead of complying, Matt just shrugged. "I think you probably should do the honors."

Michael gave Maggie a sidelong glance, one she had seen a number of times before. *Still somewhat on guard and suspicious*, she thought.

Delicately, Michael undid the tie and placed the string aside. Slowly and meticulously, he unrolled the parchment scroll.

Michael's jaw dropped suddenly and a look of astonishment spread across his face as he looked at the strange writing on the vellum.

"Well, what is it?" Maggie was now beyond curious to find out what had made Michael Sonada go speechless.

"It's in ancient Aramaic."

"What?" Maggie found his assertion incredible. "How could there be something written in Aramaic here?"

"Just wait," he commanded. Apparently not finished, he continued reading. After a few moments he looked up.

Maggie was beside herself. "Are you going to tell us what it says?"

"I—"

"Come on!" Maggie insisted. He was driving her crazy.

Michael stared at her, looking astounded. "It looks like you've discovered the third saying."

For a moment, all of them were stunned into silence. Matt was the only one present who didn't look like he had just seen a ghost.

Michael spread the parchment out in full on the table. "Hold this," he directed.

Maggie complied by pinning down the edges of the vellum with her fingers.

Matt brought over a ledger of paper and a pen. Handing them to Michael he said, "You're going to need this."

Now, equipped with the tools of his trade, Michael looked totally in his element. He scanned the scroll with a merciless intensity, appearing to magnify every corner of possibility as he interpreted the document. Then, writing with a furious burst of energy, his eyes moved back and forth from the scroll to his translation, assessing every word. When he was finished, he was breathing deeply, as if he had just had the most ecstatic experience of his life.

Well, there's no question what turns this guy on. Maggie had never thought of Michael as passionate before but guessed that if anything was going to stoke his fire, an ancient text would be the charm.

After Matt took the original parchment from under Maggie's fingers, she peered over Michael's shoulder impatiently. "So what does it say?" she implored.

Michael exhaled slowly and read his translation aloud:

Oh Jerusalem
City of Peace
The jewel laid
The city is the temple.

Architect build thy roads
Thy gates like grand arches
Rise to the East
Draw the lines of the heavenly temple
Let the stones be thy foundation.

Through the wisdom of the heart
The Pentagon in unity
The marriage of nations merge
The Star of David is complete
Jerusalem is One.

Yeshua ben Yosef

Michael turned and gave Maggie an incredulous stare.

"What?" she asked.

"Yeshua ben Yosef . . . Jesus son of Josef."

Overwhelmed, Maggie heard the words but it took her several moments to digest them. *If Christ wrote this, then it would also mean . . .* She could scarcely believe it . . . *that He wrote the inscriptions on the stones!* When she looked up, she found Michael still staring at her, but now a look of fulfillment was on his face.

"First we would have to authenticate this," Michael said, noticeably keeping his voice calm.

Maggie had no doubt. Every bone in her body felt it. "I already know it's real."

"Well, if this *is* real . . . I mean, this is a lot to take in at one time," Michael admitted, looking both elated and confused. "How could this possibly be?"

"There have always been beings that are of *the Way*," Matt said with deliberate intensity. "They are seekers and guardians of spiritual truths— not shackled by any religion, not even the one they are born into. Jesus was searching for the truth. He was seeking enlightenment. He didn't care where he had to go to find it."

Maggie detected a hint of wrath in Matt's words.

"True spirituality means that a person can belong to any religious or spiritual tradition and can still recognize the spark of enlightenment anywhere and in anyone. Jesus was born a Jew, but he went way beyond religious conformity. So what should we call him then, a Christian?"

Jampal smiled at Matt's incisive remark.

"Christ was enlightened, first and foremost," Matt said, as he rolled up the scroll. "Muhammad, Krishna, Buddha, Moses, Abraham. The mind of enlightenment does not play favorites."

With the vellum parchment again tightly wound, Matt carefully tied it with the string. He removed a small plastic tube from his desk and placed the scroll inside. "There," he said, laying the tube down next to the pile of gemstones.

Michael seemed to have sobered some since initially translating the text. He scratched his head as he spoke. "I'm still in the dark here. What does this all have to do with Jerusalem?"

"The saying is a blueprint," Matt revealed. "a *cryptic* diagram."

Maggie had realized that the saying was some sort of riddle, some kind of puzzle to decipher. She was finding it hard to comprehend that it could actually be a blueprint.

"Are you saying that it's some sort of schematic, a plan that lays out how to build something?" she asked.

"Better to say it's a framework—a visionary idea with a physical reference."

Maggie sighed. *Another enigma.*

"Allegories, myths, legends—they are themselves blueprints of ideas. Christ left this in Shambhala because it is the *Lapsis Excellis*—the Grail—the enlightened ideal needed for humankind to truly evolve this world."

"What is the ideal?" Maggie asked.

"That heaven is not some place up there," Matt said, raising his hands to the sky, "but something that you can build right here, right now, wherever you are."

Maggie felt as if something sleeping in her heart was being awakened.

"That is what Shambhala is all about," Matt said, "creating a place that is dedicated to enlightenment—an enlightenment beyond any one religion. It's about being human. It's about realizing we are all connected to a universal wisdom, and through that wisdom we can change the world."

Michael's face had softened considerably. "So how does the Kalachakra fit into all of this? What makes it so special?"

"The Kalachakra is a symbol of peace, and the teachings provide a vehicle to attain that peace." Matt took a red pencil and transliterated the word for Michael to see. "*Kala*, that means time, and *chakra* means wheel. Kalachakra means the *wheel of time*, and through its practice you will realize that what you perceive linearly as so real and substantive is really like a mist in the breeze. It's through that awareness that people can liberate themselves from the past, stop looking for retribution and get on with the business of creating peace."

Maggie sighed. She knew that so many were yearning to move past the same old arguments, frustrated by the endless cycle of blame and retaliation. Lama Jampal has said it well. *We need to make a leap.*

Matt was staring at her when she looked up. He must have noticed she had gone off into her own thoughts.

"And that is why the Kalachakra is needed," he said emphatically. "It is a teaching meant specifically for the *human community.* In Shambhala, people have devoted their entire lives to its practice. Just as a person needs to practice anything to get good at it, people need to practice peace in order to attain it. That practice involves freeing your mind from ignorance. People want to live in the illusion that they can just go about getting anything they want for themselves and ignore the suffering of others while they do it. It's delusional thinking. Like madmen, they dress up in their finest suits and gowns and ride their horses into burning stables."

As Matt spoke, Maggie looked at the stones on the table, wondering what part they would play in the blueprint. Her breath deepened.

"The world has reached a critical mass," Matt continued, "a time where no one religion or culture can claim enlightenment as its own.

To live in an enlightened world, you have to create it together. You have to plant the seed of human dignity, create a place on this earth where everyone is welcome, where spirituality is celebrated."

As Matt walked toward her, Maggie felt herself trembling. He took her hands in his as he spoke. "That is why Jerusalem is so important. Creating a space, an international zone of peace as you have suggested, allows for that seed to take a firm hold." Matt paused, his eyes filled with compassion. "There is *nothing* more powerful than an idea whose time has come."

As Matt released her hands, Maggie felt a warm rush move through her body. With it came a peace and stillness she hadn't known in a long while.

From his desk drawer, Matt removed a small, mauve-colored felt pouch embroidered in gold thread with the Kalachakra symbol. In it, he placed the twelve gems. "Just as the Kalachakra was given to the people of Shambhala to help them advance and become more enlightened, the time has come for the people of this earth to receive it for that very purpose."

Matt handed Maggie the pouch. "Take these stones back to the holy land. You'll need them to lay the foundation".

"The foundation?" Maggie asked. She found the remark curious.

"For the *new* Jerusalem."

Before she could even reply, Matt also gave her the thin plastic vial that held the parchment. "Keep it safe," he whispered, "along with you."

Maggie smiled, returning his warm glance.

Michael stepped forward then, his eyes wide with anticipation.

"As we discussed before," Matt said, addressing him, "power in the wrong hands is deadly. You must go to Tarhuna. That's where Mabus has taken the Longinus Spear. Secure that, then meet Maggie in Jerusalem. You must do this before the Peace Conference begins in four days."

Michael's jaw dropped. Maggie saw the shock in his eyes.

"And Jampal," Matt said as he turned toward the lama, who was waiting quietly. "I'll need you here with me . . . to hold my graduate rod while I do some surveying."

Every line on Jampal's face deepened as he smiled gratefully. Maggie knew he wanted nothing more in the world than to stay.

It was his wish fulfilled.

CHAPTER 59

WALKING SLOWLY through Italy's Forum Romanum, Laurel could almost see the once booming nucleus of politics and commerce as it was in the days of Rome's opulent heights. As the center of the judicial system, legal battles were waged and settled within its perimeters. *Lawyers, financiers, senators.* Just as Washington, D.C. is today, Rome had once been the pulse of the empire.

Laurel's connecting flight to Cairo would leave in four hours. Had Rosario gotten her message? Her brother-in-law had always been fond of her. Would he help her now? Laurel shook her head in disbelief. *Rosario Seline, a Catholic priest of all things, and so many years have passed.*

Along the Via Sacra, on the grounds where the Temple of Vesta had stood, Laurel looked upon the stone remains. Several of the columns were still intact on the marble-covered podium. The circular building that once hallowed the grounds had contained the sacred flame of the goddess, Vesta. A flame that was kept alight by virgin priestesses of Rome.

Women guarding the source of light, she mused.

In fact, the priestesses had been a part of the temple since the sixth century BC, keeping the flame when the temple itself was basically a hearth—a circular structure perhaps made of straw or wood—and continuing to do so through its transition into stone replicas. In addition, history would chronicle that it was *also* a woman—Julia Domna, wife of the emperor, Septimius Severus—who initiated the last true restoration of the temple back in 191 AD.

Now today, amidst the reflection of what was, festivities honoring the past would allow visitors to the site to step back in time. Standing in the courtyard, amidst ponds filled with water lilies, Laurel watched as tourists and locals came to see an enactment of the rites that kept the sacred flame alight.

Just then, six young women stepped out from behind the rose bushes. Hair flowing and adorned in the vestal garments of ancient Rome, they began making offerings of incense, flowers, cakes made of grain and salt, and straw figurines.

A few moments later, one of the women, her long yellow and white tunic flowing behind her, came forward onto the podium. As Laurel watched her standing at the microphone, she couldn't help feeling she was in the presence of an angel of time. *Do such angels have any value anymore?* Laurel wondered. *Do we ever learn from our past?*

"In the time of Rome's political dominion," the young woman addressed the audience, "one male high priest, the Pontifex Maximus, would oversee the Vestals, but it was the priestesses who were the keepers of the flame. Within the circular structure of the temple's womb, the sacred flame rested, and the order of holy priestesses initiated into the rites were responsible for always keeping it alight."

At this point, the young woman motioned to her fellow vestals to surround the flame.

"Women have always been the keepers of the hearth in their homes," she continued, "sustaining warmth, cooking food, providing light, ensuring the survival and nurturance of their households. Naturally then, what was regarded as so essential to human life was entwined with the spiritual. Thus, the flame itself was seen as containing the deity in the form of a goddess. The Greeks called her *Hestia*, the goddess of hearth and home, the virgin maiden."

One of the vestals, who was holding a long silver tray, sprinkled a powdery substance into the fire, causing the flames to rise.

"This sacred fire that sustains life rested in the womb," the principal vestal said, "first protecting the home, then growing in proportion to include community, and in the case of Rome, to be the protecting flame of the state itself, guarded by the priestess—the feminine archetype of purity and spiritual power."

A voice beside Laurel spoke quietly. "You know, if any vestal allowed the flame to die while it was in her care, the high priest would whip her."

Laurel turned. The woman standing next to her was about as beautiful as any playing the part of the vestals that day. Her high, arched brows were dark, deepening the intense look of her light brown eyes.

"And, of course," the woman added, "the priestess would then be dismissed."

"Sounds like a man," Laurel said, wondering why she was being approached.

"You must be Laurel Seline." A confident air about her, the woman addressed her with a familiar tone.

Surprised, Laurel nodded. "Do I know you?"

"My name is Valencia Coronato. Father Rosario could not come, so he called and asked me to meet you here."

She felt a sense of relief at the sound of Rosario's name. Still, she wished he could have met her himself.

"I know about your cause," Valencia said, her voice falling to a whisper. Her eyes, full of compassion and purpose, held Laurel's. "So many Italian women support you here. You will definitely see that at your talk today."

Laurel hoped that would be true. Before leaving the States, Jules had contacted Women in Black, and they arranged for Laurel to give a public talk in Rome.

"Yet, there are factions in the city, some within the church itself, that do not wish for you to speak," Valencia informed her.

"I could have guessed that. I'm not worried."

"You should be." Valencia's eyes narrowed, and her face took on a serious, no-nonsense expression. "It is dangerous, especially here in Italy. There have been certain organizations working, for quite some time, against a unified Europe. *Fascistas*, Laurel. They still lament the downfall of Mussolini and remain dedicated to his extreme ideals."

Valencia took Laurel by the arm and led her away from the crowd. Even under the umbrella of a towering poplar, Valencia's tenseness did not ease. She seemed to be readying herself to drive home a point. "This call to women—this march to Jerusalem—is already a dangerous affair," she said. "Because of the sheer number of women involved, government tolerance is rapidly disintegrating."

"But we are moving in peace," Laurel said. She counted on the basic sanity of people.

"Don't deceive yourself. Certain political and corporate entities would destroy this march right now if they could. As you get closer to your destination, those in power will become even more threatened. You'll be cornering them, Laurel, and a cornered rat turns ugly." Valencia was not mincing words. "Remember, even the empire of Rome came to be vanquished as did the Vestal Virgins themselves when a group of men, known as the Church, and the Christian emperor Constantine decided they'd had enough of female priests and feminine guardians of the State."

As Valencia's fervor flashed passionately in her eyes, Laurel found herself transfixed. Was this the new paradigm—responsible, powerful women leading the world to peace?

"But back to *this* century," Valencia said. Her eyes moved across the crowd, watchful. "The question now is how do we move forward effectively without getting crushed like our predecessors?"

After a few moments, Laurel answered. "I can see only one way." She took out a pen and a notepad from her purse. It would be her last chance to get word to her brother-in-law. She wrote quickly and handed the note to Valencia. "Please give this message to Rosario."

Valencia glanced down at what Laurel had written. A look of surprise flashed across her face. "You're certain of this?" she asked.

"Yes." Laurel was.

"Then I will get it to him as quickly as possible."

"Thank you," Laurel replied, feeling humbled by all the help she was receiving. *That's how it's been going these days*, Laurel thought. So many women were stepping forward to meet her, to connect with a movement that started with just a few steps.

"Laurel," Valencia said as Laurel was about to walk away. "I may have sounded a bit harsh before. That wasn't my intent. I want you to know I fully support this march, but I needed to let you know my concerns for you and for the other women."

Laurel didn't doubt her sincerity.

"This is for you," Valencia said softly as she retrieved an item from her bag.

Laurel accepted the curious-looking straw figurine she was being given.

"*Argei.* The Vestal priestesses would throw them into the Tiber dur- ing one of their rituals." Valencia squeezed Laurel's hand. "May it bring you protection."

Laurel watched as the beautiful woman, Valencia, walked toward the sacred shrine. There, the flames were still leaping as the circle of women took offerings from the crowd.

I have been in the presence of a Roman Vestal.

As she turned to leave the grounds, Laurel knew where she would head before her talk—to the Tiber, the river of Rome's power and passion that flowed through the city and watered the life of its people. There, she would make her offering, praying that the world would once again em- brace the female guardianship of the human hearth.

CHAPTER 60

FATHER ROSARIO SELINE would have none of it. Bishop Rudolf had called him that morning.

"We hear your sister-in-law has come to Rome. We need to see you, Father Rosario."

And what do these devils want now, he had thought.

Rosario had seen it on the news. Laurel looked frail, but frail only in body, not in mind. Her eyes were the same, fierce and blue. *Almost twenty years.* That was the last time he had spoken to her. It was at the funeral . . . her son David's.

Rosario knew Laurel had never been one to hide her feelings, not liking what she referred to as the complacency of the Church. He knew the root of her opinions and even agreed with some of them. Yet his own devotion—his commitment and loyalty to the Holy Father—was boundless.

I would give my life for this Church. But today . . . even the patience of a saint would be strained.

Father Rosario Seline walked up to the oak doors of the bishop's office, pulled them open and entered like a gush of wind into the outer parlor. Bishop Rudolf and his assistant, Father Santiago, sat facing the door. They rose pretentiously, affecting a gracious welcome. Rosario knew, however, their intentions would be far less than honorable.

After beckoning him to sit, Santiago poured him a cup of coffee. Meanwhile, the bishop wasted no time in coming to the point. "You *must* stop her, Rosario. You are family. She will listen to you."

Rosario eyed them both quizzically and laughed. "Listen to me. You do not know Laurel."

"She has led these women on a crusade. It's madness, absolute madness. This international escapade, the women of the world converging upon Jerusalem." Bishop Rudolf made the sign of the cross.

"She must be stopped before all hell breaks loose," Father Santiago warned. "This will soon grow out of control."

"And there is pressure," the bishop insisted.

"Now we get to it." Rosario could almost see the shadows of the Church's money mongers lurking in the corners of the room. "What kind of pressure? From whom?"

With one slow blink of his eyes, it appeared that Rudolf was gathering all his deceptive powers. "There are many who support our church. They have been quite generous."

"I can make a very good guess who the instigator of all this is." Rosario stared at the bishop. "This is all too obvious."

"What do you mean, Rosario? We cannot simply disregard our supporters." Bishop Rudolf's patronizing glance was dismissive.

"The Holy Father knows nothing of this, I'm sure," Rosario said, his tone accusatory.

"I cannot say," Rudolf replied.

"I can." Rosario knew the benevolence of the Pope. He would give his consent to no such agenda.

"Bishop Rudolf is acting for the good of the Church," Father Santiago said coolly, coming to the bishop's defense. "He cannot presume to bother His Holiness with every detail. The bishop does not feel it is in his interest."

"Not in whose interest? The pope's or perhaps his own?" Rosario banged his fist on the table. *I've had enough of these money changers.* "I will not be a party to your sordid schemes and plots."

"But Rosario," Rudolf implored.

"But nothing. I take my orders from His Holiness," Rosario said, his anger mounting, "and from *no one* else."

Enough, he thought as he walked quickly out of the office and across St. Peter's Square. He had heard enough slanderous talk of Maggie Seline, enough fearful rhetoric about Laurel's behavior and how to quiet her allies, enough secret discussion regarding the Church's stand.

Rosario knew the forces manipulating the direction of the Vatican, cunning and sly, were also powerful. *Wolves in sheep's clothing.* He had managed for so long to keep his observant position, weaving in and out of the net, careful not to get caught in it.

But today, it was time to slash the web.

Let the spiders fall where they may.

At his home, several miles outside the city of Rome, Guiseppe Volpi sat in his study in his favorite armchair contemplating the future of the *Fratineri*. The *fascista*, forced into a retreat after the fall of Mussolini and Hitler, had quietly increased in number, moving stealthily in the shadows for years. Bolder now, the time was coming soon when they would march into the open again, a force to be reckoned with. Propaganda Due, Volpi determined, would be in the forefront.

There is no room for disruption, Volpi thought clenching his jaw.

As Grand Master, he had been informed that morning by Bishop Rudolf that Laurel Seline had arrived in Rome and was scheduled to speak at the Piazza Colonna. Apparently, her brother-in-law, a Vatican priest, was keeping them abreast of her plans.

Volpi had also learned that it was the mayor's office that had given her permission to speak publically. *That stupid mayor and his pious idealism.* Even Governor Leosone agreed that the move was a foolish one. For now though, thwarting Laurel Seline's day in the sun would be Volpi's main concern. Dealing with the mayor would have to wait.

Bishop Rudolf had set the wheels in motion, but Volpi had many other friends he could count on. Loyal Propaganda Due members infiltrated the city. Like bees creating honey, they nested in many factions of the government including the senator's office and the judicial quarters. The stock exchange—the Palazzo Dreher—had colonies unto itself. Money, like blood, pulsed through the exchange's arteries, and Volpi saw to it that many of the wealthy moguls wheeling within its confines understood their fate relied on P2's success.

The phone in his office buzzed. Volpi picked it up.

"Signor Volpi," his secretary announced, "Frederico Bonasari is on the line."

"Tell him to hold on," Volpi ordered. "I'll be with him in a moment."

The president of the National Television System, the up-and-coming network of Italy, would have much to tell him. The exclusive coverage of Laurel Seline's speech had been directed to his channel. Based on Bonasari's past record, Volpi was confident that the media coverage was well taken care of. Mostly under Propaganda Due control, NTS was comprised of many like-minded souls. That was the way Volpi liked to think of them. Some were actually P2 members themselves, and the others, well coaxed into being sympathetic to their cause. Fear and money worked wonders.

Satisfied that Bonasari had experienced a sufficient wait, Volpi picked up the phone. "Frederico."

"It's all in place," Bonasari asserted. "The TV crew has their orders. Everything will unfold as planned."

"And what is that plan?" Volpi asked.

"Laurel Seline will go to the piazza, but as soon as she opens her mouth, she will be overridden by a barrage of detractors. At the end of it all, she'll look like the confused old fool that she is. Then the camera crew will pull the plug on her . . . no speech, no call to the masses, just an overwhelming show of disapproval from the crowd and the whole stupid scene will be over."

Volpi smiled with approval. *Let the old woman go to Jerusalem. No one will even bother with her then.*

"Let's give the old dog a good kick," Bonasari added. "No one wants to be on the side of a loser."

"I never doubted you'd come through," Volpi complimented, feeling more than pleased. "Like Caesar overseeing the Colosseum, you know people want blood . . . enjoy it. It's the perfect ingredient for exciting the masses. Frederico, you're at your best when you bring out the worst in people."

Bonasari laughed heartily. "Thank you, sir. You're too kind. And of course, the part that sweetens the pie is that the ratings will go through the roof."

CHAPTER 61

PIETRO CENTAURA SAT in the driver's seat of the Fiat, going over the prearranged sequence of events. A foot soldier in P2, Pietro had earned the position of *disseminator*, a title that aptly reflected his role when disagreeable circumstances for the *Fratineri* warranted swift action.

Today, Grand Master Volpi had given Pietro the orders himself. The Seline woman would be stopped before she even began. Pietro could count on his military training which had taught him how to sit quietly for hours tuning his instincts, enabling him to detect trouble at incredible distances and then neutralize it with one shot. The woman didn't have a chance.

Sitting beside him was another soldier of the order, Rafael Magusto. Pietro was discontent to find himself working with Rafael, who had gained a reputation as a hothead who asked too many questions. *The Spanish Inquisitor.* That was the name the older P2 members had given their comrade from Barcelona. Pietro would tolerate him, though. His intuition told him that besides his stupid arrogance, Raphael did understand one thing clearly. The men they worked for were powerful, determined . . . and willing to pay plenty.

That morning, several women had hurriedly placed posters around the Square. Although people were gathering, the numbers were nowhere near what Pietro had expected. Where were the crowds?

He could count on his own comrades, though. Soon, Pietro knew, more right-wing legionnaires would appear and their orchestration would be in place. He and Rafael would conduct the procedure, and like a fine military band, they would perform in unison to overpower the enemy.

Rafael turned on the radio but nothing happened. "Damn thing's not working," he groaned. "No music."

Pietro was glad not to be listening to some hard rock station like a teenage buffoon. *Better to sit quietly until the prey arrives.* He leaned his head back for a moment until a pop and fizzing sound made him turn.

Rafael was bringing a can of soda to his lips.

Pietro watched as the foam rose out of the can, spilled onto Rafael's pants and then the car floor. He did not bother to hide his feeling of disdain. "Coke already?"

"Yes," Rafael said. He took another gulp. "The sugar helps me to think straight."

Right.

"Ah, that was good." A look of satiation spread across Rafael's face. "When's the old woman due, anyway?"

"Soon, I imagine," Pietro answered. "Still not much of a crowd, though."

Rafael smirked. "So, what's the big deal? I say let her shoot her mouth off and be done with it."

Pietro gripped the steering wheel. His years of military training had taught him to mask his anger with a stony countenance. "Your view is somewhat limited, Rafael, and you're not considering the consequences. There are political and financial interests at stake. We can't let people go on television and radio with such ideas . . . the internationalization of Jerusalem . . . all faiths and cultures sharing the city. And the women . . . "

Rafael nearly choked on his soda. "My own mother believes this crap."

"It's just a phase." Pietro had convinced himself. "Just watch. A little trouble here, a little trouble there. No woman can withstand much of that. They are not bred for it."

"And what *are* they bred for?" Rafael smiled lecherously as he tossed the empty can into the backseat.

Close by, at the mayor's offices in Rome, Valencia sat at her desk pondering the fate of the *Seline March.* As one of the leaders of Women in Black, she had organized as much as she could, coordinating with many other European groups. *Throughout France, Germany, Spain, England, Ireland, Norway, Sweden, Denmark* . . . countless women were emerging as leaders, countless women were rising to the occasion.

The Women's Movement, which had grown over the last twenty-five years, appeared ready to make a major leap. Although women had made strides, the canyon before them had stood vast and deep. But now they had the momentum and the numbers—all conditions were ripe for the change.

"Scusi, Signora."

Valencia turned toward the doorway of her office where a young man stood, pen in hand, glasses dangling from a chain around his neck. *Smells like a reporter.* "Signor. Can I help you?"

"Donato Felipe of *La Republica*," the reporter said. "I wanted to confirm with your office that Ms. Laurel Seline will be speaking at the Piazza Colonna this afternoon, and that it was this mayor's office that gave her permission to speak there and supports her—"

"You have heard correctly," Valencia interrupted him, "but I am quite busy, Signor. I don't know how you got onto this floor, but no one, including reporters, is allowed here except through authorization from my office."

"Pardon, Signora. That's all I really wanted to know," Felipe said, backing away with feigned apology. "Thank you. We will be there at noon today. Does Signora Seline wish to make a statement to us before her talk?"

"I am not her spokesperson, Signor." Valencia's position allowed her some power over the press, and she asserted it when necessary.

"Of course. I am not suggesting—"

"You can ask all the questions you wish of her after her talk, I'm sure."

Finally accepting her tone of dismissal, Felipe, without so much as a "good day," nodded his head and left.

As the door to her office closed, Valencia's phone began to ring. She grabbed the receiver. "Yes, yes. I've informed the press of the time and place. We will be ready, Rosario."

Valencia turned off her computer and straightened out some papers on her desk. From behind a raincoat in her closet, she pulled out a suitcase and then checked her handbag for her ticket and passport.

As she headed out of the office, Valencia sighed expectantly. She would be out of the country before the next page in history was turned.

"It's after twelve. Where is she?" Pietro wondered aloud.

The organizers of the event would surely have Laurel Seline there on time. And where was the crowd? Besides the men he had set in place in the piazza, there was barely a handful of onlookers. He sensed trouble.

"Looks like we might not have needed to come after all," Rafael stated.

Soon, the few people that were standing and waiting began to move away. They were heading toward a small group that had already formed in front of *La Rinascente*, a posh trendy department store that took up nearly the whole street. Pietro observed there was a display of television sets behind the huge glass windows.

Curious now, the two men left the Fiat and ventured over to the storefront.

As Pietro tried to peer past the onlookers, a gangly wide-eyed young man approached him.

"Are you here for the talk?" the man asked. Spaced-out and disheveled, he appeared to be a typical university student.

"Yes," Pietro answered, glaring at the unkempt youth.

"They say she moved her speech."

"Moved it!" Rafael yelled, his eyes bulging. "Where to?"

"Last-minute change. Down to the Spanish Steps. See?" The young man pointed to one of the large television screens.

Pietro and Rafael hurried to push their way to the front of the crowd. When they reached the glass window where they could view the coverage, Pietro let out a muffled curse.

The Spanish Steps were filled with people, right down to the spouting waters of the Fontana della Barcaccia. Amidst pockets of beautiful orange and red flowers, the enthusiastic crowd waved flags and handkerchiefs, aiming their salutations toward the diminutive woman standing at the top of the stairs.

Laurel Seline.

"And I call upon all the women of the world to act in unison," Laurel said, coming to the end of her talk. "Let us resolve our differences and unify in a common goal. Join us in marching for peace and hope."

"What about the men?" One of the reporters yelled out from amidst the sea of microphones.

"We ask that men show their support by sponsoring those women who wish to make the journey to Jerusalem and by organizing discussions, rallies, and peaceful protests here at home," Laurel said. "But the march itself is a task for women. The voices of women may not always be as wise as we'd like, may sometimes be as unfair as any man's, but by far the women of this world are basically unified. We seek to give birth, to create, to nurture, to protect. Most of us would rather see peace than war . . . resolution and compromise rather than hatred and dissent."

The Piazza di Spagna, the magnificent Spanish steps, rippled with people and pulsated with energy. As Laurel stood in front of the Trinita dei Monti, a loud pealing from the bells of its twin towers marked the end of her speech.

A call to action, summoning the hearts of humanity to unite as one.

She hoped it would be heeded.

CHAPTER 62

THE APPIAN WAY was built along the path of Rome's first aqueduct three hundred years before the birth of Christ, a history to which Air Force General Robert Gerard was indifferent. Today was about power. Senator Malcolm Denport of Pennsylvania, beside him in the back seat of the limousine, knew he was crossing his own personal Rubicon. Hurtling away from Rome on the same road along which Paul had been led in chains in 56 AD, the Senator was more in mind of the catacombs of San Sebastiano and San Callisto, for his journey was a betrayal of his own Christian heritage.

Traffic was light on the Via Appia Antica on this early Sunday morning. The flight from Washington had been uneventful, and the driver who met them at Leonardo da Vinci Airport in Fiumicino had not spoken to them since.

There was nothing to say.

Upon sight of their destination, the driver decelerated quickly and turned left through a column of stately cypress trees. Three kilometers down the private road, they came to a massive, black wrought-iron gate and twelve-foot high brick wall painted in pastel peach. Above the arched entrance, hanging from the red tiled roof, was a gilded bronze sign: *Villa Carnuntum*.

Security guards with bomb-sniffing dogs carefully scrutinized the car and its passengers, as well as the luggage in the trunk, before opening the gate and waving them through.

Finally. Senator Denport was relieved the ride was over. A genteel man, born within a family of Pennsylvania farmers, the Senator found the general's presence disdainful. Gerard, a man whose fleshy face appeared to be stamped in a permanent scowl, had been quiet enough during the ride. But now, Denport noted as they entered the villa, the general conveyed excitement, his jowls wrapping upward into a smile. It appeared that General Gerard's emergence into the rarified air of extreme wealth and power had placed him in an orbit for which he felt suited. He certainly was a long way from the cornfields of southeast Kansas.

Senator Denport, however, did not share the general's sentiment. *Idiot*, the senator thought of himself, *better that I was dead*. But it was too late now. His invitation to attend the Providencia Especial weekend had come through Reverend Farley, one of his principal financial sponsors. Up for re-election, Denport feared his more liberal constituents, angry about his support of America's involvement in Iraq's civil war, would no longer be backing him. That, coupled with the fact that the U.S. economy was floundering in a sea of debt only made the issue of campaign funding even worse. Indeed, Denport had made his deal with the devil, and now Reverend Farley was holding him to it.

After exiting the car, he and the general were led along a curved path into a lush garden courtyard. In the center, surrounded by flowers was a white marble fountain sculpted like a tree. As they passed it, Denport anxiously noted that coiled around the fountain's base and trunk was the bronze figure of a cobra, its head twice the size of a man's, shrouded by a hood.

Others summoned to the meeting—select members of the Propaganda Due *Fratineri* and "special guests"—began to appear along the garden path. Denport was well aware that these Black Friars, as they enjoyed calling themselves, had already proven their disdain for the church, social reform and anything reminiscent of pure democratic beliefs. Within their far-reaching scope, contempt for the European Community was paid more than lip service. The breadth of their actions against such "social befriendments" was like a toxic gas, lethal, but undetectable.

"So they've arrived." From his office at the back of the house, Rinaldo Donara, Guiseppe Volpi's bull-faced head of security, surveyed General Gerard and Senator Denport on a monitor as they walked through the villa garden.

The general and the senator, now part of the eclectic group of men being summoned into the house, passed under a tall arbor of evergreens and walked down the stone path that led to the well-guarded entrance. Once they were inside, Rinaldo, observing several other monitors,

watched them move from the foyer into a large oval parlor at the end
of the hall and finally take their seats. Just then, his "waiters", all armed
security agents, served coffee and cigars to all the guests before slipping
out of sight.

Sensing that the Grand Master was about to speak, the barrel-
chested Rinaldo barked a curt direction to his assistant. "Zoom in and
give me sound. I want to hear what's being said."

"Il momento di passare, tutto." The Grand Master, Guiseppe Volpi,
pounded his puffy fist on the oak podium. "The time has come for real
action."

The sixty-two year old Volpi, short but built like an ox, was dressed
in a dark blue suit and seemed a static contrast to the rich golden hues of
the Renaissance-style décor that surrounded him. His steely black eyes
surveyed the group, demanding silence.

"As we already know, the European Community has acted against
us, and our interests have been compromised. I am here to tell you today
that this situation is about to come to an end. Not only will we derail the
socialist views of our adversaries, but we will reclaim our rightful power,
lost to these communists and clerics." Volpi leaned forward over the podium, directing his powerful gaze toward the group. "Like Garibaldi we
are relentless, recognizing no setbacks."

As Senator Denport watched Volpi speak, he could not help feeling he had walked into a timeline of Roman descent. The podium
upon which Volpi was standing, designed with a polished copper *fas-
ces*—a bundle of birch and elm branches enclosing an axe, the ancient
Roman insignia of authority—as well as the massive painting of Benito
Mussolini inspecting his army that was hanging on the wall behind the
Grand Master's head sent a shiver down Denport's spine. As he stared
at the ominous signs, Denport tried but couldn't shake the one thought
that consumed him. *My God, why have I forsaken you?*

"Gentlemen, our man is in place," Volpi assured them smugly. "The
State, our State, will crush socialist views—the rampant liberal agendas
now infecting our politics—as well as those promoting their watered-
down, communist theories. No longer will we be dictated to by *poofta-
crats* in Brussels."

After the entourage of good old boys had a laugh, Volpi allowed himself an additional satisfaction.

"The foolish few who continue to be swayed by the naiveté of FDR and the Kennedys as well as by more recently canonized Democratic saints, like Mandela, will find themselves washed away by the tide of our new state order."

The room, saturated with the powerful and elite, seemed to inflate with each breath of arrogance that Volpi released into the air. Meanwhile, Denport realized, almost none of the members of Propaganda Due knew the degree and scope of their organization's reach, the real names of agents working for them, or the intricate design of their web. Only a handful of the highest initiates and the Grand Master had that information. Denport did notice, though, the several Americans and Brits around the room and wondered what hand they were playing in the game. No matter. Amidst it all, he had an overwhelming sense that in each member's heart, which had long ached for action, one sentiment resounded: *At long last, we move.*

Volpi raised his glass of red wine in a toast. "The pieces are in place. The pundits of Islam *will* fall, and their precious oil will be ours. We will squash the aims of the elders of Zion and their American puppet state. There is only our nemesis to contend with, the lineage which has plagued us through the centuries. Finally, we shall put out the torch of Samuels and Stein and break the link of *the Way.*"

As Volpi ended his speech, the group stood in ovation. There was nothing like a good dose of arrogance to rouse the addicted to their feet. Volpi's words were like cocaine, the more power he could promise, the better the high.

The waiters, apparently having anticipated the rapacious manners of the brotherhood, emerged en masse with more coffee, pastries and Rey del Mundo cigars. One of them spoke quietly to Denport. "Follow me, Senator. Signor Volpi will see you now."

Filled with anticipation, Denport rose from his seat. He snaked through the crowded room, realizing he would soon have to be accountable for his own fate.

CHAPTER 63

GIOVANNI MABUS REALIZED that his well-crafted plan had led him to where he sat today—Villa Carnuntum—the lair of P2's most feared and secretive wolf, Guiseppe Volpi. The grandson of Mussolini's banker, Franco Predappio, Volpi had once been a military officer, and was still, to outward appearances, a bank official. He was, of course, much more. Mabus had been well aware of Volpi's ties and developed a partnership with him, gaining the leader's trust. It even turned out to be Volpi's idea for Mabus to serve as President of the EU Commission. *Brilliant*, Mabus thought at the time. *The fox in the hen house.*

But now, there was a new plan.

As Mabus sat quietly waiting for Volpi to begin their meeting, he gazed around the Grand Master's sparsely furnished den—*the strategy room*—adorned with only a few essentials . . . several tables, leather-padded chairs, and a large, antique world globe. Across from him, the faded fresco on the wall depicted a stern full-bearded Solomon glaring as, before his kingly throne, two women were remonstrating for his sage counsel, while a soldier with drawn sword held a baby by its ankle. *Volpi's aspirations.*

As always, inscrutable, Mabus gave no heed to the hard-nosed Grand Master as he paced across the Persian carpet, or to Senator Denport as he shifted uncomfortably in the chair next to him. Mabus brought the brandy snifter close to his nose as Volpi stopped and met Denport's anxious gaze.

"Senator, there are few options left for America,' Volpi stated bluntly. "Your political and energy policies have tied you to Saudi Arabia like an anchor to a chain."

Malcolm Denport drained the last of his scotch and poured himself another as he listened to the P2 leader.

"You and the vice president will now work your charms to ensure America's support of the Peace Conference."

"Just when and how am I supposed to do this, especially . . . ?" Denport, both anguished and confused, turned toward Mabus.

Mabus ignored him. Denport, he knew, was torn between his dread of what he had become involved in and his desire to hear the plan.

"I mean, the Peace Conference," Denport stuttered. "The military maneuvers taking place in the Persian Gulf. Why is Israel involved? That's never happened before, not with the Saudi military."

And won't again, Mabus thought.

"That's not for you to worry about." Volpi spoke to the Senator as if he were a child, *or an idiot*. "Just make sure General Gerard is assigned to CENTCOM Air Ops in Qatar."

Settled comfortably, Mabus struck a match and lit his Rey del Mundo cigar. Soon the billionaire Saudis with their desert robes, porno stars, playing cards, and sleek private jets would slip back under the hot rocks with the lizards and scorpions. Along with Mabus' other goals, returning Arab civilization to its rightful eminence would be a pleasure worth the price. If it took the Jew Einsof, the fascist Volpi, and the fool Denport to accomplish, then it must be so.

"Giovanni."

Mabus looked up. Volpi, now seated across from him, leaned forward. "Your energy system will be ready?"

As Volpi asked the question, Mabus noticed the anxious look on Denport's face. *Money, that's why the Senator is here.* Selling out his country wasn't such a cruel fate—for progress, commerce, industry—those were the lies Denport, no doubt, told himself, when cash in hand and more power were the real draw.

"Within the year, my engineers assure me," Mabus finally answered. "They have unlocked the missing elements Einsof thought he had kept secret."

Mabus smiled. *Einsof, the child, thinking he could hide his idealistic aims.* "A key element, as it turns out, is the use of modern technology to advance ancient knowledge. For one hundred years scientists and engineers have puzzled over how Nikola Tesla generated electromagnetic wave propagation at Colorado Springs and transmitted wireless electrical fields. Einsof, working with Tesla's notes and his own system, has designed an amplifying receiver that captures the earth's own energy.

His own peculiar contribution recognizes the benefit of incorporating additional smaller systems that will both receive as well as transmit this energy. A plasma grid, if you will." Mabus paused, feeling astonished. "Just think. Millions of households around the globe pulsing energy to and from a mother grid. Start-up time would be cut dramatically."

Denport didn't appear to be interested in the particulars. "So, we only need enough oil for perhaps another ten years?" he asked, voicing his concern.

"Perhaps *far less* than that, Senator," Volpi said, eying him intensely. "With your assistance, Vice President Bohmer will be in the position to assure our success . . . and of course, your own."

Mabus let the charade play itself out for Denport's benefit. While he was content to conquer quietly, he recognized Volpi found pleasure in toying with his victims.

"With the Saudi oil fields no longer needed, only the House of Saud and the oil companies will miss their currency. And then, of course," Volpi said, applying the final stroke, "the world will turn to us for energy."

Actually, they will turn to me.

Mabus inhaled deeply on his cigar. *Another domino set in place*, he thought.

They would fall neatly when the time was right.

THE BOOK OF WOMEN
THE SELINE MARCH

*The women will come from the twelve directions
to the central point of thirteen*

TURKEY

Across the dark, sullen expanse of water, the former Soviet Republic could not be seen or forgotten. Too many sons of Kurucasile and other villages along the Turkish coast had been lost, caught between the hazards of the coal mines and heavy factories in Zonguldak, the uncertain waters of the Black Sea fishing fleet, and the search for economic freedom in the European Community job market.

Halide Maltovitch drew her scarf close about her head and gave a kick at the geese to move them aside. She walked off the dock behind her home and slipped through the creaky wooden gate onto the rough, stone and mud street. The morning bus for Ankara was due through Bartin at six, and she had to hurry.

Halide was quite used to rushing to catch her ride. For the past eight years she worked as a domestic for Judge Bashmar. It was his daughter, Nelleke, who had called and told her of the New Jerusalem walk.

Today, she and her friend would join a long tradition of Turkish women . . . women who protested for their rights and for the humane treatment of their comrades. When Kemal Ataturk ended Ottoman rule and freed Turkey in the early 1920s, women were granted many rights but they were never fully realized. Even now, women were dismissed, not as worthy as men. They still found themselves fighting against a stubborn patriarchal society that had lived for thousands of years by a well-entrenched proverb.

Women should never be free of a child in the womb and a whip on the back.

The thought made her run. Soon, she would be with Nelleke, and they would board the bus together. *This bus will lead us all to freedom. It will take us to a land of peace.* Halide almost laughed, knowing she was going to one of the most volatile places on earth. Yet, she had to believe.

For Halide, there was no other choice.

RUSSIA

In the city of Yaroslavl, Sonia Vasilievna left early. Slowly, she closed the creaking door of her apartment, not wishing to awaken her sleeping husband. He was old and had no interest in the present turmoils of the world.

"Crimes against humanity." Her husband had scoffed at the phrase. "Crimes against humanity have always been, my dear. They've always been and they will always be. For how can you stop aggression? Almost 20 million people died under Stalin . . . collectivization, starvation, executions, the State owning everything! How do you stop men who want to possess the world and control everyone in it?"

"We start by taking steps. We begin by honoring the women," she told him, but her words had fallen on deaf ears.

"You are too old," he said, waving her away. "Leave the troubles of the world to the young and foolhardy."

Sonia had made the decision then. Her age would not stop her. After all, wasn't the woman who began the march in New York in her seventies?

SYRIA

Hoda knew she risked her father's wrath by slipping out of the house. She was jeopardizing his army career and perhaps his life, even though he was an honored soldier, having played a pivotal role in squashing the fundamentalist revolt in Hamah in 1982. The army had killed twenty-five thousand citizens then and her father's ruthlessness had won the president's favor.

Her father's fate would not be enough to stop her, though. Hoda wrapped her *hijab* around her face to conceal her identity and began walking through the streets of Damascus to meet her sister, Khadija, who had just been divorced by her husband. He had merely needed to pronounce *talaka*—repudiation—three times and their marriage was over.

Al Jazeera had been carrying stories on the Women's March for almost two weeks. With all that had happened, Hoda had not needed to spend much time convincing Khadija to become a part of it.

"Men always crush what they do not understand. They would kill us in a moment to uphold their strange beliefs."

*"But they have no concern for **our** beliefs." Khadija hung her head with sadness.*

"Exactly," Hoda confirmed, *"so we should be willing to die for them."*

Today, Hoda realized, they might have to do just that. Still, anything was better than the oppression of a man's world gone mad. She hoped their plan to cross the border nearby at El Arida by claiming to be on a shopping mission to Beirut would work.

As she spotted Khadija under the awning of her home, Hoda took a deep breath to buoy her courage. If it were not for the strange comet in the sky, she might not even attempt the journey. It was a sign, and signs and omens were messages from the angels, be they deadly or beneficent.

Only a fool would turn her back on them.

IRAN

In the streets of Esfahan, Elaheh raised her voice with the others.

"We are the women, the mothers of this country. Give us back our natural rights!"

Initially, the clerics of the Guardian Council stood on their balcony looking amused by the sight of several women protesting in the courtyard, but now Elaheh could see their wrathful contempt rearing its head as the women's group grew larger.

"We are the women, the mothers of this country. Give us back our natural rights!"

The clerics ruled with a heavy hand. Domination was the key factor in Iranian politics. Under Islamic law, women were once again being forced to cover all their hair and wear long and loose-fitting clothing. They could not even get a job without the permission of their husbands. As more and more women met in secret, Elaheh's group became emboldened, and today dared to speak out before the clerics. Yet Elaheh knew that criticizing these laws meant certain reprisal, perhaps even death.

"Enough! Enough!" The women yelled even louder.

Yes, Elaheh thought, *we've had enough.* She felt the anger that was seething in all of them. These men were pigheaded, belonging to a long lineage that for thousands of years had been dominating the women of her country, paying no heed to their humanity.

"Enough! Enough!" Some women were screaming fitfully now. It was as if they were shaking a stick at a sleeping giant.

The police answered back with their clubs. Swinging violently, their heavy batons cracked down upon backs, arms, legs. Although the streets were pealing with screams of agony, Elaheh and the other women continued to yell. "Enough! Give us back our natural rights!"

"Women and men are equal. We only wish our rights to be respected." Elaheh was now looking into the scarred face of a police sergeant. He twisted her arm and led her through the crowd.

"Human rights!" The words rushed from her lips, but the hard crack against her neck soon knocked the force of her voice from her.

TIBET

On the Tibetan plateau of Lhasa, Ling watched the Chinese soldiers as they walked down the streets. She was waiting for her Tibetan friend, Drolkar, to arrive and together they would join the great *Seline March*.

Ling had convinced her friend it was now the karma of women to stand up and come forward. *Women must bring peace,* she thought, *no matter where.* It had been many years since her government had invaded, and now Chinese and Tibetans, like the Arabs and Jews, had no choice but to move forward. Ling had recognized long ago that you cannot side with one party over another, but must work together to restore harmony.

Before leaving China, Ling lived in Sichuan close to the giant Buddha of Leshan. A magnificent sculpture carved out of the rock, the stone Buddha sat, noble and unperturbed. Ling would watch as mere humans walked over his toes and across his feet. They were of no consequence to the Buddha, though, whose gaze lanced formidably through the sky.

But then, the Chinese Army marched through the town and the questioning eyes of the Buddha became unrelenting. The soldiers paid no heed, no respect or regard, throwing their bottles of beer and their cigarettes at his feet, instead of flowers and incense.

So at seventeen, Ling had decided. She headed south toward the land of Tibet, and toward the *religious barbarians* as the Chinese government liked to call them. Ling felt an affinity with their suffering, their lonely plight. The nations of the world had turned their back on the Tibetans and their "insignificant" country so as not to upset their relations with China.

Too much money, too much power, too much greed. Ling recognized it long ago. *It makes people inhuman.*

When she had finally entered Tibet, few welcomed her, the awkward Chinese nun, and treated her suspiciously. The idea of Chinese spies watching the Tibetans was not a new one and not unfounded. It was not until the day that gunfire had exploded on the mountainside that villagers declared Ling a great heroine. Covered in the blood of a young Tibetan *ani*, Ling brought the nun to a nearby clinic. It did not take long for word of her courage to spread. Ling grew in favor with her neighbors, and the *anis* then took her into their nunnery.

But Ling soon found that life as a Tibetan nun was squalid. Shabby, with little provisions, the nunnery was barely a shelter. Electricity was practically nonexistent and the women moved about and read by candlelight in the evenings. They went without, as many felt they should. *We are women*, the others had told her, *of lower birth, so what should we expect?*

When, Drolkar, the *ani* whom Ling had saved, was well enough to return to the nunnery, she shared everything she had with Ling. It was karma, Drolkar had told her, that they should meet and care for one another. Perhaps one day their people would make amends—perhaps peace would once again fill the mountains of Tibet and China.

When Ling discovered that so many women were walking for peace, she convinced Drolkar it was time to leave their small village. Peace was all either one of them had ever hoped for their whole lives—peace between brother and sister, between their people. There was only one other thing that she and Drolkar yearned for now, and that was to receive the Buddha's teachings as men did, so freely, so much more easily—to be seen as human beings.

Ling remembered what Drolkar had said to her once. "How can a lama say enlightenment is for all beings, yet when he sees me, a woman, he does not give me the teachings as he would a man?"

But today, Ling felt the rising warmth of hope in her heart. She and Drolkar would take the train together, through northern India and the vast land of Pakistan, then travel with the trucks and cars that would caravan through Iran, along the border of Iraq and into Saudi Arabia, entering into Jordan and then, finally, Israel.

"We will march for peace—for women and for men. We go to find the pure land," Ling told Drolkar when her friend arrived.

As they waited for the bus that would take them over the border to the train station, Ling heard the voices of some of the *anis* in her head. *It can't be done. You'll be killed. The women will never succeed.*

The black chant had taken some of the wind out of her, but Ling decided to think otherwise. She realized she was not alone. So many other women had not allowed themselves to be stopped by empty voices that never uttered a sound for peace.

As the khaki-dressed soldiers eyed the crowd suspiciously with their intimidating stares, Drolkar moved closer, seeming to know her thoughts. "You must believe that good can come from good," she whispered intently. "You *must* believe."

Like the clear ringing of a bell, Ling realized the power in that one word.

It was *belief* that would get her there.

INDIA

Priti Menon sat alone in her office in Darjeeling unable to rid herself of the feeling of frustration and pain. Another day, and still her students were unable to attend school because of the gunfire and skirmishes.

She had come to know the effects of hatred and bloodshed early on. Although Priti's father was a professor at the University of Delhi, and she had grown up with the privilege of education and status, surrounding her in every direction was an antiquated caste system, branding people born within a certain community and chaining them to their fate.

But it was not only these caste divisions that caused trouble. There was now great unrest in Bhan Bhakta Sarani where she was commissioned to run the primary school. The beautiful rolling hills, filled with the rich greenery of tea plantations, proved a deceptive background as so often Muslims and Hindus would fight bitterly. *Always about land use, water rights, or religious supremacy.* Men carried rifles by day in some areas, their anger drawing blood. Although the vast majority of people were not involved in the fighting, it did not take many to create fear and chaos.

It is amazing, Priti thought, *how only a few distraught souls, whose callous hearts can find no mercy, are able to destroy the peace in an instant.*

She looked out the window toward the peaks of the majestic mountains surrounding her.

Glistening snow still clung to the top of Kanchenjunga, the highest of all mountains in India. Above and below, a misty blue sky and the green hues of the valley greeted her eyes with an explosive dance of color. How beautiful and primitive her land was, so why was it filled with so much unrest?

Her fear turned to courage as it dawned on her. Only the extraordinary could effect change.

The Great Mother has blessed this women's march, Priti thought.

Through Saraswati, Durga, Kali and others, the Great Mother had shown her face, and through all women she created the universe, including the earth itself. It is just and right that women should walk together and allow the Great Mother to appear in the midst of a most troubled land. Women had always opened up the world, and their creative spirit would give birth in Jerusalem as well.

Priti felt her heart give rise to understanding. This great march was meant to free more than just Jerusalem.

Was it really, then, only for the sake of Jews and Muslims?

No, she realized. *It's for all the people. All the daughters and the sons of this world.*

LIBYA

On the African continent, Ensala knew survival. Her homeland of Libya had its share of devastation. As she sat in an empty classroom in the Benghazi Women's College, she wondered whose life she was living. A professor of political science, she recognized that teaching about atrocities was not enough.

Pedantic abstraction. Ensala smiled to herself. That was the malady that had befallen her until the underground movement came crashing through her door one morning the previous summer. Professor Saifullah, her colleague, rushed in without even a knock, followed by several young women from the Darfur region of Sudan on the run from Janjaweed terror.

That morning had only been the beginning. Ensala then joined the movement herself and helped to liberate countless refugees from Algeria, Ethiopia, Kenya, the Sudan, and Rwanda.

So now, as a Libyan woman, a leader, and an intellectual, Ensala welcomed the new onslaught that this Jerusalem walk brought forth. When she closed her eyes, she could see them all . . . tributaries of women flowing across the continent.

From the southern tip of South Africa, from Botswana and Mozambique, from Kenya, Ethiopia, the Sudan, up along the majestic Nile, from Nigeria and Central Africa, and across Morocco and Algeria, through Libya to Egypt—they moved across the continent in great caravans, in cars and buses, in trains and automobiles. They were the women who knew the sorrow of genocide, their countries being ravaged by the onslaught of civilization, the unearthing of diamonds, gold and oil, and the hunt for the great wild animals—their skins and furs, tusks and horns, the coveted trophies of men. Desire and greed had already run through their continent like a raging river, overflowing its beds, flooding the population, killing off the species and leaving the survivors in ruin.

Ensala knew their courage and knew their pain. So many of them had walked through her door, looking for refuge. Now she would march forward with them, no longer powerless, no longer hiding their faces—crossing borders through numbers and sheer force of will. Together, they would free their voices and respond to the call of *Seline*.

Egypt

Hosanna had felt the hand groping her, pushing her, then beating her. She turned to try to face her attacker but he grabbed her groin.

"Pig of a female. Shut your mouth and tend to your family." He threw her forward then and she fell, her face slamming onto the hard, dirty street.

"Enough! Enough! You are killing your mothers!"

From the ground, Hosanna heard the voices as if they were coming over a muffled loudspeaker. The Islamic women around her railed passionately against the violence they themselves had experienced in Cairo. So many of her friends had been held captive by the police or military if their husbands were even remotely perceived to be involved in any kind of dissent against the government. Pressuring the family, taking wives and daughters into custody, had become the natural way of the regime. By coercion, the authorities imposed their will.

Hosanna and many of her friends finally reacted to the suppression. Starting their own grassroots movement, *Our Voice*, they gathered secretly throughout the city, promoting public discussion about the intimidation. When they had slashed her friend Jihan's face in the street as she was walking home from a meeting, Hosanna and the others decided they had reached the end of their veiled campaign. The time had come to step out into the open.

Now, with the blood running down from the cut on her lip, Hosanna felt the sting of retribution first-hand. Painfully, she struggled to get back on her feet.

"Come." Johassa, a friend and a member of the Muslim Brotherhood, grabbed her by the arm and pulled her up, hurrying her to the periphery of the crowd.

They barely stopped running when Hosanna heard the cries of the women. A number of men—loyal supporters of the ruling government—had surrounded the protesters. They started to scour the women with obscenities, but soon their dark mood blackened further. The men began pulling on the women's hair and dragging them down to the ground.

Hossana stood and watched in anguish as riot control officers did nothing, allowing a number of women to be beaten.

"Disgrace! You are shamed!" Bloodied and in pain, some of the women were screaming.

It was only as horrified passersby began to protest, that the riot squad felt pressured into action.

It is a bleak day for our country, Hosanna thought, *a bleak day for Islam.*

Hosanna fled, knowing the women would regroup at the bus caravan. It had only been a few days since Hosanna and her comrades had heard of the *great walk*. They had made the decision that after the protest they would press onward, no matter what, and join the women marching out of Cairo toward the Israeli border.

We have remained silent for too long, Hosanna knew. She realized that *Our Voice* was but one among a swiftly growing number of women's groups, small and large, developing the courage to speak out. With a heart filled with hope for women and for peace, she knew that her own country would play host to the masses. The fire would burn in Egypt's belly, fueled by each woman's passion, and with tens of thousands moving toward Jerusalem, Egypt would be hosting an eruption.

A blaze that men could not extinguish.

GUATEMALA

Flora DeLeyo of Mayan Indian descent was visiting her family home in Antigua on the Guatemalan mountainside. It had only been recently, merely five years ago, that the little town where she had been born and raised had acquired television reception. That great miracle, she realized, had brought with it a great curse.

The sun had always cast golden hues upon the Mayan world of sound and color, so brilliant on the mountainsides. As a child, amidst the squalling of the birds, Flora had played in the streams with the other children and ate the fruit of the grand banana. Now, over the last several years, Flora felt she was bearing witness to a slow death. What had been the country's most precious commodity, the great trees flowering with their golden banana fruits, had become her native people's deadliest.

Now, instead of laughter and gossip, she heard the babble of television sets through the windows as she passed her neighbors' homes. No longer did she see the children playing and imagining themselves to be the *caciques*, the Indian chiefs, fighting conquistadors. No longer did they pretend to ride the great horses, as she had as a child, falling into glassy pools, attempting to escape by sea from the oncoming Spaniards, while proud and courageous comrades splashed in to save them amidst laughter and screams.

Flora had grown up during the civil war that had consumed her country and ravaged her people. She left long ago, a rebellious young Indian woman, determined to make a difference. Now, using a pseud-onym, she wrote for a popular South American publication, her com-mentaries often critical of the Guatemalan government and its leaders.

Undercover in my own country. She met the thought with a painful laugh.

Some of Flora's friends had pleaded for her to return, and so now here she was, reluctant but hopeful.

"Speak to the people," Renault, her older brother's best friend prod-ded her. "They respect what you have become. They'll listen. Tell them the truth, before the television sets turn their minds to banana mush."

The platform in the middle of the town square was laced with red and white paper ribbon, and the small shops and coffee stands that lined the road were decorated with balloons. The festive colors and regalia were synonymous with her people's joyful nature. But today, Flora was not there to speak of joy. Parties, rich food and lighthearted music were not why she had traveled to the remote village.

The square was bursting with celebration and song when Renault brought her to the microphone stand, but Flora barely waited for the music to die down before she spoke.

"Guatemala has become a killing field."

The laugher stopped quickly and voices fell to a whisper. Sober faces soon replaced intoxicated smiles.

"Native Indians are being persecuted and murdered. We have lived under this madness for too long." Flora tried to keep her voice steady as she continued. "So now we cannot just watch as others, too, are tortured for their beliefs. Once again, the American government is supporting unjust policies that are doing just that. We cannot simply stand by and let it happen when this opportunity presents itself to us. We must speak out, not only for *ourselves,* the Guatemalan people, but for all indigenous peoples everywhere—all those who have been murdered in the name of big business, big religion, big government. We will no longer tolerate the BIG LIE!"

Eyes looked toward her hopefully, the light of freedom breaking through the pain.

"We must march now with our North and South American sisters, our European, Asian, Middle Eastern, and African sisters. We will all march together, no longer tolerating the sons of this earth destroying their mothers. We all belong in Jerusalem, side by side. It is for the Spirit that we must do this, the great divine Spirit which is in all of us and from which we all come."

Suddenly, there was a spray of gunfire in the distance. Renault was soon by her side. He yanked her by the arm and pulled her from the platform. "Run. You must run," he said, breathless. "Soldiers are entering the village."

Flora followed quickly, sprinting after him into a narrow alley. *Running, always running.* Maybe the gathering in Jerusalem would change all that. Maybe together, they could make some change for the good.

Just then, the whizzing sound of a bullet made her fall to the ground. *There seems to be no time anywhere for talking,* Flora thought, *but plenty of time for shooting.*

AUSTRALIA

Samantha Harris was a true child of pioneers. Although born in Alice Springs, her family was originally from England and had settled in the desert community in the 1870s. Back then, Alice Springs had been a staging point for overland telegraph lines. Her great, great grandfather, William, had worked as a telegrapher in town. His grandson, her grandfather Miles Harris, had always told her their family was like the American revolutionaries, only non-violent.

"We Aussies believe," Miles would declare with grandfatherly wisdom, "if you've got something to say, say it loud, say it large, and at least do it with some color."

Now, as Samantha sat naked under the baking sun with seven hundred other nude women on the side of a hill in Byron Bay, her grandfather's words seemed all the more poignant. Together, the all-female troop of demonstrators, all ages and all sizes—Black, White, Aboriginal,

Oriental, Latino, big breasted as well as small—creatively spelled out the phrase *No War* with their bodies.

I believe this classifies as colorful, Samantha thought, as her wide-eyed cohorts smiled and waved at an on-coming helicopter. As one of the leaders organizing the pro-peace demonstration protesting the war in Iraq, Samantha had called a local news affiliate herself. When the producer found out she was the daughter of Michael Harris, a newscaster from a rival station, he assured her a chopper would be there, and the station's photographer and videographer would be memorializing the event for primetime.

"Sammy!"

Samantha turned as she heard her name called. Her friend, Eliza was pointing westward. Another helicopter was heading their way, *Sky News* painted on its side.

Eliza's big breasts flailed from side to side as she shook with excitement. "Sammy, I think we're going national."

Indeed, Samantha thought, *national news.* Seven hundred women standing on the side streets of Canberra as the Prime Minister drove by to the capital would have been a blip on a newscaster's radar screen, but seven hundred naked women using their bodies to tell the world "No War" on a hillside in Byron Bay, now *that* was a story.

Suddenly, like a bolt from the blue an idea flashed through Samantha's mind. Why hadn't she thought of it before, she wondered, as she grabbed the bullhorn by her side.

"Now ladies," her voice boomed out over the hill, "what do we want?"

"No war!" The women answered in unison.

"What do we want?"

"No war!" they yelled even louder.

"What?"

"No war! No war! No war!"

Samantha jumped to her feet and began to turn in a circle allowing her eyes to scan the women across the grass.

"And what are we willing to do?"

Her question was met with uncertain silence.

"Are we going to march?" Samantha asked, prompting.

The women turned toward each other and toward her, looking confused.

Then one woman, part of the *N* in *No* yelled out, "We're going to march! We're going to march to Jerusalem!"

"*Where* are we going?" Samantha now flashed a look of ascent toward the crowd.

"We're going to march to Jerusalem!" they responded, yelling fervently although out of sync.

"*Where?*"

"To Jerusalem! To Jerusalem!"

The women burst out in applause and joyous laughter.

Samantha had known from the very beginning they had to say it loud and say it large. The world was too lost in *American Idol.* Not many were interested in sanity, clear thinking, or fervent pleas. Outrageous behavior . . . by God, butt-naked women, that was the way to go.

Samantha sat down once again and turned her face up toward the helicopters whirring loudly overhead. Waving and smiling at the cameras, she joined her naked sisters, each willing to play the fool in order not to be one.

ENGLAND

Cynthia Reynolds, Women for Peace London faction, stood in the pouring rain holding a sign and a banner alongside her friends as cars honked favorably, as well as sometimes . . . not so favorably.

A white Austin with rap music pumping out of its windows slowed down as it passed them. "You birds ought to take it where it belongs—to the crapper!"

Take it where it belongs. Right . . . that's right.

Cynthia had dropped off her two small children at daycare to join the other women gathered on the streets at Piccadilly Circus. Cynthia, thirty years old, a singer and songwriter had just released her first album, self-recorded in her home studio in London. It was what a lot of her musician friends were doing these days since they were all up against a conglomerate of steel-trap mindsets—the recording industry.

The bottom line was they were simply facing facts. Dominated and controlled by men, any artist not shaking her booty or who happened to be above the age of twenty-five need not bother to apply. The record moguls chose the look, they chose the kind of songs to be heard, they created the trends and then everyone followed along. In fact, good artists—males and females—were laid to waste for "what works."

Vision, artistry, creativity down the tubes for the sake of the almighty euro.

Cynthia had to admit she started going to the Women in Black gatherings because of their focus on gender equality. She just hadn't known they were talking about something more than women's rights in the music business. But slowly, she realized that even her agenda was intertwined with a larger picture. The rights she wanted to help flourish became more profound. Women's rights became human rights. And now there was something even larger to demonstrate about, something that would have an impact on the whole world, and she wanted to be a part of it.

Her group learned that Laurel Seline was in Rome and was now headed to Jerusalem. Some of Cynthia's friends already had tickets to leave for Cairo that very evening. Would their presence actually prove meaningful?

Cynthia struggled to put aside her trepidation. *Sometimes a person just has to take a chance*, she thought, the rain trickling down her face.

Perhaps just trying itself would make a difference.

FRANCE

Yvette Souvie sat in her office in Paris staring out the window that looked down onto Regnault Street. She understood that the decision she was about to make would affect her career monumentally. As a French journalist covering the United Nations, she had witnessed the diplomatic wrangling over Iraq, and like her government, disagreed with the United States and Britain.

During the year after 9/11, France maintained its position that the UN needed to perform more weapons inspections and keep a diplomatic stance. Her government disfavored any violent action and asserted that going to war had to be a last resort. At that historic time, Yvette was truly proud of her country's stance.

When it was finally revealed that *there was no evidence of weapons of mass destruction* after the invasion of Iraq, Yvette had not been surprised. Even now, with the "war president" gone and a new American administration in place, she did not trust the U.S. stance. She was frightened, like other journalists in her country, about where all of it would lead. As the war moved full steam ahead, and the relations between Jews and Muslims in the Middle East worsened, she found herself unable to shake a feeling of impending doom.

Yvette recalled the article she had written for the French newspaper, *Le Monde*, where she voiced her concern.

If we cannot take a stand that reflects sanity and fairness that will lead to peace and reconciliation, then the ticking time bomb, the city of Jerusalem itself, will be annihilated.

But at this time, Yvette realized, they were all words of the past. The world did not need any more editorials. It needed action.

The Seline March.

What better way for a journalist to know and tell the truth than to join the march herself. The thought felt radical. After all, Yvette believed in its premise, and that way she could monitor first hand how the women were met at the border.

Her heart beat quickly. It was a dangerous venture, Yvette concluded, but one that had to be journeyed. Her purpose clear, she gathered her laptop and briefcase and rushed down to the crowded street to hail a cab. If she hurried, she would be able to catch the six thirty flight out of Charles de Gaulle.

GERMANY

Monica Eder, a political science major, walked across the campus of Cologne University to meet her friends. She had just finished having an argument in class with Rolf Heitman, a watered down neo-Nazi she had grown to hate. What she found frightening was that she was meeting a growing number of people these days who resembled young Rolf—polished, smart, with pressed shirts that resembled their smooth, fascist ideas.

It seemed there was a new dawn for Hitler youth. White supremacy lived on, she knew, for she witnessed it first-hand, although in recent times in Germany those adhering to the Nazi ideals needed to blend a little differently than they did in other countries. Monica could recognize them though, by the icy shine of their eyes and what appeared to be an imprinted smirk line at the corner of their mouths.

Monica stopped walking and took a deep breath, allowing the light breeze blowing across the lawn to help her cool down from the heat of her previous argument. As she stood there breaking free from her tension, she recalled the day of reunification. Monica had only been five when that horrid wall was opened up, when East and West Germany, previously divided by hatred, became one again.

Since the time of Hitler's defeat, the horrible split between Germany's people had existed . . . a rift that separated families, friends, leaders . . . a slash upon the land. The wound had healed as much as it could. Although the body of Germany appeared whole again, Monica knew a deep scar remained. It was not only Germany's scar, though. It belonged to the whole world. Now, fascism was rearing its ugly head once again, and like an octopus with many tentacles, its varying factions were spreading across every ocean.

It's time for us to divert the power away from those without spiritual or moral conscience, who live off the blood and suffering of others for their own gain.

Monica walked forward once again toward the campus exit. With the power of her legs adding momentum to her stride, she had but one thought.

Wholeness . . . unity. The spirit of women will infuse this world with humanity, and Jerusalem will be the gateway.

SPAIN

In the Cementerio de la Almudena in Spain, Rosetta Castilla laid a small bouquet of red bougainvilleas at her sister Solar's grave. *A small remembrance for one so beautiful.* The setting sun colored the sky an orange and yellow. It was the time of day her sister had loved the most.

Rosetta remembered the awful day of Solar's death. Rosetta had been standing in the subway in Madrid, when a tremendous explosion knocked her down to the platform. She felt it must have encompassed all of Spain. Waking up in the hospital a day later, Rosetta learned the terrible truth. Her sister was gone. An Al Qaeda terrorist bombing had killed nearly two hundred people and over two thousand more had been injured.

First the 2001 attack in New York . . . then Madrid had been targeted next.

So many of her fellow Spaniards had felt Prime Minster Aznar was to blame for the horrible incident. He had insisted in supporting the U.S. and its insane war in Iraq. So what if ninety percent of the people of Spain opposed it?

Disgraceful. A tear rolled down Rosetta's face. *The time to stop this insatiable quest for power and this tremendous greed is now, with the Seline movement.* Some place on this earth needed to be a symbol, a haven for peace. Why not Jerusalem?

Rosetta would leave today. She would join the tens of thousands of others who were headed toward the Holy City. She had to admit she wasn't doing it for the Arabs or for the Jews. She wasn't even doing it for the Spaniards.

Rosetta would go for her sister, Solar, and because she would never again be able to walk with her under the yellow-orange sky.

POLAND

With a cup of tea and a stack of crackers on a plate, Barbara Panovski sat alone in the kitchen of her Krakau apartment listening to the BBC. Her tea-and-cracker ritual was an old habit, one she retained from her years of internment at Auschwitz as a child. The comfort regimen was introduced to her by a kindly old gentlemen who had managed to smuggle a bag of crackers into the camp with him. Old and stale, they were like manna from heaven to her—a young orphaned girl—alone, frightened, smelling the scent of death and sensitive to the fears of her elders.

Her aunt and uncle had found her after the war and brought her to Poland. In the years of strife that followed, unlike so many of their friends, their family chose not to immigrate to Israel. They were not alone in their decision, though. So many others, having had their fill of danger and aggression, would not be a part of this new madness.

Barbara herself, as she grew older, was happy that the state of Israel existed, but was anguished that it was built on so much blood. She prayed for her people and understood why so many wished to live there, but she would never understand, would never condone the actions and ideas of those who were willing to kill innocents for their own gain. How could she? She was a product of the camps, of Hitler's rage against the Jews. What madness that such a killer had been at large for so long and no one had stopped him.

If only people knew what was happening back then, she mused. So many were not even aware that Hitler was killing the Jews in the beginning. *But today we know*, she thought, *we know what is happening in Israel.* Some of her own people were themselves acting like monsters, treating other human being as if they had no right to live, and ironically, no right to live in *their* land. It was madness all over again.

"It must come to an end," Barbara said aloud. *The women of the world are being called forward.* She felt her own heart beat faster as if she alone was standing on a shore and a child was crying for help in the water. She would have no other choice but to jump in.

There were others, Barbara knew, many Israelis, as well as other Jewish people throughout the world, who felt the same. They wanted to stop the insanity, as she did, and would join the march for peace.

It is the only way to save our humanity, Barbara realized.

The only way to save Israel.

IRAQ

It was loud and it was deafening, but worst of all it was deadly. The driving rain made it harder, for Samia Sullah's eyes were already wet with tears. The woman in the road, blood spattered on her face like tiny speckles, would not stop screaming.

Only moments ago on the Baghdad street, the grenade had been thrown like a softball, rising high in the air. The swelling screams of the crowd had alerted Samia, and she sprang forward into a run, throwing herself behind a huge cement column. Her legs, still exposed at the time, had been cut by flying glass and debris. Even now, blood continued to leak slowly from the gashes.

"My baby!"

The chilling scream drove Samia to her knees and back onto her feet. She dismissed the stinging in her legs and tried to reach the woman as quickly as she could.

"My God, Allah, where are you? Allah! Eahhh, Allah!" the woman screamed.

It was then Samia saw the woman was carrying the torn body of a child who looked about three years old. He had been hit head on by the explosion, his skull torn in half, blood letting out from a huge opening in his neck where his small head had been. Soaked with rain and blood, the woman held her child against her body, screaming in anguish.

"My sister," Samia implored. "Come, please come."

But the woman, crying uncontrollably, could not be subdued. Samia could see the soldiers were still coming, moving down the street in teams of two, rifles and machine guns drawn.

"Leave me!" the woman screamed as Samia held out her hand, beckoning the woman to take it and run with her. "Just leave me!"

Samia had no other choice. She felt a stabbing guilt in her heart as she turned and ran. She reached a wide concrete column and slid behind it. From her position, she saw several soldiers walk up to the wailing woman. One of them poked her in the shoulder with his machine gun.

The woman then faced the soldiers and screamed. "You have killed him! Murderers! You are murderers!" Then throwing her head back to the sky once again she entreated her God. "Allah," she sobbed, her voice weak. "Oh Allah, where are you? They killed my son . . . my son. How could he harm anyone? He was just a baby. Allah . . . you have forsaken us. Come back, please, come back. Help us now."

The gunfire was swift—jolting spurts of shells that sprayed across the lamenting woman's chest. In an instant, she slumped to the ground, her hand still draped protectively over what was left of her child's body.

Muffling a scream, Samia slid further back behind the column. *Is this what my country has come to? Will there by no end?* As a child she had witnessed the madman, Saddam Hussein, come to power, torturing and killing all who threatened his petty tyranny in the slightest way. Now the tyrant was gone, his regime over, but in its place war raged like wildfire through her country.

Samia felt it welling up inside of her—a large knotted ball of pain and humiliation. She did not understand. She had nowhere to go, no place to turn for peace. Soon, the ball would suffocate her, she was certain.

For years now, everywhere she looked Shiites and Sunnis were fighting each other, and both were fighting the Americans. The insurgence still meant death—women, children, young, old. *And for what?*

Oil. Oil. Oil. Killing for oil, destroying for oil. Hatred breeding more hatred. So many now hated the American soldiers who walked through the land like it was their own, boasting their might, throwing their weight, forcing their hand.

Samia stumbled out from behind the column and moaned. The few people left in the street turned and stared but quickly dispersed as the soldiers advanced. Even though Samia saw the men and the guns, she could not stop. The ball in her throat was choking her and she had to remove it. She started to scream, a long, aching cry that made her fall to her knees.

The mothers, the sisters, the women . . . They are the only hope we have left.

"Today, we must walk!" Samia's voice broke free as the soldiers pointed their weapons at her. "We must all walk to Jerushalayim!"

BOSNIA

UN Resolutions. Octavia Stanislaus wanted to laugh. Not because they were trying, but because those good men and women on the UN Security Council thought someone in her homeland of Bosnia would listen. Octavia wiped the tears from her face.

Standing in the back room of her father's bar, she filled her sack with a change of clothing. She had to travel light for the journey ahead would be long.

How can it be, Octavia thought, *that I will leave my family and all I love?* She never dreamed she would see the day, but it had arrived nonetheless. For all of its troubles, it was there in Medjugorje that the Holy Mother had appeared to three children. *A great light had lifted the darkness.*

But how briefly? Octavia had learned that holy places were not immune from sinister intent. And it was also here that Octavia realized how much she was hated.

She did not know how the police found out, but they did. Octavia had always been so careful whenever she met her friends. The group of

Women in Black members gathered secretly, quietly arranging for safe houses to help their sisters who had been beaten by their husbands, displaced at work, or sexually harassed in the streets.

The veil of nighttime meetings apparently had not been enough as Octavia discovered several evenings before. It was late, perhaps two in the morning when she was awakened, jabbed in the side by something hard. She bolted upright in bed and found herself facing the barrel of a gun. The policeman laughed as he pushed her back down. Octavia could see in his eyes what he was about to do.

When the officer was done, Octavia felt empty, that the man had stolen her power and made it his own. The shine in his eyes as he spoke convinced her he felt the same.

"Now, little sister, you might think better of slandering the police and helping those whores leave their husbands," he had scoffed.

Three days later, and Octavia's fear was metamorphosing. The energy of her terror was now the energy of her courage. There had been no magic potion, only a shift in attitude. The world was turning, and Octavia was being pulled with the tide. Women everywhere were responding to the call.

As she stepped through the side door onto the cool street, Octavia felt the wind move through her, sweeping aside any residue of hate.

Now, no man could stop her. No man would stand in her way.

SUDAN

Sohara traveled with her ten-year-old daughter in a busload of Sudanese women heading for the Egyptian border. Although the women around her were lively and talkative, Sohara felt as if she were in a vacuum.

Female Genital Mutilation. Sohara read the title again to herself. The page in her hand was crumpled from wear, having traveled in the pocket of her purse for the past two weeks. She had found it in an American magazine in the shipping office where she worked.

When she first saw the title, she had shuddered. The pain of recognition seared through her just as the knife had done nearly twenty years earlier.

FEMALE GENITAL MUTILATION

*. . . when all or part of the female genitalia is removed.
Also known as female circumcision. It is practiced in
many African countries as well as in some Asian and
Middle Eastern locales . . .*

Sohara had been only seven when her mother took her to a dark-ened room behind the old tea shop in their village. *A lamb being led to the slaughter.* Several men eyed her as she followed her mother toward the oldest. Sohara could smell the stench of whiskey on his breath.

Her mother placed her on the table. Soon her clothes were off and the two other men were holding her down as the old man started to cut her between her legs with a penknife.

Sohara could still feel his icy fingers probing her, then the pain-ful heat of the knife as it slit her open. The pain was unbearable. She had screamed for her mother's help, but her mother stood by idly, tears streaming down her face . . . a face lined with despair, worthlessness, defeat. Finally, one man stuffed a rag in Sohara's mouth. Sohara gagged and was no longer able to scream, silenced as her own mother had been ages ago.

When it was over, Sohara was removed from the bloodied table and placed on some linens on the floor.

The old man then looked her straight in the eyes. "For your own good," he said. "Now you are clean and you will not bother your hus-band with an extra penis inside you."

The bus lurched forward suddenly, jostling Sohara back to the present.

Saddened by the old memory, she folded the article and placed it back into her purse. It was remarkable how those men and even her own mother had learned to believe that mutilating a woman was of benefit to her. Of course, Sohara had grown to know better. Making it painful for a woman to have intercourse was a tradition that men had created so they could feel safe. No pleasure meant no straying.

"Mama."

The sound of her daughter's voice softened Sohara's mind. "Yes."

"I think we are close to the Egyptian border, Mama."

Sohara pulled her daughter, Isaila, close to her and smoothed back the golden brown strands of her hair. It was because of Isaila that Sohara found her strength, and like so many other women of her village, she had decided to walk against the oppression of men and their severe ways and rites of dominance. It was because women from all over the world were standing together that she was able to join the march . . . protesting against the violence of war and the savage oppression of women, especially the brutal mutilation that she and hundreds of thousands of others had been forced to endure.

This movement was a great wind, like the fierce gale of a *ghibli* . . . a powerful spiritual force that was driving the women toward this land called Jerusalem. She had been told by the grandmothers of her village that this Jerusalem was a holy city, a place where she could beg the gods of the earth for freedom. The Mother of the World would come to the women, for were they all not human?

Sohara was glad she had taken her daughter and escaped toward the great City of Peace. It was there, Sohara knew, that her Muslim sisters would also be gathered, where the great Allah had intended her to walk.

Then a strange thought occurred to her. The spirit was bringing her and Isaila to that dangerous place to be protected. At that instant, the light in Sohara's mind grew brighter. She realized that like the old spirit walkers she had seen as a child—the old medicine men of her village who would walk into a blazing fire and not get burned—she must have faith.

It would be her best protection.

ISRAEL

Yet again, Muriel Lumina was about to speak. Although tired from another week of protests and rallies, she felt a sudden surge of adrenaline quicken her senses.

"How much longer can we go on?" Muriel asked herself and her fellow members of ONE and Women in Black. World-wide organizations, they were both dedicated to creating peaceful resolutions in the most ravaged of countries. Gathering together today, they filled their meeting hall, an artist's loft in Tel Aviv's Yemenite Quarter.

"How much longer can we have a stand-off in the Holy Land? When will it cease?" Muriel's voice shook. "It won't unless we look for an alternative solution. Governments, politicians, corporations . . . resolutions cannot arise from their usual aims. The time has come for a new paradigm, a new ideology, and the Seline March has set it into motion. It will be the women of this world who will resolve the conflict, not with guns and domination, but with spiritual wisdom. And it is *we*, the women of Jerusalem, who are at the very core of this Seline movement, for it is Jerusalem that is its soul."

Muriel saw the resolve in every woman's eyes. She took a deep breath before continuing. "Women of Israel . . . Jewish, Muslim, Christian . . . we must unite against the violence. We must unite *as women*, for it is the violence perpetrated against us which has become a definitive part of the violence raging within this sacred land.

"Although so many of us, Jews and Palestinians, are looking for peace and justice, I know that we are not all entirely in agreement. Many have called for the end of the occupation and for a Palestinian state to be formed according to the boundaries of 1967. Some feel Jerusalem needs to be shared as the capital of both states. Some of us are now in agreement with Maggie Seline's proposition for the old city of Jerusalem to become an international city. But no matter what the final outcome, we all agree on one point: Jerusalem must be free and at peace."

How often have I made that statement, Muriel wondered. She had been saying it for years, but over the last few weeks she felt as if she was a recording playing in a constant loop.

Muriel looked into the eyes of every mother, sister, daughter, friend, stranger. Every one of those eyes contained sorrow, heartfelt and unrelenting. Even if filled with rage, frustration, and anguish, each pleaded for an end to the suffering.

Being the head of one of the largest organized groups of interfaith women in Israel, Muriel had influenced other leaders to express an urgent appeal for unity. Like a finely designed tapestry, societies and groups such as Women for Jerusalem, Interfaith Women's Alliance, Women for a United World, The Jewish and Muslim Women's League, and Women in Black began to work together with ONE to weave an intricate pattern.

Throughout the week, Israeli and Palestinian women marched along the streets of Israel. Many dressed in black and lay down in the plazas. Thousands were deployed throughout Jerusalem and Tel Aviv, while others marched towards the borders of Lebanon, the borders of Egypt and Jordan, to meet other women from all over the world. Everywhere, they raised banners. *THE OCCUPATION IS KILLING US ALL . . . JERUSALEM MUST BE SHARED . . . HUMAN RIGHTS FOR ALL.*

They were women motivated by countless suicide bombings as well as the incessant retaliations. Jewish assaults on Palestinian workers entering Tel Aviv . . . Arab assaults on Israeli civilians in shopping malls or walking down city streets. Lack of compassion, civility, and human decency had created this monster, now out of control. Even government leaders had no solutions to offer, except to pour more fuel on an already blazing fire. *Kill. Destroy.* The male instinct to protect, unchecked and perverted, had left only death in its wake.

Muriel stared out into the crowd of determined women. Dressed in black, some holding black signs with white lettering that said STOP THE OCCUPATION, they had resolved to continue their work although it had become increasingly more dangerous.

Maggie Seline's ideology. Her grandmother, Laurel Seline's initiation of the march to Jerusalem. The women's movement toward peace in the Middle East mounting.

Muriel knew they had reached a boiling point and that could mean only one thing . . .

JERUSALEM

Feikra motioned to her younger sister, Rasha, to move quickly through the streets. Those in the Muslim quarter of Jerusalem knew better than to gather in groups that appeared too large. The hard, iron eyes of the Israeli military bore through them every moment, searching for some sort of horrible evil.

As a Muslim woman, Feikra was aware that her lot in Israel would always be a difficult one. Not only was she fighting against her own system that downcasted women of Islam—laws forced upon them by their own men—but she had to bear the cross of trying to live in the so-called democracy of a Jewish state.

Had to bear the cross. Her Christian sisters had introduced her to that phrase.

Suddenly, Rasha grabbed her hand and pulled her into the shadow of a doorway. Feikra felt the sweaty fear of her sister's palm as they watched several armed soldiers cross the street, then head into a tobacco shop. Once the men disappeared into the store, Rasha was dragging her forward once again. Finally, at the end of the street, they turned down a dark alleyway and stopped at a narrow wooden door. Rasha pushed it open. Feikra followed her inside and down the long corridor.

When they reached the entrance to the last apartment, Rasha knocked several times. After a few moments the door creaked open, and a small bony woman, Khalidah, motioned for them to come inside. About twelve other women were already there with her, waiting.

"What's happening?" Khalidah asked anxiously.

"They will help us move toward the borders with them." Feikra repeated Muriel Lumina's promise. Together, they had been working closely the last several months as ONE and Women in Black grew in strength and numbers. The Jewish and Palestinian women of Israel would create the peace together.

"Muriel speaks for the coalition," Feikra said. "They will help all of the Arab women members get to the borders of Lebanon, Jordan and Egypt."

"It is madness," one of the women, Dalilah, stated. She shook her head in disapproval.

Another friend, nineteen year old Sara spoke up. "We could all be killed."

The worried looks on the faces of the other women made Feikra's passion flare. "We must unite in our struggle," she implored. "There's no promise of a happy ending, but we must try."

Feikra stiffened her resolve. She had always been practical. They had to live with the Jews. They had to work, and they had to eat. Dealing with the violence and terrorism was the price they paid. There had been such tragedy, such despair, so how could they even hope for happiness? *Still*, Feikra thought, *we must hope*. It was their right as human beings to be happy, to be able to share this earth.

"We are all human," she told her companions. "In Allah's eyes, we are one and the same, our differences only shadows."

Both Dalilah and Sara smiled at her. Feikra saw the mood of her friends shifting.

"You are courageous women," Feikra implored. "Please do not let your courage fail you now. I cannot tell you not to be afraid, for there is much to fear. But I beg you to rise above your fear and join us. Our Jewish sisters will do their very best to protect us here in Israel. As for women crossing over from Jordan, Lebanon and Egypt, I've requested assistance from the League of Arab Women. They promise to do what they can at the borders."

Khalidah stood up and placed a frail hand on Feikra's cheek. "You wish to turn the darkness to light, my Feikra. Do you believe that's possible?"

"I do. I believe it in Allah's name." Feikra took her friend's hand and held it in her own.

As the women stood looking toward her, Feikra felt all the emotion from the past weeks moistening her eyes. "We have lived long enough in madness. Together, with our sisters from all nations, we will unite *here* in Jerusalem. The spirit of humankind has been waiting for us, the mothers of this world. It is the light of the mother's wisdom that will liberate the holy land from darkness."

CHAPTER 64

Time rests in oblivion where the shapeless sands of the Sahara give way to the black volcanic rock that rises quietly from the Mediterranean. How many armies have come this way? Phoenician, Romans, Turks, Berbers and the rest, leaving no trace on either soil or sand. Only builders leave their mark, not soldiers. Soldiers rip apart humanity's heart, then level the remainder. Carthage, Cyrene, Sabratha, and Leptis Magna. Their marble rubble was washed in the same moonlight that now dances on the tiny cove.

The general wonders where his mark will fall. As a professional soldier, he must do his best—kill until he himself is killed. The warm breeze rustles the date palm fronds as he brings the cigarette to his lips and inhales deeply. Erwin Rommel hears the whispering carried in the wind. He knows that he has tramped up and down this coast for countless lifetimes. *The legions of Hannibal, or Caesar, or Napoleon, or the Caliphs of Constantinople are all the same to me,* he thinks. Madman or visionary, the word of the emperor has been his only guide.

This can no longer be, Rommel muses. *This one must be stopped. Hitler is no ordinary dictator, if such a thing is even possible.* Adolph Hitler, the son of a well-to-do civil servant, had at one time even been a choir boy. Through drugs, or black magic, or both, he had fallen into

madness. Or had he simply vanished into the abyss of
eternity and his body preempted by dark forces?

The long footsteps of time disappear in the sand.
The desert has no place for them. To the west lay
Carthage where, as Hannibal, Rommel once met his
fate. Following defeat by Cornelius Scipio Africanus
at Zana in 202 BC, Hannibal had killed himself. Fifty
years later, Carthage was burned to the ground at Cato's
behest and the population sold into slavery.

Rommel wonders what his fate will be this time.
He knows of the Spear of Longinus. Which of Hitler's
generals didn't? *Is this the time to tell Abu?*

"General."

He turns at the sound of his Libyan adjutant, Abu
Nai'im Mabus . . .

By some curious twist during Michael's layover in Rome, the most interesting book he found at the newsstand was his own, *Africa's Fox*. So he
spent the one-and-a-half-hour flight from Rome to Tripoli remembering, in his own words, the fascination the land of Libya held for him.

After his plane arrived at the airport, Michael rented a Land Rover
and began his long drive to Tarhuna. Matt had to be right. Mabus would
have the Spear of Longinus taken there. Not only was it the location of
Mabus' family estate, but it was a site of mythic power. Michael wondered if perhaps Rommel himself knew of the locale, being fond of the
fresh water springs and eucalyptus groves of the mountain *jebel.*

The coastal road that led to Al Khums and Leptis was breathtak-
ing. From the thoroughfare along the shoreline, Michael viewed the
deep-blue Mediterranean as it washed onto the shore of gleaming white
sand and rough volcanic rock. Along the road, verdant citrus plantations
flourished, filling the air with the sweet fragrance of lemon and orange.
Cactus, thistle, date palms, and aloe plants competed for survival, while
barefoot boys wearing long, flowing shirts and billowy pants walked
among them, shepherding herds of goats. All the while, sanguine camels
with slow-moving mouths plodded along pulling ropes, drawing water
from artesian wells, some over a thousand feet deep.

Yet the beauty of the shoreline was still not mesmerizing enough to sway him from his objective. *Where would Mabus hide the Spear?*

Then it came to him.

Michael had learned during his last sojourn to Libya that a labyrinth of tunnels were carved underground many generations ago, possibly begun in antiquity. The Turks, he discovered, had enlarged the system. They had built a superhighway under the coast for hundreds of miles. This allowed their cavalry to ride unseen, out from under the hot sun, toward destinations where they were least expected and could arrive unheralded.

The Spear has to be in the tunnels, somewhere near Tarhuna. Michael was now certain of it. *Where else would Mabus hide it but among the ruins of his own people?*

Also, in accordance with Stephen Einsof's theories, bringing such a powerful object to a location intersecting such a large number of *ley* lines could only increase its potency, and Michael deduced, would cause a significant shift in energy as well.

Michael took a long breath. He realized he knew nothing about the *feng shui* of Tarhuna. But according to the stories told him, the tunnels from Leptis Magna led directly to the caverns below it. Finding them would be his best chance.

Michael pressed down on the accelerator, driving as quickly as possible past the dry river beds, finally reaching Al Khums to stop for provisions. The sweet scent of wild anise, *guzzah*, hung in the air as he entered a small market. After picking up a compass, flashlights, batteries and food, Michael was about to pay when his attention was drawn to the high-pitched sounds of a television set hanging off the side of the wall.

What the hell . . . ? Surprised, Michael eased himself slowly onto a wooden bench facing the TV. Al Jazeera, the famed Qatar-based network, was reporting non-stop about Laurel Seline's march toward Jerusalem.

Maggie's grandmother!

Michael immediately wondered if Maggie had gotten wind of this. He didn't have much time to contemplate as the report continued. The unbelievable footage of thousands of women moving toward the troubled city was awesome.

Lech l'cha, he thought, uttering the Hebrew words Abraham heard and understood to be from God . . . *Go forth.*

Michael's mind worked quickly. *The synchronicity of it all*—his journey with Maggie to the hidden land . . . Mabus' peace conference . . . the proposal of a new Temple . . . the women of the world moving together . . .

Everything was *going forth*, heading toward Jerusalem.

CHAPTER 65

WHEN MICHAEL FINALLY ARRIVED at the great Roman trading hub of Leptis Magna, he parked his vehicle close to the old entrance into Leptis that began at Septimus Severus' triumphal arch. From there the route proceeded down the central boulevard, the *cardo* of the city.

Michael looked around in wonder, realizing that every inch of Leptis was a historical etching. He could almost feel the thundering onrush of Roman chariots as he walked along the deeply rutted stone roads.

As he wandered down a sandy pathway, he came upon a young man squatting beside a pile of colored stones, patiently fitting them together on the ground. He was forming a mosaic—a straw basket filled with fish.

Michael squatted several feet away and watched, becoming more absorbed in the young man's work. With the heat of the sun on his neck and the sand beneath his feet, he was taken with the thought that the scene could have been similar to one experienced by a young Hannibal growing up in Carthage, several hundred miles to the west, twenty-two hundred years earlier.

"*Baksheesh.*"

Michael turned. As they seemed to everywhere in Tripoli, a ragged, young boy materialized from thin air asking for money.

Michael shook his head. "*La-ah.*"

"Cigarette."

Again Michael answered in the negative. "*La-ah.*"

"*Arabiya?*" This insistent young fellow was not going away. He wanted to know if Michael spoke Arabic.

"Yes, I do . . . *Aiwa.*"

"*Baksheesh.*" The boy was definitely used to Westerners. He tugged on Michael's shirt holding out his hand. "*Baksheesh,*" he repeated again with a wider, more innocent grin than before.

"*Half dinar,*" Michael said, grabbing the boy's hand before he could run away or invent new variations to the game. Michael pulled the coins out from his pocket and let the boy see them.

Suddenly, a thought occurred to him. Michael closed his hand quickly before the young fellow could snatch the money. "Tunnel. *One dinar,* if you find me a tunnel."

The boy smiled at him, looking happy to have found a patsy.

"*Kif halak*, Mr. Michael."

As Michael turned toward the voice, he dropped the coins. The child quickly scooped them from the ground and ran.

"You've returned." The young man addressing him, wearing a keffiyeh around his head, smiled with a familiar grin.

Michael stared. *That open face, those wide, questioning brown eyes . . .*

"*Bahi, wenti kif halak.* Jehada?" Michael felt certain it was his young friend whom he had met during his first visit to Libya. Then a thirteen-year old, Jehada had presented himself as a "tour guide to the stars."

"*Aiwa.* I am Jehada ben-Ali."

Michael found himself smiling with approval. The past several years had turned the scrawny mischievous boy into a handsome young man. What hadn't changed was Jehada's forthcoming, easy smile.

Michael realized quickly that fate may have handed him the card he needed. He explained to Jehada that he had come to Libya to find the entrance to the old tunnels that ran through the city.

"They were closed long ago by the government." Jehada eyed him suspiciously. "Why do you want to find them?"

"It's not something I can explain to you easily. I need to know if I can get to Tarhuna by using them." Michael spoke hesitantly, restraining himself from blurting out his desire to find the Mabus estate.

Fear crossed Jehada's eyes. Nervously, he looked over his shoulders. "Do not talk about the tunnels aloud. It is dangerous." He took Michael's arm. "You come with me."

Michael followed Jehada down a long narrow passage between two buildings. When they reached a door, Jehada hurried him inside.

"Father." Jehada walked toward a slight, older man, white stubble on his chin, who squinted at Michael in the dim light. "This is my father, Ali."

"I remember you," Ali stated before Jehada said another word. "The big question machine."

Michael winced at the old man's words.

"So many questions. Where is this? What is that?"

Michael didn't know whether to be amused or insulted. "Sorry to say, I am now back with another question."

Ali looked toward his son.

"Mr. Michael wishes to know the entrance to the tunnels."

Ali's eyes widened as he looked again toward Michael.

"Is it possible to reach Tarhuna through them?" Michael asked.

Ali tilted his head and his eyes narrowed slightly. "Why do you want to go to Tarhuna? And why use the tunnels?" He spoke sharply. "We are a modern country with roads."

Michael had been considering this contingency and took the path of least resistance. "I am doing further research on the German Army and Rommel."

"Germans and General Rommel," Jehada remarked. "The Germans used the tunnels during the war. They even drove their trucks through them."

"*Achtung, Herr Feld-Marshall.*" Ali's body stiffened as he spoke, spitting out the words.

Michael was numbed by the outburst.

"As you know, my father was a tunnel guide for Rommel," Ali explained. "The general used the tunnels often . . . even going to Tarhuna."

Stunned, Michael could scarcely believe what he had heard. "Why use them to go to Tarhuna?"

Ali hesitated. "Perhaps your reason is similar to what Rommel's was then . . . to see the one called Mabus." His keen insight easily penetrated Michael's bluff. "Abu Na'im Mabus was the general's aide," Ali added. "In secret, the two had met in Tarhuna many times."

Michael grew even more excited by what he had just heard. "Will you show me where to find this entrance?"

Ali stared at him for so long that Michael would have sworn that the old man could see right through him.

Finally, Ali appeared to have come to his decision. *"Ma'alish.* I know the entrance, but we must be quick before another police patrol passes."

Ali led them across the main road to a cluster of unassuming buildings whose limestone walls had long lost their shine. He stopped in front of the tall wooden door of what looked like a storage facility. After jiggling the brass knob several times, he heaved his shoulder against the door until finally, creaking and resistant, it pushed open. Michael and Jehada followed him inside. There, in the dim light, Michael could see that behind a jumble of picks, shovels, wheelbarrows and jerry cans, a flight of stairs descended into darkness.

Michael followed father and son down the steps that led through the thick limestone. When they reached the bottom, there was just enough light seeping from above for Michael to see that the stories were true. He was staring into a tunnel, wide and tall enough to drive a truck through.

They continued on through a series of passages until they came upon an old Willys Jeep. Its United States Army markings had been crudely painted over and replaced by the words *Libyan Antiquities Department.*

"It was running last time I tried it," Jehada remarked, as he began pouring gas from a jerry can into the Jeep's tank. "Let's hope it's still alive."

Michael kept his fingers crossed, the power of positive thinking his only buttress.

Ali stared down the dark passageway. He had always hated the tunnels, but still they held mystery. They were the foreigners' domain, just as Leptis Magna, the city on the outskirts of his village, had once been occupied by the Romans. Always known to him as a pile of rocks and marble columns, Leptis had never called to his soul either as a Libyan, Arab, or Muslim. The stones of Leptis were European, artifacts of colonization.

His own father, Abdul, had served the German Army for three years as a tunnel guide. He had offered his services to the Italians before that, but they had turned him down. The conquerors of Ethiopia were building their own road across the coast all the way to Egypt. No need, they said, for the tunnels.

The Germans, however, immediately understood. In fact, at seventeen, Abdul had been presented to Erwin Rommel within days of the general's arrival. The Libyan's knowledge of the coastal subterranean world played a large role in early German success. Through it, the *Desert Fox* was able to make a sudden appearance far from his anticipated location.

Ali, born years after that big war, had always sensed the shame his father felt.

Had I known . . . Had I only known . . . How often Ali heard his father repeat those words when telling the stories of the Great War. *I aided the devil's own,* Abdul once told him. *They held the great Spear, and with it, those black magicians cast their spell.*

The great Spear. It was only years later that Ali discovered what those words meant.

"Everything stops here."

Michael was stunned by Ali's words. There was no way in hell he would be able to maneuver the tunnels alone. He was helpless without Ali's guidance.

"Everything stops here," Ali repeated, "until you tell me the real reason you wish to find Mabus."

Where was this going? Michael was unsure what to say. The truth seemed so wild he was reluctant to even hint at it. But, as it turned out, he didn't need to.

"Does Mabus have the Spear of Issa?" Ali suddenly asked.

Michael couldn't believe he was hearing the words. He spoke slowly. "You mean . . . the Spear of Longinus?"

"Yes, the Spear that was thrust into the prophet's side when he was dying. Rommel told my father that with this Spear an army could conquer the world." Ali's eyes were blazing passionately, demanding an answer. "Mabus has the Spear, doesn't he, and that's why we must go to Tarhuna?"

"Yes." Michael was checkmated. He held his breath, waiting for some kind of disastrous response.

In the light, Ali's face looked troubled. Michael wondered if he was ill, but in a moment, Ali's eyes went from glazed to sharp.

"Then we must hurry," Ali said, fear creeping into his voice. "The Mabus lineage and the Spear . . . a dangerous combination."

Ali slid behind the wheel of the jeep. Michael hopped into the front next to him while Jehada jumped into the backseat.

"Andiamo!" Ali said as he turned the old key sitting in the ignition. The engine turned over hesitantly at first, before firing to life. Ali then popped the clutch suddenly, and they went rumbling off, thirty feet below the desert surface.

Ali knew his way, of that there was no doubt. With the pale yellow glow from the headlights shining against the sheer stone walls as his only beacon, Ali drove at a precarious speed. All the while Michael clutched the armrest, complimenting himself on doing an admirable job of hiding his own fear.

His eyes peeled on the "road" ahead, Michael could see that apart from the mice and rats, German Army spoor was in abundant evidence. Communication and electrical wires, broken and frayed, draped from porcelain insulators high atop the walls. Cigarette packages, rations, jerry cans and empty ammunition boxes lay scattered on the tunnel floor. As the main tunnel splintered into several, what appeared to be old tire tracks made by tandem wheeled vehicles led off into the darkness. *They're so distinct,* Michael thought, *they could have been made yesterday.*

At that moment, several bats dropped from the ceiling and rocketed out of the light. Michael smelled the foul stench of their nesting area and quickly held his hand over his nose. But their appearance did not faze Ali in the least. He kept the jeep moving forward at a steady pace, veering off onto a new branch without warning. Michael tried to make mental notes of their path, but the tunnel labyrinth was way too complex.

Turkish storm troopers on horseback, Libyan rebels harassing Italian occupiers, or Phoenician and Roman engineers . . . whoever dug these tunnels had done it well and thoroughly.

Finally, after nearly two hours, Ali slowed down and stopped the Jeep. "We are beneath Tarhuna," he announced.

At Ali's suggestion, they sat in the darkness for several minutes, allowing their eyes and ears to acclimate.

There, within the quiet tunnel, Michael felt his mood sinking. He was now cut off from the world, with only Ali and Jehada at his side.

What if it ends here? Taking several deep breaths, he tried to fight off his anxiety. *What if I can't retrieve the Spear?*

Jehada wondered at the string of events which had brought them to the darkness beneath Tarhuna. As one of the custodians of the old Roman city, his father's responsibility was to safeguard the Leptis Magna ruins for the Libyan Department of Antiquities. Why then would Ali shirk his duty and give in so quickly to Michael's desire to investigate the tunnels? Was his father's judgment impaired because of an old and tiresome legend?

From the moment of Michael's arrival at Leptis Magna that morning, Jehada had recognized him. Immediately, by the strained look on Michael's face, Jehada had known Michael was looking for something or someone. He no longer appeared the easygoing American writer, but rather a man on a mission.

Amidst the tunnel's eerie silence, Jehada felt his own ripples of fear. His first year of college and the pressure was on to join the secret militia. From its members, he heard the constant chant against Westerners, especially Americans, who they blamed for driving the Islamic people to the brink. The Arab world was being terrorized, he was told, not only by Israel, but now by the highest powers in the world. The United States Government was the all-powerful demon, the monstrous head of an unholy alliance against them.

Yet, he felt compelled to help Michael. Why was this so? With hatred toward Americans mounting, Jehada recognized his was a personal crisis. *To join the terrorists or help the infidels.* His reason told him to hate, but his instinct told him to leap, to recognize the purpose for which everyone had been sent . . . *light over darkness, love over hatred, peace over war.*

Sitting quietly, Jehada felt his fear transforming into hope. He said a prayer for himself, for his father and family.

Ins'Allah.

Jehada was certain God's will would guide them.

"*Andiamo,*" he whispered in the darkness.

It was time to go.

———

Michael's ears pricked with every sound as Ali led them down the long corridor. Beyond the glow of his flashlight, the darkness invited his imagination to fear the worst. Were Ali and Jehada really friends, or were the two men just setting him up?

I'm a fool to trust so easily.

Just then, as the tunnel veered to the right, the funky smell of bat dung was replaced by the sweet scent of eucalyptus. Michael found they were standing at the edge of a large, circular room about thirty feet in diameter. Its vaulted chamber had a higher ceiling than the tunnels themselves. Curiously, right there in the middle of the space, an old well sat under a curved stone arch, the cracked reddish-brown and cream-colored marble around its rim a testament to its age. Michael could not even imagine how long it had been there.

As Ali hurried forward, Michael noticed he touched the well reverently. Ali then turned his dim flashlight toward a tumble of boulders that was sealing the passage and motioned toward Jehada. Without saying a word, both men began scaling the rocks.

Following their example, Michael inched his way upward, grabbing at the huge stones. Suddenly, a current of fresh air moved through the passage, and Michael could see a faint light ahead. His anxiety lifted as an opening appeared, the end of their claustrophobic venture now in sight.

Michael realized he needed to make a quick decision. He turned toward Ali. "You don't have to come with me."

The older man gave him a determined look. "Yes, I do. I do need to come. My family has its own debt to be collected from Mabus." Ali turned to his son. "Jehada, go back to the Jeep. Wait for our return."

Jehada nodded. Michael noted the silent reluctance in his eyes as they left him behind.

Exiting the tunnel, Ali and Michael emerged onto a narrow dirt road that ran between two, tall limestone walls. After passing through an iron gate, Michael found they were standing in a garden. Grape arbors with light green fruit, dark leaves, and thick, bark-crusted vines encircled them. Tall bushes lined the path, small red roses budding amidst the thorns. As they crept forward, Michael saw the white stucco walls of a villa appearing between the date palms.

"Mabus," Ali said, pointing toward the house.

Michael wondered how one word could sound like an alarm, but it did.

Suddenly, a rustling from behind the gate made them both turn in fear, and Michael found himself looking down the barrel of a machine gun.

CHAPTER 66

GIOVANNI MABUS SAT QUIETLY in his office on the ground floor of his Libyan villa. After solidifying his plans with Volpi in Rome, he had come to Tarhuna to make sure all the elements of his equation were in place. Within the hour, his private jet would take him to Jerusalem. In two days the Peace Conference would convene, and his place in history would be assured. Everything he had accomplished in his life had been leading him to that crowning moment. His family would once again hold its rightful place, as powerful as any dynasty.

This is not only for my family name, Mabus thought. Although he was not much of a patriot, some old vestige of Libyan pride remained. The Phoenicians, Romans, Turks and Italians had all held his country hostage. Then the Americans and British used oil concessions as a form of control. The Americans had even maintained a huge military base on the coast, Wheelus, not far from Leptis Magna until King Idris was deposed. Mabus burned with hostility as he remembered the American hot dog fighter-pilots buzzing over the country with impunity.

It will soon be at an end.

Giovanni Mabus was going to accomplish what Gamal Abdel Nasser had tried to do and failed. *The unification of the Arab peoples across the face of North Africa.* Except, in Mabus' case, the unity of his people happened to be a necessary component for the accomplishment of his own goals. Let the fools have their religion. For him, economic power was the key.

Just then, his chief of security, Siddig Salah, also known as *the Algerian,* knocked lightly on the door as he entered. "The grounds have been penetrated. We have two prisoners."

Mabus studied his security officer's face. There appeared to be no need for concern. "Just two?" Mabus asked. Siddig was unquestionably a loyal servant, but Mabus found his clipped announcements annoying.

"One's an American, sir."

An American within the villa grounds. Mabus wondered if there had been a leak. He reviewed his precautions. "Do we know who he is?"

Siddig turned on one of the security monitors on the wall.

Mabus never allowed himself to lose his equilibrium, but the shock of seeing Michael Sonada brought him back down onto his leather chair. "What the hell is going on?" Mabus questioned. He wondered if his eyes were deceiving him. Why would Sonada come *here?*

Mabus felt a chill of anxiety move up his spine. He quickly assessed that Napesh Samuels had connected him with the Spear's disappearance. Now Sonada was probably here to wage some sort of battle. "How did they enter?"

"They were just suddenly there, sir, walking in the garden when our cameras spotted them. There was no breach in the perimeter and—"

"Just suddenly there." Mabus' anger grew. Then he remembered. *The tunnels.* It was the only way it could be possible.

"Search the tunnels immediately," he ordered. "They could not have done this alone." *Unless, the Libyan is a member of the Way.* That organization had been shadowing his family's efforts for as long as anyone could remember. Some of his own people, Arabs who were part of their brotherhood, had helped *the Way* at every turn. They would know every inch of those tunnels. Yet, the interior minister had assured him the entrances would remain sealed.

"You stopped your patrols?" Mabus questioned accusingly.

"Patrolling to the end of the tunnels was unnecessary with them shut. There was no need to think—"

"Exactly. You did not think. You didn't think that perhaps, just perhaps, the minister was less than truthful in his statements."

Siddig's large dark face filled with rage, but Mabus knew he daren't utter a word.

"They must have created an opening again," Mabus concluded. *Fools. They will pay, as will Siddig.* "Take me to them."

Michael had been standing with Ali, machines guns pointed at their heads, for what seemed like an eternity. Instead of being probed with questions, the guards stared at them icily, looking as if they were itching to pull the trigger.

"Well, what a pleasant surprise this is."

Michael turned abruptly toward the familiar voice that came from the back of the dimly lit garden area where he and Ali were being held prisoner. There, standing like a prince on his palace grounds, was Giovanni Mabus.

Here it is, Michael thought, *my confrontation, even if Mabus holds all the cards.*

"I see you brought a friend," Mabus said, staring at Ali.

Ali did not reply, but his hostile glare spoke volumes.

"And don't tell me your friend here is Special Forces, unless you mean the forces of *the Way*. He looks more like a *kaffir* boy."

"Okay, so you have us." Michael wanted Mabus to talk. "At least tell me what your plan is."

"Very good. I tell you my plan, and the wire you are carrying transmits it. Very smart." Mabus glanced at Siddig.

"No bugs," the large brute announced. "We searched them."

"No matter." Mabus stretched his arm out toward a houseboy who entered the garden holding his coat. "This entire area is jammed. No signals in, no signals out. Very efficient. Your American electronics companies will sell to anyone. Perhaps if I had told them I was North Korean, I could have gotten better prices. Libyans have too much money to get bargain rates."

Michael was not amused. "You can't possibly think everyone believes this sham of a Peace Conference you've set up?" he berated.

"Everyone but the sad old professor in Rhinebeck. I took care of him, though, and that bothersome Sheikh Wayani will see his due."

Michael was unwilling to entertain Mabus' bait tactics. Instead, he played another card, hoping Mabus would divulge his motive. "So why steal the Spear? You've set yourself up pretty well already. You can't possibly need it."

Mabus smiled insidiously. "*Barack,* good fortune." He almost stopped there, but it seemed he couldn't contain himself. "It was possessed by my family once, before the infidels took it to fight their holy wars. Besides, what would Agatha Christie call it . . . a red herring? But it only remains such to those who don't realize that an object imbued with power takes on a life of its own."

Michael felt a strange resonance with Mabus' words. The Spear's connection with events now unfolding became even clearer. "And the plan for rebuilding the Temple?" he prompted.

"That process thus far has been successful, far beyond my expectations. Any plan to build the Third Temple on Haram al-Sharif will unite the Muslim world like no other."

"But it was you," Michael fired back, "a Muslim, who presented the plan."

"That will be forgotten in the chaos," Mabus retorted icily. "Then finally, Saudi Arabia, an American puppet state until now, will revert to the true Islamic fold. Soon the American grip on oil will be broken, and so will the financial and military support of Israel, a land nothing more than a colony anyway, like Puerto Rico or Guam."

Michael felt like an overcharged battery as his mind raced to figure out Mabus' equation. His anxiety mounted as he watched Mabus preparing to leave.

Pointing a machine gun at Michael's head, Siddig took a few steps closer. "How shall I deal with them, Monsieur Mabus?" the Algerian asked.

Mabus stared at the two prisoners for a long time. "We both know your specialty, Siddig," he finally said. "Show our friends here what happens to those who interfere with progress."

Siddig looked pleased. *"Chiffon, chalumeau, or gegene?"*

"Whichever you like," Mabus said pointedly, "but wait until I am gone. I do not like the screaming. It annoys me."

Michael's heart was pounding as he realized he and Ali were being left with a sadistic killer.

"Ai'wa, al-Quds. Masalama, Michael," Mabus said as he exited the garden.

Michael turned toward his companion, hoping against hope that Ali had a plan. His friend's impassive countenance gave no such indication.

CHAPTER 67

AGAIN, LEFT ALONE *at my father's whim.* Jehada wondered when he would be trusted, given the duty of a man, instead of the errand of a boy.

Not wanting to waste the flashlight's batteries, Jehada had been waiting in the dark. Standing in the dank shadowy tunnel was beginning to unnerve him. There had to be more that he could do.

With frustration gnawing at him, Jehada began to doubt the avenue they had taken. Michael and his father had headed into the camp of the enemy. But would Mabus keep the ancient relic so close to him, in the villa itself? Unlikely. It would be hidden, but hidden in a clever way.

Then it dawned on him. Jehada stood up quickly, grazing his forehead on a low overhang. He rubbed his head, but his thoughts were more powerful than any pain. Why hadn't he recognized it before?

Jehada flicked on his flashlight, grabbed a coil of rope from the back of the Jeep and headed toward the rocky entrance. Mabus would want to keep the Spear near enough for retrieval, but far enough not to be detected. "Do not hide your jewels in the safe," Jehada's mother had told him once, "but place them in the window box at your front door."

The well.

As Jehada hurried along the corridor, he remembered the countless stories his grandfather had told him of their family's alliance with a holy brotherhood, a secret organization of men dedicated to protecting ancient, spiritual treasures.

It was this brotherhood, *the Way,* that had pledged to protect Magdalene and the Spear. For almost two thousand years that oath had gone unbroken.

Abu Na'im Mabus betrayed the pledge, one made by his own ancestors, when he told Rommel the story of the Spear's connection with Tarhuna. Abu Na'im also provided the general with other information that enabled the Germans to infiltrate and crush secret organizations that had managed to protect local spheres of mystical power across North Africa and Europe—secrets places in Jerusalem, Glastonbury, and Mount Ararat.

The payoff for the Mabus family for this betrayal continued into the present, with heavy infusions of fascist capital from those families and firms that had strong Nazi ties . . . ties that were continuously being forged anew.

When Jehada reached the well, he tied the rope to the stone arch. As he looked down the deep dark recess, he felt the blood surge through his veins.

An old bond was surfacing for him, and his purpose revealed itself like a star from behind a cloud. His father, grandfather and others before them had all known that the old well was special—that its waters had sustained Magdalene during her enlightenment . . . that the well itself had hidden and protected her. Deep beneath it were the springs that had fed the Lebda River, in those days a powerful tide that sustained Leptis.

Jehada took a deep breath and descended. He hoped the rope was long enough. If he was remembering his grandfather's story correctly, Abdul had said he had once climbed down into the Mother's Womb as he had called it, and found an entrance into a secret tunnel.

As Jehada scraped his foot against the stone wall, he felt a narrow opening. It was just large enough for him to squeeze through. When he landed on the other side, Jehada scanned the area with his flashlight and found he was staring down another dark corridor. He realized then that this must be the tunnel his grandfather had spoken of. According to Abdul, it was along this secret passage that the centurion, Longinus, had made countless trips to bring Magdalene and her followers water.

Jehada's grandfather had also shared with him the very words that had been perseveved by *the Way*, words that Longinus had spoken long ago when told that *a Roman soldier should not carry water for a woman.*

I am no centurion, or Roman. I am a simple servant of the teacher, Magdalene, for she alone holds the cup of living light from which we drink. She alone carries the message of Issa, the call of the rising sun, a vision that will one day unite mankind.

As Jehada knelt in the sand, he realized the rough earth beneath him had laid undisturbed for thousands of years—a silent witness to the

Mother's secret. Before Issa, before the Magdalene, there had been others, persecuted and pursued. But now, there would be no time to linger
and feel sorrow for their fate. The Spear awaited. Jehada felt strongly
that Mabus would have brought it here, a place where its power would
be great.

Jehada moved cautiously through the cave. As he ran his hand along
the gnarled, rough walls, he thought there was something odd about its
texture. He turned his flashlight toward the wall's surface, and could then
see clearly what had felt so unusual—the ancient root of an olive tree that
had become embedded within the rock.

Jehada stared at it in wonder. *How many thousands of years have
these enormous roots been here?* In that moment, he recognized that the
roots of the olive tree had silently absorbed the greatest of events. They
had already been powerfully embedded when the Magdalene had taken
refuge, when the great civilization in Leptis had flourished, throughout
the reign of angry kings, and through the unquenchable lust of powerful, greedy dictators.

And now, Jehada thought, *these roots will bear witness to yet another
secret unveiled.*

Jehada ben Ali of *the Way* saw it then when he shone his flashlight
on the underside of the great root talon. He felt his heart leap when
he detected the etching, barely visible in the wood—the swastika, the
great symbol of prosperity in the east. Hitler had perverted its meaning
and tarnished its use, but the Tibetan emblem still held its mysterious
power.

Jehada directed the light farther below the root, where it connected
back into a hole in the rock wall. His hand shaking, he reached into the
long, narrow opening. Jehada soon felt something cold and metallic between his fingers and wedged it out from between the rocks.

A case.

A tingling energy, like a jolt of electricity, moved up Jehada's arm.
Immediately, he knew what he had discovered.

He sat on the cave floor shining his light onto the case. After opening it, he found another container—an old and beaten leather box—lay
within. Jehada lifted the lid and looked inside, almost not believing his
own eyes. There it was, lying on a piece of red velvet cloth.

The Spear of Longinus, the great talisman!

CHAPTER 68

THE LEAR JET was warmed up and waiting at the end of the small runway. Mabus barely settled into his seat when the plane lifted off for Nicosia en route to Tel Aviv. It wouldn't do for a private plane to fly directly from Libya, even if its owner was the prominent and distinguished Giovanni Mabus.

Mabus was aware that his was a familiar name in the corridors of the Knesset, Shin Bet, and the Mossad. What was not common knowledge throughout these bureaucratic sovereignties was the degree to which he channeled classified information from the EU to Israel.

Now, as he glanced through the window of the plane as it circled over the villa, Mabus was grateful for another fact. *Americans are categorically stupid and naïve . . . way too trusting.*

How typically considerate of them.

Siddig and four of his guards pushed Michael and Ali across the lawn and around the house to a small farm storage building.

The Algerian then snapped at two of his men. "Search the grounds thoroughly. Someone must have helped them get here."

Michael held his breath as he thought of Jehada.

"Sobiai! Inside with me," Siddig commanded his main assistant. He turned to address the remaining guard. "You stay outside." Then, with a malicious smile on his face, he pointed toward the door, directing Michael and Ali into the building.

Michael curled his nose as he entered. The smell of blood and fear permeated the small room. Nervously, his eyes darted to a figure sitting in the corner with a black hood over his head—another prisoner.

"How did you get to Tarhuna? Who helped you?" Siddig, the Algerian, was a large man with beefy, oversized hands. He took a short length of rope and slowly twirled it hand over hand. With a scarred section of his lower lip turning downward, the corner of his mouth hung like a carp.

Michael, horrified, turned toward Ali who kept a stony countenance.

"Better yet," the Algerian continued, "don't tell me. I prefer finding answers my way. Since I feel generous today, I will offer you some choices. *Chalumeau*—the blowtorch—messy and loud. Monsieur Mabus is gone so noise is not a problem." He dropped the rope and picked up a rag and a can of turpentine from the table. "Or *Chiffon*. I stuff this in your mouth like a roasted pig. But, then again, that makes it hard to get intelligible answers."

Michael choked back his fear, deciding he would prefer neither.

"Since Monsieur Mabus really did not require me to offer a choice, I think maybe *gegène.*" Siddig uttered the word about as sensuously as his gruff voice would allow, as if he were describing the delicate bouquet of a fine vintage. He picked up a small black box from the counter behind him. "A wire to your wrist, the other to a breast, or perhaps to a testicle or foot. One must be creative."

As Siddig held the box lovingly in his hands, he fondled the long wire leads attached to its side. "Technology has made this a much more precise skill." He turned toward Ali. "First the *kaffir.*"

Sobiai, a black man with a shaved head and expressionless face, was even bigger than Siddig. He clenched his fist and drove it full force into Ali's midsection. The smaller man doubled over, fighting for his breath. Sobiai ripped Ali's shirt off and forced him against the wall, and then using plastic ties, secured each of his arms to iron rings.

Michael, feeling as if his own gut was wrenching, watched as Sobiai strapped a wire lead around Ali's wrist with Velcro. The black man then attached the other lead, which had a small alligator clip on its end, to Ali's right nipple.

Knowing what was about to come, Michael turned to avert his eyes.

"You must watch." Siddig grabbed the top of Michael's head and twisted it back around.

Just past Ali, Michael could see the hooded man was now twisting uncomfortably in the corner.

"The other one as well," Siddig commanded, motioning Sobiai toward the silent prisoner. "You must both understand what is *gegène.*"

Michael stared curiously as the hood was removed from Siddig's other "guest." Stephen Einsof's wide frightened eyes met his. Stunned, Michael realized his own gaze must be reflecting the same look of recognition and terror.

Siddig laughed. The moment did not appear to be lost on him. "Good, so you are acquainted. By the time I've finished extending my hospitality, you will know more about each other than your mothers did."

He pressed a button on the box in his hand. Ali screamed and his torso twisted.

"Oh, *mon petit,* that charge was so small." Siddig turned the dial and again hit the button.

Ali's scream was even louder. His body went into spasms and urine flowed down his legs.

Jehada heard the high-pitched scream. It was his father. With the case containing the Spear now in his shoulder bag, he began to run toward the tunnel opening. Exiting onto a path, he dashed through a garden gate, following the wailing cries. That's when he saw the two surly-looking men. They caught sight of him as well and instantly broke into a run. But Jehada was younger and faster. He sprinted through the maze of honeysuckle and roses till he saw his opportunity.

The rake leaning against a wheelbarrow was almost completely hidden by a profusion of thick bougainvillea shrubs. Jehada grabbed it and crouched behind the trellis and vines. He could just make out the path by peering through the shroud of shrubbery. As one of the gunmen hurried past, Jehada stepped out and hit him full force in the back of the head.

The man fell unconscious. Jehada dragged him back into the bushes, took the man's shirt off and put it over his own. He then cupped his hands over his mouth to muffle his voice. *"Ya'tee!"* he yelled, hoping the other guard would heed his call. *"Yusri!"*

When the second man came running, Jehada was waiting. He slammed the hard edge of the rake over the guard's head. The man stumbled to the ground, and again Jehada swung the rake full force. *That will quiet him.* Jehada then left the two bodies together, tying the men with their belts as best he could. He grabbed the machine gun the second guard had carried. It felt good in his hands although he had never fired anything other than old rifles and pistols. All he knew was that his father was in trouble and he, his father's son, was prepared.

What a strange fate, Stephen thought. It was certainly a strange and bizarre twist that brought both him and Michael Sonada to Tarhuna.

Events had come to the boiling point when he had gone to the police department in upstate New York to claim Tod's personal effects found in the "car wreck." Among them was a data flash drive with a label written in Arabic. Tod must have stolen it the night he went to search the guard's house.

Stephen hadn't been sure what to do. He certainly couldn't read Arabic. He also had to consider the possibility that the files on the flash drive had been coded to reveal the location of the computer used to open them.

At the time, the whole affair felt like an episode of *Mission Impossible*, and he, like Phelps, could either accept or reject the mission. After surveying the grounds around his house, he grabbed his old laptop, a computer he knew he could never use again on-line, and locked himself inside the bathroom.

While sitting on the toilet within his unlikely safe room, Stephen discovered there were several files on the drive. Since he didn't have a clue what the file names meant, he began opening them in sequence. The first three were long texts in Arabic. The fourth one caught his attention. Within the body of several pages of text was a long series of numbers:

25-22-49-34-0-27-01-50-40-30-26-12-56-15-45

A code of some sort.

Whatever Tod had discovered by reading the files, Stephen was convinced that the central message lay hidden in the number sequence within the otherwise incoherent Arabic text.

Anxious and frightened, Stephen racked his brain wondering what to do next. He didn't want to end up like Tod, nor could he very well just keep the flash drive. Mabus' security goons were constantly searching his house, clothes, car or whatever, all under the guise that they were looking for bugs, protecting themselves against industrial espionage. Stephen decided he had no other choice. Memorize the sequence and lose the drive.

Now, here he was in Tarhuna, a prisoner, with only those numbers left in his head. He searched Michael's horror-filled eyes knowing that his friend felt as helpless as he did.

Once again, the brute, Siddig, pressed the button on the small black box in his hand. The old Arab let out another loud scream, only to be topped by Siddig's insidious laughter.

Stephen tried to mentally separate himself from his circumstances. The only way to cope, he concluded, was to focus his mind on the number sequence he had memorized:

25-22-49-34-0-27-01-50-40-30-26-12-56-15-45

Over and over he repeated the numbers silently to himself. *What the hell do they mean?* They had to have value.

But his attempt at numbing himself was proving unsuccessful. The old man let out another blood-curdling scream, sending shivers up Stephen's spine.

Siddig was enjoying himself so much that Sobiai didn't even motion before going outside. He was in a hurry to relieve the pressure on his bladder. Anyway, he knew from experience, Siddig was in an advanced state of sexual arousal, and when the torture was finished, he would expect to be satiated. Sobiai was thankful he wasn't the only guard on duty today. Enough was enough.

The huge black man that entered the garden never heard his approach. Jehada struck him over the head with such force, that he brought the powerful-looking man down to his knees. As the man let out a loud groan, Jehada hit him twice more with the butt of the machine gun, leaving him in a heap on the grass.

"Capitan Sobiai?" The guard positioned by the door to Siddig's chamber called out, apparently having heard the scuffle and Sobiai's loud moaning.

Again Jehada cupped his hands to muffle his voice. *"Ta-ala,"* he said, pretending to be Sobiai.

When the guard came over to see what had happened to his superior, Jehada was ready. He stepped out from behind the grape vines and pointed the 9mm at the surprised man.

What happened next, Jehada would have never expected. With a loud scream the man lunged at him, grabbing the barrel of the machine gun, pulling both himself and Jehada down to the ground. As they wrestled on their knees, Jehada held firm to the weapon, all the while staring directly into the grimacing face of his rival. When a round of shots went off, causing them both to jerk the weapon even harder, they both fell over onto their sides, sending the gun careening through the air and landing several yards away.

Both men leapt to their feet. Still, Jehada was not quick enough and the guard was able to grab hold of him from behind, closing his arm around Jehada's neck. Jehada fought back hard, all the while gasping for air. Then, kicking backward as hard as he could, he shoved the back of his foot into the guard's knee, causing him to sink to the ground. Finally free, Jehada pounced on his opponent, punching the man until he was bloody and unconscious.

Certain the guard was incapacitated, Jehada rose to his feet. Sweating and with blood on his hands, he picked up the machine gun, feeling the heat of his own violence.

Another scream sent him racing across the lawn to what looked like a storage building. He rushed inside just as Siddig was securing Michael to the wall. As he pointed the machine gun at the ogrish man, Jehada almost smiled when he saw the look of pleasure on Siddig's face turn to one of shock.

"Jehada!" Michael yelled across the room. "There are handcuffs on the table."

Without hesitating for a moment and with his gun pointed directly at Siddig, Jehada grabbed the cuffs. He then motioned for Siddig to place his hands behind his back. With the cuffs secured, Jehada then shoved the man into a large well-lit closet at the far end of the room.

Siddig looked up at him from the floor. Jehada noticed the man, now sneering hatefully, had gained some composure.

"You son of a pig." Siddig spat onto the ground beside him. "When I see you again—"

"Ah, I do not believe you will." Jehada felt his finger moving toward the trigger.

Could he?

Instead, he flipped off the light switch. "As they say," he spoke into the darkness, "lights out." With that, he slammed the closet door shut, sliding the large deadbolt into place.

"Baba." Jehada cut the straps holding Ali who was still shaking from the shocks he had received. His father collapsed onto the floor. Jehada knelt next to him, his anger so powerful that he had a second thought about leaving the brute in the closet alive.

Hopefully, he will meet his death soon. Jehada found justice in the thought.

Quickly, he freed the two Americans, then returned to his father and helped him to his feet.

"Jehada, you and Stephen take Ali to the Jeep," Michael said as Stephen came to Ali's side to help support him. "If I'm not back soon, then leave. I *must* find the Longinus Spear."

"I have it," Jehada announced triumphantly.

Michael's jaw dropped. "*You* have it," he said. "How in God's name—"

"Exactly. By the grace of Allah, I discovered it in the well." Jehada knew that it was nothing less than God's will that brought him to the Spear. "Now quickly," he added. "We must get my father to a doctor."

The compound was eerily quiet as they made their way through the garden to the tunnel entrance. At any moment, Jehada expected someone to step out of the bushes. By the look on Michael and Stephen's faces, he knew they expected the same.

When they reached the Jeep, they placed Ali in the back and Stephen hopped in beside him. Jehada had to drive. It was up to him now to find the way back to the coast. But first . . .

Jehada handed Michael the canvas satchel. With a rush of excitement, Michael removed the case and the leather container within. He undid the clasp, his breath noticeably quickening, and opened the lid. Michael stared in awe for several moments, his eyes brightening as he looked down at the ancient relic.

The two-thousand-year-old wait is over, Jehada realized.

The heat of courage was now burning in his heart.

He had found the Spear for *the Way*. He had found it for his father.

CHAPTER 69

EBTEHAL WAS WAITING at the tunnel's entrance. She had sensed Ali's need—that he was in danger. When she saw the men holding up her husband, Ebtehal rushed toward him. Ali opened his eyes, and Ebtehal wiped his face with the hem of her skirt. She vowed never again to nag or reprimand the kindest man on earth. Never again would her unchecked spirit vent itself on him. She had loved Ali always, a love too often left unsaid.

She closed his eyes and urged him to rest before turning toward her son and the two Americans. After they told her what had happened and about the great prize in their possession, Ebtehal's feminine instinct took control. The talisman's appearance was too coincidental. Had they not heard of the great march of women?

"The Spear must go to Jerusalem," she said, sensing her own role. "We must all go."

Michael gave Stephen a questioning look.

Ebtehal knew they had to get out of the country, and fast, before Mabus' network could recover and begin searching. Nervous and wary, she urged the men to hurry as they half carried Ali home.

"Jehada," she said when they finally arrived. "Go get your uncle. And tell your cousin to drive the American's car far away and abandon it."

"Wait a second," Michael said, a look of concern in his eyes. "If the Land Rover is taken then how will I get to Jerusalem?"

"In that." Ebtehal pointed to an old, faded green Peugeot that looked as if it might make it to the next town of Misratah. Although driving it halfway across North Africa seemed a fool's dream, she hid her concern. "It's too dangerous to continue in your car. It has your name attached to it."

"One other problem . . . The police will be looking for me and Stephen," Michael informed her, "and we must get the Spear to Jerusalem in time for the Peace Conference."

Michael's feeble worries would not dissuade her. The Americans would be lucky to evade capture for twelve hours without her help.

"Listen to me," Ebtehal said firmly. "You speak Arabic and can travel as my husband. Your friend can go as my sister from the Fezzan who is too shy to speak with strangers."

Michael's eyes widened with disbelief. "Are you saying what I think you're saying?"

"Did you not hear what I said before?" Ebtehal paused. "I said *we*. I'm coming with you."

Ebtehal worked quickly. She gave Stephen a *barracan* and taught him to wrap himself properly, exposing only one eye which she then blackened with *kohl*. A light preparation of henna dye applied to Michael's hands and face, darkened him appropriately.

"We must rely on cunning." Ebtehal was aware that there was not much time. "The coastal road is the only way to drive to Egypt."

Michael, dressed in Ali's clothes, loaded the "family" into the aging Peugeot sedan for their trip. "What excuse shall we use when questioned by authorities?" he asked.

"We are joining the women's march, of course," Ebtehal retorted, believing the answer obvious. "Besides, they will be looking for two American men, not a Libyan family. The buses and cars have been coming through every day for two weeks. One more car, *ma'alish*."

As the car rumbled down the road, Ebtehal took a deep breath. *The protectors. Once again the guardians call upon their brothers.*

Ali's family had belonged to *the Way* for more generations than memory warranted. In fact, she informed them, *Ali was the Way* in Libya as far as she knew. Abu Na'im Mabus, that traitor, had abandoned their brotherhood and the war finished the rest.

"Now Jehada and I are *the Way*," she said softly, almost to herself, but she knew they had all heard her.

That is why, she thought, *I must see this to the end, no matter what that means.*

The Way, Ebtehal knew, had existed in the world long before Longinus and the Magdalene brought their mysterious relics to Tarhuna. The brotherhood's function had always been to protect the protectors.

Silent as sand, and melting back into the desert when the job was done. Recognizing the light by its shadow, they battled the darkness. And now, Ebtehal realized, she was part of the fight.

Under her direction, Michael drove through Misratah and circled the *sebkha*, the salt steppes, of Tawurgha, Umm al'Izam, and al Hayshah. When a roadside marker informed them they were ten kilometers from Bir al'Utaylah, she motioned Michael to pull off the road into the desert. They secreted themselves in the mouth of a dried river bed, *Wadi Jarif,* for the night.

While Michael and Jehada started to prepare a meal, Ebtehal took Stephen onto the *sebkha* to gather *mushrooms of Malta*. Throughout the salty field, the leafless stumpy plants were growing everywhere. "Good for cooking," she informed him.

She also used the time to correct Stephen's walk, teaching him to take shorter steps with more of a glide. "Think like a woman and your walk will follow."

Stephen rolled his eyes. "Think like a woman. You're serious."

Ebtehal laughed aloud. Her first real encounter with American men, and she felt like an army officer. "Tomorrow, *bukra,* I will start teaching you Arabic, *arab-I-yaa.*"

Evening fell, and Michael insisted that Ebtehal and Jehada sleep in the car. As he and Stephen rolled out blankets close by, Michael was amazed by the moon's effect on their surroundings. Its brilliant light, bathing the cold desert dunes, caused them to shimmer like waves.

Stephen did not appear to be as mesmerized by their environment, though. As soon as they were settled, he turned toward him, a solemn look on his face. "Several days after you took me back to Olive, Mabus' security men went ballistic. They probably realized Tod had stolen something. It turns out, they were right."

Michael waited expectantly.

Stephen's voice fell to a whisper. "Among the personal effects the police found in Tod's car, there was a data flash drive."

"Did you get a hold of it?" Michael, excited, immediately wondered what it contained.

"I did," Stephen said. "The files were in Arabic. But one of them contained a long stream of numbers that were not in Arabic script. I memorized the numbers and trashed the drive."

"Well?" Michael searched Stephen's face. "Did you figure them out? Do they have any meaning for you?"

"None. I've been going over and over them in my head," he said, frustrated. "*25-22-49-34-0-27-01-50-40-30-26-12-56-15-45*. Sounds like a long-winded quarterback calling a play. Whatever it means it must be big. When Mabus found out the drive was missing, he must have put two and two together. He ordered me taken to Tarhuna until *it* was over."

"*It?*"

"Whatever is about to take place, I imagine. I was able to gather a little more information while I was being held. Mabus wouldn't let the Algerian actually torture me. He knew I hadn't given him all the pieces to the energy puzzle. He just wanted me out of the way for the time being. Once *it* takes place, Mabus seems confident he'll be in some kind of unassailable position of power."

"25 and 22, 50 and 34," Michael repeated the numbers. "They have nothing to do with your energy system?"

Stephen responded by shaking his head.

"Give me dead languages," Michael said. "I've never been good with number codes."

Stephen laughed. "Maybe we should switch specialties," he said, looking toward the car where Ebtehal was sleeping. "At this point, a dead language is what I need."

CHAPTER 70

F ROM THE DISTANT RECESSES of her mind, Maggie heard the insistent knocking. Every muscle in her body ached as she tossed off the flimsy bed covers and sat on the edge of the bed, remembering where she was.

Amman. The Ikhbar Hotel.

Her flight to Jordan had gotten in late last night and it was after one in the morning when her driver had dropped her off at "best, first-rate hotel in big city."

"Nine o'clock! Time for to get up! Nine o'clock!" a male voice shouted from beyond the door.

Maggie guessed the Jordanian hotel clerk had taken her literally when she said she wanted a "wake-up call" in the morning.

"Coffee outside," was the next thing she heard.

Maggie threw on a shirt and her jeans. The hallway was empty when she opened the door to her room. On the floor, sitting on a plastic tray, was a carafe and a cup.

First class, she thought as she picked up the tray and brought it into her room. She placed it on the small round table by the window and poured herself some of the steaming brew. After a few sips she felt the caffeine bringing her back to life.

Sitting quietly, the sunlight filtering through the glass offering her warmth and comfort, Maggie began thinking of her father. David Seline had given her so much love. Like the sun, he had shone over her, nurturing her growth, warming her soul and awakening her ability to see her own needs. He had encouraged her to find out who she really was and what she wanted out of life.

She could almost see him sitting across from her, his sandy brown hair framing his face, his green eyes that met everyone's with inquisitiveness smiling quietly at her. If there could be such a thing as a faultless gaze, it was her father's.

His love was an invitation. Through it, Maggie discovered that traveling and exploring were exciting ways to keep open to a constantly changing world. Summer vacations often meant flying to meet up with him in some foreign country—Italy, Germany, Russia—wherever he had been assigned. When Maggie turned eighteen, and David Seline became a *Washington Post* correspondent in Israel, the world split open for her and had never been the same since. That summer, just before starting college, she joined her father in Jerusalem.

A new adventure, she had thought at the time, and it was, until that awful day. Warm tears rolled down her cheeks as she remembered.

The explosion. It sent a shockwave through her hotel room and threw her to the floor. When she caught her breath, she shot up and ran to the window. People were screaming and running down the street.

The café. Dad.

Hours later, when the police told Maggie he was killed in the bombing, she felt as if her gut had been wrenched from her body. *Dad was waiting for me. If only I had been on time, he wouldn't have left the hotel and been sitting out on the street.*

Now nearly twenty years later, she knew the truth about her father's death. Killed in his hotel room. It had been part of P2's cover-up to include him as a victim of the suicide bombing.

Yet, if I hadn't called him to delay our meeting . . .

It seemed that no matter what she believed, a lie or the truth, she would always be wondering, *what if.* Still, in the end, it had taken only a moment to end an impeccable life, to rob her of the love that had always meant so much to her.

Back home in the States, a month after her father's funeral, a cardboard box arrived, filled with David Seline's notebooks. Maggie remembered taking one of them to the woods behind her grandmother's home. Sitting on the sloping hill above the lake, she had painfully reviewed excerpts from his notes. With every word she read, she felt her father's heart pouring forth, all of his years of work and insights, his determination to explain the whole story of the Islamic-Jewish contention with honesty, still allowing for his own humanity and decency to be reflected in his reporting. Her father's words expressed his hope for peace without apology, and a belief that the strife and suffering would end one day.

Perusing the one notebook was all she had been able to take. When she brought it back to her room, she placed it with all the others, sealed the cardboard box and never looked at any of them again.

Until last month.

It had taken almost twenty years, but finally Maggie had been able to release her father's passion. She had P2's threat to thank for that.

They killed him. The rage she felt brought her to her feet. It was then Maggie decided she had to do it for him, for her father. She had to live the pure vision. She had to embody it. She had to see it all through to the end—all of her beliefs and her vision for Jerusalem. She had to continue to write about it and speak about it the way he would have wanted her to.

At that moment, she heard her father's voice in her head once again, infusing her with his tenets of reporting. "Be truthful. Go for the big picture. Strive for integrity and be well-rounded. Never divorce yourself from your feelings, rather use them to guide your style and approach. Most important of all . . . hold on to your humanity."

Gotcha Dad.

Once outside the hotel, Maggie found the street bustling with activity. Amman, today a modern metropolis, was one of the oldest cities in the world. Once called the City of Waters, in the third century BC it had also been given the name Philadelphia, a Greek word meaning "the brotherhood love," until the rise of Islam brought it back to its ancient roots again.

As she walked through the streets, past the remnants of the colonnaded walkways, the baths and the grand Amphitheater—a world filled with Roman influence and architectural design—Maggie thought of Michael. She knew that the strange confluence that had brought her to him and to this ancient city was now leading her into Israel and Jerusalem.

Soon, kebab stalls smoked the area with the smell of roasting meat. Maggie walked past them all until she came upon a café, where her senses were overwhelmed by the powerful rich scent of Arabian coffee.

"Coffee, madam?" The vendor, a soft-spoken swarthy Arab, gave her an inviting smile.

Maggie was tempted by the strong scent of the cardamom, but it was the plate of luscious pastries the vendor swept before her that made her mouth water.

"I'll take that large, sticky one over there," Maggie said, giving in to her desire.

Relishing every bite of the sweet roll, she continued down the street, passing shops that were festively decorated with colorful tiles—blue and gold, tan and green—marked with the billowing curvatures of Arabic script. Gardens abounded everywhere. Inside, men read newspapers, gossiped, shuffled cards, and tested their wits at backgammon. Groups of scruffy looking gentlemen sat together using *argeelahs*—water pipes—to smoke their tobacco.

At another time, she would have loved to stroll through the city enjoying the beautiful old villas and flowering gardens, but it wouldn't be today. Maggie stepped out into the street and waved her arms at a small yellow cab. The driver made an abrupt swerve toward her and stopped.

"Can you take me to the border?" she inquired.

The cab driver gave her a surprised look. "We're supposed to avoid that area today, madam, but you should know that."

"I should know what? What are you talking about?" Maggie asked, irritated. "Can you get me there or not?"

"I'll take you for fifty American dollars. Today is extra trouble."

Maggie sighed. *Tell me about it.*

"Fine," she said, handing over the money.

After she slipped into the back seat, the driver took off, obviously adept at scaring off pedestrians and skimming the cab on sidewalks.

Maggie was amazed by the amount of people walking about. *Tourist season must be great this year*, she thought. Soon Maggie began to notice something interesting about the crowd. Several women walking together, then ten, thirty, then several packed busloads. The crowd was moving forward and it was composed of mostly women, *massive* amounts of women.

"Do you know what's going on? What are all these women doing here?"

"Have you not heard, madam?" The cabbie looked at her inquisitively through the rearview mirror.

"I haven't heard anything," Maggie replied.

"Well, madam must have spent the last week in the middle of the desert."

"Not exactly." Maggie was growing more impatient. "So, what's happening?"

"It's a march. The women are marching to Jerusalem." The cabbie shook his head in disbelief. "Craziness. I would never have believed I'd see such a day. They are everywhere, coming from all countries, surrounding the borders of Israel. It's world news, madam."

World news. A rush of adrenalin moved through her as she began to understand what she was witnessing.

"The women are here to protest the fighting going on in the Middle East. They are demanding that old Jerusalem be declared an international city." The driver grabbed the paper, *The Jordan Times,* from the seat next to him and handed it back to her.

Maggie's eyes were riveted on the headline.

"Are you alright, madam?" the cabdriver questioned.

She was too stunned to reply. There it was in black and white, international news.

THE SELINE MARCH

CAIRO — Laurel Seline and fellow marchers request entry into the Holy Land. On the borders of Egypt, Jordan, and Lebanon nearly a hundred thousand women have gathered . . .

The magnificence of the event was truly awesome, but Maggie found her excitement quickly tempered as fear for her grandmother's safety arose. Anxious thoughts streamed through her mind. Was Laurel alright? Who was watching out for her? The dangerous nature of the women's march gave Maggie a sense of urgency.

She looked up to see the driver's black eyes staring at her.

"Madam, are you certain you want to continue? You are not looking well."

"Just get me to the border," she answered. What was an incredible and significant event could easily turn into a catastrophic nightmare. As the cab careened through the streets, Maggie tried to shake her fear.

Twenty minutes later, when the taxi finally approached the border crossing at the King Hussein Bridge, her driver slowed down. Cautiously, he proceeded forward, maneuvering the cab through the hoards of people in the street.

Astounded by the sheer number of women around her, Maggie felt the powerful karmic pull that had drawn her and thousands of others. As she stepped out of the car and into the crowd, she realized that she was now part of a mysterious movement that had shocked the world, like a tsunami suddenly growing out of the sea. How it would all end was unknown, but the waters were certainly rising.

"You have fifteen minutes."

Maggie turned toward the cab driver. "What?"

"The officials have decided to close the border today at noon. That's fifteen minutes, madam."

Her mind racing, Maggie realized she had to move fast. Hoping to avoid detection, she had decided to enter Israel through Jordan, knowing her name would undoubtedly be recognized if she had taken a flight directly into an Israeli airport. It appeared now that her plan might be all for naught. With at least thirty women waiting in line before her, it looked like she might not make it over in time for the 12 P.M. closing.

She looked at the Jordanian military guarding their post. The men were joking, a jovial brigade, not the more serious legion she expected, intent upon turning the women back.

A light went on. *God, these guys love this.* Maggie realized that if anything was going to give the Jordanian government satisfaction, it was a mass of women creating an international headache for the Israelis.

It was then that Maggie remembered her press pass. She had to take the chance. She took a deep breath and walked to the front of the line toward the border patrol. The chief guard, a massive brute with deep brown, pock-marked skin, glared at her as she approached.

Maybe this isn't such a good idea, she thought. But it was too late. Eyes looking straight at his, she walked directly up to him and presented her pass.

The guard held her gaze. What happened next surprised her. He smiled—a toothy, wide, lecherous grin. "*New York Times,*" He read off her badge. "American paper."

"Yes."

Then the guard began to sound out her name. "S . . . E . . . L, Seleeen," he said, drawing out the last syllable.

The sound of her name made her cringe. She scanned his face for any sign of recognition.

"French?" the guard questioned, apparently unaware of her notoriety.

"No, Italian," Maggie responded, the knot in her stomach beginning to unwind.

"Ah, Italian women, very luscious."

His snakelike eyes and lascivious stare made her want to slap him, but instead she smiled. *Better play up the sultry Italian number for this moron. Anything to get over the border.*

Smiling with as much wide-eyed allure as possible, she flashed her pass again. The guard indicated he liked their little exchange. *Men*, she thought.

The officer made a quick call to the Israeli border patrol. He then signaled another guard and turned back toward her. "I told them you are an American tourist who has been stranded in Amman since yesterday. Best not to mention anything about being a journalist. Those Israelis don't like foreign reporters."

Maggie assumed the guard was getting as much satisfaction duping the Israelis as he did by their flirtation.

"So I'm free to pass?"

"Yes, madam, you can go, but quickly," he directed. "We're closing the border in ten minutes."

Maggie walked over to her taxi. The driver shook his head. "No. I cannot drive you. No vehicles allowed over the bridge other than the buses."

"So how do I . . . ?

"You walk," he answered, "and you'd better hurry."

Maggie took a deep breath and began her walk over the bridge. The Israeli soldiers touting machine guns watched her approach.

Of course, she wouldn't be mentioning her reporter status, but would they buy the misplaced tourist routine? Maggie prayed that the soldiers at the border wouldn't recognize her, otherwise, it would all end there.

Fate was with her as a young, bored Israeli officer checked her American passport. After handing it back to her, he nodded his head for her to move ahead. She passed through a metal detector and was patted down by a female guard. From her position by the side of the conveyer, Maggie watched as another female officer searched her small duffle bag. Maggie had been careful to place the original pouch of stones into one of the colorful Jordanian pouches she had bought at the airport so it would look like a gift.

The officer opened the pouch and gazed at the semi-precious stones. Looking unimpressed with Maggie's collection of rocks, she tied up the pouch once again and put it back in the duffel bag. After handing the bag back to her, the officer motioned her forward, indicating they were through.

Maggie looked ahead toward the last guard in the line. Stone-faced and apparently ready for action, his was the final hoop she needed to jump through.

The guard glared at her when she reached his post. Speaking in a rough, mechanical voice, he addressed her brusquely. "What is your business?"

Okay, Maggie, you're on. "I'm here on vacation, and wouldn't you know it," she rattled, acting the complaining tourist, "all these women showed up! I took a little excursion yesterday morning to Amman, and in a few hours I was surrounded. My trip is ruined! Wait till I get my hands on my travel agent. If she thinks—"

"Secured!" With a loud bang, the guard stamped her passport. The officer waved her on, indicating he'd had enough of the rambling *goyim* from America.

Maggie hailed one of the taxis at the crossing. She directed the cabbie to drive her to El Ghazali Square in Jerusalem. She would go to her friend's house. Feikra would be able to help her.

It was nearly one o'clock when the taxi driver dropped her off at Sha'ar Ha'arayo Street, near the Square. Maggie walked down the street, then off onto a side road. Several nuns, draped in black and white dress appeared suddenly from around the corner. It was not unusual to see the sisters walking through the area, visiting St. Stephen's Gate, browsing through shops and making friends with the locals. They passed her with a flurry of light-hearted laughter.

At the end of the street, Maggie walked up to a wide wooden door. She tapped and waited. After several moments, the door creaked open slowly and a fair-skinned woman with wavy black hair poked her head out quickly. Instantly, her piercing brown eyes lit up.

"My God!" her friend, Feikra yelled, excited to see her. She grabbed Maggie by the arm and pulled her into the apartment.

Once inside, Feikra embraced her warmly. It had been months since Maggie had seen her last and she was relieved to find Feikra safe, especially after so much unrest in Jerusalem.

"What happened to you? All the newspapers, TV?" Feikra's face now conveyed her worry.

"I was laying low."

"Laying low? The media's reporting you're kidnapped, possibly even dead! What have you been doing?"

Not a time to be explaining Grail theories, Maggie realized. "Feikra, there's something I need your help with." In a rush of words, Maggie told her what she had found out about her father's death, as well as about the ensuing journey that followed, including the discovery of what she referred to, for Feikra's sake, as a "strange map."

Feikra's eyebrows lifted in astonishment. Before she could respond, the door swung open and her sister, Rasha, entered hurriedly, without glancing in Maggie's direction.

"Feikra, you must come quickly," the young woman implored. "It's a madhouse. I need you there to help give direction to the women, and then we must spin the plan into motion."

"Hello Rasha."

Rasha turned quickly. A look of astonishment on her face, she practically barreled Maggie over greeting her. "I knew you were alive." Rasha clasped Maggie tightly. "They kept telling me differently, but you're too smart."

Maggie gave her a broad smile. "If you only knew the half of what I've been through, you'd be wondering about my smarts."

Rasha ignored her comment. "As long as you're safe, that's what matters. Just stay here and you'll be alright."

"I can't."

Rasha looked at her, puzzled.

"She has a task to carry out," Feikra told her sister. Smiling, she turned her gaze toward Maggie again. "And I know just the person who can help you."

CHAPTER 71

HAVING REGROUPED IN CAIRO and determining their strategy, Laurel knew they had no time left to linger. After stocking up on rations, they rented minibuses, hired drivers and pushed forward toward the Egyptian-Israeli border.

With Lonnie and Jules sitting beside her arguing over who had counted the most herds of goats, Laurel used a paper plate as a fan as their caravan moved slowly through the rising heat. Soon, they were passing a legion of African women whose numbers seemed to swallow the dry desert terrain. But it was not only Africans that Laurel would see. By the time they got close to the border, they met up with tens of thousands of women from the Americas and Europe who mingled together with the Kenyans, Ethiopians, Sudanese and Ugandans. Laurel marveled at the tremendous number who had decided to make the harrowing journey, many crossing borders through sheer force of will.

After finally reaching the check point and exiting the bus, Laurel was happy to feel the sandy ground beneath her feet once again. But no sooner had she arrived than there appeared signs that a storm was on the way.

A strange omen that the horizon would darken so quickly, Laurel thought. The wind-driven clouds began to swirl in shadowy spirals, reminding her of a tornado she had seen once. But it couldn't be, not at the edge of the desert. *Could it?*

The first drops of rain began to fall, gently at first, but soon they were being soaked in a torrential downpour. While Jules and Lonnie rushed to unfurl a plastic tarp, Laurel could see that very few of the women had any protection. Some were pulling plastic bags from their backpacks, while others could only huddle together in circles. Several reporters who had managed to get flights into Cairo were the luckiest in the fold, their cameramen scurrying to get them under makeshift tents.

Although drenched to the skin, more and more women soon became aware of Laurel's arrival. As a swell of cheering started to rise from the group, Laurel heard one voice above the rest.

"The storm of the century is coming!"

The storm of the century. Laurel knew that the onslaught of women ready to give up everything in pursuit of peace was most definitely that storm.

But it soon became apparent to her that there were a lot more than enthusiastic marchers at the border to greet her. Soldiers were everywhere, carrying rifles and machine guns, driving the women with the butts of their weapons, taunting them. Several threatened to shoot them if they got any closer.

Laurel felt a burning fury rise in her chest but quickly realized that calm calculation was the order of the day. She knew the Egyptian military did not want to risk appearing light on the *Seline Marchers* as they were now being called. The more closely she watched, the more she could see that the soldiers' aggression seemed superficial, as if they were putting on a good show for their Israeli adversaries.

In Kerem Shalom, on the other side of the border, Brigadier General Ismael Ruffat watched closely. In charge of the Israeli border brigade, he ordered his men to stand ready for an attack, perhaps from the Egyptian military. Anything misconstrued by either side at this point would ignite a powder keg. In the pit of his stomach, he understood all too well that the explosion would be massive and could prove the catalyst for catastrophic reprisal.

And all the work of women!

Ruffat had been told that nearly a hundred thousand of them had arrived at border towns on all sides of Israel. But what exactly were they waiting for? *What kind of fiasco do we have in store?* Even he, a seasoned soldier, shuddered at the thought of having his men fire their weapons into a crowd of women. Still, as the women pressed forward inching their way closer to the border, he had to maintain his harsh exterior. Apparently, they were doing the same at the bridge crossing in Jordan and even along the hostile Lebanese frontier.

The general could see now that fear and anxiety had taken hold of his troops. Trepidation had taken its toll, and his men were worn down by the whole episode. *Armed with guns and facing women.* So many of the soldiers had likened any military assault against them to attacking their own mothers, and the women had been yelling as much at them for the last several hours.

"Shame on you! You would shoot your own mother!"

Within earshot of the verbal assaults, the Egyptians soldiers were not immune. They, too, looked shaken.

General Ruffat hated every moment of it. Standing there with the might of Israel, facing off against tens of thousands of women was an abomination, a perversity he could never have imagined to be his fate.

What would they do if the women stormed over the border?

Kill them, beat them, protect them, allow them to pass . . . join them?

Deep within the warm dry recesses of the Israeli government building, Prime Minister Mordechai Retsan was seated watching the coverage of the march from his office.

"Sir." Defense Minister Aaron Martsold addressed him. The anxious questioning in his voice was hard for him to disguise. "What do you want us to do?" Martsol needed to play this right. He understood his position was much less that of an advisor than a minion.

The prime minister motioned him to come closer. "I told you before, those women are not to cross any of the borders, not from Egypt, nor from Jordan or Lebanon. Tell the officers to shoot them if they attempt."

"But sir, they are unarmed women!"

"Who would be illegally crossing our borders," Retsan sneered.

Martsold swallowed hard. "This will not look good."

"Well, there are ways for you to make it look better, right?" Prime Minister Retsan threw a sly glance in Martsol's direction.

Martsol understood. When Israel's own troops shot up a Jewish Defense League meeting, they cleverly created a scenario that pointed the finger of blame on Arab terrorists. *The Arabs can only blame themselves,* he thought, *for making it so easy—suicide bombings, random shootings of Jewish civilians. They are only getting what is due them.*

Now, Martsol knew it would be a game of chess. The players had their pieces set in motion and those watching could never know how many steps had been preplanned. They could only view, not the planning, but the execution.

CHAPTER 72

TENSIONS WERE MOUNTING quickly, Laurel realized. The women were growing more and more restless. Tired and hungry, most of them had eaten little since they left Cairo, and the night, mercilessly long, had left them all wet from the downpour.

"Back away. Everyone is to back away and keep behind the police barricades," an Egyptian soldier blasted over a megaphone. Glaring news camera lights pointed toward the Egyptian riot squad as they pushed and taunted some of the women.

Laurel was exhausted. Although her legs felt like lead, she managed her way onto a platform of wooden crates. "We must be brave and remain peaceful," she implored the crowd, her voice booming over the loudspeaker. "We will stay here until they hear us, until they let us into Israel."

As she heard the half-hearted cheers, Laurel hoped the women's spirits could be revived. The last thing they needed was to lose their hope.

Laurel saw her then. Valencia, the beautiful woman she had met in Rome. Appearing vital and confident, Valencia climbed up onto the platform and joined her.

Is this the light we need to brighten our path?

Laurel moved aside.

"Women of the world, our time has come!" Valencia announced firmly. She felt a wave of energy move though her as she looked out onto the sea of women standing with her at the border of Israel.

"Our leaders have taken us down a road of destruction. Aggressive, masculine reflexes have created more violence and rage, have left us with little hope for remedy in the Middle East or anywhere else. Our hope of survival lies in honoring the feminine, that which a patriarchal society has tried vehemently to squelch.

"Their legacy has left us living in a deluded universe, a world that worships a fixed and righteous view. In order to feel secure, we only welcome change that men in power determine for us. Our patriarchal religions are prime examples of this, creating a one-sided world gone mad from static, brittle beliefs."

Valencia saw that some of the news reporters had their cameras on her. The soldiers themselves were watching her intently, even if most of them didn't understand a word she was saying.

"Let us remember," she continued, "that patriarchy is founded on division not unity. We concentrate on the differences instead of giving importance to the similarities. There is good and bad, there is black and white. We are constantly in a state of opposites. Where does *unity* come into the picture?

"It's no wonder women have been seen as evil, an abhorrent influence that must be destroyed. Intuition, psychic energy, spiritual force, the unknown, creation itself . . . merely feminine mockeries of sanity— or so it has been claimed by religious men in power. Women have died at the stake for challenging such beliefs, and to this day dogmatic religious views have persisted in undermining the feminine.

"Therefore it is up to us to develop a balance between the feminine and the masculine. That's the formula for a stable democracy. Wisdom and compassion working together will swing the pendulum away from aggression and fear toward peace and conciliation." Valencia paused and took a deep breath. "I'll venture to say it's already begun. We have reached a *critical mass.*"

Valencia turned her gaze upward toward the comet moving slowly across the sky. *Chiron* had been on its course all week. The comet, known as the wounded healer, appeared as if it was leading them. *How appropriate*, she thought, *that our march would occur under its direction. We must heal our wounds . . . we must heal our planet.*

Valencia took a deep breath, bringing her focus back toward the earth and the thousands of women standing on the desert sand before her. "Now," she resumed, "the energy of *woman* is being powerfully unleashed. Negative powers have reached levels where enough of us are reacting against them to instigate change. This critical mass that we have reached cannot be turned back, and the force of it will literally shift the energy of our planet, creating a new paradigm.

"And what is this new paradigm? It is the awareness that our thoughts are powerful and that each and every one of us is shaping our world. What we visualize, what we believe, will manifest. It is a paradigm that will create a spiritual renaissance, one that will take us beyond religious dogmas, one that will infuse our politics with human decency. Finally, it is a formula that will initiate an alchemical change in the Middle East, transforming the hatred and violence of a crucified land into the compassion and sanity of a City of Peace.

"This movement," Valencia said pointedly, her voice emphatic, "*our march of women*, will be the nucleus of the reactor. For those who are looking for the end of the world—the apocalypse—we will provide them that end. It will be the end of the world as we know it, the end of the power-driven *madness* that has brought us to the brink of destruction." She paused, staring into the sea of determined faces. "The apocalypse we seek is nothing less than the transformation of the human race."

Valencia watched as one by one the women stood and cheered, each one a beacon, allying with her words.

And each one lending her power to one end . . . the healing of the nations.

The burning light of Chiron moved steadily overhead. Valencia felt its presence as an omen, as if the whole march was being driven by its mysterious influence.

CHAPTER 73

I N THE MORNING, Michael climbed once again behind the wheel of the old French sedan. After the rest of his new "family" settled into the car, he drove them out of the mouth of the *wadi* back onto the coastal highway.

The sun rose like an imposing orb from the flat expressionless horizon of *Khalij Surt*, the Gulf of Sirte, bringing notice of the task awaiting them. Across the watery divide lay Benghazi, Tobruk and the Egyptian border. Michael was grateful that thus far they had only encountered an occasional lorry filled with oranges or tomatoes and a seemingly endless herd of goats munching peacefully on tufted grass.

Jehada scanned the road for danger while, in the backseat, Ebtehal continued her relentless instruction of basic Arabic to a less-than-receptive Stephen Einsof. When Stephen mimicked the words in a woman's voice, the whole car exploded with laughter.

"What?" Stephen asked incredulously.

Thank goodness for a light moment, Michael mused.

As they drove on, the new day's heat severed the cold of the night, inviting the sand scorpions, lizards, green snakes, and horned vipers to bask on rocks. Waves of heat rose from the asphalt surface, making it appear they were driving on ice. Michael looked toward his right as they passed a road sign. *Sirte 3km.*

"Look there!" Jehada said nervously pointing ahead.

Michael joined Jehada's concern when he observed army vehicles parked by the side of a checkpoint.

Ebtehal did not seem to share their anxiety. "There is nothing to worry about. It's only a small police gate."

Michael begged to differ. *A small police gate, is that all?* Anxious, his grip tightened on the steering wheel as he recalled that, besides being

Qaddafi's hometown, the municipality they were about to enter was the seat of a number of Libya's important government institutions.

A wooden barrier blocked the road, and a small, black-and-white checkered police station awaited them. Several buses sat idling, waiting to pass, while what appeared to be a large group of tourists mingled at the checkpoint.

Michael swallowed hard as they pulled in behind two, large Fiat touring coaches, brightly festooned with flags, banners and signs. There appeared to be about a hundred women—a curious mix of European and Middle Eastern—standing alongside the buses. Several wore T-shirts that had the same phrase, *Walking Toward the New Jerusalem,* written on them in different languages . . . Arabic, English, Italian and French. Michael noticed several signs on the buses made the same statement.

"What is this?" he murmured, stunned by the scene. Michael glanced nervously over his shoulder at Stephen, or what remained visible of him wrapped in the *barracan.*

Suddenly, Michael remembered. *The march. Laurel and the women.*

A self-important, young police officer wearing dark sunglasses strutted up to their car and stood by Michael's window. "Papers," he demanded.

Ebtehal did not wait for Michael to reply. Instead she stuck her head out the rear window. "We are with the buses going to Jerusalem," she cackled with defiance.

The officer puffed his chest, ignoring her. "Papers," he repeated holding his hand out to Michael.

"Idiot," Ebtehal cried. "I told you we are on our way to Israel, demanding justice." *Men, such fools always.* She climbed out of the car ready to take him on.

"Do you always let your wife speak for you?" the officer asked Michael.

"*Aiwa,* I'm no fool." Michael had been given Ali's identification card at the start of their journey. He handed it to the policeman, along with ones for Ebtehal and Jehada.

"The Leader said in the *Green Book,* 'Woman and man are equal as human beings,' " Ebtehal barked at the officer. "So why should my husband not let me speak for him?"

The young man ignored her. "There are only three sets of papers here. What about her?" He gestured toward Stephen.

Wrapped tightly within the heavy wool *barracan,* Stephen kept his one visible eye averted.

This monkey gets dumber and dumber, Ebtehal thought. Feeling the need to end the questioning, she stepped closer to the officer. No match for her height and her sharp tongue, he reluctantly shrank from her boldness.

"Moron," she said confronting him. "My sister is from the Fezzan— never away from home before. Now let us go. The buses are pulling out."

The hapless man looked toward the barrier. He then turned his gaze toward several lorries now waiting behind the Peugeot, the first one brimming with tomatoes growing ripe in the sun and attracting an armada of flies.

With the wave of his arm the officer indicated to his fellow guards to lift the barrier. He then turned back toward Michael, his face in an angry grimace. "You should watch her mouth," he hissed.

Ebtehal thought the man wanted to slap her, but his weariness appeared to outweigh his hostility. She got back into the car.

"Go!" he shouted and waved them through.

Michael accelerated the car as fast as it would go, trying to keep up with the coach buses roaring ahead. Ebtehal could see clearly that it was a futile attempt. The sedan simply didn't have the power. All they could do was maintain a dim, distant view of the buses as they continued down the road.

Several hours later, they still hadn't caught up with the coaches when they stopped for gas in Marsa al Buraygah.

"How long ago did the buses for Jerusalem come through?" Ebtehal demanded of the attendant.

"Which one? There have been hundreds in the last few days," the man said in dismay. "From Spain, Gibraltar, France, Morocco, Tunis and Algeria. They tell me they are determined to cast aside the mantle of male and political oppression." He shrugged his shoulders. "My wife joined them this morning."

CHAPTER 74

AFTER REFUELING in Nicosia on the island of Cyprus, Mabus' plane lifted off for Tel Aviv. Once airborne, Mabus realized, to his discomfort, it was time to contact the Egyptian minister.

Mabus' relations with the Egyptian government had long been strained. His father, Abu Na'im, had been a founding member of the Special Order within the Muslim Brotherhood during World War II. Organizing this group, which was authorized to carry weapons along with their Qurans, had been a major first step in anti-government activity. Then, in the 1970s, Anwar Sadat encouraged the activities of another Muslim organization, *Gama'a al-Islamiya*—the Islamic Group—in order to weaken the Muslim Brotherhood. In the tradition of Middle East politics, the Islamic Group was later behind Sadat's own assassination.

This convoluted history had already proven to be a pain in Mabus' side. Even now, after having played the card of diplomacy with Egypt's president many times, Mabus was well aware Mubarak did not trust him.

But Mabus' relationship with the Saudis was no better. His bitterness toward them traced back to his school days at *Villa Ticino*, a Swiss boarding school in Lugano that catered to rich Muslim families—the wealthier and more secular the better. As the son of a mere oil minister, Giovanni had found he was not in the social register of many of his classmates. Nor did he wish to be. With his Muslim and Christian upbringing, Mabus had been shocked at the decadent, callous Saudi princes. He found their drug and alcohol use abhorrent, and felt disgusted by the casual sexual relationships he observed among his classmates, especially those with American girls. Isolated and hostile, his ultra-conservative beliefs brought him to the conclusion that the Saudis would one day pay for their folly.

With his prejudices deeply entrenched, nothing angered Mabus more than finding himself now having to place a call to General Ali al-Hassani, the Egyptian Minister of the Interior. But what choice did he have?

This stupid women's march . . . brought about by Maggie Seline's grand-mother. The whole thing had gotten out of hand.

"*As-Salam alaikum,* my good friend, Mr. Mabus," the general responded after hearing Mabus' voice on the other end of the line, all the while wondering *Why is this double-dealing friend of Israel calling me at my home?*

"*Alaikum as-Salam,* General al-Hassani. I have a problem."

Obviously, why else would you contact me?

"As you know, there is a Peace Conference convening in Jerusalem in a few days," Mabus said. "A conference in which your government is heavily involved. This insane 'march of women' could cause a great deal of security problems."

The general knew all about security problems. His major portfolio included the State Security Investigation. The SSI was infamous for its brutality. When prisoners disappeared into the Scorpion section of Cairo's Tora Prison, they would more than likely vanish from the face of the earth. So, more than anyone, al-Hassani saw *security problems* as needing to be approached with a hand that was heavy but controlled. After all, repression was like water pressure. It was most effective when modulated. "Of course, Mr. Mabus. What would you like me to do?"

"Seal the borders." Mabus' voice was firm. "The major land route for these fanatics to reach Jerusalem from Europe is across North Africa. If they cannot enter Egypt, they will be isolated."

"That would be easier if they were first forbidden access to Libya."

"I know. I have made that request," Mabus stated caustically.

General al-Hassani was aware they both knew that Muammar al-Qaddafi was encouraging the march as a way of embarrassing both Israel and the United States. Libya had, in fact, opened its borders to a free flow of travel. He was about to state the obvious when he heard Mabus' voice once again.

"Also, there is the matter of women traveling from the south through Sudan." Mabus paused. "Any assistance you can provide will be well-compensated."

General al-Hassani was normally open to bribery, the more flagrant and generous the better. But this time he chose not to engage in that game. In this case, he realized, political maneuvering would be worth more to him than money. "I will inform my men to act with extra caution."

After concluding his conversation with Mabus, the general placed his own call to the minister of police, Suheil Tayi. *The enemy of my enemy is my friend.* "See to it that any women wishing to travel across our country toward the Israeli border are continued to be given all possible assistance. There is to be no interference from our army posts. Is that clear?"

Mabus could stew in his own juices. Later today, al-Hassani would call his cousin at the Heliopolis Presidential Palace and inform him of his action.

The general was pleased with his plan. Any harassment of Israel would be to Egypt's benefit. He would still need to analyze what tactics to employ at the border itself, though. The unknown factor—How would his Israeli counterpart react?

"What do the American's call it?" the general wondered aloud. "Playing chicken. Let's see if Israel strikes the first blow."

CHAPTER 75

A S THEY GOT CLOSER to Egypt, Ebtehal realized that their small troop had become part of a larger purpose. God's design was unfolding, and women were the warriors executing the plan.

Ebtehal was ready for the change. Her world, growing up in the small oasis of Beni Ulid, south of Tarhuna, had always been cultivated by men. Throughout her life, Ebtehal, her mother and her mother's mother before that, had to accept that women could never appear in public without their *barracan*. Gratefully, though, she had missed being condemned never to learn how to read or write. She was one of the fortunate. She could read. She knew how to drive and even voted. For her, being a woman didn't mean slavery.

As the wind blew in through the car window, Ebtehal took a deep breath. *All Muslim women must have this same taste of freedom.* It was one of the reasons why she was going to Jerusalem.

Ebtehal then thought of Ali. She had been hard on him, perhaps too hard all these years. *But there had been no other choice.* Ebtehal knew that someday he would be called upon for a great task. He knew it, and she knew it. But hers had been the greater determination. *One does not know when the messengers of Allah will call.* Ali had done his best, and her love had been his buoy. Now, it was up to her again. Once more her faith was leading her forward, driving the men in her life.

Ebtehal stared out the window. With the narrow coastal plain laying far behind them, there hadn't been a sign of a village for hours. Instead, they were now ascending yet another *jebel*, one side of the road bordering a deep ravine and the other running alongside a steep slope where hardy knobs of evergreen bushes clung to rocks, surviving through the power of sheer tenacity.

Rough country, even for the most sure-footed goat.

As they rounded a sharp curve, a bus suddenly materialized, blaring its horn angrily. It was gone from sight as quickly as it appeared. Thus far, it was their only contact with civilization during the day's long, monotonous drive.

But Ebtehal's feeling of boredom was replaced sooner than she would have wished. Before long, she noticed the sky growing steadily darker behind them, although sunset was still hours away. Moments later, what started as a light breeze quickly transformed into a strong wind. The hairs on the back of her neck stood up as she recognized the signs. "*Ghibli*," she warned the others.

Ebtehal had faced them before. Fierce, wind-blown sand that blocked the sun, choking the breath and burying roadways under drifting sand dunes. This *ghibli*, she sensed, was moving rapidly, and they were in its direct path. Ebtehal knew there was no time to waste. "Stop the car!" she insisted.

"But we're so close to the border," Michael started to argue.

"Stop the car quickly," she commanded, "or we'll die suffocating in here."

They grabbed water bottles and some food and ran up the steep rocky incline seeking shelter.

Jehada found it for them—a low rock overhang with just enough space for them to crawl under. Michael got under Stephen's *barracan* with him, and Jehada and Ebtehal wrapped themselves in hers. It became increasingly hard to breathe as the wind whipped the cloth, threatening at any moment to rip it from their fingers or whisk them each like hulls of an air blown sloop toward the rocks.

Like banshees, the *ghibli* shrieked, the rocks carried the echoes, and the sand stung their eyes. On the verge of screaming, Ebtehal held back. The *ghibli* was a maddening test of faith. Survival was everything, but death . . . She held her eyes closed tightly and prayed. Ebtehal had no delusions. *We live, we die.* But this *ghibli* was not going to claim any one of them.

She willed it so.

When the powerful winds subsided, Michael stepped out from under the overhang. Jehada and Ebtehal were quick to follow, while Stephen, looking dazed and uncharacteristically ruffled, unwound himself slowly.

God knows how we got through it, Michael thought. *If there are protectors watching over us, then more power to them.*

He let out a sigh of relief. With the dust settled, he could clearly see the deep, azure calm of the Mediterranean, and Musa'id—the Libyan-Egyptian border crossing.

Suddenly, the loud honking of a truck horn made them all turn.

"Is anyone out there?" a man's voice yelled out, echoing off the canyon walls.

Impulsively, Jehada answered, "Up here!"

Ebtehal waved her hand to silence him, but it was too late.

"We're coming up," the voice informed them.

There was no denying their presence now. Whoever had seen their car was on the way. Aching, sore, and shaking sand from every possible joint, they all waited anxiously for the first sign of a figure.

"Damn," Michael muttered when he saw them approaching. Several soldiers and an officer were making their way up the hill.

"*Kif halek.* Up here." Ebtehal waved, looking resigned to the situation.

Stephen shot Michael an apprehensive look. Anxiously, he shook the sand from his *baraccan* and wrapped himself thoroughly.

The commander, reaching them first, eyed them curiously. He demanded to know where they were headed.

"Jerusalem," Ebtehal replied in an unusually tentative manner.

Michael expected they were about to be drilled, searched, detained—the whole nine yards. Incredibly, the officer said nothing. He looked back toward two other soldiers and waved at them. "More pilgrims to Jerusalem," he called out.

Michael eyeballed his fellow travelers. They looked as bewildered as he felt.

"All of you are going together?" was the commander's next question.

Michael snapped back to attention. "Of course," he replied. "My son and I cannot allow my wife and her sister to travel alone."

Did he just see Stephen's one eye winking at him from the folds of the barracan? Michael started to doubt his own senses as he led the group back to the Peugeot, now almost totally buried in sand. Resembling a sleeping camel, it was but a forlorn dune by the roadside. Michael pulled at the door latch while Jehada scraped the windows. When Michael was finally able to peer into the tightly sealed car, he could see the interior was covered in sand.

Surprisingly, several soldiers armed with shovels walked over and offered to assist them. Together, they dug out the car and removed as much grit from around the engine as they could. Finally, when he was finished wiping down the interior enough for human passage, Michael got another surprise. The commanding officer told him they would be free to cross the border.

Apparently overhearing the edict, Stephen, who had been playing the shy sister and sitting forlornly on a distant rock, shot to his feet.

Michael was about to pile them all into the Peugeot again when he saw what looked like a roaring dust cloud advancing toward them across the sand. *Is that what I think it is?* he wondered. As the cloud got closer, it became clear that a caravan of buses, trucks and jeeps were headed their way.

Michael kept his surprise to himself. It appeared to him that the dear Libyans had figured out that it was better to ride the tide.

The worldwide onrush of women converging on Jerusalem . . . the enormous media attention. Apparently, Libyan officials had determined that it was in their best interest to allow the women passage. No doubt, their Egyptian brothers just over the border held the same belief. Maybe these officers patrolling the outskirts of the Libyan Desert had wives or sisters who had joined the march as well.

The ties that bind, Michael thought.

As the caravan moved closer, he sensed that the rest of his cohorts were thinking along the same lines as he. "Let's go," he said, and they all jumped into the Peugeot.

"*Masalama, ha-t-kun rihla,*" the Libyan soldiers said, wishing them a good trip.

As Michael drove into the middle of the stream of buses and trucks in line to enter Egypt, he couldn't help but laugh. He had finally lived to see a new dawn arrive in Arabia and women were leading the charge.

Life would never be the same in the land of the prophet.

CHAPTER 76

MICHAEL WIPED THE SWEAT from his forehead. The Egyptian sun was proving itself to be as merciless as the Libyan. Barely stopping, they drove on alongside the great *Qattara Depression*, a formidable basin of salt lakes and marshes dropping almost five hundred feet below sea level.

Michael had been wondering for some time how long the Peugeot would last. The answer came when, without warning, the car started to sputter and a puff of black smoke escaped from under the hood.

Michael held the wheel as hard as he held his breath as the Peugeot slowed down and lost steam. With a final dying sputter, the car's engine succumbed to the heat. *Le grande Peugeot* had taken them sixteen hundred kilometers. Perhaps it, like Rommel, had heard the illusive and addictive call of the *Qattara*.

Once out of the car, Stephen pointed. "Look over there."

The sign, less then fifteen yards ahead of them read *El Alamein*. Michael knew the historic landmark. It was there, where the great *Qattara Depression* met the Mediterranean, that the People's Marshal—the *Volksmarschall*—Erwin Rommel's military drive to Cairo with the German-Italian *Panzerarmee Afrika* was turned back by the British in World War II.

"Didn't Rommel run out of gas here?" Stephen asked, shaking some more sand out of the folds of his garment.

Michael was surprised Stephen knew even a hint about it. "Yes, aptly put," he answered. "Winston Churchill said the war turned after The Battle of El Alamein. What's that quote?" Michael closed his eyes and searched his memory. "Churchill said something like, 'This is not the end. It is not even the beginning of the end. But it is, perhaps, the end of the beginning.'"

So it seems, Michael thought, allowing the words to resonate with their present circumstance. *I have the Spear . . . Maggie is in Jerusalem with the foundations stones. The hard part has only just begun.*

———

It hadn't taken long before a veritable fleet of gaily-adorned buses filled with women, like an armada of gypsy wagons, stopped beside them on the road. Michael said his goodbyes to Ebtehal and Jehada who both got on to one of the buses and joined the Seline Marchers headed toward the Egyptian-Israeli border.

Michael and Stephen, after some haggling with the driver, boarded a bus bound for Alexandria. After a grueling three-hour ride, they finally made it to the famous city where, Michael knew, he and Stephen would have to part ways. He waited for Stephen's return from the bus terminal men's room where his cohort had gone to discard his feminine disguise. When Stephen was back, Michael gave him last-minute instructions.

"Get to the Alexandria Library. Darris Halakhah is the chief archivist in the manuscript department. He's there constantly. I don't think he ever leaves. Like his beloved manuscripts, he can't be taken into sunlight." Michael grinned. "I trust him totally."

"Why are you sending me to this guy?"

"Darris is a brilliant analyst. I think he can help us crack that numeric code and get an idea what Mabus is up to," Michael explained. "After I get to Tel Aviv, I plan to hook up with Raza Razain. He's an investigative reporter for *Ha'aretz*. Hopefully, he can help me find Maggie in time."

Stephen moved up against Michael's side. "Here's something for you," he said as he slipped a cell phone into Michael's jacket. "My contact number is already coded in."

"When did you manage to—?" Michael began to question him, but Stephen raised his hand.

"Right outside the men's room." Stephen shrugged, shaking his head with a sense of disbelief. "I was approached by a couple of 'salesmen.' It's amazing the kind of business transactions that can go on in a bus terminal."

"Just remember," Michael warned, "if you try to contact me, any calls in this region are monitored."

Stephen nodded and turned to leave.

Michael watched as his friend walked toward the line of waiting cabs. *This is it*, he realized.

Everyone was on their own.

CHAPTER 77

WITH THE EVENING'S DESCENT, Maggie drew the curtains in Feikra's apartment, allowing the soft glow of the lantern to warm the room as she waited.

Waited for *him*.

She remembered the year they had met. It was a year of excitement, of rising heat. Eighteen, passionate, with the world to explore, Maggie's world broke open when Ahmin entered into it. Their relationship was a rite of passage, and in fact, that whole summer abroad with her father in Jerusalem had been like a bardo—a state where she transitioned from girl to woman. During it, her childish parochial view of the Holy Land was banished. Instead, with Ahmin's help, she discovered Jerusalem was a place where you couldn't follow the stations of the cross without noticing you were wading through a cultural hotbed. She recalled how she had come to see first-hand that it was a land where spirituality met hard-ass religious dogma, where love slept side by side with hatred, and where simple human decency had been replaced with unbridled entitlement.

"Come with me." Ahmin grabbed her by the hand, and led her down the dirt road toward his home on the West Bank. He smiled at her, his presence nothing short of protective.

Maggie loved to look at him. Tall, with a deep, chestnut brown complexion and short-cropped, wavy black hair, he appeared a true gentleman. *Nineteen years old and distinguished.* Maggie liked that. On his long sloping nose, he wore a pair of gold wire-framed glasses that made him look all the more eminent.

How could there be a boy more beautiful, more intelligent, more *anything?* Smiling, she felt amazed. *I guess I really am in love.* Maggie had never gone through that experience before. The guys she knew acted so stupidly. They didn't like to think about much, except for the latest video games. And, of course, none of them took honors classes in civil engineering.

"What did your mother want to ask me?" Maggie inquired.

"She said that since we gave an interview to your father about our experiences in the occupied West Bank, then you have to give us a report on your experiences growing up in a Western country."

"She was serious?"

"Oh yes," Ahmin said, "she doesn't want me to marry anyone who is below my class."

Maggie gave him a shy smile. "She said no such thing."

"Okay, she said she wanted you over for lunch and planned to ask you about the student exchange program in your country."

"That's a far cry from marriage," Maggie said. "You've got me wondering if you're even telling me the truth *now*."

"Okay, you want me to be truthful, I'll be truthful." Ahmin took her hand in his. "I love you."

Maggie was too surprised to speak.

"What's wrong?" he asked. "Was that *too* truthful?"

Maggie felt her love for him, but telling him . . . "Well, you know I'm studying to be a journalist," she stuttered.

"I know," Ahmin said, "and you will tell the world the truth. You will tell them what you see here in Israel."

Maggie felt strong enough to do that, but expressing her love was something entirely different. *Do I actually have to tell him in words?* Maggie was sure he could feel it.

Ahmin drew her closer. Was it the excitement of his touch, the warmth of his breath on her face, his hand lovingly stroking her hair that made her love him so? At that moment, she knew it was everything . . . everything she had felt since she had met Ahmin in the garden of his home with her father.

It was then she heard the screaming, the shrill cry of a woman's voice.

"My mother!" Alarmed, Ahmin took off up the road in a full run.

Maggie sprinted after him as quickly as she could. "Ahmin!" she kept yelling, but he wouldn't stop.

As she dashed around the corner after him, Maggie saw a massive bulldozer, like a growling monster, careening into the side of Ahmin's home. His mother was holding Ahmin's youngest brother, ten-year old Muhammad, by the hand. One moment she was screaming for her son to stay beside her, and the next, screaming for the men to stop destroying her home. Maggie could feel the helplessness of it.

"What more do you want?" Ahmin's mother yelled. "We are prisoners in our own land! We carry the identity cards you force on us! We read the censored newspapers! You take our food, our land, our homes! You kill our husbands, our children, our elders! You take and take and take! My God, what is wrong with you? Can you not see you are destroying us?"

"Mother," Ahmin pleaded. "You *must* stop. It is dangerous. Please, we will find a way. For today, just come with me away from here." He coaxed her like a child. "Come, Mother."

Maggie ran toward the house. If she stood there in front of it, perhaps they would stop, listen to reason. They couldn't just destroy someone's home and belongings like that, and leave the poor family on the street. It was atrocious. The whole thing was uncivilized and wasn't even being disguised by the flimsiest veneer of fairness or justice.

Ahmin dragged her away in time. The bulldozer, moving straight forward without stopping, would have killed her.

"I'm getting my family out of here now," Ahmin told her. "You must get back to the main road. Take a taxi back to Jerusalem and find your father."

"But I can help."

"No you can't. Things will only get worse. I'm taking everyone to my family's place in Jericho."

"I don't want to leave you."

His voice softened for a moment. "You must. You must leave. It is too dangerous." He held her gaze. "Now is not our time."

Did he have to say it that way?

Before she could say a word, he turned to leave.

"Ahmin," she called after him. "I love you."

He looked back at her and smiled, a touch of longing in his eyes. Then he was gone.

But Maggie knew it would not end there for her. Although she had to let Ahmin go, circumstances dictated that she hold on to her secret. There was too much pain to be dealt with already—the sorrow of parting and of change. Her father's death, only one week later, forced her to leave Israel. She then faced the lonely journey home not only without her dad, but also wondering if she would ever see Ahmin again.

Once back in New York, Maggie knew what she had to do. She found herself walking alone to her appointment. *Why is the sun shining so much,* she wondered, *when I am feeling so low and drained?* She felt nauseous and stopped by the side of a newspaper stand hoping to ride it out.

Finally, her queasiness subsided. Maggie gained her bearings and made her way toward the clinic on Astor Place. *Village Choices* the sign read. Maggie's breath quickened. *The choice to have a child or not to have one.* Young, pregnant and alone, Maggie had to face her dilemma.

When she entered the office, the large white-haired woman behind the desk smiled but prompted her with a tone that was hurried. "Your name?"

"Maggie Seline."

"Ms. Seline, please take a seat, fill this out and bring it to me when you're done."

Maggie's hand shook as she took the clipboard. She sat in the crowded waiting room filled with women—all ages, all nationalities, *all* with the same problem.

As Maggie stared at the endless questionnaire, her eyes became blurry. She wiped a tear from her face.

Choices. *Not many*, she thought.

For her, there was only one that made sense.

CHAPTER 78

A S MAGGIE WAITED alone in the confines of Feikra's small apartment, the ticking clock on the mantelpiece made her nervous, reminding her that there was little time left. Feikra and Rasha had left nearly an hour ago—Feikra toward the Israeli-Jordanian border and Rasha toward Ya'ara, close to the border of Lebanon. Each woman had left with her Muslim and Jewish sisters from Women in Black and ONE to help the gathering masses of women who were demanding entry into Israel. *Even Laurel must be at the Egyptian border by now*, she thought.

A light tapping on the door stirred Maggie from her reverie. Sensing who it was, she held her breath as she walked over and opened it.

Although he wore a weather-beaten green jacket, jeans and army boots, the man before her still appeared distinguished. *As he always does,* Maggie thought. His warm brown eyes met hers, a glint of joy shining through them.

"Ahmin." The sound of his name always came from a deep place within her, vibrating like a cello. Smiling, Maggie held out her hands to take his, but instead he pulled her to him and held her firmly. She returned his embrace, pressing her body against his.

"Maggie." So tender, filled with pain, his voice revealed the anguish of not knowing what had happened to her, probably imagining she was lost to him, alone somewhere . . . possibly dead. She saw him as he pulled his face back from hers, swallowing back the pain he had been feeling. Maggie felt it, too. Theirs was a love that was large enough for the world, but could not be lived out in a little house together. Their worlds had always been so different, so far apart, yet their hearts had always been one, their ideals the same.

"No more questions now that your book is published?" Ahmin asked, joking half-heartedly.

"You know it was too dangerous to continue," Maggie answered. "The press was reporting about my liaison with an Arab man in Israel. So many were willing to conclude you were a PLA agent—some sort of terrorist."

"People like to jump to conclusions quickly," Ahmin responded.

Maggie noted how much more assured and confident he had become since she had last seen him.

"Americans, in particular, like their conclusions predigested for them, don't they?"

She smiled recognizing the truth in his statement. "Not everyone's on brain pabulum."

Ahmin shrugged. "In any case," he said, the look in his eyes conveying he didn't quite believe her, "Feikra told me what happened and where you've been. She said there's some sort of document you want to show me?"

Maggie opened up her purse and pulled out the small vial Matt had given her and removed the scroll.

Ahmin took it from her and sat at the pine table in the middle of the room. Within the amber glow of the Venetian lamp, he unfolded it carefully while Maggie set the small bag of jewels on the desk beside him.

"There's also a translation," she said, laying it beside the parchment.

"Now let's see here," Ahmin said. His eyes moved between the scroll and Michael's interpretation.

Maggie was familiar with the inquisitive look on his face. Even when she had first met Ahmin, then a young engineering student, he wore an aura of brilliance. At the time, he had been so full of ideas and hopes for his future and for that of his family. Maggie hated knowing he had to settle for far less than he deserved. Now a civil engineer, he worked mainly on construction projects for Israeli settlements.

While Ahmin continued to examine the parchment, Maggie poured them each a cup of strong Arabica coffee and sat next to him. Silently, she studied Ahmin's face as she waited for him to surface.

The Masons are a far older lineage than you think . . . or will ever know. As Samuels' words resonated in her mind, she caught her breath. *Ahmin.*

Ahmin looked up feeling as if he was coming out of a trance. He drew Maggie's attention to the drawing on the parchment. "Look, it contains two pentagrams." He wondered why there were two of them. What was the repetition about?

Maggie leaned over, appearing equally uncertain.

Ahmin turned back toward the cryptic poem again, this time reading it aloud:

> Oh Jerusalem
> City of Peace
> The jewel is laid
> The city is the temple.
>
> Architect, build thy roads
> Thy gates like grand arches
> Rise to the east
> Draw the lines of the heavenly temple
> Let the stones be thy foundation.
>
> Through the wisdom of the heart
> The Pentagon in unity
> The marriage of nations merge
> The Star of David is complete
> Jerusalem is One.

Ahmin took time to contemplate the meaning further. Then, after a few moments, his eyes fell upon the name of the author.

Yeshua ben Yosef

Amazed, he quickly looked up toward Maggie. The glow in her eyes affirmed his realization. "Where did you discover these writings?"

"Michael Sonada, the historian, translated the Aramaic writing we found in Shambhala," Maggie answered.

Ahmin's mind focused on one phrase in particular. "*The city is the temple.*" As he repeated the phrase, he felt a familiar resonance. "Sounds similar to the words of John in Revelation."

"But isn't that just metaphorical language, symbolic?" Maggie asked.

"That's what most have concluded to be the case, but what if we were to also read the phrases more literally?" Ahmin suggested.

Maggie raised her eyebrows.

"Architect, build thy roads," Ahmin murmured almost to himself. Suddenly, the recognition dawned on him. "In ancient times, sacred geometry was practiced, and its rites and science were passed down from master to student. In the time of Solomon, during the building of the Temple, augurs, as well as great architects and masons, divined and built using their sacred sciences."

Ahmin's breath deepened. He felt certain of their direction now. "From what I see *here*, discovering the spiritual layout of the city seems to be our task." *It has to be.*

"Our task?" Maggie was quite sure that geomancy and sacred geometry were out of her league.

"Is there a map of Jerusalem here?" Ahmin asked.

Maggie searched the bookcase until she found a text on the city. Inside the front cover was a fold-out map. She brought it to him.

Ahmin studied it for a moment alongside the translation. He looked up, his eyes intense. "First, we start with the obvious," he said, "by viewing the entire old city of Jerusalem and how the city was built up after the time of Christ. After it was destroyed, the Romans designed the city anew back in 135 AD and gave it a new name . . . Aelia Capitolina. Just like other cultures, the Romans also had their own oracles. These diviners designed the city using sacred knowledge to ensure prosperity and good fortune.

"A red pencil would work now," Ahmin said, opening his bag. "A compass and protractor would come in handy, too."

After rummaging through some papers, he pulled out all three. With the tools of his trade set squarely on the table, Ahmin appeared to be up for the challenge.

"The *Cardo maximus*," he announced, running his finger along the map for Maggie to see. "It's the first north-south axis that the Romans laid out that started and roughly began at the Damascus Gate. The street-crossing axis was called *Decumanus maximus*. The pattern of these thoroughfares seems to coincide with that of the Western Wall and the first wall of the temple."

Using his pencil, Ahmin drew lines down from the Damascus Gate and then a cross line that ran from the Jaffa Gate in the west to Absalom's Tomb in the east.

"Generally speaking," Ahmin explained, as Maggie looked over his shoulder, "the basic line of the Cardo maximus is known as Khan al-Zait Street today, and the Decumanus runs along what we now call David and Chain Streets. We can see that these streets really represent the pole and axis of the basic blueprint."

What Maggie *saw* were the furrows of contemplation on Ahmin's forehead. The lines relaxed as he began to speak again.

"Now," he said, resuming his drawing, "if we remember the idea of the original temple, we can see that if we start here at the Jaffa Gate, and we move at a right angle upward, the natural ending point is the corner of the old city wall."

Without skipping a beat, Ahmin continued marking the map. "Another line drawn straight from that point extends out and runs closely along the Via Dolorosa to St. Stephen's Gate. Then, the pattern moves to the south," he said, drawing a line down the page, "from St. Stephen's, running along the old city wall and the Golden Gate, eventually crossing the Decumanus."

"Oh! Look what we have," Maggie exclaimed as the pattern emerged, "a rectangle."

"Yes, the basic design," Ahmin confirmed. "Simple, right?"

"Maybe for you." Maggie tried to keep up with Ahmin's explanation. Although she understood the basic premise, she was beginning to see that Ahmin's knowledge was coming from a source of secret and ancient masonry, part of *the Way* that was beyond her grasp.

Ahmin seemed to sense her feeling of inadequacy. He reached for her hand, directing her to the stool next to his.

"If memory serves," he said, turning his gaze back to the map, "the ancient augers also designed a north-south orientation that is parallel to the Western Wall—intersecting the Via Dolorosa at its northern end, and at its southern end, intersecting the Decumanus, known as Chain Street, by the Chain Gate near the Western Wall."

As Ahmin studied the rectangular form, his excitement appeared to grow. "If you were to lay out a temple you would want a strong central axis. And look! My God, look it's right there!"

Maggie had no idea what his outburst was about. Nothing on the map stood out for her. "What?"

"It's not something you're going to find written on the map." His dark eyes glimmered. "It's a mystical roadway of sorts. *The messianic line.* Christians, Jews, Muslims—they all say the Messiah will enter the holy city on its path."

Maggie was mystified. She had never heard of the messianic line. "Where is the path located?"

Ahmin placed a big round dot at the Mount of Olives. "It begins here," he said, "then passes through the Golden Gate and moves over the Dome of the Spirits, thought by some to be the site of the Holy of Holies where the original tablets of the Ten Commandments had once been kept."

Maggie watched as Ahmin brought the red line further west ending it at the western side of their rectangle. She studied the line until her eyes landed on a mark that made her catch her breath.

"The Church of the Holy Sepulchre," she said.

"Yes, the messianic line extends over the Rock of Golgotha."

Maggie stared in disbelief. *The site of Christ's crucifixion.*

Ahmin appeared to have felt the power of her realization. "As you can see," he said, "this line of energy moves through very sacred and significant places."

Currents, energy lines, lung-mei, Maggie thought.

"As tradition states, the Messiah is to enter the city using this route," Ahmin explained. "The Jewish narrative also tells us that upon the Temple's destruction, the Spirit of God left through the Golden Gate and will one day reenter on this messianic path."

A light went off in Maggie's head. "It's the path that Christ also took."

Ahmin nodded in affirmation. "He entered the city on the messianic line on what is now known as Palm Sunday—from the Mount of Olives, entering the Golden Gate and ultimately moving to the Temple itself. Then, he was crucified on Golgotha, also a site along this path."

Maggie ran her finger along the esoteric pathway now lined in red on their map. The physical contact seemed to deepen her awareness.

"And what about Muslims? What do they say?"

"Islamic tenet says that on Judgment Day the angel Gabriel will blow the ram's horn. Then, everyone in the world will be standing on the Mount of Olives, and those beings who have earned the right to eternal life will pass along the messianic line through the Golden Gate."

"Strange, how the gate is kept closed," Maggie offered. "Today it's sealed, bricked up, and there's a Muslim cemetery in front of it."

"Apparently, the Golden Gate was one of the original city gates. It's been built, destroyed, rebuilt and destroyed. As far as we know it's been shut since the time Islamic forces took over Jerusalem back in 1187 and totally sealed in the 1500s. All sorts of reasons for that, both religious and political." Ahmin stared at his drawing once again, rubbing his temples as if it helped him to recollect. "But actually, there is a tradition of keeping the gate closed or blocked in some way which goes back to the period of Solomon and the first temple."

"Why's that?"

"Prophecy," Ahmin said. "It's a powerful motivator. Whatever the tradition, the symbolic essence of the messianic line is that it is a spiritual pathway, both for souls to enter paradise and as an avenue by which the divine spirit will triumph in Jerusalem." Ahmin's eyes left the map and looked up toward her. "You see Maggie, everyone is waiting for a holy presence to return to Jerusalem. If we allow our hearts and minds to perceive it, Jerusalem really is a heaven on earth."

CHAPTER 79

"SO NOW WE HAVE IT," Ahmin concluded, "the basic formula for our *temple city.*" He scanned the rectangular grid along the map, the messianic line falling directly through its center.

Maggie squirmed a bit in the seat next to him.

"Something you want to tell me?" Ahmin asked.

"Well, I hate to throw a fly in the ointment," she said, "but what about the Damascus Gate? It seems to throw off the rectangular form somewhat."

"So it does," Ahmin admitted. "Okay, we know that the Cardo is the heart line, and the Damascus Gate is basically the starting point for that central axis . . . "

As he stared at the map intently, Ahmin suddenly remembered.

The Pillar of Hadrian.

"If you look next to the gate right here," he said, pointing close to the Damascus Gate marker, "there was once a pillar there honoring the Emperor Hadrian whose town planners were laying out the city. This was actually the point where the Cardo ended—or began, depending on your point of view. You can also see that there are two other streets that also radiate out from where that marker stood. El Wad Road and this other street, Aqabat Esh Sheikh Rihan."

Looking bewildered, Maggie gave him a weak smile.

"Check this out." Using his protractor, Ahmin marked out the diagonals. "If I draw lines from this point . . . and they're both 36 degree angles . . . " His excitement grew as he measured. "They're clearly markings of the sides of what could be . . . "

"A pentagon," Maggie said, finishing his thought. Her eyes darted back toward the scroll. "Ahmin."

"I know." Ahmin was amazed as well. *Christ placed a pentacle on the allegorical map.* Ahmin felt the grip of certainty take hold of his heart. *He was depicting the sacred energies.*

Ahmin thought it simpler to start by laying out the geometrical figure of a pentagon. Using the 36 degree calculation, he marked out the lines with his protractor. As he drew, he clearly saw that each angle of the figure fell upon one of the main arteries of the old city: The Cardo, the Decumanus, David-Chain Street, and Via Dolorosa. Within the pentagon itself, a five-pointed star, a pentacle, emerged.

A rush of clarity, like an electrical charge, ran through his body. "The pentagon is a symbol of humanity," Ahmin whispered, recognizing its deeper meaning.

The glow from Maggie's eyes told him she felt the same excitement. *Pure adrenaline.* Now Ahmin knew they wouldn't stop, not until the mystery was resolved.

"There's something in the symbolism here." Maggie's gaze then shifted from the map to Christ's saying. "The pentagon is five-pointed, but the saying also refers to the Star of David."

"And that has six points," Ahmin said, still meditating on the pentagon he had just drawn.

The Star of David is complete.

Boggled, his mind kept turning in a loop as he repeated the same information to himself. The question still remained. *How do we complete the Star of David from a pentagon?*

Ahmin felt his mind straining for an answer. Needing a momentary break, he got up, went to the fridge and poured two glasses of water from the cold carafe.

"You look like you need this," he said as he handed Maggie one of the glasses and sat down.

"Calculations . . . numbers. They drive me crazy" She took a sip of water and then with a frustrated sigh, laid the glass on the table.

"I thought you liked investigating?" Ahmin taunted.

Maggie's wide-eyed stare relayed her message clearly: *Are you out of your mind?* "Yes, people, situations, myths, legends, but numbers." She brought the palm of her hand to her forehead.

"Numbers, Maggie, are part of the keys to existence," Ahmin said pointedly. "The universe is comprised of numbers. They don't exist just so we can count things in sequence. They each have their own breadth

. . . their own length. They vibrate and create. Sacred geometry is what many cities were planned on, what most temples, churches, cathedrals, mosques were based on architecturally. *Numbers* are the key."

"Spoken like a true civil engineer."

"I guess you've got my number."

Maggie rolled her eyes but couldn't hold back a smile.

"Okay, back to business," Ahmin said, reverting them both back to Michael's interpretation of the saying. "Look at these words. *The pentagon in unity*. That implies more than one, and if you look at the parchment it contains the drawing of two pentacles."

"What are you saying?" Maggie asked.

Ahmin's mind was calculating as he spoke. "There has to be more than one pentagon to this drawing." That's when the realization dawned. "The pentagon we've been able to place in the rectangular grid only spans over the right side of the diagram. The left side of the rectangle is barren."

"Perhaps . . . it needs a second pentagon." Maggie's voice shook with excitement.

"So then," Ahmin said, placing his protractor on the map again, "if we extend this line out from the Damascus gate point another 36 degrees as we did before, but now in the opposite direction, and end it just past the corner wall of the rectangle . . . then draw another 36 degree angle from that point . . . " Ahmin continued measuring and intersecting points. He stared at the result.

Another perfect pentagon and within it, another five-pointed star.

He deepened the red pencil line that ran along the Cardo. "The central line where the pentagons are joined is the Cardo, the north-south axis of the old city."

Maggie traced the line with her finger. "So, the pentagons have merged."

"*The pentagon in unity*," Ahmin said, referring back to the saying.

"Since the pentagon is a symbol of humanity, then merging two of them would mean bringing together two peoples." Maggie's eyes lit up with the insight. "It's in the saying. *The marriage of nations merge.*"

"And, you see," Ahmin said as he highlighted the sides of the new geometric figure, "the shape of the two merging pentagons creates something totally new. A six-pointed hexagram."

Maggie's eyes were transfixed on the image.

"In Pythagorean symbolism," Ahmin informed, "six is seen as the marriage number."

"Then the marriage of the pentagons . . . "

"Creates the Star of David."

"It's a reconciliation." Maggie's eyes grew soft and her voice lowered.

"And in this particular instance, it is the marriage of two nations, two peoples living harmoniously within the city," Ahmin added, a feeling of longing beginning to swell in his chest. "The sacred geometry of the two pentagons in union inspires the energy for reconciliation and peace."

Maggie took a deep breath "And with the Star of David complete, Jerusalem *is* one."

"As it should be," Ahmin noted emphatically. He felt the spacious freedom of enlightenment within his mind. "Jerusalem will be like the sun, radiating light to all the people in the world. Even within the time of Christ, there were those who understood the meaning of the *Revelation* . . . a lineage who understood Jerusalem's destiny. They have been the keepers of the flame. These guardians have watched history unfold upon Jerusalem—wars, destruction, proclamation, upheaval— and have always continued to keep its true meaning alive within the swirling undercurrents." Ahmin felt his connection to *the Way*, powerful and complete.

So here is the miracle of the Grail, he thought, *prophesied by Isaiah, Jeremiah and John . . . the vision of Jerusalem as what it was always meant to be.*

The City of Peace, the Holy Land.

CHAPTER 80

TIME WAS RUNNING OUT, Michael knew, as he ran through the Cyprus airport terminal to catch his connecting flight to Israel. He thanked his lucky stars that his six-month visa for Israel was still valid. *Thank goodness for international book tours.*

Michael took a deep breath as he hustled over to the Israeli security desk. "*Ma shlomkha,*" he greeted the stern-faced official.

The dark silent officer appeared in no mood to reply.

"I am a scholar and translator," Michael stated in the most official and businesslike tone he could muster. "Here is my security pass for the restricted areas of the *Shrine of the Book.*"

The Israeli security official's suspicious countenance turned quickly to one of respect at the mention of the famous museum and heritage center built to house the Dead Sea Scrolls.

"You are working on the Scrolls at present?"

"Yes, I am," Michael answered. "I am on one of the translation teams."

At that point, Michael showed the agent his passport, security pass and airline ticket. "I am also transporting an ancient artifact for study at the museum. Would you make sure it is secured well on the plane and returned to me promptly upon arrival in Israel?" Michael did his best to sound the dignitary as he handed over the narrow metal box containing the Spear. He was certain it would be carefully examined as well as x-rayed for explosive components.

The guard took it from Michael and tagged the cargo. Looking fairly appeased, he asked one more question. "Do you have the usual list of persons we can call at the museum to verify your status?"

Michael stopped breathing for a moment. He had almost forgotten. *Where is that damn piece of paper?* He rummaged through the side pocket of his carry-on, hoping against hope he hadn't lost it. His breath deepened with relief when he pulled out the list of authorities and scholars he knew would confirm his credentials.

"This is what you need, I believe." He handed over the list and tried to appear stoic and scholarly as the agent gave him a steady, measured look.

Dear God, make this work.

Michael was beginning to find that prayer was coming a bit easier.

A short time later, when Michael finally arrived at Ben Gurion Airport, he collected his special cargo from the security desk in Customs and hurried to the arrival area where Raza Razain was waiting for him.

"Michael, what now?" Small-boned and wiry, with short-cropped black hair, Raza shook Michael's hand with his familiar, nervous enthusiasm. "I get an early morning arrival time, not even a hello on my voice mail . . . "

Michael knew Raza's jittery appearance was deceptive. His was a keen, insightful intelligence working at broadband speed.

"We can't talk here," Michael said, scanning the airport terminal. "Let's get going."

Without another word, the two men walked quickly until they reached Raza's Volvo sedan.

"Is this really so serious?" Raza asked as they drove off.

Michael hesitated. He always had mixed feelings where Raza was concerned. He had worked with the journalist before, but still in all, he knew Raza was mainly out for the story. Although he needed to proceed cautiously, Michael felt he had no choice but to trust him now, since without Raza's help, this whole crazy venture was over. He would never be able to find Maggie and thwart Mabus before the Peace Conference convened tomorrow.

As Raza whisked along Highway One, Michael told him about Professor Samuels' poisoning. He also divulged his strange dealings with Heloff and Kumari and how that eventually brought him to Libya to find the Spear. Even though time was of the essence, Michael still didn't want to mention Maggie or Stephen Einsof and the number code he discovered, at least not yet.

All the while, Raza stared at the road, silent, his eyes widening with every additional twist in the story. Michael sensed the reporter was finding it far too incredible to believe.

He couldn't blame him.

It was.

"Bibliotheca Alexandrina," Stephen told the Egyptian taxi driver before climbing into the bright yellow Mercedes.

"Oh yes, very famous. Best in world," the cabby said, giving him a toothy grin. The taxi shot forward even before Stephen had the door closed.

As they skirted around the area, Stephen sensed the cabby was taking an indirect route to the library, but he was too tired to care. He allowed the driver to give him a mini tour of the modern cosmopolitan city.

"You know this city, she found by Alexander Great in 332. That's BC," the cabby proclaimed proudly. "Alexandria really big intelligence capital for whole world."

Stephen smiled. The cab driver's lingo made the ancient city sound like it was headquartering the CIA. What Stephen did find interesting, though, was the number of Europeans roaming the streets, certainly a lot more than Egyptians.

After circling the Western Harbor on Ras el-Tin Street, they drove around the Eastern Harbor and headed toward Chatby, where finally, the library came into view.

No amount of hype or brochures could have prepared Stephen for the Bibliotheca itself. Set less than two hundred feet from the Mediterranean shore, the massive circular structure was impressive, sporting a roof consisting of an interlocking network of glass and aluminum triangles that was pitched at a steep angle, which Stephen's cabby was more than happy to inform him was about 500 feet in diameter. Looking at it, Stephen likened it to one of his solar cells raised to the one-hundredth power. This was truly an inspired work.

Upon entering the library and mentioning Darris Halakhah's name, a security guard at the front desk quickly made a phone call and instructed his subordinate officer to escort Stephen inside. Stephen followed the guard, all the while mesmerized by the awe-inspiring architecture. The floors of the library cascaded downward. From the entrance level it was possible to see six stories of reading areas, computer work stations and art galleries.

The first elevator took them to the lowest level of the public access area, a massive reading room. There, they passed through security doors to reach another set of elevators, and the guard took Stephen down yet another four stories.

When the elevator doors opened, a pale stocky man wearing a white lab coat greeted him. "I am Darris Halakhah," he announced, and motioned for Stephen to follow him as he padded down the hallway in his Birkenstock sandals. With small tufts of white hair scattered around his broad, pink scalp, Halakhah reminded Stephen of a jellyfish bobbing in the water.

"This is the most stunning building I've ever seen," Stephen said as he hurried to Halakhah's side.

"We are actually on the site of the original library," Darris said, opening the door to his office. Removing a pile of books from a wicker-chair, he motioned for Stephen to sit. Halakhah pressed an intercom button on his desk. "Mohammed, *shahi*." Then added, "*Qahwa*."

Turning back to Stephen, Halakhah cocked his head and continued in an accent that sounded as much of Cambridge as it did of Cairo. "It was here in this library, so to speak, that Euclid discovered geometry, that Archimedes developed the principles of physics, Aristarchus first suggested that the earth revolved around the sun and Eratosthenes calculated the precise circumference of the earth. It was here, also, seventy rabbis worked together to translate the first five books of the Torah, *the Pentateuch*, from Hebrew into Greek." He paused, a whimsical look in his eyes. "Who knows, perhaps it will also be in this library that someone will discover that aliens *were* actually the true authors of the Bible."

Certainly a strange duck, Stephen thought. Strange or not, if Halakhah could help him decipher the code, Stephen couldn't care less if the guy started quacking.

A small, dark-skinned houseboy wearing a white cotton skullcap skillfully wheeled a cart into the crowded space. He removed the table-cloth, revealing silver coffee and tea carafes, and after giving Darris and Stephen a discreet bow, quietly left.

"Coffee or tea?" Darris asked.

"Coffee, please," Stephen said, craving caffeine.

"You must try these." Darris then indicated the pastries. "*Atayif* and *kunafah*. You'll never touch baklava again. As you can tell, my body is molded by them both." He patted an ample belly that seemed even more expansive when balanced on the oversized, leather swivel chair that reminded Stephen of something from the Starship Enterprise.

The coffee was flavorful, strong yet not bitter, and the sweets were to die for. Stephen, happier and definitely more relaxed was relishing his hedonistic moment. As he started to reach complacency, another sip of coffee sharpened his focus.

"Although I could expound for hours about this library site once being the center of the world's learning," Darris said, placing his pastry aside, "I'm sure you haven't come all this way just to receive a history lesson." Halakhah looked like he was going into high analysis mode as his eyes narrowed, boring into Stephen's.

As Michael had instructed, Stephen gave the librarian a quick review of the last few days, leaving nothing out. He told Halakhah of the events Michael had experienced since Professor Samuels' poisoning in Rhinecliff. Stephen then turned the conversation toward the mysterious numbers. Halakhah watched with curiosity as Stephen wrote them down.

25-22-49-34-0-27-01-50-40-30-26-12-56-15-45

"If Mabus does have something planned, it would certainly seem these numbers are an important clue. I will study them," Halakhah said as he poured himself another cup of tea. "Meanwhile, the computer in front of you has several search engines, including Nexus."

Ten stories underground, in a building shaped like a computer chip, Einsof was in his element. At last, free from goons with guns, his mind could tackle the task at hand. Before Tod's death, he would have worked on the code with abandon, not caring how long it would take, confident he would crack it. But fear had locked his brain for the last few weeks. *Kunafah* and *qahwa*, pastries and coffee, were helping him pick the lock.

The question now was where to begin.

Far below the surface of the sacred site, deep within his mind, Stephen's emotions calmed, allowing his intuitive thoughts to return. With the energies of the Alexandrian coast working on his psyche, he realized that he was actually sitting in a city that had once been a beacon for the civilized world . . . a place where for a thousand years the Pharaoh's lighthouse, one of the seven wonders, had stood rising out of the sea. That light, Stephen knew, had failed long ago. It was time for another to emerge.

Before long, Stephen Einsof experienced his own Archimedean moment. *Eureka.* The light went on.

The moment was synchronistic. Apparently, Darris was having his own breakthrough. "If you break the sequence down by a series of twos, it makes no sense," Darris concluded. His voice fell to a contemplative whisper. "25 and 22 are fine. 49 and 34 make sense . . . "

"But 0, 30 and 45 stand apart. Exactly." Stephen finished the thought. "They represent angles or a time reference."

"And the other numbers are positional," Halakhah determined.

Stephen nodded his head in the affirmative. "Yes, I think so. Latitudes and longitudes—a location."

Halakhah leaned back in his chair. "The question is *where?*"

Stephen quickly typed the numbers into the search engine.

25°22'N-49°34'E

He hit enter. Instantly, the screen displayed a map of Saudi Arabia just east of the city of al-Hufuf. "There it is, but what is it?"

Darris Halakhah looked over Stephen's shoulder at the screen. His already pale face seemed to lose even more color. "That's the middle of al-Ghawar."

"Which is?"

"The world's largest oil field."

Stephen could barely believe what he was hearing.

"Enter the other positions," Halakhah insisted.

Stephen typed in another set of numbers

27°01'N-50°40'E

A map appeared on the screen displaying al-Jubayl.

"Saudi Arabia's newest and most sophisticated oil refinery. Also the site of offshore mooring buoys capable of handling over 12 million gallons of oil a day," Darris informed.

"Last one. Here goes," Stephen said as he typed.

26°12'N-56°15'E

Halakhah stood up, nearly knocking his chair over. "That's the Strait of Hormuz at Khasab, Oman where the Persian Gulf meets the Arabian Sea. It's the narrowest point in the shipping lanes through which a great deal of Saudi and Iranian oil reaches the world. In fact, forty percent of the world's seaborne oil shipments pass through it *every day*."

"What does this mean . . . al-Ghawar at 0, al-Jubayl at 30, and Khasab at 45? Coordinates for an attack?"

"Possibly," Halakhah speculated. "Professor Samuels and I have been concerned about this region for years. If the hydro-desulfurization towers at al-Jubayl refinery were damaged, they would release enough hydrogen sulfide to kill anyone in the area within minutes. Also, sulfur dioxide acid would settle on everything for miles, behaving like a fast-acting rust and corroding the oil industry infrastructure, literally destroying it."

"That makes no sense." Stephen was doubtful. "Why would Mabus want that?"

"Why indeed?" Halakhah questioned, furrowing his eyebrows. "And all this coming up at the same time he's hosting political and business leaders from all over the world in Jerusalem." An alarmed look crossed his face. "I have to notify the Professor."

Now Stephen really was confused. "I thought Michael said he was poisoned, that he might not have survived."

"It appears that the *kaffir* with the poison ring didn't have quite enough potion to accomplish the deed," Halakhah refuted. "Luckily, Samuels is resilient."

Stephen began feeling like a player in a spy novel. No words coming to mind, he watched as Darris slid his chair back to his own computer where the screen was already flashing.

"I have an urgent e-mail," Halakhah announced. A look of surprise crossed his face as he scanned the message. "It's meant for Michael." He printed it out and handed it to Stephen.

The bride will be at the church. Meet her there.

Vocatus Atque

Stephen reread the line, then looked at the strange signature. *Vocatus Atque.* He gave Halakhah a blank stare.

"*Vocatus atque non vocatus deus*—summoned or not, the gods will be there. The message is from Samuels." Halakhah's voice grew more excited. "The man's always had a sixth sense. Do you have any way to get in contact with Michael?"

Stephen remembered the cell phone. He dug it out of his pocket and called Michael's number.

"I'll e-mail the Professor," Darris said as he began typing furiously on his computer. "I must tell him about these co-ordinates."

CHAPTER 81

"MICHAEL, THAT'S A CRAZY STORY. If I didn't know you better, I'd say you were smoking *kif* in Libya." Raza shot a surprised look over at Michael as he weaved his sedan between the other cars on the highway. "What's the sense? Why would Mabus plan something here in Israel of all places?"

Michael hesitated. "I don't know what he's up to, Raza. But I need your help. I need to know where he's staying right now."

"You *need* to know . . . " Raza shot him a curious glance. "Okay . . . He's in the permanent suite of the European Commission at the American Colony Hotel."

"By St. George's Cathedral?"

"That's the one."

"Take me there," Michael demanded.

Raza swerved off the road and stopped the car. "You really are nuts. He has a security team that hovers over him day and night. You might have a better opportunity later. He's hosting a dinner tonight at the Hyatt for the secretary of state."

At that moment, Michael's cell phone rang. Knowing it would be Stephen, he dared not answer. Instead, he ignored the ringing until it subsided.

"Think of the story you'll get once this is over," Michael said, reverting back to enticing Raza. "And it will be an exclusive." Michael's mind was racing now. "Just get me close to the hotel. I'll think of something."

"You don't have much time," Raza said, eying him now as if he had picked up the wrong baggage at the airport. "The Peace Conference begins tomorrow."

The cell phone rang again. *Damn it, Stephen.*

"Aren't you going to answer?" Raza threw him a questioning glance.

"I don't have time for small talk," Michael snapped back, getting more nervous by the second. After all, he was still taking a chance trusting Raza to begin with.

Neither of them spoke as Raza geared up the car once again and sped down the highway toward Jerusalem. All the while, Michael's mind strained to come up with a plan to smoke out Mabus' scheme.

By now, Michael was deep within his own Jerusalem Syndrome. *I am carrying an iron spearhead in my bag that was used to pierce the side of Christ two thousand years ago, an object once held by Constantine, Charlemagne, and Adolf Hitler.* It was too incredible to believe.

"We're almost there." Raza's voice brought Michael back to the dilemma at hand.

Still short of any real plan, Michael asked, "Could you use your press pass and just go into the hotel and scout around, see if Mabus is there?"

Raza gave a long sigh. He parked near the YWCA on Ibn Jubair Street. "Whatever you do, do not leave this vehicle," Raza instructed. "If you're asked, you are an assistant reporter working on a story with me. My press plates should make you appear legitimate for awhile."

Michael nodded, but he already knew he had no intention of waiting in a hot, sun-baked car. After Raza left, Michael was about to step out the passenger door when his cell phone rang once again.

This time he grabbed the phone out of his pocket and answered. "Hello."

After a brief moment of hesitation, Stephen's voice came over the line. "Michael, is that you?"

Michael's heart nearly skipped a beat. "Yes, it's me. You got to the library," he concluded, relieved.

"I did, and I located Darris." Stephen's tone became urgent. "But there's something I need to tell you. Darris received a message for you from *Vocatus Atque.*"

Michael caught his breath and felt a sudden adrenaline rush. *Samuels?*

"You still there?" Stephen queried. "Okay, here it is. 'The bride will be at the church. Meet her there.' Got that?"

"Copy that." Michael did hear it, but barely. He was still trying to digest the fact that Professor Samuels was alive.

"The other business is being clarified," Stephen said cryptically. "We are working with *Vocatus* on a solution."

"What did you find out?" Michael asked as he glanced out the car window looking for Raza.

"It could be big, but we're uncertain. We'll call you again once we've conferred with *Vocatus.*"

Wonderful. Still in the dark.

"Just remember," Stephen emphasized, "the bride will be at the church. Meet her there. We'll be in touch."

Michael was unable to get in another word as Stephen got off the line.

Wondering what to do next, a gnawing fear gripped him as he surveyed the street. With no sign of Raza anywhere, Michael's intuition kicked in. He slipped the cell phone into his pocket and dashed out of the car, nearly mowing down several old Arab women as he sprinted down the street.

CHAPTER 82

"HE IS *WHERE?* Here in Jerusalem?" Mabus' face filled with scorn and his voice had a dangerous edge that Raza had never heard before. Until that moment, he had only experienced the deceptively smooth, cosmopolitan elegance that was Mabus' trademark.

Being a man accomplished at playing both ends against the middle, Raza did not dare reveal that Michael suspected Mabus was out to sabotage the Peace Conference. If untrue, it would make him look like a fool. Besides, he wasn't about to jeopardize his relationship with a wealthy patron. If by some bizarre twist Michael's crazy tale *was* true, then Raza's life would undoubtedly be in danger just being privy to the information. Raza was certain Mabus was not a man to cross.

"How did that bastard get to Jerusalem?" Mabus asked.

Dressed in a black Armani suit, Mabus' nervous rage made him appear more a mobster than a dilettante. From his behavior, Raza felt that Mabus knew more about Michael's sudden appearance than he wished to reveal.

Mabus shot him another anxious glance. "Well, what does he want?"

Time Magazine's Man of the Year rattled. Raza found the whole exchange curious. "He wants to speak with you."

Mabus drew a breath. He took a moment to straighten his tie in the mirror. With his composure reinstated, he smirked. "Both you and I know we cannot allow him to interfere with the Peace Conference proceedings."

Raza felt the sweat on his neck building. Mabus' demeanor suddenly cooling only heightened Raza's nervousness. *What kind of sticky mess have I gotten myself into now?* he wondered.

"Perhaps, I should speak to the man," Mabus said, changing his bearing. "I'm sure I can convince Michael to temper his opinions." He turned toward Raza. "Bring him up to my suite. I'll take care of him from here."

Raza realized that if any man could play the role of Dr. Jekyll and Mr. Hyde, it was Giovanni Mabus. Raza wanted to ferret out information from Mabus as he had Michael since it appeared to him that the Libyan was not about to share tea and crumpets with his American friend and leave it at that. Perhaps, Raza thought, he could keep Michael out of trouble by just lying to him—tell him Mabus wasn't even in the hotel.

Raza had that thought in mind as he approached his sedan, but when he reached it, he saw the car was empty. Michael was nowhere in sight.

That damn fool.

Raza realized Michael was flying by the seat of his pants and taking matters into his own hands. He was probably approaching Mabus that very moment. Raza looked toward the hotel, took a step forward, but then stopped himself. He had been willing to help Michael, but not at the expense of his own life.

Michael has made his bed, he thought, *and if he wants to lie in it with Giovanni Mabus, so be it.*

Raza got into his car and started up the engine, abiding by the one golden rule that had saved his life countless times.

It was every man for himself.

Michael moved quickly, darting behind food stands as he hurried down the street. He wasn't sure what to do. A few moments later, he was on Hatem el-Tawi headed for the Muslim Quarter.

He found himself in a dark, winding labyrinth and realized he had entered a maze of *souks.* The world's original malls, these in particular were enclosed, dimly lit sensory surround-oramas. All throughout *Souks el-Qattanin, el-Lakhamin* and *el-Khawajat,* the smell of pungent spice, rich Turkish tobacco, tannin and leather, sweat, fresh slaughtered meat, olive oil, garlic, citrus and fresh baked bread fused in a waft of century-old stale air.

Michael felt as if he was walking in a place between two worlds. This *bardo* allowed him a moment to absorb the wonderful fact that Samuels was alive. Overwhelmingly relieved, the doubts he had been harboring since his arrival in Israel suddenly became bearable.

The Spear is now back in Palestine for the first time in two thousand years . . .

I will find a way to confront Mabus and discover his plan . . .

I will meet up with Maggie again . . .

Then he felt a crack in his confident armor. He had barely twenty-four hours to do it.

That incentive, along with the souk's pungent smells, revitalized his brain, and he began formulating a plan. *Mabus is hosting a dinner this evening.* That meant he would be leaving from the American Colony. He would have to confront Mabus there, Michael realized, or more than likely lose his chance.

Just then, like the breath of the Divine Spirit, a promising thought streaked through his mind.

A-la-ha Ru-hau, Michael thought, a nervous excitement quickening his stride.

There was a phone call he had to make.

Arriving late the previous night in the town of Netiv Ha'Asara, close to the Egyptian-Israeli border, Ebtehal and Jehada had been unable to proceed further in the dark. The ground was covered with camps. With a little finagling, Ebtehal had managed to find a space for them in a large tent occupied by women from Spain and Morocco.

Now, jarred from a deep sleep, Jehada awoke to the sounds of rumbling trucks and piercing cries. He rushed outside to find a convoy delivering cargos of food, as well as a group of hawkers who normally plied their trade in Cairo or Al-Arish, shamelessly yelling out to the crowd and strutting their fare of shirts, banners and hats. *Today Jerusalem Tomorrow the World, The Seline March* and *Three Religions - One Faith* seemed to be top among their prized merchandise.

Big ideas bring big commerce.

He walked past them and through the maze of bivouacs, now seeing for himself the magnitude of the march. Even the police, sent from

Cairo to maintain order, seemed to be swept up by the enthusiasm as they drank coffee, looking far more stunned than formidable.

Stopping for breakfast at a pita stand, Jehada spoke to several European women. Wary at first, they finally warmed up to him as he was certain they would—the disarming charm he relied on during his boyhood years as "tour guy to the stars" working for him even now.

With several women speaking in spurts, Jehada learned that the initial efforts to restrict the marchers from moving forward were unsuccessful, and the border at Kerem Shalom was being encroached upon by the hour. Barricades set a quarter mile from the actual border were being lifted and moved, he was informed, the women smiling surreptitiously, and through unspoken consent, the soldiers were allowing the camps to creep steadily eastward. Jehada had no doubt the tough enforcers from the SSI were simply having a hard time keeping the lid on a community composed of women who might have been their own wives, mothers or sisters. In fact, Jehada observed, it appeared that most of the men were enjoying the pressure building on Israel.

Having gleaned a good bit of information, Jehada hurried back to Ebtehal, coffee and pita in hand. Entering the tent, he found her reading her prayers.

"Mother," he said, rushing to her side. "The women tell me that Tyre in Lebanon has almost as many marchers, and the Jordanian border is being bombarded. This whole thing has become far more than anyone could have imagined." Jehada paused, taking a deep breath. "They say Laurel, the American who started this march, is already here. She will be speaking to everyone tonight."

Ebtehal's weary face lightened and the wrinkles around her eyes deepened as she smiled. Jehada had not seen her look that happy in days.

"Come," he said. "I have arranged for us to move to another tent closer to the barricade so we'll be ready when the time comes."

Ebtehal exhaled slowly. "It is finally here. We women—the mothers, the wives, the daughters, the sisters—who have cried, who have pleaded for peace will be heard." She paused, locking her gaze onto his. "Today, my son, through Laurel Seline, our voices will be as one. All of the earth will finally hear *the Great Mother of the World.*"

CHAPTER 83

T HOSE OF THE WAY *are guardians of the secret teachings.* Maggie woke up with Professor Samuels' words in her mind.

She dressed quickly. Ahmin was already in the kitchen. Coffee in hand, he turned to greet her. "Good morning."

"Good morning," Maggie responded.

It had been some time since they had spent the night in the same place together. As she looked at him, Ahmin's face revealed he was enjoying it as much as she was.

After a quick breakfast, Ahmin indicated they should proceed. "The map and the stones, are they secured?" he asked.

Along with Ahmin's temple map, Maggie had placed the twelve gemstones, the parchment and Michael's translation of the saying in a small backpack. "They're secured," she replied.

"You're certain you want to do this?" The look of concern in Ahmin's eyes only added to her anxiety.

"Yes, I am." Maggie knew it had to be done. "I've been given the task, and the precious stones must be laid."

"I'm not sure I understand that part," Ahmin said, questioning her reasoning. "Why would you actually need to lay the stones?"

Maggie looked at him incredulously. "You, of all people, should know. It's not only symbolic. The act of placing the stones at the sacred power sites creates its own energy and sets the foundation. Bringing the vision of the new Jerusalem to earth is the power of the Grail. These Kalachakra stones, marked by Christ, bring the power of his vision to Jerusalem." She paused. "He set up this last act of faith . . . for the one who finds the jewels."

"You mean for you."

Ahmin's recognition confirmed the immensity of the task.

"Sometimes we do things in faith," she said quietly, "trying to realize a vision."

"And believing in miracles?" Ahmin questioned.

Maggie caught the tone in his voice. Ahmin's rational nature had always permeated his spiritual hopes. "Why not? When all avenues have been exhausted, maybe a miracle is what we need. If people can open their minds to the idea that the Holy City of Jerusalem is the ultimate temple for all nations and all peoples then we can create that miracle together."

Ahmin grabbed hold of her then and pulled her toward him. He took her face in his hands. "I love you."

Her mouth softened and she smiled at him knowingly. The sweetness of his eyes was like warm honey, and she felt herself drawn in. "I love you, too." As soon as she said the words, her lips reached his. Maggie had never known any other touch that had made her feel so loved.

His fingers moved through her hair and she pulled him closer. With every moment they embraced, their passion deepened. Maggie knew where they were headed and slowly pulled away.

In the ensuing silence, they both gave each other a wide-eyed look, then broke down in laughter.

"Okay, come on, Ms. Protectress," Ahmin said, grabbing her by the hand. "It's time to consecrate the city."

Hand in hand, Maggie and Ahmin walked out onto the street and through El-Ghazali Square. They made their way past St. Ann's Church and the site believed to be the Pool of Bethesda where Jesus healed a paralyzed man. Maggie had been there several times before, but like so many places in Jerusalem, the richness of its history was unfathomable.

At that moment, she thought of Michael, and history then took a back seat to worry. An anxiety had been growing in the pit of her stomach for the last two days. There was no way of knowing if he had been successful. *What if he couldn't find the Spear?*

Ahmin squeezed her hand, bringing her back to the present.

When she looked up, she saw they had reached St. Stephen's Gate, the only gate on the eastern side of Jerusalem still open. Having remembered Jampal's remark about entering a holy site through the eastern door, Maggie felt it was an appropriate place to set the first stone.

"Let's act like we're in love," Ahmin whispered into her ear.

Act. Maggie smiled. She took Ahmin's arm and they strolled nonchalantly, admiring the archway, moving underneath it until they reached the outer side. There she saw what looked like the emblem of a lion decorating both sides of the entrance.

"That's why it's also called the Lion's Gate," Ahmin said. "Actually it has another name. Arab's call it *Bab Sitti Maryam*, the Gate of the Virgin Mary."

It was still early morning, and only a few tourists were moving about. They sat at the side of the gate, where they had decided she would lay the first stone. Using her fingers, Maggie felt a crack in the structure close to the ground.

After scanning the area, Ahmin nodded his ascent. Maggie opened her pack and peered into the pouch, moving the gemstones around with her fingers until she found the right one. She pulled out a clear red jasper etched with the Sanskrit letter *OM*—the first syllable of the Kalachakra mantra. She turned slightly, placed the stone into the crack and covered it with dirt.

Om, the primordial sound. The cornerstone of the mantra would be the foundation for the new city.

"*Asalama*," Ahmin whispered in her ear. "To give oneself up to God."

Om, Maggie thought, *Asalama*.

With the first stone laid, the joy of gratification began to rise in her heart. *One down*. Then, just as soon as the feeling arose, it quickly vanished. *Eleven more to go*.

Maggie and Ahmin passed back through the gate and headed toward the Via Dolorosa, celebrated as the path that Christ took as he carried the cross. Their next stop, a Muslim college, Madrasa el-Omariyya, happened to also be the site of the first station of the cross. In antiquity, it had been the location of the Roman military fortress, *the Antonia*, said to be the place where Christ was condemned to death.

When they arrived at the college entrance, Ahmin stopped and placed his hand on Maggie's shoulder. "I must go in alone."

"But—" Maggie started to protest.

"I know the imam. He's probably just finished his recitations." Ahmin then held out his hand, indicating he wanted the next foundation stone.

Maggie retrieved an exquisite sapphire, the Sanskrit letter *HAM* etched on its surface. "But where will you leave it?"

"Just trust me. I'll place it somewhere special."

Maggie did trust him, but still didn't like the idea of Ahmin heading onto the school grounds alone. As she watched him disappear around the corner, she resigned herself to the fact that she couldn't do it all by herself. It went against her grain, but the only thing she could do now was to stand and wait.

Stones as old as time crunched beneath Ahmin's sandals as he passed beneath the arched entranceway that led into the madrasa. He continued forward, drawing in a long breath, trying to steady his mind. The confidence he displayed with Maggie only moments before had been a mirage. Yes, he knew the imam. Worse, the imam, an old friend of his father, knew him and would certainly wonder about his sudden visit. Ahmin was by no means devout, the dogma of his own religion leaving him dry. Like Maggie, he held his own spiritual beliefs, but unlike her, he was uncertain he could change the world with them.

Once he had believed in Palestine, a future home for his people. As a young man he had decided to travel to California to nurture his vision, spending a semester as an exchange student and receiving what his grandfather called "a touch of heathen education." Ahmin enjoyed America's democracy, at least what he knew as democracy. At the time, he reveled in the free air of Palo Alto and the sense of world community he experienced. Those were also the early days of the World Wide Web, a wonderful new tool he learned to use and then decided to apply back in Israel. But soon, he would discover, the only web he would witness daily was one of oppression.

God, I hope Maggie is right. He tried to fight any doubt. Could it be that the power of vision would give rise to a *new* Jerusalem?

Ahmin had entered the grounds with some vague idea of wandering the halls of the school in search of a secret hiding place for the second jewel. Instead, he found himself sitting on one of the stone benches in the courtyard garden. The fresh fragrance of citrus emanated from the lemon and orange trees that surrounded him, and the stone walls felt saturated with the patience of age. *At this spot Christ was condemned to death.* Sitting there, Ahmin realized that despite appearances, so little had changed in two thousand years.

His fingers closed over the stone in his pocket. Almost in a daze, he placed it into a curved nook, where branches met the trunk of the lemon tree beneath which he now sat. He closed his eyes and sat in silence, feeling that the stone's presence had already influenced the ancient energy lines in the courtyard.

"*As-Salam alaikum,* my young friend. It's been too long."

Ahmin opened his eyes slowly as he felt the gentle pressure of long fingers close over his hand. He recognized the voice as well. Who wouldn't? It was the most widely heard in all of Jerusalem. Muezzin Jibril had been calling the faithful to prayer from atop the minaret at el-Omariyya since before Ahmin's birth. He and the imam had been his father's close associates. Ahmin felt suddenly possessed by an odd sensation of guilt. *I visit the madrasa, but not because of my faith.*

He turned to look at the ancient weathered face. Framed by a long white beard and the white cotton skull-cap of the faithful, with eyebrows as black as coal, Muezzin Jibril's face appeared even darker than usual. Ahmin was thankful he had already placed the stone.

Ahmin looked toward the muezzin, wishing the older man had not approached him. "It has been some time since I saw you last, Muezzin Jibril," he said. "I hope all has been well with you."

It appeared the muezzin recognized the small talk of one trying to slip away. With the understanding of age and insight, Jibril apparently sensed a special moment had arisen . . . an opportunity to impress Ahmin with a spiritual message.

"We both have little time, I sense." Jibril took a deep breath and sighed. "My life has been long, perhaps too long. *Ins'Allah,* I shall leave soon. Suffering, horror, fighting—I have seen it all. Yet, the light remains. God's light which shines from within can never be extinguished."

A shaft of morning sunlight broke through a gap between the tall buildings and danced upon the courtyard stones. A few moments later, the voices of boys laughing and running filled the air, and the quiet moment of reverie was severed. Now, separate in time from the events of past and future, the muezzin's message was burned into Ahmin's memory. It would rest in a silent place of honor within his mind . . . a place where the ideals of heaven met the realities of earth.

He looked into Jibril's clear dark eyes. Did they perceive his secret mission? Ahmin tried to shake the feeling. He was just being paranoid, he concluded. Ahmin quietly nodded his head and squeezed the muezzin's hand. It was time to leave.

As he was walking toward the exit, Ahmin heard the blast of car horns and the insistent cajoling of street merchants. The city was now awake. Several Franciscan monks were praying at the school gate when he passed through. Ahmin knew they would also return later, when the school closed for the day, to lead their Christian brethren onto the college grounds to the site of the first station of the cross.

One monk caught Ahmin's eye. He stood apart from the others, his cowl draped closely about his swarthy face. Ahmin glanced down and noticed the monk had on a brand new pair of black, patent leather shoes, unlike the humble leather sandals worn by the others.

This one seems to be missing the vow of poverty. Uncertain if he was being followed, Ahmin decided not to take the chance. He dashed across the path of a bus, circumventing any possible pursuit, and quickly immersed himself into the crowd.

CHAPTER 84

OUT OF BREATH, Ahmin found Maggie waiting at the end of the street. She grabbed hold of his arm and pulled him into a nearby doorway.

"Is everything okay?" she asked, concerned.

"It's probably nothing. I wanted to make sure no one was shadowing me," Ahmin said, his eyes still surveying the street.

Maggie dug the temple map out of her backpack and handed it to Ahmin. After studying it for a moment, he announced, "Next, we head to the Damascus Gate."

Peering over his shoulder at the map, Maggie saw that the gate was the high point of the united pentagons on their blueprint. "The starting point of the Cardo Maximus," she said.

Ahmin nodded. "It's a natural point of power. A perfect site to place one of the stones."

After hailing a cab, Maggie and Ahmin rode the short distance to the intersection of El Wad and Suq Khan Ez-Zeit. Their cab driver, already aiming for his next fare, dropped them off in a nervous flurry alongside a line of vendors.

"So here is where the Cardo began?" Maggie asked, feeling as if she'd been transported in time.

"Yes," Ahmin said coming up beside her, "where also Hadrian's Pillar once stood."

A powerful place, Maggie thought, *for so much to be centered around it.*

As they approached the Damascus Gate, Maggie was filled with wonder. She couldn't take her eyes off the intricate rosette carvings. Certainly, out of all those that were presently open, the principal gate of the old city was most definitely the grandest of them all.

But soon the intermingling aromas of ripened fruits, cigarettes, smoldering coals and baking pita brought her focus back to the street.

Surrounding them on all sides, the vendors were already soliciting. Stalls of trinkets and jewelry, postcards, decals, picture books at exorbitant prices, scarves, wallets, emblems, Jerusalem flags, vegetables, fruits, nuts, legumes, candies, chocolates, and, of course, coffee delighted the locals as well as the tourists. Old Arab men sat by the gate and along the stalls smoking water pipes and playing *shesh besh*, a game something like backgammon. The sound of music, streaming from the cafés and stores, accompanied the silversmiths as they hammered and shaped their metal, and the barbers who, snapping their scissors like shears, were already giving haircuts to any wandering soul in need.

"There's an excavation area over there," Ahmin said, directing her forward out the gate and toward a walkway.

"Where are we going?" Maggie pulled back when she saw the steps leading underground.

"Don't worry." Ahmin smiled as his voice dropped to a whisper. "I've been down there before. I know you'll like it."

"Why are you being so annoying? Can't you tell me what's going on before we get there?"

"No way," Ahmin shook his head. "It's part of the fun."

"So I guess living on the edge is fun."

The smile left Ahmin's face as he shrugged. "That's how we live here . . . always on the edge."

Maggie heard the regret in his voice. She remained silent as she walked down the steps behind him.

Finally, they reached the bottom, where the area was lit up by a series of bare light bulbs hanging from wires. There on the wall, Maggie saw the remains of several old Christian frescoes.

"The Crusaders," Ahmin informed her, still forging ahead.

As she stumbled over some stones, hurrying to keep up, Maggie thought they were probably walking on what used to be a road. Just then, a sign engraved with Roman lettering appeared in the center of their path. *Probably an ancient road marker.* Amazed by the sight of it, she stopped to absorb the moment, only to feel Ahmin's sudden grasp as he took hold of her arm and pulled her forward.

Another set of steps brought them down to the next level. Dim lights from the bulbs overhead fell upon a stone arch that looked like it had been part of an old entranceway.

"What's left of the old Roman gate," Ahmin said. "It's about at this point where the Roman Cardo began."

Now she understood why Ahmin was so excited about bringing her to the underground site. Here was the starting point of the Cardo Maximus, the north-south pole of the old city, also on their Jerusalem map as the common axis of their blueprint.

Ahmin found a small trowel against the wall and began to dig. Meanwhile, Maggie searched her pouch for the next stone, a white chalcedony engraved with the Sanskrit letter *KSHA*. *The central mountain . . . the axis of the universe.*

Exactly.

"Ready?" Ahmin pointed toward the hole he dug next to the arch. "Hurry," he whispered as they heard some far off voices. "Place the jewel."

Maggie set the gem inside the hole, and Ahmin quickly covered it, packing it down hard with the trowel.

With the voices almost upon them, they sprang to their feet. A moment later, a flock of Swedish tourists led by their guide came clamoring down the steps.

Maggie and Ahmin, after giving the group acknowledging nods and smiles, walked past them and sprinted up the steps, not stopping until they were back up on the street and by the gateway. As the old Arab men turned a curious watchful eye, Maggie fell into her role of pious tourist extraordinaire, touching the sacred Damascus gate reverently, all the while hoping the Swedes enjoyed low-carb chocolate.

She had dropped her candy bar by the arch.

They worked as quickly as possible to place the next three stones. Ahmin directed them to the western outskirts of the old city close to the New Gate. They placed their next stone, an emerald inscribed with the letter *MA*, by the inside corner of the city wall, at the monastery of Custodia di Tierra Santa.

They then moved toward the Jaffa Gate and *the Citadel*, the Tower of David, which Maggie knew was considered a site of rich historic significance, part of King Herod's fortress. Under a rim at the tower's base, they left a reddish brown Sardonyx imprinted with the Sanskrit letter *LA*.

After venturing to the southern part of the old city, they arrived at the Zion gate. As Maggie peered at the bullet holes—remnants of the 1948 war that pockmarked its surface—she felt the sadness and futility of peoples desperate for a home to call their own.

VA . . . Maggie let the sound permeate her soul as she took the next stone out of her bag and handed it to Ahmin. There, at *Bab el-Nabi Daud*—the Gate of the Prophet David—Ahmin placed the white and red sardius into one of the holes.

Now, with six foundation stones concealed, Maggie felt their movement through the old city like an electrical current. All the while she felt as if the circuit they were creating was already pulsing with energy. She could barely explain it to herself, but she sensed a certain rhythm . . . a cadence that was beginning to take on a life of its own.

Maggie and Ahmin headed toward David Street once again. There they were confronted with bustling shoppers and tourists, as well as street vendors who were displaying their array of religious paraphernalia and souvenirs. Although she had reservations, Maggie agreed when Ahmin came up with the idea to rent a motorcycle so they could reach their marks more quickly. With the freedom of maneuverability and speed, they weaved eastward through traffic. Maggie noticed that David soon turned into Chain Street as Ahmin directed them toward the Gate of the Chain, the entrance to the Temple Mount of Haram al-Sharif.

"Once we're outside the old Temple complex, we'll head toward the Western Wall. You'll place the seventh foundation stone there," he said.

Filled with anticipation, Maggie remained silent.

Ahmin drove them past a busy bazaar, then a long string of finely ornamented doorways, richly decorated with stone carvings. Finally, they arrived close to the entrance to the Temple Mount. Ahmin parked the motorcycle along the street and Maggie and he walked downhill toward the Western Wall plaza.

As they entered the square, Ahmin's whole countenance sobered. Maggie could feel the intense devotion as thousands of worshippers stood in prayer within the square and at the Wall itself.

"I'm going to the women's section," she told Ahmin.

He stopped her. "First, go borrow a shawl," he said, pointing to a woman in front of a long fold-out table.

After selecting a white shawl and leaving a donation, Maggie headed to the right side of the structure where the women were supposed to worship.

Upon reaching the Wall, she felt an incredible sense of awe. So precise were the Herodian masons that its huge, carefully carved rectangular stones fit perfectly onto one another. The powerful boulders spoke of ancient energy—rites and beliefs, tradition and history. Then, she noticed the bits of paper—prayers of the faithful—filling the cracks between them.

Maggie walked up to the magnificent structure and placed her forehead against it. Humbled, she felt the weighty burden that the ancient stones had absorbed—all the torment of a ruptured city. It was in that moment, perhaps more than any of the others, that Maggie knew what she and Ahmin were doing was substantial and real. She brought her hand up and touched the scarred rough surface until she found a thin fracture in the rock.

Carefully, Maggie retrieved the next foundation stone—an exquisite chrysolite marked with the letter *RA*. Clear and shining, she could see a hint of green shimmering in its depths.

When she was certain no one was watching, Maggie placed the jewel into the crack, then took a small nail file from her purse and wedged it in further.

With the stone now secured, she laid her head once again upon the great Wall, feeling the power of its wounds.

She hoped that soon they would be healed.

CHAPTER 85

I T WAS PAST three o'clock. The day was turning out to be a long one. Maggie took a sip from her water bottle as Ahmin drove around the outer perimeter of the city wall outside Dung Gate on Ma'aleh Hashalom, bringing them as close as they could get to the site of Solomon's Stables.

Ahmin pulled over across from the southwestern corner of Haram al-Sharif, by the Ophel Archaeological Garden, and Maggie hopped off the motorcycle. Self-conscious, she darted across the busy street as the traffic maneuvered around her. On the other side, Maggie came face-to-face with the remains of a huge Omayyad palace. Close to it, a tower still stood, first constructed by the Crusaders and then rebuilt by the great Muslim leader, Saladin. Beyond the tower, Maggie could see a bit of the Double Gate in the distance.

Solomon's Stables, she felt, was an important site since it not only lay on the grid of their map but had several mysterious links, one being with the Knights Templar, the other as a possible location of one of Christ's temptations. But getting inside, Maggie knew, would be impossible. The old southern entrance to the Mount, the Double Gate, had long been sealed. Even though she could go through Al-Aqsa Mosque to at least reach the old vestibule to the gate, time and prudence now dictated otherwise. Maggie quickly decided to place the next gemstone at the outskirts of the gate perimeter.

As she moved across the broken boulders to reach the tower, Maggie thought of the templar knights and the vestige of Solomon's stables, located not far from where she stood. *Christians, Jews, Muslims.* Traces of their ancestry, their beliefs and their spiritual quests were hidden in the ruins around her.

Ahmin had equipped her well. When she reached the tower's edge, Maggie pulled the small hand trowel from her belt and began digging. About a foot below ground level, she saw a crack in the tower's base.

Perfect. Maggie dropped the trowel and sifted through her bag. With only five stones left, it was easy to see the greenish blue beryl. She traced her fingers along the letter *YAM* inscribed on its surface. *The element of wind*, Maggie thought, finding it ironic she was placing the precious stone, like a breath, into the earth.

After packing the hole full of dirt, Maggie grabbed the trowel and started walking back to where Ahmin was waiting. As she scurried over the rubble, she heard a cry coming from the top of one of the buildings.

"*Qeff! Qeff!* You there, stop! What are you doing woman?"

With a quick look around, she assessed that no one else but the one guard had seen her. Instinct told her it was not the time for explanations. As if propelled by a rocket blast, Maggie launched into a full run.

"*Qeff!* Stop!"

Maggie heard the man yelling again, but his voice was becoming more distant. *Don't look back. Don't look back.* She repeated the phrase to herself until she reached the motorcycle.

With the engine already running, Ahmin was ready. As soon as Maggie hopped on, he took off like lightning down the busy street.

The wind in her hair, in the midst of traffic once again, Maggie breathed a sigh of relief.

Ahmin turned his head slightly toward her and grinned. Whatever fear he had felt had apparently turned into exhilaration. "I think Allah must definitely be with you today."

"No question," Maggie affirmed. Still, she turned to see if anyone was following. *No question at all.*

Ahmin turned the motorcycle onto Jericho Road, toward the Garden of Gethsemane. It was there that Christ had agonized over his fate and was ultimately betrayed and arrested. Maggie knew their destination, the Church of All Nations, was supposed to be built over the rock where Christ had prayed that night.

After Ahmin pulled over, they walked to the front of the beautiful Byzantine church. Maggie gazed up toward the domes on its roof.

"Twelve domes signifying the twelve nations who contributed to its building." Ahmin smiled, his rich dark hair now windblown across his forehead. "You see, Maggie, we're back to numbers again."

Twelve, twelve, twelve. Maggie's Catholic school upbringing kicked in. "In *Revelation,* John describes the New Jerusalem coming out of the sky. 'It had a great and high wall with twelve gates and at the gates twelve angels; and the names were written on them, which are the names of the twelve tribes of Israel.' "

"And the wall of the city had twelve foundation stones," Ahmin added.

That's right, twelve stones. Her hand went to the velvet pouch she was carrying.

"The number twelve," Ahmin explained, "reflects a cosmological pattern. We even order our world on it and its derivatives. Twenty-four hours in a day, twelve months in a year, twelve signs of the zodiac, and on and on. Significantly, the twelve tribes of Israel scattered throughout the world are in essence, all the people of this earth. So when the New Jerusalem is revealed these twelve *nations* will be drawn back to her."

"Ah," Maggie said as the connection dawned on her. "The twelve domes on the church, the twelve nations. . ."

"The twelve tribes returning," Ahmin added.

"The Church of All Nations!"

Maggie and Ahmin walked around the wrought-iron gate. Once on the sacred grounds, Maggie could see the beautiful arches looming above the steps of the church as well as the colorful mosaic of Christ that decorated the upper facade.

But it was the garden that was drawing Maggie. She entered, Ahmin by her side, and immediately found they were moving through a grove of olive tress, all gnarled and twisted with age. *Perhaps some of these trees have been here for over two thousand years.* The thought alone filled her with awe.

Strong thick branches arched protectively overhead as Maggie continued walking with Ahmin along the white stone pathway. When they arrived at the corner of the garden, they came upon a thick and rather unusual looking olive tree, its trunk perhaps eight feet in diameter. Oddly, three separate trunks were growing out of its base, all sprouting branches of their own. As if being drawn by a magnet, Maggie felt compelled to sit beneath it. A moment later, Ahmin joined her on the grass.

Is there anything more solid, more real than this tree? Maggie wondered. As she gazed up at its silvery green leaves, it didn't take her long to realize how special the tree was. It had to have been a witness to the extraordinary events that took place in this very garden—the drama of Christ's suffering and betrayal. This holy site, Maggie knew, was an essential part of their blueprint.

Maggie felt it strongly now. *This tree will be the refuge for the next foundation stone.*

Before she could say a word, Ahmin turned toward her, a look of understanding in his eyes. He pointed toward a lip in the gnarled surface at the base of the trunk.

Maggie removed a golden topaz from her pouch, the letter *SVA* imprinted on its surface. She maneuvered her hand under the lip and let the stone drop into the trunk.

Opening the channel.

The moment she did, Maggie felt a sense of peace. Perhaps the roots of the old olive tree would resonate with the sound of the syllable . . . a powerful vibration sinking deep into the earth.

It was nearing five o'clock. Tired and dusty, Maggie and Ahmin motored over to Derech Ha'ofel, the road which led to the Muslim cemetery. Once there, they got off their motorcycle and walked through the cemetery amidst the gravestones until they reached the Golden Gate.

Ahmin placed his hand on one of the huge stones. "As I told you, this gate has basically been shut since the twelfth century. It was finally sealed for good, bricked up, in the 1500s by the Muslim leader, Ottoman Sultan Suleiman, in part due to the prophecy of a Jewish messiah returning through it to liberate Jerusalem."

"Another power play in the Holy Land," Maggie ascertained.

Ahmin laughed. "Human nature. Here we have three religions fighting over the oldest and most famous gate of all, and all because of divine intention. The messianic line has been seen as a spiritual path, an esoteric line, and a way to a heavenly paradise for those deemed worthy to enter. There are Muslims who say when Allah gives his final judgement of mankind, all souls blessed with eternal life will enter paradise through this gate. Jews believe that the messiah will arrive through it, and Christians believe the messiah did enter it and will pass through the gate again at the second coming. So the Golden Gate has always been imbued with power—feared as well as revered. Now the gate is blocked, but at the time when the Grail is revealed, the gate shall again be opened."

"People expect some sort of miracle for that to happen, I suppose," Maggie added. Why everyone needed high drama to believe in the spiritual was beyond her.

"Seeing miracles is not the issue," Ahmin asserted. "Manifesting enlightenment is. Purifying our hearts—now that's the real feat."

Maggie felt inspired by the thought. "Compassion and wisdom infusing the world. That's enough of a *second coming* for me."

Silently, they stood before the sealed, double-arched gate. Solidly packed with what seemed an impenetrable wall of stone and brick, Maggie sensed that the temple keepers had no desire to open it up any time soon.

Realizing that Ahmin was waiting, Maggie reached again into the pouch and retrieved the tenth foundation stone, a chrysoprase, clear and green, the letter *HA* marking its surface. She turned and placed it in Ahmin's hand.

With his hands together in prayer and the gemstone in between his palms, Ahmin knelt at the foot of an old grave, bringing his folded hands down to the soft earth. Remaining on the ground, he bowed several times more in the same way before coming back to his feet. Then, after raising his folded hands toward the sky and bringing them to his heart, he walked to the blocked gate entrance.

Once at the gate wall, Ahmin planted his foot on the ground against the base and told Maggie to start digging. Using the trowel, she shoveled away the dirt until she made a hole about a foot deep. Looking pleased, Ahmin buried the gemstone, packing the earth down solidly over it with his hands.

Feeling a deep sense of respect, Maggie stood for a moment appreciating Ahmin's ritual—a beautiful blend of spirit and tradition.

"That is how it should be," Ahmin said, his eyes transfixed on the Gate. "When you make an offering, you must give your heart as well."

Maggie took his hand, her own heart warming.

Just two more stones, she thought, *and our task will be complete.*

CHAPTER 86

"WE DON'T HAVE MUCH TIME if we want to finish laying all the stones today," Maggie reminded Ahmin as they hurried up the stairs to the Temple Mount.

As they neared the top, the Dome of the Rock, gilded in gold and its façade covered in brilliant Persian blue tiles, stood dazzling in the sun. Maggie was mesmerized by the dance of colors on its surface—blue, green, turquoise, and brown. Around its perimeter, patterns of stars and flowers moved upward toward what looked like white lettering on the dark blue exterior.

"An inscription from the Quran," Ahmin said, pointing toward the area she was looking at on the parapet. "*O People of the Book! Don't be excessive in the name of your faith!*" Ahmin raised his eyebrows as if he agreed.

A ceremony in itself, they climbed the last staircase which led them to the very top of the Mount. Maggie peered across the compound and could see Al-Aqsa Mosque, the third holiest place of prayer for Muslims, as well as an array of smaller domes, fountains, prayer platforms and niches.

Ahmin gave her a nudge and tilted his head toward the northern end. Maggie's eyes landed on a miniscule structure that looked like a small gazebo.

"The Dome of the Spirits," he said.

The Dome of the Spirits . . . the shrine Ahmin told me rested directly on the Messianic line! Some believed it to be the site of the Holy of Holies in the second Temple, where the original tablets of the Ten Commandments resided in the ark.

But Maggie's excitement was soon tempered when, out of the corner of her eye, she sensed someone moving toward them. She turned to see a tall dark-skinned man dressed in traditional Islamic garb. His pockmarked face gave him a rough and worn appearance.

"*Allahu Akhbar,*" the man said, greeting Ahmin.

Nodding, Ahmin responded, "*Allahu Akhbar.*"

After the man walked past, Ahmin gave her a sidelong glance. "We're being followed."

Maggie thought he was talking about the man who had just addressed him, but Ahmin shifted his eyes in the opposite direction. She turned sideways to see who he was signaling her toward.

When she scanned the area by the Dome, she saw him—a man dressed in jeans and a cream-colored polo shirt. There was something about his manner, his small black eyes and hawk-like nose. Suddenly, she felt the bottom fall out of her stomach.

Heloff.

It was Mabus' emissary, the same man who had held Michael captive in Nepal.

"I recognize him," she said, trying to keep her demeanor calm.

Ahmin flashed her a look of alarm. "Remember what I told you."

Maggie reached casually into the pouch in her pack and removed the rose-colored Jacinth marked with the letter *E*. With his eyes intent on hers, Ahmin gave her hand a squeeze in a parting gesture. Maggie pressed the stone into his palm. He nodded, the look in his eyes sending a clear message.

Be careful.

He turned and left.

Now, standing alone in front of the Dome's entrance, Maggie felt her fear growing. She reached up and touched her locket, seeking its comfort, but she couldn't stop her breath from quickening. Determined not to look in Heloff's direction, she removed her shoes and entered the grand domain.

Inside, the beauty of the Dome was so brilliant that Maggie was immediately entranced, momentarily buffered from a reality which lay not far behind. Her eyes widened, drinking in every aspect of the intricate and lavish design and the curious ring of pillars that created what seemed another spatial dimension. Standing there, looking into the sacred space as if glimpsing into another realm, her feet sinking into the plush carpet, she reminded herself of protocol and brought her hands to her heart in prayer, instinctively giving a slight bow before walking forward.

Although still afraid, Maggie couldn't help feeling an element of exhilaration. As the sun shone through the stained glass windows that lined the ceiling, the whole interior was bathed in a beautiful, soft light. When she reached the middle of the shrine, she could see the rock over which the great sanctuary was built, claimed as the spot from which Muhammad ascended to a great paradise during a celestial journey. It was also upon this rock that Jews believed Abraham nearly sacrificed his son Isaac and around which the original Temple had been built.

It was because of these beliefs that this site had been the source of so much violence and contention. *Most of it about the location of the Temple itself.*

Now close to the sacred rock, Maggie saw that its ancient knowledge could be seen as well as felt. As her gaze fell upon the steps that had been chiseled into its worn and creviced surface long ago, she sensed an enormous power coming from it. So many had prayed deeply at this site, honored and revered it. Maggie had no doubt that the rock itself and the grounds where she stood were holy . . . blessed and protected.

From a distance, Heloff had watched as Ahmin left Maggie and walked over to another Arab man standing outside the Dome. The two had been speaking with each other for the last several minutes, and it now appeared as they shook hands that they were ready to part. Heloff then kept his eyes on Seline's boyfriend who turned and walked down the steps, heading off the Temple Mount.

Heloff's radar told him the little episode looked suspicious. *Why had Seline separated from her boyfriend and gone off on her own?* His thoughts racing, Heloff hurried across the esplanade toward the Dome, determined to find out.

Maggie peered across the inner sanctum of the sanctuary. What had become of Ahmin?

A growing anxiety pitted itself in her stomach. Without another thought, she walked back through the concentric ambulatories, passing between the marble columns and headed toward the doors. That's when she saw him again. Heloff was moving stealthily along the outer edges of the shrine. His dark eyes, surveying the room, suddenly locked onto hers.

With her heart racing, Maggie made a hasty move behind one of the pillars. Heloff advanced toward her from the opposite direction going against the circumambulating crowd. Relieved to see that he was having difficulty progressing, Maggie squeezed through the mass of people and finally made it to the exit. As she fumbled with her shoes, a large tour group was making its way toward the Dome. They paraded en masse through the main portal just as Heloff got to the door. Maggie breathed a sigh of relief when she saw that, unable to pass them, he was pushed back into the shrine.

No time to lose, she thought, her heart still pounding.

She kicked a group of shoes out of the way and bolted down the temple steps.

Fawzi Khalidi had watched as his cousin, Ahmin, left the temple mount. He waited as he had been instructed. Once Ahmin's woman companion had gone into the Dome and the sinister-looking man had followed her, Fawzi walked over to the small dome that Ahmin had pointed out to him. *The Dome of the Spirits.* He had heard that some claimed the actual Rock of Foundation lay beneath it.

Now, finally, as a group of tourists moved away from the site, he saw his chance.

The stone Ahmin had given him was still in his hand—a small red jewel bearing a strange inscription.

Fawzi leaned down and placed the gem within a fracture at the dome's base.

Silence.

He looked around him. The world had not changed.

Fawzi wondered what this intrigue was really all about. Ahmin had told him part of the secret that day. *Exactly where I stand, they wish to build a third temple.* Perhaps this strange activity he was engaged in today would help stop them. Maybe this stone he had placed held some magic that Ahmin would not reveal.

"My cousin likes mysteries," he said aloud, smiling to himself.

Sighing, Fawzi looked across the esplanade, hoping he had done more than drop a stone into a hole.

An hour later, out of breath, Maggie opened the door to Feikra's apartment. Ahmin was already inside, waiting.

"Sorry it took me so long," she said, still panting. She eased herself onto the couch. "I wanted to make sure I lost that guy. I must have zig-zagged through half the streets of Jerusalem."

"It's too late, you know, to go to the Sepulchre tonight," Ahmin informed her.

Maggie was aware that the church closed at sundown. Disappointed they hadn't made it, she kicked off her shoes, resigned. "That means we can't get in until morning."

Ahmin's face remained apprehensive.

"What?" she asked.

"I found out today that the church isn't open tomorrow."

Maggie shook her head in disbelief.

"Security reasons," Ahmin explained. "Because of the convergence of women on the borders and the Peace Conference convening, the church custodians fear there might be violence."

Maggie's heart sank. She had to place the last foundation stone in the Sepulchre. "I have to get into that church before the Conference begins. There's got to be some way—"

"There is," Ahmin said as he sat down beside her. "The gatekeeper, Walid, is a friend. He and his ancestors have been in charge of holding the key since the seventh century."

"He's willing to help us?"

"Yes. His family are protectors of *the Way*," Ahmin said with an air of discretion. "It is no accident that they have held the key for so long. We meet him tomorrow morning at 5:30 in front of the Sepulchre."

Maggie closed her eyes, trying to keep her strength intact. *Right down to the wire.* She placed her hand on the velvet pouch at her side.

One last stone remained.

Chapter 87

WHEN MICHAEL PASSED through the arched doorway into the lobby of the American Colony Hotel he found himself within a garden suitable for Eden. But the fountain, the tropical palms stretching toward the vaulted ceiling, and the guests sitting on thick padded chairs and ottomans sipping afternoon cocktails did not provide him with any ease.

His heart was racing as he approached the *concierge*. "Giovanni Mabus."

The man behind the walnut desk snapped to attention. "May I ask your name and your business, sir, and I will call his suite."

Michael needed to conjure something up fast, but before he got the chance . . .

"You asked to see me?" Mabus, dressed in his formal pleated white shirt and striped pants, surprised Michael from behind. He was flanked by two, large forbidding bodyguards, whose deadly gaze caused Michael to flinch. "My man, Siddig, informed me you departed rather abruptly from my estate. But I'm happy to see you're looking a lot better than at our last meeting." Mabus offered an insidious smile.

Michael wanted to grab hold of him, but the two thugs were closely watching his every move.

"I have a dinner engagement, and, as you can see, I'm about to leave the hotel," Mabus said curtly. "What is your business?"

"My business," Michael stressed, "is to find out *your* business."

One of the bodyguards proceeded to move toward him. Mabus, his eyes darting across the hotel lounge, subtly gestured toward the man to hold back.

"Besides your friends here," Michael said, cocking his head toward the bodyguards, "there's only the two of us. I doubt the concierge is as interested in your business as I am."

Mabus' voice fell to a whisper. "Why are you here, Michael?"

"Didn't Raza Razain tell you?" Michael asked. "He spoke to you earlier today."

"I know you brought the Spear into the country." Mabus eyes were cutting into his.

"Well done," Michael said, returning the glare. "You checked."

"You're taking quite a chance showing up here. Tell me why you believe I wouldn't just have the Spear taken from you now?"

"Because you don't know where it is, for one. And there's no way you're going to grab me right here in the hotel."

Mabus seldom looked trumped. Michael sensed that it was a feeling that would only fuel Mabus' desire for revenge.

"It's too bad Siddig didn't carry out his task." Mabus' voice sounded more controlled. "You want me to guess what happened to the Spear? Let's see, you bartered it for some apricots in the *souk*."

Michael swallowed hard. Mabus would never imagine he was stupid enough to actually carry the Spear on him. *Thank God,* Michael thought, because he had done just that.

"Not quite." Michael's anger was focused. "But I'll barter with you now. Tell me your plan, I'll tell you where the Spear is, and let the righteous man prevail."

Mabus laughed. "You have an interesting mind, Michael Sonada. I do think you've seen too many Indiana Jones movies. What makes you think I have any plan?"

"Your code has been cracked." Michael hoped his bluff wouldn't be called.

"The numbers?" Mabus said dismissively. "If you survive your stay in Israel, you may want to pursue a career as a cryptographer. The numbers are meaningless. You're on another red herring chase."

"Really," Michael pushed. "Why then would you kidnap Stephen Einsof?"

"Kidnap him?" Mabus sneered. "He works for me. I paid a fortune to develop his energy plan. How could I kidnap him?"

"Not how, why. He didn't tie himself up in Tarhuna."

Mabus ignored the remark. "Nothing you find out about those numbers will be of any help to you."

"That remains to be seen," Michael said. He took several steps backward when he saw the bodyguards making a quick scan of the area.

One of the men, pulling aside his vest, was about to reach for the pistol sitting in his holster.

At that moment, Mabus looked across the lobby. His face tightened.

"Michael, there you are. I hope I'm not late."

Michael recognized the voice. He turned toward the tall, elegant-looking woman with fine features approaching them and let out a sigh of relief.

Muriel Lumina.

Michael knew Mabus' reaction was certainly not due simply to Muriel's beauty, although her dark eyes and long black hair would have turned heads in any city.

Renowned in Israel, Muriel, along with her husband, Isaac, a retired colonel, was co-founder of *ONE*, an activist organization that proposed one Israel—non-sectarian—a home for Jews, Muslims and Christians. Michael had met Muriel at a fundraiser for the Dead Sea Scrolls project years earlier. He formed a bond with Isaac as well, over their common interest in antiquities.

Michael had left a message for Muriel on her cell earlier to meet him at the Colony. Fortunately for him, she received it.

"Giovanni Mabus, this is Muriel Lumina," he said, introducing them.

Mabus' dramatic change in posture from underlying violent to pleasantly polite made Michael's head spin.

Veiling his hostility, Mabus greeted Muriel smiling. "Delighted, madam. I recognized you immediately. The work you are doing is excellent. I hope our modest Peace Conference may be as beneficial." Mabus gave a her a deferential bow. He then turned toward Michael. "Now, if you will excuse me," he said, holding Michael's gaze for a moment before leaving.

If looks could kill.

Unnerved, Michael realized he had been holding his breath. Muriel's timely arrival had gotten him out of a dangerous predicament.

"I came as quickly as I could after your call. Did I run him off?" Muriel asked after Mabus and his bodyguards were out of the hotel.

"That was the plan." Michael breathed easier. "Now get me out of here before he changes his mind and sends those goons back."

CHAPTER 88

I N THE OLD CITY of Jerusalem, Isaac Lumina sat in his dark living room. Michael Sonada's urgent phone call had sent his wife, Muriel, hurrying to their friend's side. It had been a while since they had seen or heard from Michael, but the momentous swing in events—the women's march, the Peace Conference being held tomorrow morning, and the cryptic messages circulating through the brotherhood of *the Way*—seemed to have hastened the inevitable.

Isaac groped to turn on the light, realizing that it was now evening. He pressed the light switch and heard the click. Passing his hand over the shade, he felt the heat from the bulb.

At that moment, a shot rang out in the distance. Instinctively, Isaac reached under the couch for his pistol. He walked over to the window and stood against the frame.

Stupid, he thought. *Even now, blind, you're ready to shoot. Have you learned nothing?* If he had, he would have listened long ago. But the painful realization of his stupidity had come too late. If he had only listened to his friend, Obil, who tried to warn him of the danger of too much nationalism and pride.

Could I have averted this dark destiny?

Isaac lowered his gun and felt for the couch once again. He sank into the soft cushions, remembering the last conversation he had shared with his friend, the friend Isaac's comrades proclaimed to be "an enemy of Israel."

"*Shalom*, Isaac."

"*Alaikum as-Salam*, Obil."

The two childhood friends greeted each other and walked silently through the olive grove. As they passed beneath them, the trees' gnarled branches arched over their heads like protective arms. The olive trees, Isaac marveled, had their own spiritual lineage. A branch from one of them had been brought to Noah by a dove—a sign that the floodwaters were beginning to recede, and Moses had used the great olive tree's oil to anoint the Ark of the Covenant.

As they walked, Isaac couldn't help but wonder why his friend had been so secretive about their meeting. It was certainly known in their community that the Lumina family once had Arab caretakers living on their estate. Obil's father had tended the Lumina family's groves and when Obil was old enough he began tending to them as well.

Isaac and Obil sat on the limestone ridge of *Har Ha-Zetim* and looked across the Qidron Valley toward Jerusalem. The gold crown of the Dome of the Rock shone like a brilliant fire—a beacon radiating the prayers of all the people of the book, *Ahl al-Kitab*, to the abode of the One Without End. In return the noble *kavanah*, the aspiration that gave force to those *b'rakhah*, prayers, takes on the luminous nature of light that all who hear of the Dome or see its magnificence may understand themselves to be in the presence and under the protection of the One Without End.

"You're leaving." Isaac knew this day would come. Obil, who had worked so hard within the Arab-Israeli peace movement, had grown more and more frustrated as the years progressed. The light of hope in Obil's eyes was now darkened with despair.

Obil nodded. "I wanted to come to you today, Isaac. Although we have not agreed of late, we were once close and our families, if not our countrymen, had known peace."

"What went wrong, my friend? We were happy as children, with-out quarrel or bitterness between us." Isaac's chest tightened. The rift that had grown between himself and Obil gave him great pain.

"Yes, Isaac, we were happy you and I. Our families and communi-ties lived in peace. But now, that is only a faded memory." Obil then gestured to the ancient pillar below them, whose narrow spire was just visible. "Regard Absalom. Jealousy, anger, and the desire for power drove him to revolt against David, his own father. His vanity tempted him to build his own reliquary, perhaps knowing there would be none to do it for him. Have not our leaders followed in his path?"

Isaac surveyed the Qidron valley below. Amidst the bustle and com-merce were lemon, olive, date and orange trees bursting with delicate pastel blossoms. Rows of pomegranate trees were beginning to bare the pulpy, sweet fruit favored by King Solomon and said by Muhammad to purge the system of envy and hatred. *If only they did.*

"I suppose," Isaac remarked, "friendship alone isn't enough."

"Not without equality." Obil gave him a sad smile, but bitterness laced his voice. "Rabin promised us a real home. He promised to stop building settlements and that serious negotiations would take place for the future of Jerusalem. That vow gave us back our dreams, and we felt *the disaster* was behind us. For the first time since the 1948 *nakba*, Palestinians had hope."

Isaac tried to reach him. "Israelis, too, had hope for some peace."

"Your hope goes to sleep in warm beds," Obil qualified. "When you wake to pee, it's in a toilet, not a tin can that's dumped in the gutter in the morning."

Isaac tried to keep his patience. "That's no longer true with all the suicide bombings."

"Yes, poor Israel, how her brave citizens suffer from the evils of terrorism. Sharon, Peres, and their new puppet, 'little Bush', fear terrorism so much because they know it works. Ask the sixty-nine women and children who died inside their homes in Qibya in 1953. They were not permitted to leave while Israeli soldiers prepared the detonation explosives that ripped their bodies apart and buried them in rubble. Years later, Ariel Sharon called it a mistake. A mistake! Like the attack on the USS Liberty in 1967." He paused. "Some mistake."

"Both sides are at fault."

"No, Isaac." Obil held his ground. "Ninety people died when Jerusalem's King David Hotel was bombed in 1946. Israel was launched in a sea of blood, and Israel will die in a sea of blood."

"Never." Isaac had heard it so often now. *Mere mutterings from the infidels.*

"Look around you." Obil stretched his arms out wide. "Your dream died with ours. Why? For your stupid settlements. It could have been over after Oslo. Peace. We wanted to live, grow tomatoes, have children. Now . . . "

"It's not too late. When terrorism is defeated, we can move forward."

"Defeated?" Obil looked at Isaac incredulously. "Fool yourselves, fool America, but you can no longer fool the whole world. Israel's future is precarious. Your actions now are sealing your fate. Like grains of sand blown from the desert, my people will come after you—our children and their children. Israel will never have rest. We learned terrorism from masters, who themselves learned under the Nazi heel."

Isaac felt the flush of indignation rise to his face. He wanted to walk away, but something held him back.

"You brought this horror to Palestine," Obil accused, pointing his finger at him. "Do you really think the Jews can live as instruments of torture and hate? Your soul has been surrendered. Every day of Israel's existence destroys a moment of the harmony needed to know God."

Isaac had allowed his friend to vent his anger, but he would not allow Obil to condemn the nation he loved. "You cannot stand there and talk about harmony when your own clerics are bellowing for Muslims to kill Israelis, to kill Americans. To *kill* or *be killed*."

"Muslim life is not like that," Obil argued. "It is not natural for us to teach hate. But the world we are living in today is not natural. Natural laws, God's laws, are spat upon. So many of us have abided by the teaching of Islam—the five *arkan al-Islam*—the fundamental codes necessary for a righteous life. To bear witness before Allah, to pray five times daily, to be charitable toward the poor, to fast for one month during *Ramadan*, and to make pilgrimage to Mecca at least once in a lifetime. A simple faith for simple people. But now life is not so simple. We must fight back or perish."

Isaac wanted to knock some sense into his friend. He hated him and loved him at the same time, and the colliding emotions only posed even more confusion. "Arabs cannot simply make demands of the Jews through terrorism."

"Here you go again about Arabs." Obil flung his hands in the air. "Understand this. Your problem is not simply with Arabs. In fact, the largest Muslim nations in the world are not even Arab. This burning ember will soon be fully lit due to your intransigent policies. World pressure ended apartheid in South Africa. The same will be done to you. Not because of the world's anti-Semitic behavior but because of your own anti-Semitic conduct."

Isaac took a deep breath and thought for a moment. He wanted to stop the arguing. It sickened him to be fighting with Obil. Isaac looked into his friend's eyes. What he saw was pain, anguish, rage . . . and mixed in with all of it, a plea.

Compassion began to stir in his heart. It had been a while since Isaac had known a feeling like it. He turned toward his friend. "What can we do?"

Obil seemed to have noticed his sincerity. He bent forward further and held Isaac's gaze. "First," he said, "we must accept our unity, you and I. We are both children of Abraham. That alone will work wonders. Second, stop hating yourselves. That's what leads to your hatred of Arabs and your drive toward a 'greater Israel.' The *greatest* Israel is love of God and all other living beings as an expression of that God."

It sounded more like the Obil he knew. Although his friend sounded calmer, Isaac felt compelled to pose the question. "You ask us to do this while suicide bombers ride our buses and sit among us in restaurants?"

Obil replied with a query. "Why not ask yourselves, 'What have we done to drive these people to desire death more than life?' "

Isaac didn't answer. He was tired of it all—fighting, arguments, weapons, military raids, explaining to mothers how their sons died. Each war was the one to end them all—each battle, the one that would stomp out terrorism, which then only returned threefold. A few suicide bombers in the mid-nineties had become a few more each day. Isaac let go of his hopes.

Blue skies, cottony clouds, warm air, a white pigeon . . . His youth had been so fleeting, silky sand sifting through life's hourglass. When they were boys, Isaac had loved to swim with Obil, floating on their backs, the cool, clear water of the Tiberias suspending them between earth and sky.

Isaac realized he hadn't gone swimming in many years.

Now, as the two comrades sat quietly, Isaac knew that Obil shared his experience, each listening to the voice within. They had spoken about it many times before, a state of being absorbed, beyond listening—*fanâ*—total surrender through the elimination of self, a childhood before birth.

Just then, two spotted woodpeckers, *hud-hud,* moved across the ground, their long beaks intent and outstretched and the top of their pointed heads aimed at the sun. Murmuring voices, carried by the breeze now blowing through the valley, unsettled the quiet.

Isaac spoke first, his voice reflecting the newfound stillness of his mind. "The rabbis of old taught that a whisper is carried around the world, heard by none, but felt by all whenever a human soul leaves the body or a fruit tree is felled. I feel it and hear it." Isaac sensed his time with Obil was nearing an end.

"Far too many souls have been released through killing, and far too many fruit trees plowed under by arrogance." Obil rose to his feet and reached out his hand toward Isaac. "I must leave now."

Isaac allowed Obil to pull him up.

"The madness must stop, my brother," Obil said, still holding his hand. "We, the sons of one father, worshippers of the same God, must live in peace. It is up to you. My time is done. Few people can see the infinite or properly speak the many names, but at least those of us who have experienced the whispering must proclaim it for those who are themselves deaf to life."

Isaac hugged his friend one last time, and Obil set off down the slope toward the Mount.

As he watched him descend, Isaac finally realized a truth he could not escape.

Friendship was leaving him . . . peace was slipping away . . . and now only the dark unknown remained.

CHAPTER 89

"I T'S A LONG STORY, Muriel." Michael hardly knew where to begin.

"Fine, you can tell me and Isaac together when we get you home." Muriel maneuvered her car expertly on the fast moving Shivtei Yisrael toward the tranquil art's colony of Yemin Moshe, finally parking in front of an aged, Spanish-style building. As he exited the car, Michael could see a light was on in Isaac and Muriel's top floor apartment.

Once upstairs, they found Isaac was waiting in the middle of the living room. Looking lean and tired, he turned toward them. "Muriel?"

"Yes," she answered. "Michael's here."

It had been only five months since he had seen Isaac, but it felt like a lifetime. Michael noticed a little more gray in Isaac's sandy brown hair and a few more worry lines on his forehead. But his light blue eyes were still piercing. Once again Michael had to remind himself they were made of glass. *If you didn't know he was blind* . . . The burn marks around Isaac's eyelids were the only real reminder.

Isaac held out his hand and Michael took it. "Michael, come sit. I have some dinner made."

And he did. Rice, steaming vegetables, fresh bread and cool wine. Famished, Michael ate quickly, stopping occasionally to fill Muriel and Isaac in on his bizarre escapades. Barely eating, the couple listened intently to his account, not uttering a word. When he was finally finished and they were still silent, Michael realized they were probably overwhelmed by everything they had heard.

Then Isaac, the tactician, snapped to as if out of a dream. "There's a chance that Professor Samuels has broken the code. We should contact him right away."

Muriel was on the phone in a moment. Michael could hear her murmuring on the other side of the room. Finally, she sat down on the couch with him and Isaac and placed the phone back in its cradle, switching it to speaker.

"Michael."

It was the Professor. Michael could scarcely believe it.

"Thank God you made it," Samuels said, his voice sounding noticeably weak.

"Professor," Michael divulged, "I have it."

"The Spear?" the Professor asked excitedly.

"Yes, but I haven't located Maggie yet? Have you heard from her at all?"

"I know she arrived there two days ago, but she hasn't contacted me."

"Are you sure she's going to be at the church . . . the Sepulchre?"

Michael's question was met with momentary silence.

"I'm about as sure as I'm going to be," Samuels replied. "It's the only logical place. Everything culminates there."

Before Michael could question him further, Isaac interrupted. "Professor . . . the numbers. Were you able to discover what they represent?"

"We have," the Professor confirmed. "They're longitudes and latitudes for al-Ghawar, al-Jubayl, and the Strait of Hormuz at Khasab."

Isaac gripped the side of the couch and stood up. "Saudi Arabian oil fields, a refinery and the shipping lane connecting them to the world."

Michael exchanged an ominous glance with Muriel. She set her wine glass down slowly.

"Also," Professor Samuels continued. "Each sequence is separated by a number—zero, fifteen and thirty. Possibly, these indicate time frames."

An alarmed look passed over Isaac's face. "An attack." His voice shook. "But why?"

"Is there any indication of activity in Jerusalem?" the Professor asked.

"Security is extraordinary, even for us." Isaac replied. "The U.S. secretary of state and foreign ministers from England, France, Germany, and Italy, as well as the UN secretary-general are here . . . "

Isaac's face suddenly paled and he began to sway. Michael and Muriel rushed to his side as he slumped to the ground.

WEST BANK – 2002

The rain poured down onto the dismal streets from a dark, tumultuous sky.

"We hate you! The world hates you!" The Palestinian women were yelling from doorways, raising their arms toward the heavens. "Even God hates you!"

Colonel Isaac Lumina pressed his men forward into the refugee camp with a wary eye on every rooftop and window. Indeed, it seemed as if the very stones of the buildings hated his Israeli troops. Isaac wondered if he was beginning to hate himself for his actions, perhaps every bit as much as the Palestinians did.

It was impossible to see the tanks rolling ahead of his men without comparing this onslaught to the German destruction of Europe. Were the Israelis the sad benefactors of Hitler's legacy of terror and race madness?

Isaac wondered about Obil now as he surveyed the twisted metal and concrete refuse of Jenin.

Israel's future is precarious, Obil had warned him. *Your actions now are sealing your fate.*

Were his friend's predictions coming to pass?

Isaac's heart had broken mourning over Israel's greatest loss—*Purity of Arms*—an Israeli government ideal to only use their weapons to attack military enemies and never harm civilians. But now, it wasn't just their world image or the Arab women and children yelling after them, calling them "Gestapo" and "Nazis" that conveyed the loss. In flashes of recognition, the betrayal of that promise came from the eyes of his own troops . . . eyes dazed by fear, by death.

Beating prisoners, shooting children, exploding telephone booths, launching rockets from helicopters. All for what? So the dirty lying animals—those Arabs—could not enter the Bar Mitzvahs with bombs around their waists. So that Arab hashish vendors could be replaced by Russian Jews selling Ecstasy.

For this I've given my life, thought Colonel Lumina, *to see the once proud IDF become the private muscle for drug lords and money launderers?*

"Get out, *salibi!*"

"Butchers!"

"*Agnabi,* we hate you!"

"*Allahu akbar! Allahu akbar!*"

The sergeant riding beside Isaac on the Bradley armored personnel carrier swiveled the machine gun toward the voices. Instantly, several young boys darted down a dark alley.

"Don't these people ever tire of sounding so stupid, then dying?" the sergeant asked.

Isaac did not answer. He motioned for silence and for several of his men to proceed carefully down the alley. The Bradley followed as the men checked doorways and windows. They were just inside the entrance when the stench rose to meet them. Gasoline fumes, gunpowder, urine-soaked dry sand, and the unmistakable odor of unburied bodies swollen with gasses saturated the air.

Salty sweat soaked through his headband and ran down Isaac's face, stinging his eyes. Keeping as still as possible, he resisted the urge to wipe his hand across his forehead. Instead, he looked for movement from the enemy, his gaze sweeping across rooftops, windows, doorways, looking for shadows, lights, motion. His men proceeded cautiously past the dark doorways and blown out walls.

"Come out. You will not be harmed," Isaac said in Arabic, his voice booming through a bullhorn. There was no reply so he signaled his men to prepare tear gas and smoke grenades. "We do not wish to kill anyone. Come outside . . . unarmed."

The crashing sound of a shattering window made Isaac look up. Glass shards, like angry hornets, were flying toward them.

Alarmed, his men flung their smoke grenades.

More explosions. Gray, acrid smoke. A rifle barrel in the window. Another crash.

A large object flew out of a hole in the wall.

A bomb!

Bham, bham, bham, bham. Rapid blasts from the Bradley machine gun blew out the remaining walls.

Movement in the doorways. More shots.

Isaac's troops started yelling at each other in the street.

Then, from their hidden nests, they appeared. Shadows in doorways with arms raised overhead, one followed by another. The soldiers quickly forced their Palestinian prisoners to remove enough of their clothing to make sure none of them were wearing suicide belts. Intelligence officers wrapped the prisoners' wrists with plastic ties, and Isaac's patrol proceeded forward.

Down another street.

At first a moment of silence. Then a rumbling. The street shook and the walls around them trembled as a massive bulldozer, as tall as most houses, moved forward, ripping the buildings apart on either side of the alley. Sofas, chairs, walls filled with photos, shelves with spices, and closets of clothes still hanging on rods were left exposed in the dozer's wake.

"Killers!"

Angry cries came from the shadows.

"*Salibi, salibi, salibi!*"

"The world hates you!"

Isaac and his men moved forward, toward more alleys, more doorways, seeking to end terrorism. *But this will never end,* he realized, *never.*

Just then, the figure of a man, shrouded by smoke, rose from the dust and moved toward them.

As the man got closer, Isaac's heart began to pound. *No it couldn't be.*

A ghost . . . a memory . . . a face unchanged after so many years. *Obil.*

"No!" Isaac shouted as he jumped to the ground.

"Colonel!" the sergeant yelled in alarm. "Suicide bomber!"

"Obil!" Isaac rushed forward. "Don't!"

Now there was no time for talk, no time for listening. Isaac's troops moved quickly. Obil watched them with a blank expression, appearing to be oblivious of Isaac as well. His hand moved to his waist.

Isaac took several steps forward and screamed, "No! Obil, no!"

But it was all too fast. The explosion, the chaos, the darkness.

Olam ha-tohu. After the great noise, Isaac heard nothing, saw nothing, and felt totality, pain ripping through his body. Did the world begin this way? *Tsimtsum*—primordial chaos—our abandonment of the sacred—that moment when we were no longer in union with our own spirit.

Olam ha-tohu. The world was chaos.

The smoke became mist, the street empty space. The tension bracing Isaac's spine turned electric—an energy that could only be derailed by a hate no longer known. Within his mind he receded, the journey inward propelling him beyond the memories of Monfort, beyond his birth, to the moment when his identity began.

Isaac Lumina's spirit left his body and began a journey that was really a continuum—initiated long before this present life—suspending him between *ruach* and *adamah*, God's spirit and earth's dust. In other words, where he had always been.

That moment was *Tikkun olam*—a return to creation—the evolvement of the individual soul back to the original molecule of totality. There, beyond the separation, Isaac witnessed his reality. He finally understood that all he was doing was destroying life, destroying his dream, destroying the one ideal he thought he was fighting for—Israel.

"Medic!"

As if from down a long hollow passage, Isaac faintly heard his radioman screaming.

"Medic! Colonel Lumina is down!"

Isaac lay on the ground, his body covered with blood and burnt flesh. *The suicide bomber . . . Obil.*

Finally, Isaac understood his friend's pain. He wanted to embrace Obil, tell him of his sorrow, but it was too late.

Now, there was only emptiness.

Isaac the soldier, protector of the political Israel, had been hidden from himself by the *parachot*—the veil of separation. In an explosive flash, *bazak,* the veil had rent apart. Within its clear light, Isaac became aware . . . his death was complete.

His illusory life was over.

Isaac reached for his eyes. As he felt the blood on his face, he cried out, realizing the painful truth.

It had taken the darkness to enlighten him.

"Isaac, are you okay?" Michael stood over his friend while Muriel tried to give him a glass of water.

Isaac just waved it off. "I'm fine," he assured them both. "I was just feeling faint."

You look more like you just came back from the dead, Michael thought. He kept the observation to himself.

"You were saying security is at an all time high in Jerusalem, correct?" Professor Samuels, still on the phone, reiterated.

"Yes, but Mabus would not initiate any attack on Saudi Arabia without striking here also," Isaac noted firmly, appearing to have regained his composure.

"For what end?" Michael asked.

"Didn't you say your friend, Steven Einsof, has developed an energy system?" Isaac asked. "How soon before it can be put into effect?"

Michael wasn't sure where Isaac was headed. "I think homes and small businesses can be powered fairly soon."

"So if the world's oil supply was cut in half, then Mabus would be the immediate beneficiary," Isaac concluded.

"And an attack on the three sites in Saudi Arabia would drastically cut the oil flow, helping to accomplish that aim," Professor Samuels noted.

"That's right. It's called PSE," Isaac responded grimly. "If the Saudis thought they were under a serious attack, they would instigate a plan called Petroleum Scorched Earth, PSE. They have rigged their oil fields and refineries with RDDs—radiation dispersal devices—dirty bombs made with conventional explosive Semtex but packed with radioactive cesium and strontium." He paused. "If they can't have the oil, no one will."

Michael finally understood. "In one move, the Saudi oil industry would disappear. This would cripple the American economy."

"Not to mention leaving America as the Saudi's last asset since they own so much of it," the Professor reminded them.

"Israel would be left unprotected without American support," Muriel added.

"Worse yet," Isaac said pointedly, "with a scheme like this, I'm sure a strategy is in place to lay the blame on Israel's doorstep."

Michael felt a rush of urgency. "I need to find Maggie".

"I'll take you wherever you need to go," Muriel said, rising from the couch. "Then I'm going to Kerem Shalom. We must break the impasse and let the women into Jerusalem and stop this madness."

"Colonel Lumina." The Professor sounded strong and focused. "We have some phone calls to make. Alert your people. We must find out how the attacks will be delivered." The Professor paused and a momentary hush fell over the room. "This is going to be a *very long* night," he finally said.

Indeed, Michael thought, *it will be.*

Neither spoke as Muriel drove Michael to King David Street. Everything had moved so quickly after the conversation with the Professor that Michael felt uncertain about their plan. He knew he had to get into the Church of the Holy Sepulchre, but just how he would accomplish that was a mystery. Muriel would continue on toward Kerem Shalom to join the women marchers at the border.

But then what?

Trust. Faith. He was in need of both, he supposed. Words that had little meaning to him before now took on phenomenal proportions.

Muriel stopped in front of Jaffa Gate. Before getting out of the car, Michael leaned over and kissed her cheek. "*Mazel tov.*" He knew her ride would be a dangerous one.

Muriel squeezed his hand. "*L'Chaim,*" she responded, wishing him well in return.

As Muriel's car roared away into the night, Michael realized there was little time left. Tomorrow morning at ten o'clock, Mabus would be making the opening speech at the Peace Conference.

Michael looked at his watch . . .

It was nearly midnight. As he walked alongside the castellated walls of the Citadel, Michael realized he was not alone. Tourists, Latin Seminary students, and hashish dealers were still lingering on the sidewalks enjoying the full moon. He passed them, keeping his gaze cast to the ground and entered through the narrow tunnel of the Jaffa Gate—Bab el-Khalil—emerging within the old city.

As he passed under the shadow of David's Tower, he remembered the tale of King David. It was said he suspended a harp over his bed, and at midnight the north wind would blow and vibrate its strings, creating music. David would then rise and study the Torah until dawn.

The ritual of beginning evening prayers at midnight was a time-honored one, Michael knew. Even now, as he walked along the dark road, Kabbalah mystics were immersed in their own nightly prayers honoring *Shekhinah.*

The bride of the messiah, Michael mused. *The female principle cast out from heaven.*

It was time to reinstate her.

CHAPTER 90

THE NIGHTMARE *of this land won't end.* Would it spread even further like a raging virus, inflaming everyone's minds and hearts?

Speeding through the night, Muriel reviewed her life. At fifty-four, she was already over twice as old as her only child Benjamin had been when he was killed. His death was senseless, like so many others. Why couldn't Israel's leaders stop trying to meet death with death? Their lack of reason had led them to view Arabs as nothing more than animals, and that view had caused so many Palestinians to view Jews in the same light.

Crimes against humanity. Will they never end?

Despite what she had witnessed, Muriel still had hope . . . the same hope that had brought her back to Israel, a land under siege.

"Hello Muriel."

Muriel had only been standing in the doorway for a moment. Yet Isaac had felt her presence immediately. She smiled knowingly. *Of course he would.*

"You've come back," he said.

Isaac's deep resonant voice still struck the same chord, almost moving her to tears. Muriel walked toward him and allowed his outstretched hands to fold over hers, the same hands she had not touched since the funeral of their only child, Benjamin, killed four years earlier while on patrol in the West Bank.

After his death, Muriel found it impossible to continue to live in Israel. She blamed the government leaders, the constantly bickering politicians, and the thoughtless, arrogant settlers, so bent on stealing land that they would place the nation's youth in harm's way. Muriel had come to hate them all. And Sharon. Why did he *have* to live in Arab Jerusalem? Or visit the Temple Mount? *Why is my child dead?* For what? Her futile questioning, her unanswered fury, had driven her out of her homeland.

But now, she was back.

"Muriel, I'm so sorry." Isaac's voice cracked as the tears began to well in his eyes.

"Why would you be sorry?" Muriel asked. "I had to leave. You know that, and you know why." As she looked at Isaac, her son's face appeared in her mind. It was a painful resemblance, one she had tried to escape all these years.

"I've been blind long before now," Isaac admitted, squeezing her hand. "The army was my life. Israel, my home. I thought making one strong would ensure the survival of the other. I realize now, I've spent my life making Israel weak, destroying the soul of Judea. By demonizing Palestinians and taking and taking, we've lost our way."

Muriel brought Isaac over to the kitchen table and sat with him. "That is why I've returned," she said. "I knew it was time to come back, to work with others and try to right the wrongs."

Isaac's face contorted in anguish. "There was a moment in history, after Oslo, when we could have set so many wrongs aside. Rabin knew this. But, like so many of my compatriots I scorned his efforts and belittled him. Our conduct has made the world a far more dangerous place for us all. Even Israel itself is in jeopardy of surviving as a Jewish state. We've seen to that. If we continue on this road, perhaps in a hundred years this country's existence will merely be a small footnote in history."

Muriel realized he was serious. Isaac was not a man driven to drastic conclusions without good cause.

"The moment of creation must be approached or none of us will ever reach home," Isaac said. Even without his sight, he pointed toward the map of Jerusalem hanging on the living room wall. "Only by healing the whole do we heal any part. There can be no Jewish state or Muslim state, or even a Christian state. Israel . . . Jerusalem . . . Palestine. Our holy land must be made whole once again." He squeezed her hand.

Muriel pressed it to her cheek and allowed her tears to flow over their intertwined fingers. "I will be your eyes," she said through her tears. "I will move before you, opening the way. Together, our light as husband and wife will shine for others."

Muriel's nourishing spirit then gave birth to *ONE*. One Land, One People, One God. With her husband, Isaac, she found her purpose. Together, they began their campaign to free the Holy Land through speaking engagements on the Hyatt Hotel lecture circuit. Muriel realized early on that it would be hard to resist listening to one of Israel's most prominent military heroes preach a radical peace venue.

It was only a week later that she walked her husband to the podium of a Religions for Peace conference put together by another dominant peace force, Women in Black, which had a large following around the world and a prominent presence in Israel. Isaac's profound speech captivated the huge audience in the Rabin Auditorium.

"This is not a 'land for peace' dilemma," he proclaimed. "We have sown much disharmony and suffering. We may not even see peace within our lifetime. ONE stands for the recognition of God's light within us all. At the moment we exclude one Gentile or one Arab from our heart, we lock ourselves, our family, and our nation out of God's Kingdom.

"The God of our fathers promised this land to the descendants of Abraham. That includes all of us: Muslim, Christian and Jew. This means our most difficult days now lie before us, since we cannot avoid the trap we ourselves have set. We came into this land to escape the Holocaust and its aftermath, but it seems we brought it with us instead. By denying another's humanity and rights, we then deny our own."

Standing powerfully, his eyes transfixed in dark space, Isaac appeared even more the soldier on this day than on any other.

"So, it is not for us to bray loudly that ours is the most democratic nation in a region of dictatorial regimes. We failed ourselves by not living up to the Oslo agreements. We did not stop building settlements. We didn't even slow down. Then we accused Arafat of bad faith. He showed poor judgment, perhaps. He signed away his people's rights in return for cash, a nice office and helicopters, but that was greed and stupidity in which we were accessories."

As Muriel sat and listened, she could almost hear the old people and children as they suffered in Arab villages crying in desperation, and the agonizing despair of her own people as they lived through the terror of yet another suicide bombing. They were the whisperings of ghosts, murmuring in the night.

We will be their voice, she thought.

Sighing, Muriel closed her eyes, determined to keep her pledge.

Driving in silence, Muriel now remembered the power of that vow.

Will I see it come to fruition tonight?

After nearly two hours of being on the road, Muriel reached the southern end of the Gaza Strip. To her astonishment, when she turned off at Nir Yitzhak, still ten kilometers from the border, she came across campsites filled with women, buses and cars that lined the roadside.

Muriel drove by slowly and rolled down her window. Circles of women, arms interlocked, were dancing around fires, clapping their hands and singing.

"Muriel, Muriel!"

She stopped the car. Two figures silhouetted against the fires ran toward her.

"Shona, Sarah." Muriel was relieved to see two friends from Tel Aviv.

"You've come," Shona exclaimed, embracing her.

Sarah took her hand. "We have been waiting. Whatever needs to be done, we will do."

Muriel looked toward the campsites and fires. *So many women.* She could see the power they possessed. Then, as an idea dawned on her, Muriel took a deep breath. *Why hadn't I thought of it before?* She would call Feikra immediately. Perhaps the gloomy night still held hope.

"Quickly," Muriel said, motioning for the two women to get into the car. "There's little time left."

Their window of opportunity would soon be closed.

CHAPTER 91

SHADOWS IN THE DARKNESS. The moonlight reflecting from white-washed walls and roofs made the narrow streets appear like polarized photographs—archways too bright and alleys in complete darkness.

It was nearing one o'clock in the morning as Michael walked up Avtimos Road toward Via Dolorosa. He realized he had been rash in his judgment. In some out-of-body moment, he thought he might be able to break into the Holy Sepulchre, but the night air had brought him back to his senses. Now, he would have to wait. The church would be locked until morning.

Michael's heart nearly stopped when the cell phone in his pocket suddenly began to ring. Was it Stephen again? The street was quiet . . . unnaturally quiet. He ducked into a doorway, his eyes searching the shadows. Michael cupped his hand over the phone as he answered. "Hello."

"Michael, where are you?" Isaac's worried voice came through the receiver.

"Muristan Square," Michael whispered. He pressed his back up against the door, hoping the awning overhead would conceal him from the moonlight.

"You need to get to Johanniter Hospice at Via Dolorosa and St. Francis Street," Isaac directed. "Just above the arched doorway, you will see a large, white Maltese Cross within a red circle. Knock three times on the door, pause and knock once. Gerta is expecting you."

"What about—?"

"Go," Isaac insisted. "The rest is out of your control."

Michael stood for a moment on the moonlit street, realizing just where Isaac was sending him.

Johanniter Hospice . . . born from the carnage created when the Crusaders laid siege to Jerusalem in 1099. When the city finally fell, its thirty thousand residents were slaughtered in a sea of blood. Ten thousand Muslims were murdered on the Temple Mount alone. The massacre inspired the German knights in charge of St. John the Baptist Church to re-organize themselves as the German Hospice of the Order of St. John, a healing order. Isaac had just directed Michael to their guesthouse.

As Michael hurried past the pink stone buildings that surrounded Muristan Square's fountain, he thought their color reminded him of dried blood. Just over the rooftops, he could see the silver dome of St. John the Baptist Church glowing brilliantly in the moonlight, appearing like a halo above the city.

After crossing the square, Michael turned and headed through Souk el-Dabbagha and Souk Khan el-Zeit, stepping into the shadows to pause and scan the dark streets whenever he could. His feeling of being followed was growing stronger even though he didn't see a soul. Perhaps it was the quiet or the moonlight. *Or a very active imagination*, he thought, as he envisioned himself being wrapped in a rug and quietly disposed of.

As he continued darting through the streets, Michael tried to allay his fears. He reminded himself that it wouldn't be long before shop owners began firing up their bakery ovens. He could almost smell the hot flour and cinnamon of freshly made bagels and pastries.

Almost, but not quite.

Instead, now walking in the dark under the archways, Michael could only smell fear . . . his own.

He breathed a sigh of relief when he came upon a small knot of people . . . several pilgrims, mystics and practitioners of the *Jerusalem Syndrome*—wandering souls acting out their Biblical delusions. As he was passing them, a woman with sad eyes and long tangled brown hair dangled a towel in front of herself, offering it to him.

Stunned at first, Michael then realized what she was doing. It was here, long ago, a woman named Seraphia had stepped out from the crowd that was watching Jesus carry his cross and handed her veil to him so he could wipe his face. The true image, the *vera icon*, of Christ's face remained on the fabric when he handed it back. When sainthood was bestowed upon Seraphia by the Church, they changed her name to *Veronica*, a testament to the event.

Now, as he realized he was walking on part of the Via Dolorosa, Michael found his mood shifting even more. Although he was not religious, the path to Calvary—a place the Hebrews called Golgotha—stirred a curious passion in him. The very idea that he was headed to that locale and would have to penetrate the Church of the Holy Sepulchre to reach it seemed downright insane.

Michael felt uneasy, but his legs kept carrying him forward. He still had to get to Johanniter Hospice, although he had no idea what to expect—help or a dead end.

Only one thing was certain . . . there was no turning back.

Seven thousand miles away, Napesh Samuels sat in his Rhinecliff home watching the sunset. The glow of the early evening light glistened off the Hudson, creating shifting patterns on the river's surface.

New patterns are emerging everywhere, Samuels thought.

At that very moment, he knew that the league of men known as Propaganda Due were moving quickly, like a silent deadly wind across the planet. Theirs was a force Samuels had fought against his whole life. Would they succeed in whatever plan they were implementing? His uncle, Walter Stein, warned him long ago that *the Way's* task was difficult and dangerous. His words were etched in Samuels' mind.

The brighter the light, the darker the shadow.

The Way . . . Propaganda Due. Whatever names were placed on good and evil, the primal energies remained the same.

Samuels shivered with an unfamiliar feeling . . . fear. In what direction would the descendant of al'Mabus turn the world that evening? Like Hitler, satanic forces moved like gathering winds within Mabus, but unlike the Nazi leader, he worked without the outward display of a powerful army behind him.

Silent winds were a lot deadlier.

Mabus, it appeared, had come to that conclusion long ago. His stronghold consisted of an elite network of powerful and wealthy benefactors. *Propaganda Due.* Concealed behind corporate shades, members of the unholy allegiance made sure the world turned just the way they wanted it to, and that when the wheel of fortune spun, theirs would be a sure bet.

Just then, the Professor was jarred out of his reverie by the loud ringing of his phone. He picked up the receiver.

"Professor."

Samuels recognized Isaac's voice.

"I've learned there is a joint military exercise tomorrow around the Persian Gulf," Isaac informed him. "General Gerard of the American Air Force is in charge. The Israeli and Saudi air forces will also participate."

Samuels was disturbed by the news. The Peace Conference was starting tomorrow. Why, all of a sudden, would there be such an unusual joint mission?

Einsof's discovery! The Saudi oil fields!

Mabus' plan was beginning to unfold.

"It's a set-up!" Professor Samuels surmised. "Get your people out of it. I will call Sheikh Wayani."

"Isn't he here in Jerusalem?"

Samuels realized Isaac was right.

"I can get to him quicker," Isaac said. "Perhaps he can also help me persuade my government to cancel the exercise."

"Make sure to talk only to the Sheikh," Samuels warned. "We can't be certain who inside the Saudi camp is involved in this plot."

"Bizarre isn't it?" Isaac asked, frustration in his voice. "Burning your own house down to spite your enemies."

Bizarre indeed, Samuels thought, as he hung up the phone.

He gazed through his portico windows. Night had descended across the valley and the river's surface was now dark. With less than ten hours left before the conference, it was time to play his final card.

Below Michael's feet, worn cobblestones glistened under the light of the moon. He walked under a vaulted arch and up an inclined road until he reached a black, wrought-metal lamp set above a doorway. Just below it, set within a red circle against an old stone wall, was a white Maltese Cross. *The Johanniter Hospice.*

He climbed the twenty or so stairs, knocked three times, paused and knocked once more. The heavy oak door swung aside enough for a small hand to reach out, grab his wrist, and pull him in. Then the door was quickly shut behind him.

"Shhh, no one must see you." A short woman wearing a smock and a babushka on her head greeted him with a finger over her lips. Her round face was pleasant, though plain. She turned and scurried down the hall motioning for Michael to follow her.

As they passed through a chapel, Michael noticed the altar—a simple high table covered with a red cloth. On the cloth itself was an imprint of four lances pointing toward each other, tips meeting at the center, creating the image of the white Maltese Cross. Behind the altar itself, a series of arches set within each other formed the back wall where a large wooden figure of the crucified Christ hung at the center. Large candles, placed in niches around the room, provided the only light.

Michael expected they would speak in the chapel, but the woman did not stop. Instead, she continued through the room, exiting a side door that led into a succession of narrow hallways. Finally, they reached a plain white door. Producing a huge brass ring from her belt, his mysterious companion selected one of the tarnished keys and opened it. She shooed Michael into the room and pulled the door closed firmly behind them. In the dim light, Michael followed her cautiously down a steep set of ladder-like stairs, so narrow he had only enough room to fit the heel of his shoe on each step.

When they reached the bottom, Michael found they were standing in a storeroom. Hewn out of rock, it was lined with wooden shelves filled to the brim with provisions.

"Now we can talk," the woman said softly in a German accent. "You must be Michael. I'm Gerta."

"Isaac said you could help me," Michael said, aware of the anxiety in his voice. "That you know a secret way into the Sepulchre."

"In a city of secrets we have kept our own well," Gerta remarked cryptically. "For over twelve hundred years. Ever since Charlemagne founded a hospital at this site, right up to this very day as Johanitter Hospice. Protectors and healers, we guard those who are in need." She leaned toward him, her voice lowering further. "We even still harbor Arab refugees, here since 1947 to escape the fighting."

"That's a pretty dangerous business," Michael said. "Providing aid to Palestinians is not generally smiled upon by the Israeli government."

"Our calling is to practice the Brotherhood of Jesus, *Jesus Bruderschaft.*" Her wide eyebrows arched as she brought her face closer to his. "Colonel Lumina has been a good friend to us for a long time and believes in our work. He is also party to one of our most closely held secrets, and soon, you will be, too."

Michael held his breath in expectation.

"*Soon,*" Gerta repeated smiling, "but not yet. I will take you into the Church of the Holy Sepulchre, but we must wait."

"Wait?" Michael felt the pressure inside of himself mounting. "I don't have time to wait. I must get inside the Sepulchre."

Gerta gave him a look of warning. "It's too dangerous right now."

"Won't it be just as dangerous later?" Michael pleaded.

Gerta did not respond, but instead pointed to the floor.

Michael sighed with dismay. He saw what looked like a thick, rolled up sack at the very back of the room—his bed he supposed.

"Early morning," Gerta instructed as she backed out of the room. "Be ready by five."

CHAPTER 92

RINALDO DONARA STOOD on the Mount of Olives as one of the hand-picked agents of the Italian Secret Service sent to protect the foreign ministers. In the dark of the early morning hours, he patrolled the Seven Arches Hotel along with several other P2 members. Their elite group now supervised the security forces for the foreign diplomats who had neither trust nor confidence in the Israelis. Instead, those diplomats had elected the Italian government to be their protectors.

Their cleverness will be their undoing, Rinaldo mused.

With P2's plan in place, they would once again maneuver the political situation to their benefit, just as they had done in the past. Argentina, Chile, Greece. *But who's counting?* Rinaldo smiled. The world was not meant for those waiting for democracy to save the day. Only the ruthless had the courage to claim what they desired for their own.

In a few hours, Rinaldo would receive last-minute instructions from their leader. Captain Volpi, whose philosophy had reshaped P2's destiny, understood the ways of men. His was a philosophy that Rinaldo could comprehend. It was practical, advocated control, and had no room for frivolous emotion.

Women marching for peace . . . Israeli government leaders chomping at the bit for a stake on the Temple Mount . . . Palestinian leaders bought off or pacified by promises of the West Bank.

He had to hand it to their greatest member and benefactor. *What a magnificent scene!* Giovanni Mabus knew how to put on a show. Rinaldo smiled to himself admiring the sheer balls of it all. It was like a Vegas extravaganza—the showgirls, the bright lights, the hungry gamblers, the exploding fireworks. Mabus mesmerized, bombarded the senses, and used sleight of hand—all the clever tricks of a master magician.

But now Rinaldo's mouth was watering for the ultimate *prestigio*—the final part of an act so inconstruable that not even another accomplished magician could figure it out.

CHAPTER 93

IT WAS NEARLY 4:00 AM. Laurel sensed the time for making their move across the border was at hand. They had planned to leave early and move slowly, en masse and . . . unarmed. Feeling anxious, Laurel left her tent and walked through the light drizzle toward the covered podium.

As she got closer she saw the shadow of a figure on the platform. Suddenly, Laurel heard the soft strumming of a guitar. It grew louder, until the rhythmic music began to stir the crowd.

"Everyone. Good Morning." It was Jules. She was addressing the marchers. "I'd like to sing a song I wrote last night. I believe it expresses why we're all here and what we want to accomplish."

The sound of Jules' voice, moving and clear, brought the women to their feet, the soft rain not for one moment appearing to dampen their spirits.

As Jules motioned for the crowd to follow along, Laurel understood that the song they were singing was a call to the spirit.

> *Raising cain. Oh, I'm raising cain.*
> *I am able and I'm raising cain.*
>
> *It's been too long. Time to end the pain.*
> *'Cause I am able and I'm raising cain*
>
> *Well the skies they rumble and the clouds flash light.*
> *Now, we all fall, we stumble and we're bound to fight.*
> *But the spirit's quickening and we must unite.*
>
> *Oh, I am able and I'm raising cain.*

I see the golden dome. I hear the wailing wall.
We need a higher mind that can accept it all.
We can accept it all.

For I am able and there's no one to blame.
Oh, I am Abel and I've forgiven Cain.

Oh, I am able.
I am able.
Oh, I am able and I'm raising cain!

Thousands of women lining the border singing for peace. Laurel was in awe. As she approached the podium, Jules began to lower her voice, finally stopping when Laurel reached the platform steps.

As several women walked over to assist her up, Laurel began to tremble. She took a deep breath, hoping she could keep the fear out of her voice when she addressed the crowd.

Arriving at the border town of Kerem Shalom, Muriel Lumina was amazed to find so many Israeli women were already there keeping vigil. When she stopped her car at the edge of the road, she could also see the thousands of women on the Egyptian side—busloads and carfuls as well as those on foot—a huge campaign of demonstrators ready to enter Israel.

Facing them, Israeli tanks were rumbling. Soldiers, their guns held tightly at their sides, were standing anxiously, peering into the darkness.

As Muriel observed the scene, she understood there was no time for a rally call. Soon, their biggest fears might be realized. She wiped the light rain from her face as she walked with Shona and Sarah through the crowd. When they reached the border barricades, Muriel took a deep breath and turned toward her companions.

It was time to make their move.

At the Israeli-Lebanese border, soldiers on both sides were ready to kill each other. Captain Mustafa Tahar knew his government, having no treaty with the Israelis and hating them passionately, had taken quite a different stance regarding the women. The Lebanese president was willing to let them flood the borders and force their way across.

The Israelis deserve this justice . . . women beating them to the quick.

Tahar had to admit he liked the idea. Even more, he wanted to see Jerusalem liberated, no matter how, from the clutches of the Jews.

On the outskirts of Israel, close to the Jordanian border, Feikra pleaded with the young border policeman. She saw the look of compassion flash across his dark eyes, even as he pointed his M16 rifle at her.

"If you wish to help us, keep your distance," she told him, trying to remain calm.

The confused guard, lowering his weapon slightly, retreated, but Feikra wondered for how long.

Shooting unarmed women. Even our shameless government leaders may have some difficulty making that call. Still, as a precaution, Feikra made sure that all Arab and Christian women demonstrating were centered within a thick layer of female Jewish guardians.

But would that really ensure their safety? Feikra realized not even their circle of trust could do that.

Anxiously, she looked at her watch. She had coordinated the time with Muriel.

Four A.M.

Feikra's heart began to race, as the hour was upon them.

CHAPTER 94

ROUSED FROM SLEEP by honking horns and loud jeers, Ebtehal felt Jehada's hand on her shoulder.

"Wake up," her son was shaking her. "We cross the border tonight! Now!"

Flicking on a flashlight, she aimed it at her wristwatch. Four in the morning.

"Mother!" Jehada was panting with excitement. "The Israeli women are here! Looks like more than a thousand of them. They are still crossing the border into Egypt. They say we should return with them to Jerusalem."

As the world came back into focus, Ebtehal began to realize the importance of what was happening. "What does Laurel say?"

"She's meeting with them right now," Jehada said, pointing toward the crossing.

Ebtehal heard the diesel engines firing up as she ran with Jehada toward the border. Bus drivers, now most of them women, were preparing to move out. On the Israeli side, klieg lights were snapping on, aimed at the crossing.

Within the glare of their beams, Ebtehal saw it was true. Israeli women were now among them. Although it couldn't have been sanctioned, they apparently had not met resistance crossing over. The Israeli military certainly wouldn't be shooting Jewish women entering Egypt, but if they were to try to cross back into Israel with thousands of protest marchers, Arab women among them, that would be another issue altogether.

The unthinkable was coming to pass. A veritable army of unarmed women was preparing to march into Israel. Ebtehal observed nervous Israeli soldiers checking their weapons. It was easy shooting unarmed Arabs, but this crowd was composed of a montage of thousands of women from all over the globe—Europe, the Americas, Africa, Asia, the Middle East—women brought together for a single purpose.

As the crowd gathered closer to the crossing, Ebtehal watched Laurel being assisted onto the speaker's platform. When the older woman reached the microphone, she looked across the sea of women standing amidst campfires and tents. Some were holding candles as they waited for her to speak.

Suddenly, the Israeli Defense Force aimed the ferocious beams of their kliegs directly at the crowd. Pained by the glaring light, the women turned away quickly, covering their eyes.

Wincing, Ebtehal smirked at the attempt to intimidate them. *Do they think we have come through all of this suffering and hardship to be turned around by some halogen bulbs?* Soon, the women would shed another light onto the situation, and then, just who would blink first?

"Women of the world," Laurel began. "Tonight we wait no more. Governments may talk or stall. That is the way of men. We have come to say to them, *No More*."

Cheers and trills of excitement emanated from the densely packed crowd.

"We have stood together, sisters of all nations." Raising her hand, Laurel pointed toward the border. "Now let us move together . . . together as one."

At that moment, Ebtehal saw a young woman step up to the microphone just as Laurel backed away. The woman began to sing, her voice, powerful and strong, driving the women forward.

> *All the People*
> *All the people in the world*
>
> *Where does your heart reside?*
> *Have you lost it in your pride?*
> *The blood of children is everywhere*
> *Well, it's not here it's over there.*
>
> *We like to hear the battle cry*
> *The chant of war calls us to die*
> *We want to fight and make a stand*

So let's all fight—
Fight for the brotherhood of man

Raise the lantern, dispel your fear
Ring the bell so you might hear
When told to fight on their command
Tell them you'll fight—
Fight for the brotherhood of man

All the People
All the People in the World
All the People
All the People in the World!

Ebtehal felt swept away by a rush of adrenaline, a powerful feeling of endowment. The other women looked as if they felt the same, their faces now glowing with enthusiasm and hope. Ebtehal felt privileged to be among them—women empowered by their own courage. How fortunate she was not to be hearing the mournful cries of sobbing mothers who had lost a child to war, but instead was listening to the courageous voices of women driven by purpose.

Now, joining the others around her, Ebtehal raised her arms in a show of unity as they began to move forward.

This is history.

Ebtehal smiled to herself, reflecting on the idea.

Actually . . . it's not, she realized as they reached the crossing.

*This is **herstory**.*

CHAPTER 95

O N THE ISRAELI SIDE of the border, Sergeant Gedula overlooked the troops. His men looked anxious, disturbed.

"Sergeant, are we ready?" Captain Tzuri, in charge of
the operation, addressed him.

Ready. Ready for what? He had not heard anything from General
Ruffat. Still, his commanding officer was speaking to him. "Yes we are,"
Sergeant Gedula replied.

"Sergeant, these women must not be allowed to enter," Tzuri emphasized. "Am I understood?"

Gedula swallowed his contempt. "Yes, sir."

"Even if it means shooting them." The cold look in Captain Tzuri's
eyes left no room for doubt.

The sergeant stood ready with his orders. A moment later, the
Egyptians soldiers raised the barricades on their side of the border and
melted into the night. Just as the women began to cross into Israel,
Gedula waved three armored personnel carriers toward them.

As soon as the machine gun-armored APCs began to move, a cry
went up from the crowd.

"Nazis!"

"No more!"

Hundreds of women broke away from the main group and ran
over to the Israeli side of the crossing. Their frustration . . . their rage
and anger. Sergeant Gedula felt thousands of years of injustice finding
release in a moment. Like an unstoppable wave, more and more women
flooded the border.

"Sergeant, give the order," Captain Tzuri commanded.

Sergeant Gedula took a step back. Reality sinking in, his conscience
snapped into place. He was not going to give any such order. "They're
unarmed women."

"Sergeant, I order your men to shoot!" Captain Tzuri was yelling now.

One gunner, hearing the captain, fired a burst, raking the women in front with a heavy caliber barrage before several other officers pounced on him.

But it was too late. Reacting, a number of the troops began shooting. A slash in time became an eternity as, along with the piercing wail of gunshots, all Gedula could hear were the screams.

Laurel's heart almost stopped when she heard the shooting. Horrified, she watched as several women fell to the ground bleeding and crying while others ran forward, screaming. In the onslaught of confusion, women were yelling and running everywhere. Laurel attempted to reach the microphone, but the frightened marchers pushed her forward, making it impossible.

Caught in the powerful surge, Laurel recognized that it was now all out of her hands. The moment had decided for them all.

The time for choice was over.

After realizing the sudden burst of gunfire had come from his own troops, General Ruffat began to yell. "Hold your fire! I repeat . . . Hold your fire!"

Some of the men began to cry and throw down their weapons, while others, blinded by their own rage, continued to fire into the crowd. Ruffat knew how much some of his soldiers hated the women's display of power. *Women do not have the right to be involved in the affairs of men,* they had told him.

Now, seeing no other recourse, the general radioed a command to all his captains. A chill moved up Ruffat's spine as he saw them following his orders, raising their weapons just as he was aiming his own. Turning their guns against their own brothers, they all began to shoot any soldiers still firing at the women.

In a spray of bullets, the dissidents fell one by one to the ground. When it was over, Ruffat lowered his weapon and stared ahead in a stupor. The unbelievable had occurred and it was still not over. Now, another stream of Israeli women poured over to the Egyptian side to assist the wounded and help their fellow demonstrators enter into Israel.

No longer in control, Ruffat felt a strange sense of calm as he watched them, as if the swell of a huge tide had finally pulled him into the sea.

Shock . . . chaos . . . elation. Muriel, who had crossed over into Egypt with the other Israeli women, saw it everywhere around her all at once. Women lay bleeding. Others, crying, were lingering to help them. Even more, calling to each other triumphantly, were charging forward.

Several moments later, the atrocity over, ambulances crossed the border from Kerem Shalom. Muriel watched with relief as white-coat attendants hurried to help the wounded. She then put Shona in charge of gathering a number of English-speaking Muslim women to act as interpreters for the Arab marchers. Her next move would be to locate Laurel. The women had to proceed forward quickly.

Like a succession of waves being held back by a dam, the women who had marched to the border had been contained. Now, in the early morning hours, that dam was breached. The marchers were coursing into Israel like a raging river.

As the women moved steadily forward, the remaining Israeli military drivers backed their APCs out of the way, no longer obstructing their passage. Muriel, having finally found Laurel's bus, drove behind her, heading toward Jerusalem.

"Isaac, we're on our way. We're following Laurel Seline across the border now," Muriel said, speaking into her cell phone. The message she left on the answering machine was brief, but it had to be. Isaac would know what to do.

With Shona and Sarah in the car with her, Muriel drove forward slowly, her window open. Her attention turned to the reporters frantically phoning their editors or calling in their stories live for radio and television. One of the newsmen, microphone in hand, was giving his report just outside her car door.

"Seventeen women reported dead, and scores more wounded," he said, looking straight into the camera. "The race to Jerusalem is on. We've just received reports that the crowds on the Lebanese and Jordanian borders are also crossing over into Israel . . . "

With a sudden roar of the engine, Laurel's bus shot forward, and with the other vehicles following suit, Muriel knew they were on their way. As they sped forward, she heard the sound of singing coming from the convoy of buses, vans and trucks, including her own. The voices were jubilant, loud and clear.

All the people . . . All the people in the world!

CHAPTER 96

REPEATEDLY, ISAAC ATTEMPTED to reach Sheikh Wayani at the Seven Arches Hotel. The Sheikh was not answering his satellite phone or the e-mails Professor Samuels was sending. Isaac was about to call Samuels again, when his phone rang.

"Yes," he answered.

"Colonel Lumina, this is Sharif, Sheikh Wayani's nephew."

"I'm glad you called," Isaac said, "I need to—"

"There is no time, Colonel. I need help fast. My uncle is dead."

As if punched in the gut, Isaac felt the wind leave his body. "Dead?"

"Murdered," Sharif said, his voice shaking. "I found him in his room.

"How was he—?"

"I cannot say over the phone," Sharif stammered. "But no one must know for now. I am stalling the Italian security officials in charge."

Isaac could hear a furious banging on the other end of the line. His gut told him he had better work fast. "I will have agents over immediately. Do not let anyone in until they arrive," he instructed. "They will mention my name, so you can trust them."

It was 4:35 A.M. Everything was moving quickly now. Isaac's main task was to convince Mossad they had a problem. But an even bigger difficulty . . . how to do that without sounding like he had lost his mind.

"Go away." Sharif tried to project a confidence he didn't feel. "My uncle is not to be disturbed."

The pounding on the door continued.

"This is Captain Volpi of the Italian Military Guard. I am in command of security for this conference by the order of Signore Giovanni

Mabus and Senator Balilla. By their authority, I insist upon speaking to Sheikh Wayani. There have been reports that he has been harmed."

"That is ridiculous," Sharif retorted. *How would Volpi know that?* Then it dawned on him. Only someone involved in his uncle's death would have knowledge of his attack. *The Italian Military Guard . . . Volpi had my uncle killed.* Sharif took the small pistol from his side vest. If he needed to, he would use it.

"My uncle is resting," Sharif announced through the door.

He tried to remain calm as he looked over at Sheikh Wayani's lifeless body. Although Sharif was no stranger to beheadings—the government had made it a regular event in Riyadh—to see his own uncle mutilated in such a manner was shocking. To add to the horror, what was written on the wall in his uncle's blood sent a shiver down his spine.

Al-maoot salibi

Death to Crusaders.

Sharif had been his uncle's deputy when Sheikh Wayani had briefly headed the General Intelligence Network—Istakhbarat al Amiyyah—the Saudi espionage and intelligence arm. So it was a shock to Sharif to see *Death to Crusaders* written on the wall. Crusaders was a catch-all word for Christians and other *agnabi*—foreigners. Why would anyone refer to his uncle as such? What disturbed Sharif even more was the signature beneath the message—*Ikhwan.*

Sharif shuddered. *Fedayeen . . .* members of the Ikhwan Brotherhood. Were they behind this act?

The Ikhwan had been silent since Ibn Saud consolidated his power over the sands of Arabia and gave his name to the new kingdom. His victory had been clenched when five thousand Ikhwan were killed at as-Sabalah in 1929, the last battle of the Bedouin era . . . a victory which was followed by a blood-letting rampage of torture, amputation and beheadings. Saudi Arabia, then, had been formed on the death of the Ikhwan.

Now, like a phoenix, have they risen?

Sharif stared once again at the fated words on the wall.

Death to Crusaders.

Whoever wrote it had one very definite purpose in mind—to take an aggressive stance against the Saudi government by killing one of its representatives.

And that could mean only one thing, Sharif realized. There was something bigger in the works, and Lumina and Samuels better find out what it was, and fast.

CHAPTER 97

JARRETT WILLIAMSON hadn't been at all surprised by Professor Samuels' phone call. Of course, Maggie Seline's disappearance had been off the front pages for several weeks, but Jarrett was foremost a cop before he was an FBI agent. Although he hadn't seen Michael since their cryptic conversation about Mabus on the Brooklyn Esplanade, Jarret's intuitive sense connected Mabus with Maggie, which meant Michael was involved.

"When?" Jarret had replied to Samuel's directive to leave for Israel.

"Immediately," was the Professor's response.

It wouldn't be easy, Jarrett realized. The bureau was a hidebound bureaucracy, a massive slow-moving mastodon.

"I've already cleared it with your superiors." Professor Samuels seemed to have anticipated his thought. "There is a C-130 transport headed for Jordan leaving in an hour from Stewart Air Base. You can get to Jerusalem from there."

After the call, Jarret had jumped into his car and sped up the New York Thruway to New Windsor. An escort, waiting at the base gate when he arrived, whisked him to a massive C-130J Hercules aircraft which was already on the runway, its four massive turboprop engines idling. The soldiers and marines on board barely took notice of him.

All to his liking.

Now, hours later, listening to the steady roar of the engine as they flew over the Atlantic, Jarret sat with his laptop studying the files he had downloaded from Professor Samuels. It was all falling into place.

Mabus' Peace Conference. The Einsof energy patents. Maggie Seline's disappearance. And now this flight maneuver involving the Israeli Air Force.

Even with all that Jarrett had learned about the Professor and his involvement with a secret Masonic order, he was impressed at how quickly

Samuels and this ad hoc collection of visionaries had managed to detect and decipher such a complex scheme.

"Agent Williamson."

Jarrett turned to find the flight navigator tappping his shoulder.

"We have a message for you." The navigator then handed him a change order marked URGENT.

> *I've coordinated with CENTCOM. No time for you to land in Jordan. Your flight is proceeding to Basis Hayil-HaAvir Ramon Air Base southwest of Beersheba, Israel. Contact Colonel Lumina in Jerusalem ASAP.*
>
> *Samuels*

"I don't know what this is about, but for CENTCOM to re-route us to Israel, it must be some serious shit," the navigator said, raising his eyebrows in amazement. When Jarrett did not respond, the man's tone turned more official. "Our radio man will connect you to Jerusalem right away, sir."

Jarret understood that moving quickly was crucial. Samuels would never use his connections at CENTCOM unless it meant there was no time left for idling.

Antsy, Jarrett looked at his watch . . . a little after 5 A.M. Still two hours away from their destination.

CHAPTER 98

M AGGIE AND AHMIN moved quietly down the still dark and lonely Souk el-Dabbagha that led to the Holy Sepulchre. Maggie had called Father Luciano, a Franciscan priest who lived in the church, only the day before. A friend of Professor Samuels, she had been introduced to him a year earlier when in Jerusalem. During that time, she developed a friendship with the old priest, who told her classic tales of infighting among the Christian sects in the Sepulchre that had her both shaking her head and reeling with laughter.

Her visit to the famed church this time would not be for amusement or lectures on its history. Still, Maggie was anticipating Father Luciano's help. He had assured her he would be the one in charge of unlocking the door with the Muslim gatekeeper.

When she and Ahmin arrived at the Sepulchre's front entrance, Maggie peered at her watch. It was 5:23 A.M. The gatekeeper would be arriving soon. Barely a minute later, as they waited in the shadows, Maggie heard the sound of voices. Her heart skipped a beat when she saw a couple walking toward the church.

"It seems not everyone's aware the church is closed today," Maggie whispered nervously.

"I suppose not," Ahmin answered, his voice low. "Just play along with me."

Play along? Before Maggie knew it, Ahmin was stepping out of the shadows with her on his heels.

Just then, Ahmin's friend Walid appeared, meeting up with the couple as they reached the front of the church.

"Good morning. Are we in time for the opening?" the man asked Walid.

Wearing a suit and tie, the man was dressed rather formally for someone walking around at five-thirty in the morning. The leggy blonde he was with, wearing a tight-fitting black dress and heels seemed a bit overdone as well. But who was she to wonder, Maggie mused. She only hoped the porter would send them both packing.

"I'm so sorry," Walid said, "but the Sepulchre is not opening today."

"Oh." The man, a snooty tycoon sort turned toward his modelesque female companion. "I knew you had it wrong. The guide said they'd be closed because of all the brouhaha over this Peace Conference."

"Peace Conference," she said, turning up a long, slender nose at the idea. "People have lives to live."

"Well, my good sir, since we are here, would you be so kind as to let us in for a quick look?" the man broached. He removed his wallet from his jacket and peeled off a fifty dollar bill.

Unmoved, Walid shook his head. "No. I'm sorry, but it's not possible."

Maggie sensed he was feeling as warmly toward the couple as she was.

"The Church is not open today," Walid said firmly.

"Then why are *they* here?" the woman whined, shifting her eyes toward Maggie and Ahmin.

"Construction."

"Cleaning."

Answering at the same time, Maggie and Ahmin turned toward each other.

"Construction?" the tycoon inquired, his tone suspicious. "So early?"

Ahmin grabbed the shovel and Maggie the broom that were leaning against the side of the church.

Walid jumped in. "Yes, my construction and cleaning crews have begun to arrive."

The couple, apparently made for each other, sneered at Maggie, Ahmin, and Walid but made no show of leaving.

Modern man meets ancient history, Maggie thought.

A moment later, a small section of the door flew open. Through the portal, Maggie could see the folds of priestly garments that she recognized to be Franciscan. *Father Luciano.* She breathed a sigh of relief when, out of the basilica's doorframe, she saw a ladder being passed down to the porter.

Walid grabbed hold of the ladder and lowered it down to the ground. He then proceeded to perform the unlocking ritual, opening the lock on the lower part of the door and then using the ladder to climb up and unlock the second latch. After descending to the ground, Walid then opened the right-hand part of the door.

The two tourists watched as Maggie walked past them to enter.

"She is the supervisor of the cleaning crew," Walid informed the couple. "Wonderful person. The priests will have no other clean the Sepulchre."

The couple's whole demeanor changed as they watched Maggie entering the church. In a matter of moments, her stature had risen from mere housekeeper to that of holy purifier. All the while, Maggie hoped neither one of them would take note that the cleaning woman was wearing a pair of Gucci loafers.

As sacred holder of the broom and dustpan, Maggie thought she was entering the Sepulchre rather appropriately.

Ah, if the boys at the Times could see me now.

"Remember not to forget . . . " Ahmin smiled, shovel in hand.

With the curious, stunned couple still standing nearby, Maggie raised her eyebrows in alarm, thinking Ahmin was about to say something about the jewels or her task.

"Don't forget," he cautioned, pointing to the object in her hand. "Your broom. Last time you left it in inside, and it took us a whole day to get it out again."

Finally, looking resigned to the fact they were being denied entry, the couple began strolling away from the church.

Ahmin waited until they were out of earshot before walking over to the door.

"The last stone," Maggie sighed, feeling like the weight of the world was being lifted off her shoulders.

"Hurry," Ahmin whispered. "I'll be waiting right here for you."

He gave Maggie's hand a loving squeeze and pulled the door shut.

Michael Sonada, having barely slept, waited impatiently for Gerta to arrive. When she finally clamored down the steps, she motioned him to follow and led him down a long corridor that ended in front of a tall wooden door. Gerta then selected two keys from her ring. First she unlocked the door with one and then used the second key to open the wrought-metal gate just behind it. Michael peered into the opening ahead. A narrow passage in the rock was leading away from the Hospice.

Gerta took two flashlights off a shelf beside the door. "We will need these."

Once they were both inside the tunnel, she pulled the wooden door closed and shone her light at Michael's feet. "Sensible shoes. I like that."

Michael felt a bit of his tension subsiding. *Finally, some female approval.*

His eyes followed the beams of the flashlight as they walked forward through the passage. *How could this even be?* he wondered. In the next instant, it dawned on him.

The cisterns! The network of underground tunnels and pools were used millennia ago for transporting and storing water. He knew of their existence, of course, but had never been inside them. Michael had been told that, in this particular area of the city, they had been blocked long ago. *This tunnel must be a part of them.* Astonished, he found it hard to believe there was a passageway that actually led directly into the Sepulchre.

As Michael's eyes probed the darkness, he found the man-made tunnels reminding him of the catacombs in Rome. Although he knew of no history of the tunnels in Jerusalem ever being used for mass hiding or burial, the effect on his psyche was proving to be similar. Fascination was turning to claustrophobia. Feeling a nervous sweat building on his neck, Michael hoped their sojourn through the labyrinth would soon be over.

Gerta did not seem to notice his discomfort. She walked ahead, covering the rough ground with the steady gait of a sailor, rocking from side to side, barely fitting through the passage at times. Meanwhile, Michael noticed, they were angling slightly downward. Once the ground leveled off again, they continued ahead for about another fifty feet, before taking a sharp turn to the left. At that point, the walls widened and Gerta stopped, shining her light on the ceiling above.

"We are beneath the Convent of St. Charalampos," Gerta remarked, commanding his attention. "We don't have much further to go."

They continued down the passage, following it to a set of stairs cut into the rock. Gerta led the way up the thirty or so steps to a small landing. There, a sturdy iron gate blocked their passage.

Gerta again produced her large key ring. The oldest and most formidable looking of the them opened the gate, which swung toward them easily.

"Further down the tunnel you will find yet another set of stairs," Gerta said. "They will lead you up to the *Inventio Crucis Chapel.* Colonel Lumina said you are familiar with the church."

Michael nodded.

"He also said you are on a mission of great importance." Shining the beam of her flashlight onto Michael's face, she studied him. "Yes, I believe you have serious business about you tonight that concerns us all. God bless you and provide you with the protection you provide others."

As he stepped through the gate, Michael was certain he was not the first to use the ancient passageway as a means of entry or escape. He turned and without uttering a word, he looked into Gerta's eyes, realizing he was now part of her lineage, a lineage that guarded the secret of the Sepulchre.

Chapter 99

INSIDE THE CHURCH, Father Ramiel was waiting. He had received his instructions the previous day. That woman, Seline, was coming and he was to escort her through the Sepulchre. He had been whisked from his minor post in the Vatican library to assume his new position as replacement for Father Vitale Luciano. Bishop Rudolf had made himself clear. Ramiel's task would be simple, and he was to complete it without question.

For the Roman Catholic Church, sometimes we must tend to delicate matters with an iron fist, he thought.

It was high time, too. He loathed the way the others, the Egyptians and Greeks, the Syrians and Ethiopians had looked upon him with smiling disdain. Who were these men, but members of splintered-off sects? It was only the Catholic Church, founded by Christ's greatest disciple, Peter, that should have authority over the sacred site of his death. *These others, tolerated for so many years!* How Father Luciano put up with it for so long was beyond Ramiel's comprehension.

Still, his instructions were clear. Maggie Seline was stirring up too much sympathy. The grief she was causing to certain factions and benefactors connected with the Catholic Church would no longer be tolerated. Yet, although her ideas regarding Jerusalem had caused many of the elders in the Church to become distressed, His Holiness had not spoken out against her in any way.

A weak position, Father Ramiel observed. Such weakness had no place within the pontiff's office.

At least there were those such as Bishop Rudolf and himself who would protect the Church's interests and take matters into their own hands when necessary. It was bad enough they had to share this holiest of churches, this most sacred ground, with lesser religious orders, but the possibility that the Holy Sepulchre might be under United Nations auspices one day—included within an international city—was nothing less than sacrilege! The tumultuous uprising it would cause within the Sepulchre would make things even more dangerous than they already were. Who could tell where the power would fall?

Ramiel had also come to another conclusion. *There is no reason why the Temple should not be built.* After all, it was stated in prophecy that the Lord Christ would come when the Temple was once again erected in Jerusalem.

And no one, especially no *woman*, should get in the way of God's word.

Upon entering the Church, Maggie found she was standing in a dark entranceway. As she was allowing her eyes to adjust, a movement to her right made her turn. Silently, a robed figure stepped out of the shadows.

Maggie saw immediately that it wasn't her Franciscan friend. Surprised, she didn't know what to say to the strange priest now standing before her.

Smiling at her, he stepped closer. "Your friend, Father Luciano, fell ill. I am Father Ramiel. I've been sent here to the Sepulchre to replace him until his return or . . . ," the priest said, his voice trailing off, "well, at least until further arrangements can be made."

"What sort of illness?" Maggie asked, concerned.

"Actually, I am uncertain. I assure you he is being treated by one of the Vatican's finest physicians. But please," Ramiel said, his tone patronizing though polite. "I know you are here for a specific task."

The priest eyed her knowingly, as if aware of what she was seeking. Confused, Maggie was uncertain how to reply. *Is this priest, like Father Luciano, part of the Way?*

Father Ramiel gestured for her to follow him. He led her past the Stone of Unction, where Christ's body had been anointed before his burial. Peering upward, she saw that behind the stone, a mosaic illustrated the aftermath of Christ's crucifixion—the removal of his body from the cross, its anointment and preparation for burial, and the placement of his body in the burial tomb. Looking closely, Maggie saw a skull at the foot of the cross on the left side of the mosaic. *A depiction of the legend.* Christ was said to have been crucified on the spot of Adam's burial.

"Father, are you taking me to the Rock of Golgotha now?" Maggie realized they had just past the stairs they needed to climb to reach the site.

"Yes, but first there is something you must see," Ramiel insisted. "Come this way to the Inventio Crucis Chapel. Professor Samuels instructed me."

Maggie came to a stop. "The Professor?" She couldn't believe her ears. "But I thought—"

"He survived his ordeal, thank God, and is very much alive," Father Ramiel assured her. "His main concern is for your protection and for that which you hold."

Maggie felt relieved just hearing the Professor's name. The fact that he had contacted Father Ramiel made her feel that she could trust the priest. "You speak as if you know much, Father."

"My dear Ms. Seline, I know very little. I am but a humble servant of *the Way* at your disposal."

Feeling more at ease, Maggie began to wonder. "So, what is it the Professor wants me to see?"

"A special place, beneath the Chapel."

"Yes, I've heard of another room, but . . . "

"More even beyond that."

Quite curious now, Maggie found it hard to imagine. "You mean more rooms?"

"And more tunnels. Where the sacred relics were held . . . relics that the Templars themselves had unearthed nearly a thousand years ago . . . "

Maggie allowed herself to be swayed. *If Professor Samuels wants me to see this . . .*

She felt the pouch secured at her side, relieved the priest seemed to know something about her task. Still, Maggie had to admit, she felt a bit wary. Better to follow reservedly. Besides, the Sepulchre was closed, and whatever this priest wanted to show her would not take long to see. She would then ask for a moment alone to pray at Golgotha, the site of Christ's crucifixion, and lay the last foundation stone.

As they were passing the Chapel of Adam, Ramiel stopped suddenly. He turned toward the apse and made the sign of the cross. "That fissure was created by the earthquake that occurred when Christ died," he said.

As Maggie stared at the crack in the rock, she felt seized by a magnetic force. *Golgotha . . . Calvary*. It was directly above her.

They moved down the dark corridor, passing another chapel, until they reached a set of steps. Maggie followed Ramiel down them, marveling at the etchings of tiny Crusader crosses, carved throughout the ages, that filled the walls.

Then, when they entered St. Helena's Chapel, the whole atmosphere changed. Wafts of incense swirled eerily through the dimly lit room. The strange dichotomy in energy made her wonder. Otherwise a dazzling spectacle filled with brass lamps and chandeliers, the chapel gave her a sense of foreboding. Maggie scurried across the mosaic floor, the light tapping of her feet the only sound breaking the silence.

Father Ramiel was waiting for her by another series of steps. "Now to the old cistern," he said as he began leading the way down, "to the Inventio Crucis Chapel."

When they arrived at the lower landing, Ramiel's eyes were glowing. "Where we are standing now is the very place where Helena, the Emperor Constantine's mother, found part of the true cross of Christ."

The chapel was dark . . . darker than the previous. Brass lamps hanging down from the high arched ceiling cast a ghostly light across the floor.

Father Ramiel knelt at the altar and prayed. After a moment, he got up and walked toward her. Without saying a word, he led her to another set of stairs.

I don't believe this, Maggie thought. She had heard there was another level, but this was truly remarkable.

"It is dark," Ramiel said. "Let me light a lamp." He struck a match and lit a lantern that was sitting on a stand next to the stairs. Ramiel then walked toward an old grated-iron gate and took a key out from the pocket of his upper vestment. Unlocking the gate, he nodded toward her.

Maggie felt a fluttering of excitement as they descended the stairs, venturing deeper into the cavern. Their small lantern provided just enough light. Its flame flickering, it threw dancing shadows across the cavern walls.

As Father Ramiel led her further through the passage, Maggie noted a small iron fence running along their left, signs of the cross intertwined within the iron bars. Finally, they came to another hollow within the tunnel that seemed to be leading to yet another dark descent.

This can't be. "It goes down further?"

"Yes, there is more to see." Ramiel beckoned her to move forward.

"It looks so black down there," Maggie said as she peered down into the darkness. Instinctively, she took a step backward. "I really need to get to Golgotha now."

While holding the lantern at his side, Father Ramiel positioned himself beside her, a submissive bent to his posture. "Of course," he said, his tone now yielding.

In the flickering light, Maggie could barely see the thin line of his smile.

Ramiel then turned to lead them back out of the room. "Watch your step," he cautioned.

Maggie followed tentatively. Father Ramiel's shadow darkened the area in front of her, and she could barely see her own feet.

"Put your hand on my shoulder as you walk," Ramiel insisted.

With the light so dim, Maggie saw no other way. At least he could guide her. Just then, she felt a breeze stream through the cavern behind her, as if a door had suddenly opened. Before she could turn back, the lantern went out.

"Father. Father Ramiel."

Silence and darkness. The priest did not answer.

Maggie reached out in front of her but could feel nothing. "Father, where are you?"

The hiss was steady, like someone drawing air through a straw. She soon saw it was a cigarette lighter that had been flicked open. Expecting to see Father Ramiel, Maggie found, instead, another face illuminated by the flame.

Just then, Father Ramiel stepped into the lighted area, next to the man who was now peering directly at her. After taking the lighter from the shadowy figure, Ramiel lit his lantern once again.

"Father Ramiel, your services are no longer needed here," the man said as he continued to stare.

As the glow from the lantern brightened, Maggie caught her breath.

"Guard the main door," he said. "Make sure that none of Ms. Seline's friends find their way in."

Nodding in obedience, Ramiel bowed and began to climb the stairs.

When he was finally gone, Maggie found herself standing alone in the underground labyrinth.

With Giovanni Mabus.

Just outside the front entrance to the Sepulchre, Ahmin waited nervously. *Where is she? It's been nearly a half hour.* As the minutes ticked away, Ahmin tried to dismiss his concerns. Maggie was probably talking with the priest and taking more time in the church than initially planned.

But the gnawing fear growing in the pit of his stomach told him otherwise. Instinctively, he grabbed hold of Walid's arm. "I'm going in," he said.

Walid frowned. "You told me this might take ten minutes, no more. I cannot stand here on guard with the Sepulchre door unlocked, with you—"

"Lock it behind me," Ahmin directed as he opened the door.

"What?" Walid's jaw dropped.

"I said lock it and don't let anyone out unless it's me or Maggie." Without waiting for a reply, Ahmin slipped into the Sepulchre, closing the massive wooden door behind him.

Ahmin allowed his eyes to adjust to the dim lighting. It had been so long since he had visited the church that he needed to get his bearings. Then he remembered the stairs that led up to the Greek Chapel which had been built over Golgotha. As he turned toward his right to make his way up the steps, he felt the brunt of a hard object as it hit him on his upper arm. He fell backwards onto the floor, holding his arm in pain. As he attempted to get back to his feet, Ahmin was shocked to see who had struck him so forcefully.

A priest!

His eyes like a wild animal's, the priest was advancing toward Ahmin, ready to swing the iron bar in his hand once again.

Ahmin gritted his teeth and lunged forward. Seizing the man by the legs, Ahmin brought him down hard onto the floor. He then grabbed hold of the iron bar, battling the priest, until he was able to wrestle it out of his hands.

No longer holding a weapon, the priest scurried across the floor on his knees before lifting himself to his feet. Ahmin gripped him from behind, wrapping his arm around the man's neck.

"One false move," Ahmin warned, touching the iron bar to the priest's face, "and this comes crashing down on your skull."

Upon the threat, the frightened man stopped struggling.

"You're not Father Luciano, are you?" Ahmin was nearly choking him now.

"No," the priest blurted as he gasped for air. "I'm Ramiel."

"Tell me where Maggie is?" Ahmin insisted.

"You do not know what you are dealing with," Ramiel sputtered. "This Maggie Seline has brought the will of God upon herself. Anyone who defies the supreme authority of the Catholic Church—"

"What are you talking about? What's going on here is not the supreme will of God or the Catholic Church." Ahmin tightened his grip on Ramiel's throat. With the rage in him welling, he felt as if he could snap the priest's neck in two. "Now tell me where she is, or you'll feel the supreme will of Ahmin."

Ramiel acquiesced. "Past Helena . . . down to the True Cross," he said, between thin rasping breaths, "there's a gate . . . down stairs . . . a room."

With one long gasp, Ramiel went limp. Ahmin dragged him behind a thick drape along the wall, hiding his body from view.

Steadily, Michael moved through the cisterns, an old flashlight his only source of illumination. The torch had dimmed considerably since his sojourn began at Johanniter's Hospice, only adding to his troubles. Stumbling over loose rocks was now a commonplace occurrence, leaving his hands scratched and raw from grabbing at the rough walls while attempting to save himself from falling.

The shadows and uncertainty were catching up with him now as every bend in the cavern only led him into further darkness. His will weakened, he made himself remember. *Maggie.* The thought of her gave him strength. He rallied his resolve and pushed forward.

Finally, it looked as if his painful efforts were about to come to an end. A dim light was shining through an opening in the passageway ahead.

As he drew closer, Michael slowed his steps.

The silhouette of a man fell across the cavern floor.

CHAPTER 100

"SO WE MEET in the bowels of your beloved Jerusalem, Ms. Seline." As Mabus spoke, the lantern's light cast an eerie glow across his face.

At that moment, a flashlight turned on behind her. A large looming figure of a man stepped out from the dark portal where Maggie had just been standing with Ramiel. He planted himself underneath the cavern arch and blocked the tunnel entrance.

Maggie looked toward the exit behind Mabus that led back up to St. Helena's Chapel. She would have to knock him aside to escape. *Not likely*, she realized, as she stood trapped now on both ends.

"What is it that you want?" Maggie demanded, the crack in her voice betraying her fear.

"What I want, Ms. Seline, is for you to *shut up*."

The harshness of Mabus' tone made Maggie's blood quicken.

"Naïve optimists like yourself like to rile the public with Peter Pan philosophies that have no chance in hell of being realized. Your gibberish only succeeds in delaying the inevitable. This world is fueled by power and money. *Power and money*, Ms. Seline, not compassion and wisdom. While you dream, the world continues to run, and the powerful proceed to control your fate." Mabus eyed her as if assessing her very being. "Let's just say that for those of us who make the world turn, people like you are a liability."

Maggie's heart raced with both fear and aggression. Instinctively, she gripped the velvet pouch at her side. "You're wrong," she challenged. "It's only those who are truly spiritual who have actual power. Your power is short-lived. You offer nothing lasting to this world . . . nothing that heightens a man's spirit or leaves the world a better place."

She heard a noise behind her. Mabus' gorilla-like bodyguard had taken several steps toward her, obviously intending to end her reverie.

"No." Mabus held a hand up, a wry smile on his face. "Let her finish."

As the insidious-looking man retreated back to his post in front of the cavern, Maggie turned back toward Mabus. "You and the men you work with kill for profit. You deceive, exploit, terrorize, and demoralize, all to make an extra dime on a gallon of gas. You think nothing of all the suffering you've caused—the human tragedy." Maggie's voice began to tremble, not from fear, but from the power of her passion. "You're like a bunch of hungry ghosts starving for profit. You can make millions, but it's never enough. Even if people are starving and dying before your very eyes, you're so damn greedy you basically just don't give a shit just as long as you get yours."

Mabus stood silently for a moment, grinning. He began to clap slowly. "Bravo. Most definitely, bravo. I can see why you have so many supporters. You're quite a speaker, Ms. Seline. It's no wonder you've gotten as far as you have. But unfortunately for you, you're too much like your father. I'm afraid his sympathies for the underdog caused him a lack of judgment that proved rather unfortunate as I recall."

A fire began to rage inside of her at the mention of her father. David Seline had tried so hard to be fair to both sides, to reveal the tragedy the Arab community—Mabus' own people—had been facing. Just then, the thought streaked through her mind.

My God! P2 . . . Mabus!

"What are you saying?" Maggie's breathing quickened. "Did you have something to do with my father's death?"

"You make things so personal, Ms. Seline—or should I say Maggie at this point. I believe we're getting to know each other rather well in this little meeting of ours." Mabus then took out a pistol. Although he didn't point it at her, he examined its shiny black surface before meeting her eyes again. "Take out the personal, Maggie, and replace it with the impersonal. *Collateral damage.* Yes, that's the term. In a war, there is always collateral damage."

"My father was not at war with anyone."

"Oh, but he was. Your father's articles stirred quite a lot of trouble for us. You could say he was doing what journalists are supposed to do, but unfortunately for him he was a bit of a dinosaur. Our present league of reporters knows better. And the real absurdity of it all is that your father didn't even know he was combating something much more than terrorism among religious fools. His was a dangerous battle with a far greater power. The brotherhood of Propaganda Due is one that encompasses the globe—officials on all levels of government from countless countries, many with interests that they are unwilling to have compromised. These are men who have funded the overthrow of governments to assure that their own businesses are secure. Do you believe for one moment that your father had a chance in hell against such a formidable enemy?" Mabus' pause emphasized his question. "Unfortunately for David Seline, he seemed to believe it. In the end, Maggie, your father caused his own death."

Maggie now saw where all this was leading. Mabus would kill her as well, before she could complete her task. Filled with anguish, she realized that the vision of the *new Jerusalem*—the promise of peace among the peoples of the world—might not come to pass.

"So now I will take the last foundation stone." Mabus nodded toward his brutish guard as he approached her. "You can rest assured, Maggie, it will be kept well."

Just then, the jolting sound of a crash made her spin. Mabus' cohort was being sucked back into the dark cavern, his flashlight clattering onto the ground.

In the dark bowels of the Sepulchre, Michael had used his failing torch as a weapon, hitting the man blocking the tunnel entrance and knocking him down to the dirt floor. It was then he recognized who it was. Khan, Raciam Heloff's guard, who had held him captive in Nepal. Working quickly, Michael grabbed the side arm from Khan's holster. A moment later, with the ogre's body crumbled like a heap behind him, Michael stepped into the cavern opening.

Mabus wasted no time. He pointed his pistol straight at Maggie. Michael, in turn, aimed his at Mabus.

"Now, isn't this a sight?" Mabus said contemptuously. "It seems it's time for a reunion, Michael, or should I say a showdown."

"It's time for you to drop your pistol," Michael commanded flatly.

"You're in no position to give orders," Mabus rebuked. "All I have to do is squeeze the trigger."

Michael held Mabus' gaze even though his hand was beginning to tremble. He knew he couldn't take the chance that Mabus might make good on his threat. Although he felt his finger itching to pull the trigger, Michael gritted his teeth and dropped the gun.

"Now, kick it over to the other side of the room," Mabus ordered.

Michael brought his foot back and gave a swift kick, propelling the gun against the cavern wall.

"Good. Now come here and join your charming comrade."

Michael walked over to Maggie's side. Even in their present dire circumstance, he felt comforted to be near her.

"There is only one thing I hate almost as much as bleeding heart idealists, and that is a man who lets a woman take the lead."

Michael felt the lance in its holder under his vest. He had never had the feeling that he could kill a man. *Until now.*

"So what are you waiting for? You have us here. Kill us then," Michael taunted.

"Ever the expedient one. My man, Khan, over there is built like a mastodon. He will soon rouse from the unconscious state he's in, perhaps with a bit of a headache, but with the very clear intention of killing you both. I'll leave him his pleasures."

Mabus, stilling pointing the pistol at them, moved closer. "Now, Michael, you will give me the Longinus Spear." He leveled the gun at Michael's head. "Slowly that is, very slowly."

As Michael opened up his vest and took the sheathed lance out from his belt holder, a burning anguish gripped his heart. All the while, Mabus' ruthless sneer was cutting.

"You see, Michael," Mabus decreed, "power always finds its way back into the hands of those who command it."

Reluctantly, Michael extended his hand, feeling the pulse of the Spear's pure energy about to leave him.

Then like a forceful gust, an unfamiliar man rushed into the room. He slammed directly into Mabus, knocking him down to the ground.

"Ahmin!" Maggie yelled.

A shot rang out, missing Ahmin by inches. He managed to grab Mabus' arm and started banging it on the floor in an attempt to dislodge the gun from his grip.

"Stay back." Michael sensed Maggie was about to rush forward and grabbed her by the shoulder. No sooner had he done so, than he saw Ahmin give Mabus a hard blow to the stomach. With the wind knocked out of him, the gun fell from Mabus' hand.

Michael felt overwhelmed by the same urge he had experienced only moments before. In one quick motion, he unsheathed the Spear and dashed across the room. He saw the blade, could feel the power in his hands, and knew that with one incisive plunge he could gut a treacherous fiend . . . a deceitful spirit whose intent was not to create peace but destroy it.

"Michael! No!" Maggie was screaming now.

Her desperate plea made him stop abruptly, the point of the Spear inches from Mabus' side.

"No, Michael, please." She touched his shoulder. "He's unarmed now. We have him."

Michael stared into the dark tunnel of Mabus' eyes. Gripped again by sanity, he understood he could not kill the man, even though Mabus most certainly deserved it. "You'll have a higher price to pay when this is over," Michael whispered caustically. He then took a few steps back and resheathed the Spear.

Ahmin already had a pistol leveled directly at Mabus, whose face was now frozen in a stern grimace.

The grimace of defeat.

Maggie eyed the corner of the room and hastened across to retrieve the other pistol.

"Maggie, you must go," Ahmin directed as she handed the weapon to him. "Go and lay the last stone." Michael noticed Ahmin wasn't looking at her as he spoke, but staring directly at him as if to say *please take care of her.*

Michael understood and nodded.

"Hurry!" Maggie said, barely turning as she took off ahead of him.

Chapter 101

SITTING ON THE TARMAC at Saudi Arabia's Al Dhafra Air Base, Squadron Leader Captain Russell Dwiggins was pondering the curious order he had received that morning from CENTCOM Air Operations Center:

> Today the Israeli Air Force, under the command of their squadron leader, Captain Adam Zayin, will participate in the joint maneuver with Saudi and U.S. forces. I thank you for your professional attitude and total commitment to the successful completion of our mission.
>
> General Robert Gerard
> CENTCOM Air Operations Center
> Al Udeid Air Base, Qatar

Dwiggins had never been a part of such a joint exercise before. *Why the hell didn't those bastards at CENTCOM tell me about this sooner,* he thought.

Israelis, Saudis and Americans. Dwiggins shook his head in disbelief. If there was anything more bizarre than these countries working together on tactical procedures, Dwiggins was hard pressed to figure it out.

The flickering lights on his panel signaled that the first stage of the exercise was about to commence, and the Wing 25 Israeli air fleet would soon leave the Negev. Dwiggins had been assured that air flight control was thorough in coordinating the joint mission.

Yet, a silent alarm was going off in his brain. The unprecedented maneuvers were putting his nerves on edge.

Just one glitch, one false move . . .

Dwiggins shuddered at the consequence.

Captain Adam Zayin of the Israeli Air Force sat motionless in the cockpit of his F-16 Sufa fighter plane. In front of him stretched a three thousand-meter runway, and to his right, the sullen Makhtesh Ramon mountain range rose menacingly from the Negev Desert.

My ancestors have placed me in this position, Zayin thought. His own father had bombed Beirut to nothingness in 1982 when Zayin was just a child and his father was still his hero. It was then that he decided he would continue the family's proud tradition, finally making good on that vow years later in 2006 by bombing Beirut and the rest of Lebanon back to the Stone Age.

But that was neither here nor there, he realized. Today would be the biggest turning point of his career, and he had Giovanni Mabus to thank for it.

Zayin's association with Mabus dated to the late 1990s when Zayin served a term in Brussels as military attaché in the Israeli Mission at the European Union. Quite by accident, Zayin had thought, he one day found himself sharing an elevator with Mabus at the Italian consulate.

"You could always come to work for me, Captain," Mabus invited.

"I'm flattered Mr. Mabus." Indeed, Zayin was, to put it mildly. "I wouldn't be of much use to you, though, I'm sure."

"To the contrary, Lockheed Martin and Raytheon both do considerable business with your government." Mabus fixed his cool eyes on Zayin who did his best to return the stare. "I have sizable holdings in both those firms."

Zayin took a moment to consider the implications. Before he could answer, the elevator came to a stop.

"I will be in touch." Mabus nodded as he exited into the lobby.

And he was. The following weekend Mabus invited him to his estate outside the city.

"I'm facing a difficult choice, my friend. I want to purchase a new car, but I cannot decide between the Lamborghini, the Ferrari or the Porsche. So, I thought, who better to make the decision than a fighter pilot."

Presented with the invitation to drive all three vehicles, Zayin definitely enjoyed the opportunity to make the choice. Even pretending to wade in Mabus' lavish lifestyle was a pleasurable pastime. Zayin then decided his own inclination, had he the fortune to acquire one, would be to purchase the Porsche. He presented his suggestion to Mabus.

"No, I'm not sure I agree with your conclusion," Mabus stated, smiling easily. "Let's drive the cars some more."

Their tête-à-têtes went on for nearly three months, by which time Zayin was more comfortable in one hundred thousand dollar cars than in the tiny Fiat the embassy provided him. He also became sufficiently at ease with Mabus and his friends, including an Italian banker, Giuseppe Volpi, who seemed to be a regular guest himself. At a meeting between the three one weekend at Mabus' estate, Zayin was given his final rite of passage.

"You cannot continue, Captain." Volpi was in a feverish state.

"But we must." Zayin enjoyed arguing with Volpi, whose crude disposition insisted upon things being black or white. "We have no choice."

"You cannot continue," Volpi repeated. He set his brandy down firmly, giving Mabus a furtive glance as the latter poured himself more Evian. Volpi then turned his gaze back to Zayin. "You do have a choice. Israel has a choice. It is the Arabs who have none."

"What would that choice be then? Lay down our arms, surrender the West Bank or invade Syria and Iran?" Zayin had grown tired of the same old simpleton theories always offered, of course, by those unfamiliar with the region's complexities.

"Even better," Mabus said, his soft tone soothing Zayin's mind, "turn your back on oil."

Zayin cocked his head at the statement.

"Alternative energy is the ultimate weapon against the Arabs. Their whole economy is built on sand, and that sand floats on oil. Remove the value of the oil and they slip back into the desert . . . back to the scorpions, lizards and their goat hair tents."

Mabus' eyes bore into Zayin's as he continued. "When you flatten three generations of Palestinians under a ton of concrete and steel, all you get in return is every member of their family sworn to revenge for another generation. That is applying the work of Malthus to the creation of terrorists—a bizarre evolutionary paradigm."

"No escape," Volpi chimed at Zayin, appearing more agitated now. "Your battle isn't winnable. You fight *Hydra*, sooner or later the monster will swallow your little nation."

Mabus leaned forward, motioning almost imperceptibly with his forefinger at Volpi, but Zayin missed nothing.

"Any fool can see that killing ten Arabs for every Israeli has only spread a regional squabble in 1947 to today's worldwide conflict. We could argue indefinitely about the path forward—whether that includes peace plans or the annihilation of Syria, Iran and Pakistan." Mabus settled back in his chair. "What we are saying, Captain Zayin, is that we have a plan that will bring us all a much more palpable result. The only loser is OPEC. Let me explain."

"Captain Zayin, do you read? Over."

"Copy," Zayin relayed back to the air traffic control tower.

"Proceed to your destination. Good luck."

Beneath him, the jet engine roared to full strength as Zayin inched the throttle of the F-16 forward. But only he knew the true nature of their mission. Even his two wing mates, Yabraoth and Schtarker, did not fully comprehend the plan or its details. The former followed the captain out of blind loyalty, the latter merely to earn his million dollar payment. Such was the world of men at arms, unchanged since dawn.

Once Wing 25 was in flight, the three pilots would manually override the mission program and enter new coordinates. They would separate from the rest of the squadron moments before striking their targets. First, the oil refineries at al-Ghawar, then al-Jabayl, and lastly they would sink any oil tankers passing through the Strait of Hormuz before entering Iranian air space.

The plan was brilliant.

The first ever flight drill involving American, Saudi and Israeli planes would be a scene filled with confusion. Real alarms would be masked as part of the maneuvers.

Shades of 9/11.

Afterwards, the Iranians would be expecting three Israeli defectors to enter their air space, and in return for safe passage, Iran would get three brand new Sufa fighters. Schtarker would find contentment with his million dollars, and Yabraoth would be satisfied to have taken part in a great secret conspiracy orchestrated by Mossad. At least, that is what Zayin had led him to believe.

And finally . . . and also gratefully, Zayin himself would be free of the onerous burden of following in his hero father's footsteps.

The great Colonel Gilad Zayin had been a wing leader in the infamous Israeli air strike against Iraq's Osirak nuclear reactor at al-Tuwaitha in 1981. At the time, Zayin had seen his father as the greatest of heroes and worshipped his aggressive leadership.

But the years took more of a toll than Zayin could have imagined. His father, the staunch colonel, softened. Israel's bombing of Lebanon in 2006 totally devastated the old man. The iron will that Adam Zayin had tried to emulate his entire life wilted like a wet sponge, and his father's once great vision became hopelessly cloudy. Soon the colonel was available for every kook with a pen or microphone who wanted a witness to Israel's obsession with death and destruction.

When he thought that his shame could get no worse, Zayin then saw his father commit the ultimate treason. Gilad Zayin joined forces with Isaac and Muriel Lumina, the leaders of ONE—One Land, One People, One God.

One huge travesty!

Zayin found his father's preoccupation with peace between Jews and Arabs sickening and had not spoken to the old man since.

But now, Captain Adam Zayin's actions would speak for themselves, and Israel would finally be free. The Saudi bank that payrolled Hamas, Hezbollah and the Intifada was about to make its final transaction.

The Saudis will destroy their own oil fields. Israeli bombs would trigger Petroleum Scorched Earth, with some help from Mabus' man inside Riyadh.

Zayin clutched the plane's pressure-sensitive throttle harder. In a few moments BITS—the Built-In-Test-System—would complete its survey of the hundreds of controls necessary to propel him forward and airborne.

Zayin was ready.

I will accomplish what you lack the resolve for, Father.

CHAPTER 102

MAGGIE RUSHED UP the stairs to the pinnacle of Golgotha with Michael running closely behind her. Out of breath, she entered the Katholikon—the Greek Orthodox Chapel. Ornate, majestic, palatial, *and maybe even a bit gaudy*, Maggie had to admit she still found it mesmerizing.

Dazzling brilliantly, a huge, multi-tiered chandelier was hanging down from the high ceiling. And all around them, lights and oil lamps were creating an inviting warm glow within the otherwise reserved and formal setting.

"Take a look at that," Michael said as he pointed up toward the domed ceiling.

Maggie arched her head until she saw the circular mosaic of Christ, beams of sunlight splaying across its surface.

Illumination. She allowed it to fill her. Although Maggie's body was urging her forward, her mind was now keeping a different pace. *The final stone, and the circuit will be complete.* She called over her shoulder to Michael. "This way. We can reach part of the rock of Golgotha under the altar."

Maggie crossed the marble floor, where just before the altar, alongside an urn filled with long thin candles, the *compas* lay embedded. Traditionally known as the *navel of the world*, it looked like a sun mandala, twelve rays of light emanating from its center.

Here it is again. The number twelve, Maggie mused. *What better time for the twelve tribes to return.* What better moment for the nations of the earth to merge.

That time, that moment had arrived.

Now, just before her, brilliant silver and gold icons, shiny hanging lights, and large white candles all cast their glow upon the altar. Her heart became quiet as she looked down through the glass.

The Rock of Golgotha.

Maggie felt for the velvet pouch and the last foundation stone. She pulled out the deep violet amethyst engraved with the letter *VAM.*

Wisdom.

"Here goes," she said, taking a deep breath.

Maggie got down on her knees and crawled under the altar. There, a silver disk lay as a marker for the spot where Christ's cross was believed to have been set. Like countless others before her, she placed her hand in the hole at the center of the disk where the sacred rock could actually be touched. The gem between her fingers, Maggie maneuvered her hand to the farthest corner until she felt a small fissure in the rock. A strange sensation of longing overtook her as she slipped the final foundation stone into the crack—the realization that her task was complete.

Maggie laid her hand firmly on Golgotha's surface and closed her eyes. Within the silence, she could feel the spirit of the messianic line moving through her.

Lung-mei. Matt's description of the earth's energy meridians. With the last of the sacred Kalachakra stones laid, the foundation of the *new city* was now set.

Slowly, Maggie extricated herself out from under the altar. Michael was already smiling. She was just about to speak when suddenly, she felt the floor tremble beneath her.

"What was that?" Michael said, warily scanning the Katholicon.

Within seconds, the ground began to shake again, and a loud rumbling shattered the silence.

"My God, an earthquake!" Maggie stumbled toward Michael as they both tried to keep their balance.

"The stones." Michael eyes were fixed on hers. "There's been some sort of shift in energy."

"Come on!" Maggie yelled above the growing din. "We've got to get to the Temple Mount!"

"Sunrise in Jerusalem. Could this actually be the dawn we remember? This is Drake Harnel with CNN reporting from the gardens of the Seven Arches Hotel. In a few short hours we will see the culmination of long years of negotiations brought to fruition by the patient efforts of the president of the European Commission, Giovanni Mabus.

"As we telecast this morning from the Mount of Olives, we can see this sacred locale itself overlooks many holy sites in a city that, like no other, symbolizes the spiritual questing of mankind. Just below us in the Kidron Valley is Absalom's Tomb and the Russian Orthodox Church of St. Mary Magdalene with its multiple gold-gilded onion domes so reminiscent of Tsarist Russia. Across the valley, Islam's golden Dome of the Rock, situated on a blue-tiled, octagonal base atop the Temple Mount, is backlit by a magnificent pink sky streaked with bands of golden clouds . . . "

Harnel felt impressed with his own lofty poetic verbiage, but the rumbling tremor that shook the hotel grounds brought him back to earth.

"Holy Shit! Cut! Cut!" he yelled over to his cameraman as he tried hard to keep his balance. "Bobby, what the hell is going on?"

The CNN cameraman was still struggling to prevent his tripod from falling. "A suicide bomber maybe?"

Harnel strained to see the streets below. In the distance, he heard the wail of a siren.

Suddenly, the hotel concierge came running toward the open portico doors that led out onto the veranda. "Earthquake!" he shouted as he waved people along. "Everyone out of the hotel."

Staff members in white jackets scurried in and out of the lobby doors directing diplomats and peace conference attendees out of the Seven Arches. Then the ground shook again, noticeably stronger. Harnel heard crashing noises and cries from inside the hotel.

It took barely a moment for his instincts to kick in.

"Bobby." Harnel was back on message. "Notify Atlanta. We're going on live." He motioned the cameraman to aim toward the hotel's front exit.

Michael gave Maggie a dumbfounded stare. "Are you crazy!" He was now yelling above the noise.

Maggie sensed it as a gut feeling. They had to get to the Mount right away. All the signs were pointing to it. With no time to explain, Maggie took off like the wind. Michael hurried to keep up and was soon by her side as she raced down the stairs of the Sepulchre.

"What are you doing in here?" a black-robed Armenian priest yelled in alarm when he saw them. "By who's authority—"

Maggie flew past the priest, nearly knocking him aside.

"Excuse us," Michael apologized, running past him as well. "We got a little lost, Father. Big church and all."

Maggie dashed toward the door and pushed up against it. Realizing it was locked, she remembered the small latched portal. As she jabbed her elbow against it, it flew opened.

"What are you doing? You cannot touch the doors!" Stunned, the priest appeared more concerned with her and Michael's appearance than with the earth tremors. His eyes were nearly bugging out of his head.

Maggie glared at him before turning toward Michael. "I think I need a lift."

Without hesitating, Michael scooped her off the floor. Legs first, he lowered her out the portal until she hit the ground outside. After a few seconds of hearing what she thought was a scuffle, Michael came diving out of the opening as well.

"Oh man," he groaned as he lay on the street in front of the Church.

As Maggie helped to pull Michael up to his feet, she saw Walid staring at them both in amazement. She gave him a quick rundown of events.

"Ahmin needs help," she said. "There's been a break-in. He's holding two men at gunpoint down in the Inventio Crucis Chapel."

Maggie was certain Walid would need therapy by the time his unlikely ordeal was over.

After a momentary glaze, the shine in his eyes returned. Walid indicated he understood. As he grappled with the Sepulchre keys, he removed a cell phone from his jacket.

"Let's go!" Maggie commanded as she turned.

But Michael was gone.

Surprised, she looked down the street and saw him . . . already halfway down the block, running at full speed.

In a matter of seconds, Bobby relayed Drake Harnel's message back to the CNN newsroom and was giving Harnel a countdown. "Five, four, three, two." Bobby nodded the go-ahead.

"Good morning. This is Drake Harnel reporting to you live from the Seven Arches Hotel on the Mount of Olives in Jerusalem. The city has just been struck by a sizeable earthquake tremor several moments ago, and we have already felt one aftershock."

As his cameraman panned the front of the hotel, Harnel's initial fear turned into more of an adrenaline high. *What a shot*, he thought, as he witnessed the visible panic on the faces of high-level officials fleeing nervously from the hotel.

Harnel turned toward Bobby to give him another cue, but his cameraman was staring off in the opposite direction. Suddenly, Bobby's face turned pale. When Harnel swung around to see what was getting him so upset, he nearly dropped his microphone.

The beautiful morning sunrise had disappeared. It had given way to a massive rolling mountain of black, threatening thunderclouds that were moving west. Straight toward Haram al-Sharif!

My God, Harnel thought. Knowing there was no time to lose he waved his arms, directing Bobby to turn the camera around toward the sky just beyond the Temple Mount. As Harnel was positioning himself to resume his report, the terraced plaza where he was standing shook violently. Like a tightrope walker he tried to use his arms to gain his equilibrium, but his knees buckled and he fell to the ground. Meanwhile, Bobby was a bit luckier. He grabbed the camera in a heroic move to protect it and cradled it in his arms like a football. Then, with his prized possession secured, he fell on his butt.

The moment the trembling subsided, Harnel jumped back to his feet. Bobby, the die-hard professional, had hardly blinked. He was back in position in seconds, his camera aimed and ready.

"*This . . . is . . . unbelievable.*" Harnel dramatically emphasized each word as he looked directly into the lens. "Moments ago, the sky was pristine and pastel colored—pink, yellow and gold—a picture postcard Mediterranean morning. First an earthquake, and now what looks like a severe storm is headed our way."

Harnel pointed toward the clouds. Bobby took his cue and panned upward just as a bolt of lightning crossed the horizon, sending its skewered fingers of electricity toward the earth.

Clouds were moving swiftly across the sky when another tremor shook them. Maggie and Michael sprinted as fast as they could through the streets. Souk El-Dabbagha, then El-Saraya. There seemed to be a lot more people moving about than Maggie expected.

"What time is it?" she yelled to Michael in between breaths.

He looked at his watch. "It's 7:15."

Early morning and crowded sidewalks. It dawned on her then. *Most of these people are women.*

As they continued running, they soon came upon larger and larger pockets of women moving down the street, most looking disheveled and disoriented.

"What's happened?" Maggie yelled toward a group as she was passing them.

"You haven't heard? We got through early this morning. Most of the Seline Marchers crossed the Egyptian-Israeli border, and then, the Jordanian and Lebanese borders were breached."

Maggie was astounded. What could have happened for the Israelis to allow these women passage from all sides? Then she thought of Laurel and a shudder of fear passed through her. Maggie quickly realized she couldn't afford to think.

Instead, she tried to stay focused on weaving past the mass of people that lined El-Khalidiya Street. It began to dawn on her that it would be nearly impossible to get up to the Temple Mount with thousands of women clogging the streets. Maggie stopped suddenly. "We have to go through the Cotton Merchants Gate."

Michael jerked to a halt. "*Bab el-Qattanin?* Impossible. It's way too dangerous. They'll know in an instant we're not Muslims."

Maggie was quite aware that non-Muslims weren't allowed to enter the Temple Mount through that particular gate. "But what choice do we have?" she said, realizing their dilemma. "With crowds surrounding the whole Mount, there won't be any access through the other gates. It's the only one that will be freed up enough for us to enter."

Michael came up close to her, his face nearly touching hers. "There's a password to get in, a *new* password every day."

Maggie gave him an ardent look. "We *have* to go through that gate."

Another rumbling tremor moved beneath them. Suddenly, just as the rain came pouring down, the sound of an emergency siren sent people rushing nervously down the street.

"Come on!" Maggie urged.

But Michael, now looking determined, hardly seemed to need prodding. A piercing light came through his eyes. Maggie saw him touch the side of his soaked vest, knowing he was feeling for the lance at his side.

On the Mount of Olives, the CNN assistant cameraman held a massive umbrella over the camera as a hard driving rain and bits of hail began to fall.

Drake Harnel felt like he was back on the Kansas prairie where he had grown up. "For the sake of all of us who have had such high expectations for this conference, let us hope that this is not an ominous sign." As his own assistant tried to offer him an umbrella, Harnel waved him off with a stern look. *Dramatic effect!* Besides, he knew he appeared more seasoned without it. Anyway, it would only be a matter of moments before the wind would rip it away—CNN embossed or not.

"Drake, Drake, can you hear me? This is Barbara Taylor in Atlanta. We've just received word from the United States Geological Survey that the earthquake registered 6.1 on the Richter scale, a severe jolt by any reckoning. The thunderstorm was also unexpected. Both defy any computer forecasting model."

You're telling me, lady, Harnel thought.

Right at that moment, he heard his director, Janice Whitfield, whispering excitedly through his earpiece. "Look at monitor one," she ordered.

"What in the world?" Harnel couldn't believe his eyes.

One of CNN's secondary cameras was zooming in on the Golden Gate. The tremors had knocked down many of the enormous stone blocks, held firmly in place for over five hundred years, and it was now possible to see through the massive double arches.

The sight was causing a curious reaction in him, Harnel noted, and his Princeton studies in multi-culturalism kicked in. At that moment, he felt he was undergoing a transformation—from mere reporter to world orator.

"According to Christian, Jewish and Muslim legend," Harnel informed his audience, "this gate, the Golden Gate, would remain blocked until the Messiah, the Mahdi arrives. Today, we see that this gateway, which has been guarded and sealed over the millennia and has been a source of great contention, is now broken open by the quake."

CHAPTER 103

LAUREL SELINE WAS finding they could barely walk through the streets of Jerusalem. With the roads blocked and jammed with vehicles, most of the women had abandoned their buses and trucks and had continued by foot toward the Mount.

Laurel had not seen Rosa again since they crossed the border together. The swell of women finally flowing into Israel unleashed a media frenzy that was beyond belief. Sought after by television and radio crews, the actress had left the group, joining a team of reporters hurrying toward the Temple Mount, all desiring her commentary on the tremendous events unfolding.

But Laurel was grateful that Lonnie and Jules had managed to stay by her side. She leaned against them now for support as the marchers, wet and tired, walked into the heart of the city.

"We're almost there," Jules encouraged.

Feeling weak and dazed, Laurel felt comforted by the sound of her young companion's voice.

The ground around them had been trembling for the last ten minutes. Now, just as they reached the outer confines of the Temple Mount, a powerful jolt knocked them all down to the ground.

Laurel didn't think she could go on much longer. As she attempted to get to her feet, Lonnie grabbed hold of her arm and pulled her up. People around her were yelling, others were pointing, their eyes wide with disbelief. Finally, she understood what was causing their amazement.

With the dust still settling around it, Laurel saw the grand Golden Gate was split apart, large chunks of stone resting on the ground in front of it.

The age of the messiah.

She quickly understood the event's significance. Although exhilarated, at the same time Laurel felt something gnawing at her, like a burning ember in her chest.

Maggie is here.

CHAPTER 104

MOVING AS RAPIDLY as they could through the crowd, Maggie and Michael reached the covered street of the Cotton Merchant's Market. Slowing down their pace so as not to appear anxious, they passed through the dilapidated arched entrance.

Upon entering the market, Maggie found it was pulsing with street savvy vendors and tourists. With a dark interior dimly lit by lamps and light fixtures strung along the ceilings and walls, the bazaar reminded Maggie of the arcades she would hang out in as a kid. She hurried along nervously, Michael beside her, both searching the market for any signs of police.

As they reached the exit, daylight spilled through the gate. Maggie hurried toward the opening with Michael at her side. She thought they were home free, but then out of nowhere, a Muslim Waqf official appeared. Both she and Michael stopped dead in their tracks.

Michael glanced at her tensely. He gave her a look that told her to follow his lead.

"Kalimet al sir?" the guard asked.

"What is the password?" Michael repeated the phrase aloud for her to hear, flashing her a wary look.

Maggie knew he had dreaded this moment.

"Sir, we did not have the time today to acquire the password," Michael explained, "but we request entry. My wife and I are American Muslims, and we have come such a long way to see the Dome."

Maggie, realizing playing dumb was probably the best course to take, continued walking forward. Suddenly, she heard the guard yell.

"Qeff!"

Feigning confusion, she turned toward him and smiled. Maggie knew that in a matter of seconds they would be turned around if Michael didn't make his move.

She flashed him a furtive look. *Come on, Michael. Do something!*

In one unnaturally swift, calculated move, Michael jabbed the guard in the stomach with his fist. The soldier doubled over in pain. Stunned, Maggie watched as Michael took advantage of the guard's delayed reaction and jumped him. The two began grappling at the gate entrance. When the soldier started screaming in Arabic, another guard came dashing out of one of the sweet shops, coffee cup in hand. Throwing the paper cup against the wall, he ran toward them.

Maggie bolted to Michael's side and reached into his vest, quickly removing the Longinus Spear.

"What in God's name?" he muttered in astonishment.

"Keep them back. I'm going up to the Mount."

Just then, the second guard closed in. Gun drawn, he was about to fire when an enormous tremor shook the ground, causing him to fall and drop his weapon. Maggie stumbled to reach it and with one swift kick, sent it skidding into the crowd of frightened tourists .

With Michael still grappling with the first guard, Maggie entered the Temple Mount through the gate. What couldn't have been more than seconds seemed like a lifetime as she sprinted past a stone fountain and up the stairs that led directly to the front of the Dome of the Rock. Without knowing why, she instinctively knew the Mount was where she was supposed to be.

Maggie ran over the esplanade, all the while the wind growing stronger and dark clouds beginning to swirl overhead. As she reached the area of the Mount between the Dome of the Rock and the Dome of the Spirits, a tremendous jolt from the earth caused her to lose her footing and fall. Suddenly, only about ten feet in front of her, a huge fissure appeared across the Mount's surface.

Just then, lightning flashed across the sky, and a crashing, rumbling thunder shook her to the core.

In that instant, it became clear.

The lightning . . . the thunder . . . the lung-mei . . .

The crack in the earth.

Maggie stumbled back to her feet and headed directly toward the opening in the ground. Holding the hilt in both hands, she raised the Spear as high as she could and plunged it into the broken surface.

Then, as if stabbed with a hot iron poker, Maggie felt a searing pain rip through her shoulder. Her breath rushed from her lungs, and she collapsed backward onto the esplanade.

She lay there, the world receding. Screams and cries blended with the rumbling thunder. Soon, Maggie began to feel she was entering another dimension, where sound and movement were distant memories. A timeless sense of presence filled her, until the only thing her mind could fathom was the beautiful blue light moving like the ocean across the sky.

"Zoom in!" Janet Whitfield's voice came booming over Harnel's earpiece.

"Who was that?" Harnel asked. He had just seen a woman running through the Cotton Merchants Gate onto the Temple Mount. "Was she shot?" Harnel felt confused and excited. "Play the tape of that back. Let's see if our camera got a good view of what happened."

The video was replayed and enhanced until the woman's face was clearly visible.

Harnel was stunned. "I think that's . . . In fact, I'm certain that's Maggie Seline," Harnel relayed to his television viewers. Yes, he was sure of it. Harnel had interviewed her several times and reported on her disappearance. "What is she—?

Harnel could see she was holding something aloft, but no matter how hard he peered at the monitor, he still could not distinguish what it was. The object in Maggie Seline's hand began to glow, imperceptibly at first. Then suddenly, a brilliant flash of blue light illuminated her face.

"That's St. Elmo's fire, I'd know that glow anywhere." Harnel enjoyed appearing scientifically astute for his audience.

"What do you mean?" his anchor, Barbara Taylor, asked.

"St. Elmo's fire or St. Elmo's light. It's a plasma, a kind of ionized gas that forms during thunderstorms. It'll look like a glowing corona around an object. I saw it as a kid in Kansas on the horns of cattle during lightning storms and on the masts of ships when I was in the navy, sailing the Indian Ocean. But never, never have I seen it surround a person and seem to be virtually swallowing them up."

As they continued the video playback, Harnel saw a Waqf guard come up behind Seline and raise his pistol. Just as Seline dropped the object, the temple guard behind her fired his gun.

Shot in the back, Maggie Seline then slumped to the ground.

Harnel was about to make a comment, when Whitfield cut him off again. "Camera two, Drake, look what's coming!"

Harnel didn't need camera two. What he saw with his own eyes was enough.

Crossing the sky, like a swirling ocean, was something that looked like a phosphorous blue mist. As it moved across the city, Harnel shivered.

His mind went numb.

Michael didn't realize he had it in him. The thought of Maggie running up the Temple Mount, alone and vulnerable, triggered a profound protective impulse. His fists felt like iron balls as he punched the guard in the face, finally knocking him out cold.

The previous tremor had sent the crowd into a panic, and people were dashing in all directions. Michael charged through the same gate Maggie had passed through only moments before, but he was not alone as other non-Muslims caught in the confusion and fear followed suit.

Just as he reached the upper level of the Temple Mount, a flash of lightning made him look up toward the sky, and what he saw next held him spellbound.

A milky patch of blue light, nearly a mile long, moved slowly across the sky above the city. As a sudden cold wind sent a chill through his body, Michael realized the temperature must have dropped drastically. Barely a moment later, the distinct smell of ozone permeated the air.

Then, like a fluorescent blanket, the cloud of light descended from the sky toward the earth, enveloping everyone and everything. Looking beyond the Mount in every direction, Michael could see the holy city of Jerusalem was now within a halo of light. Sparks appeared to jump from object to object as the whole area became charged with electricity.

When the hazy blue light began to clear, everything around him glowed with brilliance. Just when he thought the phenomenon was over, a large, luminous orange ball of light appeared in the sky.

Ball lightning. Michael watched the brilliant mass of plasma, like a miniature sun, grow brighter and denser.

Then Michael saw it.

The Spear. It was sticking out of the esplanade ground. Before he could even think another thought, the strange anomaly shot down from the sky toward it.

A sudden tremendous explosion sent Michael reeling backward. In his prone position, he shielded his eyes and watched as the cracked ground beneath the Spear widened further, turning into a chasm, and the great talisman—prized by the most powerful leaders in history—was swallowed into the earth.

Dazed and exhausted, Michael lay back onto the ground, allowing the full brunt of what he had witnessed to permeate his body. All that phenomenal electrical energy, he realized, had passed from sky to earth.

And the Spear was the conductor.

By the time Michael got to his feet again, he felt as if he was standing in a well of silence. The tens of thousands within the city and looking down from the Mount of Olives had witnessed it all along with him.

He took a deep breath. Then, as his mind began to focus again, he saw her.

Maggie lay crumpled on the ground close to the chasm . . . her blood mixing with the chalky broken marble.

CHAPTER 105

CAPTAIN ZAYIN WAS PRIMED. His last mission. He hadn't felt like this in years—his adrenaline pumping, his mind wound as tight as the powerful Pratt & Whitney engine he was strapped to. This was real. Bombing the West Bank and Gaza had simply been a ride in the park. Even Beirut had been fairly sedate. The sophisticated detection electronics on his Sufa had made it far too easy to evade Hamas rockets, much less automatic rifle fire.

Today, if all went according to plan, Zayin would have several minutes in which to carry out his attack before the Saudis and Americans realized it was no drill. But Volpi had also said he had several men within the Saudi command who would continue the deception. What had been his words? *Just like 9/11.*

"Captain Zayin, stand down." He heard the voice coming over his earpiece.

Zayin was astounded by the command. *What nonsense is this?*

"We have an American plane making an emergency landing."

"On my runway?" he questioned.

"Affirmative."

Damn it. "Hold that plane," Zayin directed. "I'll be out of here in two minutes."

"Captain Zayin." He recognized the stern voice. It was the base commander, General Magnes. "STAND DOWN."

Zayin glanced toward his wing-men, Yabraoth and Schtarker, flanking him on the runway in their F-16s. They looked as if they knew his thoughts. He had seconds in which to decide. If he took off now the entire IAF might scramble after him.

But then again, if he didn't . . .

Zayin released the wheel brakes, and his fighter began to move forward.

As the C-130 neared the Negev airstrip, the flight navigator approached Jarret.

"Please sir, come with me."

Jarret unstrapped himself and followed him into the cockpit. Captain Timberg, piloting the plane, turned around and motioned for Jarrett to come closer. As he looked through the cockpit window, Jarret saw a squadron of Israeli F-16s on the runway.

"Are we on the proper approach?" the co-pilot asked, looking confused.

Still staring through the window, Jarret could see the fighter planes positioned at the back of the airfield were gearing up for take-off. The lead fighter was already taxiing down the runway.

This is it! These are the planes!

Jarret nearly grabbed the controls himself. "Take her down!" he yelled at Timberg. "Those planes must not take off."

As the pilot maneuvered the C-130 for a landing, Jarrett got into the seat behind him and secured his safety belt. He gripped the armrest hard as the transport shuddered with the pressure of a quick descent. All the while Jarret prepared himself, acknowledging that if the fighter jet below lifted off, it would never clear their aircraft.

"Captain." It was Yabraoth speaking to him over the radio. "We have a problem."

Six military police jeeps, their yellow lights flashing, were racing toward the tarmac.

Zayin's posture stiffened. *No time left.* He inched the computerized throttle forward as quickly as he could. As the jet engines flamed to full power, the plane jumped. "We go!" he yelled toward his fellow conspirators.

From his semi-prone position inside the cockpit, which he laughingly referred to as *the glass coffin*, Zayin could see the eyes of his wingmen widen like saucers as they both glared out their cockpit windows.

"Captain, twelve o'clock. Look out!" Yabraoth alerted.

That's when Zayin saw the fortress-sized C-130 touching down. His heart sank as he comprehended the meaning of the aircraft's landing. If he didn't divert off the runway, he would be dead.

Zayin veered the F-16 Sufa hard to starboard. But it was too late. With a shuddering force the oncoming plane shattered his port wing. He spun his head quickly to look out the window. Flames were shooting across the glass. A moment later smoke filled the cockpit.

As he watched the light from the fire intensify, Zayin wondered if perhaps it was for the best.

Death before shame.

All that he had hoped for was lost.

CHAPTER 106

"**D**RAKE! DRAKE!" Whitfield was yelling at Harnel through his earpiece again.

Uncharacteristically, Harnel was speechless. Almost everyone around him had fallen to the ground when the strange sphere of golden yellow light suddenly sped rapidly toward the Temple Mount. For a few moments after the explosion, Harnel felt as if he were in a vacuum. There was no sound, no motion, only a palpable stillness.

Bobby pointed toward the monitor. The body of Maggie Seline lay prone on the Mount, and a man was kneeling over her. A fissure several feet wide had split open on the stone esplanade. A Temple guard was standing close by, a look of disbelief on his face, a pistol still in his hand.

As Harnel stood on the veranda of the Seven Arches Hotel staring down into the valley below, he could hardly believe the phenomenon he had just seen. Fellow reporters from all over the world that were stationed on the Mount of Olives with him were giving each other knowing looks, appearing to have realized they had witnessed an event of historical magnitude.

As Bobby panned the camera, Harnel looked out upon the entire vista himself—from the broken doorways and debris-filled front gardens of the Seven Arches, down toward the Kidron Valley, to the tens of thousands surrounding the Temple Mount and stretched out across the avenues and souks, and finally back toward the Mount itself and the Golden Dome, glowing even more brilliantly in the aftermath of the earthquake and electrical storm.

Harnel took a deep breath before he spoke. His lungs felt as if they needed more oxygen than he could muster. "Onlookers, hundreds of thousands throughout the city, including the women marchers from around the globe as well as the retinue of world delegates here for the Peace Conference, have observed the mysterious phenomenon which has taken place here in Jerusalem . . . "

EPILOGUE

ON THE MOUNT of Olives, on the terrace of the Seven Arches Hotel, Maggie stood with Michael looking out onto the old city and the Temple Mount. For the first time in days, the hoards of press finally receded back into the conference hall and were waiting for the Peace Conference to begin.

A clear sky, traced with a wisp of clouds, provided a serene backdrop to the crowded city below. In the valley, the golden dome magnetized the sun's rays and exuded its powerful aura over the city. Huge crowds of women marchers, having lingered over the last several days, filled the streets and markets, adding their powerful current to an already charged atmosphere. Seeing them, Maggie was in awe. What Laurel had accomplished was beyond comprehension. Maggie felt incredibly grateful for her grandmother's unwavering belief in her ideas and her extraordinary determination to bring them to fruition.

As Maggie allowed her gaze to settle on the Golden Gate below, she still could scarcely believe her eyes. Completely sealed for hundreds of years, it now stood broken apart. The centuries old dam had collapsed, and Maggie could feel the energy flowing through the gate and washing over the Temple Mount like a rushing river. From the Mount of Olives, moving along the messianic line, a divine presence had once again entered Jerusalem, confirming the city's sacred inheritance as the *Mother of the World*.

Suddenly, a searing pain ripped through Maggie's shoulder, cutting through her feeling of serenity. She nearly doubled over. Maggie now wondered if she had done the right thing by refusing the heavier dose of painkillers her doctors had wanted to prescribe. Being doped up on medication, though, was not exactly how she wanted to attend what she knew would be a monumental event.

Michael's face was lined with worry as he leaned over. "Are you alright?"

"Not exactly. The pain in my shoulder is acting up," Maggie confessed. She clenched her teeth as she waited for another wave of pain to subside.

"Well, that's what you get for taking that Lara Croft thing too far," Michael smiled. "Taking a bullet for peace will be your legacy."

"Funny," she said, smiling.

"Besides that, it appears your heroism and Mabus' indictment has caused your *Times'* publisher to have a change of heart." Michael reached into the pocket of his jacket and pulled out a folded piece of paper. "Read this. I took it off the internet this morning."

As soon as Maggie opened up the page, her jaw dropped.

In bold lettering on the front page of that morning's *New York Times* was the story homeland security squelched nearly a month ago.

THE MABUS CONNECTION

By Maggie Seline

"Your story is even more explosive now, with everything unraveling here in Israel. Some congressmen are already calling for impeachment proceedings against the vice president."

Maggie's mind was trying to keep up with all the implications.

"Who would have thought we could have accomplished what we did." Michael sighed, looking about as astonished as she felt. "What a bizarre twist of events."

Maggie had to agree. Over the last several days both she and Michael had witnessed the extraordinary. They had learned the extent of Mabus' plan—both to hijack the conference as well as execute an attack on the Saudi oil fields. The Mossad, with CIA assistance, had arrested the infamous Propaganda Due leader, Guiseppe Volpi, along with other high-level P2 members, including a U.S. Senator and military officials.

"In a way, we have Mabus' deception to thank for all of this," Maggie said, realizing the strange truth as she looked out over the sea of delegates. "What started as a sham has now turned into a real platform for peace."

"Definitely not his intention," Michael commented.

"But certainly ours," Maggie said, smiling, "and that of the Grail's." Maggie brought her hand to his for a moment. She was touched by his shyness as he looked away.

"Yes, the lung-mei, the energy flow that helped create this event," Michael added. "It's extraordinary."

"And we all created it together." Maggie still found herself amazed at what she had experienced.

Michael's eyes widened, fixed on a horizon Maggie could only imagine. "It's the manifestation of the third saying of Christ," he said, "what Thomas had known all the while:

> *Oh Jerusalem, City of Peace. The jewel laid, the city*
> *is the temple. Architect build thy roads. Thy gates like*
> *grand arches rise to the East. Draw the lines of the*
> *heavenly temple. Let the stones be thy foundation.*
> *Through the wisdom of the heart, the Pentagon in*
> *unity, the marriage of nations merge. The Star of David*
> *is complete. Jerusalem is One."*

The Pentagons in unity, Maggie thought, *the marriage of nations*. "Arabs and Jews living in peace, side by side. Do you think that day is getting closer?" Maggie's felt the rise of hope in her heart.

"The foundation for the Star of David is present because of you." Michael's eyes held hers with a certainty and confidence that left no room for doubt.

As Michael took her arm to head back into the hotel, Maggie caught sight of Ahmin standing in the far corner of the garden. They had agreed there would be no contact between them. Too dangerous, too much room for media distortion.

Apparently, though, Ahmin had seen her on the terrace and decided to take the opportunity to be close by. As he smiled, Maggie felt his warmth embrace her.

Soon, his eyes were telling her, and her eyes answered in return, *soon*. Maggie knew that might mean months, but in terms of a lifetime, it was only a moment.

The Peace Conference was just about to commence as she and Michael walked into the back of the dimly lit conference hall. Maggie felt grateful for the darkened environment, preferring what she knew would be a short-lived anonymity, as she took a seat next to several Indian delegates at the back of the room. Michael slipped into the chair beside her.

Just then, the secretary general of the UN, Akanis Arran, walked onto the stage. His assurance and dignity were greeted by enthusiastic applause.

"Welcome, ladies and gentlemen, delegates, representatives from all nations of the world," Arran began. "Not long ago in the scheme of history, Franklin Delano Roosevelt spoke these very poignant words. *The only thing we have to fear is fear itself.* We have seen how true that is. Through fear we misunderstand, we terrorize, we destroy. Only a few short days ago, totally unexpected and incredible events occurred that we have all been a part of. They have given us the courage to move forward with renewed hope.

"It is with this hope and courage that I announce that the world leaders present today have decided to include in the conference agenda an examination of an alternative solution to the ongoing Middle East crisis, one that has been inspired by these truly awesome events, one that is widely supported by the tens of thousands of women who have marched to Jerusalem advocating this solution as well as millions of others throughout the world, both men and women, who have come to realize that warring over God leaves no survivors.

"This proposal—to create an international zone of peace in Jerusalem—has been kindled by one of us, a truly remarkable woman who said 'No More' until we joined her in her resolve. I present to you, ladies and gentlemen, Maggie Seline."

Nearly seven thousand miles away, within the quiet recesses of New York's Hudson Valley, Napesh Samuels took a sip of port from his glass as he watched the news. Having just heard the UN Secretary General Akanis Arran's speech initiating the opening ceremony of the Peace Conference, he turned down the volume.

As Samuels saw Maggie was about to take the podium, he took a deep breath and closed his eyes. Thankfully, she had survived the shooting, and with Mabus' plans thwarted, the far-reaching and sinister aims of Propaganda Due had been leveled . . . at least for now.

Still, Professor Samuels had lived long enough to know that the world of good and evil was in constant play, and real victory lay beyond its reach. That realization, in fact, was one known to every member of *the Way*, to all the true spiritual architects and masons who honor the divine above any religion, even their own.

There lies the path of enlightenment, the path of the Grail.

Samuels knew it to be so, deeply, with every fiber of his being. How else could the holy and divine be drawn into the physical but through the powerful elements of one's own mind. *It was belief and intent*, Samuels realized. Belief and intent were the alchemical keys that unlocked the mystery. Therein lay the magic.

Within the mystical science of the Grail, a seed had been planted, and a new Jerusalem revealed. An earthshaking event had brought the collective consciousness of millions of people to bear on one pressing issue.

Peace and human decency above all else . . . peace within this very lifetime.

The Professor looked back at his silenced television screen once again. As he viewed the dignitaries listening to the speeches, Napesh Samuels realized that in every face he saw a seeker . . . each searching for the Grail, each yearning to find their own Shambhala, and like Christ, Muhammad and Abraham before them, each questing for the highest vision.

The pure vision of the sun.

Breinigsville, PA USA
29 September 2009
224980BV00003B/6/P